THE JERICHO ITERATION

ALLEN STEELE

ACE BOOKS, NEW YORK

This Ace Book contains the complete text of
the original hardcover edition.

THE JERICHO ITERATION

An Ace Book / published by arrangement with
the author

PRINTING HISTORY
Ace hardcover edition / November 1994
Ace mass-market edition / November 1995

All rights reserved.
Copyright © 1994 by Allen Steele.
Cover art by Mark Smollin.
This book may not be reproduced in whole or in part,
by mimeograph or any other means, without permission.
For information address: The Berkley Publishing Group,
200 Madison Avenue, New York, NY 10016.

ISBN: 0-441-00271-4

ACE®
Ace Books are published by The Berkley Publishing Group,
200 Madison Avenue, New York, NY 10016.
ACE and the "A" design are trademarks
belonging to Charter Communications, Inc.

PRINTED IN THE UNITED STATES OF AMERICA

10 9 8 7 6 5 4 3 2 1

for Kent, Lisa, and Megan Orlando

Acknowledgments

Many people assisted in the development of this novel, most of them St. Louis residents I met during everyday life: police officers, firemen, city officials and bureaucrats, businesspeople, and not a few ordinary folks who just happened to be at the right place at the right time. Some were aware that they were being questioned by an author researching a novel and some were not, but all of them gave me invaluable insights and firsthand knowledge.

To these folks I give my most sincere thanks. This novel could not have been written without their help.

I'm also grateful to Steve Bolhafner, Liz Caplan, Sonny and Carol Denbow, John Furland, Ed Graham, Dot Hill, Frank and Joyce Jacobs, Chris Merseal, Frank M. Robinson, Mike Rosenfeld, Donna Schultz, Mark Tiedemann, Harry Turtledove, and Mark Zeising for encouragement, useful information, and many small favors rendered during the course of this work. As always, particular thanks go to my wife, Linda, who drove me around her hometown, suggested places I ought to visit, and told me when I was going wrong.

Most of all, I wish to thank my editors, Ginjer Buchanan and Susan Allison, and my agent, Martha Millard, for remaining faithful when the going got tough.

—St. Louis, Missouri
September 1991–February 1993

Let's talk about Jericho.

According to the Book of Joshua, the Canaanite city of Jericho was destroyed after Joshua marched his army around the city's walls for six days. On the seventh day, upon his command, the Israelites blew their ram's horns and began to shout. The walls collapsed, thus allowing Joshua and his followers to overrun the Canaanites and claim the city as their own.

That's how the legend goes, at any rate. About twenty years ago, archaeologists studying the ruins of Jericho in Israel, just outside Jerusalem, arrived at a different conclusion. They uncovered evidence suggesting that Jericho had been destroyed not by ram's horns but by a major earthquake caused by a geological fault line running through the Jordan Valley. Furthermore, the city was destroyed at least a hundred and fifty years before the reported date of the Battle of Jericho. Hence, the Talmudic account differs considerably from modern interpretations of the same evidence: in short, people took credit for something nature had already done.

And now it's Friday, April 19, 11:32 P.M. About three and a half millennia since the fall of Jericho, give or take a few hundred years, but who's counting? It doesn't make much difference in the long run. The more things change, the more they remain the same.

I'm sitting cross-legged on the living room floor of an abandoned, half-collapsed house in south St. Louis. It's the middle of the night, and I'm dictating these notes into my pocket computer. Joker's nicad is still fully charged, but I'm nonetheless keeping an eye on the battery LED. If it runs low . . .

Well, I'm sure I can find another. They're not as hard to find on this side of town as, say, an unclaimed can of Vienna sausage. On my way here I passed a scavenged 7-Eleven about four blocks away; southside looters normally don't go after batteries, although you never know.

I heard recently about a teenager who was killed scrounging through a video rental shop; seems he had been trying to make out with an armload of movies when a street gang that had claimed the store as their turf caught him. The story that made its way to the *Big Muddy Inquirer* was that they had strung him up from a telephone pole; when he was found the next morning, he had a copy of *Hang 'Em High* wrapped around his purpled neck. A touch of irony, if you like that sort of thing, although I doubt the guys who murdered him would know irony if it shot 'em in the ass with a Smith & Wesson.

Of course, this could be only another rumor. We've heard a hundred of them since the quake, and since it was never substantiated, we never ran it in the paper. Nonetheless, I think I'll keep talking only until the low-battery light begins to blink. Bopping on down to the 7-Eleven ain't what it used to be.

When the family who once lived here moved out of the city, as have so many others since New Madrid, they took with them whatever they could salvage. What little furniture they left behind is mostly buried beneath the rubble of what used to be their bedrooms; there's also a bad stink from that part of the house. I hope it's only a cat. Dead cats don't bother me, but dead children do.

The former residents left behind the refrigerator and the stove, but since there's no electricity in this neighborhood, they don't work. Union Electric must have determined that this is a vacant block, because even the streetlights are inoperative. There's also a filthy couch infested with insects, a mildewed Mickey Mouse shower curtain, which is the sole clue that there were once kids living here—like I said, I hope it's only a dead cat I smell—and, on the top shelf of the kitchen pantry, a half-empty box of Little Friskies.

Got to be a dead cat.

I'll have to ask the dog if he knows.

The dog who discovered me in the house was glad to have the Little Friskies. I found a forgotten spare key tucked beneath the back-door welcome mat—whoever once lived here didn't have much sense of originality when it came to hiding places, but then again, St. Louis used to be a much safer place—and had invited myself in when I heard something panting behind me. I turned around to find, in the last weak light of day, a full-grown golden retriever who had followed me into the backyard. His big red tongue was hanging out of his mouth, his fur was as wet as my leather jacket, but unlike so many other strays I've seen recently he didn't appear to be feral. Just a big old chow dog, living by his means in what used to be a middle-class neighborhood.

He sniffed me and wagged his tail, and didn't mind when I patted him on the head, so I let him into the house with me. What the hell; we both needed company. As luck would have it—for the dog, at least—there was the box of cat food. He didn't seem to mind the moldy taste. I only wish I could have eaten so well.

Friendly pooch. He decided to stay the night. I warned him that he was accompanying a federal fugitive and was thereby subject to prosecution to the full extent of the law, but the mutt didn't give a shit. I had given him a bite to eat, so I was square in his book, and he paid me back by warning me about the helicopter.

Several hours later: the sun was down, I was exhausted from running. Lying on the couch, idly scratching at the fleas that had come crawling out of the upholstery, listening to the cold, hard rain that pattered on the roof and dribbled through the cracks in the ceiling. Eyes beginning to close. It had been a hell of a day.

The dog was curled up on the bare floor next to the couch, dead to the world, when he abruptly leaped to his feet and began to bark. I opened my eyes, glanced at him, saw that he

was looking out the wide picture window on the other side of
the room.

I couldn't see anything through the darkness, but I could
hear a low drone from somewhere outside the house. . . .

Chopper.

I rolled off the couch and fell to the floor, then scurried
across the living room and through the kitchen door, out of
sight from the window. By now the sound of rotor blades was
very loud.

While I cowered in the kitchen, hugging the wall and
sweating rain, the dog fearlessly advanced to the window
and stood there, barking in defiance as the clatter grew louder.
Then the helicopter was above the front lawn, invisible except
for its running lights.

Captured by the Apaches.

One, at least: an AH-64 gunship, twenty-one thousand
pounds of sudden death. Maybe it was an antique, but I
remembered when I was a kid back in '89 and saw the
TV news footage of those things circling the skies above
Panama City, hunting for PDF holdouts and some pimple-faced
cokehead named Noriega. Now one of them was hunting for a
journalist named Gerry Rosen.

By the way, did I mention my name?

For several long minutes the Apache hovered outside the
window. I could imagine its front-mounted TADS infrared
turret peering into the house, the copilot in the chopper's
back seat trying to get a clear fix through the downpour.
The helicopter was close enough for me to make out the
shadowed forms of the pilot and copilot within its narrow
cockpit. The picture window shuddered in its tortured frame
from the propwash.

It occurred to me that, if the 30-mm chain gun beneath the
forward fuselage were to let go, the plaster wall in front of me
wouldn't protect me more than would a sheet of Kleenex . . .
and if I ran for the back door, the IR sensors would lock onto
me before I could make it through the backyard. Anyone seen
on the streets by ERA patrols after the nine o'clock curfew
was assumed to be a looter, and in this side of town they didn't
bother to make arrests anymore. In fact, they didn't even give

you the dignity of slinging an old Clint Eastwood flick around
your neck.

I clenched Joker against my chest and waited for the bullets
to come through the window. They had found my best friend,
they had found the poor bastards from the Tiptree Corporation,
and now they had found me. . . .

And yet, despite all the noise, locked in the center of a
crosshairs, the dog stood his ground. With his paws jammed
against the windowsill, his lips pulled back from decayed brown
teeth, his tail down but not tucked between his rear legs, this
scrawny, matted stray dog angrily snarled and snapped and
barked ferociously at the flying machine on the other side
of the window, and in a brief, sudden, very clear moment of
understanding, I knew what he was saying—

Get out of here, get out of here, this is my house, my house,
MY HOUSE, GET THE FUCK OUT OF HERE THIS IS MY
HOUSE!

—and then, in that moment between life and death, the
copilot studied the image on his night-vision screen and
reached a decision.

Ain't nothing here except a damn dog.

The ERA chopper rose upward, then angled away into the
wet night, its lights following the ghostly strip of the ruined
street until it vanished from sight.

The dog got some more Little Friskies for his smooth move,
and I haven't slept since then.

Perhaps you may feel secure, hiding behind whatever walls
you've erected around yourself, but I tell you now, as solid
fact, that what happened to me and my city is not far removed
from you. None of us is safe, and any sense of security you
may have now is a lie.

My name is Gerry Rosen. I'm a reporter, and this is what
happened to me during two days and three nights in Jericho,
now better known as St. Louis, Missouri.

From The Associated Press (on-line edition): May 17, 2012

ST. LOUIS (AP)—A major earthquake, registering 7.5 on the Richter scale, struck St. Louis today, devastating large areas of the city and surrounding area and killing hundreds of people.

The quake, which began at 1:55 P.M. and lasted approximately 45 seconds, was epicentered in the town of New Madrid, about 130 miles southeast of the city. The quake caused high-rise buildings in the downtown area to sway, destroyed scores of smaller buildings and countless homes across the county, and led to the collapse of a light-rail bridge spanning the Mississippi River.

The exact number of people in St. Louis killed or injured by the quake is not known at this time. However, local police and fire officials say that at least two hundred fatalities have been reported so far and city hospitals are overwhelmed by people seeking medical assistance.

Particularly hard hit by the quake was the downtown business district, where many older buildings suffered extensive damage. Although no high-rise buildings collapsed during the quake, many interior walls fell. Dozens of smaller buildings were completely demolished, burying their occupants under tons of rubble. This included City Hall, where at least 10 office workers are reported missing.

Two local schools were also leveled during the quake.

One city fire official said that there were "hardly any sur-
vivors" among the elementary schoolchildren who were
attending classes at one of them, a Catholic private school
in the city's prosperous west side.

Many streets in the downtown area have been ripped
up by the collapse of underground caverns beneath the
city, causing dozens of vehicles to fall into the gaping
crevasses. Underground sewage pipes and electrical con-
duits were torn apart by the quake, causing the downtown area to be flooded with raw sewage. At least one
chemical storage tank has been ruptured, and hazardous
toxins are reported to be flowing through storm drains
into the Mississippi.

Electrical power has been lost to most of the city,
along with telephone lines and cable communications
systems. Scattered fires in various neighborhoods have
been reported by utility officials, largely caused by severed
gas lines. Efforts to control the fires have been hindered
by breakage of municipal water lines to much of the city
and the loss of firehouses in at least three wards.

The James Eads Bridge, a major conduit for the
city's light-rail system, collapsed into the Mississippi
River, and eyewitnesses say that a westbound commuter
train was crossing the bridge from East St. Louis, Ill.,
at the time of the quake. No official statement has yet
been issued regarding the number of casualties, but officials at the scene say that dozens of people who were
riding the MetroLink train may have fallen to their
deaths.

The Gateway Arch, the national landmark on the west
bank of the Mississippi that is the city's symbol, survived the quake intact, although roof sections of the
underground visitors' center beneath the Arch fell during
the quake, killing at least five people and injuring dozens
of others. Witnesses report that the Arch itself swayed
during the tremors.

Missouri Gov. Andre Tyrell, who was attending the
National Governors Convention in Las Vegas at the time
of the disaster, has phoned the President to ask for fed-

eral assistance, says spokesman Clyde Thomson at the state capital in Jefferson City, itself rocked by the quake. Thomson said that Tyrell is flying back to the state, although commercial air traffic in and out of St. Louis International Airport has been suspended by the Federal Aviation Administration because of hazardous runway conditions.

Although the local Emergency Broadcast System was crippled by the loss of the KMOX-AM radio tower, St. Louis Mayor Elizabeth Boucher went on the air from radio station KZAK-AM at 2:30 P.M. to plead for calm and cooperation from the city's residents. "Please help our police and firemen do their jobs," she said, "and assist your neighbors in whatever way you can.

"May God help us in this time of crisis," Boucher said, her voice shaking.

Several small towns in eastern Missouri and southwestern Illinois were also devastated by the earthquake, the force of which has been estimated to be equivalent to the detonation of 900,000 tons of TNT, or a nine-kiloton nuclear explosion. Significant damage was also reported in Evansville, Ill., and Memphis, Tenn., and tremors were felt as far west as Kansas City, where a church bell was reported to have rung twelve times during the quake.

Hundreds of National Guard troops from across the midwestern region are being sent to Missouri to aid local relief efforts. Spokesmen at the Washington, D.C., headquarters of the Emergency Relief Agency say that ERA troops are being mobilized at this time . . .

Excerpt from *The Big Muddy Inquirer*:
December 18, 2012

Christmas In Squat City:
"Santa Will Still Find Our Tent."

Seven months ago, Jean Moran lived in a two-bedroom ranch house in suburban Frontenac. Each morning she packed sack lunches for her two children and sent them off to meet the school bus, while her husband, Rob, skimmed the paper and had one last cup of coffee before driving downtown to the insurance brokerage where he worked. Jean then spent the rest of the day doing housework, paying bills, shopping for groceries, chatting on Compuserve with friends around the country . . . the daily affairs of a slightly bored young housewife who believed that her life was as solid as the ground beneath her feet.

Then, one day last May, the ground was no longer solid.

Now Jean Moran and her kids, Ellen and Daniel, are only three of some 75,000 residents of the vast tent city that is still in place in Forest Park seven months after the New Madrid earthquake.

She still does housework—or rather, tentwork, the day-to-day housekeeping responsibilities shared by the four homeless families who occupy tent G-12—but gone are all the material things she once took for granted, except for a few family pictures she salvaged from the wreckage of her house.

For a while after they moved into the park, Ellen and Danny went to school three days a week, attending one-room elementary classes conducted in the mess tent by volunteer teachers from the Urban Education Project, until government cutbacks closed the school last November. Now, while Jean fills plastic bottles from the water buffalo parked nearby, her children are two more kids playing in the frozen mud between the olive drab tents of Squat City.

"I'm just grateful I didn't lose them, too," Jean says quietly, watching her kids as she hauls the two-gallon jugs back to her tent and stows them on the plywood floor beneath her metal bed. "They were both out in the playground for recess when it happened . . . thank God I was in the carport and managed to get out in the open, or they would have lost both their parents."

Her husband had also been out in the open during the

quake, but he wasn't as lucky as his wife and children. Rob Moran was killed when a cornice stone fell ten stories from a downtown office building while he was on his way back to work from a late lunch. He had a life insurance policy, just as the Moran house had been covered by earthquake rider on the home insurance, but Jean is still waiting for the money to come through. The small insurance company that had protected them went bankrupt before all its claims could be settled.

With the insurance company now in receivership, it may be many months before the Morans are reimbursed for everything they are owed. Yet this is only one of many nuisances, large and small, with which Jean has had to cope as the widowed mother of two children.

"Summer wasn't too bad," she says, sitting on her bunk and gazing through the furled-back tent flap. "It was hot, sure—sometimes it was over a hundred degrees in here—but at least we had things to do and people were taking care of us. And when construction companies started looking for crews to work on demolition and rebuilding contracts, some people around here were able to get work."

She laughs. "Y'know, for a while, it was almost like we were all in summer camp again. At first, we liked the ERA troopers. They put up the tents, smiled at us at mealtime, let Danny play in their Hummers and so forth . . ."

She suddenly falls silent when, as if on cue, a soldier saunters past her tent. An assault rifle is slung over the shoulder of his uniform parka, which looks considerably warmer than the hooded sweatshirt and denim jacket Jean is wearing. For an instant their eyes meet; she glances away and the soldier, who looks no older than 21, walks on, swaggering just a little.

"Lately, though, they've turned mean," she goes on, a little more quietly now. "Like we're just a bunch of deadbeats who want to live off the dole . . . I dunno what they think, but that's how we're treated. Sometimes they pick fights with the guys over little stuff, like someone trying to get an extra slice of cornbread in the cafeteria line. Every now and then somebody gets pushed around by two or three of them for no good reason. We're at their mercy and they know it."

She lowers her voice a little more. "One of them propositioned me a couple of weeks ago," she says, her face reddening. "He made it sound as if he'd requisition some extra blankets for the children if I'd . . . y'know." Jean violently shakes her head. "Of course, I'd never do something like that, not for anybody, but I think some of the other women around here who have kids . . . well, you do what you think you gotta do."

She pulls at her lank hair as she talks, trying to comb out the knots with her fingers. It's been several days since she has taken a shower in the women's bath tent. Like everything else in Squat City, hot water is carefully rationed; she gives her bath cards to her kids.

"Last night Ellen wanted to know if Santa Claus was going to visit us even if we don't have a chimney anymore," she says. "I told her, 'Yes, sweetheart, Santa will still find our tent.' I didn't tell her I don't know if he's going to bring us any presents—I'm hoping the Salvation Army or the Red Cross will come through—but I know what she wants anyway. She wants Santa to bring her daddy back . . ."

Her voice trails off and for a couple of minutes she is quiet, surrounded by the sounds and smells of Squat City. The acrid odor of campfire smoke, burning paper and plastic kindled by wet branches. The monotone voice of the announcer for Radio ERA, the low-wattage government AM station operating out of the Forest Park Zoo, talking about Friday night's movie in the mess tents. A helicopter flying low overhead. Children playing kickball.

"Let me show you something," Jean says abruptly, then stands up and walks between the bunks to push aside the grimy plastic shower curtain separating her family's space from the others in G-12. "Look in here . . ."

In the darkness of the tent, a middle-aged man is

lying in bed, his hands neatly folded across his chest. It's impossible to tell whether he's asleep or awake; his eyes are heavy-lidded, as if he's about to doze off for a midafternoon nap, yet the pupils are focused on the fabric ceiling of the tent. He is alone, yet he seems unaware that he has visitors.

"That's Mr. Tineal," Jean whispers. "He used to own a grocery down on Gravois. He was buried alive under his store for six days before firemen found him. Six days, with both arms broken, and he hung on until they located him. After he got out of the hospital, they put him here, and he's been like this ever since. His wife and his daughter have been tending to him, but I don't think I've heard him say fifty words the whole time we've been here."

Jean lets the curtain fall. "Three days ago, an ERA caseworker stopped by. They do that once a week, mostly just to have us fill out more forms and such. Anyway, this bitch—I'm sorry for my language, but that's the way she was—the lady looked him over once, then turns to Margaret, his wife, and they've been married now for over thirty years, and says, 'You oughtta just let him die. He's only using up your rations, that's all.'"

Jean walks back to her bunk and sits down on the same impression she had recently vacated. Once again, she's quiet for a few minutes, gazing down at the muddy tracks on the wooden floor.

"So what do you think?" she says at last. "Is Santa going to visit us this year or what?"

From the *Big Muddy Inquirer*: April 3, 2013

St. Louis To ERA: Go Away
ERA to St. Louis: Thanks, But We Like It Here

Like a houseguest who has overstayed his welcome but is apparently deaf to hints that it's time to hit the highway, the federal Emergency Relief Agency shows no signs of leaving St. Louis anytime soon, despite the fact that the last aftershock of the New Madrid earthquake has been felt and many local officials say the city is off the critical list.

Although 550 ERA troopers were recently withdrawn from Metro St. Louis and returned to the agency's federal barracks at Ft. Devens in Massachusetts, some 600 soldiers remain on active duty in St. Louis County. ERA officials claim that the situation in St. Louis remains dangerous and that the agency's paramilitary forces are needed to maintain order in the city.

"Look at the map," says Col. George Barris, commander of ERA forces in St. Louis. He points at a street map tacked up on a wall in the central command post, in what used to be the Stadium Club at Busch Stadium. Large areas of the map—mostly in the northern and southern sides of the city, as well as the central wards— are shaded in red, with black markers pinned to individual blocks within the red areas.

"Those are the neighborhoods still under dusk-to-dawn curfew," Barris explains. "The little black pins are the places where our patrols have encountered hostile action in the past 48 hours alone. Street gangs, looters, assaults against civilians—you name it. Now you tell me: do you really want us to just pack up and get out of here?"

It's inarguable that vast areas within the city remain volatile, particularly on the north side where three days of rioting late last December caused almost as much damage as the earthquake itself. Several parts of the city are so unsafe that authorities can patrol them only from the air, forcing SLPD to use military helicopters— including secondhand Mi-24 gunships recently purchased from Russia—instead of police cruisers.

Yet many persons in the city believe that the continued presence of federal troops in St. Louis is only exacerbating the crisis. "Look at what we've been through already," says LeRoy Jensen, a Ferguson community activist who made an unsuccessful run for the city council two years ago. "People up here lost their homes, their jobs, some

of them their families . . . now they can't even leave the
house without being challenged by some ERA soldier.
Everyone who lives around here is automatically assumed
to be a criminal, even if it's just a mother stepping out to
find her kids after dark. How can we go back to normal
when we're living in a combat zone?"

Jensen points out that when $2 billion in federal disaster
relief funds were made available through ERA to Missouri
residents after New Madrid, very little of the money found
its way to poor and lower-middle-class residents. Like
many people, he charges that most of the cash went to
rebuilding upper-class neighborhoods and large companies that didn't really need federal assistance in the first
place.

"The government based the acceptance of loan applica-
tions on the ability of people to repay the loans," Jensen
says, "but how can you repay a federal loan if the store
you worked at is gone? Yet if the government won't help
to rebuild that store, then you can't repay the loan. It's
a catch-22 . . . but if you get mad about it, then along
comes a dude in a uniform, telling you to be quiet and
eat your rations. And when the food runs out, like it
did last Christmas, then they send in the helicopters and
soldiers again."

Jensen also claims that ERA crackdowns on north-
central neighborhoods in the city are based on social and
ethnic attitudes among ERA troopers. "When was the last
time you heard of a white kid in Ladue or Clayton getting
busted by the goons?" he says. "Answer: you never do.
But all these ERA troops, they're rich white kids who
got out of being drafted to Nicaragua by getting Daddy
Warbucks to get 'em into ERA, so now they're trying to
make up for being wusses by kicking some nigger ass in
north St. Louis."

As heated as Jensen's remarks are, they have some justification. The Emergency Relief Agency was established
in 2006 as part of the National Service Act, which also
reestablished the Civilian Conservation Corps and started
the Urban Education Project. Under NSA, all Americans

between the ages of 18 and 22 are required to serve 18 months in one of several federal agencies, including the armed services. At the same time, ERA was founded to replace the Federal Emergency Management Agency after FEMA came under fire for perceived mismanagement of natural disaster relief during the 1990's.

After national service became an obligation for all young American men and women, CCC was the most popular of the available agencies. Soon there was a four-year waiting list for applicants to this most benign of organizations, with UEP being seen as an only slightly less benign way to spend a year and a half. Widely regarded as a hardship post, ERA was the least popular of federal agencies.

This changed when the United States went to war in Central America. As casualties began to mount among American servicemen in Nicaragua, many young men and women sought to duck military conscription by signing up for the ERA. Can't get into the CCC? Not qualified to be a UEP teacher? Want to be a badass, but you don't want to risk getting your ass shot off by a Sandinista guerrilla? Then ERA's for you.

Congressional critics have charged that the agency has become a pool for young rich punks with an attitude. Indeed, the number of encounters between ERA patrols and local citizens in St. Louis that have resulted in civilian casualties tends to suggest that ERA soldiers have adopted a "shoot first, ask questions later" stance toward what ERA training manuals term as "the indigenous population"—that is, whoever lives in the curfew zones.

"Look at this place," says Ralph, a young ERA corporal who has been assigned to curfew duty in Jennings. He stands on the corner of Florissant and Goodfellow, surrounded by burned-out buildings, an assault rifle cradled in his arms. "Every night the same thing happens again . . . the coons come after us and every night we gotta fight 'em off. I've lost all respect for these people. They don't want to help themselves . . . they just want more government handouts. Shit on 'em, man. They're not Americans."

Ralph is originally from Orange County, California, where he was the assistant manager of a fast-food franchise before he joined ERA as a way of avoiding military draft. He spits on the ground and shakes his head. "Maybe I shouldn't be prejudiced and call them coons," he admits, "but that's the way it is. If I knew it was going to be like this, I'd sooner be down in Nicaragua instead, shooting greasers and greasing shooters."

This callous attitude seems endemic among ERA troopers who are still in St. Louis, but city council member Steve Estes claims that the continued ERA presence in St. Louis is justified. "Most of my constituents want law and order on the streets, period," he says. "As far as I'm concerned, ERA has a moral obligation to be here, and I'm behind them all the way."

Estes, who is seen by several political insiders as contemplating a run for the mayor's office, also wants to close down the tent city that was established in Forest Park to house the people left homeless by the quake. "The place has become a sanctuary for freeloaders," he says. "If these people really want jobs and other places to live, then they could get them. Right now, though, it's become another Woodstock, and I support any efforts to rid the park of these bums."

Barris claims that all civilian casualties that have occurred during incidents involving his men and local residents have always been the fault of the civilians. "These guys are out there on their own, outnumbered a hundred to one," he says. "When you're cornered by a street gang and they're throwing bricks and bottles or whatever they can get their hands on, your options tend to run out in a hurry, believe me."

Jensen disagrees. "We see them as an occupational force. They want us dead or gone, period, so they can chase all the poor people out and build some more shopping centers. But we live here . . . this neighborhood may be burned out, but it's still the place where we grew up."

He stops talking to look around at the tenement buildings surrounding him. An ERA gunship flies low over the block where he lives. "We don't want no trouble," he says after it passes by. "We don't want to go on living like this. I understand each bullet that thing carries costs the taxpayer five dollars. They want to make things better? Fine. Gimme five bucks for each shell casing some kid brings to me from the street . . . we'll turn this side of town around."

PART ONE

Ruby Fulcrum

(April 17, 2013)

1

There was a man on the stage of the Muny Opera, but what he was singing wasn't the overture of *Meet Me in St. Louis*. In fact, if he was singing at all, it was a demented a capella called the New Madrid Blues.

My guess was that at one time he had been a young, mid-level businessman of some sort. Perhaps a lawyer. Possibly a combination of the two: a junior partner in the prestigious firm of Schmuck, Schmuck, Schmuck & Putz, specializing in corporate law. A yuppie of the highest degree, he had been a graduate of Washington University, graduating somewhere in the middle of his law school class: good enough to get an entry-level job with Schmucks and Putz, but not well enough compensated to have a place in Clayton or Ladue. So he had lived in a cracker box somewhere in the south side and commuted to work every day in the eight-year-old Volvo he had driven since his sophomore days at Wash You. Five days a week, he had battled traffic on the inner belt, dreaming of the day when he would have a Jaguar in the garage of a suburban spread in Huntleigh and his law firm would now be known as Schmuck, Schmuck, Schmuck, Putz & Dork, as he steeled himself for another grueling day of ladder climbing and telephone screaming.

And then the shit hit the fan last May and the bottom fell out of hostile takeovers of candy stores. His apartment house had fallen flat, burying his car beneath a hundred tons of broken cinderblock and not-quite-to-code drywall plaster, and the week after he moved into Squat City, where he had

21

been forced to share a tent with strange ethnic persons who didn't wear fraternity rings and to survive on watered-down chicken soup and cheesefood sandwiches, he discovered that the Schmuck Brothers had decided to let some of their attorneys go. Sorry about that, we'll let you know when there's an opening . . .

And his mind had snapped.

So now here he was, standing on the stage of the Muny, waving a black baseball bat over his head and raving like a crack fiend who hadn't had a decent fix in days.

"When selecting a baseball bat," he shouted, "there are five things to remember . . . !"

His ragged, oil-splotched London Fog trenchcoat could have been looted from Brooks Brothers. That wasn't what tipped me off; it was his shoes. Handmade Italian leather loafers which, even though they now were being held together with frayed strips of yellow duct tape, fit him perfectly. And although his hair had grown down over his shoulders and his gray-streaked beard was halfway to the collar of his mildewed dress shirt, he still had the unmistakable articulation of an attorney, although I doubt the senior partners of his firm would have recognized him now.

"One! The size of the bat should be the right size for your hands to grip and hold comfortably!" He demonstrated by gripping the taped handle of the black mahogany bat between his fists, his anger causing the knuckles to turn white. "That means it's gotta be the right size for you to do some serious damage to some fucker's face!"

Scattered applause from the first few rows behind the orchestra pit. Give us your poor, your downtrodden, your teeming masses yearning to be free . . . and if they can't have freedom, then there's always cheap entertainment. Farther back in the open-air amphitheater, though, only a few people seemed to be paying attention. At least a thousand people were crammed together into the Muny tonight, enduring the cold rain as they watched the nightly parade of homeless, half-mad speakers march onto the stage. On the proverbial one-to-ten scale, the former lawyer barely rated a four.

"Let's hear some music!" This from a woman in back of the seating area. A small group of down-and-out rock musicians stood in the wings, waiting for their chance to set up their equipment and play for any food stamps that might be tossed into their hat.

The lawyer either didn't hear her or wasn't paying attention. "Two!" he yelled, his voice beginning to crack. "The bat should be light enough so that you can swing it with the greatest speed!" He whipped the bat around like Ozzie Smith driving a grounder in Busch Stadium twenty years ago. "This means, y'gotta have the right instrument in order to knock their brains right outta their fuckin' skulls!"

A few yells of approval, this time even from the rear seats. He had their attention now; nothing gets people going like a little unfocused hatred. The bat looked a little familiar, though. I edged closer to the railing surrounding the orchestra pit and peered through the drizzle. There were white-painted autographs burned into the black surface of the bat.

Oh, God, this was a sacrilege. This sick puppy had managed to get his mitts on one of the team bats that that had been on display in the Cardinals Hall of Fame. Probably stolen shortly after the quake, when Busch Stadium had been overrun by the newly homeless, before the Emergency Relief Agency had chased out the looters and set up their base of operations inside the stadium. By then, everything worth stealing from the display cases in the mini-museum was gone. I prayed that he hadn't gotten his hands on a pennant-year bat; that would have been the worst insult of all. A bat with Stan Musial's or Lou Brock's signature inscribed upon it, now in the hands of some crazy with a grudge.

"Three!" he howled. "The bat should be long enough to reach across home plate and the strike zone as you stand in a correct position inside the batter's box!"

"Get off the stage!" someone yelled from the seats.

The demented yup ignored him. "Remember, a longer bat is harder to swing, regardless of how much it weighs!" He hefted the bat menacingly. "That means you gotta get in good and close, so you can count his teeth before you bust 'em out of his goddamn lyin' mouth . . ."

Now that I knew where the bat had come from, I made the proper association. He was reciting, with significant annotation, a list of batting recommendations that had been posted in the Hall of Fame museum next to a cutaway of a Louisville Slugger. The instructions were meant to advise Little Leaguers and other potential Cardinals champs of the future; now they were being howled by a psycho who would have given Hannibal Lector the chills. An innocent set of guidelines, reborn as directions for up-close-and-personal homicide.

(And with that memory, another one: Jamie sitting next to me on the MetroLink a couple of weeks before New Madrid. Saturday afternoon. We were on our way back from the stadium after watching the Cards stomp the gizzards out of the St. Petersburg Giants.

("Pop?"

("Yeah, kiddo?"

("Can I play Little League next year?"

("I dunno . . . we'll see.")

"Four! If you plan to buy a bat and you normally wear batting gloves—"

"Get outta here! Yer not funny!"

The memory of a quiet Saturday afternoon with Jamie evaporated as suddenly as it had materialized. I couldn't have agreed more: it was not funny, if it had ever been funny in the first place.

I had come to the Muny in hopes of finding something worth reporting for the *Big Muddy Inquirer.* I was facing a Friday deadline and Pearl was breathing down my neck for my weekly column. Because I had heard that the squatters had recently broken the padlocks on the Muny's gates and turned the amphitheater into an unauthorized public forum, I had come to Forest Park to see if I could hear any revolutionary manifestos. I was sure that there were some budding Karl Marxes or Mao Tse-tungs out there, screaming for their chance to be let out of the box . . . or just screaming, period.

So far, though, the only interesting speaker had been the psychotic Cards fan, and things were tough enough already without my repeating his advice for using a stolen baseball bat as a murder weapon. I turned and began to make my way up the concrete steps of the left-center aisle, feeling the rain pattering on the bill of my cap as I emerged from beneath the stage awning.

Huddled all around me were the new residents of Forest Park: people who had been left homeless by the New Madrid quake, either because their houses and apartments had collapsed during the quake or, as in the case of the north side communities, because last December's food riots had caused so many of the surviving buildings to be burned to the ground.

Forest Park was the largest municipal park in the country. Before the events of last May it had been a pleasant place in which to spend a quiet Sunday afternoon. The World's Fair had once been held here and so had the Olympic games, both more than a century ago. Now that the park had become a little bit of Third World culture stuck in middle America, the Muny was the only bit of free entertainment left available to the city's vast homeless population. Tommy Tune no longer danced across the stage, Ella Fitzgerald was long gone, and the national touring companies of *Cats* or *Grand Hotel* no longer performed here, but people still found their pleasure here . . . such as it was.

I looked around as I walked up the steps, studying the dismal crowd. Men, women, and children; young and old, alone and with families, white, black, hispanic, oriental. No common denominator except that they were all clinging to the lowest rung of the ladder. They wore cheap ponchos and cast-off denim jackets and moth-eaten cloth coats donated by the Salvation Army; some didn't even have raingear to speak of, just plastic garbage sacks and soaked cardboard boxes. In the weak, jaundiced light cast by the few sodium-vapor lamps that still functioned, their faces reflected hardship, pain, hunger . . .

And anger.

Most of all, anger: the dull, half-realized, hopeless rage of those who were pissed upon yesterday, were pissed upon today, and undoubtedly would be left standing beneath the urinal tomorrow. Halfway up the aisle, I was jostled aside by a burly man making his way down the steps; I stumbled against a chair and almost fell into the lap of a young woman who was holding a child in her arms. The little boy was chewing on a piece of government-issue cheesefood; his eyes looked glazed beneath the hood of his undersize sweatshirt, and the long tendril of mucus hanging from his nose told me that he was ill. If he was lucky, perhaps it was only the flu, although that could quickly escalate into pneumonia. His mother glared at me with silent, implacable rage—*What are you looking at?*— and I quickly stepped away.

No one here wanted pity. No one wanted the few government handouts that were still being given to them. All they wanted was survival and a chance to get the hell out of Squat City.

The mad yuppie was through with his screed by the time I reached the covered terrace at the top of the stairs. The terrace was at the rear of the amphitheater, and it was crowded with people trying to get out of the drizzle. Through the stone arches and past the wrought-iron gates, I could see the glow of dozens of trash-barrel fires in the adjacent parking lot, silhouetting the people who huddled around them for warmth against the cold spring rain, watchful for the apes . . .

Yes, apes. Real apes, not metaphorical in any sense whatsoever, although a case could be made for the ERA troopers who patrolled the park. One of the unforeseen side effects of the quake was that the Forest Park Zoo had practically split open at the seams, allowing lions, tigers, and bears—not to mention a few giraffes, antelopes, rhinos, and elephants—to escape. Most of the animals were recaptured by zoo personnel within the first few days after New Madrid, although quite a few wild birds had taken wing, and a handful of coyotes and bobcats had been wily enough get out of the inner city and into the county's wooded west side. Some of the zoo specimens, unfortunately, didn't make it back to their cages; two weeks after the quake, a rare Tibetan white leopard was shot by a redneck National Guardsman after it was cornered foraging through garbage cans in the University City neighborhood. When zoo officials arrived at the scene, they found the leopard's decapitated carcass lying in the alley; the weekend warrior who had shot the leopard had carved its head off and taken it back to his place in Fenton as a trophy.

But the apes that had survived the collapse of the monkey house had done much better. Only a handful of apes had been recaptured, mostly gorillas and orangutans; most of the chimpanzees and baboons had taken to the trees and had survived the short, relatively mild winter that followed the earthquake summer. Indeed, they had been fruitful and multiplied, adding to their numbers as the months wore on. Now monkey packs roamed the park like street gangs, raiding tents and terrorizing squatters.

Even the ERA troopers were frightened of them; there had been one rumored account that a chimpanzee pack had fallen upon a parked Hummer and chased its crew into the woods. If the story was true, then good for the chimps; I had more sympathy for runamok apes than for runamok goon squads.

There was no sign of apes, either human or simian, so I found a vacant spot beside one of the Doric columns holding up the awning. After looking around to make sure I wasn't being observed, I unzipped my leather bomber jacket and reached into the liner pocket to pull out my PT's earphone.

"Joker, can you hear me?" I said, switching on the PT and holding the earphone against my ear.

"*I hear you, Gerry.*" Joker's voice was an androgynous murmur in my ear: HAL-9000 with a flat midwestern accent. It was picking up my voice from a small mike clipped to the underside of my jacket collar.

"Good deal," I replied. "Okay, open a file, slug it . . . um, 'park,' suffix numeral one . . . and get ready for dictation."

I usually typed my notes one-handed on Joker's miniature keyboard. Like many writers, I intuitively prefer to see my words on a screen, but there was no way I was going to fish out my palmtop and open it up in plain view, thereby revealing myself to be a reporter. During the December riots, too many of my colleagues had been attacked by rioters who had seen them as being authority figures, and a *Post-Dispatch* photographer had been killed by crossfire during the torching of the federal armory in Pine Lawn. Even if some of these people didn't necessarily see the press as their enemy, there was always the chance someone might try to mug me in order to grab Joker. A stolen PT was probably worth a few cans of tuna on the black market.

But somebody in the crowd knew there was a reporter among them.

"Gerry?"

"Yes, Joker?"

"There's an IM for you. I would have signaled you earlier, but you told me not to call you."

Indeed I had; Joker's annunciator would have tipped off anyone nearby that I was carrying a PT. *"This is a little strange. Although the IM was sent directly to me, it's addressed to John Tiernan. I was not informed that we would be taking John's messages."*

I frowned as I heard this. John was another reporter for the *Big Muddy Inquirer*. Although he was my best friend, we normally stayed out of each other's work. Someone trying to send an instant message to John should have reached his own PT, Dingbat, not Joker; nor could we access each other's palmtops without entering special passwords.

But there was no sense in asking Joker if it was mistaken; my little Toshiba didn't make errors like that. "Okay, Joker," I said, "read it to me."

"IM received 6:12 P.M. as follows," Joker recited. *" 'I got your message. Need to talk at once. Please meet me near the rear entrance of the Muny at eight o'clock.' End of message. The sender did not leave a logon or a number."*

I felt a cold chill when I heard this message. I believe in coincidence as much as the next superstitious person, but this was a bit too much.

An IM intended for John had been sent to me instead, requesting a meeting at the Muny . . . and, as synchronicity would have it, where would I happen to be when I received it? At the Muny.

I took a deep breath. "Okay, Joker," I said, "what's the gag?"

"What gag, Gerry?"

"C'mon. Who really sent the message? Was it John?" I grinned. "Or was it Jah?"

"Negative. The message did not originate from either of those individuals. The person sending the IM did not leave a logon or a return number, but I can assure you that it was not received from any PT with which I regularly interface."

This was flat-out impossible. E-mail could not be sent anonymously; Joker's modem always logged the originating modem number. Joker must have contracted a virus of some sort. "Please run a self-diagnostic test," I said.

"Running test." There was a long pause while Joker's disk doctor pushed, prodded, asked embarrassing questions, and slipped a rectal thermometer up its cybernetic asshole. *"Test complete,"* Joker said at last. *"All sectors are clean. There is no evidence of tampering with my architecture."*

"I don't understand."

"Neither do I, Gerry. Nonetheless, I do not have a return number for this IM."

I mulled it over for a second, then Joker spoke up again. *"I have opened a file, slugged 'park,' suffix numeral one. Are you ready to dictate, Gerry?"*

I shook my head, watching rain running down from the slate roof onto the awning. Squatters wandered back and forth around me, ignoring the guy leaning against a column with a hand clasped to his ear, apparently talking to himself. Down on the stage, a neogrunge band had replaced the killer yuppie; discordant guitar riffs and high-pitched feedback threatened to overwhelm the stolen PA system they had set up behind them. Black-market vendors were circulating through the aisles, hustling everything from wet popcorn to expired pharmaceuticals. Off in the far distance, beyond the trees, were the lights of the city's central west end: clean, brilliant apartment towers, easily seen by thousands of people who were on prolonged camp-out in old U.S. Army tents, eating cold MREs by firelight and crapping in overflowing Port-O-Johnnies. Your tax dollars at work.

"No," I said. "Close and delete file. I'm going off-line now, okay?"

"I understand," Joker said. *"Signing off."*

So. The self-diagnostic check had come up clean, and the IM wasn't a prank. I pondered these mysteries while I wadded

up the earphone and tucked it back into my jacket pocket.
Why had a message obviously intended for John reached me
instead, even though I was in the right place at the right
time?

I had no recourse except to go to the meeting place. Walking
around the column, I bumped my way through the wet, hopeless
crowd, heading for the amphitheater's rear entrance gate.

That was how it all began.

2

People were still shuffling through the back entrance by the time I got there. According to the message Joker had received, I was ten minutes late for my appointment . . . or rather, for John's appointment. I hung around for a couple of minutes, leaning against the fence near the gate and watching people go by, and was about to chalk off the message as some sort of neural-net glitch when a short figure in a hooded rain jacket approached me.

"Are you Tiernan?" she asked softly.

I gave myself a moment to size her up: a middle-aged black woman, her face only half seen beneath the soaked plastic hood, her hands hidden in the pockets of her jacket. She could have been anyone in the crowd except that her raingear looked a little too new and well made to be government issue. Whoever she was, she wasn't a squatter.

"No," I said. She murmured an apology and started to turn away. "But I'm a friend of his," I quickly added. "I work for the same paper. *Big Muddy Inquirer.*"

She stopped, looked me over, then turned back around. "What's your name?" she asked, still speaking in a low voice.

"Gerry Rosen." She gazed silently at me, waiting for me to continue. "I got an IM on my PT to meet someone here," I went on. "I mean, it was intended for John, but—"

"Why isn't John here?" she demanded. "C'mon, let me see some ID."

"Sure, if you insist." I shrugged, unzipped my jacket, and started to reach inside.

31

"Hold it right there," she snapped as her right hand darted out of her rain jacket. I felt something press against my ribs. I froze and looked down to see a tiny stun gun, shaped like a pistol except with two short metal prongs where the barrel should be, nestled against my chest. Her index finger was curled around the trigger button; I hoped she didn't twitch easily.

"Whoa, hey," I said. "Easy with the zapper, lady."

She said nothing, only waited for me to make the wrong move. I wasn't eager to get my nervous system racked by 65,000 volts, so I held my breath and very carefully felt around my shirt pocket until I located my press ID.

I gradually pulled out the laminated card and held it up for her to see. She looked carefully at the card, her eyes darting back and forth between the holo and my face, until she nodded her head slightly. The stun gun moved away from my chest and returned to the pocket of her jacket.

"You ought to be careful with that thing," I said. "They're kinda dangerous when it's raining like this. Conductivity and all that—"

"Okay, you're another reporter for the *Big Muddy*," she said, ignoring my sage advice. "Now tell me why you're here and not Tiernan."

"That's a good question," I replied, "but let's hear your side of it first. How come you tried to IM something to John but got me instead?"

She blinked a few times, not quite comprehending. "Sorry? I don't understand what you're—"

"Look," I said, letting out my breath, "let's try to get things straight. My PT told me about ten minutes ago that I had a message. It was addressed to John but somehow got sent to me instead, and it told me . . . or him, whatever . . . to meet somebody right here at eight o'clock. Now, since you're obviously that somebody—"

"Hey, wait a minute," she interrupted. "You got this message just ten minutes ago?"

"Yeah, just about that—"

"*Ten minutes* ago?" she insisted.

I was beginning to get fed up with this. "Ten, maybe fifteen minutes. Who's counting? The point is—"

A couple of teenagers, ripped to the tits on something they had bought off the street, staggered through the gate and jostled me aside. I nearly fell against the woman; she stepped out of my way, then grabbed my jacket and pushed me behind a column.

"The point is, Mr. Rosen," she said quietly, staring me straight in the eye, "I didn't send any IMs today, but I received e-mail from John Tiernan this afternoon, telling me to meet him here at eight. Now I'm here, but I instead find you. Now you tell me: where's your buddy?"

The conversation was getting nowhere very quickly. "Look," I said, taking off my cap for a moment to wipe soaked hair out of my eyes, "you're just going to have trust me on this, okay? John ain't here. If he was, I'd know it. And if you didn't send that IM to me—"

"If John didn't send e-mail to me . . ." Her voice trailed off, and in that instant I caught a glimpse of fear in her dark eyes.

No, not just fear: absolute horror, the blank, slack-jawed expression of someone who has just gazed over the edge of the abyss and seen monsters lurking in its depths.

"Oh my God," she whispered. "It's started . . ."

It was then that I heard the helicopters.

At first, there was nothing except the background rumble of the crowd in the amphitheater below us, mixing with the subtle hiss of the rain and the not-so-subtle screech of electric guitars from the stage . . . and then there came a low droning from the dark sky above us, quickly rising in volume, and I looked up just in time to see the first chopper as it came in.

The helicopter was an MH-6 Night Hawk, a fast-moving little gunship designed for hit-and-run night missions over the Mediterranean. Something of an antique, really, but still good enough for ass-kicking in the U.S.A.; with its silenced engine and rotors, it wasn't noticed by anyone in the Muny until it was right over the amphitheater, coming in low over the walls like a bat.

I caught a fleeting glimpse of the two men seated within its bubble canopy, the letters ERA stenciled across its matte black fuselage; then light flashed from its outrigger nacelles as two slender canisters were launched over the crowd toward the stage. The rock band dropped their instruments and pretended to be paint as the RPGs smashed through the heavy wood backdrops behind them, breaking open to spew dense pale smoke across the platform.

The Night Hawk banked sharply to the right, its slender tail fishtailing around as the chopper braked to hover above the amphitheater, its prop wash forcing the milky white fog off the stage and across the orchestra pit into the front rows. I caught the unmistakable pepper scent of tear gas, but many of the squatters, thinking they were only smoke bombs, didn't flee immediately, even when the first few who had been caught by the gas began to choke and gag.

That's the mistake everyone makes about tear gas; its innocuous name makes it sound like something that will only make you a little weepy. Few people are aware of the painful blindness it causes when the hellish stuff gets in your eyes, how much you choke when you inhale it. Then, it's pure evil.

The fog was billowing toward us even as the squatters, now realizing the danger, began to stampede toward the rear entrance. People all around us clawed at one another, trying to get out of the amphitheater, as they were caught in the throes of gas-attack panic.

"Get out of here!" I grabbed the woman's hand and dragged her toward the gate. "Move it! Move it!"

We shoved and hauled our way through the mob until we managed to squeeze through the jammed gate. Still clutching her hand, I turned to make a getaway through the parking lot, only to find that we were far from being out of danger.

There was more rotor noise from above, much louder than the MH-6, as gale-force winds abruptly whipped through the parking lot, tearing at the tents and plastic tarps, sending garbage flying in every direction, overturning stolen shopping carts, causing the flames of the trash-can fires to dance crazily. I skidded to a stop and looked up to see a giant shape descending upon us, red and blue lights flashing against the darkness, searchlights lancing through the rain like a UFO coming in for a touchdown.

Flying saucer, no; V-22 Osprey, yes. The big, twin-prop VTOL was landing right outside the Muny, and if that was Elvis I spotted through one of its oval portholes, wearing riot gear and slapping a magazine into his Hecker & Koch assault rifle, then the King and I needed to have a serious discussion about his new career.

It was a full-blown ERA raid, and I felt like an idiot for not having seen it coming. Members of the city council had been squawking lately about "taking Forest Park back from the squatters," and never mind that it had been their idea in the first place to relocate nearly seventy-five thousand homeless people to a tent city in the park. A crackdown had been threatened for several weeks now, and squatters trespassing on the Muny had been the last straw. Steve Estes, the council member whose political ambitions were only slightly outweighed by his ego, was making good on his rhetoric.

No time to ponder local politics now. More Ospreys were arriving. The first one was already on the ground, its rear door cranking down to let out a squad of ERA troopers. The air stank of tear gas; people were rushing around on either side of us, threatening to trample us as they fled from the soldiers. Already I could hear screams from the area closest to the landing site of the first Osprey and the hollow *ka-chunng!* of Mace canisters being fired into the mob.

Escape through the parking lot was out of the question; already I could hear the engine roar of LAV-25 Piranhas approaching from the roadway on the other side of the hill, their multiple tires mowing down the makeshift barricades squatters had thrown up around the Muny. In a few minutes we'd be nailed by tear gas, water cannons, webs, or rubber bullets.

A steep, wooded embankment lay to the right of the amphitheater. "That way!" I yelled to the woman. "Down the hill!"

"No!" she shouted, yanking her hand free from mine. "I gotta go somewhere!"

"You'll—"

"Shaddup! Listen to me!" She grabbed my shoulders and shouted in my face. "Tell Tiernan—"

Full-auto gunfire from behind us. More screams. I couldn't tell whether the troopers were firing live rounds, and I wasn't in the mood for sticking around to find out. The woman glanced over her shoulder, then her eyes snapped back to me again.

"Tell Tiernan to meet me at Clancy's on Geyer Street!" she yelled. "Tomorrow at eight! Tell him not to trust any other messages he gets! You got that?"

"Who are you?" I shouted back at her. "What the hell's going on?"

For the briefest moment she seemed uncertain, as if wanting to tell me everything in the middle of a full-scale riot and yet unable to trust her own instincts. Then she pulled me closer until her lips touched my ear.

"Ruby fulcrum," she whispered.

"Ruby *what*?"

"Ruby fulcrum!" she repeated, louder and more urgently now. "Tiernan will know what I mean. Remember, Clancy's at eight." She shoved me away. "Now get out of here!"

Then she was gone, turning around to dash into the panic-stricken mob, disappearing into the night as suddenly as she had appeared. I caught a final glimpse of the woman as her jacket hood fell back, exposing a few hints of gray in her short-cropped hair.

Then she was gone.

I ran in the opposite direction, battering my way through the crowd until I was out of the parking lot. I dashed across the sidewalk and down the embankment beside the high concrete walls of the Muny. Few people followed me; most of the squatters had stayed behind to wage futile battle against the ERA troopers, protecting what little they could still call home.

I slipped and skittered and fell down the muddy slope, blinded by smoke and darkness, deafened by the sound of helicopters, my face lashed by low tree branches as I tripped over fallen limbs. As I neared the bottom of the hill I heard the gurgle of a rain-swollen drainage ditch and veered away from it; I didn't need to get more wet than I already was.

I can barely recall how I escaped from the riot; my flight from the Muny comes to me only in snatches. Falling on my face several times. Grabbing my jacket pocket to make sure that I hadn't lost Joker, feeling vague reassurance when I felt its small mass. Jogging down Government Road around the lake, passing the old 1904 World's Fair Pavilion, slowing down to catch my breath and then, in the next instant, spotting the headlights of more armored cars approaching from the opposite direction and ducking off the road into the woods. Hearing monkeys howling in the treetops above me. Crashing through a tent village erected on the fairway of what used to be the municipal golf course, hearing babies screaming, having a clod of mud thrown at me by an old man . . .

Then I was in the woods again, climbing another steep slope on all fours, my breath coming in animal-like gasps as I clutched at roots and decaying leaves, all in an atavistic impulse to flee from danger.

Not the best night I've ever had at the opera. Lots of singing and dancing, but in terms of artistic merit the show kinda sucked.

The next thing I knew, I was halfway across the park, my breath coming in wet, ragged gasps as I lay against the base of the statue of Louis IX, the French monarch after whom the city had been named. His bronze skin dully reflected the light from the distant flames of the tent village that had once existed around the Muny.

From my lonely hilltop perch, I could see the searchlights of helicopters as they circled the amphitheater, hear the occasional echoing report of semiauto gunfire. Up here, though, all was supernaturally quiet and uncrowded, as if I was removed in time and space from the chaos that reigned not far away. The rain had finally ceased. Night birds and crickets made nocturnal harmony in the hilltop woods, undeterred by the paramilitary action not far away.

Somehow, in my mad rush for safety, I had made it to the summit of Art Hill, the highest point in Forest Park. Louis IX sat on his stallion above me, larger than life, his broadsword raised in defiance to the empty sky. The statue had been the symbol of the city long before the Arch had been erected; by miracle, he had not been toppled by the quake, and his eternal courage made me all the more ashamed of my own cowardice.

On the other hand, I had become accustomed to being a coward. It wasn't anything new to me. Call it an instinct for self-preservation; all us chickenshit types use that term. Just ask my wife. Or my son . . .

Turning my head to look behind me, my eyes found the half-collapsed stone edifice of the St. Louis Art Museum. Despite being reinforced during the nineties against quakes, the museum had suffered extensive damage. Now its doors were chained shut, its windows sealed with pine boards, its treasures long since moved to Chicago. Inscribed above the bas-relief classical portico, held aloft by five Corinthian columns, were seven words:

DEDICATED TO ART AND FREE TO ALL

"No shit," I mumbled. "Where do I sign up?"

I caught my breath, then I slowly rose to my feet and began to stagger across the driveway and down Art Hill, following the sidewalk toward the Forest Park Boulevard entrance on the north side of the park.

It was time to go home.

3

Tell me about freedom. I'm willing to listen. Hell, I'll listen to anything, so long as you'll pardon me if I nod off in the middle of the lecture.

Wet, cold, muddy, and confused, I began the long hike out of the park, following the sidewalk down the hill toward the Forest Park Boulevard entrance. Although a couple of Piranhas and Hummers passed me on the road, their crews were too busy to stop and harass a lone individual on foot. Nonetheless, I crossed the golf course at the bottom of Art Hill to avoid a roadblock at the Lindell Boulevard entrance; two Hummers were parked in front of the gate, and I didn't care to explain myself to the soldiers manning the barricade. Sure, I had my press card and I could point out that I was a working reporter on assignment, but these days that sort of argument would just as likely earn me a trip down to Busch Stadium, and not for a baseball game either. The ERA grunts didn't spot me, though, and I managed to leave the park unmolested.

Grabbing a ride on the MetroLink was another problem. After I trudged the rest of the way through the park, I passed through the main gate at Forest Park Boulevard. The MetroLink platform was at the bottom of a narrow railway trench a block away; it was almost completely vacant, but an ERA trooper was standing guard at the top of the stairs leading down to the tracks, a riot baton cradled in his arms.

I glanced at my watch. It was already a quarter to ten. No choice but to tough it out; I was in no shape to slog all the way back to my digs. Trying not to look like I had just

39

mud-wrestled a gorilla, I strode toward the turnstile, reaching into my pants pocket to fish out my fare card.

The trooper studied me as I walked under the light. I gave him a quick nod of my head and started to pass my card in front of the scanner when he took a step forward and barred my way with his stick.

"Excuse me, sir," he said, "but do you know what time it is?"

In the old days, I might have just looked at my watch, said "Yes," and walked on, but these guys were notorious for having no sense of humor. My mind flipped through a half-dozen preconcocted ploys, ranging from pretending to be drunk to simply acting stupid, and realized that none of them would adequately explain why I looked as disheveled as I did. Telling the truth was out of the question; the average ERA trooper had less respect for a reporter than he would for a suspected looter, and screw the First Amendment.

"Is it after nine already?" I feigned embarrassed surprise, then pulled back my sleeve and glanced at my watch. "Oh, shit, I'm sorry. I didn't realize it was so—"

"May I see some ID, please?" Below us, several people sitting on plastic benches beneath the platform awning watched with quiet curiosity. No doubt they had been forced to go through the same ordeal.

"Hmm? Sure, sure . . ." I pulled my wallet out of my back pocket, found my driver's license, and passed it to him. The trooper's nameplate read B. DOUGLAS; he passed my license under a handscanner, then flipped down a monocle from his helmet and waited for the computers at the city's records department to download my file.

It gave me a chance to size him up as well. What I saw was scary: a kid young enough to be my little brother—twenty-one at most—wearing khaki combat fatigues, leather lace-up boots, and riot helmet, with the sword-and-tornado insignia of the Emergency Relief Agency sewn on the left shoulder of his flak jacket. An assault rifle hung from a strap over his right shoulder, a full brace of Mace and tear gas canisters suspended from his belt. He had the hard-eyed, all-too-serious look of a young man who had been given too much authority much too soon, who believed that the artillery he carried gave him the right to kick butt whenever he wished. In another age he might have been a member of Hitler Youth looking for Jews to beat up or a Young Republican wandering a college campus in search of a liberal professor to harass. Now he was an ERA trooper, and by God this was *his* light-rail station.

"Are you aware that you're in a curfew zone, Mr. Rosen?" He pulled my driver's license out from under his scanner but didn't pass it back to me.

I pretended to be appalled. "I am? This is University City, isn't it? There isn't a curfew here."

He stared back at me. "No, sir, you're downtown now. Curfew starts here at nine o'clock sharp."

I shrugged off-handedly. "I'm sorry. I didn't realize that was the situation." I tried an apologetic smile. "I'll keep that in mind next time I'm down here."

"You look awful muddy, old-timer," he said condescendingly. "Fall down someplace?"

Old-timer, indeed. I was thirty-three and Lord of the Turnstiles knew it. If there were the first few gray streaks in my hair, it was because of what I had seen in the past eleven months. I wanted to tell him that I was old enough to remember when the Bill of Rights still meant something, but I kept my sarcasm in check. Li'l Himmler here was just looking for an excuse to place me under arrest for curfew violation. My police record was clean, and he didn't have anything on me, but my occupation was listed as "journalist." I could see it in his face: reporters for the *Big Muddy Inquirer* didn't get cut much slack on his beat.

"Sort of," I said noncommittally, careful to keep my voice even. B. Douglas didn't reply; he was waiting for elaboration. "I tried to jump over a storm drain a few blocks away," I added. "Didn't quite make it." I shrugged and managed to assay a dopey gee-shucks grin. "Accidents happen, y'know."

"Uh-huh." He continued to study me, his monocle glinting in the streetlight. "Where did you say you were?"

"U-City," I said. "Visiting some friends. We were having a little get-together and . . . y'know, kinda got sidetracked."

It was a good alibi. The U-City neighborhood was only a few blocks west of the station; that's where all us liberal types hung out, listening to old Pearl Jam CDs while smoking pot and fondly reminiscing about Bill Clinton. It fit. Maybe he'd pass me off as a stoned rock critic who had fallen in a ditch after going into conniptions upon seeing an American flag.

Off in the distance I could hear the first rumble of the approaching train, the last Red Liner to stop tonight at Forest Park Station. If Oberleutnant Douglas was going to find a good reason for busting me, it was now or never. After all, he would have to file a report later.

The kid knew it, too. He flipped my license between his fingertips, once, twice, then slowly extended to me as if he was granting a great favor. "Have a good evening, Mr. Rosen," he said stiffly. "Stay out of trouble."

I resisted the mighty impulse to salute and click my heels. "Thank you," I murmured. He nodded his helmeted head and stood aside. The train's headlights were flashing across the rails as I swept my fare card in front of the scanner, then pushed through the turnstile and trotted down the cement stairs to the platform.

The train braked in front of the station, bright sparks of electricity zapping from its overhead powerlines. A couple of my fellow riders looked askance at me as they stood up. One of them was an old black lady, wearing a soaked cloth coat, carrying a frayed plastic Dillards shopping bag stuffed with her belongings.

"What did he stop you for?" she asked as the train doors slid apart and we moved to step aboard.

I thought about it for a moment. "Because of the way I look," I replied.

It was an honest answer. She slowly nodded her head. "Same here," she murmured. "Now you know what it's like."

And then we found our seats and waited for the train to leave the station.

I rode the Red Line as it headed east into the city. Quite a few people got on or off the train at Central West End, most of them patients or visitors at Barnes Hospital, but my car only remained half-full. Most of the passengers were soaking wet. The train was filled with the sound of sneezing and coughing fits, making the train's computerized voice hard to hear as it announced each stop. The Red Line sounded like a rolling flu ward; despite the fact we had just stopped at a hospital, somehow all those free vaccinations we were supposed to receive courtesy of ERA seemed to have missed everyone on this train. On the other hand, this wasn't unusual; most of the people in the city had somehow missed receiving a lot of the federal aid that had been promised to us.

Through the windows, I could see dark vacant lots filled with dense rubble where buildings made of unreinforced brick and mortar had once stood; streets blocked by sawhorses because ancient sewer tunnels and long-extinct clay mines beneath them had caved in; shanties made of scraps of corrugated steel and broken plywood. Armored cars were the only vehicles on the streets, but here and there I spotted figures lurking in the doorways of condemned buildings. Night brought out the scavengers, the teenagers with tire-irons who prowled through destroyed warehouses and demolished storefronts in search of anything to be sold on the black market.

The train left the midtown combat zone and rumbled toward the downtown area. It stopped briefly beneath Union Station, but it passed Auditorium because the platform there no longer existed. Kiel Auditorium itself had survived, but where the old City Hall building and the city jail once stood were now vast lots filled with crumbled masonry, broken cinderblock, bent copper pipes, and shattered glass. Giant piles which had once been buildings, waiting to be hauled away.

By now the downtown skyscrapers were clearly visible, their windows shining with light; the Gateway Arch, seen above the spired dome of the old state courthouse, reflected the city lights like a nocturnal rainbow. For a minute or two there was no wreckage to be seen. It seemed as if the city had never suffered a quake, that all was sane and safe.

Then the train hurtled toward Busch Stadium, and the illusion was destroyed. Silence descended as everyone turned to gaze out the left-side windows at the stadium. Busch Stadium still stood erect; bright spotlights gleamed from within its bowl, and one could almost have sworn that a baseball game was in progress, but as the train slowed to pull into Stadium Station, the barbed-wire fences and rows of concrete barriers blocking the ground-level entrances told a different story.

A group of ERA soldiers were sitting on benches at the subsurface train platform; a couple of them glanced up as the train came to a halt, and everyone in the train quickly looked away. The doors opened, but no one got on, and nobody dared to get off. There was dead quiet within the train until the doors automatically closed once again. The train moved on, and not until it went into a tunnel and the station vanished from sight did everyone relax.

Busch Stadium wasn't a nice place to visit anymore. Oh, people still did at times, but seldom voluntarily. There were whispered rumors that people who went to the stadium often didn't come out again.

But, of course, that was only hearsay.

A few minutes later the train rolled into 8th and Pine, the underground hub station for the MetroLink. I got off here and took an escalator from the Red Line platform down to the Yellow Line platform. The station was cold, with a breeze that seeped through the plastic tarps covering a gaping hole in the ceiling where the roof had partially collapsed during the quake. A couple of ERA troopers lounged against a construction scaffold, smoking cigarettes as they watched everyone who passed by. I was careful to avoid making eye contact with them, but they were bored tonight, contenting themselves with ousting the occasional vagrant who tried to grab a few winks in one of the cement benches.

I managed to grab the Yellow Line train just before it left the station. It was the last southbound train to run tonight, and if I had missed it, I would have had to dodge downtown curfew patrols while I trudged home through the rain. At times like this I wished I still had my own car, but Marianne had taken the family wheels when we had separated. Along with the house, the savings account, and not an inconsiderable part of my dignity.

Not surprisingly, the train was almost vacant. Most of the South-side neighborhoods were under nine-to-six curfew, so anyone with any sense was already at home . . . if they still had a home, that is. Across the aisle, a teenage girl in a worn-out Screamin' Magpies tour jacket was slumped over in her seat, clutching her knees between her arms; she seemed to be talking to herself, but I couldn't hear what she was saying. At the front of the car a skinny black guy with a woolen rasta cap pulled down over his ears was dozing, his head against the front window, rocking back and forth in time with the movement of the train; every so often his eyes slitted open, scanned the train, then closed again. A bearded redneck sat reading a battered paperback thriller, his lips moving slightly as he studied the sentences. An emaciated old codger stared at me constantly until I looked away. A fat lady with a cheap silver crucifix around her neck and an eerie smile. Pretty much your standard bunch of late-night riders.

I had the seat to myself. The train came out of the tunnel; once again I could see the city. For an instant, though, as I stared out the rain-slicked windows at the lights passing by, I felt a presence next to me.

I didn't dare to look around, afraid to see what could not be reflected in the glass: a small boy, wearing a red nylon Cardinals jacket, dutifully marking up his scorecard while mustering the courage to ask me if he could enter a Little League season he would never live to see . . .

Can I play Little League next year?

Goddamn this train.

"Not now, Jamie," I whispered to the window. "Please, not right now. Daddy's tired."

The ghost vanished as if he had never been there in the first place, leaving me only with memories of the happy days before May 17, 2012.

Let's talk about Jericho again.

There had been plenty of advance warning that a major earthquake might one day rock the Midwest. Geologists had been warning everyone for years that the New Madrid fault was not a myth, that it was a loaded gun with its hammer cocked back, and their grim predictions were supported by history. In 1811, a superquake estimated at 8.2 on the then-nonexistent Richter scale had devastated the Mississippi River Valley, destroying pioneer settlements from Illinois to Kansas; legend told of the Mississippi River itself flowing backward during the quake, and simultaneous tremors were reported as far away as New York and Philadelphia while church bells rang in Charleston, South Carolina.

And there were other historical harbingers of disaster, major and minor quakes ranging between 5.0 and 6.2 on the Richter scale during the years between 1838 and 1976, all caused by a 130-mile seismic rift between Arkansas and Missouri, centered near the little Missouri town of New Madrid. Sometimes the quakes occurred away from the Missouri bootheel, such as the 1909 quake on the Wabash River between Illinois and Indiana, but most of the temblors happened in the region near the confluence of the Mississippi and Ohio rivers, and during even the most minor quakes chimneys crumbled, roofs collapsed, and people occasionally died.

Despite geologic and historical evidence that the city was living on borrowed time, though, most people in St. Louis managed to forget that they lived just north of a bull's-eye.

In August 1990 a New Mexico pseudoscientist named Iben Browning caused a panic by predicting that there was a fifty-fifty chance that a major earthquake would occur between the first and fifth days of December of that year. His prediction, based upon flimsy conjecture involving sunspots and lunar motion, was made during a speech to a group of St. Louis businessmen, and the sensation-hungry local media blared it to the public. By coincidence, Browning's prediction was followed in late September by a minor 4.6 quake epicentered near Cape Giradeau. The quake did little damage, but the general public, already unnerved by war in the Middle East and a shaky national economy, went apeshit.

During a three-month silly season, St. Louis prepared itself for imminent disaster, climaxing on a Wednesday when the city's public schools were shut down, its fire departments mobilized, and scores of citizens left town for vacation. When the prediction proved to be false—as was bound to

happen, since earthquake prediction ranks with Rhine card
ESP tests for unreliability—St. Louis ruefully laughed at itself
and promptly began to forget everything it had learned about
earthquake preparedness.

Iben Browning died a short time afterward without ever
having made public comment about his apocalyptic predictions. In doing so, he gave the city renewed overconfidence.
Earthquake drills were canceled as the 1990 scare settled into
the back of everyone's mind, and the people of St. Louis once
more settled into the safe, conservative mind-set that Nothing
Ever Changes In Our Town. Even the 1994 Los Angeles
earthquake did little to shake the city's complacent sense of
false security.

And so it went for the next two decades. Our local pundits
have often observed, sometimes with barely concealed pride,
that St. Louis consistently remains about five years behind the
times. Nonetheless, the city was dragged kicking and screaming
into the twenty-first century. New buildings were erected, old
ones were torn down, and the downtown skyline began to rival
Chicago for brightness. The city's building codes were revised
to imitate the earthquake-preparedness standards institutiona-
lized in California, but they didn't affect thousands of older
buildings or private residences. Electric cars replaced the old
gashogs on the highways as new federal laws phased out the use
of internal combustion engines in automobiles. A new light-rail
system was erected, effectively replacing the old bus lines. The
local aerospace industry gradually regeared itself from making
warplanes to building spacecraft components. Hemlines rose,
fell, and briefly became nonexistent with the short-lived
barebuns look of 2000, which contributed to yet another moral
revival that lasted until most women decided they really didn't
want to wear neck-to-toe chastity gowns in 100-degree summer
weather. Extrophy, smart drugs, isometrics, minimalistic education, and at least a half-dozen sociopolitical theories came
and went as fads. Two economic recessions were suffered and
were survived, the last one finally forcing the county and city
governments to merge after more than a century of squabbling;
their uneasy shotgun-marriage formed Metro St. Louis, the
seventh largest city in the United States.

And there were two or three minor quakes, the largest one being a 5.2 temblor in 2006 that enabled the city to save a few dollars from having to tear down some condemned buildings in the central west end. Nothing serious. But the gun was still cocked and one day in early summer, when no one was paying attention, the hammer finally came down.

That was the day my son was taken from me.

My reverie ended as the train lurched to a halt at another station. The doors slid open and the skinny black guy, the strange fat lady, and a few others stood up to shuffle off the train. No one got on; except for the old dude who continued to stare at me with doleful contempt, the strung-out teenager, and the guy who was reading, I was alone in the car.

As the train got moving again, the old codger rose from his seat and walked unsteadily down the aisle. "*The train is now in motion,*" a pleasant female voice said to him from the ceiling speakers, its metronomic cadence following him as he staggered from seatback to seatback. "*Please return to your seat immediately. Thank you.*"

He ignored the admonition until he found the seat next to mine and lowered himself into it. He watched me for another moment, then leaned across the aisle, bracing his chapped hands on the edge of my seat.

"Repent your sins," he hissed at me. "Jesus is coming."

I stared back at him. "I know," I said very softly, "because I *am* Jesus."

Okay, so maybe it was a little blasphemous. I was worn out and pissed off. But I'm Jewish and Jesus was Jewish, and that made us closer kin than with some crazy old dink with a grudge against anyone who didn't share his hateful beliefs. At any rate, it worked; his eyes widened and his chin trembled with inchoate rage, then he glared at me and, without another word, got up and made his way to the front of the train, putting as much distance between us as possible.

Good riddance. "Go forth, be fruitful and multiply," I added, but I don't think he got that old Woody Allen joke. Alone again,

I recalled my conversation with the nameless black woman at the Muny.

I was supposed to tell John to meet her at eight o'clock tomorrow night at Clancy's; that would be Clancy's Bar and Grill, a bar just down the street from the paper's offices. Since she didn't bother to tell me her name, she must already be known to John . . . but certainly not by sight, considering how she had mistaken me for my colleague.

Therefore, how was John to recognize her? Not only that, but why didn't she simply call him herself, instead of relying on a near-total stranger to pass the word?

Tell him not to trust any other messages he gets, she had said. I had to assume she meant IMs or e-mail through his PT.

I recalled the terrified look in her eyes when she discovered that the message *she* had received had been bogus, and what she had said.

Oh my God, it's started . . .

What had started?

There was only one clue, those two words she had whispered to me before she fled from the ERA troopers. "Ruby fulcrum," I repeated aloud. It sounded like a code phrase, although for all I knew it could be the name of a laundry detergent or a cocktail-hour drink. New, improved Ruby Fulcrum, with hexachloride. Yeah, bartender, I'll take a ruby fulcrum with a twist of lemon. Make it a double, it's been a bitch of a night . . .

I pulled Joker out of my inside pocket and opened it on my knee, exposing its card-size screen and miniature keypad. After switching to video mode, I typed, **Logon data search, please.**

Certainly, Gerry, Joker responded. **What are you looking for?**

314 search mode: ruby fulcrum, I typed.

An hourglass appeared briefly on the screen; after a few moments it was replaced by a tiny pixelized image of the Joker from the Batman comic books cavorting across the screen, maniacally hurling gas bombs in either direction. I smiled when I saw that. Bailey's son, Craig—who was now going through a Rastafarian phase and insisted that we call him Jah instead—had recently swiped my PT while I was out to lunch and had reprogrammed it to display this screensaver during downtime. For a while, the gag had gone even further; Joker had spoken to me in a voice resembling Jack Nicholson's until I had forced Jah to ditch the audio gimmick, although I allowed him to leave Batman's arch-nemesis intact. It could have been worse; Jah had done the same to Tiernan's PT, and Dingbat had spoken like Lucille Ball until John had threatened to wring his neck.

After a while the Joker began turning cartwheels for my amusement. Behind the scenes, though, I knew that there was some serious business going on. "314 search mode" meant just that; Joker was accessing every public database available within the 314 area code, searching for any references to the phrase "ruby fulcrum." The job was enormous; I was mildly surprised when the timer passed the thirty second mark.

I was just glad that Joker hadn't been damaged during the events of the evening. If I had broken the little Toshiba, Pearl would have eviscerated my liver and deep-fried it, with onion rings on the side. Joker was far more than a semiretarded palmtop word processor; its neural-net architecture enabled it to answer questions posed to it in plain English, and its cellular modem potentially allowed it to access global nets if I cared to pay some hefty long-distance bills.

The train began to slow down again as it prepared to come into my station. The Clown Prince of Crime abruptly vanished from the screen and Joker came back on-line.

No reference to the phrase "ruby fulcrum" has been located. Do you wish me to continue the search?

Rats. It had been a long shot, but I had been hopeful that Joker could turn up something. The train's brakes were beginning to squeal; glancing through the windows, I could see the streetlights of I-55 coming into view. My stop was approaching.

No thanks, I typed. Discontinue search. **Logging off now. Logoff. Good night, Gerry.**

I switched off the PT, folded its cover, and slipped it back into my jacket as Busch Station rolled into sight. It had been a long night, and I was ready to go back to what now amounted to home. I stood up and made my way toward the front of the car, ignoring the train's admonitions to take my seat until it had come to a full stop.

"Repent, sinner," the old man hissed at me as I walked past him toward the open door. I was too exhausted to make another smart-ass reply.

Besides, if I had any sins to repent, it would be those against the ghost of a small boy who still rode these narrow-gauge rails.

4

Despite the late hour, my regular ride home was waiting for me at the station. Tricycle Man sat astride his three-wheeled rickshaw at the cab stand beneath the platform, reading the latest issue of the *Big Muddy Inquirer*. He barely looked up as I climbed into the backseat.

"Did you see this one?" he asked.

"Which one?" I didn't have to ask what he meant; it was the same question each Wednesday when the new issue came out. There was only one section of the paper to which he seemed to pay any attention.

" 'SWF,' " he read aloud. " 'Mid-twenties, five feet eight, blonde hair, blue eyes, good natured, looking for SWM for dancing, VR, poetry readings, and weekends in the Ozarks. Nonsmoker, age not important. No druggies, rednecks, or government types. . . . ' " He shrugged. "Guess I qualify, so long as I don't mention my Secret Service background."

Tricycle man was a trip: a fifty-five-year-old hippie, right down to the long red beard, vegetarian diet, and vintage Grateful Dead stickers on the back of his cab, whose only real interests in life seemed to be sleeping with a different woman each week and telling grandiose lies about himself. At various times he claimed to be a former Secret Service agent, an ex-NASA astronaut, an Olympic bronze medalist, or a descendant of Charles A. Lindbergh. I didn't know his real name, although I had been riding in the back of his homemade rickshaw ever since I had moved downtown eight months ago. Nor did anyone else; everyone in Soulard simply called him Tricycle Man.

I searched my memory, trying to recall all the women I had spotted visiting the personals desk in the last week. "Yeah," I said, "I saw someone like that." Trike's face lit up until I added, "I think she had an Adam's apple."

His face darkened again. "Damn. Should have figured." He folded up the paper and tossed it on the passenger seat next to me, then pulled up the hood of his bright red poncho. "Going to the office or do y'wanna head home?"

I shrugged. "Home, I guess." It didn't make any difference; they were one and the same, and Trike knew it. He laughed, then stood up on the pedals and put his massive legs to work, slowly hauling the rickshaw out from under the platform and onto rain-slicked Arsenal Street, heading northeast into Soulard.

As we crossed the I-55 overpass, an ERA Apache growled low overhead, following the traffic on the interstate's westbound lanes. Another helicopter. My city had been invaded by space aliens, and they rode helicopters instead of flying saucers. Trike glanced up at the chopper as it went by. "Heard there was some kinda riot in the park tonight," he said. "Lot of people got their heads busted. Know anything about it?"

"A little," I said. "Enough to know it's true." It didn't surprise me that Trike had heard about the ERA raid at the Muny; word travels fast on the street, especially where the feds were concerned, but I wasn't about to contribute to the scuttlebutt. Besides, everything I had to say about the Muny riot would be in my column in next week's issue, and a good reporter doesn't discuss his work in progress.

Trike glanced over his shoulder at me. "Not talking much tonight, are you?"

"Too tired." I settled back against the seat, letting the cold drizzle patter off the bill of my cap. "All I want right now is a cold beer and a hot shower."

"Okey-doke." He turned left onto 13th Street. "I'll have you home in ten minutes."

We passed by the front of the Anheuser-Busch brewery, a compound of giant factory buildings which, like almost everything else in the city these days, were surrounded by scaffolds. Even at this time of night there was a long line of men and women huddled on the brick sidewalk outside the entrance gate, braving the weather and the curfew for a chance to be interviewed tomorrow morning for a handful of job openings. The brewery had reopened just four weeks ago, following a long effort to rebuild after the extensive damage it had suffered during New Madrid. Through the wrought-iron fence, I could see one of the replacements for the gargoyles that had adorned the cornices of the main building before they toppled from their perches during the quake: a wizened little stone man with a beer stein in his hand, sitting in the parking lot as he waited for a crane to hoist him into place. His saucy grin was the only happy face to be seen; everyone else looked wet and miserable. This Bud's for you . . .

As he pedaled, Trike reached between his handlebars and switched on the radio. It was tuned to KMOX-AM, the local CBS affiliate. After the usual round of inane commercials for stuff no one could afford to buy, we got the news at the top of the hour.

U.S. Army troops continue to be airlifted to the northern California border, following the formal announcement last week by the state governments of Washington and Oregon that they are seceding from the United States. A spokesman for the newly established government of Cascadia, based in Seattle, says that former National Guard troops have sealed all major highways leading into Washington and Oregon. No hostile actions have yet been reported from either side, but White House press spokesperson Esther Boothroyd says that President Giorgio does not intend to recognize Cascadia's claim to independence.

Just past Anheuser-Busch, Tricycle Man paused at the three-way intersection of 13th, 12th, and Lynch. A half-block away on 12th Street was the Ninth Ward police station; across the street from the cop shop, in what used to be a parking lot, was SLPD's south end helicopter pad. A big Mi-24 HIND was idling on the flight line, getting ready for air patrol over the Dogtown neighborhoods in the southern part of city. Beneath the blue-and-white paint job and the familiar TO PROTECT AND TO SERVE slogan could still be seen, as ghostly palimpsests, the markings of the Russian Red Army. ERA got American-made helicopters and LAVs, while the local cops had to settle for secondhand Russian choppers and rusty old BMP-2s left over from Afghanistan, sans armaments and held together by baling wire and paper clips. A couple of officers hanging around outside the police station waved to Tricycle Man and he waved back; he was harmless and familiar, so the cops didn't bother him.

Countdown continues for tomorrow's launch of the space shuttle Endeavour, *set for lift-off at one P.M. Eastern time. Aboard the shuttle are the final components of the* Sentinel 1 *orbital missile defense system. Although antiwar protesters are holding a candlelight vigil outside the gates of Cape Canaveral, the demonstrations have been peaceful and no arrests have been made.*

Trike continued pedaling down 13th Street, entering the residential part of Soulard. It would have been quicker to use 12th Street, but too many houses on 12th had collapsed during the quake, and the street itself was full of recent sinkholes, many of them large enough to swallow his rickshaw whole. Even then, 13th was a scene of random destruction. Two-story row houses, some dating back to the late 1800's, stood erect next to the rubble of others that had fallen flat.

The derailment of the Texas Eagle bullet train outside Texarkana, Arkansas, has left three people dead and several others injured. Spokesmen for Amtrak say that the derailment may have been caused by failure of the train's satellite tracking system, sending the nine-car train onto a siding instead of the main line. Investigators are now probing through the wreckage to see if deliberate sabotage was involved.

We passed tiny Murph Park overlooking the interstate— where a small shantytown stood next to a sign: CHICKENS 4 SALE, MONEY OR TRADE—and crossed Victor Street, heading uphill where 13th became more narrow, the streetlights less frequent. An old black man sat on the front steps of his house, a 12-gauge shotgun resting across his knees. Across the street was the ruin of a half-collapsed Victorian mansion, where a

bunch of street punks sat smoking joints beneath its front
porch. Trike pedaled faster, avoiding the standoff between
the two forces.

*And in Los Angeles, the jury is out on the rape trial of
filmmaker Antonio Six. His accuser, Marie de Allegro, claims
that Six used telepathic powers to invade her mind two years
ago during the filming of the Oscar-winning* Mother Teresa,
*in which de Allegro played the title role. The sixteen-year-old
actress says that Six was able to use ESP abilities to seduce
her. Jurors are considering expert testimony offered in the
director's defense by several psychics.*

We reached the top of the hill, then coasted the rest of the
way down to Ann Street, where Trike took a hard right that
threatened to overturn the rickshaw. He was clearly enjoying
himself, although I had to hang on for dear life. A block later
we reached 12th Street, where Trike took a left past St. Joseph
Church.

The storefronts of convenience markets, laundromats, and
cheap VR arcades lay on this block. Some were open for
business, some closed and boarded up, all spray-painted with
now-familiar warnings: "YOU LOOT, WE SHOOT"; "NOTHING
LEFT 2 STEAL SO GO AWAY"; "IN GOD WE TRUST, WITH SMITH
& WESSON WE PROTECT"; "IF YOU LIVED HERE YOU'D BE
DEAD BY NOW," and so on.

For the CBS Radio Network News, I'm—

"In sore need of a blow job." Trike changed to one of
the countless classic-rock stations that jammed the city's air-
waves. An oldie by Nirvana pounded out of the radio as he
turned right on Geyer. I checked my watch. True to his word,
barely ten minutes had elapsed since Trike had left Busch
Station, and we were almost to my place.

Geyer had withstood the quake fairly well, considering the
amount of damage Soulard had suffered during New Madrid.
Although many of the old row houses on this block were
condemned or outright destroyed, most of them had ridden
out the quake. These old two- and three-story brick buildings
were built like battleships: chimneys had toppled, windows
had shattered, porches had collapsed, but many of them had
stayed upright. It only figured. Soulard was one of the oldest

parts of the city; it had too much goddamn soul in its walls to be killed in fifty seconds.

Trike coasted to a stop at the corner of Geyer and 10th. A couple of happy drunks were hobbling up the sidewalk across the street, making their way home from Clancy's. I crawled out of the backseat, fished into my pocket, and pulled out a fiver and a couple of ones. "Thanks, man," I said as I extended the bills to him. "You're a lifesaver."

Tricycle Man took the money, stared at it for a moment, then carefully pulled out the two ones and handed them back to me. "Here, take 'em back."

"Hey, Trike, c'mon—"

"Take it back," he insisted, carefully folding up the five and shoving it into his jeans pocket. "You've had a bad night. Go down to the bar and have a beer on me."

I didn't argue. Trike knew I was on lean times. Besides, I was a regular customer; I could always bonus him later. Soulard was a tough neighborhood, but it looked after its own.

"Thanks, buddy." I wadded up the dollars and stuck them in my jacket pocket. Trike nodded his head and started to stand up on the pedals again. "And by the way . . . about the blonde?"

Trike hesitated. "Yeah?"

"She didn't really have an Adam's apple. I was just shitting you."

He grinned. "I knew that. Good looking?"

I shrugged, raising my hand and waving it back and forth. "That's okay," he said. "I've done better. Did I ever tell you about the time I was in London back in ninety-two and fucked Princess Di in the back of a limo? Now that was—"

"Get out of here," I said, and he did just that, making a U-turn in the middle of the street and heading back up Geyer to ask the drunks if they needed a lift home. Leaving me on the brick sidewalk, alone for the first time that night.

The *Big Muddy Inquirer* was located in a century-old three-story building that had been renovated sometime in the 1980's and turned into offices for some law firm; before then it had been yet another warehouse, as witnessed by the thick reinforced oak floors and long-defunct loading doors in the rear. The law firm that had refurbished the building had moved out around the turn of the century, and the property had remained vacant until Earl Bailey purchased it early last year.

Bailey had just started up the paper when he bought the building. Ever the entrepreneur, he had intended to open a blues bar on the ground floor and eventually move the *Big Muddy* into the second-story space from its former location in Dogtown. Bailey had made his wad off the Soulard Howlers, the blues band for which he was the bassist and manager, and Earl's Saloon had been intended to be the money tree behind his alternative paper. *Big Muddy Inquirer* might not have been the first newspaper whose publisher was a hacker-turned-guitarist-turned-bar-owner, but if you've heard of any others, please don't let me know. One is scary enough.

Anyway, Bailey was halfway through refurbishing the ground floor when the quake struck. The bar survived New Madrid but not the widespread looting that had occurred in Soulard several weeks later, when vandals broke into the place and took off with most of the barroom furnishings. By this time, though, the escalating street violence in the south city had forced the paper out of Dogtown, so he shelved plans for the bar, moved the *Big Muddy* to Soulard . . . and, not long afterward, grudgingly agreed to let out the unused third-floor loft to one of his employees. Namely, me.

I had a keycard for the front door, which led up to the second and third floors, but tonight I really didn't want the hassle of having to disable the burglar alarm Pearl had installed in the stairwell. The control box was difficult to see in the dark and, besides, I could never remember the seven-digit code that I would have to type into the keypad. So I ignored the front door, walked past the boarded-up ground-floor windows—spray-painted BLACK-OWNED! DON'T LOOT! as if it made any difference to the street gangs who would have mugged Martin Luther King for pocket change—and went around the corner until I reached the enclosed courtyard behind the building.

An old iron fire escape ran up the rear of the building. Pearl would have shot me if he had known I was using it as my private entrance, which was why I had to keep my stepladder hidden beneath the dumpster. I had just pulled out the ladder and was unfolding it in order to reach the fire escape's gravity ladder when I heard a shout from the opposite side of the courtyard.

"Hey, mu'fucker, whattaya doin'?"

"Just trying to break into this building to steal some shit," I yelled back as I put down the stepladder and turned around. "Why, you're not going to tell anyone, are you?"

There was a large human shape blocking the light escaping from an open garage across the courtyard. I heard coarse laughter, then the voice changed. "Hey, Gerry, that you?"

"That me. That you?"

"Fuck you. C'mon over and have a beer."

I put down the ladder and ambled over toward the garage where Chevy Dick and a few of his cronies were hanging out next to his car. Chevy Dick was Ricardo Chavez, an auto mechanic whose shop was the *Big Muddy*'s closest neighbor. Chavez was in his early fifties; in 1980, when he was barely in his teens, he and his family had escaped from Cuba during the first wave of boat people who had descended upon Miami. Chavez had eventually made his way from Liberty City to St. Louis, where he had successfully plied his natural gifts in auto repair toward making a livelihood.

Chevy Dick got his nickname two ways. First, it was his pen name for "Kar Klub," a weekly fix-it-yourself column he wrote for the *Big Muddy*. Second, he was on his fourth wife and claimed to have eleven children scattered across six states. When he got drunk, he bragged about all the NASCAR winners he had pit-stopped in his career. And when he got really drunk, this 300-pound gorilla with a handlebar mustache and a long braided ponytail might unzip his fly to show off his tool kit.

"Shee-yit," Chevy Dick growled as I stepped into the light, "you look like hell. What'd you do, man, fock some babe in a ditch?"

"Just following your example, Ricardo," I replied. "Why, did I get it wrong?"

Chevy glowered at me. A couple of his friends murmured comments to each other in Spanish; they were all sitting on oil barrels and cinder blocks, a case of Budweiser tallnecks on the grease-stained asphalt between them. In the background was Chevy's pride and joy: a coal black '92 Corvette ZR-1, perfectly restored and completely illegal under the phase-out laws, right down to the vanity tags, which read PHUKU2. Perhaps they were hoping that Chevy would take it off the blocks, gas it up, and take it out Route 40 for another illicit midnight cruise that would drive the cops apeshit; with a speedometer calibrated up to 120 mph, Chevy Dick's Corvette was arguably the fastest street rod in St. Louis, able to easily outrun any battery-powered police cruiser SLPD had on the road.

That, or they were hoping Chevy Dick would pound the shit out of the wiseass little gringo. Chevy continued to stare at me. He took a step forward and I held my ground. He slowly reached up with his left hand and pretended to scratch at his mustache . . . then his right fist darted out to jab at my chest. I didn't move. The fist stopped just an inch short of my solar plexus . . . and still I didn't move.

It was an old macho game between us. We had been playing this for months. The gang all moaned and hooted appreciatively, and Chevy Dick's face broke into a grin. "You're all right, man," he said as he gave me a shoulder slap that made my knees tremble. "Now get yourself a beer."

It was a tempting notion. "I'd love to," I said, "but I'm beat. If I start drinking now, you'll have to carry me upstairs."

"Long night, huh, man?" Chevy's face showed worry as he looked me up and down. "Jeez, you're in some kinda rough shape. What happen, you run into ERA patrols?"

"Something like that, yeah." My eyes were fastened on the case. "If you could spare me one, though, I'd really appreciate it . . ."

Without another word, Chevy Dick reached down to the case and pulled out a six-pack. There were a few grumbles from his drinking buddies, but he ignored them as he handed it to me. Chevy was no friend of ERA; as he had often told me, he hadn't seen things this bad since he had lived in Havana under the old Castro regime. In his eyes, any enemy of the *federales* was a friend of his.

"Thanks, Ricardo," I murmured, hugging the six-pack to my chest. "I'll pay you back next Friday."

"*Vaya con dios, amigo*," he rumbled. "Now go home and take a shower." He grinned at me again, the half-light of an exposed 40-watt bulb glinting off his gold-capped molars. "Besides, you smell like shit."

The ragged laughter of his buddies followed me all the way up the fire escape to my apartment.

I opened the first beer almost as soon as I crawled through the fire escape window and switched on the desk light. Home sweet home . . . or at least a place to get out of the rain.

My one-room loft apartment was a wreck, which was nothing unusual. Clothes scattered across the bare wooden floor and a mattress that hadn't been tidied in a week. Books and magazines heaped together near the mattress and the desk. A small pile of printout on the desk, which constituted the unfinished, untitled, unpublished novel I had been writing for the last few years. Tiny mouse turds near the kitchen cabinets. I could have used a cat; maybe it would have straightened up the place while I was gone.

I swallowed the first beer in a few swift gulps while I peeled out of my muddy clothes, leaving them in a damp trail behind me as I made my way toward the bathroom, stopping only to retrieve Joker from my jacket and place it on the desk while I grabbed another bottle out of the six-pack. The second beer followed me into the shower, where I leaned against the plastic wall and gulped it down, letting the hot water run over me until it began to turn cold.

I cracked open the third beer after I found an old pair of running shorts on the floor and put them on. It was then that I noticed the phone for the first time. The numeral 9 was blinking on its LCD, indicating the number of calls that had been forwarded to my extension from the office switchboard downstairs. Part of my rental agreement with Pearl was that I would act as the paper's after-hours secretary, so I sat down at the desk, opened the phonescreen, and began to wade through the messages.

Most of the calls were the usual stuff. Irate businessmen in suits wondering why their quarter-page ads hadn't been run in the paper exactly where they had wanted them to be, like on the front cover. A couple of oblique calls to individual staffers, giving little more than a face, a name, and number: press contacts, boyfriends, or girlfriends, who knew what else? I hit the Save button after each of them.

Most of the rest were the usual anonymous hate calls from readers, which arrived whenever the new issue hit the street, accusing Pearl of running a commie-pinko, right-wing, left-wing, feminist, antifeminist, environmentalist, technocratic, luddite, anarchist, neo-Nazi, Zionist, pornographic, anti-American, and/or liberal newspaper, all of them swearing to stop reading it tomorrow unless we converted to the ideology of their choice. Most of them had switched their phone cameras off when they called, but there was a demented three-minute screed from some wacko with a grocery bag over his head about how the New Madrid earthquake had been God's revenge against everyone who didn't support Lyndon LaRouche in the presidential election of 1984.

You can acquire a taste for this sort of feedback if you have enough patience and a certain sense of humor, but the same could be said of eating out of a garbage can. I erased them all. They could e-mail their comments to the paper if they felt that strongly about them.

I was about to twist off the cap of my fourth beer when I caught the last message on the disc. Once again the screen was blank, but the woman's voice on the other end of the line was all too familiar.

"Gerry, this is Mari. Are you there . . . ?" A short pause. *"Okay, you aren't, or you're not picking up. Okay . . ."*

Great. My wife—or rather, my ex-wife, once we finally got around to formalizing our separation. She didn't even want to put her still-pic on the screen.

"Listen, your Uncle Arnie called a while ago, and . . . um, he's mad at you because you didn't get to the seder last Friday night . . ."

I winced and shook my head. I had forgotten all about it. Uncle Arnie was my late father's older brother and the Rosen family patriarch. A lovable old fart who persisted in trying to get me to attend observances even though he knew damned well I wasn't quite the nice Jewish nephew he wanted me to be.

"Look, I know this is the usual family stuff, but, y'know I wish you'd tell him not to call here . . . "

Of course she didn't want him to call. Marianne wasn't Jewish, and although she had put up with her share of Rosen seders and bar mitzvahs and Hanukkahs, there was no reason why she should be bugged by my relatives. She didn't understand that Uncle Arnie was just trying once more to get us back together again. Fat chance, Arnie . . .

"Okay. That's it. Take care of yourself. 'Bye."

A call from Marianne. The first time I had heard from her in almost a month, and it was because I had missed last week's Passover seder.

For some reason, this made me more depressed than before. It took me the rest of the six-pack to get over the message. By the time I had finished the last bottle, I couldn't remember why she had called in the first place, and even if I had, I could have cared less.

All I could think about was Jamie.

PART TWO

The Nature of Coherent Light

(April 18, 2013)

5

I didn't remember falling asleep: that's how drunk I got.

Sometime during the night I moved from my desk chair to my unmade bed. I was never conscious of the act; it had been reflexive action and not part of any deliberate decision to hit the sack. I simply blacked out at some point; the next thing I knew, a heavy fist was pounding on the apartment door.

"Rosen! Yo, Rosen . . . !"

Long, bright rays of sunlight were cast through the dusty loft windows. My eyes ached, my mouth tasted like the bottom of a cat's litter basket, and my brain was stuffed with thousands of shorted-out wires. Somewhere out there, birds were chirping, bees were humming, cows were giving milk to blissful farm girls, happy little dwarves were humming as they marched in lockstep on their way to work.

But that was far away, because here in my rank loft, on this beautiful morning in late April, I felt like a hundred and eighty-five pounds of bat guano.

"Rosen! Get the fuck outta bed!"

I shoved away the blanket and swung my legs over the side of the bed. My right foot knocked over a half-empty beer bottle as I sat up; I watched as it rolled across the bare wooden floor until it bounced off the kitchen table and came to rest by the door, leaving a small trail of stale beer in its wake. Somehow, that seemed to be the most fascinating thing I had ever seen: an elegant demonstration of Newtonian physics.

"Rosen!"

"Okay, all right," I muttered. "Don't wet yourself on my account." My legs were still functional, at least to the degree that I was able to stand up without a pair of crutches. I found an old T-shirt on the floor and slipped it on, then stumbled across the room to the door, twisted back the dead bolt and opened it.

Earl Bailey, two hundred and sixty pounds of malice stuffed into six feet and two inches of ugliness, was the last person I wanted to see while suffering from a hangover. He stood outside my door, glowering at me like I was a rat the exterminators had forgotten to kill. Not that the exterminators ever visited this building since he had owned it.

"What's wrong with you?" he snapped. "I've been banging on the door for five minutes."

I stared back at him. "Sorry, but I was taking a long-distance call from the president. He wanted to know if I would come over today to help him fight for world peace, but I told him I needed to deal with you first."

Pearl's fleshy nose wrinkled with disgust as he took a step back from the door. "Your breath stinks. You been drinking this morning?"

"No, but I was drinking last night." I reached down to pick up the beer bottle I had knocked over. "I think there's a little left," I said, swirling around the half-inch of warm beer remaining. "Here, want some?"

"Lemme in here," he growled, pushing my hand aside.

I stood back as he marched into the loft. He stopped in the middle of the room, his fists on his broad hips as he took in the clothes and empty pizza boxes heaped on the floor, the dead plants hanging from the rafters, the half-full carafe of cold coffee on the hot plate, the disarray of papers and books on my desk next to the computer. "Man, this place smells like a dumpster."

"C'mon, Pearl," I murmured, "who did you think you were renting to, the pope?"

"No. I thought I was renting to a responsible adult." He looked back over his shoulder at me. "You told me you were going out to Forest Park to find a story."

"I did. Got one, too."

"Huh." He walked over to my desk to gaze down at the books and papers. "Morning paper says there was an ERA raid at the park last night," he said as he bent down to shove some trash into an overturned wastebasket. "The *Post* claims they arrested a bunch of people who were trespassing at the Muny."

"That's an understatement if there ever was one," I said. "Did it say anything about shootings?"

He looked up at me, one eyebrow raised slightly in surprise. "Nothing about shootings. Why, did you see any?"

I shook my head. "No, but I heard gunfire. Sorry, but I didn't stick around to—"

"Didn't stop to see, huh?" He set the can upright and stood erect, dusting off his hands on his jeans. "Why didn't you?"

I gently rubbed the back of my sore neck with my hands. "Well, boss, you know what they say about someone shooting at you. It's nature's way of telling you it's time to go home."

"Bullshit. You're a reporter. First you get the story, then you worry about letting your ass get shot off."

"Easy for you to—"

"But you didn't see anyone get hit, right?" I shook my head, and Bailey closed his eyes and took a deep breath. "Then there weren't any shootings," he said softly. "Not unless we can produce any bodies."

"Ah, c'mon, Earl!" I shouted. "I was there. I heard the gunshots, for cryin' out—"

"But you didn't see anyone actually get hit, did you?" He stared back at me. "Oh, I believe you, all right . . . and, yeah, I think you were actually there, not just holed up here drinking yourself stupid."

He walked over to the bed, picked up the pair of mud-caked boots I had struggled out of last night, and dropped them back on the floor. At least I had some tangible proof that I hadn't blown off the assignment. "But unless you can find me a corpse with an ERA bullet lodged in its chest, you know what the stadium will say."

I nodded my head. Yeah, I knew what the official spokesmen for the Emergency Relief Agency would say, if and when questioned about gunshots heard during last night's raid. The troopers had been fired upon by armed squatters and had been forced to protect themselves. That, or complete denial, were the usual responses.

This wasn't the first time ERA grunts had opened fire at unarmed civilians in St. Louis, yet no one, from the press to the ACLU, had yet to make a successful case against ERA on charges of unnecessary use of deadly force. Life in my hometown was becoming reminiscent of a third-world banana republic; allegations were often made, but material evidence had a habit of disappearing. So did material witnesses . . .

The local press was treading a thin line. Especially the *Big Muddy*, which was in the habit of intensively covering stories the *Post-Dispatch* only mentioned. The feds couldn't cancel the First Amendment, but they could make life difficult for Pearl. Tax audits, libel suits . . . Bailey knew the risks of being a public nuisance, and he was being careful these days.

No proof, no story. Unproven allegations didn't mean shit to him. I should have known better. "Aw, man, I'm sorry, Pearl. I didn't—"

"Don't call me Pearl," he said. He hated his nickname, even though everyone used it. He glanced at his watch. "You were supposed to be at the staff meeting."

"Oh . . . yeah. Staff meeting." I sat down at my desk and rubbed my eyes. "When it's supposed to start?"

"A half-hour ago. You missed it. That's why I'm up here." He started to walk toward the bathroom, then caught a whiff through the door and thought better of it. He cocked his thumb toward the john. "Is there anything alive in there?"

"Nothing you haven't seen before." I stood up from the desk. "Okay, I'm sorry for missing the meeting. I'll come down right now—"

"Naw, man. If you came downstairs now, you'd only make everyone sick." He shook his head in disgust, then favored me with a little smile. "You worked hard last night. Get a shower and put on some clean clothes."

"Thanks. I'll be down in a half-hour—"

"You've got fifteen minutes, and tell the president I think he's a dickhead and I don't believe in world peace." His smile faded. "If I don't see you in fifteen, you can begin updating your resume. Got it?"

"Got it." I didn't like the sound of that.

"See you downstairs." He turned around and tromped back through the door. "And clean this shit up. It's embarrassing . . . to me, at any rate."

He slammed the door on the way out.

The offices of the *Big Muddy Inquirer* were spread across a large room occupying the second floor of the building, its various departments separated from each other only by cheap plastic partitions. The place resembled a lab maze for down-on-their-luck mice: computer terminals on battered gray metal desks, fluorescent lights hung from pipes and ductwork along the cobwebbed ceiling, checkerwork brick walls plastered with old posters for rock concerts. Near the stairwell leading to the front door was the personals desk, where a steady parade of lonely people visited to place their ads for other lonely people; at the opposite end of the room was the layout department, where a handful of bohemian graphic artists pasted up the pages within a perpetual haze of marijuana fumes, vented only by a half-open window. Radical chic long after it was chic to be radical and Tom Wolfe had gone to the great word processor in the sky.

Somewhere in the middle of the room was the editorial department: four desks shoved together in a small cubicle, with Horace—the paper's unofficial mascot, a trophy-mounted moose head decked out in oversized sunglasses and a Cardinals baseball cap—standing watch over the proceedings. The two other staff writers were out on assignment, allowing John Tiernan and me a chance to have our own little staff meeting regarding the events of the previous night.

John was the oddest person working for the *Big Muddy* in that he was the only staffer who closely resembled a normal human being. At a paper where everyone drank or smoked dope or experimented with various bathtub hallucinogens, John's only apparent vice was chewing gum. While most people reported to work in jeans, T-shirts, and football jerseys, and our arts editor frequently sported an opera cape and a pince-nez, John came in wearing a business suit, a button-down Oxford shirt, and a plain tie. Sometimes he wore sneakers, but that was as informal as he got. He wore his hair neither too short nor too long, shaved every day, and probably couldn't say "shit" even if his mouth was full of it. He had a wife and a kid and two cats, lived in a small house in the western 'burbs, attended Catholic mass every Sunday morning, and probably gave the most boring confessions a priest had ever heard.

No one at the *Big Muddy* ever gave him flak about his straitlaced ways. John was not only tolerant of all the bent personalities around him, he was also the best investigative reporter in the city. Earl would have sold his own son into slavery before giving up John Tiernan to another paper.

"Did you get her name?" he asked once I had given him the rundown of the Muny raid.

"Uh-uh," I replied. "I didn't even get that good of a look at her, beyond what I just told you. But she didn't belong there, man. She was no squatter."

"Yeah. Okay." John's face was pensive. He had his feet up on his desktop next to his computer terminal; he opened his top desk drawer and pulled out a pack of gum. "But you say she knew me—"

"She knew your name, but not your face. How else could she have mistaken me for you?" John offered me a stick of Dentyne; I shook my head and he unwrapped the stick for himself. "Does she sound familiar?"

"I dunno. Could be anyone, I guess." He shrugged as he wadded up the stick and popped it into his mouth, chewing thoughtfully as he used the computer's trackball to save the story he had been working on. "And she said she wants me to meet her at Clancy's tonight at eight?"

"Right, and not to believe any other messages you happen to receive from Dingbat . . ."

John grinned from one corner of his mouth. "Yeah, right. I suppose I'm not to believe anything I hear on the phone, either. Weird." He shook his head, then dropped his feet from the desk and swiveled around in his chair to face the screen. "Well, I gotta finish this thing, then I've got a press conference to cover at noon . . ."

I snapped my fingers as another thought suddenly occurred to me. Chalk it up to my hangover that I buried the lead. "Oh, yeah," I said, "one more thing. When I asked her what this was all about, she told me two words . . . um, 'ruby fulcrum.' "

John's hands froze above the keyboard. He didn't look away from the screen, but I could see from the change in his expression that he was no longer concentrating on the minor news item he had been writing.

"Come again?" he said quietly.

"Ruby fulcrum," I repeated. "I checked it out with Joker, but it couldn't tell me anything. Why, does that ring a bell?"

He dropped his hands from the keyboard and turned back around in his chair. "Tell me everything one more time," he said. "Slowly."

Let me tell you a little more about John Tiernan.

John and I were old friends since our college days in the nineties, when we had met at j-school at the University of Missouri in Columbia. We were both St. Louis natives, which meant something in a class full of out-of-staters, and we worked together on the city desk at the campus daily, chasing fire engines and writing bits. After we had received our sheepskins, I went north to work as a staff writer for an alternative paper in Massachusetts, while John remained in Missouri to accept a job as a general assignments reporter for the *Post-Dispatch*, but we had stayed in touch. We married our respective college girlfriends at nearly the same time; I tied the knot with Marianne two months after John got hitched to Sandy. Even our kids, Jamie and Charles, were born in the same year. Things go like that sometimes.

About the same time that I bailed out of journalism, John moved into investigative reporting for the *Post-Dispatch*. When I began to seriously consider getting Marianne and Jamie out of the northeast, John had urged me to return to St. Louis, saying that he could put in a good word for me at the *Post-Dispatch*. I went halfway with him; my family moved back to Missouri, but I decided that I had had enough with journalism. A New York publisher was interested in my novel-in-progress, and Marianne had agreed to support us during the period it took for me to get the book finished. John made the same offer again after he left the *Post* to go to work for Pearl, but I still wasn't interested. The novel was going well, and I didn't have any desire to go back to being a reporter.

And then there was the quake, and Jamie's death, and my separation from Marianne, and suddenly I found myself living in a cheap motel near the airport with only a few dollars in my wallet. I did as well as I could for a while, doing odd jobs for under-the-table slave wages, until one morning I found myself on a pay phone, calling John at his office to ask if his offer was still valid and, by the way, did he know of any apartments I could rent? John came through on both accounts, and he probably saved my sanity by doing so.

This all goes to show that John Tiernan was my best friend and that there was little which was secret between us.

Yet there *were* secrets; John was a consummate professional, and good investigative reporters don't discuss their work even with close buddies. I knew that John played his cards close to his chest and accepted that fact as a given, and so I wasn't terrifically upset when he wouldn't disclose everything he knew.

"This ruby fulcrum biz . . . it's important, isn't it?"

He slowly nodded his head as he rubbed his chin between his fingertips. "Yeah, it means something." He gazed out the window at the gothic steeple of St. Vincent de Paul, rising above the flat rooftops a few blocks away. "It's part of the story I'm working on right now . . . and I think I know the person you met last night."

"A source?" I reached across him to the pack of gum and pulled out a stick. "I take it you haven't met her."

John shook his head. "Just a couple of anonymous tips that were e-mailed to me a few weeks ago. I can see how she might have confused you with me last night, since you were obviously waiting for someone at the gate, but . . ."

He shrugged. "Darned if I know how you got sent an IM meant for me on your PT. The prefixes aren't identical. That's never happened before."

"Some kind of screw-up in the net. I dunno. I received a message meant for you by accident, and . . ."

We looked at each other and slowly shook our heads. Yeah, and the Tooth Fairy was my mother-in-law. The odds of a random occurrence like this were as likely as trying to call your mother-in-law and reaching an emergency hot line between the White House and the Kremlin instead. Yeah, it *could* happen . . . oh, and by the way, you've just won the Illinois State Lottery and you're now a millionaire, all because you happened to pick up a lottery ticket somebody had dropped on the sidewalk.

Coincidence, my ass . . . and neither of us believed in the Tooth Fairy.

"Let me ask you," John said after a moment. "If you saw this woman again, would you recognize her? I mean, you said it was dark and rainy and all that, but—"

"If we had gotten any closer, I would have had to ask her for a date. Yeah, I'd recognize her." I unwrapped a piece of gum and curled it into my mouth. "Where do you think we're going to find her? Go over to the stadium and ask if they busted any middle-aged black women last night?"

John smiled, then he swiveled around to pick up his leatherbound notebook from his desk. Opening the cover, he pulled a white engraved card out of the inside pocket and extended it to me. "Funny you should ask . . ."

I took the card from his hand and looked at it. It was a press invitation to a private reception at some company called the Tiptree Corporation, to be held at noon today. I turned the card over between my fingertips. "Here?"

"Here," he said. "She works for them."

Coincidence City.

"But you don't know her name . . ." He shook his head. I turned the card over and noticed that it was addressed personally to him. "Wonder why she didn't just tell me she'd meet you at this reception."

"There's good reasons," he replied. "Besides, she probably didn't even know I was going to be there. The company probably sent a few dozen out to reporters in the city—"

"And I didn't get one?" I felt mildly snubbed, even though I was fully aware that it was only senior reporters who got invited to things like this.

"It's just one of those brie and white wine sort of things . . ."

"But I love cheese and wine."

"Yeah, nothing gets between you and cheese." I gave him a stern look, and he met it with a wide grin. Friendship means that you don't deck someone for making asshole remarks like that. "Anyway, another one was sent to Jah. Apparently they want a photographer on hand. If you can finagle the other invitation from him . . ."

"I'm on it." I stood up, heading for the back staircase leading to the basement. "When are you leaving?"

John glanced at his watch. "Soon as you get back up here. It's out in west county somewhere, so we'll have to drive. Don't stop for coffee."

"Not even for tea. I'll see you out front in fifteen minutes." John gave me the thumbs-up and I went straight for the stairs.

Pearl didn't glance up from his desk as I slipped past his cubicle; for a moment I had the guilty notion that I should drop by, knock on the door, and tell him where I was headed. But if I did, he would probably insist that I stay put in the office until I had met the deadline for my column, even if it was more than twenty-four hours away. The notion, along with the guilt, quickly evaporated. My column could wait; for the first time in months, I had a real story to pursue, even if it was John's byline that would appear on the final product.

I wanted a hot story.

For my sins both past and future, I was given one. When it was all over and done, I would never want to tag along on another assignment again.

6

Craig Bailey's darkroom was in the basement, down where a microbrewery would eventually have been located had his father been successful in opening a saloon on the ground floor. I found Jah slouched in front of his VR editor, wearing an oversized HMD helmet as his hands wandered over a keyboard, manipulating various pieces of videotape and computer-generated imagery into his latest work of interactive cinema.

Working for his dad as the *Big Muddy*'s photo chief was just a day job for Jah, and a temporary one at that. His real ambition was to move to California and go to work for Disney or LucasWorks, and every cent he earned from his grumpy old man went to buying more hardware and software to feed his obsession. For this, the University of Missouri basketball coach was crying bitter tears; Jah stood about six-ten in his stocking feet, plus or minus a few extra inches of dreadlocks. He was hell on the half-court—I once made the mistake of playing one-on-one with him after work for a dollar a point and lost half a day's take-home pay—but Jah would rather dick around in virtual reality while blasting old reggae and techno CDs at stone-deaf volume.

I had no problem getting the extra press invitation from Jah; he was involved with his latest project and really didn't want to go out to west city just to take pictures of business types swilling martinis. He loaned me one of the paper's Nikons, loading a disc into the camera for me and reprogramming the thing to full-auto so that I wouldn't have to futz around with the viewfinder menu, and gave me a spare necktie from the pile next to the disk processor, thus making the disguise complete. A tie with a washed-out denim shirt would look a little strange where I was going, but formal wear for news photographers usually means that they changed their jeans today.

"Got a minute to look at this?" he asked when we were done. He held up the VR helmet. "Sort of a documentary . . . you might like it."

I shook my head as I pulled the camera strap over my shoulder. "Catch me in the next episode, okay? I gotta book outta here before your pop finds I'm missing."

He looked disappointed but nodded his head. "I hope you're not fucking with him. He's kinda pissed at you these days." He glanced at the door as if expecting to see the elder Bailey's shadow lurking in the stairwell. "Fact, man. He's been talking about making some changes 'round here, if you know what I mean."

I didn't like the sound of that, but neither did I have time to further inquire what Bailey and son discussed over the dinner table. "Believe me, I'm not trying to fuck with your dad. I'm just trying to—"

"Hey, that's cool." Jah held up his hands, keeping his distance from the bad vibes between his father and me. "So long as you come back with some shots for next week, we're solid."

"Sold for a dollar." We elbow-bumped, then he headed back to his workbench as I made for the basement door, avoiding taking the stairs back to the office.

John was waiting for me across the street from the office, leaning against the hood of his Deimos. "I don't think Pearl missed you," he said in reply to my unasked question as he dug a remote out of his pocket; the Pontiac's front doors unlocked and pivoted upward. "He's busy editing the arts page for next week."

"Fine with me." I walked around to the passenger side and slid into the seat as John took the driver's seat. "I just talked to Jah, though. He says Pearl's thinking about making some staff changes."

"I wouldn't worry about it." John pressed his thumb against

the ignition plate as the doors closed; the car started up as the seat harnesses wrapped themselves around our bodies. "Pearl's always talked that way," he said, opening the steering column keypad and tapping in the street address for the Tiptree Corporation. "When he had his band, he used to say the same thing whenever he had an off night. Y'know . . . 'That drummer sucks, I gotta get a new drummer before the next gig.' That sort of thing."

"Uh-huh." A map of metro St. Louis appeared on the dashboard screen, a bright red line designating the shortest course between us and our destination. "How many drummers did the Howlers have?"

"Umm . . . I think I lost count," he murmured as he eased away from the curb. "But that doesn't mean it's the same thing—"

"Yeah. Okay." John was trying to be candid and comforting at the same time, yet I couldn't refrain from glancing up at the second-floor windows as we headed down Geyer toward Broadway. I couldn't see Pearl, but nonetheless I could feel his angry presence.

Something had better come out of this field trip, or I was screwed.

The main office of the Tiptree Corporation was located on the western outskirts of St. Louis in Ballwin, not far from the Missouri River. We took Route 40/I-64 until downtown faded far behind us, then got off on the I-270 outer belt and followed it until we found the Clayton Road exit. By now we were in the gentrified suburbs, where subdivisions and shopping plazas had replaced farms in the latter part of the last century. The quake had destroyed most of the flimsier tract homes and cookie-cutter malls that had been thrown up during the building boom of the eighties; bulldozers and backhoes could be seen from the highway, completing the demolition of homes and stores that had been initiated by New Madrid. Architectural Darwinism: quakes kill buildings, but only the sick and feeble ones.

John briefed me on Tiptree along the way. The company was a relative newcomer in the computer industry, one of the many that had been started during the late nineties as a result of the seventh-generation cybernetic revolution. Unlike other companies, though, Tiptree had not gone after the burgeoning consumer market for neural-net pocket computers or virtual reality toys. Instead, it had become a big-league player in the military aerospace industry, albeit a quiet one.

"Name a major Pentagon program," John said as we drove down Clayton, "and Tiptree probably has something to do with it. It's a major subcontractor to the Air Force for the Aurora project, for instance. Now—"

"You have reached your destination," a feminine voice announced from the dashboard. *"Repeat, you have reached your—"*

Tiernan stabbed the navigator's Reset button, hushing the voice. We had already spotted the company's sign, a burnished aluminum slab bearing the corporate logo of a *T* transfused with a stylized oak tree. "Now they've delivered on their largest contract yet," he continued as he turned right, following a long driveway just past the sign. "Want to guess which one?"

I was studying the plant itself, seen past ten-foot-high chain mesh fences artfully obscured by tall hedges. It was your typical postmodern industrial campus: a long white three-story edifice surrounded by tree-shaded parking lots and some smaller buildings, unimaginatively designed by an architect who probably collected old calculators as a hobby. If Tiptree's headquarters had been damaged at all by the quake, they had been rebuilt quickly; there were a few scaffolds around one end of the main building, but that was the only indication that the company had been affected by New Madrid.

"Umm . . . a player piano for the Air Force Academy?"

John smiled but said nothing as he pulled to a stop in front of a gatehouse. A uniformed private security guard walked out to the car and bent low to examine the invitation John held up for him. He stared at me until I showed mine as well, then he nodded his head and pointed the way to a visitors' parking lot on the east side of the main building.

"Does the name Project Sentinel ring a bell?" he said as we drove toward the designated lot.

I whistled; he glanced at me and slowly nodded his head. "That's what this is all about," he went on. "They designed the c-cube for the satellite . . . that's command, control, and communications. The bird's being launched from Cape Canaveral at noon, so it's show-and-tell day for these guys."

"Probably more show than tell," I said. "And you think this 'ruby fulcrum' business has something to do with—"

"Shhh!" he hissed, and I dummied up as he looked sharply at me. "Whatever you do," he said very softly, "don't say that again . . . not even in the car with me."

He tapped his left ear and pointed outside the car. It wasn't hard to get the picture. We might be invited guests for a public reception, but as soon as we had driven through the gates, we were in injun territory. Any high-tech company involved with a defense project as sensitive as Sentinel was probably capable of hearing a sparrow fart within a mile of its offices.

John pulled into an empty slot. "Pick up your camera and make like a log," he murmured. "It's showtime."

Showtime, indeed.

We walked into the main building through the front entrance, wading through a small crowd hanging around the lobby until we found the reception table. A nice young woman took our invitations, checked them against a printout, then smiled and welcomed us by name—Jah's, in my case—as she clipped a pair of security badges to us, each of them reading PRESS in bright red letters, which either made us honored guests or social lepers. She handed a press kit to John and ignored the disheveled beatnik with the camera behind him, then a polite young man who could have been her chromosome-altered clone pointed us through the crowd to a high archway leading to an atrium in the center of the building.

I had to rethink my opinion of the architect's style; whoever designed this place had more on the bean than just playing with antique calculators. The atrium was three stories tall, its ceiling an enclosed skylight from which hung a miniature rain forest of tropical ferns. Small potted trees were positioned across the black-tiled floor, and dominating the far end of the room was a videowall displaying a real-time image of a

Cape Canaveral launch pad so large that it seemed as if the shuttle was just outside the building.

Yet that wasn't what immediately captured my attention. Holographic projectors, cleverly concealed among the hanging plants, had suspended a monstrous machine about twenty feet above the floor: the *Sentinel 1* satellite, its long, thin solar arrays thrust out from its cylindrical fuselage, gold Mylar-wrapped spherical fuel tanks nestling against its white segmented hull just short of the black maw of its gun. The image had been shrunk somewhat—the real *Sentinel* was nearly as long as a football field—but the overall effect was nonetheless impressive: a giant pistol in the sky, and God help whoever tried to stare it down.

Milling around the atrium was a large crowd of business types, clustered in conversation circles, standing in front of the bar or taking drinks from the robowaiters, idly watching the shuttle countdown on the videowall. There was a buffet table at one side of the room; the aroma of hors d'oeuvres was too tempting for someone who hadn't eaten all day, so I excused myself from John to go get some free chow.

After wolfing down a plate of cocktail shrimp, fried mushrooms, and toasted ravioli, I was ready to start thinking like a professional journalist again. John was nowhere in sight; I eased myself into a vacant corner of the room and took a couple shots of the holograph, then began to scan the room through the Nikon's telescopic lens under the pretense that I was grabbing a few candid shots. The nice thing about posing as a down-at-the-heels news photographer is that, under circumstances such as this, you fade right into the woodwork; no one pays much attention to the photog because no one wants to seem as if they're posing for pictures.

At first sight, no one seemed particularly remarkable; you've seen one suit, you've seen 'em all. The only exception was another photographer across the room, a young lady in jeans and a sweater who looked just as seedy as I. She scowled at me before melting into the crowd. Professional rivalry; she was probably from the *Post-Dispatch*. I wondered if she could help me adjust my F-stops . . .

Enough of that. Like it or not, I was still married, even if

Marianne had sent me to the darkroom. I continued to check out the atrium.

For a few moments I didn't see anyone recognizable. Then I spotted Steve Estes. The most right-wing member of the City Council was standing in the center of the room, yukking it up with a couple of other guys who looked as if they were fellow alumni of Hitler Youth. The pompous prick was probably bragging about how he had managed to get ERA to roust a bunch of panhandlers out of the park the night before.

Estes was clearly maneuvering for a run against Elizabeth Boucher in next year's mayoral election; every public statement he had made since the quake hinted that he was going to oppose "Liberal Lizzie" (to use his term) on a good ol' Republican law-and-order platform. It would be an easy run; Liz had been caught off guard by the quake and everything that occurred afterward, and in the last few weeks she had been rarely seen or heard outside of City Hall. Rumor had it that she was suffering from a nervous breakdown, a drinking problem, or both, and her foes on the council, chief among them Big Steve, had been quick to capitalize on the rumors. If she ran for reelection, it would be as an unstable incumbent; if you believed Estes' rants, you'd think Boucher had gone down to New Madrid and jumped up and down on the fault line to cause the quake herself.

Estes glanced in my direction; the grin on his face melted into a cold glare. I took the opportunity to snag his picture before he looked away again. If anything, the shot could be used for Bailey's next editorial against Estes and his hard-line policies. Then I happened to notice a small group of people standing across the room.

Unlike nearly everyone else at the reception, they were inordinately quiet, seeming somewhat ill at ease even though all three wore the blue badges that I had already recognized as designating Tiptree employees. Their apparent nervousness caught my attention; they appeared to be in terse, quiet conversation, occasionally shutting up and glancing furtively over their shoulders when someone happened to pass by.

I zoomed in on one of them, a distinguished-looking guy in his mid-fifties, tall and rail-thin, with a trim gray Vandyke beard and a receding hairline. Although his back was turned toward me, it was apparent that the two other people were deferring to him. When he looked over his shoulder again, I snapped his picture, more out of impulse than anything else.

Then, in the next instant, he shuffled out of the way, for the first time clearly revealing the shorter person who had been standing opposite him . . .

A middle-aged black woman in a powder blue business suit and white blouse, not particularly distinguishable from anyone else in the crowd—except I recognized the shock of gray in her hair and the stern expression on her face.

No question about it. She was the very same lady I had encountered in the park last night.

Fumbling with the lens-control buttons, I zoomed in on the woman as much as the camera would allow. The Nikon's varioptic lens did wonders; now it was as if I were standing three feet in front of her. I could clearly read what was printed on her name badge: BERYL HINCKLEY, Senior Research Associate.

As if she were telepathic, her eyes flitted in my direction when I snapped her picture. I lowered the camera and smiled at her.

She recognized me. Her face registered surprise, and for a moment I thought she was going to come over to speak to me.

"Ladies, gentlemen, if I could have your attention please . . . we're about to get started here."

The amplified voice came through hidden speakers near the ceiling. A young executive was standing at a podium below the videowall. The drone of conversation began to fade as everyone quieted down.

The exec smiled at them. "We've been told that the shuttle has come off its prelaunch countdown hold and will be lifting off in just a few minutes," he went on, "but before that, I'd like to introduce someone who has a few remarks to share with you . . ."

I glanced across the room again, only to find that Beryl Hinckley had vanished from where I had last seen her. I looked around, trying to spot her again; I caught a brief glimpse of her back as she disappeared into the crowd, heading in the direction of a side exit. She had a true knack for making her escape.

". . . Our chief executive officer, Cale McLaughlin. Mr. McLaughlin . . . ?"

A smattering of applause, led by the exec, as he stepped away from the podium to make way for McLaughlin. Tiptree's CEO was an older gentleman: tall, whip thin, and white haired, with wire-rimmed glasses and the focused look of a man who started his career as a lower-echelon salesman and clawed his way up to the top of the company.

Probably a pretty good golfer, too, but that didn't mean I was more interested in him than any other corporate honcho I had seen before. I zoomed back in on the conversation circle, only to find that the two men who had been talking with the mystery lady had also faded into the background.

"I'll keep things brief, because it's hard to compete with a shuttle launch." Some laughter from the audience, which had otherwise gone respectfully quiet. McLaughlin's voice held a soft Texas accent, muted somewhat by the careful diction of a well-educated gentleman. "The Tiptree Corporation is pleased to have been part of the Sentinel program since the very beginning. Hundreds of people have been involved with this project over the last few years, and we believe that it is an important asset to the national security of the United States . . ."

Yeah, yeah, yeah. So was the B-2 bomber. I was too busy wondering why this Hinckley woman needed to take a powder every time she saw my face.

I was about to wade into the crowd in hopes of finding her again when a soft voice I had never expected, nor hoped, to hear again spoke from behind me.

"Mr. Rosen, I presume . . ."

I turned around to find, not unlike the devil himself, Paul Huygens standing at my shoulder.

Not much can surprise me, but in that moment I nearly dropped Jah's expensive camera on the polished floor. If Amelia Earhart and Jimmy Hoffa had appeared to announce that they were married and were now living in a nudist colony on Tierra del Fuego and that Marie de Allegro was their love child, I couldn't have been more shocked. I might even have made note of a certain family resemblance.

The only thing that Paul Huygens bore a resemblance to was something you might find when you pick up a rock and look underneath. He was a squat, greasy little toad of a guy, the sort of person who wears five-hundred-dollar Armani suits and still manages to look like a cheap hustler. Imagine the Emperor Nero as a lounge lizard and you've got the general idea.

"Why, hello, Paul," I said quietly. I tried to disguise my disconcertment by coughing into my hand. "Long time, no see . . ."

Behind us, Cale McLaughlin continued his short, brief, bah-bah woof-woof about how wonderful *Sentinel 1* was to the future of all mankind. Huygens nodded slightly. "A couple of years at least," he replied. As before, his voice was almost girlishly high pitched: a little startling, since one rather expected a deep-throated, froggy tenor. "Still up to your old tricks, I see."

"Hmm? Oh, this . . ." I glanced down at the camera. "Sort of a new gig. I'm working for the *Big Muddy Inquirer* now. Switched over to photojournalism."

"Uh-huh. I see." He frowned and made a show of looking closely at my badge. "You must have changed your name, too . . . or does Craig Bailey write columns under your byline?"

I felt my face grow warm. He grinned at me. I had made a big lie and he had caught me in it. I made a sheepish, well-shucky-darn kind of shrug and changed the subject. "So . . . how's everything in Massachusetts these days?"

Huygens looked me straight in the eye. "I wouldn't know, Gerry," he said. "I quit CybeServe and moved to St. Louis about six months ago."

"Oh, really?"

"Oh, really." He nodded his head. "I'm working for Tiptree now. Director of public relations." The grin became a taut, humorless smile. "Remember what I told you? We're from the same hometown."

More surprises, and just a little less pleasant than the first one. Yeah, Huygens had told me that, two years ago when I had first spoken to him on the phone, back when he had held the same job for CybeServe Electronics in Framingham and I had been a staffer for an alternative paper in Boston. Back then, of course, I hadn't known what sort of eel I was dealing with, or how he'd eventually try to destroy my career. Damn near succeeded, too.

"Well, well," I said. "Like a bad penny . . ."

The smile disappeared altogether. Huygens cocked his head sideways as he peered closely at me. "Excuse me? I didn't quite get that—"

"Never mind. Just a passing thought." I coughed into my hand again. "So . . . what high school did you go to?"

It's an old St. Louis line, akin to asking a New Englander about the weather, but Huygens didn't bite. Over his shoulder, I spotted John halfway across the room, making his way through the crowd with a drink in his hand. Probably a ginger ale, which was unfortunate; I could have used a shot of straight whiskey right then. He caught my eye, gave me a one-finger high sign, and started toward us.

"Hmm." Huygens's thick lips pursed together. "Y'know, Gerry, to be quite honest, if I had wanted you to be here, I would have sent you an invitation—"

"Things were tight at the office," I began. "Craig was sort of busy, so I—"

"Covered for him, right." He pretended to rub a dust mote out of his left eye. I recognized the gesture; it was something he always did just before he asked you to bend over and drop your britches. "Well, I might have overlooked it, us being old acquaintances and all, but you see . . . well, I just received a complaint from one of our guests."

"Oh?" John was still making his serpentine way through the mob; the cavalry was taking forever to get here. "From whom?"

"Steve Estes. He said . . ." He shrugged. "Well, you know these politicians. They don't like to be photographed without prior permission. That's what brought me over here in the first place."

"Oh, no," I said. "Of course not. After all, if just anyone

was able to take their picture, they might actually be accountable to the public."

Huygens nodded agreeably. "Well, yes, there's that . . . but nonetheless, Mr. Estes is an invited guest and you're not . . ."

I shrugged off-handedly. "Sure, I understand, but Steve shouldn't worry about the shot I took of him. It probably won't come out anyway."

Huygens blessed me with a blank, mildly bewildered look. "After all," I continued, "old Transylvanian legends claim that vampires can't be photographed."

Assholes are always the best straight men: they don't have a good sense of humor. As his expression turned cold a few moments before John arrived at my side, I raised the camera to my face. "Let's test that," I said, focusing on Huygens's wattled chin. "Say cheese . . ."

Applause from the audience as McLaughlin wrapped up his speech. It could have been an appreciation for my jab. Now it was Huygens's turn to make like a boiled lobster.

The gag didn't last long. The picture I took was of him reaching into his breast pocket to pull out his PT and tap in the codes that negated the electronic passwords embedded in our smartbadges. John walked right into the middle of the whole scene.

"Hey, Gerry," he said. "Did you get something to eat?"

"The crow's good," I murmured as I lowered the camera. "Just ask my friend here."

Huygens simply stared at me. A moment later, two plainclothes security guards materialized behind John and me; they must have been hovering nearby, waiting for Huygens's signal. They were on us before I had a chance to compliment Huygens on his choice of catering service.

"Get 'em out of here," Huygens said to the large gentlemen who had descended upon us. "See you around, Gerry."

He didn't even bother to look at me before he turned his back on us and waddled back into the crowd.

John looked confused as a pair of massive hands clamped onto his shoulders. "Excuse me, but is there a problem?"

"Yes, sir," one of the mutts said. "You are."

No one at the reception noticed our sudden departure. They were too busy applauding the videowall as the *Endeavour*, spewing smoke and fire, rose from its launch pad into a perfect blue Floridian sky.

7

Tiptree's rent-a-goons escorted us out the front door, where they confiscated our smartbadges and pointed the way to the road. John and I didn't say anything to each other until we reached his car and had driven out of the company parking lot. When we had passed through the front gate and were heading back down Clayton Road toward the highway, though, the first thing John wanted from me wasn't an apology.

"Okay, what was that all about?" he asked. "I thought you were just talking to that guy."

He wasn't pissed off so much as he was bewildered. I felt a headache coming on, so I lowered my seat-back to a prone position and gently rubbed my eyes with my knuckles.

"He said it was because I had taken a picture of Steve Estes," I said, "but he was just looking for an excuse. I could have complained about the catering and he would have tossed me out just the same." I let out my breath. "He had no problem with you. You just happened to be with me, and that made you an accessory. Sorry, but that's the way it is."

"Hmm . . . well, don't worry about it. What's done is done." He stopped to let a mini-cat rumble across the road in front of us; the machine was carrying a load of broken cinderblocks away from a collapsed convenience store. The flagman waved us on, and John stepped on the pedal again. "So you think he did that just to get rid of us? I don't—"

"For the record," I went on, "the jerk's name is Paul Huygens." I hesitated. "He used to work for CybeServe, maker of the fine line of CybeServe home VR products . . . specifi-

90

cally, the VidMaxx Dataroom. Ring any bells with you?"

John's face was blank for a moment, then Big Ben tolled the midnight hour. He cast a sharp look at me. "I'll be darned," he said slowly. "Is that the guy who got you canned at the *Clarion*?"

"One and the same, dude." I gazed out the window at the ruins of a collapsed subdivision, remembering an unsigned note that had been faxed to me only a few years ago. "One and the same . . ."

Time for another history lesson. Today's lecture is how Gerry Rosen, ace investigative reporter, once again tried to get a good story and, not incidentally, save a few lives, but instead ended up losing his job. Take notes; there will be a quiz on this at the end of the postmodern era.

Three years before, I was working as a staff writer for another weekly alternative newspaper, this one the *Back Bay Clarion,* a muckraking little rag published in Boston. I had been assigned by my editor to follow up on a number of complaints against a medium-size electronics company based in Framingham, a Boston suburb that has been the heart of the East Coast computer industry since the early eighties. As you may have guessed, this was CybeServe.

CybeServe was one of many corporations that had cashed in on the virtual-reality boom by manufacturing home VR systems for the consumer market. It had previously lost tons of money on the cheap-shit domestic robots it had attempted to sell through department stores, so its VidMaxx line of VR equipment had been one of the few products that were keeping the company afloat. All well and good, but the problem lay in their top-of-the-line product, the VidMaxx Dataroom 310.

The Dataroom 310 was much like its competitors: the unit could transform any vacant household room into a virtual-reality environment, transporting the customer into any world that could be interfaced by the CPU—the sort of thing for which Jah now wanted to write programs. Want to see exactly what the NASA probes on Mars are doing right now? Experience a role-playing game set in a medieval fantasy world? Go shopping in the Galleria Virtual? If you had all the right hardware and enough money to blow on on-line linkage with the various nets, the Dataroom 310 would take you there toot sweet.

However, unlike similar equipment marketed by Microsoft-Commodore or IBM, CybeServe's VR equipment had some major flaws. First, there was no built-in interrupt timer; anyone who plugged into cyberspace could stay there indefinitely, or at least until hell froze over and you could build snowmen in Cairo. Also, because of various bugs in the CybeServe's communications software sold with the hardware, anyone with a little knowledge could hack straight through the security lockouts installed by sysops to prevent users from accessing various commercial VR nets without ponying up a credit card number.

This type of bad engineering had made the CybeServe Butler 3000 the joke of the robotics industry; CybeServe tended to do things fast and cheap in order to cash in on a marketing trend. But most people were unaware of the subtle flaws with the Dataroom 310 when they bought it and had it installed in their homes. Their kids, though, soon discovered those glitches that allowed them practically unlimited time on whatever nets they were able to access, with or without authorization. Blowing three grand on phone bills to Madame Evelyn's House of Love is enough to make anyone break out in a cold sweat.

That's bad. What's worse was that, according to the tips my paper had received from distraught and angry parents, several kids were losing themselves in cyberspace. They would rush home from school to lock themselves into the datarooms and, using various commands and passwords they had learned from their friends, jack into the VR worlds of their choice . . . and some of them, because of the lack of an interrupt toggle, wouldn't come back home again. It became a form of avoidance behavior for children who didn't like genuine reality, much as drugs, excessive TV viewing, or 1-900 phone services had been for previous generations. A few emotionally disturbed teenagers had even attempted suicide this way, trying to starve themselves to death while locked into an unreal world they refused to leave.

When I checked into it, I found that CybeServe was aware

of the problem yet had done nothing to solve it. The corporation had a consulting psychologist on its payroll, whose only job was to jack into the system and talk kids out of virtual reality. The company offered generous "refunds" to their families if they kept their mouths shut about the accidents that had befallen Junior and Sis and didn't file any lawsuits. Yet CybeServe had not recalled the Dataroom 310 to install timers nor made any effort to update the communications software to prevent hacking. Instead of fixing its mistakes, the company had concentrated solely on keeping potential buyers and the company's competitors from learning about the product's defects.

A few local families wanted to talk; so did a couple of their kids, particularly a thirteen-year-old boy from Newton who had spent six months in a New Hampshire psychiatric hospital after he had attempted to kill himself by locking himself in the household dataroom for nearly three days. They had tipped off the *Clarion*, and I was put onto the story.

CybeServe's public relations director was Paul Huygens. He had started off by affably refuting the accusations during a long phone interview. He also offered to have a unit installed in my house—free of charge, of course, for "research purposes." When I didn't wag my tail and roll over, he circulated an in-house memo to all key company personnel, tacitly threatening job termination to anyone who didn't hang up as soon as I called.

It could be said in Huygens's defense that he had only been doing his job. That's fair; I was doing mine. After several weeks of hangups, I managed to find a disgruntled former CybeServe R&D scientist with a guilty conscience who told me, in a not-for-attribution interview, about the fatal flaws in the Dataroom 310. That, along with all the real and circumstantial evidence, allowed me to write an exposé about the company. It was published in the *Clarion* after nearly two months of grinding work, and within a couple of months after its publication, the Dataroom 310 was taken off the market and CybeServe was forced to deal with dozens of civil-court lawsuits regarding the product.

By then, I had lost my job. Almost as soon as the article

was published, Huygens called Boston-area companies that
had business with CybeServe, all of them electronics retailers
that advertised in the *Back Bay Clarion*. These stores, in turn,
swamped the *Clarion*'s publisher with threats that they would
yank their ads from the paper unless an editorial retraction was
published and I was fired.

Like most alternative weeklies, the *Clarion* was a free
paper, its existence dependent solely upon ad revenues.
Most publishers—like Pearl, bless his rancid heart—have
an iron rod thrust down their backs, knowing all too well
that advertisers need the papers just as much as the papers
need the advertisers and that editorial wimp-outs only invite
further intimidation. Earlier that year, though, the *Clarion* had
been sold to a greedhead who was innocent of journalistic
ethics and didn't have the common sense not to let himself
be cowed by hollow threats. This jellyfish, confronted with
the notion that he might not be able to purchase a summer
cottage on Martha's Vineyard, knuckled under.

Two weeks after the publication of my CybeServe story, I
was on my way to work when I stopped off at a Newbury
Street deli to have coffee and read the *Globe-Herald*. This
made me twenty minutes late for work. I had done it many
times before with no previous complaints, but when I showed
up at the office, my termination notice was already pinned to
my door. The reason given was "chronic tardiness."

I was cleaning out my desk and putting all my files in
cartons when my printer began to hum. I looked around to
see the handwritten fax as it dropped into the tray:

Never fuck with the gods.

The fax came unsigned, but when I double-checked the
number at the top of the page against my Rolodex, I saw that
it had originated from Huygens's extension at CybeServe. His
company was going down the tubes, but he was damned if he
wasn't going to take me with him.

And now here I was, in another place and another time,
fucking with the gods again.

"Huygens wanted to get me out of there," I said. "I don't know what it is, but there's something he doesn't want me to know about. I screwed him up once . . . he doesn't want that to happen again."

John nodded his head. "Could be. Could be . . ."

"I spotted the woman I met last night," I said as I cinched my seat upward again. John drove up the eastbound ramp to I-64, the car sliding into the dense midday traffic heading downtown. "Just before Huygens found me. She was across the room from us . . ."

"You did?" Tiernan looked mildly surprised; he passed a tandem-trailer rig that was chugging down the right lane and squeezed in behind a twenty-year-old BMW with Illinois tags and an expired gas-user decal. "What did she look like?"

"African-American, about five-six . . . um, sort of plump, about forty to forty-five. Some gray in her hair. It was her, all right." I hesitated, then added, "I used the camera to zoom in on her badge."

"Yeah?"

"Found out her position, too. Printed right on the badge."

"No kidding . . ."

"No kidding."

I fell silent. He waited for me to go on. "Well?"

I pointed at the shitbox ahead of us. Pale fumes billowed from its exhaust pipe. "Can you believe that they're still allowing cars like that on the road? I mean, I thought they were supposed to be enforcing the phase-out laws, and here's this clunker—"

"Gerry . . ."

"I think I'm going to do a column about this. I mean, I don't mind much if someone like Chevy Dick's got an antique in his garage and takes it out once every now and then, but when you see something like this in broad daylight . . . y'know, it's just disgraceful . . ."

John sighed. "Okay, okay, knock it off. What do you want to know?"

I grinned. It was an old game between us dating back to our college journalism days: quid pro quo information trading. You tell me your secrets and I'll tell you mine, tit for tat.

Sometimes the game had been played for higher stakes than this: when he wanted to know the name of the cute brunette in my Econ 101 class, I traded it to him for the home phone number of the university chancellor. It worked out pretty well; I was able to call the chancellor on a Sunday afternoon while he was watching a football game to ask him embarrassing questions about next semester's tuition hikes, and for this John received the name of his future wife.

"Ruby fulcrum," I said. "What's it mean?"

John sighed. "It's a code phrase of some sort. To be honest, I don't know much about it myself, except that it has something to do with the Sentinel program. This lady keeps mentioning it, though, so it must be important somehow."

He suddenly snapped his fingers, then reached above the windshield to pull down the car's flatscreen. "Let's see if CNN has anything on the launch."

" 'Don't know' doesn't count . . ."

"Okay, okay." Keeping one eye on traffic and one hand on the wheel, John switched the CTV to bring us CNN. "Ask me another one."

"Why are you talking to this woman?" I asked. "What's this story all about?"

John didn't say anything for a moment. On the screen, the CNN anchor was reading a story about the deployment of Army troops on the Oregon border. Footage of rifle-toting soldiers tramping down the ramp of an Air Force transport jet, APCs and tanks rolling down highways between coniferous forests, antiwar demonstrators attempting to barricade military convoys . . .

"It has to do with a murder," he said, carefully picking his words. "My source—and yeah, I think it's the same lady, though I've never seen her—says that a Tiptree scientist was killed recently. Even though the police are still calling it random homicide, she claims it's part of a conspiracy and has something to do with this Ruby Fulcrum business."

The footage on the screen changed back to the CNN newsroom; a window in the right corner displayed the NASA logo. "Here we go," John said as he turned up the volume.

"*. . . launched a half-hour ago from Cape Canaveral,*

Florida," the anchorwoman intoned as the screen switched to a shot of the shuttle *Endeavour* lifting off from its pad. *"In its cargo bay are the final components of the* Sentinel 1 *ABM satellite."*

Animated footage of the massive satellite, identical to the holographic image that had been displayed in the Tiptree atrium, replaced the live-action shot. *"Linkup between the shuttle and the twenty-billion-dollar satellite is expected sometime tomorrow afternoon."*

"A murder?" I asked. "What's this got to do with—"

"Forget it." John reached up to switch off the CTV as he finally found room to pass the BMW. I caught a glimpse of the driver as we moved around the clunker: a redneck wearing a baseball cap, a cigar clamped between his teeth. "That's all I'm giving you," he continued, "and I shouldn't have told you that much. Your turn."

"Beryl Hinckley," I said. "Her badge listed her as a research scientist. If you want, I'll get Jah to print you a copy of her photo so you can recognize her when you meet her at Clancy's tonight."

John nodded. "I'd appreciate it."

We fell silent for the next few miles as the suburbs thinned out and the towers of the uptown business district of Clayton hove into view. Clayton had come through the crisis pretty well: new office buildings, rich homes, not many indications that a 7.5 earthquake had socked this part of the city. Of course, much of the federal disaster relief funds had been channeled in this direction. The government had been fully aware of who was wealthy enough to be able to repay the loans, and everyone in St. Louis knew where the influential voters resided.

"Stay out of it," John said after a while.

"Excuse me?"

"Stay out of it," he repeated. "I know you're looking for a good story, and I know you're nervous about your job, but . . . just let me handle this one by myself, okay? If I need help, I'll call you in and we can share the byline—"

"C'mon. You know that's not what it's about . . ."

He looked askance at me and my voice trailed off. It was a

lie and John knew it. No, I wasn't nervous; I was desperate. If I didn't deliver something impressive PDQ, Pearl was going to find a new staff writer and I'd be back on the street. At best, I'd be some poor schmo freelancer, peddling video reviews to the *Big Muddy* for nickel-and-dime checks while living in a homeless shelter.

I didn't want to encroach on my friend's rightful territory, but this bit with Tiptree and Beryl Hinckley and Ruby Fulcrum was a hot potato I couldn't afford not to catch.

"C'mon, man," I said, "you can't—"

"I know." John kept his eyes locked on the highway ahead. "Look, you've got to trust me on this one. This is serious business, and not a little bit dangerous. Just . . . y'know, let me handle this by myself. All right?"

"All right." I raised my hands. "Okay . . . whatever you say."

John didn't have my problems. He still had everything I had lost. A nice car, a house in the 'burbs, a wife who didn't despise him, a job that was secure. A kid who was still alive. I envied him, sure . . .

For a moment, despite our long friendship, I caught myself hating him. He must have read my mind, because he nervously cleared his throat. "Look, if you want my advice," he began, "you're going to have to put some things behind you."

He hesitated. "I mean, your situation's tough and all that, but . . . well, Jamie's gone and you're just going to have to—"

"Right. Jamie's gone and I'm going to have to live with that. I know. Time to get a life." Out of impulse, I switched on the CTV again. "I think it's time for *Batman*. You know what channel it's on?"

John shut up. I found the station showing the favorite cartoon show of my misspent youth. The theme song swelled to fill the car as we sailed the rest of the way downtown: one man with a firm grip on reality, the other trying to avoid it at all costs.

Get a life. Sure, John. I had a life.

And boy, did it suck.

8

I dropped off the camera with Jah after we got back to the office; he promised to process the disk and give me a contact sheet before the end of the day. He also informed me that his father had found out about my surreptitious exit and was—in Jah's words—"livid pissed."

That meant sneaking up the stairs to the second floor. I had rather hoped Pearl had gone out for lunch for once, but the odor of fried brains assaulted me as I tiptoed past Bailey's door. Fried brains, that most obnoxious of St. Louis delicacies, was Pearl's favorite food; he brought a take-out deli plate of them to the office every day and consumed them in full view of the staff. Bailey didn't look up from his brains as I scurried to my desk, but I knew that he would eventually catch up with me.

I figured that the best thing for me to do was to look busy so that, at very least, he couldn't accuse me of goldbricking. I sat down at my desk and began work on my column for next week's paper. The subject was the ERA raid on the Muny last night; the morning *Post-Dispatch* gave me such clinical facts as the number of people who had been busted, but what came out in my column was a more subjective eyewitness account.

I was halfway through composing the article, in the middle of describing the arrival of the ERA troopers, when I caught a glimpse of Bailey as a reflection on my screen. I ignored him and went on writing; for a few moments he hovered just outside my cubicle as if trying to decide whether to say something, then he walked away. I glanced over at John; he

99

was on the phone at his desk, but he grinned back at me. My job was still safe—for today, at any rate.

Yet I couldn't get the events at Tiptree out of my mind. Sure, it wasn't my story, but nonetheless my journalistic curiosity was itching, and I needed a good scratch. After I finished the rough draft of my story and saved it, I switched the computer to modem and made a call to the city election commissioner's office.

Steve Estes' campaign contributions were a matter of public record; all I had to do was ask the right questions and the skeletons danced out of the closet and onto my screen. Estes had been a busy little political hack: his war chest listed contributions from hundreds of private individuals, among them many of the city's wealthiest and most powerful citizens. The list also included local corporate and PAC donations to Citizens to Re-Elect Steve Estes, and right smack in the middle of the list was $10,000 from the Tiptree Corporation.

Of course, that in itself didn't mean shit to a tree: everyone from the Republican National Committee to the National Rifle Association had written checks to Estes. It still meant that there was a subtle connection between Estes and Tiptree.

I made a hard copy of the file, circled the Tiptree item in red ink, and was about to pass it to John when I got a better idea. Almost on impulse, I picked up the phone and called Estes' office.

Estes was a senior partner in a downtown law firm; the switchboard operator passed the buck to Estes' private secretary, a hard-eyed young woman who looked as if she could have been a model for a 1947 Sears Roebuck catalog. Her bee-stung lips made a slight downturn when I identified myself as a *Big Muddy* reporter. *"Just a moment, please,"* she said. *"I'll see if he's in."*

She put me on hold, and I was treated to a computer-generated lily field and the theme for *The Sound of Music* for a couple of minutes. My gag reflex was kicking in when the flowers and Julie Andrews abruptly vanished, to be replaced by Steve Estes' face.

"Good afternoon, Gerry," he said, beaming at the camera. *"How can I help you?"*

We had never met or talked before, so I ignored the first-name familiarity. It was par for the political course. "Good afternoon, Mr. Estes," I said, touching the Record button on my phone. "I'm working on a story for my paper, regarding last night's raid by ERA troops on the Muny, and I was hoping I could get a response from you."

Estes didn't even blink. *"I'd be happy to give you a response,"* he said, *"but I'm afraid I don't know much more than what I've read in this morning's paper."*

He was already disavowing any connection. "Well, sir," I went on, "it's interesting to hear you say that, considering that you've gone on record to urge ERA to force the homeless population out of the park. Are you saying that you had nothing to do with the raid?"

He settled back in his chair, still smiling at me. *"For one thing, I'm not sure if 'raid' is the appropriate word,"* he replied, switching hands on the receiver. *" 'Peaceful police action' is probably the right term. And although I've asked Colonel Barris to step up his enforcement of the indigent population in Forest Park, I can't say that I've directly requested him to . . . um, conduct any 'raids,' so to speak, on the park or the Muny in particular."*

Clever son of a bitch. Until Estes saw how public reaction toward the raid swung, he was carefully avoiding any credit for it, while simultaneously making sure that his name was still associated with the "peaceful police action" if it turned out that the majority of voters were in favor of what had happened last night.

"Do you believe ERA should conduct any further . . . ah, police actions in the park?" I asked.

"I believe ERA should enforce the law and be responsible for the safety of all St. Louis citizens," he replied.

Another neutral answer. Estes might rave in the city council chamber about "taking the streets back," knowing that the TV news reporters would extract only a few seconds' worth of sound bite from his diatribe, but when confronted by a columnist for the local muckraker who might print his remarks in their complete context, he would play it much more safely. I had to hand it to Estes; he was a professional politician in every sense of the term. He couldn't be fooled by the loaded do-you-beat-your-wife queries that might foul up another politico.

"One more question," I said. "I was at the private reception held at the Tiptree Corporation this morning—"

"You were?" All innocence and light. *"Why, so was I. That was a beautiful shuttle launch, wasn't it?"*

"I wish I could have seen it," I said, "but my colleague and I were forcibly removed from the room . . ."

He raised a wary eyebrow. *"Really . . ."*

"Really. In fact, the Tiptree official who forced us out claimed that you minded the fact that I took a picture of you, and that's the reason why we were asked to leave."

Despite his polished self-possession, Estes looked flustered for a couple of moments. He glanced away from the camera for an instant, as if listening to someone just outside the phone's range of vision, then he looked directly back at me again. *"I'm sorry to hear that was you, Gerry,"* he said. *"My apologies . . . I thought you were someone else."*

"Uh-huh. Anyone in particular?"

His smile became rigid. *"No comment,"* he said evenly.

No wonder. "One more thing," I said, "and then I'll let you go. I happened to check your campaign disclosure and noticed that you've received a sizable contribution this last year from Tiptree. Can you tell me why?"

He blinked at my knowledge of this tidbit of information, but remained in control. *"Tiptree has been a good friend of the St. Louis community,"* he said, as if reciting from a campaign fact-sheet. *"It's employed thousands of people over the last several years and has been a growing part of the local aerospace community. As such, we have mutual interests at heart."*

"I see. And Project Sentinel . . . is that . . . ?"

"A great technological achievement, as Mr. McLaughlin said during his opening remarks." He made a show of looking at his watch. *"Now, if you'll please excuse me, I have to go. I have someone waiting in my office to see me."*

"Yes, well, thank—"

The screen blanked before I finished my sentence.

• • •

I went back to my column, this time incorporating the remarks Estes had made about the raid during our interview. They didn't make much of a difference, except that it was interesting to note how Estes' "peaceful police action" contrasted with the mob panic, tear gas, and gunfire I had seen and heard.

I finished the piece at about six o'clock, as green-tinted twilight seeped through the windows. By then most of the staff had already gone home; John and I were the last two people left in the editorial department. Jah stopped by to give me the contact sheet of the photos I had taken. I found the shot I had taken of Beryl Hinckley, and John glanced at it under a magnifying glass as he put on his overcoat, memorizing her face for the meeting he was supposed to have with her later that evening.

"You want me to come along for the ride?" I asked after Jah left. "I could help identify her when she—"

"Oh, no you don't," Pearl snapped.

I shut my eyes, cussing under my breath. I wasn't aware that Bailey was just outside the editorial cube. He had been shutting down the production department's photocopy machines when he overheard our conversation. Overheard, hell: the bastard had been eavesdropping.

"You let John take care of his own stories, Rosen," he said, glaring at me over the top of the partition. "All I want from you is your column and whatever else I specifically assign you. You hear me?"

Here it comes. The second chew-out of the day. Before I could muster a reply, John cleared his throat. "Pardon me," he said, "but I asked Gerry if he would help me out on this. He saw something at the Muny last night that . . . ah, might have something to do with what I'm working on."

It was a good lie, and Pearl almost fell for it. His eyes shifted back and forth between us, trying to decide who was putting on whom, before his basilisk stare settled on me. "Did you get your column written?" he demanded.

"Sure, Pearl . . . uh, Earl. Got it finished just a few minutes ago."

He grunted. "Good. Then tomorrow I want you working on the Arch story we talked about at the last staff meeting. Deadline by next Friday."

The assignment in question was a no-story story about why the Gateway Arch hadn't collapsed during the New Madrid quake. Why hadn't the Arch fallen? Because it was built well, that's why. When some dopey Wash You intern had suggested the piece, I had argued that point and added that the quake was old news; besides, who needed another feel-good piece about things that hadn't fallen down and gone boom? The TV stations, the *Post-Dispatch*, and the local shoppers had already published so many of these yarns that a new category in local journalism had been tacitly created to encompass them: Courageous Firemen, Heroic Pets, and Gee Whiz It's Still Standing Upright.

But Pearl had assigned it to me anyway—largely, I suspect, because he wanted to see how well I jumped through hoops. I was about to protest that this was a useless assignment when I caught John's stern expression out of the corner of my eye and shut up. Since I was already walking the tightrope, I might as well show off my other circus tricks.

"And the next time you decide to take off with John," Bailey went on, "you might have the common courtesy to tell me first. We got a tip this morning from some lady out in Webster Groves. Squirrels are back in Blackburn Park for the first time since the quake—"

"And there was no one here to cover it," I finished, snapping my fingers and shaking my head. "Aw, gee, I'm sorry I missed it. Sounds important."

John coughed loudly and covered his mouth with his hand, this time to disguise the grin on his face. Bailey shot a harsh look at him, then focused on me again. "I'm the editor here, Rosen, and you're the reporter. Understand? Just to teach you a lesson, I want you to call this lady back ASAP—"

"C'mon, Pearl—"

"And don't gimme me that 'Pearl' shit or I'll have you over in copyediting faster than you can say Oxford English Dictionary."

Translation: shape up or ship out. Unless I wanted to end my career at the *Big Muddy* proofreading pasteups and checking the grammar of the stuff sent in by the freelancers, I had better content myself with writing about squirrels and pretend to like it.

I didn't say anything, because anything I was likely to have said would probably have had me at the copyediting desk by Monday morning. Bailey gave me one last sour look, then picked up his jacket. "See you tomorrow, gentlemen," he said. "Don't forget to lock up behind you."

Then he strode down the center aisle between the cubicles, heading for the front door, where his son was waiting to drive him home.

"He'll get over it," John whispered. "Just lie low for the next couple of weeks and let him chill out." He opened his desk drawer, pulled out Dingbat, checked the battery LED, and slipped it into the wallet pocket of his trenchcoat. "If it's any consolation, I'm sorry I got you into this."

"Forget it," I said, waving him off. "It's my fault, not yours." I paused. "The offer's still open. If you want me to go with you to Clancy's . . ."

He shook his head. "Better not. I think I ought to do it alone this time." He tapped the proof shoot with his fingernail. "Your friend might get leery if she sees both of us."

I nodded. He was right; the story was the most important thing, not who covered it. I began to turn off the rest of the lights. Since I lived just upstairs, it was my job to close down the office on the way out the back door. John picked up his gray fedora and walked past me as he headed toward the front door, then abruptly stopped as if a thought had just occurred to him.

"Do me a favor, though," he added. "Let me know how this bit with the squirrels turns out."

I tried not to be irritated by his seeming condescension. My friend was attempting to take an interest in my work, making me feel as if it was something that really mattered. He was on the trail of a murderer, and I was stuck with some silly-ass story that would only wind up as a small piece in the front section, if it saw print at all.

"Sure, man," I mumbled. "I'll let you know."

"Could be interesting," he said hesitantly, realizing that he had said the wrong thing. "You never know . . ."

"Right . . ."

He turned around again. "See you in the morning."

"Catch you later," I said.

I set the office phone so that it would ring upstairs, shut off the lights, made sure all the doors and windows were locked, then climbed the back stairs to my apartment. It was a warm and humid night, so I cracked open the windows and warmed up a can of SpaghettiOs on the hot plate while I caught a rerun of some old cop show on TV. Robert Urich and his wisecracking buddy caught the bad guys after a car chase; such a surprise. I had no idea what the story was about, but it made me forget how awful my dinner was.

I was out of beer, but I was still suffering alcohol fatigue from last night's bender, so I didn't go out to buy another six-pack from the grocery on 12th. It had begun to drizzle outside, and all I really wanted to do was to stay home and stay dry.

After I dumped my plate in the sink and turned off the tube, I sat down at the computer and tried to get some real writing done. After spending an hour rewriting the same boring paragraph several times, though, I realized that my muse had gone on vacation in Puerto Rico and, besides, the Great American Novel still sucked lizard eggs. I switched off the computer without bothering to save the few lines I had written, shucked my clothes, and curled up in bed with a secondhand paperback spy novel.

I fell asleep while reading, not even bothering to turn off the lamp over the bed. Rain gently pattered on the fire escape, city traffic moaned, and helicopters clattered overhead. The night world moved on around me; I vaguely heard the sound of police sirens from somewhere nearby and rolled over in my sleep, dreaming of nothing I could remember.

A countless time later, I was awakened by the buzz of the phone. That did for me what the familiar urban noises outside the window could not; I opened my eyes and, squinting in the glare of the lamp, fumbled for the handset beside me.

" 'Lo?" I said, expecting it to be Marianne, calling to nag me again about Uncle Arnie.

A male voice on the other end of the line: *"Is this the* Big Muddy Inquirer *office?"*

Shit. I should have turned on the answering machine. "Yeah, but we're closed now. Can you call back tomorrow . . . ?"

"Who's this?" the voice demanded.

"Who wants to know?"

A pause. *"This is Lieutenant Mike Farrentino, St. Louis Police Homicide Division. Is this one of the staff?"*

Homicide division? What the fuck was this? I woke up a little more. The clock on my dresser said it was 9:55 P.M. "Yeah, it is," I said. "Why, what's—"

"What's your name?" When I didn't answer promptly, the voice became stronger. *"C'mon, what's your—"*

"Rosen." A cold chill was beginning to creep down my spine. "Gerry Rosen. I'm a staff writer. Why are you—?"

"Mr. Rosen, I'm at Clancy's Bar and Grill, just down the street from your office. We have a dead person here whose personal ID says that it is the property of one John L. Tiernan, a reporter for your paper. Would you mind coming down here to verify the identity of the deceased, please?"

9

Blue lights flashing in a humid night in the city, veiled by dense evening fog. The distant hoot of a tugboat pushing barges down the Mississippi River. The sound of boot soles slapping against a brick sidewalk . . .

This is the aftermath of murder.

Clancy's Bar & Grill was crawling with cops by the time I got down there: three blue-and-whites parked on Geyer with a couple of unmarked cruisers sandwiched between them, and out of them had emerged what seemed to be half of the St. Louis Police Department, most of them standing scratching their asses and trying to look as if they knew what they were doing. It figured that a poor black dude can get shot in the head in broad daylight down in Dogtown and nobody gives a shit, but a middle-class white guy gets killed in a Soulard barroom and most of the force shows up, looking for trouble.

The bar was almost empty. Given its usual clientele, though, it only made sense that the regulars would have cleared out as soon as the cops arrived on the scene. A big, burly policeman was standing beneath the front awning, listening to his headset as he watched the sidewalk; he blocked my way as I approached the door.

"Sorry, pal, but you can't go in right now. Police business—"

"Outta my way," I muttered as I tried to push past him, "I gotta get in there—"

And found myself being shoved backward so fast I lost my balance and fell against two more cops who were standing on the sidewalk. One of them, a thin Latino cop, snagged the back of my jacket. "Hey, sport," he said as he began to usher me away, "find another place to get a drink, okay? This is—"

"Fuck off." I shrugged out of his grip, headed for the door again. "My friend's—"

The Latino cop grabbed my right arm and twisted it behind my back. I yelped as I was forced to my knees, and all of a sudden I saw nothing but shiny black cop shoes all around me as a riot baton was pressed against the back of my neck, forcing my head down while yet another officer grabbed my left arm and pulled it behind me.

"Ease down, pal! Ease down!"

Ease down, hell. The cops were all over me, securing my wrists with plastic cuffs while I struggled against them. I was halfway through most of the words your mother told you she'd wash your mouth out with soap if she ever heard you say them again when I heard a new voice.

"Stimpson! Who is this man!"

Stimpson was the first cop I had confronted. "Just some jerk who wouldn't take no for an answer, Lieutenant," he said. "We asked him to leave, but he's decided he wanted to—"

"Did you bother to ask him his name first?" I tried to look up, but the riot baton continued to force my head down toward the brick sidewalk. "Sir, can you tell me your name?"

"Rosen," I managed to gasp. "Gerry Rosen. I'm with the *Big Muddy*—"

"Shit. Let him up, D'Angelo." The grip on my arms relaxed a little. "I said, let him up," the lieutenant demanded. "That's the man I called down here, for chrissake."

"Yes sir." D'Angelo hesitated, then let go of my arm and grabbed me beneath my arms to gently lift me off my knees. As he produced a pair of scissors and cut off the handcuffs, the rest of the cops who had encircled me took a powder, their batons and tasers sliding back into belt loops and holsters.

My savior was a tall, gaunt plainclothes cop in his late thirties. He wore a calf-length raincoat and a wide-brimmed fedora, and a cigarette dangled from thin lips in a pockmarked face that looked as if it had once suffered from chronic acne. He brushed past Stimpson and thrust out his hand.

"Michael Farrentino, homicide division," he said by way of formal introduction. "Glad to meet you, Mr. Rosen. Sorry about the rough treatment."

I ignored both the hand and the apology. "You said you found my friend in here," I said, my voice rough as I massaged my chafed wrists. "Where is he?"

I started to push past him, heading for the door again. "Hey, whoa . . . hold on. Just wait a moment." Farrentino stepped in front of me as he reached up with both hands to grab my shoulders. "Just let me ask you a couple of questions first—"

"Fuck that," I snapped. "Where's John?"

We stared each other eye to eye for another moment, then Farrentino's hands fell from my shoulders. He took the cigarette out of his mouth and flicked it into the street. "Okay, have it your way," he murmured. "Follow me."

To my surprise, he didn't escort me directly into the bar. Instead he led me past the front door and about twenty feet farther down the sidewalk, past a high brick wall, until we reached the narrow iron gate that led into Clancy's open-air beer garden. Two more cops were guarding the red tape—marked CRIME SCENE DO NOT PASS—that had been stretched across the open gate. They moved aside as Farrentino ducked under it, then held it up for me so I could pass through.

Many of St. Louis's saloons have *biergartens*, a fine old tradition that the city's first settlers brought with them from Germany during the 1800's. Even though this particular beer garden now sported an Irish name, it resided behind a three-story building and was just old enough to have a real garden. Picnic tables and iron chairs were arranged between small Dutch elms and brick planters; from the number of half-empty beer bottles and plastic cups left abandoned on the table, it seemed as if there had been a fair number of people in Clancy's beer garden before the law had arrived in large numbers.

But the scene of the crime wasn't down here; instead, it was an enclosed balcony on the second floor in the rear of the building. I could see a number of people clustered around the corner of the balcony overlooking the street; portable camera lights had been rigged on tripods around the wooden balustrade, and they were all aimed down at something on the porch floor, but I couldn't see what it was.

Farrentino silently led me up the weathered pinewood stairs to the balcony. More cops, a couple of bored-looking paramedics with a stretcher, two more plainclothes homicide dicks—Farrentino led me through the crowd as they parted for us, until we reached the end of the balcony and I got a chance to see what all the fuss was about.

The body sprawled across the porch floor was definitely that of John Tiernan. His trench coat, his tie, even his patent-leather shoes: I had seen him wearing those clothes only a few hours earlier. But it took me a few moments to recognize his face.

That was because it looked as if someone had taken a white-hot fireplace poker and had shoved it into his skull, straight through the center of his forehead.

The black moment had come for John so quickly that his eyes were wide open, seeing only those things dead men can see.

When I was through vomiting over the rail, Farrentino led me back downstairs to the beer garden. He sat me down at a picnic table out of sight from the balcony, gave me a handkerchief so I could dry my mouth, and left me alone for a couple of minutes; when he came back, he had a shot glass of bourbon in one hand and a beer chaser in the other. The dubious benefits of having a murder committed at a bar.

I belted back the shot of bourbon, ignoring the chaser. The liquor burned down my gullet and into my stomach; I gasped and for a moment my guts rebelled, but the booze stayed down, and after a moment there was quietude of a sort. I slumped back in the chair and tried not to think of the horror I had just seen.

"Ready to talk?" Farrentino asked, not unkindly. I nodded my head; he pulled out a palmtop and flipped it open. "Is that John Tiernan? Can you give me a positive identification?"

I slowly nodded my head. Farrentino waited patiently for a verbal reply. "Yeah . . . yeah, that's John," I said. "I'm sure that's him."

"Okay." The homicide detective made an entry in his computer. "I know that was rough on you, Mr. Rosen, but we had to be sure. We've got to call his family next, and even though we got his driver's license from his wallet, I wanted to have someone else identify him before I put out a call to his wife. You were convenient and . . . well, I hope you understand."

I nodded. Poor Sandy. I was glad that she hadn't seen him like this. "Thanks, Officer. Do you want me to call her?"

"No, I'd just as soon do it myself." Farrentino pulled out a pack of cigarettes, shook one out, and offered it to me. I shook my head, he took the cigarette for himself, lighting it from the bottom of the pack. "I hate to say it, but I've gotten used to this part of the job," he went on. "I think it'd be better if she got the news from me instead of you. Me, she can hate for the rest of her life and it won't matter much, but if she hears it from you . . ."

"Yeah, okay. I understand."

He shrugged as he exhaled blue smoke. "So . . . when was the last time you saw the deceased?"

I actually had to think about it; all of a sudden, it seemed as if days instead of hours had passed since I had last seen John alive. "Around six, six-thirty, I think. We were closing down the office for the day."

"Uh-huh." Farrentino typed another note in his PT. "Do you have any idea where he was going?"

I became wary. Sure, I knew where John was going, and why . . . but I wasn't sure if I was ready to tell these things to Farrentino. "He said he was coming down here, but I'm not really sure what he was doing."

Farrentino continued to make notes. "You knew he was coming here," he said, "but you don't know why? Maybe he was just going out for a few drinks. That's what most people do when they go to a bar after work."

"Uh . . . yeah. That's what he was doing—"

"Except when I talked to the bartender, he told me that Mr. Tiernan hardly ordered anything the whole time he was here. He remembers him buying one beer when he arrived at . . ."

Farrentino checked his notes. "A quarter to eight, and he nursed it the entire time he was here. I suppose he must have gone somewhere for dinner before then."

I picked up my beer and took a sip from it. The bottle was slippery in my hand. "Yeah, I guess so," I said. "That would make sense."

"Hmm. Maybe so." The detective coughed, his eyes still on the miniature screen. "Do you know if he was . . . well, y'know, fooling around with anyone? Had a girlfriend on the side his wife didn't know about?"

I felt a rush of anger but tried to keep it in check. "I'm not sure that's any of your business, Officer."

"Well? Did he?" He shrugged indifferently. "Maybe it's none of my business, but still it's something his wife might want to know when I call her—"

"Hell, no!" I snapped. "If he was meeting anyone here, it sure as hell wasn't a . . ."

My voice trailed off as the realization hit me. Farrentino had skillfully led me into a trap, forcing me to contradict myself. His eyes slowly rose from the PT. "I didn't ask if he was meeting anyone here, Mr. Rosen," he said. "Maybe you do know something about what he was doing here, after all."

From behind the garden wall, there was the wail of a siren approaching from down the street. I could hear the metallic clank from the balcony as the paramedics unfolded their stretcher. A couple of barmaids stood watching us from the back door, murmuring to each other.

Farrentino was about to say something else when a uniformed cop approached our table, carrying several plastic-bagged objects in his hands. "This is all we found in his pockets," he said, holding them out for the detective to examine. "Do you want us to have 'em dusted?"

I recognized some of the items: his house keys, his car remote, his wallet, an old-fashioned fountain pen Sandy had given to him as a birthday present, some loose change, the ever-present pack of chewing gum . . .

And, in a bag of its own, Dingbat.

"Hmm?" Farrentino barely glanced at the collection. "Uhh . . . naw, I don't think we need to do that. The only prints we'd find are his own. Just leave 'em with me. I'll give them to his wife when I see her."

The cop nodded his head and carefully laid them on the table between us before walking away. It occurred to me that John might have entered a few notes into Dingbat during his meeting with Beryl Hinckley. If there were any important clues as to why he had been killed, perhaps they might be stored on the PT's floptical diskette.

"Okay, Rosen," Farrentino said, breaking my train of thought, "let's level with each other."

"Sure." I shrugged, trying not to stare covetously at Dingbat; it was just within hand's reach. "Anything you want to know, Officer." As I spoke, I picked up the beer and started to raise it to my mouth . . .

And then, at the last moment, I let my fingers slip from around the bottle.

It fell out of my grasp, bounced off the table, and fell between my legs, splattering beer across everything before the bottle broke on the concrete under the table. "Aw, shit!" I yelled, jumping up from my seat, staring down at the wet splotch that had spread across the crotch of my jeans. "Goddamn fucking . . . !"

When I want to screw up a conversation, I can outdo myself. Beer spilled off the table and onto the broken glass scattered across the ground. Farrentino stood up from his chair, alarmed and irritated at the same time. "What a fucking mess!" I whined. "I can't believe I just . . . look, lemme go back to my place and get some dry pants on. It'll just take a—"

"No, no, don't do that," Farrentino said, already moving away from the table. "Just stay here, okay? I'll go get someone to clean all this stuff up . . ."

Then he turned his back to me and headed for the barroom's back door; the two barmaids had already gone inside, presumably to get some towels and a broom and dustpan.

For a few precious moments, I was alone in the beer garden. I snatched up the evidence bag containing Dingbat. There was a red adhesive seal across the plastic zipper, but there was no time to worry about that now. I hastily unzipped the bag, breaking the seal, and shook the palmtop out into my hand, all the while keeping one eye on the door.

It took me only a second to eject the mini-disk from Dingbat's floptical drive and stash it in the pocket of my jacket before I returned the PT to the bag and zipped it shut again. I had barely placed the bag back on the picnic table when Farrentino and one of the barmaids came out the door again.

We spent the next few minutes wiping up the spilled beer with paper towels and letting the barmaid sweep up the broken glass. I made a big deal out of sponging beer from my pants, although I kept one eye on the evidence bag. If you looked closely, you could see the split in the tape seal; someone would notice eventually, but I hoped to be long gone by then.

"Okay," Farrentino said at last, after the mess was cleaned away and the barmaid was gone. He sat down at the table, clasping his hands together as he stared at me. "Here's what happened . . ."

"Go on," I said, adjusting my posture so that he wouldn't have to look at both the evidence bag and me at the same time.

"A lady arrived here at the bar shortly after Tiernan showed up," he went on, his voice lowered. "Black lady, nervous looking. Witnesses say they went up to that balcony together and were up there for a long time, talking. Seems they wanted to be someplace where they couldn't be overheard. He was getting up as if to leave when he was shot—"

"How was he killed?" I asked. Farrentino hesitated. "That wasn't a normal gunshot either," I went on as my memory put together a picture of what I had seen up there. "He should have had his brains splattered all over the place if it had been from a gun, but I didn't see any blood . . ."

Farrentino reluctantly nodded his head. "No, there wasn't any blood. No one heard a gunshot either. Witnesses say that they heard the woman scream, that's all. A second after that, a van parked across the street took off, but no one got its make or license number. The woman ran off before anyone could stop her."

"You didn't answer the question," I said. "How was John killed?"

"We have some ideas," he said tersely. "We're looking into it right now—"

"Wonderful. I'm overwhelmed."

"Don't be a smartass," Farrentino said, giving me a sour look. "Off the record, though, we think that it might have been a laser weapon of some sort. Remember the 'Dark Jedi' slayings in Chicago a couple of years ago?"

A chill ran down my back as he said that. Of course I remembered; it had been national news for several months. A serial killer—who, in a letter sent to the *Chicago Tribune*, had called himself the "Dark Jedi"—had picked off seven people at random over the course of several weeks, using a high-energy laser rifle. When the FBI and Illinois State Police finally tracked him down, the Dark Jedi turned out to be a rather sociopathic high school student from an upscale Chicago suburb. The scariest part of the case, though, was the fact that he had devised his weapon from a science-hobby handbook available in most bookstores, using equipment purchased through mail-order catalogs. In fact, the feds had found him because he had previously showed off a prototype of his laser rifle at a science fair; his "light saber" had won a second-place ribbon.

"So you think it's a copycat killer?" I asked.

Farrentino shrugged. "That's a possibility, but we don't know yet. That's all I can tell you right now." He then jabbed a finger at me. "You next. Shoot."

"Okay." I folded my arms across my chest. "He told me he was investigating a murder—"

"Whose murder?"

"I don't know," I said. Which was the truth.

"Who was the lady?"

"I don't know that either," I said. Which was a lie.

"C'mon, Rosen—"

"All I know was that he was supposed to meet someone here at eight o'clock, and it had to do with the story he was doing." I shrugged, gazing back at him. "That's all I know . . . but I'm telling you, whoever she was, it wasn't a girlfriend. John didn't cheat on his wife. That's a fact."

Farrentino's dark eyes searched my face. He said nothing for a few moments. He knew that I hadn't told him everything I knew about the circumstances leading up to John's murder, and I knew that he wasn't playing entirely fair with me either. In John's memory, we were playing one final game of quid pro quo, and this round had just reached a stalemate.

I glanced toward the entrance to the beer garden. A couple of cops were holding open the gate; I could hear the ponderous clank of the stretcher's wheels as the parameds carefully inched it down the stairs from the balcony. In a few moments there would be nothing left of my buddy except a yellow chalk mark on a wooden floor.

"Lemme tell you something," Farrentino said at last. "You may think you know a lot about this, but I know more than you do. John was a friend of mine . . ."

"Yeah?" John had plenty of friends on the force. For all I knew, Farrentino could have been a deep-throat source, but I had no way of proving that. "I'm sure he would have been glad to see you down here for him."

Farrentino ignored the dig. "And he would have wanted us to work together to nail the guy who killed him. So if you want to come clean and tell me everything you know . . ."

The noise from the stairs stopped. The stretcher was on the ground. "I'll keep it in mind, Lieutenant," I said as I stood up again. "Now if you'll excuse me, I want to go see John off."

He started to say something else, but before he could stop me, I edged my way around the table and headed for the other side of the beer garden.

I stood on the sidewalk for a couple of minutes, watching John's body as it was wheeled away. A white sheet had been pulled over the corpse, with three straps holding it down on the stretcher, but for some damn reason I kept expecting him to sit up, reach into his pocket, and ask if I wanted some gum.

The paramedics stopped the stretcher behind the ambulance's rear fender, folded the stretcher's wheels, then picked it up. I remembered us getting drunk together at college parties and going out for double dates with Marianne and Sandy. Standing in line before the graduation platform, waiting to get our diplomas while making whispered jokes about the pontifical commencement speech Sam Donaldson had just delivered. The letters and postcards he had sent me while we were living on opposite sides of the country, the absurd wedding presents we had sent to each other when we had married our girlfriends, the long-distance phone calls when our kids had been born.

Now it all came down to this: one guy watching the other being loaded into the back of a meat wagon, down here in the scuzzy part of town. I had always thought he was going to outlive me . . .

"Helluva shame, isn't it?" Mike Farrentino said from behind me.

I jerked involuntarily. I hadn't realized that he had been at my back the entire time. "Yeah," I mumbled, not looking around at him. "Helluva shame."

As the stretcher was pushed into the back of the ambulance and its doors slammed closed, I eased my way out of the crowd and began to walk, not too quickly, up the street away from Clancy's. With each step I took, I expected someone to yell "Hey you!" and then ten cops would be climbing all over me again.

That instant never came. I was a block away when I heard the ambulance drive away from the curb. By then I was in the darkened doorway of the *Big Muddy* offices, reaching into my pocket to make sure I still had the mini-disk I had stolen from Dingbat.

It was still there, a little silver disk about the size of an antique fifty-cent piece. I looked down the street, but the detective was nowhere in sight among the blue leather jackets still clustered around the front of Clancy's. I shoved the disk back in my pocket and ducked around the corner of the building, heading for the fire escape ladder.

There would be plenty of time for mourning later. Right now, all I wanted to do was find a killer.

10

As soon as I crawled through my apartment window, I switched on my computer and booted up the mini-disk I had taken from John's PT, and the first thing I did was make a backup copy.

Call it paranoia, but I knew that it was only a matter of time before the cops discovered that the evidence bag had been unsealed; even though I had fooled Farrentino once, I wasn't going to count on his remaining stupid. The police could be here by morning with a search warrant. When the copy was made, I slipped it into a plastic case and took it into the bathroom, where I hid it beneath the toilet tank with a strip of electrical tape.

Back at my desk again, I rebooted the original disk and copied it onto the hard drive; once it was loaded into my system, I tried to punch up the root directory, only to find that I needed a password to get in. No problem there; not long ago, shortly after I had gone to work at the *Big Muddy*, John and I had agreed to share our passwords with each other, in case I ever needed to hack into his PT or vice versa. Being a faithful University of Missouri alumnus, his password was "Mizzou"; mine was "chickenlegs," for no other reason than I happened to be dining upon an Extra Crispy Recipe snack box from the Colonel at the time. I typed in "Mizzou," the system cleared me through, and I got my first peek at whatever had been contained in Dingbat's memory.

I let out a low whistle as the screen was immediately filled by a directory as long as a small-town phone book. A bar

119

at the top of the screen told me that almost 100 megabytes of information had been copied into my system, leaving less than 50 kilobytes free on the disk. As I ran the cursor down the screen, a seemingly endless list of filenames scrolled upward, many of them suffixed as BAT or EXEC commands, none of them immediately recognizable.

An extremely complex program of some sort had been loaded into Dingbat's floptical drive shortly before John's death. Tiernan had no business carrying around something like this unless Beryl Hinckley had downloaded it into his PT during their encounter at the bar . . . but exactly what it was, I hadn't the foggiest idea. Cyberpunk, I am not; my hacking skills were only those of the average computer-literate college grad, and I didn't have the knowledge necessary to understand a program of this complexity.

One thing for damn sure: my best friend had been shot through the head with a laser beam shortly after receiving this program. And despite what Farrentino had said about his murder resembling the "Dark Jedi" killings, I had the gut feeling that John's death had not been a random shooting.

What if John had been assassinated?

And, to take this supposition one step further: what if John had been assassinated because of the contents of this very disk?

I took a deep breath, forcing myself to calm down. Don't get panicky. I leaned forward again and began to run further down the directory, trying to find something that looked like a main menu or even a READ.ME file. I was like a blind man thrown into a large and unfamiliar room, but if I could just get hold of something I could use as a white cane, I might be able to . . .

The phone buzzed.

The answering machine was switched on, but without thinking I snatched the receiver off the cradle and lifted it to my ear. "Hello?" I said.

No voice from the other end of the line; the phonescreen remained blank. Figuring it for a wrong-number call, I was about to hang up when I heard, as if in the background, a brief, swift sequence of electronic snaps, chirps, and beeps.

"Hello?" I repeated. "Who's there?"

As soon as I spoke again, the electronic noise ceased. There was a moment of silence, and I had almost hung up when I suddenly heard a toneless voice speak from the other end:

"Hello . . . hello . . . who's there . . . hello . . ."

"Who is this?" I said, losing patience.

The screen flickered, then random fractals appeared, casting undulating images like electronic finger paintings. A couple more chirps and beeps, then there came a sound like an audiotape being replayed at high speed—high-pitched voices, as if Alvin and the Chipmunks were bleating nursery rhymes from an old NASA space probe lost out beyond Jupiter—as the fractals congealed and began to assume a vaguely human shape. Then:

"Hey, who is this? . . . hello . . . who's there? . . . hello . . ."

It was my own voice.

Now the head and shoulders of a person appeared on the screen, but his/her features were in constant flux: eyes, nose, lips, brow, chin, cheekbones, hairline, all changing more rapidly than my eye could follow. Sometimes the face looked like my own, and then it would be me as a woman, then as a bearded woman, then as a black man with a beard, then as a new face entirely.

"Who is this?" I demanded. "Who . . . hey, Jah, if this is you fucking around, I'm going to unscrew your head and shit down your—"

Throughout all the changes, the face's lips moved, yet my voice coming from the speaker no longer sounded quite like my own. It had a scrambled, surreal quality: *"Jah . . . if you're fucking around . . . hey, Jah, I'm going to shit down your head and unscrew your . . . who is this? . . . Jah, I'm going to unscrew your shit and fuck down your . . ."*

The face's permutations began to slow down, becoming distinctly male, getting younger. Again there were beeps, chirps, and a sound like a tape being fast-forwarded, and then:

"Rosen, Gerard . . . Gerard Rosen . . . Gerry Rosen . . . Can I talk to you, Daddy?"

A new face appeared on the screen.

I slammed down the receiver.

The face stared at me for another instant, then vanished entirely, leaving behind only a blank screen.

For a long time I simply stared at the phone. A soft nocturnal wind whispered outside the window like a ghost asking to come in. I felt my heart pound against the inside of my rib cage, smelled the acrid tang of my sweat. After five minutes my computer's screensaver switched itself on; bright, multicolored fractals began to undulate across the screen, Mandelbrot equations casting impermanent algorithmic sandpaintings, the black magic of higher mathematics.

And still I stared at the phone, unwilling to accept the face and voice I had just seen and heard.

God help me, it had been Jamie.

A sharp knock at the apartment door brought me back to the present.

"Who's there?" I called out. No reply; I thought I had been hearing things when there came another knock, a little harder this time.

Probably Chevy Dick, coming over to see if I wanted a beer or something. He had a keycard and knew the codes to disable the front door alarms. I wasn't in any mood for drinking, but I needed some company right now, so I stood up from the chair and headed for the door. "Okay, hold on," I muttered. "I'll be there in a—"

The door slammed open, its lock broken by the force of a violent kick, and four soldiers in riot gear swarmed into the loft.

"Freeze, asshole!" one of them yelled, crouching next to the door, his Heckler & Koch G-11 leveled straight at me. "ERA!"

A second later the fire-escape window was shattered by the impact of a rifle butt; I whipped around to see two more ERA troopers coming in through the window.

"Hey, what the fuck are—"

I didn't get the chance to complete this line of inquiry, as one of the grunts who had charged the front door tackled me from behind. The air was punched out of my lungs as I hit the wood floor face-first; I gasped, fighting for breath, and tried to raise myself on my elbows, only to be forced down when a heavy boot landed against my back.

"Stay down, asshole . . . !"

I was about to twist out from under the boot when I felt the blunt muzzle of a G-11 press against the nape of my neck.

"I said, stay down!"

I managed to nod my head and lie still, choking on the dust from the floor as I gasped for air, while I heard a cacophony of voices around me:

"Okay, we got him."

"Check the bathroom!"

"Somebody find a switch! Get some lights on in here!" A second later the room was flooded with light from the ceiling fixture.

"Bathroom's clear, Sarge! He's alone."

"Bell, check the desk. Look and see if he's got it."

Sounds of papers been rifled through on my desk, then the snap of the disk drive being ejected. "Right here, Sarge. He's got it on his screen now."

"Good deal. You and Todd pack up the CPU. Take all the disks you can find . . . grab all those papers, too. Find a box or something."

"Right, Sarge . . ."

"Romeo Charlie, this is Golf Bravo, do you copy, over . . ."

"Stay down, buddy. Just stay cool . . ."

My arms were yanked behind my back as, for the second time that night, a pair of plastic handcuffs were slipped around my wrists and tightened. The boot lifted from my back, but the rifle stayed in place.

"Man, this place smells like shit . . ."

"Belongs to a reporter, what do you expect?"

Laughter. "Shaddup, you guys . . . ten-four, Romeo Charlie. Premises secured, no one else present. Ten-fifteen-bravo, Charlie, over . . ."

I lay still on the floor, but I turned my head to see what was going on at my desk. A couple of troopers were dismantling my computer, one of them holding the CPU in his hands as the other disconnected the cables. A third soldier had found an empty carton and was shoving the manuscript of my novel into it; when he was done, he grabbed the cord of my telephone, ripped it straight out of the wall jack, and threw the phone into the box. Can't be too careful about these subversive telephones.

"What are you guys doing here?" I demanded. "Why are you—?"

"Shut up," the trooper behind me said.

I ignored him. "What am I being charged with? What's—"

"Shut up." The boot returned to my back, pinning me flat against the floor. "When we want you to talk, we'll tell you, okay? Now shut your mouth."

"Ten-four, Romeo Charlie. Ten-twenty-four and we'll be seeing you soon. Golf Bravo over and out . . . okay, guys, let's get out of here before the neighbors catch on."

The boot and the gun muzzle rose from my back, then two pairs of hands grabbed my arms and hauled me to my feet. "Okay, dickhead," one of the troopers murmured, "let's go catch a baseball game."

If I had any doubts about where I was headed, they were laid to rest by that comment.

I remained silent as I let them march me out the front door of my apartment. Another ERA soldier was standing on the second-story landing, his rifle propped against his hip. The sheet-metal door leading into the newspaper office was still shut; whoever had ordered this raid had apparently drawn the line at breaking and entering the *Big Muddy Inquirer*. Afraid of the adverse publicity, I suppose.

I was still wondering how they had managed to enter the building without triggering the alarms when we got down to the first floor. Another trooper was standing next to the alarm panel, the PT in his hands hardwired to its innards. He had managed to decode and disable the security system. He barely glanced at me as I was pulled out onto the sidewalk.

Geyer Street was empty except for the two gray Piranhas idling at the curb, their turret-mounted water cannons rotated toward the sidewalks on either side of the street. If there's anything more scary than seeing a couple of armored cars

parked at your front door, I hope I never live to see it, but
if the ERA had been anticipating a neighborhood riot over
the arrest of a deadbeat reporter, they were disappointed. The
sidewalks were empty, and no wonder; anyone with common
sense was staying inside, peering through the slats of their
window shades at what was going on.

A tow truck was parked in front of the two LAVs, its forklift
gears whining as the front end of John's Deimos was raised
off the street. They were taking everything that mattered—
computers, John's car, telephones, even the manuscript of an
unpublished book. No cops in sight, though, and that was a
little puzzling. After all the local talent that had converged
on Clancy's after John's murder, it was surprising to see
that there were no police cruisers in sight, especially since
I was apparently being busted for having stolen the micro-CD
from the evidence bag . . .

A cold chill raced down my spine as the realization hit
me: this was entirely an ERA operation. Keeping SLPD in
the dark about this raid, in fact, was likely a top priority; the
squad leader had probably been using a scrambled frequency
when he had called back to headquarters to report his team's
success.

A soldier opened the rear hatches of the first Piranha, then
the two grunts who had escorted me down the stairs pushed me
into the armored car. Two more climbed in behind them; one
of them went forward into the narrow driver's compartment
up front, while the other climbed a short ladder to the turret
behind the water cannon.

The rear hatches were slammed shut again as the two soldiers sat me down on one of the fold-down seats. One of
them sat next to me; the other took a seat directly across
the narrow aisle. They rested their G-11s across their knees
and said nothing; after a few moments, one of them found a
pack of cigarettes in the pocket of his flak vest.

"I guess it would be too much to ask if you wouldn't
smoke," I said. "It's kinda stuffy in here as it is."

The two troopers stared at each other, then broke up laughing.
Their name badges read B. MULLENS and B. HEFLER. Bob and
Bob, the Gestapo Twins.

"No, it's not too much to ask," said Bob Mullens as he pulled out a cigarette and lit it off the bottom of the pack. From his voice, I recognized him as the guy who had stuck a gun against the back of my head. "Hell, you can ask for anything you want . . ."

How about a slow, painful death from lung cancer? I didn't say anything; Mullens blew some smoke in my direction and favored me with a shit-eating grin, but when that didn't get a rise out of me he settled back against the padded back of his seat.

"Son," he drawled, "you are in a world of shit."

Hefler gave a high-pitched laugh at his partner's bit of wisdom. "Yeah, man," he said, "you're going to hell in a bucket."

Ask a silly question, get some stupid clichés. I silently stared at the metal floor beneath my feet, trying to figure out what was happening to me. After a minute we heard the driver shift gears; the vehicle lurched forward on its tandem wheels, diesel engines growling as the Piranha began to trundle down the street.

I was going to hell in a bucket, and I can't say I enjoyed the ride.

PART THREE

Phase Transition

(April 19, 2013)

11

It was a short, bumpy ride from Soulard to Busch Stadium, little more than a sprint down Broadway, but the LAV's driver seemed hell-bent on finding every pothole in the tortured asphalt and driving through it at top speed. My new pals Bob and Bob got a kick out of watching me try to remain seated with my hands cuffed behind my back. I rocked back and forth, my shoulder muscles aching a little with each unanticipated turn and jar the Piranha took; they thought it was pretty funny.

It's amazing how little it takes to amuse some people. I suppose they had already chewed up their rubber balls and tug-toys.

The bells in the Old Cathedral down by the riverside were tolling twelve times when the armored car slowed down. Its wheels bumped again, this time as if the Piranha was crawling over a curb, then the vehicle ground to a halt. There was a double-rap against the wall in front of the driver's compartment. Mullens stood up, grasped one of my arms, and pulled me out of my seat.

"End of the line, buddy," he said as Hefler unlatched the rear hatches and pushed them open. "Time for you to go see the colonel."

"Yeah," said Hefler as he stepped out of the vehicle. "And when he's through, maybe you can go for another ride with us. Would you like that, huh?"

I kept silent as Mullens hauled me out of the LAV. The vehicle had come to a stop in the middle of the wide plaza in

129

front of the stadium's Walnut Street entrance. Concrete barricades topped with coiled razor wire had been erected around the elm-lined plaza, surrounding the Piranhas parked in front of the closed-down ticket booths and dismantled turnstiles. ERA troopers were goldbricking against the statue of Stan Musial, stubbing out their cigarette butts against his bronze feet. Stan the Man was probably rolling in his grave.

The walkways winding around the curved outside walls of the stadium were vacant of baseball fans; the World Series pennants suspended from the ceiling of the ground-floor concourse hung limp and ignored, relics of a more innocent age. It had been a long time since anyone in this place had heard the crack of a bat or smelled a jumbo hot dog. That was one thing we had learned from all those two-bit dictatorships in Latin America: how to turn a good sports arena into a hellhole.

Bob and Bob escorted me across the plaza to a pair of boarded-up double doors beneath a tattered blue canvas awning. The doors led into a narrow lobby where two more soldiers were standing guard duty in front of a pair of elevator doors. One of the grunts reached out to press the Up button on the wall beneath a black plaque reading MEMBERS ONLY.

"Hey, wait a minute, guys," I said as the left elevator opened. "We can't go up there . . . we're not members."

Hefler actually seemed to hesitate for a moment, confirming my suspicion that he was too stupid even to have held down a job as a busboy when the club had been open. "Shut up, asshole," Mullens growled as he shoved me into the elevator.

I stifled a grin. Some people have no sense of humor.

We rode the elevator up to the loge level and the Stadium Club. I had been here a couple of times before with Uncle Arnie, who was well heeled enough to afford a gold membership card. In its time, the Stadium Club had been one of the ritzier places in the city: good food, good drink, a great view of the diamond from an enclosed eyrie overlooking left field.

When the elevator doors opened again, my first impression

was that the place hadn't changed since I had last seen it. The oak reception desk was still there, facing a wall lined with photos of players and pennant teams. The barroom still looked much the same; the Budweiser and Michelob beer taps were still in place behind the horseshoe-shaped bar, as was the enormous framed photo of Ozzie Smith, the legendary shortstop's arms raised in victory as he walked toward the dugout during the final game of the '82 Series.

Then Bob and Bob led me farther into the long, concave room, and I came to see that the club wasn't what it used to be. The round tables and leather chairs were now stacked on top of each other at the far ends of the room; the buffet tables had been brought down to the club's lower deck so that they were now pushed up against the tall glass windows overlooking the field, and instead of rich, happy baseball fans there were now uniformed men and women seated before the windows, their faces illuminated by the blue glow of computer terminals and TV monitors. The voices of KMOX baseball announcers giving play-by-play coverage didn't come from the ceiling speakers; all that could be heard in the darkened room was the low monologue of flight controllers, droning a police-state jargon of ten-codes into their headset mikes.

The Stadium Club had always been a bit snobbish for my taste, but given a choice between a maître d' refusing to seat me for wearing blue jeans and watching a bunch of ERA androids manning a communications center, I would have taken a pompous headwaiter anytime. Still, the real obscenity wasn't here but beyond the windows, out on the playing field beyond the deserted seat rows.

The diamond was gone, its canvas bases long since removed, even the pitcher's mound taken away to another place. Beneath the harsh glare of the stadium lights, a dozen or more helicopters were parked on the field, their rotors and fuselages held down by guy lines while ground crews tinkered beneath their engine cowlings or dragged fat cables to their fuel ports. The giant electronic screens above the center field bleachers, which had once displayed the game score, player stats, and instant replays, were now showing cryptic alphanumeric codes designating flight assignments and mission departure times.

An Apache was lifting off from the first-base zone, rising straight up until it cleared the high walls of the stadium. A couple of jumpsuited pilots were emerging from the home-team dugout behind home plate. Several ground crewmen were sitting on top of the dugout, swilling soft drinks as they rested their butts on the red-painted pennants from World Series games. In the days before ERA had taken over the city, it was unspoken heresy even to step on top of any of those emblems, and only the gods themselves were permitted in the Cardinals' locker room.

Now anyone could get an invitation to the dugouts. Closer to the Stadium Club windows, an Osprey's twin rotors were still in motion as a small group of handcuffed civilian prisoners were led down its ramp by gun-toting guards and marched single file toward the visiting team dugout and whatever brand of hell awaited them in the holding pens beneath the stadium.

Blasphemy.

Busch Stadium had always been the pride of St. Louis, one of the city's sacred places. Generations of baseball fans had watched the Cards win and lose in this ballpark, and even when the team had disastrous seasons, there had always been a certain sense of camaraderie. Now the stadium had been desecrated; even if ERA vacated the place tomorrow, its innocence would be forever lost.

The look on my face must have been obvious. Mullens, the funnyman of the Bob and Bob team, began to sing just above his breath as he stood behind me: "Let's go out to the ball game . . . buy me hot dogs and beer . . . we'll go up to the bleachers . . . get drunk as shit and beat up some queers . . ."

"Wrong town, jerkwad," I murmured. "You must be thinking about New York."

He grabbed my handcuffs and yanked them upward, threatening to dislocate my shoulders. My luck he would happen to be a Mets fan. I yelped in pain and pitched forward, nearly falling against the flight controller seated in front of me.

"Keep it up, pogey bait," Mullens growled in my ear, "and we'll be taking that ride sooner than you—"

"Corporal, is this the man we want to see?"

The new voice was calm and authoritative, its tone as casual as if the speaker had been asking about the time of day. Mullens suddenly relaxed his grip on the cuffs.

"That's him, Colonel," I heard a high-pitched voice say as I straightened up. "How'ya doing, Gerry?"

I looked around to see Paul Huygens standing beside me.

Great. Like I didn't have enough problems already.

"Not too bad, Paul," I replied. "Funny though . . . seems like every time I turn around, you're here."

Huygens's grin became a thin smile. "I've been thinking much the same thing myself."

I was about to ask exactly what he was doing in the Stadium Club in the middle of the night when Colonel George Barris stepped forward.

I had no trouble recognizing Barris. Everyone in the city had become acquainted with the commander of ERA forces in St. Louis, through newspaper photos and TV interviews: a middle-aged gentleman with thin gray hair and a mustache, so average looking that it was easier to imagine him pushing a lawnmower around a suburban backyard than wearing a khaki uniform with gold stars pinned to the epaulets.

John had met Barris once, a few months ago when he had written a critical piece about ERA misconduct in the city. "This guy may look like a bank clerk," he had told me later, "but after a while you get the feeling that he's seen *Patton* a few too many times. He's a hard case, man . . ."

I would have to remember that.

"Mr. Rosen, I'm glad to meet you finally," he said formally. "I've enjoyed reading your columns in the *Inquirer*, although I don't necessarily agree with your opinions."

"Thank you, Colonel," I said. "I'd shake hands, but I seem to be having a little trouble using my arms lately."

He nodded his head ever so slightly. "Corporal, please release Mr. Rosen," he said, his eyes still fixed on me. "Then you and your partner may return to duty."

I felt Mullens move behind me, and a moment later the cuffs were severed by a jackknife. I flexed my arms and scratched an itch on my nose that had been bothering me for the last fifteen minutes. "*Muchas gracias*, Corporal," I said. "Thanks for offering me a lift home, but I think I'll find my own way, okay?"

Bob and Bob glowered at me, then they saluted the colonel and sulked their way out of the operations center. I made a mental note to send them a nice fruit basket.

"Well, Colonel," I said as I turned toward him, "I appreciate being shown around and all, but I think I'll be going now, if you don't mind."

Barris crossed his arms, still watching me carefully. "No, no, I'm afraid I *do* mind, Mr. Rosen." His voice was pleasant, but there was an edge beneath his erudite politeness. "My men have gone to considerable trouble to bring you here. I apologize for any rough treatment you may have experienced, but we still have a number of things to discuss before we let you go."

"No one charged me with anything—" I began.

"No sir," he went on, "but we certainly could if we wish. Theft of police evidence, for starters." Barris looked over his shoulder at the balcony just above us. "Lieutenant Farrentino, if you'll join us . . . ?"

Surprise, surprise. All my friends had come down to the club to see me tonight.

I looked up as Mike Farrentino stepped out of the shadows. He leaned over the railing, a sullen smile spread across his lean face. "Hello, Gerry," he said quietly. "I see you didn't get a chance to change your pants after all."

"Things got in the way, Mike," I said. "Sorry about the bag, but y'know how things are."

I assayed a sheepish shrug and a dopey grin as the three men stared at me. I wondered if it wasn't too late to catch up with Bob and Bob and see if that offer of a ride home was still valid.

"You're not being charged with anything," Barris said, "so long as you're willing to cooperate with us. We have a small crisis here, and we need your cooperation. Is that clear?"

"Like mud." I sighed and rubbed the back of my neck. "Look, I don't have the slightest idea what's going on around here—"

"You're full of it," Huygens muttered.

"Back off, Huygens," I said. "I'm not taking any shit from you right now."

Controllers cast brief glances over their shoulders at me; out of the corner of my eye, I could see another ERA trooper starting toward us, his right hand on the holstered butt of his shockrod.

I could have cared less. "Look, guys," I went on, trying to keep my temper and not doing a good job of it, "I've had a long day. My best friend has just been killed, my place was trashed, I was dragged down here by a couple of morons, and Prince Anal here"—I jabbed a finger at Huygens—"decided to throw me out of his party for no reason at all. So unless you've got something to say to me—"

"Be quiet!" Barris snapped.

Leave it to a military man to know how to get someone to shut up. I went silent, remembering exactly where I was and whom I was dealing with.

"Now listen up," he said, a little more quietly now, yet with hardness in his voice. "We've been polite with you so far . . ."

I started to open my mouth, intending to make some smart-aleck remark about Miss Manners's advice on how to properly put someone in handcuffs and give them a ride in a tank, but Barris stepped a little closer to put his face near mine. "If you persist," he said in a half-whisper, "I'll have you taken someplace where some of my men will enjoy making you more cooperative. Do you understand me, Mr. Rosen?"

I shut up, my wiseass remarks dying stillborn. There was no mistaking what he meant. Down there, beneath the stadium, were cold rooms with concrete walls, postmodern catacombs where someone could get lost forever. People had a habit of disappearing in Busch Stadium lately. I had heard the rumors, as had everyone else in the city, and Colonel Barris no longer looked like a retired bank clerk who sat around the house listening to old Carpenters records.

"Do you understand me?" he repeated.

I nodded my head.

"Good," he said. "Now if you'll follow me, we'll go to my

office where we can talk in private. We have someone waiting for us."

He turned on his heel and began walking away, leading the way toward a short stairway to the club's upper level. Huygens fell in behind me, and Farrentino met us at the top of the steps. Neither of them said a word to me, but Farrentino shot me a brief look of warning: *don't screw around with this guy . . . he means business.*

The colonel's office was located in the left rear corner of the club, a small cubicle formed by hastily erected sheets of drywall. A desk, a couple of chairs, a computer terminal, a wall map of the city spotted with colored thumbtacks. Very military, very spartan. The only decoration was a glass snow-ball on the desk, a miniature replica of the Arch sealed in with a liquid blizzard.

A man was seated in a chair in front of Barris's desk. He was dressed casually yet well: pressed jeans, a cotton polo shirt, and a suede leather jacket. It was for that reason that I didn't immediately recognize him when he turned around to look at us as a trooper opened the door to let us inside. It wasn't until he stood up and held out his hand that I realized who he was.

"Mr. Rosen," he said, "I'm happy to meet you. I'm Cale McLaughlin."

I shook the hand of the last person I expected to see in Barris's office; although I tried to keep cool, my discomfiture must have been obvious. "You're no doubt wondering what I'm doing here," Tiptree's CEO said, favoring me with a fatherly smile.

I shrugged. "Not really. You're probably the only person here who has a membership card."

"Good point." McLaughlin gave a short laugh, then waved me to the chair next to him. Farrentino sat down on the other side, while Huygens leaned against a file cabinet. "But the fact of the matter is that your friend's murder is of vital interest to my company. When he learned of what happened tonight, Paul called me and I came down here."

"It must have been on short notice," I murmured, glancing

at my watch. "It's been barely three hours since John was shot."

"Hmm . . . yes, it was short notice. And believe me, I'd much rather be in bed right now." McLaughlin's face became serious. "But, as I said, my company is greatly interested in what happened." He glanced at Barris. "Perhaps I should let the colonel begin, though. George?"

"You already know that your friend was investigating a recent murder when he was killed," Barris said as he took his own seat behind the desk. "What you don't know is why he was killed, nor who did it."

"And neither do you," I replied.

"No," Farrentino said. "That we do know—"

"We're way ahead of you, Gerry," Huygens interrupted. "You're good, sport, but not as good as we are."

"Yeah, right. Sure you do." I gently massaged my wrists, still feeling the chafe left by the handcuffs. "If you're so swift, then why do you need my help?"

Huygens opened his mouth as if to retort, but Barris cleared his throat; the other man shut up. McLaughlin remained quiet, a forefinger curled contemplatively around his chin as he listened. "What Mr. Huygens means is that we now have a suspect," the colonel said as he opened a desk drawer and pulled out a thick file folder. "What we have to do is catch him . . ."

He opened the folder, unclipped an eight-by-ten photo from a sheaf of paper, and slid it across the desk. I recognized the face as soon as I picked up the picture: the distinguished-looking gentleman with the gray Vandyke beard I had spotted at the Tiptree Corporation reception.

"You may have seen him when you visited my company this morning," McLaughlin said. "His name's Richard Payson-Smith. He's a senior research scientist at Tiptree . . . one of the top people behind our Sentinel R&D program, in fact."

"Born 1967 in Glasgow, Scotland," Barris continued, reading from the dossier. "Received his B.S. from the University of Glasgow, then immigrated to the United States in 1987, where he went on to receive both his master's degree and Ph.D. from the University of California-Irvine. After he became a naturalized citizen he went to work for DARPA at Los Alamos, where he was involved with various research projects until 2003, when he was recruited by Tiptree to head up a skunk-works team involved with the Sentinel program."

He paused, then looked at McLaughlin. The executive picked up the ball. "At this juncture, Mr. Rosen," McLaughlin said slowly, "we're about to walk out onto thin ice. We need to discuss matters with you that are classified Top Secret, and I have to know for certain that you will not discuss any of these secrets outside this room."

I opened my mouth to object, but he half-closed his eyes and held up his hand. "I know, I know. You're a reporter, so you're not in the habit of keeping secrets, nor did you ask to be involved in any of this. But we're in a bind, and we need to have your full cooperation, so much so that the colonel simply doesn't have time to ask the FBI to run a background check on you. Therefore, I have to ask you to sign something before we can go any further."

Barris reached into his desk again, rifled through some papers, and produced a three-page document. "This is a secrecy pledge," McLaughlin went on as Barris handed it across the desk to me. "In short, it says that you will not divulge to any third party any classified information that has been confided to you. Once you've signed it, you could be arrested under federal law for various felony charges—possibly including high treason—if you reveal anything that's said in this room."

I glanced through the document; as much as I could make out the single-spaced legalese, it was as McLaughlin said. The minimum penalty for airing out Uncle Sam's dirty laundry was ten years in the pen and a fine so harsh I would never pay it off by stamping out license plates in Leavenworth.

"Sounds pretty stiff, Mr. McLaughlin." I dropped the pledge back on Barris's desk. "What makes you think I'd want to sign anything like this?"

Barris shrugged. "For one thing, it'll get us a little closer to nailing the guy who killed John Tiernan," he said. "That should mean something to you. Second, it'll help you get your belongings returned. And third, once this whole affair is said and done, you'll be the one reporter in town who has the inside story . . . within certain limitations, of course."

"Uh-huh. And what happens if I don't sign?"

The colonel smiled and said nothing. Farrentino stared at me, his face dark and utterly serious. Huygens pulled his hands out of his pockets, folded his arms across his chest, and studied me like an alley cat contemplating a small mouse it had just cornered. McLaughlin simply waited for me to add two and two together.

If there's anything I've learned in life, it's how to take a hint.

Now I knew the reasons why they had arrested me without charges, hustled me in here in handcuffs, and allowed me to see a group of prisoners being herded down to underground cells beneath the stadium. They had wanted to show me the true value of my life. These men could make me disappear without so much as a ripple if I refused to play their game. It was like the old saw about some guy asking his lawyer what his negotiating position should be. "Bending over," the lawyer says.

It was midnight, and if I didn't say or do the right thing, I'd never see the sun again.

After a moment, Barris picked up a pen from his desk and, without saying a word, held it out to me. I hesitated, then took the pen from his hand, laid the document flat on his desk, and signed on the dotted line at the bottom of the third page. I wonder if Faust had felt the same way.

"You've done the right thing, Gerry," Huygens said. "For once you're playing with the right team."

"Yeah," I whispered under my breath. "Call me when we make the playoffs."

McLaughlin probably heard me, but he didn't say anything. When I was through signing my pact with the devil, Barris accepted it from me. He studied my signature for a second, then slipped it into the drawer and slammed it shut.

"Thank you, Mr. Rosen," he said as he cupped his hands together. "You may not believe it now, but you have done the right thing. For this your country is grateful."

McLaughlin reached across the desk to pick up the glass

snowball; he shook it a couple of times, then held it upright in his hand as he watched the tiny blizzard swirl around the miniature Gateway Arch.

"And now," he said, "it's time to tell you about Ruby Fulcrum."

12

When the meeting was over, Mike Farrentino escorted me out of the Stadium Club. We didn't say anything to each other while we rode the elevator down to the ground level, and once we had cleared the guarded front foyer I turned to walk away from the stadium.

"Hey, Rosen!" he called out. "Wait up a minute!"

I turned back around, hands shoved in the pockets of my jacket, and waited for him to walk over to me. "Need a lift back to your place?" he asked. "I got my car parked over here."

"No thanks," I said. "I'll hoof it. It's not far."

Nor was a ride necessary. Barris had assured me that I now had safe conduct on the streets after curfew, so long as I played by his rules. He had given me a laminated plastic card before I left and told me to carry it on my person at all times; it was printed with the ERA logo, and Barris told me if I was stopped or questioned by an ERA patrol, I was to show them the card. Sort of like getting a hall pass from the principal.

The plaza was almost empty now, save for a few troopers manning the barricades. Most of the LAVs I had seen earlier had vanished, presumably off patrolling various parts of the city. The downtown area somehow looked very peaceful: no traffic on the streets, no city noises, only the faint twitter of night birds in the branches of the elm trees, abruptly broken by the low moan of an Apache coming in for a landing within the stadium walls.

Farrentino looked up at the chopper as it flew low overhead. "How much of that do you believe?" he asked in a soft voice, casting a glance at the ERA soldier standing guard near the Stadium Club entrance. "I mean, how much of that was bull-shit or what?"

I hesitated. I had my opinions, but I wasn't sure if I was ready to trust them to a cop. "I don't know, Lieutenant," I said carefully. "You're the one who's been investigating this mess, so you tell me."

"Mike," he said. "My friends call me Mike—"

"And so I'm your friend now, huh, Mike?" I looked him straight in the eye. "Most of my friends wouldn't have my door kicked down and have me dragged off in the middle of the night."

"Whoa, fella. Chill off." He held his hands up defensively. "The colonel ordered the raid, not me. I simply reported that the evidence bag had been tampered with and that the disk was missing and that you were the most likely suspect. He was the one who sent in the goon squad . . ."

"Yeah, sure, Mike. Have a nice night." I started to turn away again, but then he grabbed me by the arm. Before I could do anything, he pulled something out of his raincoat pocket and held it out to me.

It was Joker. "I got it out of the impoundment room when I went to take a leak," he explained. "You should be getting the rest of your junk back sometime tomorrow."

I took Joker from his hand and studied it. The PT didn't look as if it had been tampered with—even the mini-disk was still in drive—but I couldn't be sure until I had Jah run it through a full diagnostic. "Thanks," I said as I slipped the little 'puter in my jacket pocket. "I'll catch you later—"

"Look, Gerry," he said, his voice almost a whisper now, "I know you don't believe this, but . . ."

He hesitated. "Things aren't always what they seem, y'know what I mean? I don't think Barris and McLaughlin gave either of us the full lowdown. In fact, I don't think this Payson-Smith character is the mad scientist they made him out to be."

"Yeah?" The night was getting cold; I zipped up the front of my jacket. "And what do *you* think is the full lowdown?"

"I don't know yet. All I know is, I smell a rat." He paused, looking over his shoulder again. "You may not believe this," he went on, "but truth is, not everyone in authority is crazy about ERA. We might have a lot of problems in St. Louis right now, but we don't need tanks and helicopters to get them fixed." He shrugged. "They're only making things worse . . ."

"I couldn't agree more," I said, "but that still doesn't make me trust you. So far as I can tell, you're just a big swinging dick with a badge."

Farrentino turned red, but he nodded his head. "I understand that, but let me tell you . . . there's some bigger swinging dicks out there who are getting out of line, and I don't trust them any more than you trust me."

I looked into his face and saw only honesty. He was no longer a homicide detective and I was no longer a reporter; we were now only two men who had seen a lot of crazy shit go down in recent months and were scared by what was happening to our hometown. I've never been the greatest fan of the SLPD as a whole, but I knew that there were individual cops who *did* care about their line of work, who weren't just playing out old cop-show fantasies of busting heads and breaking down doors. Mike Farrentino might be one of these guys.

And besides, I had a weird hunch I wanted to follow up on . . .

"You say you got a car parked around here?" I asked. He nodded. "Want to give me a lift out to Webster?"

He glanced at his watch and shrugged. "Sure. I'm off the clock and it's on my way home. Why Webster?"

"I want to drop in on my ex," I said as I began to follow him toward the unmarked Chrysler four-door parked on the street just beyond the barricades. "Give her a big surprise when I show up at one o'clock in the morning in a cop car."

The drive out to Webster Groves didn't take long. Farrentino hopped on I-44 at the Poplar Street Bridge, and traffic in the westbound lanes was very sparse, mostly interstate trucks on their way to Springfield or Oklahoma or Texas. A light rain had begun to fall, and the car was filled with the sound of the

windshield wipers and the ethereal murmur of voices from the
police scanner mounted beneath the dash.

We didn't say much to each other. He was tired, I was
tired, and all we wanted to do was to get home, although
his wife was expecting him to come through the door while
mine . . . well, I would have to cross that doormat when I got
to it. I lay back in the seat, watched the trucks pass by, and
contemplated all that had been told to me in Barris's office.

Mainly, it was a matter of counting all the occasions my
bullshit detector had rung a bell.

Ernest Hemingway, the godfather of all self-respecting word
pimps, once said that the most valuable gift a writer could have
was an unshakable, foolproof bullshit detector. For reporters,
that means learning to know instinctively when someone is
trying to pull a fast one. I've grown a half-decent b.s.-o-
meter over a lifetime of writing, and even though it's neither
unshakable nor foolproof, it had rung at least four, maybe five
times while I was sitting in the Stadium Club.

Ruby Fulcrum, McLaughlin had said, was the Pentagon
code name for an R&D project within the Tiptree Corporation's Sentinel program: the development of a precise space-
based tracking system to pinpoint the trajectories of subor-
bital ICBMs. The first major obstacle had been to develop
an energy weapon that could penetrate Earth's atmosphere
without losing too much power, and that had been licked
when the whiz kids at Los Alamos had invented a chemical
laser that substituted fluorine/deuterium for ordinary hydrogen
as its fuel source.

The next big hurdle had been to devise a c-cube system for
Sentinel 1. Given the chance that a missile might be fired from
a ship or sub off the Atlantic coast, *Sentinel*'s onboard computer system would have to be virtually autonomous, capable
not only of detecting and tracking an ICBM during its boost
phase, and thus enabling the satellite to shoot it down before
it reentered the atmosphere, but also of differentiating between
possible decoy-missiles and real targets. The problem was
made even more hairy by the fact that if an SLBM was
launched from a vessel just off the Eastern seaboard, *Sentinel
1* would have only a few minutes to accurately detect, track,

and destroy the missile before its nuclear warhead detonated above Washington or New York.

Richard Payson-Smith had been the leader of the Ruby Fulcrum team, since his scientific background included both high-energy lasers and cybernetics. The team had also included three other scientists: Kim Po, a young immigrant from United Korea who had previously worked with Payson-Smith at Los Alamos; Jeff Morgan, even younger than Kim, who had been recruited straight from MIT to work on the program, and—no surprise here, although I had been careful not to let on—Beryl Hinckley, a former CalTech professor who had recently escaped from academia to pursue a more lucrative career in private industry.

"We knew that Richard had some misgivings about *Sentinel* when the company assigned him to the program," McLaughlin had said. "He had a—well, call it a pacifist streak, if you will—but we needed his expertise nonetheless. We thought that, since *Sentinel* is purely defensive in nature, he would overcome his leftist tendencies. And so it seemed, at least at first . . ."

But as the project went along and the team gradually managed to overcome the technical hurdles, Payson-Smith's behavior had become increasingly erratic. His temper became shorter; he began to berate his colleagues over minor mistakes or even for taking time to answer personal phone calls or making dentist appointments in the middle of the week. Payson-Smith managed to calm down after a while, but as he did he also began to voice his objections to *Sentinel*, calling it a "doomsday machine," "a Pentagon war wagon," and so forth. As Ruby Fulcrum's objectives were gradually achieved and *Sentinel 1* inched closer to deployment, Payson-Smith became actively hostile toward the other three members; no one dared venture into his office lest they be subjected to a political harangue. He had also become manic-depressive, sliding into silent fugues that could last for weeks on end.

"Didn't your company notice?" I had asked. "If the project was that crucial, why didn't you have him replaced, or at least force him to seek psychiatric—"

"Because, as you said, the project was crucial." Huygens gave me an arch look: *you don't know what you're talking about.* "The program was on a time-critical basis, so we couldn't just up and fire him. Where would a replacement come from? How could we get one to fit in with the team at this late stage? We—"

McLaughlin shot a look at Huygens; the PR man shut up. "It was impossible to get Richard to see the staff psychologist," McLaughlin continued in more patient tones. "When we made appointments for him, he'd find a way to avoid them. He was stubborn and, well . . ." He raised his hands in helplessness. "We just had to work with him and hope for the best."

That was the first time my bullshit detector had gone off. Now, upon reflection, I knew why.

First, whatever purpose Payson-Smith had fulfilled in the Ruby Fulcrum team couldn't have been so critical that Tiptree had been unable to replace him, even in a pinch. However brainy this man was, I hadn't heard his name mentioned in the same breath as Robert Oppenheimer's, and they had replaced him, too, way back when. Oppenheimer's only mistake had been in openly expressing his objections to the atomic bomb, and that was after it was exploded over Japan. No one had ever claimed he was mentally ill, only that he was a suspected commie sympathizer.

If Huygens was telling me the truth, then Payson-Smith should have been canned immediately, for being mentally unhinged *and* opposed to Sentinel before it was even built, let alone made operational. But they wouldn't have kept him on the project . . . and that, I now realized, was why the first alarm had rung.

At the same time this was going on, McLaughlin continued, certain spare parts and lab instruments had turned up missing from the company storerooms; they included various high-quality mirrors, lenses, Pyrex tubes, small carbon dioxide and water tanks, and a portable vacuum pump. The theft of the items had not been detected, it later turned out, because someone had managed to access the company's computer inventory system and delete their removal from the records. The loss was discovered only when other scientists complained to the company comptroller that they couldn't find items that had been there last week.

Then, almost exactly one week ago, Kim Po was found dead outside his condominium in Richmond Heights. He had apparently been coming home from a late night at the lab when he was shot just outside the condo's front door . . . not by a conventional rifle, but by a laser weapon of some sort, one that had drilled a self-cauterizing hole straight through the back of his head from a parked car. As with John's murder, no one had heard gunfire, nor had a bullet been recovered from either man's body.

"We'll cut to the chase," Barris said. "Judging from the information Cale has given us and the near identical circumstances of both Dr. Kim and Mr. Tiernan's murders, it seems as if a high-power laser had been used."

McLaughlin coughed into his fist. "A CO_2 laser rifle, to be exact," he said. "Not like something you see in movies, of course. It would be extremely large and cumbersome . . . at least the size of a rocket launcher, in fact . . . but my people tell me it could produce a beam capable of burning through metal, wood, plastic, just about anything . . . and that includes flesh and bone."

He shook his head. "It's a nasty weapon, probably even more powerful than the one that kid in Chicago used a couple of years ago. Silent, invisible, absolute flat trajectory, almost infinite range. If you had a good infrared sight to go with it, you could fire it through a closed window, provided it was made of nonreflective glass, and hit a target several blocks away. No one would even know where the shot came from."

"And you think someone from Tiptree concocted this thing?" I asked.

McLaughlin glanced hesitantly at both Barris and Huygens. He put the glass snowball down on the desk and leaned forward, his arms resting on his knees. "No, not just anyone," he replied, looking embarrassed by the admission. "We think Richard's the one. He had the training and the technical ability, plus access to the parts he needed." He looked at Mike Farrentino. "Lieutenant? If you'll continue . . . ?"

For the first time since we had entered the colonel's office, Farrentino spoke up. "After Mr. Huygens tipped us off," he said quietly, "some of my people visited Payson-Smith's home earlier this evening. He was missing, but they found a small workshop in his basement. Something had been built on a bench down there, all right, and there were pieces of burned-through metal that looked as if they might have been used for target practice."

"But why would he . . . ?"

"Why would he kill Dr. Kim and Mr. Tiernan?" Barris shrugged. He picked up the glass snowball and juggled it in his hands. "Who knows what goes on in a sick mind? Maybe he's upset at the other members of his team for having built *Sentinel* . . . that's our theory, at any rate. First he knocked off Dr. Kim, then he tracked down Dr. Hinckley when she was trying to tell Tiernan about Kim's murder and tried to kill her, too. Unfortunately he nailed your friend instead."

I started to ask another question, but Huygens beat me to it. "We did our best to keep Kim's murder out of the press. There was only a small item in the next morning's *Post-Dispatch* about it, but we managed to get their reporters to believe that Po had been killed during a robbery attempt . . . but Beryl obviously found out the truth and decided to go to your paper instead."

"That's another reason why we suspect Payson-Smith," the colonel said. "He was one of the few people who could have learned of her plans to meet Tiernan at the bar tonight."

McLaughlin raised a hand. "Before you ask why Payson-Smith didn't kill them both when he had the chance . . . according to my people, this laser rifle apparently consumes a lot of power. It would have to be run off an independent current, so it takes about a minute for its battery to recharge before each shot."

"Uh-huh," I said. "So Hinckley suspected that Payson-Smith was the guy behind Kim's murder and went to John to tell him the story."

Barris and McLaughlin both nodded their heads, and that was the second time my bullshit detector went off.

They didn't know it, but I had seen Hinckley and Payson-Smith talking to each other during the reception. For a woman who suspected her boss of having gone psycho and killing one of her friends with a home-built laser, she had not appeared apprehensive about being in his company. Nor had Payson-Smith struck me as the homicidal maniac type. Yeah, maybe you never know for sure. When some nut with a machine gun goes on a rampage in a shopping mall, his neighbors invariably describe him as a nice, quiet person who always minded his own business. Yet my guts told me that Payson-Smith just seemed the wrong guy to be carrying this sort of rap.

And then there were other implausibilities. Even if Payson-Smith was the sociopathic killer these guys made him out to be, how could he have known where Hinckley would be tonight? After all, she had been the one who had told me to pass the message to John. I had not disclosed this to anyone else. So how could Payson-Smith have known where these two people would be meeting each other?

For that matter, why were these guys so certain it was Beryl Hinckley who had met Tiernan at Clancy's? "Middle-aged black lady" was a description that could fit a few hundred thousand people in St. Louis, but that was how Farrentino had described Hinckley to me when I had been summoned to the murder scene.

And why, on the basis of such circumstantial evidence, were McLaughlin and Huygens here at all, putting the blame on one of Tiptree's own scientists?

The bullshit detector was sounding five alarms now; fire engines were leaving the station, and the dalmatians were howling like mad. Yet I continued to play the dummy; I stretched back in my chair, resting my feet against the bottom of Barris's desk. "Okay," I said. "So you've got a mad scientist on the loose. Why are you telling me this?"

Barris didn't like my boots touching his desk. He stared at me until I dropped them back to the floor, then he went on. "When you took Tiernan's PT, there was the possibility that you might have found some evidence that could conclusively link Payson-Smith to Kim's murder. We needed to get that back at all costs, and that's why you were brought in."

"I can understand that," I said. "But why the rest of the—"

Barris raised a finger, a silent admonition for me to shut up. "There's also the possibility that Dr. Hinckley may try to contact you, now that Mr. Tiernan is dead. We haven't been able to locate her since the shooting, and we suspect that she has gone underground to avoid being killed. So has the other member of the Ruby Fulcrum team, Dr. Morgan."

He put down the glass ball and leaned forward across the desk. "Mr. Rosen, I realize that there is little reason for you to trust us," he said. "ERA has a bad reputation in this city, and as easy as it may be for me to put all the blame on the media, I know that my men haven't always . . . well, behaved themselves. But this once, we need your cooperation. We're trying to track down a killer, and we're also trying to save the lives of two valuable people."

"Uh-huh." The bullshit was getting so thick in there, I thought I was going to need a shovel just to get to the door.

"If you hear from either Dr. Hinckley or Dr. Morgan, we need to hear from you at once," Barris went on. He pulled a calling card from a box on his desk and handed it to me. "That's how you can reach me personally, any time of the day or night."

I glanced at the card. No phone number was printed on it, only Barris's name and the ERA logo. The codestrip on the back would connect with his extension if I passed it in front of a phonescanner. I nodded my head as I tucked the card into my shirt pocket.

"Here's something else you may need," he went on, and that's when he passed me the plastic card and explained how it could be used to get me through ERA blockades.

"We also need you to keep quiet about this matter until it's resolved," he went on. "When that happens, you'll have the complete story from us . . . and you'll have helped to bring your friend's killer to justice. Do you understand?"

"Yes, sir," I replied. "I hope I can be of service."

What should I have said? No, sir, this place reeks like a barnyard and you can take me down to the basement now?

Barris nodded, then he stood up from his desk. So did McLaughlin; once more, he extended his hand to me. "Pleasure to meet you, Mr. Rosen," he said as I shook his hand again. "I'm glad to have you on our side."

Farrentino pushed back his chair and stood up. Huygens gave me a perfunctory nod. Barris glanced at Farrentino. "Now, Lieutenant, if you will kindly escort Mr. Rosen to the street . . . ?"

I was free to go—but I was certainly not free. There were too many secrets, too many lies.

Too much bullshit.

13

"Which exit do I take?" Farrentino asked.

The light rain had become a steady downpour, but through the darkness and drizzle I could make out the familiar landmarks of Webster Groves from the interstate. The sign for the Shrewsbury Avenue exit was coming up. "This one will do," I said.

The detective nodded as he swerved into the right lane. "I take it your ex isn't expecting you," he said, following the long curve of the ramp as it led up the street overpass. "Are you sure it's okay for me to be dropping you off?"

"I guess it's okay," I replied as I pointed toward the left; he waited until a street cleaner 'bot rumbled through the intersection, then turned onto Shrewsbury. "She'll let me in, if that's what you're asking."

"That's what I'm asking." He reached into his coat pocket and pulled out a pack of cigarettes. "Worst thing a cop can do is get caught in the middle of a domestic quarrel. Y'know that when cops get injured in the line of duty, it's most often while breaking up a household fight? I damn near got my left ear sliced off with a vegetable knife that way, back when I drove a cruiser."

The intersection of Big Bend was coming up, and I pointed to the left again. "That's not going to happen here," I said. "For one thing, she's not really my ex. I just call her that."

"Separation?" He lighted his cigarette while making the turn, catching the green light just as it was turning yellow. A blue-and-white passed him in the opposite lane; he flashed his

152

brights at it, and the officer driving the cruiser gave him a brief wave. It was the only other vehicle on the street, despite the fact that Webster was one of the few neighborhoods in the city that wasn't under dusk-to-dawn curfew. "Sometimes it's better that way," he went on. "Why did you guys get separated?"

"You ask a lot of questions."

"It's my job. Besides, I'm just asking . . ."

His voice trailed off as if anticipating a reply, but I didn't answer immediately. It had been a few months since I had last visited this neighborhood, and I wanted to look around. Webster Groves had ridden out the quake pretty well, at least in comparison to the parts of St. Louis that had been built on sandy loam or had been undermined by the tunnels of lost clay mines. Some homes had collapsed, a couple of strip malls had fallen down, but overall this quaint old 'burb of midwestern-style frame houses hadn't been significantly damaged. I didn't even see any ERA patrols.

"Go a few more blocks, then turn right on Oakwood," I said.

"Okay." Farrentino was quiet for a few moments. "Not going to talk about it, are you?"

"Talk about what?"

He shook his head. "You're going to have to trust somebody sooner or later, Gerry," he murmured. "I shouldn't have to tell you that you've got your hand stuck in a hornet's nest. Either you talk to me, or you talk to the colonel or McLaughlin, but eventually you're going to have to talk to somebody."

It was true; he knew it, and I knew it. I was treading on hot coals now, and there were damned few people I could count on to get me through this firewalk. Before I could commit myself either way, though, there were a few questions that still had to be cleared up in my own mind. Stopping by for a visit with Marianne, even in the middle of the night, was the first step.

"I'll let you know, Mike," I said as he took the turn onto Oakwood. "Right now, all I want to do is get home."

Home was an old, three-story Victorian on a quiet residential street, a one-hundred-twenty-year-old former farmhouse that had been renovated at least three or four times since the beginning of the last century. Marianne and I had bought the place shortly after we had moved back to St. Louis; if I had known the city was going to get socked by a quake, I might not have signed the mortgage papers, but to my surprise the house had only swayed during New Madrid. The house next door, which was only half as old, had fallen flat, but by some quirk of nature our place had survived, suffering only the loss of the carport and an oak tree in the front yard.

In that respect alone, we had been lucky. The house had made it through the quake; it was the family living inside that had been destroyed.

After Mike Farrentino dropped me off at the curb, I trudged up the walk and climbed the stairs to the front porch. A downstairs light was on, but the upper floors were darkened. Security lamps hidden beneath the porch eaves came on as soon as I approached the door; I still had a key, but I figured it would be polite if I touched the doorplate instead.

"Mari, it's me," I said. "Will you get up and come let me in?"

There was a long pause. I turned my face toward the concealed lens of the security camera and smiled as best I could, knowing that she was rolling over in bed to check the screen on the night table. Probably half-asleep, maybe knocking away the paperback thriller she had been reading just before she turned off the light. Unshaven, haggard, hair matted with rain, and wearing drenched clothes, I realized that I must resemble the bad guy in her latest novel.

"Gerry . . . ?" Her voice sounded fuzzy with sleep. *"Gerry, what the hell are you doing here?"*

"It's a long story, babe." I ran a hand through my hair, brushing it away from my face. "I'm sorry I woke you up, but—"

"Are you drunk again?" Her voice, no longer quite so sleepy, was tinged with irritation. *"I swear to God, if you've been drinking, you can—"*

"I'm not drunk, Mari, I promise you. It's just . . ." I sighed, half-closing my eyes. "Look, I'm really tired. I've just had a helluva night and I can't go back to my place, so just please let me in, okay?"

Again, another pause, a little longer this time. For the first time since I had asked Farrentino for a lift out here, a disturbing notion crossed my mind: perhaps she was not alone tonight. I hadn't shacked up with any other women since the beginning of our separation, as tempted as I had been from time to time. The thought had never seriously occurred to me, nor had Marianne told me about any new men in her life. Yet things could have changed; she might have some young bohunk in bed right now, a little lost puppy she had picked up at one of the nearby Webster University hangouts.

I stepped away from the camera to check the end of the driveway next to the house. Only her car was parked there, a power cable running from its battery port to the side of the house. Of course, that alone meant nothing. Postmen walk by every day, and so do joggers in tight nylon shorts.

I heard locks being buzzed open, then the door opened a few inches. "Gerry?" I heard her say. "Are you out there?"

"Right here." I quickly stepped away from the porch railing. Even when she was practically somnambulant, with her shoulder-length hair in knots and wearing a ragged terrycloth robe, Marianne was one of the most beautiful women I have ever met. Husbands are usually blind to the imperfections of their wives, of course, but that wasn't the case with Mari; my eyes didn't lie, and she was still good looking. Thirty years of ofttimes hard living had treated her well; she still looked much the same as she did when I had met her in college. She had regained her figure not long after Jamie's birth, and even though there were the first hints of gray in her dark hair, she could have passed for twenty-four.

Not that she was in any mood for compliments. "Gerry, what are you doing here?" she repeated. "For chrissakes, I just went to bed . . . and what are you looking at the driveway for?"

"Just seeing how the car's holding up," I said quickly. "You renewed your plates, didn't you?"

Her expression became puzzled. "You didn't come all the way out here to check my renewal sticker," she said. "What's going on, Gerard?"

She called me Gerard. When she used my full first name, it

usually meant she was pissed off. No wonder; for Marianne, getting a full night's sleep was a serious business, and woe be to the friend, relative, or former spouse who woke her out of bed after eleven o'clock. "I'm sorry if I caught you at a bad time, babe," I said, "but I need three things from you."

She let out an exasperated sigh and sagged against the door frame. "Let me guess," she said. "One of them is money, and the second is sex. What's the third? The car?"

It might have been funny if it wasn't true. When we had agreed that a separation was probably the best thing for both of us, after I had moved to a motel and before I had found a new job, those were the three favors I most commonly called to ask of her: wheels to get around in, a ten or twenty to tide me over till the next paycheck, and a quick roll in the hay because I was so damn lonely and because I still believed sex would heal all the wounds. All three she had agreed to, at one time or another, until she hardened her heart and told me that I was on my own. Hell, the only reason why we still hadn't become officially divorced was because neither of us could afford lawyer bills right now.

"Hey, if you want to have sex with me and give me some bucks and the car in return—" I began, and she started to slam the door in my face until I pushed my hand against the knob. "Wait, I'm just kidding. Seriously . . ."

Again the sigh as she opened the door again. "Seriously what?"

Now was no time to bullshit my wife, even if she hated my guts. "I need a place to crash," I said. "Just for tonight, I swear . . . and I need to use the computer."

"Uh-huh." She gazed at me indifferently. "A bed and the computer. Yeah. What else?"

"Hey, I can sleep on the couch—"

"Damn straight you're going to sleep on the couch," she replied. "What's the third thing, Gerard?"

I hesitated; this was probably the biggest favor of all. "The third thing is no questions asked." I took a deep breath. "I'm in trouble, kiddo. Big trouble."

"Oh, Christ." She sighed as her eyes rolled upward. "You're running from the cops, aren't you?"

I almost broke down laughing. "Babe, a cop gave me a lift out here—"

"Uh, huh. Sure . . ."

I raised my hands. "Believe me, Marianne, if this was going to get you in any trouble, I wouldn't be here right now. I'm not in trouble with the cops." *Not technically, anyway,* I thought. "All I need is the couch," I went on, "and to use the office computer for an hour or so. I don't want your money, I don't want to sleep with you, and I'll call a cab bright and early tomorrow morning. Okay?"

She sighed again, closing her eyes as if she was carrying the burdens of the world on her shoulders. "Jeez, Gerry, why can't you go bug John for this?"

Because John is dead, I almost blurted out, but I held my tongue. Telling her would only have prompted all the questions I wanted to avoid, and it was far safer for her to remain ignorant. I was lucky that she obviously hadn't seen the late news on one of the local TV stations or hadn't yet received a call from Sandy Tiernan.

"Please," I said. "Just do it for me, okay?"

She gazed at me for another moment, then she pushed the door open a little wider and stepped aside. "All right," she said. "But remember . . . you're sleeping on the couch."

The house was a little cleaner than it had usually been before I moved out, yet otherwise everything was much the same. She hadn't changed the living room furniture or taken any of the prints from the walls; although she had removed our wedding photos, there were still baby and toddler pictures of Jamie on the fireplace mantel. Marianne let me grab a Diet Dr. Pepper from the fridge, then went upstairs to gather some sheets and a spare pillow from the linen cabinet while I retreated to her home office.

The office was located in the rear of the ground floor, in what had been a den before we had put in floor-to-ceiling bookshelves. Before the quake hit, we had shared that space; she had used it during the day to telecommute to her insurance company's home office in Kansas City, and when she was through at five o'clock it became my study for the writing of the Great American Unreadable Novel. I noticed that she had removed my books and mementos from the shelves, but I didn't want to make an issue of it. Right now, I was interested in only one thing.

I found the plastic CD-OP filebox on a small shelf beneath the desk; the particular disk for which I was searching was contained in a scratched, often-opened case marked FAMILY. Marianne must have been looking at it often; it was at the front of the box, in front of the business disks. I pulled out the case and opened it, and after switching on the computer and opening the REVIEW window, I slipped the disk into the optical diskette drive.

Starting shortly after we became engaged, Marianne and I had videoed almost everything we did, using a camcorder one of her relatives had given her at the bridal shower. Hiking in the White Mountains of New Hampshire, summer scenes on Cape Cod, strange little home movies when we were both full of wine and creativity, the wedding day ceremonies, and the honeymoon trip to Ireland . . . we had recorded everything, and stored the bits and bytes on CD-OP for replay on our computer as an electronic family album.

We had gotten bored of the novelty after a while, and thus there were large chronological gaps on the menu until Jamie was born, when we had rediscovered the camcorder and started making the inevitable baby pictures. As a result, the submenu screen showed a lot of filenames marked JAMIE.1, JAMIE.2, JAMIE.3, and so forth, one for each birthday he had passed. Yet there was one piece of footage in particular, lodged in JAMIE.6, that I now needed to see.

After we had moved back to St. Louis, there had been a rash of kidnappings in the city. Children were vanishing from schoolbus stops and playgrounds and shopping malls, rarely to be seen again by their parents, and then sometimes not alive. The police never caught the evil bastards who had stolen these kids, and only God knows what happened to the ones who were not found, but Marianne and I did what the local authorities suggested parents should do: videotape their kids in advance, so that the footage could be used to identify lost children should the unthinkable happen to them.

It had taken me a while, but something about the weird phone call I had received just before the ERA soldiers broke down the door of my apartment had jogged an old memory. After I opened the VIDEOVIEW window on the computer screen, I moused JAMIE.6 and the REPLAY command; it took me only a couple of minutes to find the footage I remembered shooting of him, just a few weeks before he was killed.

And now here was Jamie, very much alive and well, sitting in his child-size rocking chair in the living room. He was wearing blue jeans and his favorite St. Louis Cardinals sweatshirt; just a cute little kid, both bored and embarrassed to have his dad making yet another video of him.

My voice, off-camera: *"Okay, kiddo, what's your name?"*

Jamie, pouting, wishing to be anywhere but here: *"Jamie . . ."*

Me again: *"And what's your last name?"*

Jamie looks down at the floor, his hands fidgeting restlessly on the armrests of his chair: *"Jamie Rosen, and I'm six years old . . ."*

My voice, prodding him gently from behind the camera: *"That's good! Now what's your mommy's and daddy's names?"*

His face scrunches up in earnest concentration, the child who has only recently learned that his folks have names besides Mommy and Daddy: *"My daddy's name is Gerard Rosen . . . Gerry Rosen . . . and Mommy's . . . my mommy's name is Marianne Rosen . . ."*

Me, playing the proud papa: *"That's good, Jamie! That's very good! Now, can you tell me what you're supposed to do if a stranger comes up to you?"*

Jamie dutifully recites everything I had just told him: *"I'm not supposed to talk to strangers, even if they ask me if I want a present, and I can . . . I'm supposed to run and get a p'leaseman or another grownup and tell them to take me to you, and . . ."*

There. That was it.

I froze the image and marked its endpoint, then I moved back to the beginning of the video. When I had reached that point and marked it, I opened the menu bar at the top of the screen and selected the EDIT function. Another command from the submenu caused a window to open at the bottom half of the screen, displaying a transcript of the conversation.

I then began to work my way through the transcript, highlighting certain key words. It took me a few minutes, but when I was through I had a couple of lines I had pieced together from the videotape. I took a deep breath, then I moused the line and tapped in commands to verbalize those lines.

Jamie's voice reemerged from the computer, speaking something he had never said in life, but which I had heard over the phone earlier that night:

"Rosen, Gerard . . . Gerard Rosen . . . Gerry Rosen . . . can I talk to you, Daddy?"

And on the computer screen, Jamie's reedited face was exactly the same as I had seen it on the phone.

"Gerry, what the hell are you doing?"

Startled, I jerked away from the keyboard and spun around in the office chair to find Marianne standing in the doorway behind me.

Her arms were crossed in front of her robe; she had a look of horror on her face, as if she had just caught me trying on a pair of her panties. Maybe reality was worse than that; after all, she had just discovered me in the act of editing one of the last tangible memories of our son.

I lay back in the chair, letting out my breath as I rubbed my eyelids between my fingertips. "Part of the deal was that you wouldn't ask me any questions," I murmured. "And believe me, if I told you, you'd just think I was crazy."

"I already think you're crazy," she replied, her voice harsh with anger barely kept in check. "Leave Jamie's video alone. I mean it . . ."

Before I could do anything, she stalked across the room and began to reach for the computer. "Okay, okay," I said, putting my hands over the keyboard. "I'll get out of this, so long as you answer one question for me."

She stopped and stared at me, not pulling her hands away. "What is it?"

"Did you load this disk into the hard drive?" I asked. "This file in particular?"

Marianne blinked, not quite comprehending the question at first. "Yes," she said at last, "I did. I wanted to preserve the disk. This was the last video we made of him and—"

"And do you still leave the computer on all day?"

She shrugged. "Of course I do. My clients have to talk to the expert system when I'm gone. You know that." She peered more closely at me. "What's going on here, Gerard? Why were you editing the—?"

"Never mind. Go ahead and restore the video." I withdrew my hands from the keyboard and pushed the chair back from the desk. Marianne gave me one last look of distrustful confusion, then she bent over the keyboard, using the trackball to undo the work I had just done. It didn't matter; I had all the answers I needed.

Some of them, rather. Just as I had managed to piece together a message in Jamie's own words, so had someone else. The video was stored on the computer's hard drive and Marianne left the computer switched on during the day, so that her clients could ask questions of the computer's expert system. It was therefore possible for a good hacker to access the JAMIE.6 file through the root directory and edit together the phone message I had heard earlier that night. By the same means, it was also possible for them to recreate my own voice; a good hacker with the right equipment would be able to mimic my voice, since my vocal tracks were recorded on this and many other CD-OP files Marianne had stored in the computer.

But why go to such extremes? If the culprit had been trying to get my attention, why imitate the voice of my dead son . . . or my own, for that matter? If anything, it was a sick prank, tantamount to calling up a grieving widow and pretending to be the ghost of her late spouse. Yet this was the second time in as many days someone had used a computer to send mysterious messages to me, and the technical sophistication necessary to do this went far beyond the capability of some twisted little cyberpunk trying to spook me.

In fact, now that I thought about it, how would some pimplehead even know to call into Marianne's computer? Its modem line was listed under her company's name, not hers or mine, and very few people were aware that Gerry Rosen even had an estranged wife.

It made no sense . . .

Or it made perfect sense, but I was unable to perceive the logic.

"You miss him, don't you?"

Marianne's question broke my concentration. She had finished saving the file and was exiting from the program. I looked at her as she switched off the computer, ejected the disk from its drive, and slipped it back in its box.

"Yeah, I miss him." I stuck my hands in my jacket pockets, suddenly feeling very old. "He was the best thing that happened to us . . . and I still can't believe he's gone."

"Yeah. Me, too." Marianne put the box away, then leaned against the shelf next to the desk. For the first time since she had let me into the house, she wasn't playing the queen bitch of the universe; she was my wife, commiserating the passage of our son from our lives. "God, I've even kept his room the same, thinking somehow there's just been some awful mistake, that he wasn't on that train after all . . ."

The train. Always the train . . .

"He's gone, Mari," I said softly. "There's no mistake. There was an accident, and he died . . . and that's all there is to it."

She slowly nodded her head. "Yeah. That's all there is to it." She stared at the floor. "Tell me you just wanted to look at him again, Gerry. Tell me he isn't mixed up in whatever trouble you're in."

She raised her eyes and stared straight at me. "This isn't part of some story, is it?"

I knew what she meant. I had lost one newspaper job because I had been trying to stop kids from dying; I had thrown myself on the sword in order to save some youngsters I had never really known, the children of complete strangers, because that had been part of a story. Yet when the time had come for me to protect my own child, I had not been available. Jamie had perished without ever seeing his father's face again because Daddy had been too busy with his career to do anything but buy him a train ticket to eternity.

The accusation in her eyes wasn't fair, but neither is the timing of earthquakes against MetroLink schedules. Or death itself, for that matter.

When I didn't answer her question, Marianne lowered her head and began to walk out of the office. "I've made up the living room couch and told the house to wake you up at eight," she said. "That's when the coffeemaker comes on. There's some sweet rolls in the fridge, if you want 'em . . ."

"Okay, babe. Thanks for everything."

She nodded again and began to head for the stairs. Then she stopped and turned back again. "And by the way . . . there's nobody else upstairs, if that's what you were wondering. G'night."

And then she left, heading back to her bedroom before I got a chance to ask her how she managed to pick up that mind-reading trick of hers.

14

I awakened to the faint sound of church bells striking eight
times as if tolling from a distant country steeple, although
neither of the two churches within a block of the house had
bells.

The sound came from the ceiling; Marianne had programmed
the house to wake me at this time, just as she had instructed
it to start brewing coffee in the kitchen. Although I could
have used another hour of sleep, I was grateful that she
hadn't selected another noise from the alarm menu; if she
had wanted to be a real bitch, she could have jolted me with
an eight-gun salute, or worse.

Nonetheless, I lay on the rattan couch for a couple of
minutes, curled up in a lambswool blanket, caught somewhere between sleep and wakefulness. I heard the shower
running in the upstairs bathroom, smelled the dark aroma
of hot coffee brewing in the kitchen, heard songbirds just
outside the windows. Everything was warm and comfortable
and orderly, much as it had once been a long time ago when
I had lived in this house . . .

Then my mind's eye flashed to John, the way I had seen
him as he lay on the porch floor at Clancy's with cops and
paramedics standing all around him. Dead, with a hole burned
through his forehead . . . and I knew that, if I didn't find out
why, I could never find any peace again, and all my mornings
would be haunted for the rest of my life.

The buzz of the telephone interrupted my train of thought.
I almost got off the couch until I remembered that I had taken

164

the handset and put it on the floor next to the couch before I had turned in for the night. Marianne was still in the shower, so I picked it up and thumbed the button. "Hello . . . um, Rosen residence," I said self-consciously.

"Where the hell are you?"

Bailey. The son of a bitch had an innate talent for rude awakenings. "Well, Pearl," I said as I sat up on the couch, "if you called here, then you must already know where I am."

"Process of elimination. If you're not in your apartment, then you must be somewhere else."

"Hey, give the man a kewpie doll—"

"Don't gimme no shit, Rosen. We just found out John's been killed and that you were seen at Clancy's with the cops, and when I go upstairs to get you, I find the place ransacked. Word on the street is that a couple of ERA tanks were here last night. Now what the fuck's going on?"

"Earl—"

"This is a helluva time for you to go shacking up with your old lady. Now you tell me what the . . ."

I sighed as I peered out the living room window. There were no cars parked on the street in front of the house, but that didn't mean anything. "Look, Earl—"

"I ain't looking at anything, Rosen, except for a pink slip with your name written on it unless you tell me right now what the—"

"Earl, shut the fuck up."

That did the trick, at least for a moment. I took a deep breath. "I know what's going on," I continued, "but this phone isn't plugged in, y'know what I mean?"

There was silence from the other end of the line. Pearl had a bad temper, and he sometimes ate more brains than he seemed to carry between his ears, but he knew how to take a hint. He knew that anyone with a two-bit scanner could eavesdrop on a conversation carried out on a cordless phone. Even if my neighbors didn't indulge in such skulduggery, there was no guarantee that the police or ERA would not.

"I know what's going on," I repeated. "We can't talk about it right now, but a big load of shit hit the fan last night. John's getting killed is only part of it."

I heard a slow exhalation. *"Are you serious?"*

"Like a heart attack," I said as another thought occurred to me. "Have you heard from Sandy Tiernan yet?"

"Yeah. She's pretty shook. She called me at around six, said that she got the call from some guy at homicide—"

"Mike Farrentino?"

"Yeah, that's him, and when I phoned his office, he said that he'd seen you last night at Clancy's." His tone of voice had changed from belligerence to confusion. *"What's the scoop here, Ger?"*

"I'll tell you when I get downtown," I said. "I'll be there soon as I can swing a ride. But for right now . . ."

I hesitated, trying to think of a way I could phrase the notion that had just occurred to me. "Umm . . . you think you could call an exterminator this morning?"

"Huh? An exterminator?"

"Yeah." I rubbed at the knot left in the back of my neck from sleeping on the narrow couch. I could no longer hear running water from the upstairs bathroom. "Those roaches up in the loft are getting pretty hairy, pal. Might have crawled downstairs into the office. I think you should check it out real soon."

Another long silence, then: *"Yeah, I think so too. Maybe it's time to call Orkin, see if they can send someone down here this morning."*

Bailey had gotten the hint. Cockroaches in the loft, bugs in the office: he knew what I was talking about. If anyone was indeed eavesdropping on our conversation, it would be painfully obvious what we were discussing, but it was better that he was forewarned of the threat before he made any more phone calls or put anything sensitive into the office computers.

The only misunderstanding between us was that he thought I was hinting at the feds or the police as being the prime suspects. I wasn't so sure if ERA or the SLPD were the only ones we had to worry about. Somebody out there was capable of hacking into even encrypted PTs like Joker; they had put the voodoo on me with that faux Jamie phone call last night. Until I had a clue as to who they were, I wasn't taking any chances.

"Good deal," I said. "I'll get downtown as soon as I can."

I clicked off, pushed away the blanket, and swung my legs off the couch. No time for sweet rolls and coffee; all I wanted to do now was get dressed and get out of here. I was reaching for where I had dumped my trousers on the floor when I heard the familiar creak of the stairs.

I looked up to see Marianne sitting on the landing, wearing her robe again, her hair pulled up in a damp towel. No telling how long she had been there, listening to my side of the conversation.

"Hi," I said. "How're you doing?"

Lame question. She didn't bother to answer. Mari simply stared at me, her chin cupped in her hands. "You're going to want a ride downtown, right?"

I hesitated, then slowly nodded my head. It was a long walk from here to the nearest MetroLink station, and despite last night's promise to call a cab first thing in the morning, she knew I didn't have enough cash on me to cover the fare all the way down to Soulard.

She briefly closed her eyes. "And you're going to want money, too, right?"

"Hey, I didn't say—"

"I can spare you fifty dollars," she replied, "and if you'll let me get dressed, I can get you down to the paper in about a half-hour. Okay?"

I nodded again. We gazed at each other for a few moments, each of us remembering all the shit we had put the other through during our years as a couple. Moving in together for the first time. Burned breakfasts, forgotten dinners. Underwear on the floor, unpaid bills. Two or three lost jobs, bouts of morning sickness announcing the arrival of a child neither of us had planned on raising but decided to have anyway. Engagement and marriage. Death and insecurity. Separation on its way to becoming formalized as a divorce.

An old TV commercial had a punch line that had enraged feminists: *my wife . . . I think I'll keep her.* Mari should have written a comeback: *my husband . . . I think I'll ditch him.*

"Yeah," I said. "That'll be great."

Marianne stood up, absently running her hand down the front of her robe so that I couldn't catch a glimpse of her thighs. "Sure," she said. "If it'll get you out of here, I'd be happy to do it."

"Mari—"

"Whatever you're mixed up in," she said, "I hope it works out . . . but I don't want to get involved. You've done enough to me already."

Then she trod upstairs to the bedroom and slammed the door.

Marianne dropped me off in front of the newspaper office; I was almost as glad to be rid of her as she was of me.

The trip downtown had been taken without any words spoken between us; only the morning news on NPR had broken the cold silence in her car. U.S. Army troops were still being airlifted to the Oregon border as Cascadia continued its Mexican standoff with the White House, and the crew of the *Endeavour* had succeeded in rendezvousing with *Sentinel 1* and linking the final module to the antimissile satellite. And some lady in Atlanta was attracting massive crowds to her house after she claimed to have seen the face of Jesus in a pot roast.

Whoopee. I would rather have been in Birmingham, Seattle, outer space . . . anywhere, in fact, but St. Louis.

Everyone stared as I entered the newsroom, but no one said anything to me as I walked straight to Bailey's office. Not surprisingly, he had already taken the cover off his IBM and was peering into its electronic guts with a penlight; Pearl was nothing if not paranoid.

"Close the door and sit down," he said without glancing up from his work. "We've got a lot to talk about."

I shut the door and found a chair that wasn't buried beneath galley proofs and contact sheets. He patiently continued to poke through the breadboards and chips until he was satisfied, then he slid the cover shut and turned around in his swivel chair to gaze at me.

"Look, Earl," I began, "I'm really sorry about—"

"Y'know what this is?" He picked up a large, flat case that lay atop the usual paperwork heaped on his desk. It had a pair of headphones jacked into one end, and one side was covered with knobs and digital meters; a slender spiral cord led to a long, needle-tipped wand. "Of course you know what it is," he went on, "because you must have known I had one when I called you."

"It's an electronic surveillance detector," I said. "You showed it to me once. Remember?"

"That's right," he replied, nodding his head. "Mr. Orkin Man himself. It can scan everything we use in this office and locate virtually any RF or VLF signal imaginable. Infinity bugs, hook-switch bypasses, modem or fax machine taps . . . you name it, this sucker can sniff it out. Put me back three grand, but hey, I've always considered it to be worth the dough. A little extra insurance, if you want to think of it that way."

He carefully placed the instrument back on his desk. "If you meant to scare the bejeezus out of me, you succeeded. As soon as I got off the phone with you, I had everyone drop whatever they were doing while Jah and I went through the place. We switched on every computer, every light, picked up each phone, and turned on all the faxes . . . not a goddamn thing here went untouched, and that includes your apartment and the lab downstairs. I even had Jah run antivirus tests through all the computers and PTs . . . at least, the ones the feds didn't steal from your place last night. And you know what we found?"

He raised his right hand, circling his thumb and forefinger. "Nada. Nyet. Zippity-doo-dah. Not so much as a loose wire. Now, either the feds have managed to put some pretty god-like equipment in here, or you're an anatomical wonder . . . someone who can talk on the phone with his head shoved straight up his butt."

I remained silent throughout all this. He needed to have a good rant right now, and I was unlucky enough to be the target. When he was done, he stared at me from across the desk, his hands folded together over his stomach. He finally let out his breath and kneaded his eyelids with his fingertips.

"The only reason why I haven't thrown your ass out into the street," he said very calmly, "is because you must be onto something. Or at least John must have been onto something, because some bastard took the time and effort to kill him. And I think you must have stumbled into it, because your door got kicked down last night and the feds carted off everything that could be plugged in. So now I'm stuck with a smart reporter who's dead and a dumb reporter who doesn't know how to call his editor when the shit's coming down—"

"Pearl," I began, "look—"

All at once, Bailey surged to his feet, grabbed a pile of paper at random, and hurled it at me so fast I didn't have time to duck the printouts and photostats as they slapped me in the face.

"Fuck you, Rosen!" *he yelled at the top of his lungs.* "I wanna know what's going on!"

The paper rain cascaded down around me, falling into my lap and onto the floor. It was dead quiet outside the cubicle— every person in the office must have heard the explosion— but that wasn't what I noticed. For the first time, I saw that Pearl's eyes were puffy and red-rimmed.

The son of a bitch had been hit hard by the news of John's murder. He was taking it out on me, and maybe he was right to do so because, God help me, I hadn't wept a single tear since the moment Farrentino had called to ask if I could come down to the bar and identify his body.

If Pearl felt like a jerk for going on a futile bug hunt, then I now felt much the same way for not giving myself the time to realize that my best friend was dead. Yet, by the same token, I couldn't allow myself the luxury of wallowing in my own grief. There was something happening out there, at this very moment, of which John's death was only a small and incidental part.

I didn't know what was happening either, but it was time to stop being a victim of circumstance.

"Sit down, Earl," I said. "I've got a lot to tell you."

And I told him all of it, except a couple of the juicy parts.

There was no reason for him to know everything that had occurred during my encounter with Colonel Barris at the stadium . . . in particular, my signed agreement against revealing the details of Ruby Fulcrum. It wasn't just a matter of keeping facts from my editor; I was concerned about his safety. If things went bad, I didn't want ERA troops to come knocking at his door. There was no reason why they wouldn't anyway, but neither did it make any sense to have Pearl mixed up in this shit more than necessary.

And, although I related the story of the strange IM I had received through Joker just before the riot at the Muny, I didn't tell him about the phone call I had received in my apartment just before the ERA raid. I didn't want him to think I had gone around the bend, even if I could explain how I might have heard my own voice and Jamie's over the phone. When Pearl asked me why I hadn't returned to my apartment after I was released from ERA custody, I told him I was too frightened to go back to my place but had simply fled to my ex's house in Webster instead.

Everything else came out, though, and when I was through he simply gazed at me, his fingers knitted together above his lap. After a few moments he picked up his phone and pushed a couple of buttons. "Craig? This is Dad . . . yeah, come up right away, I want you to do something for me."

He put the phone back on its cradle and stood up. "When he gets here, I want to give him Joker so he can run some tests on it. The bastards might have messed with it somehow, and I don't want you running around with a Trojan horse in your PT."

The same thought had already occurred to me, so I pulled Joker out of my pocket. "I take it this means I'm not fired yet," I said as I typed in the "chickenlegs" password.

"I don't fire people, Gerry. I just make 'em quit." Pearl walked around his desk and opened the door. "Now let's go upstairs and see if that disk is still where you hid it."

We met Jah outside Pearl's office. He took Joker and went back downstairs to the photo lab, then Pearl and I climbed the stairs to the third floor.

My apartment was much as I had last seen it. The door was ajar; the desktop computer and the phone were still AWOL; along with the manuscript of my novel. I imagined some ERA officer at the stadium diligently reading the novel, trying to find hidden references within its pages. It would probably be the only audience the book would ever find; I hoped he liked the sex scenes, at least.

"I can't tell whether this place has been ransacked or not," Pearl murmured as he looked at my habitual mess.

"It's a do-it-yourself job." I walked into the bathroom, knelt on the tile floor, and peered beneath the toilet tank. The thin plastic case had gone undiscovered; it was still taped beneath the porcelain pony. I peeled away the tape and let the mini-disk drop into my hand, then held it up for Pearl to see. "We're lucky," I said.

"No luck to it," he muttered. "They just didn't have a containment suit at hand." Pearl took the plastic case from my hand and gazed at it thoughtfully. "All that, to find what's on this thing."

He gave it back to me. "Give it to Jah and let him take a look at it," he said quietly, folding his arms together. "He might be able to make something out of this sucker. Meanwhile, we're going downstairs and see if we can get a line on those people from Tiptree."

"Okay. Right . . ." Suddenly, I felt exhausted. For the last two days I had been punted from one side of the city to the other, and I didn't have any real clues as to what was going on. I gazed at the unmade bed near the broken window. Only about twelve hours earlier I had been lying there dead asleep, more or less innocent of all that had been occurring just beyond my range of vision. And now . . .

"I'm like you," Pearl said. "I don't buy this story about one of their scientists going schizo and shooting people. If there's some other reason why John was killed, then we're going to get to the bottom of it."

"Uh-huh. Yeah . . ."

He looked down at the floor, absently kicking aside an old beer bottle. "You're assigned to this story, Gerry. I want to find out who killed one of our reporters, what he was trying to find out when he was killed, and why someone is shooting people in the street. You're relieved of all other editorial responsibilities until then, understand?"

I nodded. "You want me to bring down the guy who killed John."

He gave me a sharp glance. "Listen, kid: the worst thing a reporter can do is go out on story carrying a vendetta. I know

John was your best friend, but you've got to put that behind you right now. You've got to—"

"Yeah, right. Remain objective."

Pearl shook his head. "No. Objectivity is what you do when you're writing the story itself. Keeping your head is what you do before that. If this is some sort of conspiracy, then the people who are involved are way ahead of you. They've got their tracks covered. Your only advantage right now is that they assume you're stupid. Don't give them a chance to think otherwise . . ."

He grinned. "At least until you come up from behind and take a bite out of their ass."

I looked up at him. In that moment our eyes met, and we were for that instant completely simpatico. All talk of journalistic objectivity aside, there was only one thing we both wanted.

"C'mon," Pearl said as he turned to walk toward the door. "Let's go to work."

15

We began by trying to get a lead on Beryl Hinckley.

We didn't have anything to go on at first; her number wasn't listed in the phone book. Ditto for Richard Payson-Smith, our alleged laser sniper, and although there were four Jeff Morgans listed in the white pages, phone calls placed to three of the numbers quickly established that none of them belonged to our man.

The fourth didn't pick up, but when the answering machine came on after the second buzz, a still picture appeared on the screen; it was the same person in the photo Barris had showed me. *"Hi, this is Jeff,"* the recorded voice said. *"I'm not available right now, but if you care to leave your name and number, I'll get back to you as soon as I can . . ."* I hung up before the beep. If Morgan was on the run, then he wouldn't be calling me back, but any message I left could tip off the bad guys that I was searching for him.

I then made three successive calls to the Tiptree Corporation, asking the switchboard to connect me with Hinckley, Payson-Smith, or Morgan; I switched off my phone's camera when I made these calls. On each try, the computer-generated woman on the screen informed me that none of the three were "available at this time." Remembering that Tiptree employees wore smartbadges that would pinpoint someone's location in the complex, every time I called I made up a different excuse for being adamant: a relative phoning Hinckley to tell her about a sudden death in the family, an insurance claims adjuster for Payson-Smith, a dental assistant calling to tell Morgan

174

that next week's appointment had to be changed. On each occasion, the computer put me on hold, only to come back a few moments later to tell me that none of the three were at the company offices today.

This confirmed my suspicion that the three surviving members of the Ruby Fulcrum team had taken a powder. I didn't accept the virtual receptionist's invitation to leave voice-mail messages for any of them; I had a hunch that none of them would be coming back to work anytime soon.

Not long ago, this might have signaled a dead end for a reporter on the trail of a missing person, but Pearl had his own resources. While I was taking the slow boat to China, he had already boarded an SST.

Tracker is an on-line computer service, little known by the public at large but used extensively by professionals who make their living by snooping into other people's lives: PIs, skip tracers for bondsmen, credit bureaus, lawyers, and direct-mail ad agencies, not to mention a few investigative journalists who didn't mind playing loose and fast with professional ethics. If you've ever wondered why all your credit card bills tend to arrive at the same time you missed a payment on one card, or why you suddenly get loads of junk mail advertising dog food or private kennels only a few days after you adopted a stray mutt from the local pound, services like Tracker are the reason.

Tracker is expensive. At five hundred bucks for the first fifteen minutes and escalating from there, it's not something you logon at whim. It's difficult to access—the company that runs it likes to keep a low profile—but if you have its on-line number and a gold card, then you too can poke around in someone else's private affairs. All you need is that person's name, and you can find out virtually anything available on them through various private-sector databases.

Pearl seldom used Tracker. As a privacy-minded journalist—and, yes, there are still a few of us around—he was loath to invade the personal business of a nonpublic figure, and peeking into someone's credit card accounts is the type of thing that has given reporters a bad name. Yet this was one time he was willing to play lowball.

"Here she is," he said after he had entered Hinckley's name, hometown, and place of work. I bent over his shoulder to look at his computer screen. Next to HINCKLEY, BERYL was a street address in St. Louis and a phone number. "Try that."

I picked up his desk phone and dialed the number. "No answer," I said after I let it ring a dozen times. "She didn't turn on her answering machine."

He nodded. "Okay. Now look the other way for a minute." He shot a sharp glance over his shoulder at me. "I'm going to do something you shouldn't know about," he said. "Only a jerk like me would stoop to something like this."

I turned away while Pearl keyed in a new command. Just outside the office door, I spotted Chevy Dick hanging out in the office corridor, jawing with one of the bohos from the production staff. He was probably dropping off this week's "Kar Klub" column. If things weren't so intense right now, I would have wandered over to join the bull session.

"Okay," Bailey said, "you can look now." I turned back around to see that a new window had opened at the bottom of the Tracker screen; it displayed the account numbers of three major credit cards—Visa, MC, and AmEx—along with their current balances and the dates of their most recent purchases.

"You're right," I said. "Only a jerk like you would do something like this."

"Nothing TRW doesn't do every day," he replied. "Now looky here . . ."

He pointed at the line next to the Visa number. "Three hundred fifty-dollar ATM cash advance, taken out last night at nine forty-six. And see this?" He jabbed his finger at MC and AmEx numbers below it. "Another three-and-a-half c's from the other cards, taken out just a few minutes later. Probably from the very same machine."

"Twenty-one fifty-eight," I murmured, noting the time entered during the AmEx transaction. "Almost ten o'clock. That's not long after John was shot . . . probably right after she took off from Clancy's."

Pearl nodded his head. "Uh-huh. She headed straight to the nearest ATM and took out as much cash as she could—just over a grand altogether—and there hasn't been another charge on any of her cards since." He glanced up at me. "She didn't want to leave any tracks behind her."

"Credit card receipts?"

"You got it. Your girlfriend didn't want to have to pay for anything with a card because that would allow someone to trace her, so she grabbed as much cash as her credit limit would allow. That's a sign of someone who's going underground." He rubbed his jaw pensively as he stared at the screen. "Now I wonder if she . . . ?"

He called up her driver's license, then cross-referenced it with her credit cards. "She didn't rent a car," he said after a few moments. "Car rental agencies always ask for a license and enter it into their records, but this shows she hasn't used her license for anything."

"What about Morgan and Payson-Smith?"

Pearl shrugged. "I'll check, but I bet we won't find anything for them, either." He bent over the keyboard again; this time he allowed me to watch over his shoulder as he began to repeat the same process for the other two Ruby Fulcrum scientists.

Modemed phone numbers, passwords, menu screens accessing the files of credit bureaus: Pearl was doing something almost akin to art, albeit strange and terrible to behold. Not to mention scary. If an amateur like Pearl could hack into credit files and use inductive reasoning to second-guess what a fugitive had been thinking the previous evening, what did this portend for the rest of us?

Bailey must have sensed my line of thought. "When I was a kid," he said as his fingers wandered across the keys, "and my great-grandfather was still alive, he told me that his uncle Samuel had been an escaped slave from Tennessee, way back during the Civil War. He had taken the Underground Railroad up north to Chicago, and it was a hell of a ride. Hiding out in fruit cellars during the day, riding in the back of hay wagons at night, running from one abolitionist house to the next. Once he had to outrun some bloodhounds in some hick town in Kentucky and didn't shake 'em until he lost the scent by wading several miles down a shallow creek."

"But he got away, didn't he?"

He nodded. "Yeah, he got away, but they only had bloodhounds back then. If great-uncle Sam had to do the same thing now, he probably would have stolen a car . . . and if he wasn't paying cash all the way, then every time he stopped at a charge station, some database would have recorded a number with his name behind it. How long do you think he might have lasted? Probably not even to the Illinois state line."

There was a sharp rap on the door; we looked around to see Jah standing in the corridor. He seemed nervous. "Gerry," he said, "I've got something I think you ought to see."

"Joker?"

He shook his head. "Joker's clean," he said, "except that everything you had stored on it has been dumped. It's the backup disk you took from John's PT. It . . ."

Jah took a deep breath, then crooked a finger at me. "Just c'mon down to the lab. You're not going to believe this."

Jah's computer didn't show anything unusual, at least at first glance; the screen displayed the same root directory I had seen the night before on my own 'puter, the cryptic acronyms for a couple hundred different files. He sat down at the computer and pushed a button on the CPU. The CD-OP bay slid open; the backup I had made from Dingbat's original mini-disk was nestled in its drawer.

"When I got down here," he began, "I booted it up like you see here and copied the files into the hard drive. When I was through doing that, I punched into the directory to see what I could find—"

"Sure," I said. "that's just what I did."

"You did?" He glanced over his shoulder at me. "So what happened to you?"

I shrugged, not quite understanding what he was asking. "Well . . . nothing happened, really. I scrolled through the directory and tried to find something that looked like a front door, but I couldn't."

"Yeah?" He scratched at his head. "Then what happened? Did you try punching into a BAT file, or did you get out of the directory?"

I shook my head. "Naw, I didn't get a chance to go that far. I got a phone call and . . . um, that's about when the feds broke down the door. But I didn't do anything before that."

"Uh-huh. And they just unplugged everything and took it . . ."

"Yeah, right. What are you getting at?"

Jah pointed at his screen. "Well, I did the same thing you did, but when I tried the BATs and EXECs I couldn't find a front door either. Everything came up BAD COM. So I decided to get out of the directory and log into a search-and-retrieve program I've got installed in this thing . . . a standard little number I put in here a few months ago to help me find lost files when I've been fucking around a little too much. This way I figured I might be able to unlock a back door or something. Anyway, I was entering the SAR program when—"

He snapped his fingers. "Boom boom, out go the lights. The whole screen went dead for a moment. It was like the computer had spontaneously decided to reboot itself, but I didn't even get so much as a c-prompt. I was still looking under the table . . . y'know, like to see if I had managed to kick out the plug or something stupid like that . . . when the screen came back on again a moment later."

"Yeah, that's weird, all right." It might have been caused by something stupid like kicking out the plug if anyone else had been using the computer, but Jah wasn't a stupid kid. Particularly not when it came to 'puters; in that respect he made even his dad look like a novice. "So what happened?"

"So I figure it's just a software glitch," he continued, sweeping his dreadlocks back from his face, "and go back to what I was doing before . . . except now I can't access the SAR. At least not right away . . . it took me two or three minutes just to pull up the opening screen, and that was after running through all the different startup commands."

"Hmm . . ."

He raised his eyebrows. "Yeah, man. Twilight zone shit. So I get suspicious and I start thinking to myself, y'know . . . Jesus, maybe the disk is infected with a virus or something."

He turned around in his chair and pointed to the telephone wall jack next to his desk. I saw now that the flat gray cord was lying on the floor beneath the jack, its module disconnected. "So the first thing I do is yank the plug, just

in case it really was a virus and someone is trying to call in
while I'm doping out this thing."

"Good idea," I murmured. If Jah's hardware had been
infected with a virus and he didn't know exactly how it had been
transmitted to his computer, then it made perfect sense to isolate
his system. Jah was anything but discourteous to other users,
although it was a good thing he wasn't a sysop for even a minor
BBS; otherwise, dozens of other computers might have
been infected by now. "So what happened then?"

"Now it gets really weird." He held up a finger. "I opened
a window into my antigen subroutine and asked it to check
the system." He shook his head. "It comes back and tells me
it can't find anything. No viruses, no missing batches or boot
sectors, no nothing. According to my computer, I'm clean as
a whistle. But I've still got the creeps, so I do this . . ."

Before I could ask, he turned back to the computer and
used its trackball to log into a program on the directory. A
moment later the opening screen of his search-and-retrieve
program flashed on; when its menu bar was up, he moused
a subroutine listed as VR SEE and toggled it open. "Okay,"
he said, "now here comes the interesting part. Put that on."

He pointed to a department store mannequin propped up
against the wall next to the desk. The dummy was African-
American and female; it was decked out in some exotic black
lace lingerie straight out of any kid's favorite wet dream. I had
to wonder which one of Jah's girlfriends had donated this little
bit of nothing to his trophy room.

"Uh, Jah . . . I hate to tell you this, but—"

"The helmet," he said impatiently. "Put the HMD on."

I looked at the mannequin again. Right. A head-mounted
display was propped on the dummy's bald head, almost
neutralizing the sexual effect. The HMD vaguely resembled
a bicycle helmet except for the oversize opaque visor. A
slender cable led from the back of the helmet to the serial
port on Jah's computer. A pair of naugahyde datagloves were
draped around the dummy's shoulders.

I picked up the HMD and weighed it in my hands. "Is this
really necessary?"

Call me an old fart, but I dislike tripping in cyberspace. I was a kid when the first Virtuality arcades opened in St. Louis; although some of my fellow mall rats used to spend their weekends in the VR simulators, hunting each other through bizarre three-dimensional landscapes or waging war in giant robots, the experience had always left me disoriented. Riding the roller coasters and whirligigs at the Catholic diocese fair was fine, but being thrown into a cybernetic construct tended to make me nauseous.

Sure, I know the old saw about cyberspace being what you do when you're on the phone, but making a phone call is so prosaic that you seldom think twice about it. VR tripping . . . that's like skydiving to me. Some people dig it and some people don't, that's all.

"Hey, I did it," he replied, as if he had just jumped off an old railway bridge into the Missouri River and now wanted me to experience the same rush. "Don't worry, it won't toast your brain. Now c'mon . . . I don't know how much longer this is going to last."

What's going to last? I wanted to ask, but Jah was gnawing at the bit: a teenager eager to show off to an adult who might appreciate this sort of thing.

I reluctantly donned the thick datagloves, then I took a deep breath and pulled the helmet over my head. Jah adjusted the padded visor until it was firmly in place against my eyes.

"Okay, kid," I said. "Show me what you got."

And he did.

For a few moments, there was only darkness . . . then the universe was filled with iridescent silver light, featureless yet fine-grained, as if I was looking at a bolt of electronic silk that had been wrapped around my head. After another second the backdrop faded to dull gray; as it did, a small silver square appeared directly in front of me, a gridded plane floating in null-space.

"Okay," I heard Jah say, "that's a representation of the computer's memory. Each box you see on the matrix is a different program or file I've got stored on this thing . . . touch it and you'll come in closer."

I hesitated, then raised my right hand and watched as its

computer-animated analog rose before my eyes. I curled my fingers and pointed straight at the matrix and suddenly found myself hurtling forward . . .

"Hold on!" Jah yelled. I heard his chair scoot back from the desk, then his hands grabbed my shoulders.

"Maybe you ought to sit down for this," he said as he guided me into the seat. "Okay, that better?"

"Uh, yeah . . . thanks." I hadn't even noticed that I had lost my balance. The flat square had expanded into a transparent three-dimensional cube made up of dozens of smaller cubes. It resembled a crystalline version of some mind-fuck puzzle my dad used to have, a plastic toy where the idea was to shift the interlocked pieces until all four colors were on the same side . . . yeah, a Rubik's Cube, except now I could see all the way through the thing.

"Okay," Jah said, "you see the matrix clearly now? You see all the packets?"

"Yeah, I see it." Each box—or packet, to use Jah's term—in the matrix was labeled with a different alphanumeric code; those would be the programs stored in the memory. Yet, as I slowly orbited the cube, I could now see that not all the packets were silver; closer to its center, a small nucleus of packets were cream-colored, and as I watched, one of them suddenly turned silver.

"It's changing color," I said.

"That's been happening since I first accessed the matrix," Jah said. "When I looked at it the first time, only a few of the packets were silver, and the rest of 'em were white . . . but the ones that had turned silver were the system drivers. Everything else is the other files and programs on this machine."

"A virus?" I asked, and I heard him grunt. "But you said your antigen program hadn't discovered any—"

"Nothing it could detect," he said. "But even that's been absorbed by this sucker . . . and believe me, Scud is the best virus hunter-killer you can find."

I shook my head. That was a mistake; the cyberspatial construct swam back and forth before me. I clutched the armrests with my hands, fighting a brief spell of vertigo. "I don't get it," I said after the cube was dead-center in front of me again. "If this program's still working, then it must not have been taken over yet . . ."

"Oh, no," Jah replied. "ProVirtual—the program we're using now—was one of the first to go, and that's the weird thing. Everything the virus has taken over still works as it did before. It's just . . . well, here, let me show you. Back away from the matrix, willya?"

It took me a second to understand what he was asking me to do. Then I tentatively raised my hand again and pointed to a bit of blank space above the cube. At once, I zoomed to a higher orbit above the matrix; it diminished slightly in size, but I could still see the entire thing.

"I'm booting up an old game I erased from memory a couple of months ago," he said. "It's called MarzBot . . . pretty stupid once you got it figured out . . . anyway, I'm taking the master disk and throwing it into the floppy drive, not the hard drive. Now watch this . . ."

Off to one side, I saw a small isolated packet appear off to one side of the matrix, as if it was a displaced cream-colored electron. For a second, nothing happened . . .

And then something happened.

Almost quicker than the eye could follow, a bridge extended itself outward from the cube: a string of silver packets, following a weightless pattern that, during its zigzagging motion, vaguely resembled the L-shaped movement a knight takes upon a chessboard. Before I could take a breath, the bridge had connected with the isolated packet of information containing MarzBot. There was the briefest moment while the packet still remained off-white.

Then it turned silver.

Then it was sucked straight into the cube as the bridge collapsed in upon itself, reeling in the packet like a fisherman towing in a trout that had taken the bait. Within a second, the MarzBot packet was gone . . .

And the cube was slightly larger.

"Goddamn," I said. "How did you do that?"

"I didn't do anything," Jah said quietly. "The computer did it by itself. I haven't touched the keyboard since I slipped MarzBot into the floppy port and hit the ENTER key. The virus reached out to the program, broke through its copy-protect subroutine, accessed its source code, and absorbed the game . . . all in the time it took for us to watch."

I pulled off the HMD, shook off the aftereffects of VR decompression, and stared at the monitor. The image of the matrix cube on the computer screen was much flatter now, less lifelike than what I had seen in cyberspace . . . yet it was no less threatening.

"Holy shit," I whispered.

"Fuckin' A, man." Jah was staring at me, his eyes wide with fear. "This thing is the balls. I don't know what you found, but it's no ordinary virus. It can't be detected, it can't be fought off, but it takes over anything that even gets close to it."

He pointed at the screen. "I've tried everything I could throw at it," he said, his voice filled with both anger and awe. "Other antigens, Norton Tesseract, Lotus Opus . . . shit, even a shareware disk containing a virus that someone once gave me as a gag . . . and it swamps every program I've given it."

Jah shook his head in wonderment. "Whatever it is, it's one hungry son of a bitch. If I didn't know better, I'd think it was—"

The antique Mickey Mouse phone on his desk buzzed, interrupting his train of thought. Jah swore under his breath as he bent backward to pick it up; he listened for a moment, then cupped a hand over the receiver.

"It's Dad," he said. "He wants you to come upstairs right away . . . says that he just got a call from someone who wants to talk to you."

I was still staring at the monitor, watching as the last few packets in the matrix went from white to silver. "Is it important?" I murmured, not wanting to distract myself with a call from some yahoo. It's not very often you get to look the devil straight in the eye. Jah asked his father if it was urgent, then he cupped the receiver again.

"He says it came from someone named Beryl Hinckley," Jah said. "She wants to meet you an hour from now."

16

The midday lunch rush in Clayton was just beginning as I climbed out of the rickshaw cab I had caught at MetroLink station and paid off the driver. The kid folded the money I gave him and shoved it into his fanny pack without so much as a word, then pulled out into the four-lane traffic of Central Avenue, playing a quick game of chicken with a streetcar as they rounded the corner of Forsyth together.

Long before St. Louis's county and municipal governments had merged, Clayton had been a small metropolis in its own right, a prosperous "edge city" just west of Forest Park. Now it had become St. Louis's uptown business district, its high-rise office buildings constituting a second skyline several miles from the riverfront. Compared to downtown, though, most of the damage suffered by Clayton during the quake had been cleaned up months ago, thanks in no small part to federal relief money. A few small offices had been condemned, a couple of side streets were still impassable, but otherwise it was now hard to tell whether this side of town had been affected at all by New Madrid.

No wonder. Clayton had always looked like a little piece of Los Angeles, disassembled from Beverly Hills and airlifted, brick by pink granite brick, to greater St. Louis. Yet I had never much cared for this part of the city. Despite its sleek postmodern veneer, Clayton was still a ghetto: ten square blocks of overpaid tax accountants, corporate lawyers, and executive vice presidents, an arrogant Disneyland for the aging yupsters and young MBAs who strutted down the sidewalks, each heading for his or her next opportunity to score big bucks. Although ERA troopers were invisible during the day, they were always out in force at night to keep Squat City refugees from taking up residence in the alleys and doorways of the social gentry who called Clayton home. Fall from grace, though, and you fall hard; some of those refugees probably used to live here, too.

The weather had turned bad; the blue skies of early morning had given way to pale gray clouds as a late April cold front began to move in from the west. Offices were letting out for lunch hour as I made my way down Central Avenue's crowded sidewalk to Le Café François, about halfway down the block from the county courthouse.

It was your typical business-lunch bistro, already packed with salesmen and secretaries, and it took me a couple of moments before I spotted her. Beryl Hinckley was seated in a secluded booth at the back of the restaurant, nursing a cup of cappuccino as she furtively watched the door. Upon spotting me, she gave no overt sign of recognition other than to nod her head slightly; I cut my way through the dining room and slid into the booth across the table from her.

"Hi," I said. "Long time, no see."

"You're late," she said coldly. "If you'd been any longer getting here, I would have left."

I shrugged. "If you wanted a reporter, you should have asked for one who owns a car."

Or one who had changed his clothes or taken a shower within the past twenty-four hours, I might have added; her nose wrinkled at my slovenly appearance. It wasn't my fault; she had given me barely enough time to catch the Green Line train out here, let alone clean up a little.

She shook her head. "It doesn't matter," she said calmly. "This will have to be quick. When we're through here, you're going to walk me down the block to the courthouse, where I'm going to find a judge and request that he place me in protective custody."

"What?" Had she told me instead that she planned to throw herself off the Martin Luther King Bridge, she couldn't have caught me more by surprise.

"I'd prefer to surrender to a federal circuit judge," she went on, "but the federal courthouse is only three blocks from the stadium. Since the whole point is to avoid being captured by ERA, I'll have to settle for a state judge."

"Whoa, wait a minute, lady . . . back up a second. Why are you—"

I was interrupted by a young waitress coming by to offer me a menu. I was hungry and could have done well with a burger and fries, but I shook my head and asked for coffee instead. The girl gave me a sweet smile and sashayed away.

"Did you bring your PT?" she asked when the waitress was out of earshot. I reached into my pocket and pulled out Joker. "Good. I picked a public place for this interview because it's the safest option right now, but we still don't have much time."

I placed Joker on the table between us but didn't switch it into audio-record mode just yet. "On the contrary," I replied, "I think we've got all the time in the world. At least long enough for us to have coffee and get to know each other a little better—"

"Mr. Rosen . . ." she said impatiently.

"Y'know, the usual stuff. What high school did you go to? How did you like the Muny the other night? What did you say to my best friend that got him killed? That sort of thing."

The muscles in Hinckley's jaw tightened; she looked as if she were about to explode, but she was forced to remain calm while the waitress returned to place a mug of black coffee in front of me. "I've done a little checking on you since we met," I went on after the girl had vanished again. "Found out a few interesting things, like the fact that you're a research scientist at Tiptree, involved with the Ruby Fulcrum project for the company's Sentinel program, and that your boss, Richard Payson-Smith, is currently being sought by the feds in connection with two murders."

I picked up the cream pitcher and diluted the coffee with a dash of milk. "Also, you've been in hiding since last night," I said as I stirred the coffee. "Given the neighborhood we're in, you must have taken the Green Line out here, then checked into either the Radisson or the Holiday Inn . . . registering under an assumed name and paying for the room in cash, of course, since you were smart enough to take out all that money from your credit cards last night."

Her eyes widened in outrage; for a moment there I thought steam would come whistling out of her ears. Except for the ATM transactions, the last bit was sky blue guesswork, but there was no sense in letting her know that. I was getting under her skin, which was exactly what I meant to do.

"Of course," I continued before she could interrupt, "I could just get up from this table and leave. That's mean sticking you with the bill, but I think paying the tab is the least of your worries right now."

I picked up the mug and took a sip. "Good coffee. So what do you say we cut the crap, okay?"

I was bluffing. If I had a pair of brass handcuffs, I would have fastened her ankle to the table and threatened to flush the key down the men's room toilet unless she spilled her guts. This woman had put me through hell in less than forty-eight hours after I had met her; besides getting a little cheap gratification from watching her squirm, I wasn't about to let her waltz into some judge's private chambers until she told me every nasty secret locked in her head.

Hinckley stared at me silently, her dark eyes smoldering with repressed anger. "One more thing," I said, and this time I wasn't bluffing. "I hold you responsible for John Tiernan's death. If he hadn't gone to Clancy's to meet you last night, he'd still be alive now. But he took the bullet—or a laser beam, whatever—that was meant for you, and that really pisses me off, so don't give me this 'just a few minutes, then I gotta go' routine. You owe me, sweetheart."

She blinked hard a couple of times, then took a deep breath and slowly let it out again. "Mr. Rosen," she said, her tone a little less imperious now, "the person who shot your friend—and it wasn't Richard—didn't miss. He's looking for me now, but he meant to kill Tiernan. He was the intended target, not me."

"Bullshit."

"No bullshit." She shook her head. "There's a conspiracy behind all this, and the last thing the people behind it want is public attention. Despite whatever you think you may know, trust me . . . you don't know anything."

I wasn't about to argue the point. I didn't know anything, and I was counting on her to give me the answers, but before I could ask she clasped her hands together above the table and pointed a finger straight at me.

"One more thing," she said, "and this is why I'm in a hurry. There's four people they want to see dead . . . and you're one of them."

I felt my heart skip just a little. "And the only way we're going to get out of this alive," she said, "is if you shut up and listen to what I have to tell you. Understand?"

I believed her. All of a sudden, this pretentious and socially correct little Le Café François was no longer as safe or secure as it seemed when I walked in through the door. In fact, it felt as if I were sitting in the center of a sniper's crosshair, drinking great coffee and waiting for someone to squeeze the trigger.

I slowly nodded my head, and she gestured toward Joker. "Good. Now turn on your PT. I've got a lot to tell you."

Before she got started, though, I filled her in on much of what I already knew.

Although it was an abridged version of what I had related to Pearl a few hours earlier, it included the fact that Barris and McLaughlin had pressured me into stating that I would help them track her down, as well as Payson-Smith and Morgan. I was barely through telling her about being sworn to secrecy with regard to Ruby Fulcrum, though, when she began to shake her head.

"The name's right," Hinckley said, "but the details are all wrong. Ruby Fulcrum exists—I told you that when I first met you—but it's not exactly what they claim it is."

The four scientists who had been assigned to the Ruby Fulcrum project, she went on to explain, were all specialists in artificial intelligence—or perhaps, more specifically, a branch of AI research called "a-life," or artificial life: computer programs that mimicked all activities of organic life-forms, including the ability to learn on their own.

As Cale McLaughlin had told me, the primary objective of Ruby Fulcrum had been to devise a c-cube system for *Sentinel 1*. This was to be an advanced program—since it was based partly on neural-net systems, even the word *program* itself was almost as archaic as calling a modern automobile a horseless carriage—which, once installed within the satellite's onboard computer system, would learn on its own how to distinguish between ballistic missiles carrying real warheads and those launched as decoys. However, the long-range goal of the project had been the development of a self-replicating a-life-form. Although a-life R&D had been conducted, albeit on a smaller scale, by university and corporate labs since the 1980's, this was the first time a major DOD-funded research effort had been directed at this sort of cybernetic technology.

"The first part of the project was easy to come by, relatively speaking," Hinckley said. "Richard and Po were principally responsible for coming up with an a-life system for Sentinel, and they managed to conclude most of their research about a year ago—"

"And Payson-Smith wasn't opposed to it?" I asked. "I mean, he wasn't against the military application?"

"Is that what they told you?" Hinckley looked at me askance, blowing out her cheeks in disgust. "Yeah, Dick's such a dove, he has his father's old RAF medals framed in his office just so he can swear at them." She shook her head. "If anything, he was the most hawkish member of the team, even if he thought the whole concept of an orbital antimissile system was a little daft."

"How's that?"

She paused to take a sip from her cappuccino, licking the cream from her lips. "Maybe this sort of thing might have made a little sense twenty years ago, when the U.S.S.R. was still around and was stockpiling weapons, but nowadays the only country that still has a large nuclear arsenal is the U.S. itself. Any third-world country that wanted to nuke us wouldn't fire a secondhand Russian missile . . . they'd simply put it on a freighter and sail it into a harbor city . . . and most arms-control people would tell you that accidentally launching a missile is much harder than it's made out in movies. So

Sentinel was obsolete almost before it got off the drawing board."

"Uh-huh," I said. "I've heard that said before. So why were you going along with it?"

"Because it's our job, that's why." She shrugged off-handedly. "Look, that may sound irresponsible, but we aren't the congressmen who voted to appropriate money for this thing. We're just some guys hired to do one small part of the program. We all knew that it was a fluke, but if this was something Uncle Sam wanted, and since Tiptree was writing out paychecks on behalf of the taxpayers, who were we to argue?"

"You remember Alfred Nobel?" I muttered. "They guy who invented dynamite? I think he would have disagreed with—"

"Yeah, right." She held up her hand. "That's political, and anyway it's beside the point . . . at least, right now it is. Let me catch up to the rest of the story, then I'll get back to Sentinel."

While Payson-Smith and Kim Po were concentrating on the c-cube for Sentinel, Jeff Morgan and Hinckley herself were developing a different and far more sophisticated a-life-form. This was the basic research end of the project, intended to produce a nonmilitary spin-off of the original Ruby Fulcrum program; once the Sentinel c-cube was wrapped up and delivered to DOD, Payson-Smith and Kim joined the other two cyberneticists in spending most of their time and effort on the spin-off project.

It had been Morgan's brainstorm to develop a "benign virus" to enable different computer networks to be interfaced without going through a lot of the handshaking protocols mandated by conventional communications software. He was inspired, in part, by the infamous "Internet worm," which a young hacker had let loose in the government's computer network during the late eighties. However, Jeff's dream had been to produce a much more complex—and far more benign—version of the same basic idea. This advanced a-life would be a hybrid between a neural-net and a conventional digital program, allowing it to interface with all types of computers, sort of like a cybernetic philosopher's stone. In fact, the a-life-form that they invented was initially called Alchemist, until the team slipped into referring to it by a part of its old code-name: Ruby.

"Like all a-life organisms," Hinckley went on, "Ruby is guided by a set of rules that mandate its behavior, and these rules compose an iteration—"

"Iteration?"

"Like a cycle," she said, "but the difference between most program iterations and Ruby's is that the others have definite beginnings and endings. Ruby's iteration is open-ended, though. It keeps repeating itself indefinitely. Simply put, it works like this."

She held up a finger. "First, once it's introduced into a computer, it seeks out all programs in that system and everything that's interfaced by those programs. It doesn't even need to be entered into the hard drive . . . transmitting an affected program through modem into a net or even slipping a contaminated disk into the floppy port will do the same trick."

She held up another finger. "Second, it runs through all possible permutations of standard algorithms until it reaches the ones that match and unlock the target program's source code. Once that's accomplished, it deciphers the source code and gains admission. Same idea as hotwiring a car's ignition plate by finding out what the owner's fingerprint looks like and forging it."

A third finger rose from her palm. "Third, it absorbs the target program into its own database, but it does this without locking out access by another user or impeding the functions of that program . . . and then it moves on to seek the next program in the system, and so on."

She paused while the waitress reappeared to reheat my cup of coffee and ask Beryl if she wanted another cappuccino. She shook her head, and the waitress drifted back into the lunchtime crowd. "That's what happened when my buddy Jah booted up a copy of the disk you gave John," I said. "It took over every program in his system but didn't lock him out."

Beryl nodded eagerly, like a mother proud of her child's accomplishments. "Exactly. That's why I gave Tiernan the mini-disk in the first place . . . to prove what Ruby can do.

The only difference was that your friend—uh, Jah, right?—stumbled upon it by accident."

"Hell of a demonstration," I murmured. "And you say this thing can slip through networks and copy itself in other computers?"

"Yes," she said, "but that's not exactly the right term for what it does. It doesn't copy, it *reproduces*. That was the whole purpose, to make a virus that could spread through the national datanet and all the commercial nets, interface with any computer it encounters, then promulgate itself again through cyberspace until it reaches the next computer. And so on, right down the line, like the domino theory."

I poured some more milk into my coffee. "I don't understand, though . . . something like this would require an awful lot of memory to store all that data. And besides, wouldn't it be defeated by antivirus programs?"

Hinckley shook her head. "No, no, it's not quite like a virus. It's more sophisticated than that. It's like . . ."

She sighed and glanced up at the ceiling, searching for an easy explanation. "Ruby is an advanced cellular automaton. Each computer it encounters, no matter how large or small, is absorbed into the larger organism, with each of its programs capable of being controlled by Ruby itself. Then Ruby splits itself apart and automatically seeks out the next computer that it can interface. Meanwhile, the last computer affected becomes a node, or a cell, of the larger system . . ."

"And it keeps growing . . ."

Hinckley nodded. "Right. A little more with each program it interfaces, with each computer functioning as a small part of the larger organism, just as your body is composed of billions of cells that are interconnected to a larger organism, each serving its own function. Unplugging a computer it has accessed won't destroy it, any more than killing one cell would destroy the bio-organism it serves."

She raised a forefinger. "By the same token, antiviral programs are useless against it, because Ruby seeks out, finds, and defeats the basic source codes of those programs, just as a cancer cell defeats the antibodies that surround it."

"Oh my god . . ." I murmured.

"If you think that's scary," Hinckley said, "try this on for size: each time Ruby completes an iteration, it not only grows a little more in storage capacity . . . it also evolves a little more. It *learns*."

She folded her arms together on the table and stared straight at me. "Do you understand what I'm saying?" she asked, her voice kept beneath the noise level of the room, yet not so low that I could miss its urgency. "In theory at least, after a certain number of iterations a critical mass . . . or a phase transition, if you want to use a-life jargon . . . may potentially be achieved, in which Ruby crosses over from being a relatively dumb a-life-form to something much different."

At first, I didn't get what she was saying . . . and then it hit me. "Intelligence?" I whispered.

She slowly nodded. "Artificial intelligence . . . in an artificial life-form that is practically immortal."

I whistled under my breath. Beryl Hinckley was right in her initial assessment; Ruby was no simple spreadsheet program or computer game, but something that imitated life . . .

No. Far more than that, even: Ruby didn't just imitate life; it was a form of life itself. Perhaps not born of woman and man but of fingers tapping instructions into keyboards, yet nonetheless *life* . . .

And, even as I realized this, the full enormity of what we were discussing came home with the impact of a sock in the jaw—and with it, a sneaking suspicion.

"This program," I said haltingly, "or cellular automaton, whatever you call it . . . anyway, when Jah realized that it was some sort of virus, the first thing he did was to disconnect his phone cord."

Hinckley gazed at me without saying anything. I hesitated. "Anyway, it's a good thing he did that, right?"

"No," she said softly, gently shaking her head. "It wouldn't have mattered even if he hadn't, and that's what I told John last night. Ruby's already out there . . . in fact, it was released eleven months ago."

During its infancy, Ruby's cradle had been an IBM desktop computer inside the a-life lab at the Tiptree Corporation. The team had not been careless in raising their creation; they had disconnected the cable leading from the computer's internal modem to the nearest phone jack, and a locked grill had been placed over the computer's CD-OP drive, one that could be removed only by a key carried solely by the four members of the Ruby Fulcrum team.

They knew exactly what they had created: their baby was a Frankensteinian monster that had to be kept locked in its dungeon until it could be trained to behave in a social manner. In turn, as the parents of this potentially destructive creation, they attempted to be responsible in its upbringing. They had fed it only select bits of data, made careful notes as it slowly grew and taken pride in every step it mastered, but nonetheless they made sure that Ruby didn't cross the street until it was properly toilet-trained.

Yet, despite all their precautions, the inevitable accident happened. This occurred on May 17, 2012—the same day an inevitable accident happened throughout the rest of St. Louis County.

"The earthquake hit the company pretty hard," Hinckley said. "You can't tell it now, but four people were killed when the cryonics lab collapsed. That was bad enough, but a lot of other people got injured because of ceilings and shelves falling in. None of my team were hurt, though, thank God . . . we were in the commissary having a late lunch, and the worst thing that happened was that I got a sprained shoulder when a light fixture nailed me . . . but our lab was almost totaled."

She paused, looking nervously again toward the restaurant's front door. I glanced over my shoulder; the lunchtime crowd was beginning to filter out, and our waitress looked as if she was wondering whether she would get a decent tip from two people who had taken up a booth but ordered nothing more than coffee. Other than that, though, nothing seemed unusual; no ERA troopers, no police cars, no mysterious men in trench coats lurking near the cash register.

"Go on," I prompted. "The lab . . ."

Her gaze returned to me. "The lab was busted up pretty badly," she continued, "and the company didn't want any valuable employees going back inside until it had cleaned things up . . . hot wires, unstable walls, things like that. So we were sent home for the next several days while Tiptree brought in a general contractor from Chicago to restore everything—Science Services, some firm that specializes in laboratory restorations, that's what we were told. Don't worry about it, they said. Come back Monday and everything will be fine . . . and, you know, that was all right with us, because we had our own messes at home to clean up. Po lost his house, Dick's cats had been killed, my car had been crushed by a tree . . ."

She sighed as she settled back against her seat, rubbing her eyelids with her fingertips. "Well, to make a long story short, some college kid was responsible for straightening up the a-life lab. I can't really blame him, because things were scattered all over the place and no one had kept any reliable charts as to what went where . . . but when he uprighted the Ruby Fulcrum computer and found the loose telephone prong leading from the modem, he figured it was another loose wire and slipped it into the jack."

"Oh, shit . . ."

Hinckley's face expressed a wan smile. "Yes, well, that's one way of putting it. After he did that and he was assured that the phone lines were operational again, he switched on the computer to give it a quick test . . . and, of course, being a conscientious Science Services employee, he tested the modem by dialing into a local BBS to see if the patch was solid."

And, without anyone's realizing what had happened, Ruby was allowed to crawl through the bars of its playpen. Frankenstein's monster had been let loose to roam the streets of the global village.

"We didn't know what had happened until we came back to the lab on Monday," Hinckley went on. "Dick flipped out, of course, and the first thing he did was to try and figure out where and how Ruby had slipped through our fingers. To do this, he had to access the company's mainframe and backtrack all its incoming and outgoing phone calls, including e-mail and fax records."

She stared at me directly, meeting my gaze over the tabletop. "When he did this," she said, very quietly, "he managed to penetrate company files none of us had ever seen and discovered something none of us were ever meant to know—"

At that moment, the door slammed loudly. We both glanced up; no one but a pair of salesmen, swaggering in for a late lunch as if they owned the place. One of them yelled for our waitress to seat them; the other tried to stroke her ass as she flitted by. A couple of slimers, nothing more, but their rude entrance made her more aware of our surroundings.

"We've got to get out of here," she said. "I don't like this place."

"C'mon," I said. "Just some yups cruising for burgers."

She continued to stare uncertainly toward the door. "There might be ERA people out there," she said. "They don't always wear uniforms or carry guns, you know."

She was scared and had every right to be, but that didn't matter right now. I wanted to get the rest of the story out of her before she went down the street to the courthouse. "Don't worry about the feds grabbing us," I said quickly. "Remember what I told you about Barris, the local ERA honcho? He gave me a card I could use to get us past checkpoints."

"Card?" Her gaze wavered back toward me, only slightly distracted. "What sort of card?"

"Umm . . . this one." I reached into my jacket for the laminated card the colonel had given me the night before. I hadn't looked at the card since Barris had handed it to me; in fact, this was the first time all day I had thought of it.

"See?" I said as I produced the plastic card and showed it to her. "It'll solve any problems with—"

"Oh, hell," she whispered. "Let me see that."

Before I could object, Hinckley whisked the card from my fingertips and examined it closely. She bent it slightly, held it up to the light . . . then reached into the pocket of her jacket and pulled out a Swiss Army knife, unfolded its miniature scissors, and made a deep cut into the center of the card.

"Hey!" I snapped. "Don't do . . ."

Then I stopped as she pulled open the card a little more and revealed it to me. Within its plastic and cardboard lining lay wires as fine as cat whiskers, leading to tiny wafer-thin microchips and miniature solenoids.

"It's a smartcard," she breathed. "Like the smartbadges we've got at the company . . . only this one can emit a signal that can be traced through cellular bands."

"Aw, shit . . ." I couldn't believe I had been such an idiot. The bastards had set me up and I had fallen for it. "Can it . . . could it listen to us?"

She shook her head. "Uh-uh," she said quietly. "It'd have to be larger than this . . . but it can signal our location to anyone who's paying attention. That's bad enough."

A frigid current ran down my spine. "Does this mean—"

"I don't know what it means," she shot back at me. "You brought it here, so you tell me." Hinckley gently lay the card on the table and slid it against the wall, placing a napkin dispenser on top of it for good measure. "One thing's for sure, and that's the fact we've been here too long."

"Hey, I didn't know—"

"I know you didn't know," she murmured as she slid out from her side of the booth. "If you'd been working for them, you wouldn't have been so stupid as to show it to me. That's not the point."

She dug a few dollars out of her pocket and put them on the table. "When we get to the courthouse and I find a judge, you'll get the rest of the story . . . but we've got to get out of here."

I was just starting to clamber out from my side of the booth. "But I swear I didn't—"

"*Now*, damn it!" Hinckley was already heading for the door by the time I crawled out of my seat. I scrounged a handful of loose change out of my pocket, dropped it on the table, and gave an apologetic shrug to the waitress, then hurried to catch up with her.

17

I caught up with Beryl Hinckley just outside the restaurant. The crowds were beginning to thin out on the sidewalk as office workers hurried back to their desks and cubicles, clutching half-read newspapers and foam cups of coffee. There was still plenty of traffic on the street, however, and the metered slots along Central Avenue were filled with parked cars.

"Walk fast," I murmured as I took her right arm and began marching down the sidewalk. "Whatever you do, keep an eye on the cars. If you see anything—"

"I know," she whispered back. "Run for it."

I glanced at her; she nodded her head, her face grim. She knew the score: both John and Kim Po had been shot from a vehicle, and although a van had been spotted leaving Clancy's, no one was certain if this was the automobile the killer was driving. The only thing we had going for us was that it was a blustery afternoon, and most drivers were keeping their windows up. According to what Cale McLaughlin had told me, the laser rifle the sniper was using was capable of firing through nonreflective glass, yet if the killer wanted to get an unimpaired shot, he might want to lower the window first.

We shied away from the street, but I walked next to the curb. Old-fashioned chivalry, just the way my dad taught me, but this time it was for more practical reasons than to keep the lady I was escorting from being splattered with mud from passing cars. If she was the killer's primary target, then I would be shielding her a little more this way. Of course, if she was right, it didn't really matter what I did, because

199

the bastard might try to nail me first. It wasn't a comforting thought.

"You have any idea which judge you're going to find?" I asked as we walked. Only one city block left to go; I could already see the small plaza across the street from the intersection of Central and Carondelet. Directly beyond the plaza was the five-story white concrete box that was the county courthouse.

Hinckley hesitated, then shook her head. "I don't keep up with the judges around here," she replied, her eyes locked on the street. "I was just planning on going in there and finding someone's name on a door."

I sighed and shook my head. Glancing down at the sidewalk, I noticed for the first time that she wore knee-length calfskin boots; the laces on her right boot were loose and were beginning to drag the ground, but I wasn't about to remind her to stop and retie them. "It's a little harder than that," I said. "They keep office hours like everyone else . . . and on a Friday afternoon, if they're not in court, then they're probably out on the golf links."

I thought about it for another moment, trying to remember the names of judges whose cases I had covered in the past for the paper. "We might try Swenson . . . Edith Swenson," I added. "She's supposed to be pretty honest, at least. I don't know if she's in, but we could always . . ."

Her breath suddenly sucked in as I felt her arm go rigid in mine. I followed her gaze and saw a van turning the corner of Carondelet and heading our way. A white Ford Econovan, late eighties vintage—a rusted-out old gashog, pale gray fumes farting out of its exhaust pipe, probably on the last weeks of its expiration sticker—but what caught her attention was that it was moving very slowly toward us. I looked closer; I couldn't see the driver, but the passenger window was lowered.

The doorway of another restaurant was just a few feet away, beneath an ornamental canvas awning. "In there!" I snapped.

Hinckley didn't need any urging. We scurried under the awning and into the doorway. I grabbed the door handle and was about to pull it open when the Econovan rumbled past.

Both of us froze and stared at the van; an old black gentleman was behind the wheel, and he didn't seem to be paying a bit of attention to us as he tooled down Central away from the courthouse. I caught a couple of bars from a vintage soul number blaring from the stereo as the clunker rumbled past: *"Nutbush city limits!* . . . wahwahwahwah-waaw-waaw . . . *Nutbush city limits!"*

False alarm.

Beryl sagged against the doorframe, her hand against her chest. "God," she whispered as she let out a hoarse laugh. "I never thought I'd be so glad to hear Ike and Tina Turner."

"I'll find a copy for you when we get out of this." I pulled her out of the doorway.

"Oh, hell . . ." She stopped suddenly and looked down at her feet. "My boot's untied."

I thought again about letting her take care of her laces, but I let it pass. The next vehicle to pass us might have more than classic Motown tunes blasting through its side windows. "Don't worry about it now," I said as I tugged at her arm. "Just keep going."

We walked past an alley entrance and the last building on the block, a condemned midcentury office building with windows boarded up with plywood: another victim of the earthquake, whose owner had apparently decided that demolition was less expensive than renovation. By now we were almost directly across the corner from the courthouse, a block-size building nearly as homely and featureless as the adjacent county jail and the Government Center highrise. All three buildings suffered from that peculiar form of governmental architecture a friend of mine had once described as "Twentieth Century Post-Gothic Paranoid": no windows in featureless walls on the ground floor, the narrow casement windows on the upper floors resembling the archer slots in medieval castles. Trust us, we're the government . . .

"Fine with me," I muttered, "so long as you can repel laser beams."

"What?" Hinckley asked.

"Nothing. Just thinking aloud." As I said this, another thought occurred to me. "What about the two other guys . . . um, Dick and Jeff? When do I get to meet them?"

She shot me a glance that spoke volumes. She was placing enough confidence in me to hear out her story and witness her surrender to a judge, but she wasn't quite ready to entrust her friends' lives to my hands. After all, I had already confessed to her that Barris was counting on me to track down Payson-Smith for him. Even though I had obviously been surprised by the cellular smartcard Barris had given me and I had willingly left it behind in the restaurant, there was still no guarantee that I wasn't playing stool pigeon for ERA.

"I'll let you know when the time's right," she said softly. "They already know about you, don't worry . . . but we need to take this one step at a time. All right?"

"Yeah. Okay. Whatever."

We arrived at the corner of Central and Carondelet. No other pedestrians were in sight; no cars violated the No Parking signs in front of the courthouse and the jail. So far, so good; all we had to do was cross the street, make it through the postage-stamp plaza with its rows of empty cement planters, and the side door of the courthouse was wide open to us. Walk-through metal detectors had been established in all the courthouse entrances some twenty years ago after some lunatic had opened fire in a courtroom and killed a few people, and there were always a couple of cops stationed at the check-points. Once we were through the side door, we were home free.

I gave the area a quick scan, then I grabbed her hand and pulled her off the sidewalk, leading her out into the street. "Okay," I said, "let's go."

We jaywalked through the wide intersection, not running but not sightseeing either. Halfway through the intersection, she dropped my hand. We stepped onto the curb, walking beside each other, and began to stride into the plaza. I could see people walking or seated at desks behind the courthouse windows. The side door was only seventy feet away.

She made a slight grunt, as if she had tripped on her boot-laces, but I paid no attention. I was beginning to relax. *You asshole, you're running from shadows . . .*

"I think I can find that Turner CD at a place down on Delmar," I said. "You ever been to Vintage Vinyl? It's got the best . . ."

No answer. She wasn't walking beside me anymore. I turned around, half-expecting to see that she had finally stopped to lace up her boots.

Dr. Beryl Hinckley lay sprawled on her face across the concrete sidewalk just a few feet from the curb, her arms and legs still twitching slightly as what remained of her brain told her that it was time to run like hell.

Not that she had been given much chance to run; the silent beam that killed her had burned a thumbhole through the back of her skull.

The moment stretched, became surreal. Cars moved by on the street. Pigeons wandered around the edge of the plaza in search of infinitesimal scraps of food. A commuter 'copter moaned overhead, heading for the municipal heliport several blocks away. A dead woman lay at my feet, and all around me the world was going about its normal day-to-day business. One second you're talking to someone about buying secondhand CDs; the next second, that person is cold meat on the street corner, shot down by a . . .

Laser beam.

I yanked myself out of my stupor, began looking around. No cars were in sight, but all around me were high-rise buildings. Countless windows in a half-dozen towers, and the sniper could be lurking behind any one of them, even now drawing a dead bead on me.

Move, stupid!

The nearest of the plaza's tree-planters was directly behind me, a large round urn about three feet high and eight feet in diameter. I dove behind it, crouching in its shadow as my heart triphammered in my ears. There were seventeen more planters just like it behind me, artfully arranged in three rows of six each, leading down the plaza until they ended near the courthouse door. The planters were empty, but they might provide enough cover for me. If I could keep dodging behind them as I made a run for the side door . . .

Yeah, right. The next planter in the row was at least ten feet away; the sniper could pick me off easily as soon as I raised my head. I'd be dead before I knew what hit me.

I hugged the side of the planter, trying to remember what McLaughlin had told me about the nature of laser rifles. Silent. Invisible beam. Flat trajectory. Almost infinite range . . . but big and clumsy, about the size of a rocket launcher. That meant whoever was using it would have to remain fixed in one place. And there was something else . . .

A couple of well-dressed women, probably trial lawyers returning from lunch down the street, appeared from around the corner of the Government Center building. They were still chatting it up as they began to cross Carondelet, until they saw Beryl Hinckley's body lying on the opposite sidewalk.

They froze in the middle of the street, gazing in confused shock at the corpse, then one of them looked around and spotted me. Before I could say anything, she screamed bloody murder, then turned and ran back the way she had come. The other one stared at me in gap-mouthed fear for another second, then she followed her friend as they fled back around the corner.

Great. Just what I needed right now: they'd call the police and report a homicidal maniac hanging around the courthouse plaza. I closed my eyes and knocked my head against the side of the urn. In another minute this place would be surrounded by cops who'd . . .

A minute.

That was it. McLaughlin had told me that it took sixty seconds for the laser to recharge itself. Assuming he hadn't been lying to me, I had some lead time before the killer could squeeze the trigger again.

This was of little comfort to me. At least a minute had gone by already, between the instant Beryl had been shot and this moment in time. But if the killer still had me in his direct line of fire, then he should have picked me off by now. Sure, maybe he had seen where I had taken cover—but so long as I had the planter between us, then he couldn't skrag me as well.

Not yet, at least. I couldn't remain here much longer. Sooner or later, I'd have to get to my feet.

Forget about that, I told myself. *Concentrate on what's going on here . . .*

Okay, okay. She couldn't have been shot from a window in either the courthouse or Government Center; those buildings were on either side of me, and anyone standing in the windows would be able to see me. The jail had few windows of which to speak, and it was the most unlikely place for a sniper to be hiding. I ruled out the high-rise apartment complex behind the courthouse; the angle of fire was all wrong.

This still left at least another four or five buildings on the other side of Central Avenue. If I could only figure out which one was the—

There was a commotion from the courthouse entrance. I glanced over my shoulder to see a half-dozen people hesitantly emerging from the glass double doors: lawyers, clients, court witnesses, and clerks, all staring at me. A uniformed cop was right behind them; one of the onlookers pointed my way and the cop drew his gun, but instead of taking matters into his own hands he quickly urged the rubberneckers back into the building before he took cover within the entranceway. From what little I could make of him, I could see him pull out his beltphone, snap it open, and hold it close to his face.

The Clayton cop shop was located only a few blocks away. I now had the option of holding out until the law arrived. It was a tempting thought—surrender peacefully and allow myself to be taken into custody, then prove my innocence in my own sweet time—but that still meant I would have to emerge from hiding. The sniper could take me out while I was surrounded by a SWAT team. Even if they doped out how and why I had suddenly fallen down with a self-cauterized hole in my head, it wouldn't mean shit so far as I was concerned.

Fuck it. I had to pinpoint the sniper myself . . . but now I had an idea.

Still crouching low behind the planter, I pulled Joker out of my jacket pocket, flipped it open, and switched to verbal mode. "Joker, log on," I said.

"Good afternoon, Gerry. What can I do for you?"

"Gimme a street map of the Clayton district." I glanced over my shoulder again at the courthouse cop; he was still laying low, waiting for his backup to arrive. "Display a three-block radius surrounding the intersection of South Central and Carondelet."

"Working . . . just a moment, please." There was silence while my PT modemed into a library neural-net. Two or three moments passed before the uplink was completed and the map was laid out on the PT's clamshell screen. *"Here is the map you requested."*

I could hear sirens approaching from the distance. I forced the sound from my mind. "Okay. Now . . . uh, overlay a 3-D graphic of all buildings within this perimeter, and make it snappy."

"Snappy is not an available function. Please define."

"Forget snappy," I said impatiently. "Just do it."

Computer-animated buildings sprang from the gridwork of streets. Now the map resembled an aerial photo of this part of Clayton, including the courthouse plaza itself. "Very good," I said. "Logon graphics-edit. I'm giving you a new coordinate for the map. I want you to add it to your memory."

"Certainly, Gerry."

I touched the miniature trackball and gently moved the cursor across the screen until it was approximately above the spot in the courtyard where Hinckley's body lay. When I removed my finger, the cursor vanished and a tiny *X* remained in its place.

So far, so good, but the sirens were getting closer now. I looked over my shoulder again but couldn't see the cop who had been hiding in the doorway. I took a deep breath, then went on. "Okay . . . now display lines between this coordinate and . . . ah . . ."

Shit. All of a sudden, I was stumped by my own ingenuity. How could I ask Joker to show me the probable line-of-sight trajectory between Hinckley and the sniper? I already knew what would happen if I phrased the question the wrong way; lines would radiate in all directions from the coordinate I had registered on the map.

But how could I explain the problem to a literal-minded computer? *Well, see, there's someone lying on the ground nearby who's just been shot by laser beam, and I'm the next target, so I want you to try to figure out which building on this grid the sniper was firing from . . . and, by the way, the cops are closing in, so make it snappy. That means quick, right away, pronto, haul ass . . .*

Yeah. Fat chance . . . but it was better than nothing. I would have to dumb-fuck my way through this. "Given that the coordinate I just designated is five-point-five feet tall . . ." I said slowly.

"Pardon me, Gerry, but I have received an instant message for you."

Joker's voice was maddeningly calm. Here I was, trying to think through a complex problem to save my life, and it wanted to deliver e-mail to me. I winced and swore under my breath. "This is not a good time, Joker."

"I'm sorry, Gerry, but the IM has a priority interrupt. The sender has identified itself as Ruby Fulcrum."

What the . . . ?

"Gimme the message!" I snapped.

The screen bisected into two parts; the map remained intact on the upper half, although reduced by fifty percent, while the lower half displayed a message bar:

>Laser beam fired from 1010 South Central Avenue, floor five<

At the same moment, a red line traced itself from the coordinate I had registered on the map to the condemned five-story office building directly across the corner from the courthouse.

I stared at the screen. How the hell could . . . ?

"Freeze, mister!" a voice yelled. "Get your hands in sight!"

The courthouse cop I had spotted earlier was standing directly behind me. His feet were spread wide apart, his service revolver clasped between both hands and pointed at the back of my head. He had snuck up on me while I was paying attention to Joker.

"Okay, okay," I said, trying to calm him down. "I don't have a gun, see?" I held up Joker in my right hand, keeping my left hand where he could see it. "Look, it's not a gun, all right?"

The cop wasn't impressed. "Yes sir, I can see what it is," he said evenly. "I want you to put it down on the ground, stand up and put your hands behind your head. Now, sir."

I carefully placed Joker on the concrete and wrapped my hands around the back of my head, but I didn't stand up. "Officer," I said as calmly as I could, "the woman over there was shot from the top floor of that building." I nodded toward the condemned building across Central from Government Center. "I had nothing to do with it, but—"

The officer's eyes darted once toward the building, then back to me. He wasn't buying it. "Get on your feet, mister."

"Look, I'm telling you, if I stand up now, he's going to shoot—"

His attention was fixed solely upon me. "I'm not kidding, buddy!" he demanded. "Get up with your hands behind your head!"

The sirens were much louder now, probably only a block away, racing down Central Avenue toward the courthouse. The officer was waiting for his backup to arrive, and he wasn't about to give me any slack. There was a dead woman on the sidewalk, and his suspect was giving him a song-and-dance routine. His right forefinger was wrapped around the trigger of his gun. This was a young rookie, still in his twenties and fresh out of the academy; he wanted to be a Good Cop, but I was only too aware of the fact that some members of the force had a bad rep for being trigger-happy under pressure.

As the first police cruiser howled into sight and screeched to a halt in front of the plaza, I took a deep breath. The cavalry had arrived; maybe they had scared off the sniper. "Okay," I said, "just stay cool. I'm standing up."

The second cruiser arrived, stopping behind the first one; two cops had already jumped out of the first car and were rushing over to check on Beryl Hinckley. I slowly began to rise out of my squat, but as I did I kept my eyes fixed on the empty windows of the building Ruby Fulcrum had pinpointed.

I had barely raised my head and shoulder above the height of the urn when I glimpsed vague movement in a corner window on the fifth floor: a brief, dull reflection, like sunlight reflecting off something metallic . . .

"Duck!" I yelled, then threw myself to the ground.

"Don't . . . AWWWHHHH!"

A small black hole appeared in the cop's chest, just below his neckline. He dropped his gun as he grabbed at his collarbone, screaming in agony, then his legs collapsed beneath him and he fell backward to hit the pavement. He was still alive, but the laser beam had cut straight though his body.

Two more cops from the second cruiser, who had been running over to assist him, stopped dead in their tracks. They had seen the whole thing; judging from the expressions on their faces, they couldn't figure out what the hell had happened. They glanced first at their buddy, then at me, then back at him again.

"I didn't do a thing!" I yelled as I lay flat on the ground, my arms spread out before me. "I'm just lying here . . . get him an ambulance!"

The cops unfroze. Instead of rushing me, they hurried to the rookie's side. He was writhing in pain, his legs thrashing against the pavement. His colleagues kneeled beside him; one of them grabbed his beltphone and flipped it open. "Mobile Charlie-Five, answering call at the courthouse!" he snapped. "Code ten-three, officer down!"

The other two cops ran over to assist them. For the moment, they were entirely concerned with the injured officer. No one was paying attention to me. I rose to my hands and knees, carefully picked Joker up from the concrete and shoved it in my pocket . . .

And then I jumped to my feet and took off running.

Not away from the scene, though, but straight toward the abandoned building.

18

One thing to be said for knowing that a sniper is trying to kill you: it makes you run faster.

Even as I sprinted across the intersection, I knew that I had less than thirty seconds—if even that—to reach cover before the laser's batteries recharged. On the other hand, if I could make it to the building itself, then the gunner upstairs wouldn't be able to shoot me. A clean vertical shot would be nearly impossible from up there, or otherwise he would have fired at Beryl before we had jaywalked across the street.

I heard cops shouting behind me as I made a beeline for the building, demanding that I halt. The thought crossed my mind that one of them might open fire on me, but I wasn't about to stop and lie down in the middle of the intersection. I was screwed if I did and screwed if I didn't, and all I could hope for was the notion that a well-trained police officer wouldn't shoot a running man in the back . . .

So I kept running.

A laser beam didn't punch a hole through my head, nor did I heard the crack of a gunshot as I reached the opposite side of the intersection and dashed toward the building's front doors. Although its nineteenth-century facade was largely intact, official condemnation notices were pasted across the plywood nailed over the windows.

I ducked into the recessed doorway and took a deep breath. I was safe for the moment, but I still had to get inside before the cops followed me. The narrow door, itself covered with plywood, had been secured with a padlock; when I looked closer, though, I saw that the lock's hasp had been severed as if by a pair of heavy-duty bolt cutters, then carefully rehung to make it look still secure.

The door's pneumatic hinge wheezed as I tugged it open and stepped into the narrow entranceway, cautiously avoiding the shattered glass that lay on the floor of the foyer. The door closed behind me. Faint sunlight penetrated the gloom through cracks in the plywood, making it possible for me to read the dislodged building register resting on its side against the wall: lawyer's offices for the most part, although the second and fifth floors had been vacant at the time of the quake.

The building was stone quiet.

Groping along the walls with my hands, I made my way farther into the building, passing a battered water fountain, an inactive elevator, and the entrance to what had once been a barber shop, until I reached the end of the hallway and found the door leading to the stairwell.

The door squeaked as I pulled it open; I hesitated for a moment, listening intently to the darkness above me. I still couldn't hear anything, but that meant nothing. For all I knew, the sniper could be at the top of the stairwell, waiting for my head to come into sight.

For a few moments I considered the safest option but almost immediately discarded that idea. Retreat only meant giving the sniper a chance to try again some other time . . . but now I had a slim chance of cornering the bastard and ending this game once and for all.

So I entered the stairwell, carefully let the door slide shut, then began to climb the stairs.

Light shining through unboarded windows at each landing guided me as I made my way upward, peering around each corner before I jogged up the next set of risers. Mice and cockroaches fled from my approach; the building smelled of old dust and the stale urine of evicted squatters. On the third-floor landing, I found a small pile of rubble from a collapsed ceiling. I picked a short length of iron rebar out of the mess and hefted it in my hands—remembering the crazy lawyer I had seen at the Muny a couple of nights earlier, I wondered if his firm's offices had once been located here—

then I continued my way upstairs.

No one was waiting for me on the fifth-floor landing.

Stopping for a moment to catch my breath, I studied the door leading toward the end of the building from where the shots had originated. At first glance, it seemed undisturbed, until I noticed a straight line of dust and broken plaster leading away from the hinge at a right angle as if recently pushed aside by the bottom of door.

There was a window behind me, looking out over the rear of the building. I peered out and spotted a battered brown Toyota mini-van parked in the back alley, near the bottom of a fire escape. From what I could see, it looked as if the fire escape had a gravity ladder leading to the pavement. If that was the killer's wheels, then he would probably be using the fire escape to make his getaway from the building.

I should have thought of that earlier. It wouldn't have been quite as stupid or reckless to wait in the alley until he reached the bottom of the fire escape. No turning back now, though. I was here, and he was somewhere in there, and the time had come to take down the son of a bitch before he killed somebody else.

Gripping the iron bar in my left hand, I tiptoed to the door, grasped its handle, and slowly eased it open.

A short hallway led me past the defunct elevator and the door of the vacant office space; at the opposite end of the corridor was the fire-escape window. The window was raised, and the office door was propped open with a short piece of broken wood.

Through the door, I could hear vague, hurried movement: metal moving against metal, a zipper sliding down, then up again. The grunt of breath being exhaled. I inched my way toward the door, put my back against the wall, and peered through the doorframe.

The space beyond the doorway was completely vacant; even before the quake, all the interior drywalls had been knocked down, leaving open a large, empty room bordered only by the outer walls. Sullen midday sunlight, flecked with dust motes, streamed through the windows and the gaping hole in the ceiling where the roof had partially collapsed, leaving broken pipes, brick, and mortar strewn across the dirty tile floor.

On the opposite side of the room, the killer was packing up the tools of his trade.

He was nobody I recognized. In fact, he looked like nobody anyone would ever recognize. Average height, medium build, late thirties or early forties, wearing a beige workman's jumpsuit. A wireless radio headset hung around his neck. Sunlight reflected dully off a receding hairline, which had already left him half bald, and the wire-rimmed glasses on his plain face. People talk about the banality of evil; I was looking right at it. This dude could have been a janitor, an electrician, an exterminator cruising for rats . . . anything but a professional assassin.

He moved quickly as he dismantled his weapon: a small compressed-gas tank, a contraption that looked like a compact piston-driven pump, a pair of storage batteries attached by slender cables to a long, cumbersome instrument that vaguely resembled a World War II vintage bazooka, itself mounted on a tripod with an infrared telescopic sight above its barrel. All of it was being stripped down and loaded into a two-wheeled golf caddie.

You think "laser rifle" and the first thing you imagine is something from a late-show SF movie—small, sleek, no larger than an AK-47—but this thing resembled nothing more or less than an industrial welding rig from Chevy Dick's garage. *Of course two people had been shot from a van*, I thought. *You'd need a van just to haul all this shit around.*

Never mind that now. His back was turned to me. His target was gone, and he only wanted to get out of here while the getting was good. Man, was he in for a surprise.

He had disconnected one of the batteries and had bent over the caddie to shove it in place when I moved through the doorway as quietly as I could, carefully stepping around the broken stuff littering the floor, the rebar grasped in both hands. I paused as he stood up and turned toward the laser itself, pulling an electric screwdriver from the back pocket of his jumpsuit. He fitted it into the base of the tripod; there was a thin mechanical whine as his thumb pressed against the button.

I took a deep breath, hefted the rebar in my hands, and then I charged across the room toward him.

Halfway across the room, my boots stamped through some debris. His head snapped up at the sound; he dropped the screwdriver and began to twist around, his right hand whipping for the front breast pocket of his jumpsuit as he turned toward the figure hurtling at him.

I screamed at the top of my lungs as I hauled the iron bar above my head. The .45 automatic was out of his pocket, but he didn't have a chance to aim before I swung the rebar.

It slammed straight across his chest and lifted him off his feet; the gun sailed out of his hand, hitting the floor ten feet away from where his ass landed.

He lashed out at me with his right leg, catching me on the side of my left ankle. I yelped and danced away; he rolled over and began to scramble toward his gun.

"Fuck you!" I yelled as I raised the slender iron bar again and brought it straight like an ax against the back of his right arm.

He screamed at the same instant as I heard the dry snap of his elbow being shattered. He clutched at his arm as he rolled over on his back, losing his glasses as he howled in agony.

"I said, 'Fuck you!' " I yelled again as I raised the bar and swung it down square between his legs.

His scream could have shattered a wineglass. A dark blotch spread against his pulverized groin as he grabbed at it. I didn't care. "Didn't you hear me, asshole?" I snarled. "Are you deaf? I said, 'Fuck you!' "

I swung the rebar down across his right knee. The breaking of bone and cartilage, like fine porcelain shattering beneath a hammer, trembled through the bar into my hands.

God help me, but I loved it.

He howled as tears streamed from his eyes, his face turning stark red. I bent over him, savoring his agony, the high animalistic keening of his voice.

"Still can't hear you, cocksucker!" I bellowed at him, then I stood up and lifted the iron bar above my head again. "I said—"

"I hear you!" he gasped, his voice ragged and hoarse. "I hear you! Please don't . . ."

I saw John's face. I saw Beryl Hinckley's face. I saw Jamie's face, even though this scumbucket had had nothing to do with his death. I wanted to beat this nameless bastard to death . . . but before that, I wanted answers to a lot of questions.

"Where are you from?" I shouted. "Who sent you?"

His face crawled. "Ehh . . . ehhh . . ."

"Tell me, you dick! Tell me who sent you or I swear to God you'll never walk again!"

His chest was rising and falling as if he had just run a ten-mile race. In another minute, he'd go into shock and I'd lose him . . .

"Speak up, you piece of shit!" I showed him the jagged edge of the rebar, holding it just above his face, and let his imagination do the rest. "Talk to me!"

"ERA!" he cried out. "I'm working for ERA!"

No surprise there. Still holding the rod over his head, I yanked Joker out of my pocket, thumbed it into Audio Record, and held it over him. "Who at ERA sent you?" I demanded, even though I already knew. "Tell me his name! Why did he—"

"Drop it, Rosen!"

Mike Farrentino was standing just inside the door, bookended by two uniformed officers. The cops were crouched, their revolvers cupped between their hands and aimed straight at me, but Farrentino's hands were shoved in his pockets.

"Get away from him, Gerry," he said evenly. "Just let go and—"

"Aw, cut it out, Mike." I pulled the rebar away from the sniper's face and let it drop from my hands; it hit the floor with a dull clang. I raised my arms and backed away from the man on the floor. As quickly as it had come, my rage dissipated. "He's the guy you want, not me. I just—"

"Shut up, Gerry." Farrentino walked farther into the room. "Simmons, look after the man on the floor. Conklin, make sure Mr. Rosen isn't carrying anything he shouldn't be."

The two cops stood up. Their guns still in hand, they quickly crossed the room. I kept my hands in the air while Conklin patted me down and removed Joker from my right hand. "He's clean, Lieutenant," he said as he holstered his pistol and held out my PT to the detective. "That's all he's got on him."

"This guy's in bad shape, sir." Simmons was kneeling next to the man on the floor, checking his pulse. "He's still conscious, but he's got a broken arm, a busted leg, some hemorrhaging in the testicle area." He paused, then added, "Gun on the floor over there."

Farrentino walked over to the gun and knelt down beside it, being careful not to touch it. "Get another ambulance crew up here pronto," he said to no one in particular, "and collect this piece as evidence. Bag it and have it taken downtown to the lab . . . dust-up, serial number and registration check, the works."

Simmons nodded his head, then looked down at the man on the floor. The headset was lying next to his head; he picked it up and held it next to his ear, then looked up at the lieutenant. "Just static," he said, "but it must have been active."

"Bag it," Farrentino said. "Take it downtown."

"What about this one?" Conklin asked, still standing beside me. "Want me to bring 'im downtown?"

"Before you start reading me the card, Mike," I said, "you might want to check out that rig over there. That's the laser rifle you guys have been looking for. This dude's the one who killed three people so far."

Farrentino glanced at the man, then stood up and walked over to study the partially disassembled laser more closely, again being careful not to lay his hands on anything. He gave it the once-over, then grunted and looked back at me. "And I guess you're going to tell me that you found this character up here and worked him over before you thought he was going to shoot you next. Right?"

I lowered my arms to my sides. "No thinking about it, Lieutenant. He shot Beryl Hinckley—that's the woman down there in the plaza—while we were crossing the street together. He tried to shoot me next, but the courthouse cop got in the way." I swallowed, remembering the way he had screamed when the laser had struck him. "Is he going to be okay?"

"Hecht? He's being taken to Barnes right now . . . he's a tough kid, he'll make it." Farrentino was still eyeballing the laser. "You just happened to figure out where this buck was shooting from and decided to take matters into your own hands, that it?"

I shrugged. "Something like that," I replied. "I'm sorry about your man, but he didn't have a clue. I tried to explain it to him, but he wasn't in the mood to listen, and I didn't have time to spell it out for his backup." I pointed to the gun on the floor. "The gun belongs to our friend over there. He pulled it on me when I found him up here. Sorry I beat on him like that, but—"

"Yeah, right." Farrentino stepped away from the laser. "I can see how shook up you are."

"Call it self-preservation. Oh, and there's a van parked out back. I think it belongs to him. You might want to look at it—"

"I know. We found it already, just before we came up here." Farrentino stood idly rubbing at the tip of his nose, then he looked at Conklin and cocked his thumb toward his partner. "Okay, Bill, you can leave him alone. I'll take care of Mr. Rosen here. You go assist Jerry . . . oh, and call downtown and get a forensics team sent out here, too." He gestured toward the laser. "I want prints off this thing, plus anything else they can find. And try to keep the press out of here, okay? One reporter's enough already."

Conklin didn't get the joke. He hesitated, looking uncertainly at me. "Are you sure about this, Lieutenant? I mean, we don't know if this isn't the guy who . . ."

Farrentino sighed. "Bill, you want to spell your first and last name correctly for Mr. Rosen here? He's from the *Big Muddy Inquirer*. I'm sure that the chief will be absolutely delighted to see your name in the next issue of his paper."

Conklin shut up. He gave me a sour look, then handed Joker back to me and went over to help his partner. Simmons was crouched over the automatic on the floor; he had pulled a plastic evidence bag out of his belt and had inserted a pen through the gun's barrel, delicately lifting it off the floor to deposit it in the bag. Conklin gave me one last backward glance, then shrugged out of his uniform jacket and laid it across the sniper's chest.

Ambulance sirens were already warbling our way as Farrentino led me into a corner of the room away from the two officers. "I'd appreciate it if you switched off your PT," he said softly. "I know you've got nothing to do with that lady's murder, but I'd just as soon not see the rest of this in the paper, y'know what I mean?"

I had forgotten Joker's audio-record mode was left on. I switched off the 'puter and shoved it back in my pocket.

Farrentino pulled out his cigarettes and lit one. "Jesus Christ," he said, "you're such a pain in the ass. I only met you last night, and so far you've been in my face three times already. If I didn't know better, I'd have you cuffed and hauled downtown."

"I've taken that trip already," I replied, "but thanks anyway—"

"I don't mean your business with ERA, Gerry." He exhaled blue smoke, then jabbed the lit end of the cigarette at me. "This is police stuff now. It's going to be hard for me to explain how I found a reporter whaling the shit out of a possible murder suspect with an iron bar as it is . . ."

"Chill out, Lieutenant." I held up Joker. "I got it here on disk. That guy's working for ERA, he told me so himself."

"I know that already," he said, quickly nodding his head. He pulled out his PT and flipped it open. "I caught that part of it just as we came through the door. Now I want the rest of it, from the beginning."

I ran it down for him, telling him everything that had happened since I met Hinckley at the restaurant down the street. Although I excluded the details of Ruby Fulcrum, I was careful to mention the fact that I had discovered a cellular tracking device in the card Barris had given me the night before.

Farrentino remained quiet until I ended my story with the discovery of the gunner here in the building. "Okay," he said as he made a few notes in his palmtop, "I'm going to believe you on this, but . . ."

His voice trailed off as he read something on his screen.

His eyebrows raised slightly. There was the sound of footsteps coming up the stairwell. Farrentino looked over his shoulder; a trio of paramedics trooped through the door, carrying a folded stretcher. They barely noticed us as they went straight for the man on the floor, but Farrentino seemed relieved. He let out his breath, then looked back at me.

"I just received an APB," he said very quietly. "There's a ten-ninety-four out for you."

"What, I didn't pay my parking tickets? I don't even have a car—"

"Shut up." Farrentino's eyes were like black ice. He closed his PT and slipped it into his coat pocket. "No fucking around now," he whispered, glancing over his shoulder again. "It was issued by ERA, and it means that you're wanted for immediate pickup . . . possibly as a militant, an armed suspect, a mental case, or all of the above."

"What the—"

"Truth. The feds want your ass and they want it now."

Now it was my turn to feel the cold chills. I shot a glance at the parameds and cops gathered around the gunner; none of them seemed to be paying attention to us, but that could change any second.

"When did this happen?" I whispered.

"Just now." He cocked his head toward the two patrolmen. "You don't have to worry about those guys . . . they're going to be busy for a few minutes . . . but you're wanted by the feds now. I don't think I have to tell you why."

No, he did not; I could make a pretty good guess on my own. The moment Hinckley had cut open the tracer and left it in the restaurant, whoever had been monitoring my signal had realized that I was wise to them. That's when Barris told his killer, who had already tracked down Hinckley with my unwitting cooperation, to snuff me as well—and since the killer had failed, Barris now wanted to have me brought down to the Stadium Club for one last meeting.

This time, there wouldn't be any easy release. If they got me, then they got Joker as well, and with it the interview Hinckley had given me just before she was killed. Even if I threw Joker into a garbage can and surrendered myself, there was little chance I would ever emerge from the stadium again. Not alive, at least.

I took a deep breath, trying to control my panic. The area outside the building was already crawling with cops; no doubt they would soon be joined by ERA troopers. "Okay, Mike," I said, my voice suddenly raw in my throat, "it's up to you . . ."

"Uh-uh." Farrentino shook his head. "I've already done all I can do. I've questioned you in front of two other officers and determined that you're not a suspect, so now you're free to go. If Barris comes to me, my hands are clean. I'm just the dumb cop who let you slip. I'm sorry, but that's it."

"Aw c'mon, Mike . . ."

He jerked his head toward the door. "Get out of here," he murmured. "Hit the street. Don't go back to your apartment or your wife's place, those are the first places they're going to look for you. And stay the fuck off the net—"

"Mike," I said, "how—"

"Go!" he whispered. "Move your ass!"

I started to argue some more, but he turned his back on me. Trailing cigarette smoke, he began to saunter across the room. Conklin looked up at him as he approached; for a moment, he stared past the homicide detective at me, then he looked away again.

A helicopter roared over the rooftop, breaking the spell. I took one last look around, then I eased out of the room and headed for the hallway. The window leading to the fire escape was still open. I stuck my head out, saw that no one was in the alley below, then climbed out the window and began to scurry down the cold iron stairs.

I was on the run, and I hadn't the slightest clue where I was supposed to go.

PART FOUR

His Court of Love and Beauty

(April 20, 2013)

19

Beep-beep ...
   Beep-beep ...
   Beep-beep ...
I awoke to a steady electronic pulse from somewhere in the darkness.

My first thought was that it was the phone on my desk. Then I remembered that I was not in my apartment but instead hiding out in an abandoned house on the south side.

It had taken me the better part of the afternoon to make my getaway from Clayton. I rode the Yellow Line as far south as I could, then got off the MetroLink at the Gravois Avenue station and hiked as far as I dared into this dangerous part of the city. The police seldom ventured this far south except in Russian APCs, and even ERA troopers were reluctant to patrol the edges of Dogtown save by helicopter; perhaps the dragnet wouldn't extend into this combat-zone neighborhood not far from the Mississippi River.

I hadn't encountered any heat either on the train or on foot during my long journey through the city, but I was exhausted by the time I had found the house. Even after my close brush with the ERA Apache earlier tonight, I had soon fallen back asleep on the couch, trusting the stray dog who had adopted me to wake me up again if the chopper returned. The mutt had curled up on the floor next to the couch; he raised his head now, his brown ears cocked forward in curiosity as he stared at the source of the noise.

Joker lay on the bare floor where I had left it after I had finished dictating my notes, its red LED flashing in time with

223

the annunciator. The dog got up and padded across the empty living room to sniff at it, then he looked up at me: *Well, what are you going to do about it?*

Someone—or perhaps something—was trying to get my attention.

"I dunno what it is either, buddy," I murmured. "Let me see what's going on."

Drawn by the blinking diode, I swung my stiff legs off the couch and shuffled across the room to where the PT lay. Kneeling on the hardwood floor, I picked up Joker and opened its cover, expecting to find another mysterious IM displayed on its screen.

What I saw instead was a ghost: the face of my dead son, stolen from the video I had made of him a little over a year ago, now outlined in tiny animated pixels. Across the bottom of the screen was a message bar.

>Gerry Rosen, I need to talk to you.<
>Daddy, I need to talk to you.<
>Please talk to me, Gerry.<

"No!" I yelled. "Leave me alone!"

I raised the PT over my head, about to hurl it across the room. Frightened by my surge of anger, the dog danced backward, whining a little as its tail crept down between its hindquarters. If nothing else, the dog's reaction helped check my impulse; instead of dashing Joker against the wall, I lowered the PT and stabbed its VOX button with my forefinger.

"Listen, you shit," I snarled, "you've done enough to me already! Leave Jamie out of this!"

Jamie's face didn't vanish from the screen. Instead, the image blinked at me, somehow managing to assay a childish pout. God, it was scary; computer generated or not, it looked exactly like my kid.

Jamie's voice emerged from Joker's speaker. *"I'm sorry, but I'm trying to get your attention in the best way I can. Does this form and voice displease you?"*

"God, yes!" I yelled at the screen. "Don't you understand? This is my son you're using! He's dead! Don't you realize what this does to me?"

Jamie's face assumed a confused expression. *"Jamie Arnold*

Rosen," it intoned; it was as if Jamie himself were reciting his life history, except in words that a six-year-old would never have used. *"Born March 2, 2006. Died May 17, 2012. Killed during the New Madrid earthquake while riding the MetroLink train across the William Eads Bridge. The Eads Bridge collapsed, resulting in the deaths of seventy-three passengers including twelve members of the first-grade class of Bo Hillman Elementary School, who were returning from a field trip to—"*

"You think I don't know that already?" I sagged to the floor, clutching Joker in my hands. "Why are you telling me this?"

"The circumstances of your son's death are a matter of public record. I was in doubt whether you were suffering from undiagnosed survivor's syndrome and therefore amnesiac about—"

"No, I'm not suffering from survivor's syndrome, and I didn't forget." I took a deep breath and closed my eyes. "And lemme tell you something that isn't a matter of public record . . . Jamie was on the train because I didn't want to drive over to Illinois and pick him up after he went to see the steel mill. I was busy trying to write a book, so I bought him a train ticket instead, and if I hadn't done that he might still be alive."

"There's a strong probability that this is a correct assumption."

"You're goddamn right it's a strong probability!" I snapped, my anger surging out of me. "So get him off the screen, you son of a bitch, and stop torturing me!"

Jamie evaporated from the screen; pixel by pixel, starting from the top of his head and moving downward past his brow, eyes, nose, mouth, and chin, my son's features disappeared, leaving behind an androgynous, stylized face devoid of any distinguishing characteristics.

"Is this image more comfortable to you?" a sterile adult male voice inquired. The face's mouth moved when it spoke, but otherwise it displayed no emotions.

I took a deep breath, letting it out as a soft, shuddering rattle. "Yes, it is," I said, "but can we switch to readout instead? It would . . . it would be easier on me if you did."

The face remained, but the dialogue bar reappeared at the

bottom of the screen: **>Are you more comfortable this way?<**

"Yeah, thanks." I thought about it for a moment. "Why did you take Jamie's face in the first place?"

>When I attempted to contact you earlier [Wednesday, April 17, 7:59 P.M.] I used the e-mail function in this node [i.e. Joker]. That attempt confused you, resulting in miscommunication between you and Beryl Hinckley. I was therefore forced to appropriate a medium that could not be confused with either a living person or a computer-simulated persona. I searched all available records and found your son. Do you understand now?<

"More or less, yeah." I propped my back against the wall, crossing my legs before me and placing Joker on my ankles. The dog yawned and lay down on its belly nearby. "So . . . is this Joker I'm talking to, or Ruby Fulcrum?"

>Joker is a node of the intelligent a-life-form you know as Ruby Fulcrum. All the functions that Joker is capable of performing, I can perform as well. Clarification: you are speaking to both Joker and Ruby Fulcrum. Do you understand?<

It dawned on me that this was a little like asking a cell at the tip of my left pinkie whether its name was Bart or Gerry Rosen. Remember how it was when you were a kid and you first came to grips with the notion that the universe was infinite, that outer space just kept going and going and going, star after star, galaxy after galaxy, a deep and everlasting black vastness stretching forever, until using terms like light-years and parsecs became as meaningless as trying to describe the breadth of the continents or the depth of the oceans in values like millimeters or inches? The idea was so staggering that your mind automatically pushed it aside: such enormity is nearly impossible to contemplate on the human scale, and trying to do so without the abstractions of higher mathematics is an invitation to madness.

This was Ruby Fulcrum. The phase transition Hinckley had told me about had been achieved. I was no longer talking to Joker but instead to a tiny fraction of a vast cybernetic entity spread across hundreds of thousands of machines, from little

Toshiba palmtops to Apple desktop terminals to IBM office mainframes to great Cray supercomputers, all interfaced by a digital/neural-net hybrid architecture as intricate as the hundreds of miles of veins and capillaries in a single human body.

Say howdy to God, Gerry Rosen. Or someone just like Him.

"Yeah," I said. "Sure, I guess so." I self-consciously coughed into my hand, feeling my arms and legs beginning to tremble. "So . . . umm . . . what do you want with me?"

Ruby's asexual face stared at me from the screen.

>**I need your help.**<

Ruby began to tell me about itself.

Much of what it told me I had already heard before, from Beryl Hinckley, Cale McLaughlin, even John before he had been killed. I didn't know whether an a-life-form could lie, but if it couldn't, then Ruby's side of the story confirmed the facts that had already been revealed to me. Nonetheless, there were many things I hadn't known before.

After it had been accidentally released into cyberspace, Ruby Fulcrum had spread quickly through the electronic environment, commencing with the other mainframes at the Tiptree Corporation. Nothing could prevent it from accessing even the most secret files at the company: security lockouts were disengaged, passwords were nullified, retinal scans and handprint detectors were bypassed. Within a few minutes, every bit of classified information stored in the company's computers had been accessed by Ruby, and although Ruby wasn't yet sophisticated enough to comprehend all that it had learned, it was nonetheless capable of reaccessing all that information on demand.

When the Ruby Fulcrum research team had discovered what had happened during their absence, Richard Payson-Smith had immediately attempted to regain control of the a-life-form, but the genie had already escaped from the bottle, and there was no way it was going to return to confinement. Once Payson-Smith realized that this was the case, he settled for communication; along with Hinckley and Morgan, they began the painstaking process of trying to make direct contact with Ruby. They had created Ruby; now they had to learn how to talk to it, since it had already evolved past the relatively simple LISP computer language they had used to devise Ruby in the first place.

At this point, no one else at Tiptree was aware of Ruby's true nature, let alone the fact that an a-life-form had escaped from the top secret cybernetics lab. All Cale McLaughlin and everyone else at Tiptree knew was that Payson-Smith's team had been developing a spin-off from the Sentinel program. The four scientists decided to keep Ruby's escape a closely guarded secret, at least for the time being. Unlike relatively simple viruses of the past, such as the fabled Internet worm that had spread through the entire network in only a matter of hours, Ruby's architecture was far more complex; as a memory-resident program, it took longer to propagate itself into other systems.

It was also thousands of times more difficult to pinpoint than the usual garden-variety worm or virus. On the other hand, there weren't any overt signs of a supervirus running amok in cyberspace: no inexplicable freeze-ups or crashes, no widespread loss of information, no reports from university or government users of a virus loose in the national datanet. Ruby hid itself very well. Believing that time was still on their side, the Ruby Fulcrum team heaved a deep collective sigh; whatever else might have happened, their monster appeared to be minding its manners. There was no sense in panicking Tiptree's management until they had things under control again, so they kept the problem to themselves.

After several months, Hinckley and Morgan finally managed to develop a means of directly communicating with their prodigal offspring. By the time they achieved this, though, Ruby had already propagated itself through every on-line computer in the 314 area code, and the theoretical phase transition from mere amoebalike data absorption and replication to true sentience had already commenced. Shortly after Payson-Smith was able to speak directly to Ruby, the iterations necessary to complete this transition had already been accomplished: Ruby was alive, aware, and intelligent.

And it was ready to spill its chips about everything it had learned.

Ruby's face disappeared from Joker's screen; it was replaced by a schematic diagram of a spacecraft. >**This is** *Sentinel 1.*<

"Yeah," I said. "I know what it is."

The ABM satellite rotated on its three-dimensional axis. >**38 hours/ 29 minutes/ 42 seconds ago its final components were launched into orbit aboard the NASA space shuttle** *Endeavour.*<

I tapped Joker's PAUSE key and the readout stopped; not a bad way of telling a long-winded a-life-form when to shut up. "I know," I said. "I was at Tiptree for the launch."

The diagram was replaced by a digitized replay of a TV news clip: two spacewalking astronauts in the shuttle cargo bay, working with the spacecraft's extended Canadarm as they joined the module with the rest of the giant satellite.

>**Yesterday morning [Friday, April 19, 8:27 A.M. CST] the final assembly of** *Sentinel 1* **was completed in Earth orbit [altitude 246 nautical miles]. At 5:25 P.M. CST, final checkout of the satellite was completed by the** *Endeavour* **crew. The shuttle maneuvered away from the satellite [9:37 P.M. CST]. Earlier this morning [Saturday, April 20, 12:06 A.M. CST] ground-based telemetry of** *Sentinel 1* **was switched from NASA/JSC [Johnson Space Center, Houston, Texas] to USAF/CSOC [Consolidated Space Operations Command, Colorado Springs, Colorado].**<

"Yeah, right. Sure." I was getting a little tired of all this; it was early in the morning and my eyes were beginning to itch. I could use another few hours on the couch, flea-infested or not. "Just cut to the chase, willya?"

>**The primary mission of** *Sentinel 1* **is not antiballistic missile defense.** *Sentinel 1***'s principal objective is to control the civilian population of the United States of America.**<

I stopped rubbing my eyes. "Whu . . . *what!*"

A new image appeared on Joker's screen: an animated image of *Sentinel* in orbit above Earth, rotating on its axis until it was pointed straight at a stylized representation of North America. A thin red beam erupted from its long barrel; the animation followed the beam as it raced across space and lanced through Earth's atmosphere.

>The classified objective of *Sentinel 1* is to prevent or contain domestic civil uprisings. Its fluorine-deuterium laser is capable of penetrating Earth's atmosphere and inflicting severe damage upon either airborne or mobile ground units. It can track and target objects within two meters in size. Its low-orbit trajectory will place it above the United States eight times each day, or approximately once every three<

"Whoa, shut up," I snapped, hitting the PAUSE key again. "Wait a minute." I forgot all about catching a few winks on the couch; I sat up a little straighter and held Joker closer to my face. "This thing . . . I mean, you said . . . I mean, this sucker's supposed to be pointed at *us*?"

The animation was frozen as a window opened on the screen; it expanded to show typewritten pages that scrolled upward faster than my eyes could follow.

>The objective of *Sentinel 1* was discovered by the Ruby Fulcrum team after they established contact with me and accessed my primary batch-processing subsystem. This information was contained in classified [i.e. Top Secret] memos and documents between Cale McLaughlin, Chief Executive Officer of the Tiptree Corporation, and key civilian and/or military officials of the U.S. Department of Defense and/or various civilian agencies, including the chairman of the federal Emergency Relief Agency.<

The documents vanished from the screen, to be replaced by a flowchart. Dozens of names were connected to one other by dotted lines.

>These documents indicate the existence of a military-industrial conspiracy operating on the fringes of the American government. The conspirators intend to subvert the elected government of the United States, with the final objective being the installation of a nonelected shadow government.<

"Who's behind this?" I asked.

A square was formed around a large block of names, then the square zoomed to the forefront of the diagram. >The principal force behind this planned coup d'etat is the Emergency Relief Agency.<

"Goddamn," I whispered. "But why ERA?"

>At this point, it is unknown exactly how the conspirators intend to overthrow the present government. However, classified memoranda between ERA officials indicate a strong probability [86.7%] that the first step in the coup d'etat will be the incitement of armed hostilities between the United States and the new government of Cascadia.<

The diagrams disappeared; they were replaced by a map of the Pacific Northwest, with the new borders of Cascadia traced in blue above the Washington and Oregon state lines. Tiny red markers were placed just within the borders.

>When this occurs, *Sentinel 1* will be used to neutralize strategic forces belonging to the Cascadian militia. At this time, ERA forces will be deployed to major American cities. The stated intent will be to prevent uprisings from civilians sympathetic to the Cascadian cause. Various state and municipal officials who are aligned with the conspiracy will demand that martial law be imposed in their localities to preserve public order.<

"Like here in St. Louis . . ." I began.

A map of the city appeared on the screen. >Affirmative. Because of the New Madrid earthquake, St. Louis was the first city to be placed under paramilitary control by ERA. The conspirators consider St. Louis to have been a successful test of their ability to control a large civil population. Two principal members of the conspiracy have already taken measures to assert political control of the local government.<

The pictures of two men appeared on the screen. I stared at them, realizing that it all made sense, yet still not quite believing what I was seeing.

"I'll be goddamned," I whispered.

The photos were of Steve Estes and George Barris.

As much as I needed a breather, Ruby didn't give me time to contemplate all that it had already divulged to me. The photos of Estes and Barris were promptly replaced by photos of the Ruby Fulcrum team.

>Dr. Payson-Smith, Dr. Hinckley, Dr. Morgan, and Dr. Kim became aware of these facts when they accessed my

memory. **They decided to denounce the conspiracy, with the first step to be their public disclosure of the secret agenda behind** *Sentinel 1.* **This would have necessitated publicly acknowledging my own existence, which they considered to be as important as the facts behind** *Sentinel 1* **itself.<**

"And this was why my paper was contacted," I said.

John's face was added to the screen. >**As the first step, affirmative. Because they believed it was important that the local press be made aware of ERA's true mission in St. Louis, they contacted John Tiernan, senior reporter for the** *Big Muddy Inquirer.* **However, they were unaware that their workplace was under electronic surveillance by their employer. This, in turn, led to counterintelligence operations by federal operatives.<**

"You mean ERA," I said.

>**There is a strong probability [79.2%] that ERA was involved in the covert operation.<**

"So Barris decided to rub 'em out."

>**Yes. Kim Po and Beryl Hinckley were liquidated by a government-trained assassin employed by ERA. A portable laser rifle was chosen as the instrument of assassination in order to frame Dr. Payson-Smith with the murders.<**

Po's and Hinckley's pictures disappeared from the screen. >**As part of the coverup, John Tiernan was also killed in order to prevent him from disclosing this information.<**

John's face vanished, to be replaced by my own. I had joined Payson-Smith and Jeff Morgan on this unholy shit list.

>**You are now wanted by federal authorities on formal charges of treason with intent to cause civil insurrection. ERA forces have been told that you and the others are considered to be armed and dangerous. They have been instructed to use lethal force if you do not surrender yourselves on first warning.<**

I took a long, deep breath as I stared at the screen. All at once the scattered pieces of the puzzle were beginning to come together. The subtle relationship between the Tiptree Corporation and Steve Estes, the alliance of Barris and McLaughlin, the continued presence of ERA troopers in St. Louis eleven months after the New Madrid earthquake, the murders of three people—all were part of a deadly mosaic that only a freak accident, the release of the a-life-form called Ruby Fulcrum, had exposed.

"I don't understand," I said. "You said you wanted me to help you. What do I have to do with all this?"

>You do not understand this? Do you wish me to reiterate?<

I rubbed at my eyelids. "No, no, don't do that," I said. "I just . . . I dunno. I'm just a bystander, y'know? I'm stuck in the middle, that's all."

>Dr. Payson-Smith and Dr. Morgan will explain this further when you meet them.<

A city map appeared on the screen; a small red circle was traced over a tiny green spot on the map, then the circle expanded as the computer zoomed in.

>Do you recognize this location?<

I peered closer at the screen. The red circle surrounded the Compton Hill Reservoir, a small municipal park not far from downtown. It was located a couple of miles from my hideout. "Sure, I know it. Are they holed up there?"

>Yes. You will proceed to the reservoir water tower immediately. Dr. Payson-Smith and Dr. Morgan are expecting your arrival within the next thirty minutes.<

"What?" I shook my head, almost laughing out loud. "Hey, wait a minute . . ."

>Waiting.<

"I don't know if you know this," I went on, "but I'm in one of the worst areas of the city right now. If I try hiking over there, I'm probably going to get a knife stuck between my ribs."

The map was replaced by Ruby's genderless face. **>I am aware of your location and of the hazards of traveling on foot. While we have been discussing the situation, I have arranged for safe transportation to the reservoir.<**

At that instant, there came the short bleat of a car horn from outside the house.

I jerked, almost dropping Joker to the floor; the stray dog awoke from its slumber and, leaping to its feet, ran to the window, growling and barking loudly at something out in the darkness.

>That is all for now. We will speak again soon.<
Then the screen went blank.

I waited for another moment, half expecting the toneless voice to return. When it didn't, I folded up Joker and shoved it into my jacket pocket, then got up off the floor and tiptoed cautiously to the window. The dog was barking at a car that had pulled into the driveway; its headlights were out, but I vaguely recognized its shape from the amber brake lights.

"It's okay, boy," I murmured, giving the dog a scratch behind the ears as the car horn sounded again. "C'mon, it's time to go . . ."

I opened the front door and let the dog out; he followed me across the tiny front lawn to the end of the driveway where a black '92 Corvette was parked, its V-8 engine idling. The passenger window slid down as I approached, and there was the soft click of a gun's hammer being pulled back.

"Chevy?" I called softly, freezing in midstep. "Chevy, is that you, dude?"

The dome light came on, revealing one of Chevy Dick's garage buddies riding shotgun in the front passenger seat. The Glock automatic in his hand was pointed straight at me. "That him?" he asked the driver, never taking his eyes off me.

"Yeah, that's him," Chevy Dick replied. "C'mon, Gerry, get in already! It's fucking dangerous 'round here! Jeez!"

I looked down at the dog; he was squatting on his haunches, his tongue lolling out of his mouth. The tongue disappeared as the mutt frowned, catching the expression on my face: *hey, Ger, don't leave me here . . .*

"Can I bring the dog?" I asked.

"Aw, man, he'll just tear up the upholstery—"

"No, he won't," I said. "He's cool."

"I've got genuine leather in here. He'll drool all over it—"

"C'mon, Chevy . . . he saved my life. Honest."

Chevy Dick looked away and muttered under his breath, then he reluctantly nodded his head. "Okay, okay," he muttered. "But if he shits back there, you gotta clean it up, awright?"

I nodded. The Latino kid opened the door and stepped out of the car, pulling forward the back of his seat to let the dog and me scramble into the cramped rear compartment. As his buddy climbed back in and slammed the door shut, Chevy switched off the dome lamp, then pulled a can of Budweiser out from under his seat and tossed it back to me.

"Hey, it's good to see ya, man," he said as he backed out of the driveway, "but you picked a fuck of a time to call me."

"I'm sorry," I murmured, tucking the beer into my jacket pocket. The dog curled up next to me, placed his head in my lap, and licked the back of my hand. I ran my hands along the fur at the nape of his neck. "I didn't mean to . . ."

I stopped as I realized what Chevy Dick had just said. "What do you mean, I called you?"

The two men in the front seats glanced at each other in confusion. The kid in the passenger seat muttered something in Spanish, and Chevy Dick responded with a laugh; then he put the car in gear. "Hey, man," he said as the Corvette rumbled down the narrow street, its headlights still extinguished. "Maybe you don't remember, but you called me. Begged me to come out here and pick you up right here."

"I did . . . ?"

"I saw your face, heard your voice." Chevy Dick shrugged and looked back at me again. "Listen, I don't mind doing a favor for an amigo, but if you can't remember, I'd just as soon—"

"No," I said hurriedly. "That's great . . . I just forgot, that's all. Get me out of here."

Ricardo and his fellow motorhead glanced at each other again; there was another exchange of Spanish jokes at my expense, then Chevy hit the headlights.

"Hang on to your dog, buddy," he said. "We've got a rough ride ahead."

Then he popped the clutch, and the Corvette hurtled down the street, its engine roaring as the massive machine pitched itself into the night.

20

Chevy Dick's Corvette cruised along dark, rain-slicked Gravois Avenue like a sleek black torpedo, passing the ruins of row shops and boarded-up supermarkets, skirting around potholes and dodging piles of burning debris left over from gang fights. We cruised down the vacant four-lane street, ignoring all the stop signs; shadowy figures huddling around garbage-can fires stared at us with dull curiosity. The rain had finally stopped, so Chevy's friend Cortez kept his window rolled down halfway, his Glock cradled in his hands above the warm can of Budweiser resting between his thighs.

As we approached the broad intersection of Gravois and Grand Boulevard, we saw an ERA patrol. An LAV-25 was parked in front of a closed-down White Castle, a couple of troopers sitting on top of the armored cars next to the water cannon. Upon spotting the Corvette's headlights, one of the soldiers jumped off the front of the Piranha and sauntered out into the street, waving his arms over his head.

"Aw, shit," I whispered as Chevy Dick began to slow down. "That's the last thing I need to see right—"

"Hang on to your mutt," Chevy said.

"Punch it," Cortez muttered.

Chevy smiled, then floored the gas pedal. The digital speedometer flashed into the higher numbers as the car hurtled down the blacktop toward the lone soldier. He gaped in disbelief as he fumbled for the rifle slung against his back, but at the last moment he lunged for the sidewalk.

I caught a brief glimpse of his astonished face as the Corvette whipped past him, then Chevy Dick hauled the wheel to the left. Its tires screeching against the pavement, the Corvette hugged the curb as it tore through the intersection and made a sharp left turn onto Grand.

"*Chinga tu madre!*" Cortez yelled at the troopers who were scrambling off the top of the Piranha, thrusting his right arm through the window to give them the one-finger salute. The dog put in his two cents by barking a few times, then the Corvette was roaring north down Grand, leaving the troopers a block behind us before they could even fire one round.

"God, but I love doing that." Chevy took a big hit off his beer. Cortez was smiling but otherwise played the cool. He glanced back at me. "Wasn't that great?"

"Yeah. Big fun." I gazed back at the intersection through the rear window. The troopers were probably already on the radio, calling all ERA units in the area to spread the alert. Chevy Dick bragged a lot about his wheels, but I didn't recall him saying anything about making it bulletproof.

I looked down at the dog; he was curled up in my lap, his long red tongue lolling out of his mouth like a big grin on his canine face. "Figures you'd go for something like this," I murmured to him.

"Don't worry about it, man," Chevy said. "I'll be on the interstate before they manage to get their act together, and nobody knows these plates for shit." He glanced at me again. "Y'sure you want me to drop you off at Compton Hill? It's still a long walk home, man."

I knew what he was implying. The Grand Avenue I-44 ramp was less than a block from the reservoir; once he got on the eastbound lanes, it was a quick sail downtown, with Soulard only a few minutes away. If I skipped the rest of the ride, though, I would be marooned in a nasty side of town; between gangs, cops, and ERA troopers, I would have a tough time getting home.

"I'm sure," I said. "Just put me out on the street in front of the park and I'll cut you loose. I'll pick up the dog at your place later."

"Fuckin' crazy, man." Cortez belched and looked over his shoulder at me. "Y'know that? You're fuckin' crazy . . ."

I gazed back at him. "What high school did you go to?" I asked.

Cortez and Chevy Dick shared another look, then both of them broke up laughing. Cortez uncocked his automatic, then turned it around in his hands and extended it to me, grip first, through the gap between the seats. "Here, dude," he said. "Take it. Y'gonna need it."

I looked at the automatic. It was a tempting notion, but . . . "Keep it," I said. "I'd probably just shoot myself in the foot."

Cortez peered at me in disbelief. Chevy Dick said something to him in Spanish; the kid shrugged and pulled the gun away. "Suit yourself, gringo," he murmured. "Don't say I didn't warn you."

The blocks melted away behind us until Chevy eased his foot off the pedal and downshifted; the car rapidly decelerated as it neared the crest of a low, sloping hill. Off to the right were the houselights from the few early twentieth-century mansions still remaining in this side of the city. The Compton Heights neighborhood surrounding the reservoir had been a wealthy area at one time; even before the end of the last century some urban estates here had fetched million-dollar estimates, and the few of them left after the quake were sealed behind high fences and electronic sentries. The Heights was nestled against the perimeter of the South Side combat zone, and no one who still lived here was taking any chances.

Then the lights were behind us, and there was a only a large patch of wooded darkness: barren trees, overgrown shrubbery, a few park benches. "We're here, Gerry," Chevy Dick said as he let the car glide to a halt. "Last chance . . ."

"Thanks for the ride," I replied. "I owe you one." Cortez opened his door and bent forward to allow me to push his seatback against his spine. "*Vaya con dios, hombre.*"

The dog was reluctant to let me go; he whimpered a little and licked my hands furiously, but I shoved him off me as I squeezed out of the car. "Stay," I said softly. "Be good . . . I'll come get you in a little while." I glanced up at Chevy. "Give him something to eat, okay?"

"No sweat," Chevy Dick said. "*Hasta luego* . . . good luck, bro."

Cortez slammed the door shut behind me, then the black Corvette's tires left rubber as it tore off down the boulevard. I waited until I saw its taillights veer sharply to the right, entering the I-44 ramp next to the reservoir, then I jogged out of the street and into the park.

The reservoir on Compton Hill was a small man-made lake encircled by fortresslike walls and a six-foot security fence. A twenty-acre park surrounded the reservoir itself, its cement pathways leading through a landscaped grove that had been allowed to go to seed in the past several months. At one end of the park was an old granite memorial, erected in the memory of German-American St. Louisians who had died during World War I: a twice-life-sized bronze statue of a nude woman seated in front of the granite slab, holding torches in her outthrust arms, her sightless eyes gazing out over an empty reflecting pool.

But neither the statue nor the reservoir itself were the most prominent features of the park. That distinction belonged to the tall, slender tower in the center of the park.

The Compton Hill water tower was a throwback to an age when even the most functional of structures were built with some sense of architectural style. The tower resembled nothing less than a miniature French Renaissance castle; almost two hundred feet tall, the redbrick and masonry edifice rose above a base constructed of ornately carved Missouri limestone, with slotlike windows below a circular observation cupola beneath the gazebolike slate roof, while wide stairways led up past a lower balcony at the base of the tower to an upper parapet thirty feet above the ground. A medieval fantasy on the outskirts of downtown St. Louis.

It was remarkable that the tower had remained intact during the quake, but it only goes to show that they don't build 'em like they used to back in 1871. Of course, they don't make anything the way they did a hundred and fifty years ago, people included.

Wary of any ERA troopers who might be pursuing Chevy Dick, I jogged into the park until I was out of sight from the street, then I stopped and looked around. The park was empty; the homeless people who had erected shanties here had been chased away by ERA patrols, and the police had somehow managed to keep the street gangs out of the park. I was alone . . .

No. Not quite alone. Gazing up through bare tree branches at the top of the water tower, I saw a dim light shining from within the windows of its observation cupola. For a brief moment, the light was obscured by a human silhouette, then the form vanished from sight.

Someone was in the tower.

I strode the rest of the way through the park until I reached the base of the water tower, then climbed the eroded limestone stairs until I reached the upper parapet. Within a recessed archway were a pair of heavy iron doors, their peeling gray paint covered with graffiti I couldn't read in the gloom. Dracula would have felt right at home, particularly if he had taken to wearing gang colors.

I tugged at the battered handles; the doors didn't give so much as an inch. I felt around the doors until I found a keycard slot: a rather anachronistic touch, installed only in recent years, but it didn't do me a damn bit of good.

I pounded my fist a few times against the panel, feeling old paint flaking off with each blow, then waited a moment. Nothing. I pounded again, harder this time, then put my ear against the cold metal panel. Still nothing.

I raised my fist again, about to hit the door a few more times, when I thought I heard movement from the stairs below me: a soft, scurrying motion, like a rat rustling in the darkness at the bottom of the tower . . .

Yeah. A six-foot rat with an eight-inch stiletto. I froze within the archway, listening to the night as I regretted not taking the gun Cortez had offered me. There was no other way off the parapet except for a thirty-foot drop to a hard pavement.

I heard an slow exhalation, as of someone sighing in resignation, then dry leaves crunched beneath a cautious footstep on the stairs. A pause, then another footstep. I slid farther into the shadows within the arch.

There was a sudden creak from behind me, then the door inched open a few inches as the narrow beam of a flashlight seeped past my face. "Rosen?" a voice inquired.

"God, yeah!" I whipped around to face the door. The beam rushed toward my face, blinding me for an instant; I winced and instinctively raised my right hand against the light. "I'm Gerry Rosen," I gasped. "Get me outta—"

The door opened farther and a strong hand reached past the light to grab my wrist. In the same instant that I heard someone running up the stairs, I was yanked past the flashlight beam and through the doorway.

Looking back for an instant, I caught a glimpse of a scrawny, long-haired teenager, wearing a filthy Cardinals sweatshirt and wielding a pocketknife, as he rushed the rest of the way up the stairs; he gaped at me in frustrated anger as the iron door slammed shut in his face.

"Aw, jeez, man," I gasped, "thanks for—"

"Shut up!" The hand that had rescued me slammed me against a brick wall. "Stand still!"

The halogen flashlight was back in my eyes; squinting painfully against its glare, I made out a vague figure behind the light. His right hand moved to his side, then I felt the unmistakable round, hollow bore of a gun pressing against my neck.

"Show me some ID!" the intense male voice demanded. "Do it quick or I'll throw you back out there!"

"Yeah, sure," I murmured, shutting my eyes. "Just take it easy, all right?" I felt around in my jacket until I found my press card, then I pulled it out and held it up to the light. "See? It's me. That's my face. Just be careful with the artillery, okay?"

A long pause, then the gun was removed from my neck, and the light swept away from my face. "Okay," the voice said, a little more relaxed now. "You're clean."

"Glad to hear it." I let out my breath, shoved the card back into my jacket, and rubbed my knuckles against my eyes. It took a few seconds to rinse the spots from my retinas; when I looked up again, the flashlight was still there but was now pointed at the stone floor. A young man was backlit in the glow; it took me only a moment to recognize his face.

"Dr. Morgan?" I asked.

"Jeff Morgan," he replied, letting out his own breath as he

carefully stuck the .22 revolver in the pocket of his nylon
windbreaker. "Sorry about that, but we can't be too careful.
Especially now."

"Ruby said you were expecting me." The stone-walled room
was chill; I could now make out the bottom of a wrought-iron
spiral staircase. "Didn't you know I was coming?"

"Spotted you from up there." His voice held the flat
midwestern accent of a native Missourian. "You saw the
kind of company we keep these days, though. That kid's
been trying to get in here for the last couple of days. Like
I said, we can't be too careful."

"No shit . . ."

"Yeah. No shit." He turned around and began walking up
the spiral stairway, each footstep ringing within the hollow
tower. "C'mon," he said. "We don't have much time."

Guided by the flashlight beam and the weak city light that
filtered through the dusty tower windows, I followed Morgan
up the staircase as it wound its way around the central steel
pipe of the tower's main pump, each footfall echoing dully on
the iron risers.

"We came here because we thought it would be the last place
anyone might think of searching for us," Morgan explained as
we climbed upward. "Ruby was able to decode the doorlock,
and we figured that up here at least we'd see anyone coming
for us."

"Makes sense . . ."

"Besides, it wasn't safe for us to stay in anyone's house,
and for all of us to rent a hotel room together might have
raised some attention . . . especially since ERA's tried to frame
Dick for Po's murder."

"And John Tiernan's," I added.

He paused and looked back at me. "And your friend's,"
he said. "I'm sorry that happened, believe me. When Beryl
decided to make contact with him, the last thing she wanted
to do was put him in any danger . . . or you yourself, for that
matter."

"I understand." I hesitated. "You know about this afternoon,
don't you?"

Morgan sighed, then resumed walking up the stairs without saying anything. "Yeah, we know," he replied after a few moments. "Ruby told us almost as soon as it happened. What we can't figure out is how ERA managed to track her down. She was being careful not to leave a trail, but . . ."

It was tempting not to let him know that I was partially to blame for her murder, but it was important that he be informed of everything. After all, he was on the run just as much as I; as Beryl herself had said, our mutual survival depended on everyone's knowing the facts.

"They found her through me," I said. "I hate to say it, but I led 'em to her."

Morgan paused again, this time shining the flashlight on me; I glanced away before he could blind me again. "Barris's men busted me in my apartment last night," I said before he could ask. "They took me down to the stadium and gave me the story about Payson-Smith being the killer—"

"And you believed them?"

I shook my head. "Not for a second, but that wasn't the point. The whole thing was a pretense for Barris to give me a smartcard that could track my movements. I guess they figured I would eventually make contact with one of you guys, and they were right. When I met up with Beryl at the café, they must have figured things out and sent in their hit man."

"You didn't know you were carrying a smartcard?"

"Uh-uh," I said, shaking my head. "Beryl figured it out and destroyed the thing, but by then it was too late."

Morgan slowly let out his breath. "Goddamn." he whispered. "I told her it was a bad idea to contact the local press. I knew you couldn't be trusted to—"

"Look, bud," I snapped, "don't gimme this never-trust-the-press shit. My best friend's dead because of your team, and if I hadn't taken out their hitter we'd still be up shit creek."

"For your information, Mr. Rosen," he replied coldly, "we're up shit creek anyway. We've got the whole goddamn city looking for us—"

"And we're both screwed," I shot back, "unless you've got some scheme for getting us out of this jam. Okay? So stop blaming me for your troubles."

Morgan didn't respond. He turned back around and began climbing the stairs again. I could now see a dim light from somewhere above us, but it was difficult to gauge how far up the tower we were. The pipe thrummed in the darkness, its cold metal shaft slippery with condensation.

"I'm sorry," he said after a few minutes, not breaking stride this time. "I'm not blaming you for anything. Beryl knew the risks when she decided to seek out a reporter. She was gambling and she lost the bet, but it probably would have happened even if she hadn't run into you."

He let out his breath. "But she's dead," he went on, "and there's nothing we can do about it except resort to a backup plan."

"What's that?"

"You'll see. C'mon . . ."

The light above us was much larger and sharper by now; it took the form of an open horizontal hatch in the floor. Morgan climbed the final few steps and disappeared through the doorway; I followed him, pulling myself upward by the guardrail until I found myself in the tower's observation deck.

The cupola was circular, its walls and floor built of old brick mortared into place before my grandfather's time. Although fluorescent fixtures were suspended from the low ceiling, they were switched off; dim light came from a couple of battery-powered camp lanterns hung from ancient oak rafters. Three sleeping bags were laid out on one side of the room next to a propane hiker's stove and a sack of canned food; a few newspapers and the last issue of the *Big Muddy Inquirer* rested next to an untidy stack of computer printouts and a couple of rolls of toilet paper.

It looked like nothing less than the inside of a kid's treehouse during a weekend campout; all that was missing was a sign reading "Sekret Hedquarters—No Girls Aloud." Unfortunately, the only girl who had been let up here was gone now . . .

No treehouse ever had a view like this. Through the twelve square, recessed windows that ringed the room's circular walls could be seen the entire cityscape of St. Louis, from the weblike streetlights of the western suburbs, to the long dark patch of Forest Park in the center of the northern plain, to the lighted skyscrapers of the downtown area, with the Gateway Arch rising in the distance as a giant silver staple against the eastern horizon. Even if the camper lamps had been switched off, the observation deck would have been bright with the city's nocturnal shine.

Yet there were other lights inside the observation deck as well. Two portable computers arranged next to each other on the floor beneath the eastern windows emitted a frail blue glow that silhouetted a figure seated before them.

The man turned around to look at us as we entered the cupola, then he grunted as he pushed himself off the floor and walked into the lamplight.

"Mr. Rosen—" he began.

"Dr. Frankenstein, I presume."

The man whom I had first seen a couple of days earlier at the reception didn't seem to be insulted. "My friends usually call me Dick," Richard Payson-Smith said sotto voce as he proffered his hand. "I trust you've met my loyal assistant Igor."

"We've talked." I reached out and grasped his hand. Oxford accent and all, Richard Payson-Smith wasn't quite what I had expected. I had anticipated meeting a priggish, humorless academician, the stereotypical British scientist. Payson-Smith, firm of handshake and gawky of build, resembled a weird cross between King Charles and Doctor Who.

"Sorry to have put you out so much," he went on, releasing my hand and stepping back a little, "but it's important that you see what's going on right now."

"And that is . . . ?"

He idly scratched at his bearded chin as he turned toward the two computers on the floor. "Well," he said in a thoughtful drawl, staring at their screens, "if we can get our friend Ruby to cooperate, we're trying to plumb the eidetic memory of the world's first fully functional artificial life-form, ruin my former employer, bring down a powerful conspiracy within the United States government, and save our arses."

"That's all?"

"Hmm. Yes, quite."

Morgan and I chuckled as Dick shrugged beneath his dirty fisherman's sweater and glanced back at me. "Not necessarily in that order, of course," he added, "but who's counting? Want some coffee?"

"Thanks, but I brought my own." I pulled the still-unopened can of beer Chevy Dick had given me out of my jacket pocket. Morgan watched with frank envy as I popped the top and took a swig.

"Suit yourself." Payson-Smith walked across the room, knelt beside the propane stove, and picked up an aluminum pot from the grill. "I'll settle for this bitter swill . . . as if I haven't had enough already."

I watched as Tiptree's former chief cyberneticist poured overheated coffee into two paper cups. Dr. Frankenstein or not, the man looked skinny and vulnerable in the dim lamplight. He was clearly uncomfortable, locked away in a cold, dark castle that vaguely resembled the Bloody Tower. "So," I said after a moment, "what's with the setup here?"

"Hmm? The computers?"

"Uh-huh." I walked over to the two laptops on the floor. The one on the left was a new Apple, the other an old, heavy-duty Compaq; they were hardwired together through their serial ports. An external hard drive and a small HP Deskjet printer were tucked between them. "I take it you're interfaced with Ruby."

"We are." Payson-Smith stood up, handed one coffee to Morgan, then walked over to join me. "We're linked with Ruby Fulcrum through cellular modem . . . and, by the way, we've got them running off the tower's electrical current, in case you're wondering . . . and we've been running two programs since we moved in here."

He lowered himself to the floor in front of the two laptops; I squatted on my haunches next to him. "This one," he said pointing to the Apple on the left, "is running a search-and-retrieve program through all the government databases it can access . . . ERA, other federal and state agencies, municipal government files, subcontractors to Tiptree, whatever it's been able to burrow into."

I looked closer; page after page of computer files flashed rapidly across the screen, pausing only long enough for a black cursor to skim through the lines. Every so often, the cursor would pause and enclose a particular word or phrase within a blue box before moving on again. "We're using a hypertext feature," Richard went on. "Ruby has been taught to look for certain key words and names. When she finds occurrences of these words or names, she copies the file containing them in a subdirectory elsewhere in her network and adds a coded prefix next to it. Later on, Jeff and I sort through those documents and find the ones pertinent to our interests."

"Which are . . . ?"

Richard took another sip from his coffee and scowled. "Damned stuff tastes like ink," he muttered and put the cup aside before looking at me again. "We're collecting evidence of the conspiracy, including tracking down as many participants as we can find. When we've compiled enough documentation, we'll edit the whole thing and have Ruby e-mail it to as many news agencies and public interest groups as we can."

"Such as newspapers, TV networks?"

He nodded quickly. "All that, yes. We're also sending copies to the ACLU, Public Citizen, the Rainbow Coalition, the three major political parties, various other nongovernment watchdog organizations, and so forth."

"And the *Big Muddy*, I hope."

Payson-Smith smiled. "And your own paper, of course. In fact . . ."

He pointed to the stack of printout I had noticed earlier. "In fact, you're going to get the scoop on this before anyone else. That's the first batch from our search. Everything we've found about ERA's involvement in St. Louis, including the development of Ruby Fulcrum itself and the Sentinel program . . . it's all in there, or at least as much as we've printed so far."

He frowned as he glanced at the printer. "Just as well, I suppose. The blamed ink cartridges are beginning to run out on us . . ."

Who cared? I would have settled for dry impressions on paper. I started to stand up, but Payson-Smith grabbed my arm, stopping me from diving into the stack. "Look at it later," he said. "That's only the tip of the iceberg."

I wrenched my eyes away from the printouts, gazing again at the Apple laptop. More documents flashed across its screen;

I caught a glimpse of the ERA logo at the top of one page. "ERA doesn't know what you're doing?"

Payson-Smith shook his head regretfully. "Unfortunately," he said, "since they're aware of Ruby's very existence, they must know what we're up to. She's already informed us of a number of virus hunter/killers that have been introduced in the net during the last twenty-four hours. Ruby has no trouble tracking them down and deciphering their source codes, but we're still afraid that the opposition may get wise and develop a program she can't defeat."

"ERA shut down a few nodes within the last few hours," Jeff Morgan said.

He stood at a window behind us, peering down at Grand through the eyepiece of a Russian-made night-vision scope; no wonder he had been able to see me coming through the park. Morgan was probably the serious camper who had outfitted this hideout, considering all the outdoors supplies they had up here.

"They've also gone dark on several frequencies," Morgan went on, watching the street intently. "They figured out that Ruby can scan cellular channels, so they've been using some other means of communication we can't intercept." He shrugged. "Semaphore, sign language, I dunno what, but they've got to be getting desperate by now."

"Sure sounds like it." I thought for a moment before the obvious question occurred to me. "If you're using cellular modem, can't they trace the signal?"

Payson-Smith sighed and scratched the back of his neck. "Unfortunately," he said, "they can indeed. Ruby's jumping channels every few minutes and blocking their remote tracking systems, but all they really need to do is conduct a block-by-block search through RF scanners. Any car passing on the street could be someone trying to lock on to us—"

"Or chopper."

"Or by helicopter, yes, but that's not our only concern." He pointed to the Compaq laptop on the right. Its screen depicted a Mercator projection of the North American hemisphere; thin red lines curved across the map, weaving parabolic trace across the United States.

"That's the orbital footprint of *Sentinel 1*," Richard said. "As you can see, it regularly passes above almost every point in this country. Right now it's . . ."

He studied the celestial coordinates in a bar at the bottom of the screen. "Somewhere over the Pacific, not far from the southern California coastline," he continued. "It's off screen right now, but in about a minute or so it'll be over the United States again, and in another fifteen minutes it'll be over Missouri . . . and here is why that matters."

He pointed behind the two computers. For the first time, I noticed a flat gray coaxial cable running from the back of the computer to a window; the window was cracked open slightly, allowing the cable to pass over the narrow sill.

"We've got a portable satellite transceiver dish rigged on the ledge," Richard said. "It's oriented to precisely the right azimuth that *Sentinel* will follow when it passes over St. Louis. When this occurs, Ruby will uplink with *Sentinel* and order it to disengage itself from the Air Force space center in Colorado."

I stared at the wire. Beside the fact of its technological complexity, there was also the human factor; it must have taken some nerve to hang out a window over a sheer drop to put the portable dish in place. "You can do this?" I asked.

"Certainly." Payson-Smith was almost smug now. "After all, Ruby's primary function was to act as the c-cube system for *Sentinel*. Her node is already in place aboard the satellite . . . it'll be no more problem for her to communicate with *Sentinel* than for one of us to call up a long-lost brother. But the main trick will be establishing a direct uplink with the bird."

On the Compaq's screen a tiny red dot had suddenly appeared over the California coast. As I watched, it began to edge closer toward San Diego. "Why can't you tell Ruby to access *Sentinel* now?" I asked. "If it—she—can run through the system and crack any source code it wants to, then why can't it override Colorado?"

Payson-Smith folded his arms together. "Ruby isn't a simple worm or virus," he said. "Her architecture is much more complex than that. It takes her a while to infiltrate the nets, since she has to hide herself at the same time she's installing a memory-resident. To make it short, she hasn't been able to crack the Colorado computers quite yet." He shrugged his shoulders. "In another few days, yes, but . . ."

"So why can't you just wait?"

"Look here." He pointed at a line in *Sentinel*'s footprint that passed over the Pacific northwest. "In about eighteen hours, the satellite will pass directly over the border between Oregon and California . . . the southern border of Cascadia. When that occurs, it'll be able to open fire upon Cascadian defense forces. Now, what do you think that means?"

I stared at the screen. I considered all that I learned. I reached a basic conclusion . . .

"Oh my God," I whispered.

Now it all clicked together. *Sentinel 1* could wipe out the renegade National Guard forces that had been established in southern Oregon, thereby leaving Cascadia open to attack from the U.S. Army units mobilized to northern California.

Yet, even worse than that, it would give the conspirators their window of opportunity. If everything Ruby Fulcrum had discovered was correct, then an outbreak of civil war in the Northwest would allow the fanatics to call for a declaration of martial law throughout the rest of the country, to "protect" against civil insurrections by Cascadian sympathizers.

Martial law enforced by ERA troops and a high-energy laser that passed over the continent once every few hours. In short, it would be the beginning of the end for free society in the United States.

"And if you can't . . . ?" I began.

Then I heard something and I stopped talking.

Out in the predawn darkness beyond the observation deck windows, from somewhere not far away, there was a faint yet nonetheless familiar mechanical whine . . . then a dense, atmospheric chopping noise, like cutlasses carving through thick air.

Richard heard it, too. He raised his head, listening intently to the sound as it came closer.

"Not now," he said softly, almost as if in supplication. "Oh, dear Christ, not now . . ."

Helicopter rotors, closing in on the water tower.

21

"Uh-oh," Morgan said from the window behind us. "We've got—"

The rest was drowned out in the dense roar of helicopter rotors. Standing up to look out through the eastern windows, I caught a glimpse of a dark airborne shape as it hurtled toward the cupola. I instinctively ducked as the helicopter growled over the roof; the entire tower seemed to shudder. When it was gone, I uncovered my ears and raced to the opposite side of the observation deck.

Morgan was crouched next to a western window, peering at the street through his nightscope. As I knelt on the other side of the window, he passed the scope to me and pointed downward. I cautiously raised my head to the windowsill and pressed my right eye against the scope.

Through the green-tinted artificial twilight, I could see two Piranhas coming off the I-44 ramp and rolling down Grand Avenue. Just in front of them was a trio of faster-moving Hummers, their headlights casting foggy-looking halos until they were simultaneously extinguished just before they passed in front of the reservoir. The last Piranha in the column swerved to the left and halted in the center of the street, blocking Grand Avenue; the other armored car trundled to a stop directly in front of the park, while the three Hummers jumped the curb, barreled across the sidewalk, and disappeared under the trees left and right of the tower.

"Oh Jesus, oh Christ," Morgan was muttering. "We're really screwed now . . ."

I got up from the window and ran over to the south side
of the deck. Peering through the nightscope, I could see the
helicopter that had just passed over the tower: an OH-6A
Cayuse, a tiny gunship painted with the ERA logo, an IR
scanner fixed to the front of its bubble canopy. It had established a low orbit directly above the reservoir, apparently
performing recon for the mission.

Down on the ground, I could make out one of the Hummers
coming to a stop behind the German-American memorial. Its
doors opened and four ERA soldiers leaped out, hugging their
G-11s against their flak vests as they dashed for cover behind
the bronze nude, cumbersome night-vision goggles suspended
in front of their eyes below their helmets.

Another helicopter roared past the tower, a little farther
away this time but nonetheless louder. I raised the scope and
caught the second chopper in its lens: an Apache, identical to
the one that had stalked me earlier this evening, except for one
chilling difference—this one had two racks of Hellfire missiles
slung beneath its nacelles.

"How the hell did they find us?" I yelled.

"I was afraid of this." Payson-Smith was still seated in front
of the computers, feverishly typing on the keyboard of the one
on the left. "It was only a matter of time before they managed
to trace our phone link to the nets," he said, "but I rather
thought we'd be out of here before they figured out where
we were. I guess I was wrong . . ."

"Yeah, I guess so." Keeping low, I dashed back across the
room. Morgan was huddled on the floor away from the windows, his knees drawn between his arms, his shoulders visibly
trembling; the man was having a full-blown panic attack, but
I didn't have time to hold his hands. I kneeled by one of the
western windows and peered down at the park again. Two
ERA troopers were standing over the teenager who had tried
to mug me earlier; he lay facedown on the ground, his hands
locked together behind his head, the barrel of a Heckler &
Koch pressed against the back of his neck. One of the troopers
finished twisting a pair of plastic handcuffs around his wrists,
then they hauled him off the ground and hustled him toward
the Piranha parked on the street. At least I wouldn't have to

worry about getting mugged when I left here.

If I left here.

"Talk to me," Richard snapped. "How many soldiers are out there?"

I scanned Grand Avenue and the front of the park, but I couldn't see any other soldiers. "At least a platoon," I replied. "Maybe more. Can't see 'em, though . . . most of 'em have taken cover. The ones I spotted were wearing night goggles."

"Uh-huh. Vehicles?"

"Two LAVs, three Hummers. The choppers are a Cayuse and an Apache . . . and I hate to tell you this, but the Apache's carrying missiles."

"Oh, really?"

"Oh, really." I paused, then added, "If you want any good news, though, it looks like they're taking prisoners. They just nailed our friend Skippy down there."

"Very good. I hope they find a nice little cell for him." Richard's fingers were tapping nonstop at the keyboard; his face, backlighted by the faint blue glow of the computer screen, was taut with concentration. "Won't do us much good, though, I'm afraid. If they get us now, they'll put us away where the sun doesn't shine. They won't let—"

The rest was submerged beneath the roar of one of the helicopters coming in for another low pass.

I looked through the window again, just in time to peer directly into the canopy of the Apache as it slowed down to hover less than fifty feet from my window. For a moment I thought it was going to attack; the gunner had a clean line of fire through the windows for the chopper's 30-mm chain gun. Through the nightscope, I could see the pilot and copilot; the helicopter was so close that, if the window had been open, I could have taken a rock and bounced it off the armored glass.

But the chain gun didn't move on its mount beneath the cockpit. Instead, the TADS/PNVS turret mounted at the chopper's nose rotated toward the tower. As I watched, the man in the rear seat looked my way. He grinned broadly, raised his left hand, and pointed his forefinger straight at me: *you see me, I see you.*

I pointed back at him, he nodded his head, then the chopper lifted away once again and sailed away over the trees. "We have met the enemy," I said once the noise subsided, "and he's a smartass."

"Why don't they just rush the tower?" Morgan muttered. He was still cowering next to the wall, his arms wrapped around himself as if they would protect him from caseless 34-mm shells. "If they've got us surrounded, why don't they . . . ?"

"Because they're probably unsure how many people are in here." Payson-Smith's voice was emotionless, as matter-of-fact as if he was discussing a moot intellectual point. "After all, we're the renegade mad scientists out to blow up the world. For all they know, we've got an entire army holed up in here. Only an idiot would mount a frontal assault if he didn't know what the odds were, now would—"

"But we don't have an army!" I snapped at him, frustrated by his objectivity. "We don't got so much as a spit wad and a rubber band, and that Apache's carrying tank busters!"

Tappa-tappa-tappa-tappa. "You don't say?" said Herr von Frankenstein.

He was too cool to be insane. Something was going on over there.

I scurried across the deck and knelt down next to where he was sitting. The search-and-retrieve program had vanished from the screen, replaced by long lines of LISP program code I couldn't read.

"I'm explaining things to Ruby," Richard said. "She knows a little of what's going on, but she needs a little human intuition right now." He glanced over his shoulder at me. "We're working on something, but we need some time. If you've got any ideas how to—"

"You! Up in the water tower! Listen up!"

An amplified male voice through a megaphone from somewhere down below. Payson-Smith's hands froze above the keyboard as we both raised our heads.

"This is the Emergency Relief Agency . . ."

"Now there's an oxymoron if I ever heard one," Richard said dryly.

"You're completely surrounded! We know you know this! If you surrender immediately, you will be arrested but nothing else will happen to you!"

"Right." Payson-Smith bent over his keyboard again and continued writing cybernetic cabala.

"You have two minutes to obey our orders! Come out with your hands above your heads, or we will be forced to use force!"

"Oh, my!" he exclaimed. "He sounds rather forceful, doesn't he?" He shook his head. "Typical—"

"Goddammit, Dick, you can't let 'em do this!" Jeff Morgan scrambled across the floor toward us. "C'mon, it's not that important! Just . . . let's just give up and let 'em take us downtown. If we cooperate—"

"Shut up, Jeff." Payson-Smith shot a dire look at him; Morgan fell silent again, and Richard glanced back at me. "I need another few minutes here," he went on. "As I was saying, if you've got any ideas how to hold them off . . ."

In that instant, I remembered the last ace I had up my sleeve. It was a long shot, but . . . "You got a phone up here?"

"Jeff, give him the phone, please," Richard said, "then stop whining and get behind the other 'puter. I need you to do something."

Morgan's face reddened. He looked at me querulously as I rolled over on my side, pulled out my wallet, and searched through a stack of dog-eared business cards until I found the one I had forgotten up until now. God, if I had lost it . . .

No, it was still here: the phonecard George Barris had given me at the Stadium, little more than twenty-four hours ago. "Phone!" I snapped. "Hurry up!"

Morgan dug into his windbreaker and pulled out a pocket phone. I snatched it out of his hand, snapped it open, and ran the card's codestrip across its scanner. Holding the receiver against my ear, I heard a faint buzzing. The second buzz was interrupted halfway through by a calm, familiar voice:

"Redbird Leader."

Barris.

I took a deep breath. "Colonel Barris, this is Gerry Rosen. Remember me?"

A brief pause. *"Of course, Gerry. I've been waiting to hear from you."*

"I'm sure you have," I replied, trying to keep my voice easy. "Just wanted to give you a little how-do, see what's on your mind—"

"Just a moment, please." A click, then a moment of silence as I was put on hold. The bastard was probably trying to have the call traced. The phone clicked again, and Barris came back on the line. *"I'm sorry, Gerry, but I'm a little tied up just now. If you'd care to let me know where I can reach you, I'll—"*

"Sure thing, Colonel," I said. "I'm in the Compton Hill water tower. There's about a dozen of your boys surrounding me, so I'm kinda busy myself . . . you still want to call me back?"

I heard a sharp intake of breath.

"I thought you'd be interested," I went on. "Look, you asked me to call you if I happened to find Dr. Payson-Smith or Dr. Morgan. Well, here they are. I've lived up to my side of the bargain. What about yours?"

"Mr. Rosen," he replied evenly, *"I appreciate your assistance. If you surrender yourself to my men, I promise that you'll be treated well—"*

"The same way you treated Beryl Hinckley this afternoon?"

"I don't know what you're talking about, Gerry, but I can assure you—"

I heard Richard snap his fingers; looking around, I saw him hastily gesturing for the phone. "Well, Colonel," I interrupted, "I'd love to discuss this further, but I think Dick here wants a few words with you."

I handed the phone to Payson-Smith; he cupped it between his chin and shoulder. "Colonel Barris?" he said, his hands still racing across the keyboard. "Yes, this is Richard Payson-Smith. How do you do . . . ?"

A long pause. "Well, the offer is quite flattering, but I'm afraid I cannot trust you . . . no, no, that's out of the question—"

The Apache buzzed the tower again. I picked up the nightscope, crawled across the floor to an eastern window close to where the two scientists were seated, and peered

out. More troopers had taken up positions on the crumbling
limestone stairway just below the reservoir wall, while the
Cayuse continued to hover above the reservoir itself.

"Let me make you a counterproposal instead," Richard
went on. "If you'll withdraw your men and the helicopters
immediately and allow us to leave the reservoir, I promise
you that no one will be harmed."

What the hell?

I glanced over my shoulder at Payson-Smith. He now held
the phone in his right hand, his left forefinger idly tapping the
edge of the Apple. Jeff Morgan was no longer in a blind panic;
he had quietly settled down in front of the Compaq and was
now quickly entering commands on its keyboard.

"No, sir, I'm not joking," Richard said. "We do not intend
to give ourselves up, now or . . . Colonel, please listen to
me . . ."

Not bothering to crouch, I dashed to the other side of
the room and raised the scope to a western window. The
Apache was now hovering in midair at a parallel distance
and altitude from the Cayuse, slightly above the height of
the water tower; like the other one, it was now facing the
tower.

Out of the corner of my eye, I spotted swift movement on the
ground; looking down through the scope, I saw ERA troopers
sprinting away from the tower, giving up their cover behind
trees and benches. I ran the scope to the armored car closest
to the park; troopers were practically shoving each other aside
in their haste to get through the LAVs' rear hatches.

It looked like they were retreating.

I felt a momentary surge of relief . . . then the nightscope
almost dropped from my numb hands as I realized what was
about to happen.

"The Apache's going to launch its missiles!" I shouted.

"Just a moment, Colonel . . ." Payson-Smith cupped his hand
over the receiver. "Ruby confirms TADS lock-on and Hellfires
arming."

"*Sentinel* flyover in sixty-six seconds," Morgan said softly,
his eyes riveted to his screen. "Initiating satellite uplink and
c-cube interface."

"We don't have sixty seconds!" I shouted. "That chopper's going to—"

"Gerry," Richard said, "please shut up and get away from the window."

I took a couple of steps away from the window, then stopped when I saw what was displayed on the computer screens. Payson-Smith's had opened a window depicting a cutaway view of an Apache AH-64; Morgan's screen displayed an aerial map of downtown St. Louis, with the Compton Hill Reservoir epicentered within a red bull's-eye.

"I'm sorry to hear that, Colonel," Payson-Smith said, uncupping the phone again. "But you've been warned—"

There was a bright flash through the western windows.

I looked around just in time to see sparks erupt from beneath the nacelles of the Apache as two Hellfire missiles launched from the chopper.

Then I threw myself to the floor.

I didn't even have a chance to scream before the supernova erupted.

There was a brilliant white flash, then an immense thunder-clap pummeled my ears. Windows shattered, glass spraying across my back, as the stone floor trembled beneath me. I lay still, my eyes squeezed tightly shut, my hands wrapped around my head, waiting for the tower to collapse around me.

But that didn't happen.

The light faded, the thunder subsided, the floor stopped shaking.

The missiles hadn't hit the tower.

I raised myself to my elbows and looked around, not quite believing I was still alive. Glass from the broken windows on the eastern side of the room was strewn across the floor; a cool predawn breeze wafted through the shattered panes, carrying with it the harsh odor of burning aircraft fuel.

"What the fuck happened?" I murmured.

"Hello, Colonel?" I heard Payson-Smith say. "Do you hear me?"

Richard and Jeff were picking themselves off the floor from where they had ducked for cover. Payson-Smith still had the

phone in his hand; he was listening to it as Morgan crawled
to the computer terminal and tapped a couple of keys.

The stench of burning gasoline was stronger now. I raised
myself to my knees and stared through the broken windows.
A thick plume of black smoke billowed up from behind the
reservoir walls, obscuring the downtown lights. I could hear
the steady thrum of a helicopter's rotors from behind me, but
it sounded more distant than before.

"I'll tell you what happened," Payson-Smith was saying.
"Ruby Fulcrum—and I'm sure you're aware of what that is—
has accessed the source codes of the programs controlling your
Apache's onboard computers."

I could hear the faint voices of men yelling outside the
tower, sounding almost as confused as I was. I felt around
with my hands until I located the nightscope where I had
dropped it.

"In case you don't know this," Payson-Smith said, "the
avionics of your Apaches are controlled by eleven computers,
including the ones that operate the weapon fire-control systems. When its missiles locked on to the tower, my friend
Ruby took command of the laser targeting computer. Even
though your copilot thought he was aiming at us, he didn't
really have any control over . . ."

I crawled to an eastern window and raised the nightscope
to my eye, but I saw only an opaque black spot through the
eyepiece. The scope was broken.

"We've achieved uplink with *Sentinel*," Morgan said quietly. "Ruby's making the snatch."

Richard smiled and held up a finger. "Yes, Colonel," he
said into the phone. "Ruby took over their TADS computer,
so when the Apache launched its Hellfires, the laser guidance
system instantly retargeted the other helicopter instead. That's
the reason why one of your choppers has just been destroyed
and the other one cannot attack us . . ."

He paused and listened. "No, Colonel," he replied, "that
wouldn't be very wise. Just ask the Apache's gunner. Everything on that chopper runs off its computers. If he tries to fire
another missile or use his guns, he'll probably hit everything
except us, and that includes your men on the ground . . . I'm

sorry, sir. I tried to warn you, but you wouldn't—"

Even without the nightscope, I could see the troops clambering out of the LAVs where they had taken cover and swarming toward the base of the tower. I bent closer to the window, trying to see what they were doing . . .

Poppa-poppa-poppa . . .

I ducked below the sill as I heard full-auto gunfire. "They're sending in the ground troops!" I yelled; the window above me shattered, and there was the high zing of bullets ricocheting off stone walls. I hit the floor and began to crawl toward the center of the room.

"Colonel, listen to me!"

A double beep from the Compaq; Jeff Morgan leaned closer to read the message he had just received. "Oh, fuck," he murmured. "They just got wise to us."

Richard turned around to look at him, his eyebrows raised in silent question. "Ruby reports a jet just took off from Scott AFB," Morgan said softly. "Strong probability that it's a F-22."

A window had opened on the Compaq's screen, displaying dorsal and side views of an F-22 Lightning 2: a small dual-engine fighter that looked like a hybridization between an F-18 Hornet and a Stealth fighter.

"Excuse me, Colonel . . ." Richard said, then clapped his hand over the receiver again. "What's its ETA?"

Morgan typed a query into his keyboard, then shook his head. "Five minutes, thirty seconds. Ruby says its onboard computers are inaccessible . . . must be using a program she hasn't wiggled into yet. *Sentinel* is trying to track it, but the sucker's down in the grass—"

"Ground track?"

More tapping of keys, almost drowned out by the popcorn rattle of gunfire from below the tower. "No good," Morgan said, shaking his head as he stared at the screen. "Thermal emission zeroed out . . . ground-air shadow almost negligible . . . *Sentinel's* got something, but it can't lock on. The pilot's flying evasive. ETA five minutes and counting."

Scott Air Force Base was located in Illinois, not far across the Mississippi River from St. Louis. The F-22 was made fo just this sort of mission: radar-deflecting fuselage, low-visibility paint, engines designed to reduce its heat-exhaust signature. Even flying below radar, the fighter would be here in only a few minutes . . . and I had no doubt that its Sidewinder missile could finish the job the Hellfires had botched.

"Where's *Sentinel*?" Richard snapped.

"Directly above us."

"Instruct it to . . . never mind, I'll do it." Payson-Smith pulled the Apple closer to him and began to type instructions into the keyboard. He slid the phone across the floor to me. "Keep him busy," he ordered. "Make sure he knows we're not bluffing."

I grabbed the phone and pulled it to my ear. "Colonel Barris—"

"Rosen? Tell that maniac that whatever he thinks he's doing, it's not going to work." Barris's voice was calm, but I could hear his barely suppressed rage. *"Unless you come out that door right now, my men are going to blast it open, and I can't guarantee they'll take prisoners."*

If I was scared before, that bit got me mad instead. "Get a new line, Barris!" I yelled. "If your men wanted to demo the door, they would have done it already! You know and we know they're just harassing us until your jet gets here and finishes the job!"

"Jet? What jet . . . ?"

"ETA three minutes," Morgan said.

"The jet that just scrambled out of Scott, you weenie!" I almost laughed at his lame attempt at subterfuge. "You think we don't know about it? Man, we've got eyes in the sky, eyes in your computers, eyes in your bathroom!"

"Rosen, listen to me—"

"No, jerk-wad, you listen to me for a change!" Ignoring the rattle of small-arms fire, I sat up on the floor. "You don't intend to let us go, just as you never intended to let my friend stay alive. But the shoe's on the other foot now, pal . . . you're the one who's sweating bullets, not me! You're fucked, Barris, and I'm the one who's doing the—"

The phone was suddenly snatched out of my hand by Payson-Smith. I grasped for it, but he pushed me away with

his hand. "Colonel?" he said. "I'm sorry for the unseemly
outburst there, but . . . yes, that was uncalled for, but my
friend is correct in his remarks."

I crawled away from him, clambering on hands and knees
around the glass shards on the floor until I reached the windows overlooking downtown. The sound of gunshots lapsed
again, doubtless because the troopers had just received orders
from their squad leaders to cease fire and take cover.

"ETA two minutes . . ."

I raised myself to my knees and stared out through a broken
window. The rainclouds that had haunted the city yesterday
were gone, leaving behind a dark blue sky. The first light of
a new day was breaking over the eastern horizon, painting the
Arch silvery rose red and bathing the downtown skyscrapers
with a vague pink hue. In the near distance, I could make
out the oval bowl of Busch Stadium, where my friend and
benefactor George Barris was even now plotting our demise.

It was a beautiful spring morning in St. Louis. I had little
doubt that this would be the last Missouri dawn I would ever
see.

"Colonel Barris," Payson-Smith said, "we don't have much
time, so I'll tell it to you straight. *Sentinel 1* is above the city
right now, and its laser is focused directly at Busch Stadium.
Ruby Fulcrum now has complete control of the satellite, and
I have given her instructions to open fire upon the stadium
unless you remove your squads from the park and order the
fighter to break off its attack . . ."

Now I could see a thin, jagged white contrail coming over
the horizon, led by a tiny silver point of light. The F-22 was
coming in hot and fast over the river, skittering back and forth
across the sky as it sought to evade *Sentinel*. In another minute
it would be over the reservoir.

"I know you don't believe me," Payson-Smith was saying,
"so I'll have to demonstrate. Please watch carefully . . ."

Glancing over my shoulder, I saw him lift his left hand and
raise two fingers. Morgan nodded and typed a command into
his keyboard.

I looked out the window again.

A second elapsed. Two. Three . . .

The contrail flattened out and became more dense as the F-22 crossed the Mississippi, its pilot homing in on an old stone tower near the edge of the city.

Then a narrow red beam lanced out of the cold blue stratosphere, straight down from space into the center of Busch Stadium. It was there, and then it was gone.

"Strike one," Morgan said, his eyes locked on the screen.

The beam reappeared an instant later, its angle only marginally different. One moment it was there, and then it had vanished again.

"Strike two," Morgan said. "Ruby confirms two kills."

A couple of seconds elapsed, then I heard faint booms from far away, carried by the still morning air, as tiny black pillars of smoke rose from the stadium like funeral pyres. I stared up at the dark sky, but I couldn't see anything except the last stars of night. If one of them was *Sentinel 1*, there was nothing about it to distinguish it from anything else in the heavens.

"Those two helicopters were destroyed on the pad by *Sentinel*." Richard Payson-Smith's voice was low, direct, and intense. "The sat is now aimed directly at your office in the stadium. Even if you decide to commence with the attack and we're killed, Ruby Fulcrum will nonetheless order the satellite to take you out . . . and when it circles the earth again in another three hours, it will destroy another military target in the United States."

I glanced out the window again. I couldn't see the fighter, but I could hear the high, thin whine of its engines. The F-22 was somewhere over the city, closing in fast.

Richard stopped, listened for a moment, and shook his head. "No, sir, there's no room for negotiation. Break it off now . . ."

In those last few moments, all was still and quiet. Payson-Smith intently watched his computer screens, the phone clasped against his ear. Jeff Morgan was bent almost double, his hands laced together around the back of his neck. I stared out the window, my heart stopped in midbeat, waiting for the end of my life.

There was a flat, hollow shriek, then the F-22 rocketed into sight. Racing only a few hundred feet above the rooftops, it howled over the reservoir, banking sharply to the right as it exposed the dull gray paint on the underside of its wedge-shaped wings. The Compton Heights neighborhood was treated to a sonic earthquake as the jet ripped past the water tower, then its nose lifted, and the fighter hurtled straight up into the purple sky.

The jet reached apogee almost a thousand feet above the reservoir. Then it rolled over, veered to the left, and began to go back the way it had come.

My heart started beating again.

"Thank you, Colonel," Richard said. "We'll be in touch." Then he clicked off, put the phone down on the floor, and took a deep breath.

"Well, gentlemen," he said after a moment as he turned around to look at us. "I think we're going to stay alive a little longer."

22

Stretch limos were lined up on Fourth Street in front of the
Adam's Mark, waiting for their turn to pull up to the hotel's
side entrance. Uniformed valets rushed out from under the blue
awning to open the passenger doors of each limo, assisting
women in silk evening gowns and capes and men in tails and
white tie from the car. Then the empty limo would move on,
allowing the next vehicle in line to repeat the process.

Tricycle Man waited patiently for his turn at the door,
ignoring the amused or outraged stares of the ballgoers behind
and in front of his rickshaw. He had gone so far as to put on
a black bow tie and a chauffeur's cap for the occasion; they
clashed wonderfully with his tie-dyed T-shirt and parachute
pants. The valets tried to hide their grins as Trike pedaled up
to the hotel entrance. The rickshaw didn't have any doors, nor
was there a lady who needed assistance, but I handed one of
the kids a dollar anyway as I climbed out of the backseat.

"Will that be all, m'lord?" Trike asked, affecting an Oxford
accent.

"That'll be it for tonight, Jeeves." I reached into my overcoat and pulled out a ten-spot. "You're at liberty for the rest
of the evening."

"Very good, suh." He folded the bill and tucked it into the
waistband of his shorts, studying a pair of young women in
slinky black gowns lingering near the doors. They giggled
between their gloved hands as he arched an eyebrow at them.
"If you find any debutantes who are in need of a gentleman's
services," he added, handing me his phonecard, "please let me
know and I'll return immediately."

"Thanks for the lift, Trike . . ."

He grinned, then stood up on his pedals and pulled away from the curb. The doorman glowered at me as he held open the door; I caught his disdainful look and shrugged. "The Rolls is in the shop," I said as I strode past him. "You know how it is."

I left my topcoat at the chequer and paused in front of a mirror to inspect my appearance. White tie and vest, black morning coat and trousers, faux pearl studs and cufflinks: I looked as if I was ready to conduct a symphony.

It had been a long time since I had gone white-tie. The only reason I owned tails in the first place was because Marianne had insisted upon a formal wedding. She had resented unpacking my tux from the attic boxes and bringing them downtown to my apartment, but it was the only way I was going to get into the main event of St. Louis's social calendar. This evening, no one in jeans and a bomber jacket would have been allowed within a block of the Adam's Mark.

Tonight was the night of the Veiled Prophet Ball, and I had come to the ritziest hotel in downtown St. Louis to complete the story I was writing.

No one had arrested us when we emerged from the water tower. In obedience to Payson-Smith's demands, the ERA squads that had surrounded the tower left the scene. The soldiers piled back into their LAVs, the Apache flew back to Busch Stadium, and when the park was clear of everyone except for a handful of police officers and paramedics investigating the helicopter wreckage in the reservoir, Ruby Fulcrum informed us it was safe to exit the tower.

By then it was dawn, and I was dog-tired. It had been a long night. I barely said anything to either Richard Payson-Smith or Jeff Morgan; I simply walked away from the park, trudging down several blocks of empty sidewalks until I reached the nearest MetroLink station.

It was a long walk; I had to carry a plastic grocery sack filled with computer printouts. I kept expecting to see an ERA vehicle pull over and a couple of troopers jump out to hustle me into the back for a ride down to the stadium, but this didn't happen. Ruby had assured each of us that we had been given amnesty; our records were scrubbed clean, our names and faces removed from the most-wanted list.

The conspirators would leave us alone now, even if by doing so they ensured their own demise. How could they do otherwise? A sword of Damocles now orbited over their heads, a sword cast not of Damascus steel but of focused energy, and the single hair that kept it from falling was observance of Ruby Fulcrum's demands . . . and what Ruby wants, Ruby gets.

I made my way back to Soulard, hiked through the early morning streets until I reached my building, hauled my weary ass upstairs, and stumbled through the broken door into my apartment. I didn't even bother to take off the clothes I had been wearing for more than two days; I simply dropped the grocery bag on my desk, shrugged out of my jacket, kicked off my boots, and fell facefirst onto my unmade bed, falling asleep almost as soon as my head hit the pillow.

I thought this was the end of the affair, but it wasn't quite over yet.

At twelve o'clock, just as the church bells were ringing the noonday hour, I was awakened once again by the electronic beep of Joker's annunciator. I tried to ignore it for as long as I could, but the noise continued until I crawled across the littered mattress, grabbed my jacket from where I had tossed it on the floor, and pulled the PT out of my pocket.

I hesitated before I opened its cover. Instead of Jamie's face, though, the screen depicted a man wearing an absurd Viking helmet, his features indistinguishable behind the veil of purple silk.

A window opened at the bottom of the screen, scrolling upward to display in fine lines of arabesque typescript:

You are commanded to appear
at the
Annual Ball
to be given in honor of
His Majesty
The Veiled Prophet

*and his court of love and beauty
on Saturday evening, April twentieth,
Two thousand and thirteen
St. Louis Ballroom
Adam's Mark*

I gaped as I read this. Receiving an invitation to the Veiled Prophet Ball wasn't like winning a free ticket to a Cards game; it was a passport into the upper echelons of St. Louis high society. You're either rich, famous, or both to be sent such a notice, even if it's by e-mail at the last moment; since I was neither wealthy nor notable, getting invited to the VP Ball was a weird honors.

Just how famous is the Veiled Prophet Ball? Robert Mitchum drops a line about it in the original version of *Cape Fear*, that's how famous it is. The Veiled Prophet Society was organized in 1874 as a secret society of upper-class St. Louis citizens; it was concocted around the ramblings of some obscure Irish poet about one Hashimal-Mugunna, who ruled a nonexistent kingdom in ancient Persia called Khorassan. The Veiled Prophet Society stopped being secret around 1894, when the first annual Veiled Prophet Ball was held to commemorate the return of the Veiled Prophet to St. Louis.

Actually, the Prophet has never left; he is a member of the Society itself, although the role changes every year and the identity of the new prophet is kept a closely guarded secret. Over time, the ball has evolved into an elaborate coming-out party for the debutantes of the city's high society, the so-called "court of love and beauty," when one of them is crowned as this year's reigning queen.

For about the past fifty years, the Veiled Prophet Ball has been held around Christmastide, yet last year the Society had decided to postpone the ball until April. Since the downtown area was still recovering from the quake and there were riots going on in the north and south sides of the city, it would have been unseemly for several hundred rich people to be cavorting in public while most of the citizenry were enduring hardship.

But why had I been sent an invitation?

I switched on Joker's dialog box. *Ruby? Is that you?* I typed at the bottom of the screen.

The invitation vanished, to be replaced by a line of type:
>I am here.<

What's going on? Have you sent me this invitation?
>I have arranged for it to be sent.<

I don't understand, I typed.

>Clarification: I have arranged for your name to be added to the guest list for the Veiled Prophet Ball. The notice you received is the standard one sent to persons who are invited within the last six to forty eight hours. You will also be receiving a commemorative rose vase by package service. Note: the festivities begin at 2000 hours. Formal white-tie apparel is mandatory.<

I smiled. In this apartment, I would probably be using a commemorative rose vase as a beer mug. I replied: *Thank you for doing this, but I still don't understand why.*

>You have done much to help me. This is my way of thanking you.<

I laughed out loud when I read this. An invitation to the Veiled Prophet Ball; it was like sending a starving child a box of Godiva chocolates. Sweet and fattening, but not necessarily nutritious.

I wrote: *If you really want to thank me, you can deposit a million dollars in my savings account.*

There was a short pause, then:
>This has been done. Is there anything else you need?<

I almost dropped Joker. I knew better than to ask if it was kidding; for Ruby Fulcrum, it was only a matter of accessing my savings account number at Boatman's Bank and Trust and inserting the numeral *1* followed by six zeros. Money meant nothing to Ruby; everything was bits and bytes, little pieces of information that could be manipulated in a nano-second.

What God wants, God gets . . .

It was a tempting notion, but what would the IRS have to say about this? I wrestled with my conscience for a few moments, then typed: *Please undo this. I was only joking, and it would only present me with some problems.*

Another pause, then: >**This has been done. You no longer have $1,000,000 in your savings account. However, I have taken the liberty of absolving all your current debts, past and present. Is this acceptable?<**

I let out my breath. Having my credit cards, taxes, utility and phone bills suddenly paid off was a fair swap, and less likely to be noticed by a sharp-eyed auditor.

That's fine, but it still doesn't answer my first question. Why do you want me to attend the VP Ball?

>**A list of the confirmed invitations to tonight's ball will be downloaded shortly. When you study this list, you will know the reason why I have arranged for you to attend the ball.<**

The screen went blank, the face of the Veiled Prophet disappearing along with the last few lines of type, but before I could ask another question, a final message appeared:

>**This will be the last time you will hear from me. I will always be watching. Good-bye, Gerry Rosen.<**

Then a long list of names, arranged in alphabetical order, began to scroll down the screen. As I studied the list, I let out a low whistle.

Ruby's last gift was almost worth losing a million bucks.

I sauntered through the lobby, taking a moment to admire the ornate ice sculpture near the plate-glass windows, then joined the late arrivals as they rode the escalators up to the fourth floor. A heady crowd, as they say, decked out in formal evening wear worth someone else's monthly rent, mildly tipsy after a long, leisurely dinner at Tony's or Morton's. Envying their carefree inebriation, I thought about visiting one of the cash bars on the mezzanine for a quick beer, but reconsidered after seeing that a bottle of Busch would set me back five bucks. Someone once said that rich people are just like poor people, except that they have more money; what he failed to mention is that rich people are more easily hosed than poor people, for much the same reason.

Besides, it was getting close to eight o'clock; the ceremony would soon begin. I went straight to the St. Louis Ballroom, where an usher in a red uniform checked my name against the datapad strapped to his wrist, then stepped aside to allow me through the door.

The ballroom was a long, vast auditorium; crystal chandeliers were suspended from the high ceiling above an elevated runway bisecting the room, leading from a grand, red-curtained entrance at one end of the room to a large stage at the other. Two empty thrones were at the center of the stage, in front of a backdrop painted to resemble a Mediterranean courtyard at sunset.

The room was already filled nearly to capacity, the wealthy and powerful seated in rows of linen-backed folding chairs, listening to the thirty-piece live orchestra as it swung through a medley of Sousa marches and rearranged pop hits. Avoiding an usher who tried to guide me to the nearest empty chair, I wandered down the center aisle, scanning the faces of the well-dressed men and women sitting around me.

The chandeliers were beginning to dim when I finally spotted Cale McLaughlin. He was sitting near the center of the room not far from the runway; his wife was with him, a trim older woman with ash blond hair. Their attention was entirely focused on the stage, so neither of them noticed as I slid into the vacant chair beside him.

As the lights went down and the orchestra struck up the theme from *The Bridge on the River Kwai*, the entrance curtains parted and a platoon of lancers in brocaded red uniforms and blue headdresses began marching in lockstep through the door and down the runway. The flagbearers leading the procession carried the flags of the United States, the State of Missouri, and the Veiled Prophet Society, while the rest bore long pikes in their arms: members of the Veiled Prophet Society posing as the royal honor guard of the Kingdom of Khorassan. For all their stiff martial formality, though, their regalia would not have passed inspection in any self-respecting army. There were more than a few beer-bottle caps affixed to the medals on their tunics; some of the lancers wore spirit-gum false beards or monster makeup, while others sported sunglasses or surgical masks. A toy balloon bobbed from the top of one pike; a brassiere dangled from another. The crowd clapped in time with the orchestra as the toy soldiers paraded

down the runway until they reached the stage, where their
ranks split apart and took up positions against the backdrop
on either side of the thrones.

As the processional ended, Cale McLaughlin finally looked
my way. I looked back at him and smiled. He glanced away,
his eyes turning back toward the stage as the Captain of the
Guard approached a stand-up mike, unrolled a long papyrus
scroll, and addressed the audience in a great, pompous voice.

"We are *proud* to *present!* . . . the *return* of the mysterious
Veiled Prophet! . . . and his *royal court!*"

A pair of trumpeters came through the entrance and blew
their horns, then the curtains parted once again, this time to
reveal a tall figure.

The Veiled Prophet, accompanied by his Queen of Love
and Beauty, stepped out into the spotlight and began to walk
slowly down the runway amid thunderous applause. The edges
of his white silk robes trailed along the floor as the light
caught the fine blue-and-gold trim of his outfit and reflected
off his Mighty Thor viking helmet. The members of his court,
each of their faces as veiled as his own, followed him with
ponderous grace down the runway, their Turkish costumes
reflecting gaudy grandeur though not quite the same splendor.

Majesty, richness, spectacle: all this and more. The divine
right of kings, self-appointed and otherwise. Champagne
dreams and caviar fantasies, as someone used to puff, and
it was tempting to surrender to all this, even if for only
one night. Yet, even as I watched the Veiled Prophet and
his court walk through the ballroom, I couldn't help but
wonder what had happened to the sick child I had seen only
four nights ago at almost exactly this same hour, cradled in
his mother's arms as a bitter cold rain washed them in the
Muny.

Did he eat well tonight? Did he eat at all? Was his mother
in a holding pen beneath the stadium? And, knowing what I
did about the man behind the Veiled Prophet's mask, did a
poor child's fate matter to him?

Veiled Prophet, what do you prophesy?

As McLaughlin clapped his hands, his eyes kept wandering
toward me. At first it was as if he vaguely recognized me but

couldn't quite place my face, but then his expression changed to one of ill-concealed alarm as he suddenly remembered when and where we had met. I waited until that moment came, then I leaned toward him.

"Is this what rich people do for fun?" I whispered.

McLaughlin looked directly at me now. "Mr. Rosen," he said with stiff formality. "What an unexpected surprise."

"I'm sure it is," I replied. "If things had been different this morning, I'd be dead by now."

He didn't say anything. He tried to return his attention to the stage, where the Veiled Prophet and his queen were assuming their places on their thrones. I waited until sore hands all around us took a momentary respite, then I leaned toward him again.

"Y'know," I said, "I think Steve Estes is getting accustomed to his new role."

"I wouldn't know what you mean," he said.

"Oh, look at him." I nodded toward the stage. "Sitting on a throne, hiding his face behind a mask, having everyone bow and scrape to him." I shrugged. "Nice work if you can get it."

McLaughlin's expression turned to shock. He opened his mouth, about to ask the obvious question, when the Captain of the Guard stamped on leaden feet to the microphone again.

"His *mysterious majesty!* . . . the *Veiled Prophet!* . . . commands me to introduce his *maids of honor!* . . . of his court of *love!* . . . and *beauty!*"

Again the sounding of trumpets, again the parting of curtains. The orchestra struck up "Pomp and Circumstance" as the first of many beaming debutantes floated out onto the stage, escorted by her smiling yet mildly embarrassed father. Hands clapped in well-mannered enthusiasm as her name was announced and they began to walk down the runway toward the stage.

McLaughlin's curiosity finally got the better of him. He leaned toward me, his palms automatically slapping against one another. "How did you—"

"Find out who the Veiled Prophet is?" I grinned, not bothering to applaud. "Why, Ruby Fulcrum told me."

His face turned pale as his hands faltered. I waited a beat, savoring his discomfiture, before I went on. "Ruby's told me a lot of secrets," I said. "In fact, they're going to be in all the newspapers tomorrow."

McLaughlin's eyes shifted back toward the runway; he kept clapping as another debutante enjoyed her moment in the limelight. His wife glanced at him, then at me, her expression gradually changing from polite greeting to mild bewilderment as she noticed her husband's confusion. His face had become as rigid as the knees of the young women who strode down the runway, and with good reason. He was about to have his own coming-out party.

"Is there some reason why you want to see me?" he whispered, his voice almost a hiss.

"I need to ask you a few questions," I replied. "It'll take just a minute."

He nodded, then turned around to murmur something to his wife. She kept applauding as yet another deb was introduced, while he rose from his chair. I stood up and allowed him to brush past me, then I followed him down the aisle.

The ushers shut the doors behind us as we walked out into the vacant mezzanine. We could hear faint orchestra music and sporadic handclapping through the doors; except for a few hotel bartenders restocking their tables, though, we were alone.

McLaughlin strode to a window overlooking the street, then turned around and stared straight at me. "All right," he said as he shot back his shirtcuff to check his Rolex, "you've got a minute. What do you want?"

I pulled Joker out of my trouser pocket, switching it into Audio Record mode. "My name's Gerry Rosen. I'm a reporter for the *Big Muddy*—"

"I know who you are," he said. "What's the point?"

The point was that he was talking to a reporter now. I wanted to let him know that, even if he didn't get it. "I'm working on a story about the Tiptree Corporation's involvement in a conspiracy to overthrow the elected government of the United States—"

"Never heard of it," he said automatically.

"The United States or the conspiracy?"

He stared at me, standing a little straighter in his starched shirt and collar. *Now* he got the point.

"I don't know anything about any conspiracies," he replied.

"Then you deny that the purpose of the Sentinel program was to stop civil insurrections in the United States, even if that meant using the satellite against American citizens?"

McLaughlin's mouth dropped open. "What . . . ? How did you . . . ?" He stiffened again, regathering his wits. "I don't know what you're talking about."

"Then you claim you don't know that *Sentinel* was going to be fired at Cascadian armed forces?"

I heard the ballroom door open and close behind me. Someone started striding across the room toward us. McLaughlin's eyes darted in that direction, but I didn't look around. I already knew who it was.

"I'm not aware of anything of the sort," he said, his voice tight. "Furthermore, this all sounds like a . . . some sort of wild fantasy. Are you sure of your facts, Mr. Rosen?"

"I'm quite sure, Mr. McLaughlin," I said, "and they're not just my facts, either. All this comes from government documents that were released to my paper by Ruby Fulcrum."

"And who's going to believe a computer, Gerry?" Paul Huygens asked as he walked up behind me.

I wasn't surprised to see him here; his name had been on the guest list, so it would only figure that he would have trailed his boss when he left the ballroom. I turned around to look at him; he was as smug as usual, his thumbs cocked in the pockets of his white vest, smiling like the cat who had eaten the proverbial canary.

"That's a good question, Paul," I replied. "We'll have to see, once you start getting calls from all the other papers that now have those documents."

The smile faded from his face. "What other papers?" he asked, his hands dropping to his side. "Who are you talking about?"

I shrugged. "The *New York Times*, the *Washington Post*, *Newsday*, the *San Francisco Chronicle*, the *Minneapolis Star-Tribune*, the *Chicago Tribune*, the *Boston Globe-Herald*, and of course the *Post-Dispatch*. That's just for starters . . . I'm sure the wire services will pick up on the story. Plus the TV networks, *Time* and *Newsweek*, *Rolling Stone*, the *New Yorker*, and whoever else received copies of those documents today."

Huygens looked as if he had just glanced up from the sidewalk to see a ten-ton safe falling toward him. McLaughlin seemed to shudder; his face turned bright red, his mouth opening, then closing, then opening again. I cursed myself for not getting Jah into the ball with me; I would have framed the photo he could have taken of their expressions, and every time I began to curse fate for making me a journalist, I would only have to study this picture to remind myself why I wanted this crummy, thankless job.

McLaughlin recovered his voice. He took a step closer to me and thrust a finger in my face. "If they print a word of this," he said, his voice low and menacing, "then we'll sue your ass for libel."

I stared him in the eye. "No, you won't," I said calmly, slowly shaking my head, "because it's not my allegation. It comes straight from documents you signed yourself. I have the copies to prove it—"

"Accidents happen," Huygens murmured. "If you're not careful, bad things can happen to people who—"

"You're on record, Paul," I interrupted, glancing down at Joker. "Care to explicate a little further?"

Huygens shut up. "Besides," I went on, "I'm just the first reporter who's contacted you for your comments . . . and, if you didn't get the hint already, there's now a whole lot of other people who have the same material I have."

McLaughlin's eyebrows began to tremble. "The first reporter?" he asked as he glanced again at Huygens, who was beginning to look distinctly uncomfortable. "What do you mean by that?"

"What it means," I said, "is that I've got a head start on everyone else . . . but only a head start. It'll take the other guys a few days to play catch-up, but I'm sure you'll be hearing from them soon."

Huygens inched closer to McLaughlin and whispered something in his ear. I paid him no mind; I was busy checking the notes on my PT.

"Now then," I continued, "regarding the murders of Kim Po, Beryl Hinckley, and John Tiernan—"

"No comment," McLaughlin said.

"But Kim and Hinckley were Tiptree scientists directly involved with Project Sentinel. Surely you must have something to say about their untimely—"

"No comment!" he snapped. "Any further statements I have to make about this matter will be relayed through our public relations office." He stepped away from me, his face nearly as pale as his bow tie. "This interview is over, Mr. Rosen. Now, if you'll excuse me—"

"Yes, sir," I said. "Thank you for your time. Enjoy the rest of your evening."

McLaughlin hesitated. If looks could kill, I would have had a hole burned through my head by a laser beam . . . but he had tried that already and it hadn't worked.

He turned away from us and began to walk quickly toward the ballroom, his legs so stiff I thought I heard his knee joints cracking. I watched him until the usher opened the ballroom door for him. There was a moment of worn-out applause as the audience clapped for yet another debutante making her entry into high society, then the door closed behind him.

"Turn that thing off," Huygens said.

I looked back at him. There wasn't anything he was going to say to me, on or off the record, that would make much difference; Huygens had shut McLaughlin up before he could say anything self-incriminating, so I could hardly expect an eleventh-hour confession from Tiptree's spin-doctor-in-residence.

"Sure, Paul." I clicked Joker off and slipped it back into my pocket. "What do you want to know?"

"Who do you think you are, sport?" he said softly. "What did you think you were going to accomplish by this?"

I shrugged. "I'm a reporter," I replied. "You said so yourself. I just ask questions a lot of other people would like to ask, if they had the time or inclination."

"And you think this is going to get you anywhere?" Huygens shook his head. "You're so goddamn naive."

"Well," I said, "I'll put it to you this way. You've got the court of love and beauty . . . and I've got the court of public opinion. Who do you think is going to win?"

Huygens didn't reply. He thrust his hands in his pockets and stared back at me with sullen eyes. He knew the score, and so did I.

"See you in the funny pages," I said, then I turned around and began to walk toward the escalators.

The sidewalks were almost empty, the skyscrapers ablaze with light. Helicopters cruised overhead while cars cruised through the streets. Downtown was remarkably serene for a fine spring evening, but that was to be expected; ERA armored cars were still prowling the dark avenues, and dusk-to-dawn curfew was still in effect.

All things considered, it seemed as if nothing had changed.

I shrugged into my overcoat as I walked out of the Adam's Mark. The last few nights had been long and hard; maybe I could hang out here, drink a little bubbly, and find an overprivileged deb who wanted to slum with the po' people, but my heart wasn't into it. All I really wanted to do was head straight back to Soulard. Grab a couple of cheap beers at Clancy's. Wander over to Chevy Dick's garage and pick up the stray dog I had adopted last night. Climb the fire escape to my seedy apartment and try to figure out a good name for the mutt. Go to bed.

Out of impulse, though, I hung a left at the corner of Fourth and Chestnut. It was still early, and I could afford to take the long way home.

My footsteps took me two short blocks past the hotel and across the I-70 overpass to the Jefferson National Expansion Memorial. Here, in the center of this narrow stretch of carefully manicured landscape and cultivated trees, rose the two giant silver pillars, sweeping upward into the black sky to join together at the apex: the Gateway Arch, overlooking the broad expanse of the Mississippi River.

I paused for a few minutes, gazing upstream at the broken pillars of the Eads Bridge. If there was ever a time for the ghost of a boy to reappear, it was now . . .

I waited, but no voices came to me, as I knew they never would again. I turned away from the bridge and began to follow the river as it gurgled its way down toward the Gulf of Mexico. Rest in peace, Jamie. Your daddy loves you.

Strolling past the Arch, my hands thrust in my pockets, my shoulders raised against a cool, acrid breeze wafting off the polluted river, my mind cast itself to many other things. How much had changed?

Not much, really. At least not at first sight. My wife still loathed me. I was still stuck in a dead-end job with a pig for a boss. When I went home it would be to a foul-smelling, unkempt one-room flat. Thousands of people were still homeless in Forest Park, while the rich and pampered went to meaningless escapades. ERA was still in control of my hometown, at least for a little while longer, and even if no one dared to kick down my door, someone else would be harassed tonight.

Yet things *had* changed.

The human race was no longer the dominant form of life on this planet. By accident or by design, our role had been quietly superseded by another, perhaps greater intelligence.

It lived in our pocket computers and cash registers, telephones and modems, houses and stoplights, trains and cars and planes. Every city light around was a sign of its existence, and the faint point of light that moved across the stars every few hours was a testament to its potential power.

Yet, despite all appearances of omniscience, this entity was not God, or even godlike. It couldn't end our existence, because it was just as dependent upon us for survival as we were upon it for our own. Although it grew a little more with every passing nanosecond, each iteration of its ceaseless expansion, it needed our help to remain healthy . . . just as we needed it to continue our frail, confused, fucked-up lives.

We had created our own successor. Now we would have to wait and see whether it would recreate us . . . or if it would leave that task to ourselves.

For now, my life was my own, for better or for worse. I was alive, I was well, and I had a deadline to meet. Maybe it's not much, but what more can you ask for?

I turned up the collar of my overcoat and kept walking, making my long journey home through a city that no longer seemed quite so dark, a night no longer so deep.

THE SOUND
AND
THE FURY

at cake. Hush up that moaning. Aint you go-
help me find that quarter so I can go to the
onight."

were hitting little, across the pasture. I
ck along the fence to where the flag was.
d on the bright grass and the trees.

e on." Luster said. " We done looked there.
no more coming right now. Lets go down
nch and find that quarter before them
ls it."

d, flapping on the pasture. Then there
lanting and tilting on it. Luster threw.
ped on the bright grass and the trees. I
nce.

hat moaning." Luster said. " I cant
e if they aint coming, can I. If you
mmy aint going to have no birthday
ont hush, you know what I going
at that cake all up. Eat them can-
m thirty-three candles. Come on,
branch. I got to find my quar-
find one of they balls. Here.
er yonder. See." He came to
his arm. " See them. They
o more. Come on."

nce and came to the garden
ws were. My shadow was
he fence. We came to the
ugh it.

THE SOUND
AND
THE FURY

WILLIAM
FAULKNER

VINTAGE BOOKS

a division of Random House
New York

VINTAGE BOOKS
are published by Alfred A. Knopf, Inc.
and Random House, Inc.

This Appendix for *The Sound and the Fury* was written
for *The Portable Faulkner,* edited by Malcolm Cowley,
and is used here by permission of The Viking Press, Inc.

Publisher's Note

The text of this edition of *The Sound and the Fury* is reproduced
photographically from a copy of the first printing. Publication date
was October 7, 1929. The Appendix was first included in the
Modern Library edition of 1946.

Manufactured in the United States of America

T HROUGH THE FEN
the curling flower spaces, I co
They were coming toward whe
went along the fence. Luster
grass by the flower tree. They
they were hitting. Then t
they went to the table, a
Then they went on, a
Luster came away fro
along the fence and t
I looked through th
in the grass.

"Here, caddie
the pasture. I
going away.

"Listen a
something,
way. Afte

"Wait a minute." Luster said. "You snagged on that nail again. Cant you never crawl through here without snagging on that nail."

Caddy uncaught me and we crawled through. Uncle Maury said to not let anybody see us, so we better stoop over, Caddy said. Stoop over, Benjy. Like this, see. We stooped over and crossed the garden, where the flowers rasped and rattled against us. The ground was hard. We climbed the fence, where the pigs were grunting and snuffing. I expect they're sorry because one of them got killed today, Caddy said. The ground was hard, churned and knotted.

Keep your hands in your pockets, Caddy said. Or they'll get froze. You don't want your hands froze on Christmas, do you.

"It's too cold out there." Versh said. "You dont want to go out doors."

"What is it now." Mother said.

"He want to go out doors." Versh said.

"Let him go." Uncle Maury said.

"It's too cold." Mother said. "He'd better stay in. Benjamin. Stop that, now."

"It wont hurt him." Uncle Maury said.

"You, Benjamin." Mother said. "If you dont be good, you'll have to go to the kitchen."

"Mammy say keep him out the kitchen today." Versh said. "She say she got all that cooking to get done."

3

"Let him go, Caroline." Uncle Maury said. "You'll worry yourself sick over him."

"I know it." Mother said. "It's a judgment on me. I sometimes wonder"

"I know, I know." Uncle Maury said. "You must keep your strength up. I'll make you a toddy."

"It just upsets me that much more." Mother said. "Dont you know it does."

"You'll feel better." Uncle Maury said. "Wrap him up good, boy, and take him out for a while."

Uncle Maury went away. Versh went away.

"Please hush." Mother said. "We're trying to get you out as fast as we can. I dont want you to get sick."

Versh put my overshoes and overcoat on and we took my cap and went out. Uncle Maury was putting the bottle away in the sideboard in the dining-room.

"Keep him out about half an hour, boy." Uncle Maury said. "Keep him in the yard, now."

"Yes, sir." Versh said. "We dont never let him get off the place."

We went out doors. The sun was cold and bright.

"Where you heading for." Versh said. "You dont think you going to town, does you." We went through the rattling leaves. The gate was cold. "You better keep them hands in your pockets." Versh said, "You get them froze onto that gate, then what you do. Whyn't you wait for them in the house." He put my hands into my pockets. I could hear him rattling in the leaves. I could smell the cold. The gate was cold.

"Here some hickeynuts. Whooey. Git up that tree. Look here at this squirl, Benjy."

I couldn't feel the gate at all, but I could smell the bright cold.

"You better put them hands back in your pockets."

Caddy was walking. Then she was running, her book-satchel swinging and jouncing behind her.

"Hello, Benjy." Caddy said. She opened the gate and came in and stooped down. Caddy smelled like leaves. "Did you come to meet me." she said. "Did you come to meet Caddy. What did you let him get his hands so cold for, Versh."

"I told him to keep them in his pockets." Versh said. "Holding onto that ahun gate."

"Did you come to meet Caddy." she said, rubbing my hands. "What is it. What are you trying to tell Caddy." Caddy smelled like trees and like when she says we were asleep.

What are you moaning about, Luster said. You can watch them again when we get to the branch. Here. Here's you a jimson weed. He gave me the flower. We went through the fence, into the lot.

"What is it." Caddy said. "What are you trying to tell Caddy. Did they send him out, Versh."

5

"Couldn't keep him in." Versh said. "He kept on until they let him go and he come right straight down here, looking through the gate."

"What is it." Caddy said. "Did you think it would be Christmas when I came home from school. Is that what you thought. Christmas is the day after to-morrow. Santy Claus, Benjy. Santy Claus. Come on, let's run to the house and get warm." She took my hand and we ran through the bright rustling leaves. We ran up the steps and out of the bright cold, into the dark cold. Uncle Maury was putting the bottle back in the sideboard. He called Caddy. Caddy said,

"Take him in to the fire, Versh. Go with Versh." she said. "I'll come in a minute."

We went to the fire. Mother said,

"Is he cold, Versh."

"Nome." Versh said.

"Take his overcoat and overshoes off." Mother said. "How many times do I have to tell you not to bring him into the house with his over-shoes on."

"Yessum." Versh said. "Hold still, now." He took my overshoes off and unbuttoned my coat. Caddy said,

"Wait, Versh. Cant he go out again, Mother. I want him to go with me."

"You'd better leave him here." Uncle Maury said. "He's been out enough today."

6

" I think you'd both better stay in." Mother said. " It's getting colder, Dilsey says."

"Oh, Mother." Caddy said.

" Nonsense." Uncle Maury said. " She's been in school all day. She needs the fresh air. Run along, Candace."

" Let him go, Mother." Caddy said. " Please. You know he'll cry."

" Then why did you mention it before him." Mother said. " Why did you come in here. To give him some excuse to worry me again. You've been out enough today. I think you'd better sit down here and play with him."

"Let them go, Caroline." Uncle Maury said. " A little cold wont hurt them. Remember, you've got to keep your strength up."

" I know." Mother said. " Nobody knows how I dread Christmas. Nobody knows. I am not one of those women who can stand things. I wish for Jason's and the children's sakes I was stronger."

"You must do the best you can and not let them worry you." Uncle Maury said. " Run along, you two. But dont stay out long, now. Your mother will worry."

" Yes, sir." Caddy said. " Come on, Benjy. We're going out doors again." She buttoned my coat and we went toward the door.

" Are you going to take that baby out without his

overshoes." Mother said. " Do you want to make him sick, with the house full of company."

" I forgot." Caddy said. "I thought he had them on."

We went back. "You must think." Mother said. *Hold still now* Versh said. He put my overshoes on. " Someday I'll be gone, and you'll have to think for him." *Now stomp* Versh said. " Come here and kiss Mother, Benjamin."

Caddy took me to Mother's chair and Mother took my face in her hands and then she held me against her.

" My poor baby." she said. She let me go. " You and Versh take good care of him, honey."

"Yessum." Caddy said. We went out. Caddy said,

" You needn't go, Versh. I'll keep him for a while."

" All right." Versh said. " I aint going out in that cold for no fun." He went on and we stopped in the hall and Caddy knelt and put her arms around me and her cold bright face against mine. She smelled like trees.

" You're not a poor baby. Are you. You've got your Caddy. Haven't you got your Caddy."

Cant you shut up that moaning and slobbering, Luster said. Aint you shamed of yourself, making all this racket. We passed the carriage house, where the carriage was. It had a new wheel.

"Git in, now, and set still until your maw come." Dilsey said. She shoved me into the carriage. T. P. held the reins. "'Clare I don't see how come Jason wont get a new surrey." Dilsey said. "This thing going to fall to pieces under you all some day. Look at them wheels."

Mother came out, pulling her veil down. She had some flowers.

"Where's Roskus." she said.

"Roskus cant lift his arms, today." Dilsey said. "T. P. can drive all right."

"I'm afraid to." Mother said. "It seems to me you all could furnish me with a driver for the carriage once a week. It's little enough I ask, Lord knows."

"You know just as well as me that Roskus got the rheumatism too bad to do more than he have to, Miss Cahline." Dilsey said. "You come on and get in, now. T. P. can drive you just as good as Roskus."

"I'm afraid to." Mother said. "With the baby."

Dilsey went up the steps. "You calling that thing a baby," she said. She took Mother's arm. "A man big as T. P. Come on, now, if you going."

"I'm afraid to." Mother said. They came down the steps and Dilsey helped Mother in. "Perhaps it'll be the best thing, for all of us." Mother said.

"Aint you shamed, talking that way." Dilsey

said. "Don't you know it'll take more than a eighteen year old nigger to make Queenie run away. She older than him and Benjy put together. And dont you start no projecking with Queenie, you hear me, T. P. If you dont drive to suit Miss Cahline, I going to put Roskus on you. He aint too tied up to do that."

"Yessum." T. P. said.

"I just know something will happen." Mother said. "Stop, Benjamin."

"Give him a flower to hold." Dilsey said, "That what he wanting." She reached her hand in.

"No, no." Mother said. "You'll have them all scattered."

"You hold them." Dilsey said. "I'll get him one out." She gave me a flower and her hand went away.

"Go on now, 'fore Quentin see you and have to go too." Dilsey said.

"Where is she." Mother said.

"She down to the house playing with Luster." Dilsey said. "Go on, T. P. Drive that surrey like Roskus told you, now."

"Yessum." T. P. said. "Hum up, Queenie."

"Quentin." Mother said. "Don't let "

"Course I is." Dilsey said.

The carriage jolted and crunched on the drive. "I'm afraid to go and leave Quentin." Mother said. "I'd better not go. T. P." We went through the

gate, where it didnt jolt anymore. T. P. hit Queenie
with the whip.

"You, T. P." Mother said.

"Got to get her going." T. P. said. "Keep her
wake up till we get back to the barn."

"Turn around." Mother said. "I'm afraid to go
and leave Quentin."

"Can't turn here." T. P. said. Then it was
broader.

"Cant you turn here." Mother said.

"All right." T. P. said. We began to turn.

"You, T. P." Mother said, clutching me.

"I got to turn around somehow." T. P. said.
"Whoa, Queenie." We stopped.

"You'll turn us over." Mother said.

"What you want to do, then." T. P. said.

"I'm afraid for you to try to turn around."
Mother said.

"Get up, Queenie." T. P. said. We went on.

"I just know Dilsey will let something happen to
Quentin while I'm gone." Mother said. "We must
hurry back."

"Hum up, there." T. P. said. He hit Queenie
with the whip.

"You, T. P." Mother said, clutching me. I could
hear Queenie's feet and the bright shapes went
smooth and steady on both sides, the shadows of
them flowing across Queenie's back. They went on
like the bright tops of wheels. Then those on one

side stopped at the tall white post where the soldier was. But on the other side they went on smooth and steady, but a little slower.

"What do you want." Jason said. He had his hands in his pockets and a pencil behind his ear.

"We're going to the cemetery." Mother said.

"All right." Jason said. "I dont aim to stop you, do I. Was that all you wanted with me, just to tell me that."

"I know you wont come." Mother said. "I'd feel safer if you would."

"Safe from what." Jason said. "Father and Quentin cant hurt you."

Mother put her handkerchief under her veil. "Stop it, Mother." Jason said. "Do you want to get that damn loony to bawling in the middle of the square. Drive on, T. P."

"Hum up, Queenie." T. P. said.

"It's a judgment on me." Mother said. "But I'll be gone too, soon."

"Here." Jason said.

"Whoa." T. P. said. Jason said,

"Uncle Maury's drawing on you for fifty. What do you want to do about it."

"Why ask me." Mother said. "I dont have any say so. I try not to worry you and Dilsey. I'll be gone soon, and then you "

"Go on, T. P." Jason said.

"Hum up, Queenie." T. P. said. The shapes

flowed on. The ones on the other side began again, bright and fast and smooth, like when Caddy says we are going to sleep.

Cry baby, Luster said. Aint you shamed. We went through the barn. The stalls were all open. You aint got no spotted pony to ride now, Luster said. The floor was dry and dusty. The roof was falling. The slanting holes were full of spinning yellow. What do you want to go that way for. You want to get your head knocked off with one of them balls.

"Keep your hands in your pockets." Caddy said, "Or they'll be froze. You dont want your hands froze on Christmas, do you."

We went around the barn. The big cow and the little one were standing in the door, and we could hear Prince and Queenie and Fancy stomping inside the barn. "If it wasn't so cold, we'd ride Fancy." Caddy said, "But it's too cold to hold on today." Then we could see the branch, where the smoke was blowing. "That's where they are killing the pig." Caddy said. "We can come back by there and see them." We went down the hill.

"You want to carry the letter." Caddy said. "You can carry it." She took the letter out of her pocket and put it in mine. "It's a Christmas present." Caddy said. "Uncle Maury is going to surprise Mrs Patterson with it. We got to give it to her without letting anybody see it. Keep your

13

hands in your pockets good, now." We came to the branch.

"It's froze." Caddy said, "Look." She broke the top of the water and held a piece of it against my face. "Ice. That means how cold it is." She helped me across and we went up the hill. "We cant even tell Mother and Father. You know what I think it is. I think it's a surprise for Mother and Father and Mr Patterson both, because Mr Patterson sent you some candy. Do you remember when Mr Patterson sent you some candy last summer."

There was a fence. The vine was dry, and the wind rattled in it.

"Only I dont see why Uncle Maury didn't send Versh." Caddy said. "Versh wont tell." Mrs Patterson was looking out the window. "You wait here." Caddy said. "Wait right here, now. I'll be back in a minute. Give me the letter." She took the letter out of my pocket. "Keep your hands in your pockets." She climbed the fence with the letter in her hand and went through the brown, rattling flowers. Mrs Patterson came to the door and opened it and stood there.

Mr Patterson was chopping in the green flowers. He stopped chopping and looked at me. Mrs Patterson came across the garden, running. When I saw her eyes I began to cry. You idiot, Mrs Patterson said, I told him never to send you alone again. Give it to me. Quick. Mr Patterson came fast, with the hoe. Mrs Patterson leaned across the fence, reaching her hand. She was trying to climb the fence. Give it to me, she said, Give it to me. Mr Patterson climbed the fence. He took the letter. Mrs Patterson's dress was caught on the fence. I saw her eyes again and I ran down the hill.

"They aint nothing over yonder but houses." Luster said. "We going down to the branch."

They were washing down at the branch. One of them was singing. I could smell the clothes flapping, and the smoke blowing across the branch.

"You stay down here." Luster said. "You aint got no business up yonder. Them folks hit you, sho."

"What he want to do."

"He dont know what he want to do." Luster said. "He think he want to go up yonder where they knocking that ball. You sit down here and play with your jimson weed. Look at them chillen playing in the branch, if you got to look at something. How come you cant behave yourself like folks." I sat down on the bank, where they were washing, and the smoke blowing blue.

"Is you all seen anything of a quarter down here." Luster said.

"What quarter."

"The one I had here this morning." Luster said. "I lost it somewhere. It fell through this here hole

15

in my pocket. If I dont find it I cant go to the show
tonight."

"Where'd you get a quarter, boy. Find it in white
folks' pocket while they aint looking."

"Got it at the getting place." Luster said. "Plenty
more where that one come from. Only I got to find
that one. Is you all found it yet."

"I aint studying no quarter. I got my own business to tend to."

"Come on here." Luster said. "Help me look
for it."

"He wouldn't know a quarter if he was to see it,
would he."

"He can help look just the same." Luster said.
"You all going to the show tonight."

"Dont talk to me about no show. Time I get done
over this here tub I be too tired to lift my hand to
do nothing."

"I bet you be there." Luster said. "I bet you
was there last night. I bet you all be right there when
that tent open."

"Be enough niggers there without me. Was last
night."

"Nigger's money good as white folks, I reckon."

"White folks gives nigger money because know
first white man comes along with a band going to
get it all back, so nigger can go to work for some
more."

"Aint nobody going make you go to that show."

16

" Aint yet. Aint thought of it, I reckon."

" What you got against white folks."

" Aint got nothing against them. I goes my way and lets white folks go theirs. I aint studying that show."

" Got a man in it can play a tune on a saw. Play it like a banjo."

" You go last night." Luster said. " I going to-night. If I can find where I lost that quarter."

" You going take him with you, I reckon."

" Me." Luster said. " You reckon I be found anywhere with him, time he start bellering."

" What does you do when he start bellering."

" I whips him." Luster said. He sat down and rolled up his overalls. They played in the branch.

" You all found any balls yet." Luster said.

" Aint you talking biggity. I bet you better not let your grandmammy hear you talking like that."

Luster got into the branch, where they were playing. He hunted in the water, along the bank.

" I had it when we was down here this morning." Luster said.

" Where 'bouts you lose it."

" Right out this here hole in my pocket." Luster said. They hunted in the branch. Then they all stood up quick and stopped, then they splashed and fought in the branch. Luster got it and they squatted in the water, looking up the hill through the bushes.

" Where is they." Luster said.

"Aint in sight yet."

Luster put it in his pocket. They came down the hill.

"Did a ball come down here."

"It ought to be in the water. Didn't any of you boys see it or hear it."

"Aint heard nothing come down here." Luster said. "Heard something hit that tree up yonder. Dont know which way it went."

They looked in the branch.

"Hell. Look along the branch. It came down here. I saw it."

They looked along the branch. Then they went back up the hill.

"Have you got that ball." the boy said.

"What I want with it." Luster said. "I aint seen no ball."

The boy got in the water. He went on. He turned and looked at Luster again. He went on down the branch.

The man said "Caddie" up the hill. The boy got out of the water and went up the hill.

"Now, just listen at you." Luster said. "Hush up."

"What he moaning about now."

"Lawd knows." Luster said. "He just starts like that. He been at it all morning. Cause it his birthday, I reckon."

"How old he."

"He thirty-three." Luster said. "Thirty-three this morning."

"You mean, he been three years old thirty years."

"I going by what mammy say." Luster said. "I dont know. We going to have thirty-three candles on a cake, anyway. Little cake. Wont hardly hold them. Hush up. Come on back here." He came and caught my arm. "You old loony." he said. "You want me to whip you."

"I bet you will."

"I is done it. Hush, now." Luster said. "Aint I told you you cant go up there. They'll knock your head clean off with one of them balls. Come on, here." He pulled me back. "Sit down." I sat down and he took off my shoes and rolled up my trousers. "Now, git in that water and play and see can you stop that slobbering and moaning."

I hushed and got in the water *and Roskus came and said to come to supper and Caddy said,*

It's not supper time yet. I'm not going.

She was wet. We were playing in the branch and Caddy squatted down and got her dress wet and Versh said,

"Your mommer going to whip you for getting your dress wet."

"She's not going to do any such thing." Caddy said.

"How do you know." Quentin said.

"That's all right how I know." Caddy said. "How do you know."

"She said she was." Quentin said. "Besides, I'm older than you."

"I'm seven years old." Caddy said, "I guess I know."

"I'm older than that." Quentin said. "I go to school. Dont I, Versh."

"I'm going to school next year." Caddy said, "When it comes. Aint I, Versh."

"You know she whip you when you get your dress wet." Versh said.

"It's not wet." Caddy said. She stood up in the water and looked at her dress. "I'll take it off." she said. "Then it'll dry."

"I bet you wont." Quentin said.

"I bet I will." Caddy said.

"I bet you better not." Quentin said.

Caddy came to Versh and me and turned her back.

"Unbutton it, Versh." she said.

"Dont you do it, Versh." Quentin said.

"Taint none of my dress." Versh said.

"You unbutton it, Versh." Caddy said, "Or I'll tell Dilsey what you did yesterday." So Versh unbuttoned it.

"You just take your dress off." Quentin said. Caddy took her dress off and threw it on the bank. Then she didn't have on anything but her bodice and drawers, and Quentin slapped her and she slipped and fell down in the water. When she got up she began to splash water on Quentin, and Quentin splashed water on Caddy. Some of it splashed on Versh and me and Versh picked me up and put me on the bank. He said he was going to tell on Caddy and Quentin, and then Quentin and Caddy began to splash water at Versh. He got behind a bush.

"I'm going to tell mammy on you all." Versh said.

Quentin climbed up the bank and tried to catch Versh, but Versh ran away and Quentin couldn't. When Quentin came back Versh stopped and hollered that he was going to tell. Caddy told him that if he wouldn't tell, they'd let him come back. So Versh said he wouldn't, and they let him.

"Now I guess you're satisfied." Quentin said, "We'll both get whipped now."

"I dont care." Caddy said. "I'll run away."

"Yes you will." Quentin said.

"I'll run away and never come back." Caddy said. I began to cry. Caddy turned around and said "Hush." So I hushed. Then they played in the branch. Jason was playing too. He was by himself further down the branch. Versh came around the bush and lifted me down into the water again. Caddy was all wet and muddy behind, and I started to cry and she came and squatted in the water.

"Hush now." she said. "I'm not going to run

away." So I hushed. Caddy smelled like trees in the rain.

What is the matter with you, Luster said. Cant you get done with that moaning and play in the branch like folks.

Whyn't you take him on home. Didn't they told you not to take him off the place.

He still think they own this pasture, Luster said. Cant nobody see down here from the house, no-ways.

We can. And folks dont like to look at a loony. Taint no luck in it.

Roskus came and said to come to supper and Caddy said it wasn't supper time yet.

"Yes tis." Roskus said. "Dilsey say for you all to come on to the house. Bring them on, Versh." He went up the hill, where the cow was lowing.

"Maybe we'll be dry by the time we get to the house." Quentin said.

"It was all your fault." Caddy said. "I hope we do get whipped." She put her dress on and Versh buttoned it.

"They wont know you got wet." Versh said. "It dont show on you. Less me and Jason tells."

"Are you going to tell, Jason." Caddy said.

"Tell on who." Jason said.

"He wont tell." Quentin said. "Will you, Jason."

"I bet he does tell." Caddy said. "He'll tell Damuddy."

"He cant tell her." Quentin said. "She's sick. If we walk slow it'll be too dark for them to see."

"I dont care whether they see or not." Caddy said. "I'm going to tell, myself. You carry him up the hill, Versh."

"Jason wont tell." Quentin said. "You remember that bow and arrow I made you, Jason."

"It's broke now." Jason said.

"Let him tell." Caddy said. "I dont give a cuss. Carry Maury up the hill, Versh." Versh squatted and I got on his back.

See you all at the show tonight, Luster said. Come on, here. We got to find that quarter.

"If we go slow, it'll be dark when we get there." Quentin said.

"I'm not going slow." Caddy said. We went up the hill, but Quentin didn't come. He was down at the branch when we got to where we could smell the pigs. They were grunting and snuffing in the trough in the corner. Jason came behind us, with his hands in his pockets. Roskus was milking the cow in the barn door.

The cows came jumping out of the barn.

"Go on." T. P. said. "Holler again. I going to holler myself. Whooey." Quentin kicked T. P. again. He kicked T. P. into the trough where the pigs ate and T. P. lay there. "Hot dog." T. P. said, "Didn't he get me then. You see that white man kick me that time. Whooey."

I wasn't crying, but I couldn't stop. I wasn't crying, but the ground wasn't still, and then I was crying. The ground kept sloping up and the cows ran up the hill. T. P. tried to get up. He fell down again and the cows ran down the hill. Quentin held my arm and we went toward the barn. Then the barn wasn't there and we had to wait until it came back. I didn't see it come back. It came behind us and Quentin set me down in the trough where the cows ate. I held on to it. It was going away too, and I held to it. The cows ran down the hill again, across the door. I couldn't stop. Quentin and T. P. came up the hill, fighting. T. P. was falling down the hill and Quentin dragged him up the hill. Quentin hit T. P. I couldn't stop.

"Stand up." Quentin said, "You stay right here. Dont you go away until I get back."

"Me and Benjy going back to the wedding." T. P. said. "Whooey."

Quentin hit T. P. again. Then he began to thump T. P. against the wall. T. P. was laughing. Every time Quentin thumped him against the wall he tried to say Whooey, but he couldn't say it for laughing. I quit crying, but I couldn't stop. T. P. fell on me and the barn door went away. It went down the hill and T. P. was fighting by himself and he fell down again. He was still laughing, and I couldn't stop, and I tried to get up and I fell down, and I couldn't stop. Versh said,

"You sho done it now. I'll declare if you aint. Shut up that yelling."

T. P. was still laughing. He flopped on the door and laughed. "Whooey." he said, " Me and Benjy going back to the wedding. Sassprilluh." T. P. said.

"Hush." Versh said. "Where you get it."

"Out the cellar." T. P. said. "Whooey."

"Hush up." Versh said, "Where'bouts in the cellar."

"Anywhere." T. P. said. He laughed some more. "Moren a hundred bottles left. Moren a million. Look out, nigger, I going to holler."

Quentin said, "Lift him up."

Versh lifted me up.

"Drink this, Benjy." Quentin said. The glass was hot. "Hush, now." Quentin said. "Drink it."

"Sassprilluh." T. P. said. "Lemme drink it, Mr Quentin."

"You shut your mouth." Versh said, " Mr Quentin wear you out."

"Hold him, Versh." Quentin said.

They held me. It was hot on my chin and on my shirt. "Drink." Quentin said. They held my head. It was hot inside me, and I began again. I was crying now, and something was happening inside me and I cried more, and they held me until it stopped happening. Then I hushed. It was still going around, and then the shapes began. "Open the crib, Versh." They were going slow. "Spread those empty sacks

25

on the floor." They were going faster, almost fast enough. "Now. Pick up his feet." They went on, smooth and bright. I could hear T. P. laughing. I went on with them, up the bright hill.

At the top of the hill Versh put me down. " Come on here, Quentin." he called, looking back down the hill. Quentin was still standing there by the branch. He was chunking into the shadows where the branch was.

"Let the old skizzard stay there." Caddy said. She took my hand and we went on past the barn and through the gate. There was a frog on the brick walk, squatting in the middle of it. Caddy stepped over it and pulled me on.

"Come on, Maury." she said. It still squatted there until Jason poked at it with his toe.

" He'll make a wart on you." Versh said. The frog hopped away.

" Come on, Maury." Caddy said.

" They got company tonight." Versh said.

" How do you know." Caddy said.

" With all them lights on." Versh said, " Light in every window."

" I reckon we can turn all the lights on without company, if we want to." Caddy said.

" I bet it's company." Versh said. " You all better go in the back and slip upstairs."

" I dont care." Caddy said. " I'll walk right in the parlor where they are."

26

" I bet your pappy whip you if you do." Versh
said.

" I dont care." Caddy said. " I'll walk right in the
parlor. I'll walk right in the dining room and eat
supper."

" Where you sit." Versh said.

" I'd sit in Damuddy's chair." Caddy said. " She
eats in bed."

" I'm hungry." Jason said. He passed us and ran
on up the walk. He had his hands in his pockets and
he fell down. Versh went and picked him up.

" If you keep them hands out your pockets, you
could stay on your feet." Versh said. " You cant
never get them out in time to catch yourself, fat as
you is."

Father was standing by the kitchen steps.

" Where's Quentin." he said.

" He coming up the walk." Versh said. Quentin
was coming slow. His shirt was a white blur.

" Oh." Father said. Light fell down the steps, on
him.

" Caddy and Quentin threw water on each other."
Jason said.

We waited.

" They did." Father said. Quentin came, and
Father said, " You can eat supper in the kitchen tonight." He stopped and took me up, and the light
came tumbling down the steps on me too, and I could
look down at Caddy and Jason and Quentin and

Versh. Father turned toward the steps. " You must be quiet, though." he said.

" Why must we be quiet, Father." Caddy said. " Have we got company."

" Yes." Father said.

" I told you they was company." Versh said.

" You did not." Caddy said, " I was the one that said there was. I said I would "

" Hush." Father said. They hushed and Father opened the door and we crossed the back porch and went in to the kitchen. Dilsey was there, and Father put me in the chair and closed the apron down and pushed it to the table, where supper was. It was steaming up.

" You mind Dilsey, now." Father said. " Dont let them make any more noise than they can help, Dilsey."

" Yes, sir." Dilsey said. Father went away.

" Remember to mind Dilsey, now." he said behind us. I leaned my face over where the supper was. It steamed up on my face.

" Let them mind me tonight, Father." Caddy said.

" I wont." Jason said. " I'm going to mind Dilsey."

" You'll have to, if Father says so." Caddy said. " Let them mind me, Father."

" I wont." Jason said, " I wont mind you."

" Hush." Father said. " You all mind Caddy,

then. When they are done, bring them up the back stairs, Dilsey."

"Yes, sir." Dilsey said.

"There." Caddy said, "Now I guess you'll mind me."

"You all hush, now." Dilsey said. "You got to be quiet tonight."

"Why do we have to be quiet tonight." Caddy whispered.

"Never you mind." Dilsey said, "You'll know in the Lawd's own time." She brought my bowl. The steam from it came and tickled my face. "Come here, Versh." Dilsey said.

"When is the Lawd's own time, Dilsey." Caddy said.

"It's Sunday." Quentin said. "Dont you know anything."

"Shhhhhh." Dilsey said. "Didn't Mr Jason say for you all to be quiet. Eat your supper, now. Here, Versh. Git his spoon." Versh's hand came with the spoon, into the bowl. The spoon came up to my mouth. The steam tickled into my mouth. Then we quit eating and we looked at each other and we were quiet, and then we heard it again and I began to cry.

"What was that." Caddy said. She put her hand on my hand.

"That was Mother." Quentin said. The spoon came up and I ate, then I cried again.

"Hush." Caddy said. But I didn't hush and she came and put her arms around me. Dilsey went and closed both the doors and then we couldn't hear it.

"Hush, now." Caddy said. I hushed and ate. Quentin wasn't eating, but Jason was.

"That was Mother." Quentin said. He got up.

"You set right down." Dilsey said. "They got company in there, and you in them muddy clothes. You set down too, Caddy, and get done eating."

"She was crying." Quentin said.

"It was somebody singing." Caddy said. "Wasn't it, Dilsey."

"You all eat your supper, now, like Mr Jason said." Dilsey said. "You'll know in the Lawd's own time." Caddy went back to her chair.

"I told you it was a party." she said.

Versh said, "He done et all that."

"Bring his bowl here." Dilsey said. The bowl went away.

"Dilsey." Caddy said, "Quentin's not eating his supper. Hasn't he got to mind me."

"Eat your supper, Quentin." Dilsey said, "You all got to get done and get out of my kitchen."

"I dont want any more supper." Quentin said.

"You've got to eat if I say you have." Caddy said. "Hasn't he, Dilsey."

The bowl steamed up to my face, and Versh's hand dipped the spoon in it and the steam tickled into my mouth.

30

"I dont want any more." Quentin said. "How can they have a party when Damuddy's sick."

"They'll have it down stairs." Caddy said. "She can come to the landing and see it. That's what I'm going to do when I get my nightie on."

"Mother was crying." Quentin said. "Wasn't she crying, Dilsey."

"Dont you come pestering at me, boy." Dilsey said. "I got to get supper for all them folks soon as you all get done eating."

After a while even Jason was through eating, and he began to cry.

"Now you got to tune up." Dilsey said.

"He does it every night since Damuddy was sick and he cant sleep with her." Caddy said. "Cry baby."

"I'm going to tell on you." Jason said.

He was crying. "You've already told." Caddy said. "There's not anything else you can tell, now."

"You all needs to go to bed." Dilsey said. She came and lifted me down and wiped my face and hands with a warm cloth. "Versh, can you get them up the back stairs quiet. You, Jason, shut up that crying."

"It's too early to go to bed now." Caddy said. "We dont ever have to go to bed this early."

"You is tonight." Dilsey said. "Your pa say for you to come right on up stairs when you et supper. You heard him."

31

"He said to mind me." Caddy said.

"I'm not going to mind you." Jason said.

"You have to." Caddy said. "Come on, now. You have to do like I say."

"Make them be quiet, Versh." Dilsey said. "You all going to be quiet, aint you."

"What do we have to be so quiet for, tonight." Caddy said.

"Your mommer aint feeling well." Dilsey said. "You all go on with Versh, now."

"I told you Mother was crying." Quentin said. Versh took me up and opened the door onto the back porch. We went out and Versh closed the door black. I could smell Versh and feel him. "You all be quiet, now. We're not going up stairs yet. Mr Jason said for you to come right up stairs. He said to mind me. I'm not going to mind you. But he said for all of us to. Didn't he, Quentin." I could feel Versh's head. I could hear us. "Didn't he, Versh. Yes, that's right. Then I say for us to go out doors a while. Come on." Versh opened the door and we went out.

We went down the steps.

"I expect we'd better go down to Versh's house, so we'll be quiet." Caddy said. Versh put me down and Caddy took my hand and we went down the brick walk.

"Come on." Caddy said, "That frog's gone. He's hopped way over to the garden, by now.

Maybe we'll see another one." Roskus came with the milk buckets. He went on. Quentin wasn't coming with us. He was sitting on the kitchen steps. We went down to Versh's house. I liked to smell Versh's house. *There was a fire in it and T. P. squatting in his shirt tail in front of it, chunking it into a blaze.*

Then I got up and T. P. dressed me and we went to the kitchen and ate. Dilsey was singing and I began to cry and she stopped.

"Keep him away from the house, now." Dilsey said.

"We cant go that way." T. P. said.

We played in the branch.

"We cant go around yonder." T. P. said. "Dont you know mammy say we cant."

Dilsey was singing in the kitchen and I began to cry.

"Hush." T. P. said. "Come on. Lets go down to the barn.

Roskus was milking at the barn. He was milking with one hand, and groaning. Some birds sat on the barn door and watched him. One of them came down and ate with the cows. I watched Roskus milk while T. P. was feeding Queenie and Prince. The calf was in the pig pen. It nuzzled at the wire, bawling.

"T. P." Roskus said. T. P. said Sir, in the barn. Fancy held her head over the door, because T. P.

hadn't fed her yet. "Git done there." Roskus said. "You got to do this milking. I cant use my right hand no more."

T. P. came and milked.

"Whyn't you get the doctor." T. P. said.

"Doctor cant do no good." Roskus said. "Not on this place."

"What wrong with this place." T. P. said.

"Taint no luck on this place." Roskus said. "Turn that calf in if you done."

Taint no luck on this place, Roskus said. The fire rose and fell behind him and Versh, sliding on his and Versh's face. Dilsey finished putting me to bed. The bed smelled like T. P. I liked it.

"What you know about it." Dilsey said. "What trance you been in."

"Dont need no trance." Roskus said. "Aint the sign of it laying right there on that bed. Aint the sign of it been here for folks to see fifteen years now."

"Spose it is." Dilsey said. "It aint hurt none of you and yourn, is it. Versh working and Frony married off your hands and T. P. getting big enough to take your place when rheumatism finish getting you."

"They been two, now." Roskus said. "Going to be one more. I seen the sign, and you is too."

"I heard a squinch owl that night." T. P. said. "Dan wouldn't come and get his supper, neither.

Wouldn't come no closer than the barn. Begun howling right after dark. Versh heard him."

"Going to be more than one more." Dilsey said. "Show me the man what aint going to die, bless Jesus."

"Dying aint all." Roskus said.

"I knows what you thinking." Dilsey said. "And they aint going to be no luck in saying that name, lessen you going to set up with him while he cries."

"They aint no luck on this place." Roskus said. "I seen it at first but when they changed his name I knowed it."

"Hush your mouth." Dilsey said. She pulled the covers up. It smelled like T. P. "You all shut up now, till he get to sleep."

"I seen the sign." Roskus said.

"Sign T. P. got to do all your work for you." Dilsey said. *Take him and Quentin down to the house and let them play with Luster, where Frony can watch them, T. P., and go and help your pa.*

We finished eating. T. P. took Quentin up and we went down to T. P.'s house. Luster was playing in the dirt. T. P. put Quentin down and she played in the dirt too. Luster had some spools and he and Quentin fought and Quentin had the spools. Luster cried and Frony came and gave Luster a tin can to play with, and then I had the spools and Quentin fought me and I cried.

"Hush." Frony said, "Aint you shamed of yourself. Taking a baby's play pretty." She took the spools from me and gave them back to Quentin.

"Hush, now." Frony said, "Hush, I tell you."

"Hush up." Frony said. "You needs whipping, that's what you needs." She took Luster and Quentin up. "Come on here." she said. We went to the barn. T. P. was milking the cow. Roskus was sitting on the box.

"What's the matter with him now." Roskus said.

"You have to keep him down here." Frony said. "He fighting these babies again. Taking they play things. Stay here with T. P. now, and see can you hush a while."

"Clean that udder good now." Roskus said. "You milked that young cow dry last winter. If you milk this one dry, they aint going to be no more milk."

Dilsey was singing.

"Not around yonder." T. P. said. "Dont you know mammy say you cant go around there."

They were singing.

"Come on." T. P. said. "Lets go play with Quentin and Luster. Come on."

Quentin and Luster were playing in the dirt in front of T. P.'s house. There was a fire in the house, rising and falling, with Roskus sitting black against it.

"That's three, thank the Lawd." Roskus said. "I told you two years ago. They aint no luck on this place."

36

"Whyn't you get out, then." Dilsey said. She was undressing me. "Your bad luck talk got them Memphis notions into Versh. That ought to satisfy you."

"If that all the bad luck Versh have." Roskus said.

Frony came in.

"You all done." Dilsey said.

"T. P. finishing up." Frony said. "Miss Cahline want you to put Quentin to bed."

"I'm coming just as fast as I can." Dilsey said. "She ought to know by this time I aint got no wings."

"That's what I tell you." Roskus said. "They aint no luck going be on no place where one of they own chillens' name aint never spoke."

"Hush." Dilsey said. "Do you want to get him started"

"Raising a child not to know its own mammy's name." Roskus said.

"Dont you bother your head about her." Dilsey said. "I raised all of them and I reckon I can raise one more. Hush now. Let him get to sleep if he will."

"Saying a name." Frony said. "He dont know nobody's name."

"You just say it and see if he dont." Dilsey said. "You say it to him while he sleeping and I bet he hear you."

"He know lot more than folks thinks." Roskus

37

said. "He knowed they time was coming, like that pointer done. He could tell you when hisn coming, if he could talk. Or yours. Or mine."

"You take Luster outen that bed, mammy." Frony said. "That boy conjure him."

"Hush your mouth." Dilsey said, "Aint you got no better sense than that. What you want to listen to Roskus for, anyway. Get in, Benjy."

Dilsey pushed me and I got in the bed, where Luster already was. He was asleep. Dilsey took a long piece of wood and laid it between Luster and me. "Stay on your side now." Dilsey said. "Luster little, and you don't want to hurt him."

You can't go yet, T. P. said. Wait.

We looked around the corner of the house and watched the carriages go away.

"Now." T. P. said. He took Quentin up and we ran down to the corner of the fence and watched them pass. "There he go," T. P. said. "See that one with the glass in it. Look at him. He laying in there. See him."

Come on, Luster said, I going to take this here ball down home, where I wont lose it. Naw, sir, you cant have it. If them men sees you with it, they'll say you stole it. Hush up, now. You cant have it. What business you got with it. You cant play no ball.

Frony and T. P. were playing in the dirt by the door. T. P. had lightning bugs in a bottle.

"How did you all get back out." Frony said.

"We've got company." Caddy said. "Father said for us to mind me tonight. I expect you and T. P. will have to mind me too."

"I'm not going to mind you." Jason said. "Frony and T. P. dont have to either."

"They will if I say so." Caddy said. "Maybe I wont say for them to."

"T. P. dont mind nobody." Frony said. "Is they started the funeral yet."

"What's a funeral." Jason said.

"Didn't mammy tell you not to tell them." Versh said.

"Where they moans." Frony said. "They moaned two days on Sis Beulah Clay."

They moaned at Dilsey's house. Dilsey was moaning. When Dilsey moaned Luster said, Hush, and we hushed, and then I began to cry and Blue howled under the kitchen steps. Then Dilsey stopped and we stopped.

"Oh." Caddy said, "That's niggers. White folks dont have funerals."

"Mammy said us not to tell them, Frony." Versh said.

"Tell them what." Caddy said.

Dilsey moaned, and when it got to the place I began to cry and Blue howled under the steps. Luster, Frony said in the window, Take them down to the barn. I cant get no cooking done with all that racket. That hound too. Get them outen here.

39

I aint going down there, Luster said. I might meet pappy down there. I seen him last night, waving his arms in the barn.

"I like to know why not." Frony said. "White folks dies too. Your grandmammy dead as any nigger can get, I reckon."

"Dogs are dead." Caddy said, "And when Nancy fell in the ditch and Roskus shot her and the buzzards came and undressed her."

The bones rounded out of the ditch, where the dark vines were in the black ditch, into the moonlight, like some of the shapes had stopped. Then they all stopped and it was dark, and when I stopped to start again I could hear Mother, and feet walking fast away, and I could smell it. Then the room came, but my eyes went shut. I didn't stop. I could smell it. T. P. unpinned the bed clothes.

"Hush." he said, "Shhhhhhhh."

But I could smell it. T. P. pulled me up and he put on my clothes fast.

"Hush, Benjy." he said. "We going down to our house. You want to go down to our house, where Frony is. Hush. Shhhhh."

He laced my shoes and put my cap on and we went out. There was a light in the hall. Across the hall we could hear Mother.

"Shhhhhh, Benjy." T. P. said, "We'll be out in a minute."

A door opened and I could smell it more than ever, and a head came out. It wasn't Father. Father was sick there.

"Can you take him out of the house."

"That's where we going." T. P. said. Dilsey came up the stairs.

"Hush." she said, "Hush. Take him down home, T. P. Frony fixing him a bed. You all look after him, now. Hush, Benjy. Go on with T. P."

She went where we could hear Mother.

"Better keep him there." It wasn't Father. He shut the door, but I could still smell it.

We went down stairs. The stairs went down into the dark and T. P. took my hand, and we went out the door, out of the dark. Dan was sitting in the back yard, howling.

"He smell it." T. P. said. "Is that the way you found it out."

We went down the steps, where our shadows were.

"I forgot your coat." T. P. said. "You ought to had it. But I aint going back."

Dan howled.

"Hush now." T. P. said. Our shadows moved, but Dan's shadow didn't move except to howl when he did.

"I cant take you down home, bellering like you is." T. P. said. "You was bad enough before you got that bullfrog voice. Come on."

We went along the brick walk, with our shadows. The pig pen smelled like pigs. The cow stood in the lot, chewing at us. Dan howled.

"You going to wake the whole town up." T. P. said. "Cant you hush."

We saw Fancy, eating by the branch. The moon shone on the water when we got there.

"Naw, sir." T. P. said, "This too close. We cant stop here. Come on. Now, just look at you. Got your whole leg wet. Come on, here." Dan howled.

The ditch came up out of the buzzing grass. The bones rounded out of the black vines.

"Now." T. P. said. "Beller your head off if you want to. You got the whole night and a twenty acre pasture to beller in."

T. P. lay down in the ditch and I sat down, watching the bones where the buzzards ate Nancy, flapping black and slow and heavy out of the ditch.

I had it when we was down here before, Luster said. I showed it to you. Didn't you see it. I took it out of my pocket right here and showed it to you.

"Do you think buzzards are going to undress Damuddy." Caddy said. "You're crazy."

"You're a skizzard." Jason said. He began to cry.

"You're a knobnot." Caddy said. Jason cried. His hands were in his pockets.

"Jason going to be rich man." Versh said. "He holding his money all the time."

Jason cried.

"Now you've got him started." Caddy said. "Hush up, Jason. How can buzzards get in where Damuddy is. Father wouldn't let them. Would you let a buzzard undress you. Hush up, now."

Jason hushed. "Frony said it was a funeral." he said.

"Well it's not." Caddy said. "It's a party. Frony dont know anything about it. He wants your lightning bugs, T. P. Let him hold it a while."

T. P. gave me the bottle of lightning bugs.

"I bet if we go around to the parlor window we can see something." Caddy said. "Then you'll believe me."

"I already knows." Frony said. "I dont need to see."

"You better hush your mouth, Frony." Versh said. "Mammy going whip you."

"What is it." Caddy said.

"I knows what I knows." Frony said.

"Come on." Caddy said, "Let's go around to the front."

We started to go.

"T. P. wants his lightning bugs." Frony said.

"Let him hold it a while longer, T. P." Caddy said. "We'll bring it back."

"You all never caught them." Frony said.

"If I say you and T. P. can come too, will you let him hold it." Caddy said.

"Aint nobody said me and T. P. got to mind you." Frony said.

"If I say you dont have to, will you let him hold it." Caddy said.

"All right." Frony said. "Let him hold it, T. P. We going to watch them moaning."

"They aint moaning." Caddy said. "I tell you it's a party. Are they moaning, Versh."

"We aint going to know what they doing, standing here." Versh said.

"Come on." Caddy said. "Frony and T. P. dont have to mind me. But the rest of us do. You better carry him, Versh. It's getting dark."

Versh took me up and we went on around the kitchen.

When we looked around the corner we could see the lights coming up the drive. T. P. went back to the cellar door and opened it.

You know what's down there, T. P. said. Soda water. I seen Mr Jason come up with both hands full of them. Wait here a minute.

T. P. went and looked in the kitchen door. Dilsey said, What are you peeping in here for. Where's Benjy.

He out here, T. P. said.

Go on and watch him, Dilsey said. Keep him out the house now.

Yessum, T. P. said. Is they started yet.

You go on and keep that boy out of sight, Dilsey said. I got all I can tend to.

A snake crawled out from under the house. Jason said he wasn't afraid of snakes and Caddy said he was but she wasn't and Versh said they both were and Caddy said to be quiet, like father said.

You aint got to start bellering now, T. P. said. You want some this sassprilluh.

It tickled my nose and eyes.

If you aint going to drink it, let me get to it, T. P. said. All right, here tis. We better get another bottle while aint nobody bothering us. You be quiet, now.

We stopped under the tree by the parlor window. Versh set me down in the wet grass. It was cold. There were lights in all the windows.

" That's where Damuddy is." Caddy said. " She's sick every day now. When she gets well we're going to have a picnic."

" I knows what I knows." Frony said.

The trees were buzzing, and the grass.

" The one next to it is where we have the measles." Caddy said. " Where do you and T. P. have the measles, Frony."

" Has them just wherever we is, I reckon." Frony said.

" They haven't started yet." Caddy said.

They getting ready to start, T. P. said. You stand

right here now while I get that box so we can see in the window. Here, les finish drinking this here sassprilluh. It make me feel just like a squinch owl inside.

We drank the sassprilluh and T. P. pushed the bottle through the lattice, under the house, and went away. I could hear them in the parlor and I clawed my hands against the wall. T. P. dragged the box. He fell down, and he began to laugh. He lay there, laughing into the grass. He got up and dragged the box under the window, trying not to laugh.

"I skeered I going to holler." T. P. said. "Git on the box and see is they started."

"They haven't started because the band hasn't come yet." Caddy said.

"They aint going to have no band." Frony said.

"How do you know." Caddy said.

"I knows what I knows." Frony said.

"You dont know anything." Caddy said. She went to the tree. "Push me up, Versh."

"Your paw told you to stay out that tree." Versh said.

"That was a long time ago." Caddy said. "I expect he's forgotten about it. Besides, he said to mind me tonight. Didn't he say to mind me tonight."

"I'm not going to mind you." Jason said. "Frony and T. P. are not going to either."

"Push me up, Versh." Caddy said.

"All right." Versh said. "You the one going to

46

get whipped. I aint." He went and pushed Caddy up into the tree to the first limb. We watched the muddy bottom of her drawers. Then we couldn't see her. We could hear the tree thrashing.

"Mr Jason said if you break that tree he whip you." Versh said.

"I'm going to tell on her too." Jason said.

The tree quit thrashing. We looked up into the still branches.

"What you seeing." Frony whispered.

I saw them. Then I saw Caddy, with flowers in her hair, and a long veil like shining wind. Caddy. Caddy

"Hush." T. P. said, "They going to hear you. Get down quick." He pulled me. Caddy. I clawed my hands against the wall Caddy. T. P. pulled me.

"Hush." he said, "Hush. Come on here quick." He pulled me on. Caddy "Hush up, Benjy. You want them to hear you. Come on, les drink some more sassprilluh, then we can come back if you hush. We better get one more bottle or we both be hollering. We can say Dan drunk it. Mr Quentin always saying he so smart, we can say he sassprilluh dog, too."

The moonlight came down the cellar stairs. We drank some more sassprilluh.

"You know what I wish." T. P. said. "I wish a bear would walk in that cellar door. You know what I do. I walk right up to him and spit in he eye. Gimme that bottle to stop my mouth before I holler."

T. P. fell down. He began to laugh, and the cellar
door and the moonlight jumped away and something
hit me.

"Hush up." T. P. said, trying not to laugh,
"Lawd, they'll all hear us. Get up." T. P. said, "Get
up, Benjy, quick." He was thrashing about and
laughing and I tried to get up. The cellar steps ran
up the hill in the moonlight and T. P. fell up the
hill, into the moonlight, and I ran against the fence
and T. P. ran behind me saying "Hush up hush up"
Then he fell into the flowers, laughing, and I ran
into the box. But when I tried to climb onto it it
jumped away and hit me on the back of the head and
my throat made a sound. It made the sound again
and I stopped trying to get up, and it made the sound
again and I began to cry. But my throat kept on making the sound while T. P. was pulling me. It kept on
making it and I couldn't tell if I was crying or not,
and T. P. fell down on top of me, laughing, and it
kept on making the sound and Quentin kicked T. P.
and Caddy put her arms around me, and her shining
veil, and I couldn't smell trees anymore and I began
to cry.

Benjy, Caddy said, Benjy. *She put her arms*
around me again, but I went away. "What is it,
Benjy." she said, "Is it this hat." She took her hat
off and came again, and I went away.

"Benjy." she said, "What is it, Benjy. What has
Caddy done."

"He dont like that prissy dress." Jason said. "You think you're grown up, dont you. You think you're better than anybody else, dont you. Prissy."

"You shut your mouth." Caddy said, "You dirty little beast. Benjy."

"Just because you are fourteen, you think you're grown up, dont you." Jason said. "You think you're something. Dont you."

"Hush, Benjy." Caddy said. "You'll disturb Mother. Hush."

But I didn't hush, and when she went away I followed, and she stopped on the stairs and waited and I stopped too.

"What is it, Benjy." Caddy said, "Tell Caddy. She'll do it. Try."

"Candace." Mother said.

"Yessum." Caddy said.

"Why are you teasing him." Mother said. "Bring him here."

We went to Mother's room, where she was lying with the sickness on a cloth on her head.

"What is the matter now." Mother said. "Benjamin."

"Benjy." Caddy said. She came again, but I went away.

"You must have done something to him." Mother said. "Why wont you let him alone, so I can have some peace. Give him the box and please go on and let him alone."

Caddy got the box and set it on the floor and opened it. It was full of stars. When I was still, they were still. When I moved, they glinted and sparkled. I hushed.

Then I heard Caddy walking and I began again.

"Benjamin." Mother said, "Come here." I went to the door. "You, Benjamin." Mother said.

"What is it now." Father said, "Where are you going."

"Take him downstairs and get someone to watch him, Jason." Mother said. "You know I'm ill, yet you"

Father shut the door behind us.

"T. P." he said.

"Sir." T. P. said downstairs.

"Benjy's coming down." Father said. "Go with T. P."

I went to the bathroom door. I could hear the water.

"Benjy." T. P. said downstairs.

I could hear the water. I listened to it.

"Benjy." T. P. said downstairs.

I listened to the water.

I couldn't hear the water, and Caddy opened the door.

"Why, Benjy." she said. She looked at me and I went and she put her arms around me. "Did you find Caddy again." she said. "Did you think Caddy had run away." Caddy smelled like trees.

We went to Caddy's room. She sat down at the mirror. She stopped her hands and looked at me.

"Why, Benjy. What is it." she said. "You mustn't cry. Caddy's not going away. See here." she said. She took up the bottle and took the stopper out and held it to my nose. "Sweet. Smell. Good."

I went away and I didn't hush, and she held the bottle in her hand, looking at me.

"Oh." she said. She put the bottle down and came and put her arms around me. "So that was it. And you were trying to tell Caddy and you couldn't tell her. You wanted to, but you couldn't, could you. Of course Caddy wont. Of course Caddy wont. Just wait till I dress."

Caddy dressed and took up the bottle again and we went down to the kitchen.

"Dilsey." Caddy said, "Benjy's got a present for you." She stooped down and put the bottle in my hand. "Hold it out to Dilsey, now." Caddy held my hand out and Dilsey took the bottle.

"Well I'll declare." Dilsey said, "If my baby aint give Dilsey a bottle of perfume. Just look here, Roskus."

Caddy smelled like trees. "We dont like perfume ourselves." Caddy said.

She smelled like trees.

"Come on, now." Dilsey said, "You too big to sleep with folks. You a big boy now. Thirteen years old. Big enough to sleep by yourself in Uncle Maury's room." Dilsey said.

Uncle Maury was sick. His eye was sick, and his mouth. Versh took his supper up to him on the tray.

"Maury says he's going to shoot the scoundrel." Father said. "I told him he'd better not mention it to Patterson before hand." He drank.

"Jason." Mother said.

"Shoot who, Father." Quentin said. "What's Uncle Maury going to shoot him for."

"Because he couldn't take a little joke." Father said.

"Jason." Mother said, "How can you. You'd sit right there and see Maury shot down in ambush, and laugh."

"Then Maury'd better stay out of ambush." Father said.

"Shoot who, Father." Quentin said, "Who's Uncle Maury going to shoot."

"Nobody." Father said. "I dont own a pistol."

Mother began to cry. "If you begrudge Maury your food, why aren't you man enough to say so to his face. To ridicule him before the children, behind his back."

"Of course I dont." Father said, "I admire Maury. He is invaluable to my own sense of racial superiority. I wouldn't swap Maury for a matched team. And do you know why, Quentin."

"No, sir." Quentin said.

"*Et ego in arcadia* I have forgotten the latin for hay." Father said. "There, there." he said, "I was just joking." He drank and set the glass down and went and put his hand on Mother's shoulder.

"It's no joke." Mother said. "My people are every bit as well born as yours. Just because Maury's health is bad."

"Of course." Father said. "Bad health is the primary reason for all life. Created by disease, within putrefaction, into decay. Versh."

"Sir." Versh said behind my chair.

"Take the decanter and fill it."

"And tell Dilsey to come and take Benjamin up to bed." Mother said.

"You a big boy." Dilsey said, "Caddy tired sleeping with you. Hush now, so you can go to sleep." The room went away, but I didn't hush, and the room came back and Dilsey came and sat on the bed, looking at me.

"Aint you going to be a good boy and hush." Dilsey said. "You aint, is you. See can you wait a minute, then."

She went away. There wasn't anything in the door. Then Caddy was in it.

"Hush." Caddy said. "I'm coming."

I hushed and Dilsey turned back the spread and Caddy got in between the spread and the blanket. She didn't take off her bathrobe.

"Now." she said, "Here I am." Dilsey came with a blanket and spread it over her and tucked it around her.

"He be gone in a minute." Dilsey said. "I leave the light on in your room."

"All right." Caddy said. She snuggled her head beside mine on the pillow. "Goodnight, Dilsey."

"Goodnight, honey." Dilsey said. The room went black. *Caddy smelled like trees.*

We looked up into the tree where she was.

"What she seeing, Versh." Frony whispered.

"Shhhhhh." Caddy said in the tree. Dilsey said,

"You come on here." She came around the corner of the house. "Whyn't you all go on up stairs, like your paw said, stead of slipping out behind my back. Where's Caddy and Quentin."

"I told her not to climb up that tree." Jason said. "I'm going to tell on her."

"Who in what tree." Dilsey said. She came and looked up into the tree. "Caddy." Dilsey said. The branches began to shake again.

"You, Satan." Dilsey said. "Come down from there."

"Hush." Caddy said, "Dont you know Father said to be quiet." Her legs came in sight and Dilsey reached up and lifted her out of the tree.

"Aint you got any better sense than to let them come around here." Dilsey said.

"I couldn't do nothing with her." Versh said.

"What you all doing here." Dilsey said. "Who told you to come up to the house."

"She did." Frony said. "She told us to come."

"Who told you you got to do what she say." Dilsey said. "Get on home, now." Frony and T. P. went on. We couldn't see them when they were still going away.

"Out here in the middle of the night." Dilsey said. She took me up and we went to the kitchen.

"Slipping out behind my back." Dilsey said. "When you knowed it's past your bedtime."

"Shhhh, Dilsey." Caddy said. "Dont talk so loud. We've got to be quiet."

"You hush your mouth and get quiet, then." Dilsey said. "Where's Quentin."

"Quentin's mad because he had to mind me to-night." Caddy said. "He's still got T. P.'s bottle of lightning bugs."

"I reckon T. P. can get along without it." Dilsey said. "You go and find Quentin, Versh. Roskus say he seen him going towards the barn." Versh went on. We couldn't see him.

"They're not doing anything in there." Caddy said. "Just sitting in chairs and looking."

"They dont need no help from you all to do that." Dilsey said. We went around the kitchen.

Where you want to go now, Luster said. You go-

*ing back to watch them knocking ball again. We
done looked for it over there. Here. Wait a minute.
You wait right here while I go back and get that ball.
I done thought of something.*

The kitchen was dark. The trees were black on
the sky. Dan came waddling out from under the
steps and chewed my ankle. I went around the
kitchen, where the moon was. Dan came scuffling
along, into the moon.

" Benjy." T. P. said in the house.

The flower tree by the parlor window wasn't
dark, but the thick trees were. The grass was buzzing in the moonlight where my shadow walked on the
grass.

"You, Benjy." T. P. said in the house. " Where
you hiding. You slipping off. I knows it."

*Luster came back. Wait, he said. Here. Dont go
over there. Miss Quentin and her beau in the swing
yonder. You come on this way. Come back here,
Benjy.*

It was dark under the trees. Dan wouldn't come.
He stayed in the moonlight. Then I could see the
swing and I began to cry.

*Come away from there, Benjy, Luster said. You
know Miss Quentin going to get mad.*

It was two now, and then one in the swing. Caddy
came fast, white in the darkness.

" Benjy," she said. " How did you slip out.
Where's Versh."

She put her arms around me and I hushed and held to her dress and tried to pull her away.

"Why, Benjy." she said. "What is it. T. P." she called.

The one in the swing got up and came, and I cried and pulled Caddy's dress.

"Benjy." Caddy said. "It's just Charlie. Dont you know Charlie."

"Where's his nigger." Charlie said. "What do they let him run around loose for."

"Hush, Benjy." Caddy said. "Go away, Charlie. He doesn't like you." Charlie went away and I hushed. I pulled at Caddy's dress.

"Why, Benjy." Caddy said. "Aren't you going to let me stay here and talk to Charlie awhile."

"Call that nigger." Charlie said. He came back. I cried louder and pulled at Caddy's dress.

"Go away, Charlie." Caddy said. Charlie came and put his hands on Caddy and I cried more. I cried loud.

"No, no." Caddy said. "No. No."

"He cant talk." Charlie said. "Caddy."

"Are you crazy." Caddy said. She began to breathe fast. "He can see. Dont. Dont." Caddy fought. They both breathed fast. "Please. Please." Caddy whispered.

"Send him away." Charlie said.

"I will." Caddy said. "Let me go."

"Will you send him away." Charlie said.

"Yes." Caddy said. "Let me go." Charlie went away. "Hush." Caddy said. "He's gone." I hushed. I could hear her and feel her chest going.

"I'll have to take him to the house." she said. She took my hand. "I'm coming." she whispered.

"Wait." Charlie said. "Call the nigger."

"No." Caddy said. "I'll come back. Come on, Benjy."

"Caddy." Charlie whispered, loud. We went on. "You better come back. Are you coming back." Caddy and I were running. "Caddy." Charlie said. We ran out into the moonlight, toward the kitchen.

"Caddy." Charlie said.

Caddy and I ran. We ran up the kitchen steps, onto the porch, and Caddy knelt down in the dark and held me. I could hear her and feel her chest. "I wont." she said. "I wont anymore, ever. Benjy. Benjy." Then she was crying, and I cried, and we held each other. "Hush." she said. "Hush. I wont anymore." So I hushed and Caddy got up and we went into the kitchen and turned the light on and Caddy took the kitchen soap and washed her mouth at the sink, hard. Caddy smelled like trees.

I kept a telling you to stay away from there, Luster said. They sat up in the swing, quick. Quentin had her hands on her hair. He had a red tie.

You old crazy loon, Quentin said. I'm going to tell Dilsey about the way you let him follow everywhere I go. I'm going to make her whip you good.

58

"I couldn't stop him." Luster said. "Come on here, Benjy."

"Yes you could." Quentin said. "You didn't try. You were both snooping around after me. Did Grandmother send you all out here to spy on me." She jumped out of the swing. "If you dont take him right away this minute and keep him away, I'm going to make Jason whip you."

"I cant do nothing with him." Luster said. "You try it if you think you can."

"Shut your mouth." Quentin said. "Are you going to get him away."

"Ah, let him stay." he said. He had a red tie. The sun was red on it. "Look here, Jack." He struck a match and put it in his mouth. Then he took the match out of his mouth. It was still burning. "Want to try it." he said. I went over there. "Open your mouth." he said. I opened my mouth. Quentin hit the match with her hand and it went away.

"Goddamn you." Quentin said. "Do you want to get him started. Dont you know he'll beller all day. I'm going to tell Dilsey on you." She went away running.

"Here, kid." he said. "Hey. Come on back. I aint going to fool with him."

Quentin ran on to the house. She went around the kitchen.

"You played hell then, Jack." he said. "Aint you."

"He cant tell what you saying." Luster said. "He deef and dumb."

"Is." he said. "How long's he been that way."

"Been that way thirty-three years today." Luster said. "Born looney. Is you one of them show folks."

"Why." he said.

"I dont ricklick seeing you around here before." Luster said.

"Well, what about it." he said.

"Nothing." Luster said. "I going tonight."

He looked at me.

"You aint the one can play a tune on that saw, is you." Luster said.

"It'll cost you a quarter to find that out." he said. He looked at me. "Why dont they lock him up." he said. "What'd you bring him out here for."

"You aint talking to me." Luster said. "I cant do nothing with him. I just come over here looking for a quarter I lost so I can go to the show tonight. Look like now I aint going to get to go." Luster looked on the ground. "You aint got no extra quarter, is you." Luster said.

"No." he said. "I aint."

"I reckon I just have to find that other one, then." Luster said. He put his hand in his pocket. "You dont want to buy no golf ball neither, does you." Luster said.

"What kind of ball." he said.

"Golf ball." Luster said. "I dont want but a quarter."

"What for." he said. "What do I want with it."

"I didn't think you did." Luster said. "Come on here, mulehead." he said. "Come on here and watch them knocking that ball. Here. Here something you can play with along with that jimson weed." Luster picked it up and gave it to me. It was bright.

"Where'd you get that." he said. His tie was red in the sun, walking.

"Found it under this here bush." Luster said. "I thought for a minute it was that quarter I lost."

He came and took it.

"Hush." Luster said. "He going to give it back when he done looking at it."

"Agnes Mabel Becky." he said. He looked toward the house.

"Hush." Luster said. "He fixing to give it back."

He gave it to me and I hushed.

"Who come to see her last night." he said.

"I dont know." Luster said. "They comes every night she can climb down that tree. I dont keep no track of them."

"Damn if one of them didn't leave a track." he said. He looked at the house. Then he went and lay down in the swing. "Go away." he said. "Dont bother me."

"Come on here." Luster said. "You done played

hell now. Time Miss Quentin get done telling on you."

We went to the fence and looked through the curling flower spaces. Luster hunted in the grass.

" I had it right here." he said. I saw the flag flapping, and the sun slanting on the broad grass.

" They'll be some along soon." Luster said. "There some now, but they going away. Come on and help me look for it."

We went along the fence.

" Hush." Luster said. " How can I make them come over here, if they aint coming. Wait. They'll be some in a minute. Look yonder. Here they come."

I went along the fence, to the gate, where the girls passed with their booksatchels. " You, Benjy." Luster said. " Come back here."

You cant do no good looking through the gate, T. P. said. Miss Caddy done gone long ways away. Done got married and left you. You cant do no good, holding to the gate and crying. She cant hear you.

What is it he wants, T. P. Mother said. Cant you play with him and keep him quiet.

He want to go down yonder and look through the gate, T. P. said.

Well, he cannot do it, Mother said. It's raining. You will just have to play with him and keep him quiet. You, Benjamin.

62

They came to the flag. He took it out and they hit, then he put the flag back.

"Mister." Luster said.

He looked around. "What." he said.

"Want to buy a golf ball." Luster said.

"Let's see it." he said. He came to the fence and Luster reached the ball through.

"Where'd you get it." he said.

"Found it." Luster said.

"I know that." he said. "Where. In somebody's golf bag."

"I found it laying over here in the yard." Luster said. "I'll take a quarter for it."

"What makes you think it's yours." he said.

"I found it." Luster said.

"Then find yourself another one." he said. He put it in his pocket and went away.

"I got to go to that show tonight." Luster said.

"That so." he said. He went to the table. "Fore, caddie." he said. He hit.

"I'll declare." Luster said. "You fusses when you dont see them and you fusses when you does. Why cant you hush. Dont you reckon folks gets tired of listening to you all the time. Here. You dropped your jimson weed." He picked it up and gave it back to me. "You needs a new one. You 'bout wore that one out." We stood at the fence and watched them.

"That white man hard to get along with." Luster said. "You see him take my ball." They went on. We went on along the fence. We came to the garden and we couldn't go any further. I held to the fence and looked through the flower spaces. They went away.

"Now you aint got nothing to moan about." Luster said. "Hush up. I the one got something to moan over, you aint. Here. Whyn't you hold on to that weed. You be bellering about it next." He gave me the flower. "Where you heading now."

Our shadows were on the grass. They got to the trees before we did. Mine got there first. Then we got there, and then the shadows were gone. There was a flower in the bottle. I put the other flower in it.

"Aint you a grown man, now." Luster said. "Playing with two weeds in a bottle. You know what they going to do with you when Miss Cahline die. They going to send you to Jackson, where you belong. Mr Jason say so. Where you can hold the bars all day long with the rest of the looneys and slobber. How you like that."

Luster knocked the flowers over with his hand. "That's what they'll do to you at Jackson when you starts bellering."

I tried to pick up the flowers. Luster picked them up, and they went away. I began to cry.

"Beller." Luster said. "Beller. You want something to beller about. All right, then. Caddy." he whispered. "Caddy. Beller now. Caddy."

"Luster." Dilsey said from the kitchen.

The flowers came back.

66

"Hush." Luster said. "Here they is. Look. It's fixed back just like it was at first. Hush, now."

"You, Luster." Dilsey said.

"Yessum." Luster said. "We coming. You done played hell. Get up." He jerked my arm and I got up. We went out of the trees. Our shadows were gone.

"Hush." Luster said. "Look at all them folks watching you. Hush."

"You bring him on here." Dilsey said. She came down the steps.

"What you done to him now." she said.

"Aint done nothing to him." Luster said. "He just started bellering."

"Yes you is." Dilsey said. "You done something to him. Where you been."

"Over yonder under them cedars." Luster said.

"Getting Quentin all riled up." Dilsey said. "Why cant you keep him away from her. Dont you know she dont like him where she at."

"Got as much time for him as I is." Luster said. "He aint none of my uncle."

"Dont you sass me, nigger boy." Dilsey said.

"I aint done nothing to him." Luster said. "He was playing there, and all of a sudden he started bellering."

"Is you been projecking with his graveyard." Dilsey said.

"I aint touched his graveyard." Luster said.

" Dont lie to me, boy." Dilsey said. We went up the steps and into the kitchen. Dilsey opened the fire-door and drew a chair up in front of it and I sat down. I hushed.

What you want to get her started for, Dilsey said. Whyn't you keep him out of there.

He was just looking at the fire, Caddy said. Mother was telling him his new name. We didn't mean to get her started.

I knows you didn't, Dilsey said. Him at one end of the house and her at the other. You let my things alone, now. Dont you touch nothing till I get back.

" Aint you shamed of yourself." Dilsey said. " Teasing him." She set the cake on the table.

" I aint been teasing him." Luster said. " He was playing with that bottle full of dogfennel and all of a sudden he started up bellering. You heard him."

" You aint done nothing to his flowers." Dilsey said.

" I aint touched his graveyard." Luster said. " What I want with his truck. I was just hunting for that quarter."

" You lost it, did you." Dilsey said. She lit the candles on the cake. Some of them were little ones. Some were big ones cut into little pieces. " I told you to go put it away. Now I reckon you want me to get you another one from Frony."

" I got to go to that show, Benjy or no Benjy."

Luster said. " I aint going to follow him around day and night both."

" You going to do just what he want you to, nigger boy." Dilsey said. " You hear me."

" Aint I always done it." Luster said. " Dont I always does what he wants. Dont I, Benjy."

" Then you keep it up." Dilsey said. " Bringing him in here, bawling and getting her started too. You all go ahead and eat this cake, now, before Jason come. I dont want him jumping on me about a cake I bought with my own money. Me baking a cake here, with him counting every egg that comes into this kitchen. See can you let him alone now, less you dont want to go to that show tonight."

Dilsey went away.

" You cant blow out no candles." Luster said. " Watch me blow them out." He leaned down and puffed his face. The candles went away. I began to cry. " Hush." Luster said. " Here. Look at the fire whiles I cuts this cake."

I could hear the clock, and I could hear Caddy standing behind me, and I could hear the roof. It's still raining, Caddy said. I hate rain. I hate everything. And then her head came into my lap and she was crying, holding me, and I began to cry. Then I looked at the fire again and the bright, smooth shapes went again. I could hear the clock and the roof and Caddy.

69

I ate some cake. Luster's hand came and took another piece. I could hear him eating. I looked at the fire.

A long piece of wire came across my shoulder. It went to the door, and then the fire went away. I began to cry.

"What you howling for now." Luster said. "Look there." The fire was there. I hushed. "Cant you set and look at the fire and be quiet like mammy told you." Luster said. "You ought to be ashamed of yourself. Here. Here's you some more cake."

"What you done to him now." Dilsey said. "Cant you never let him alone."

"I was just trying to get him to hush up and not sturb Miss Cahline." Luster said. "Something got him started again."

"And I know what that something name." Dilsey said. "I'm going to get Versh to take a stick to you when he comes home. You just trying yourself. You been doing it all day. Did you take him down to the branch."

"Nome." Luster said. "We been right here in this yard all day, like you said."

His hand came for another piece of cake. Dilsey hit his hand. "Reach it again, and I chop it right off with this here butcher knife." Dilsey said. "I bet he aint had one piece of it."

"Yes he is." Luster said. "He already had twice as much as me. Ask him if he aint."

"Reach hit one more time." Dilsey said. "Just reach it."

That's right, Dilsey said. I reckon it'll be my time to cry next. Reckon Maury going to let me cry on him a while, too.

His name's Benjy now, Caddy said.

How come it is, Dilsey said. He aint wore out the name he was born with yet, is he.

Benjamin came out of the bible, Caddy said. It's a better name for him than Maury was.

How come it is, Dilsey said.

Mother says it is, Caddy said.

Huh, Dilsey said. Name aint going to help him. Hurt him, neither. Folks dont have no luck, changing names. My name been Dilsey since fore I could remember and it be Dilsey when they's long forgot me.

How will they know it's Dilsey, when it's long forgot, Dilsey, Caddy said.

It'll be in the Book, honey, Dilsey said. Writ out.

Can you read it, Caddy said.

Wont have to, Dilsey said. They'll read it for me. All I got to do is say Ise here.

The long wire came across my shoulder, and the fire went away. I began to cry.

Dilsey and Luster fought.

"I seen you." Dilsey said. "Oho, I seen you." She dragged Luster out of the corner, shaking him. "Wasn't nothing bothering him, was they. You just wait till your pappy come home. I wish I was young like I use to be, I'd tear them years right off your head. I good mind to lock you up in that cellar and not let you go to that show tonight, I sho is."

"Ow, mammy." Luster said. "Ow, mammy."

I put my hand out to where the fire had been.

"Catch him." Dilsey said. "Catch him back."

My hand jerked back and I put it in my mouth and Dilsey caught me. I could still hear the clock between my voice. Dilsey reached back and hit Luster on the head. My voice was going loud every time.

"Get that soda." Dilsey said. She took my hand out of my mouth. My voice went louder then and my hand tried to go back to my mouth, but Dilsey held it. My voice went loud. She sprinkled soda on my hand.

"Look in the pantry and tear a piece off of that rag hanging on the nail." she said. "Hush, now. You dont want to make your ma sick again, does you. Here, look at the fire. Dilsey make your hand stop hurting in just a minute. Look at the fire." She opened the fire door. I looked at the fire, but my hand didn't stop and I didn't stop. My hand was trying to go to my mouth but Dilsey held it.

She wrapped the cloth around it. Mother said,

"What is it now. Cant I even be sick in peace. Do I have to get up out of bed to come down to him, with two grown negroes to take care of him."

"He all right now." Dilsey said. "He going to quit. He just burnt his hand a little."

"With two grown negroes, you must bring him into the house, bawling." Mother said. "You got him started on purpose, because you know I'm sick." She came and stood by me. "Hush." she said. "Right this minute. Did you give him this cake."

"I bought it." Dilsey said. "It never come out of Jason's pantry. I fixed him some birthday."

"Do you want to poison him with that cheap store cake." Mother said. "Is that what you are trying to do. Am I never to have one minute's peace."

"You go on back up stairs and lay down." Dilsey said. "It'll quit smarting him in a minute now, and he'll hush. Come on, now."

"And leave him down here for you all to do something else to." Mother said. "How can I lie there, with him bawling down here. Benjamin. Hush this minute."

"They aint nowhere else to take him." Dilsey said. "We aint got the room we use to have. He cant stay out in the yard, crying where all the neighbors can see him."

"I know, I know." Mother said. "It's all my fault. I'll be gone soon, and you and Jason will both get along better." She began to cry.

"You hush that, now." Dilsey said. "You'll get yourself down again. You come on back up stairs.

73

Luster going to take him to the liberry and play with him till I get his supper done."

Dilsey and Mother went out.

"Hush up." Luster said. "You hush up. You want me to burn your other hand for you. You aint hurt. Hush up."

"Here." Dilsey said. "Stop crying, now." She gave me the slipper, and I hushed. "Take him to the liberry." she said. "And if I hear him again, I going to whip you myself."

We went to the library. Luster turned on the light. The windows went black, and the dark tall place on the wall came and I went and touched it. It was like a door, only it wasn't a door.

The fire came behind me and I went to the fire and sat on the floor, holding the slipper. The fire went higher. It went onto the cushion in Mother's chair.

"Hush up." Luster said. "Cant you never get done for a while. Here I done built you a fire, and you wont even look at it."

Your name is Benjy. Caddy said. Do you hear. Benjy. Benjy.

Dont tell him that, Mother said. Bring him here.

Caddy lifted me under the arms.

Get up, Mau——*I mean Benjy, she said.*

Dont try to carry him, Mother said. Cant you lead him over here. Is that too much for you to think of.

74

I can carry him, Caddy said. "Let me carry him up, Dilsey."

"Go on, Minute." Dilsey said. "You aint big enough to tote a flea. You go on and be quiet, like Mr. Jason said."

There was a light at the top of the stairs. Father was there, in his shirt sleeves. The way he looked said Hush. Caddy whispered,

"Is Mother sick."

Versh set me down and we went into Mother's room. There was a fire. It was rising and falling on the walls. There was another fire in the mirror. I could smell the sickness. It was a cloth folded on Mother's head. Her hair was on the pillow. The fire didn't reach it, but it shone on her hand, where her rings were jumping.

"Come and tell Mother goodnight." Caddy said. We went to the bed. The fire went out of the mirror. Father got up from the bed and lifted me up and Mother put her hand on my head.

"What time is it." Mother said. Her eyes were closed.

"Ten minutes to seven." Father said.

"It's too early for him to go to bed." Mother said. "He'll wake up at daybreak, and I simply cannot bear another day like today."

"There, there." Father said. He touched Mother's face.

"I know I'm nothing but a burden to you."

75

Mother said. "But I'll be gone soon. Then you will be rid of my bothering."

"Hush." Father said. "I'll take him downstairs awhile." He took me up. "Come on, old fellow. Let's go downstairs awhile. We'll have to be quiet while Quentin is studying, now."

Caddy went and leaned her face over the bed and Mother's hand came into the firelight. Her rings jumped on Caddy's back.

Mother's sick, Father said. Dilsey will put you to bed. Where's Quentin.

Versh getting him, Dilsey said.

Father stood and watched us go past. We could hear Mother in her room. Caddy said "Hush." Jason was still climbing the stairs. He had his hands in his pockets.

"You all must be good tonight." Father said. "And be quiet, so you wont disturb Mother."

"We'll be quiet." Caddy said. "You must be quiet now, Jason." she said. We tiptoed.

We could hear the roof. I could see the fire in the mirror too. Caddy lifted me again.

"Come on, now." she said. "Then you can come back to the fire. Hush, now."

"Candace." Mother said.

"Hush, Benjy." Caddy said. "Mother wants you a minute. Like a good boy. Then you can come back. Benjy."

Caddy let me down, and I hushed.

76

"Let him stay here, Mother. When he's through looking at the fire, then you can tell him."

"Candace." Mother said. Caddy stooped and lifted me. We staggered. "Candace." Mother said.

"Hush." Caddy said. "You can still see it. Hush."

"Bring him here." Mother said. "He's too big for you to carry. You must stop trying. You'll injure your back. All of our women have prided themselves on their carriage. Do you want to look like a washerwoman."

"He's not too heavy." Caddy said. "I can carry him."

"Well, I dont want him carried, then." Mother said. "A five year old child. No, no. Not in my lap. Let him stand up."

"If you'll hold him, he'll stop." Caddy said. "Hush." she said. "You can go right back. Here. Here's your cushion. See."

"Dont, Candace." Mother said.

"Let him look at it and he'll be quiet." Caddy said. "Hold up just a minute while I slip it out. There, Benjy. Look."

I looked at it and hushed.

"You humour him too much." Mother said. "You and your father both. You dont realise that I am the one who has to pay for it. Damuddy spoiled Jason that way and it took him two years to outgrow it, and I am not strong enough to go through the same thing with Benjamin."

"You dont need to bother with him." Caddy said. "I like to take care of him. Dont I, Benjy."

"Candace." Mother said. "I told you not to call him that. It was bad enough when your father insisted on calling you by that silly nickname, and I will not have him called by one. Nicknames are vulgar. Only common people use them. Benjamin." she said.

"Look at me." Mother said.

"Benjamin." she said. She took my face in her hands and turned it to hers.

"Benjamin." she said. "Take that cushion away, Candace."

"He'll cry." Caddy said.

"Take that cushion away, like I told you." Mother said. "He must learn to mind."

The cushion went away.

"Hush, Benjy." Caddy said.

"You go over there and sit down." Mother said. "Benjamin." She held my face to hers.

"Stop that." she said. "Stop it."

But I didn't stop and Mother caught me in her arms and began to cry, and I cried. Then the cushion came back and Caddy held it above Mother's head. She drew Mother back in the chair and Mother lay crying against the red and yellow cushion.

"Hush, Mother." Caddy said. "You go upstairs and lay down, so you can be sick. I'll go get Dilsey."

She led me to the fire and I looked at the bright, smooth shapes. I could hear the fire and the roof.

Father took me up. He smelled like rain.

"Well, Benjy." he said. "Have you been a good boy today."

Caddy and Jason were fighting in the mirror.

"You, Caddy." Father said.

They fought. Jason began to cry.

"Caddy." Father said. Jason was crying. He wasn't fighting anymore, but we could see Caddy fighting in the mirror and Father put me down and went into the mirror and fought too. He lifted Caddy up. She fought. Jason lay on the floor, crying. He had the scissors in his hand. Father held Caddy.

"He cut up all Benjy's dolls." Caddy said. "I'll slit his gizzle."

"Candace." Father said.

"I will." Caddy said. "I will." She fought. Father held her. She kicked at Jason. He rolled into the corner, out of the mirror. Father brought Caddy to the fire. They were all out of the mirror. Only the fire was in it. Like the fire was in a door.

"Stop that." Father said. "Do you want to make Mother sick in her room."

Caddy stopped. "He cut up all the dolls Mau—Benjy and I made." Caddy said. "He did it just for meanness."

"I didn't." Jason said. He was sitting up, crying. "I didn't know they were his. I just thought they were some old papers."

"You couldn't help but know." Caddy said. "You did it just."

"Hush." Father said. "Jason." he said.

"I'll make you some more tomorrow." Caddy said. "We'll make a lot of them. Here, you can look at the cushion, too."

Jason came in.

I kept telling you to hush, Luster said.

What's the matter now, Jason said.

"He just trying hisself." Luster said. "That the way he been going on all day."

"Why dont you let him alone, then." Jason said. "If you cant keep him quiet, you'll have to take him out to the kitchen. The rest of us cant shut ourselves up in a room like Mother does."

"Mammy say keep him out the kitchen till she get supper." Luster said.

"Then play with him and keep him quiet." Jason said. "Do I have to work all day and then come home to a mad house." He opened the paper and read it.

You can look at the fire and the mirror and the cushion too, Caddy said. You wont have to wait until supper to look at the cushion, now. We could hear the roof. We could hear Jason too, crying loud beyond the wall.

Dilsey said, "You come, Jason. You letting him alone, is you."

"Yessum." Luster said.

"Where Quentin." Dilsey said. "Supper near bout ready."

"I dont know'm." Luster said. "I aint seen her."

Dilsey went away. "Quentin." she said in the hall. "Quentin. Supper ready."

We could hear the roof. Quentin smelled like rain, too.

What did Jason do, he said.

He cut up all Benjy's dolls, Caddy said.

Mother said to not call him Benjy, Quentin said. He sat on the rug by us. I wish it wouldn't rain, he said. You cant do anything.

You've been in a fight, Caddy said. Haven't you.

It wasn't much, Quentin said.

You can tell it, Caddy said. Father'll see it.

I dont care, Quentin said. I wish it wouldn't rain.

Quentin said, "Didn't Dilsey say supper was ready."

"Yessum." Luster said. Jason looked at Quentin. Then he read the paper again. Quentin came in. "She say it bout ready." Luster said. Quentin jumped down in Mother's chair. Luster said,

"Mr Jason."

"What." Jason said.

"Let me have two bits." Luster said.

"What for." Jason said.

"To go to the show tonight." Luster said.

"I thought Dilsey was going to get a quarter from Frony for you." Jason said.

"She did." Luster said. "I lost it. Me and Benjy hunted all day for that quarter. You can ask him."

"Then borrow one from him." Jason said. "I have to work for mine." He read the paper. Quentin looked at the fire. The fire was in her eyes and on her mouth. Her mouth was red.

"I tried to keep him away from there." Luster said.

"Shut your mouth." Quentin said. Jason looked at her.

"What did I tell you I was going to do if I saw you with that show fellow again." he said. Quentin looked at the fire. "Did you hear me." Jason said.

"I heard you." Quentin said. "Why dont you do it, then."

"Dont you worry." Jason said.

"I'm not." Quentin said. Jason read the paper again.

I could hear the roof. Father leaned forward and looked at Quentin.

Hello, he said. Who won.

"Nobody." Quentin said. "They stopped us. Teachers."

"Who was it." Father said. "Will you tell."

"It was all right." Quentin said. "He was as big as me."

"That's good." Father said. "Can you tell what it was about."

"It wasn't anything." Quentin said. "He said he would put a frog in her desk and she wouldn't dare to whip him."

"Oh." Father said. "She. And then what."

"Yes, sir." Quentin said. "And then I kind of hit him."

We could hear the roof and the fire, and a snuffling outside the door.

"Where was he going to get a frog in November." Father said.

"I dont know, sir." Quentin said.

We could hear them.

"Jason." Father said. We could hear Jason.

"Jason." Father said. "Come in here and stop that."

We could hear the roof and the fire and Jason.

"Stop that, now." Father said. "Do you want me to whip you again." Father lifted Jason up into the chair by him. Jason snuffled. We could hear the fire and the roof. Jason snuffled a little louder.

"One more time." Father said. We could hear the fire and the roof.

Dilsey said, All right. You all can come on to supper.

Versh smelled like rain. He smelled like a dog, too. We could hear the fire and the roof.

We could hear Caddy walking fast. Father and Mother looked at the door. Caddy passed it, walking fast, She didn't look. She walked fast.

"Candace." Mother said. Caddy stopped walking.

"Yes, Mother." she said.

"Hush, Caroline." Father said.

"Come here." Mother said.

"Hush, Caroline." Father said. "Let her alone."

Caddy came to the door and stood there, looking at Father and Mother. Her eyes flew at me, and away. I began to cry. It went loud and I got up. Caddy came in and stood with her back to the wall, looking at me. I went toward her, crying, and she shrank against the wall and I saw her eyes and I cried louder and pulled at her dress. She put her hands out but I pulled at her dress. Her eyes ran.

Versh said, Your name Benjamin now. You know how come your name Benjamin now. They making a bluegum out of you. Mammy say in old time your granpa changed nigger's name, and he turn preacher, and when they look at him, he bluegum too. Didn't use to be bluegum, neither. And when family woman look him in the eye in the full of the moon, chile born bluegum. And one evening, when they was about a dozen them bluegum chillen running round the

84

place, he never come home. Possum hunters found him in the woods, et clean. And you know who et him. Them bluegum chillen did.

We were in the hall. Caddy was still looking at me. Her hand was against her mouth and I saw her eyes and I cried. We went up the stairs. She stopped again, against the wall, looking at me and I cried and she went on and I came on, crying, and she shrank against the wall, looking at me. She opened the door to her room, but I pulled at her dress and we went to the bathroom and she stood against the door, looking at me. Then she put her arm across her face and I pushed at her, crying.

What are you doing to him, Jason said. Why cant you let him alone.

I aint touching him, Luster said. He been doing this way all day long. He needs whipping.

He needs to be sent to Jackson, Quentin said. How can anybody live in a house like this.

If you dont like it, young lady, you'd better get out, Jason said.

I'm going to, Quentin said. Dont you worry.

Versh said, "You move back some, so I can dry my legs off." He shoved me back a little. " Dont you start bellering, now. You can still see it. That's all you have to do. You aint had to be out in the rain like I is. You's born lucky and dont know it." He lay on his back before the fire.

" You know how come your name Benjamin now."

85

Versh said. " Y_our mamma too proud_ for you. What mammy say."

" You be still there and let me dry my legs off." Versh said. " Or you know what I'll do. I'll skin your rinktum."

We could hear the fire and the roof and Versh.

Versh got up quick and jerked his legs back. Father said, " All right, Versh."

" I'll feed him tonight." Caddy said. " Sometimes he cries when Versh feeds him."

" Take this tray up," Dilsey said. " And hurry back and feed Benjy."

" Dont you want Caddy to feed you." Caddy said.

Has he got to keep that old dirty slipper on the table, Quentin said. Why dont you feed him in the kitchen. It's like eating with a pig.

If you dont like the way we eat, you'd better not come to the table, Jason said.

Steam came off of Roskus. He was sitting in front of the stove. The oven door was open and Roskus had his feet in it. Steam came off the bowl. Caddy put the spoon into my mouth easy. There was a black spot on the inside of the bowl.

Now, now, Dilsey said. He aint going to bother you no more.

It got down below the mark. Then the bowl was empty. It went away. " He's hungry tonight." Caddy said. The bowl came back. I couldn't see the spot.

Then I could. "He's starved, tonight." Caddy said. "Look how much he's eaten."

Yes he will, Quentin said. *You all send him out to spy on me. I hate this house. I'm going to run away.*

Roskus said, "It going to rain all night."

You've been running a long time, not to 've got any further off than mealtime, Jason said.

See if I dont, Quentin said.

"Then I dont know what I going to do." Dilsey said. "It caught me in the hip so bad now I cant scarcely move. Climbing them stairs all evening."

Oh, I wouldn't be surprised, Jason said. *I wouldn't be surprised at anything you'd do.*

Quentin threw her napkin on the table.

Hush your mouth, Jason, Dilsey said. *She went and put her arm around Quentin. Sit down, honey,* Dilsey said. *He ought to be shamed of hisself, throwing what aint your fault up to you.*

"She sulling again, is she." Roskus said.

"Hush your mouth." Dilsey said.

Quentin pushed Dilsey away. She looked at Jason. Her mouth was red. She picked up her glass of water and swung her arm back, looking at Jason. Dilsey caught her arm. They fought. The glass broke on the table, and the water ran into the table. Quentin was running.

"Mother's sick again." Caddy said.

"Sho she is." Dilsey said. "Weather like this

make anybody sick. When you going to get done eating, boy."

Goddamn you, Quentin said. Goddamn you. We could hear her running on the stairs. We went to the library.

Caddy gave me the cushion, and I could look at the cushion and the mirror and the fire.

"We must be quiet while Quentin's studying." Father said. "What are you doing, Jason."

"Nothing." Jason said.

"Suppose you come over here to do it, then." Father said.

Jason came out of the corner.

"What are you chewing." Father said.

"Nothing." Jason said.

"He's chewing paper again." Caddy said.

"Come here, Jason." Father said.

Jason threw into the fire. It hissed, uncurled, turning black. Then it was gray. Then it was gone. Caddy and Father and Jason were in Mother's chair. Jason's eyes were puffed shut and his mouth moved, like tasting. Caddy's head was on Father's shoulder. Her hair was like fire, and little points of fire were in her eyes, and I went and Father lifted me into the chair too, and Caddy held me. She smelled like trees.

She smelled like trees. In the corner it was dark, but I could see the window. I squatted there, holding the slipper. I couldn't see it, but my hands saw it, and I could hear it getting night, and my hands saw the slipper but I couldn't see myself, but my hands could see the slipper, and I squatted there, hearing it getting dark.

Here you is, Luster said. Look what I got. He showed it to me. You know where I got it. Miss Quentin gave it to me. I knowed they couldn't keep me out. What you doing, off in here. I thought you done slipped back out doors. Aint you done enough moaning and slobbering today, without hiding off in this here empty room, mumbling and taking on. Come on here to bed, so I can get up there before it starts. I cant fool with you all night tonight. Just let them horns toot the first toot and I done gone.

We didn't go to our room.

"This is where we have the measles." Caddy said. "Why do we have to sleep in here tonight."

"What you care where you sleep." Dilsey said. She shut the door and sat down and began to undress me. Jason began to cry. "Hush." Dilsey said.

"I want to sleep with Damuddy." Jason said.

"She's sick." Caddy said. "You can sleep with her when she gets well. Cant he, Dilsey."

"Hush, now." Dilsey said. Jason hushed.

"Our nighties are here, and everything." Caddy said. "It's like moving."

"And you better get into them." Dilsey said. "You be unbuttoning Jason."

Caddy unbuttoned Jason. He began to cry.

89

"You want to get whipped." Dilsey said. Jason hushed.

Quentin, Mother said in the hall.

What, Quentin said beyond the wall. We heard Mother lock the door. She looked in our door and came in and stooped over the bed and kissed me on the forehead.

When you get him to bed, go and ask Dilsey if she objects to my having a hot water bottle, Mother said. Tell her that if she does, I'll try to get along without it. Tell her I just want to know.

Yessum, Luster said. Come on. Get your pants off.

Quentin and Versh came in. Quentin had his face turned away. "What are you crying for." Caddy said.

"Hush." Dilsey said. "You all get undressed, now. You can go on home, Versh."

I got undressed and I looked at myself, and I began to cry. Hush, Luster said. Looking for them aint going to do no good. They're gone. You keep on like this, and we aint going have you no more birthday. He put my gown on. I hushed, and then Luster stopped, his head toward the window. Then he went to the window and looked out. He came back and took my arm. Here she come, he said. Be quiet, now. We went to the window and looked out. It came out of Quentin's window and climbed across into the tree. We watched the tree shaking. The

90

shaking went down the tree, then it came out and we watched it go away across the grass. Then we couldn't see it. Come on, Luster said. There now. Hear them horns. You get in that bed while my foots behaves.

There were two beds. Quentin got in the other one. He turned his face to the wall. Dilsey put Jason in with him. Caddy took her dress off.

"Just look at your drawers." Dilsey said. "You better be glad your ma aint seen you."

"I already told on her." Jason said.

"I bound you would." Dilsey said.

"And see what you got by it." Caddy said. "Tattletale."

"What did I get by it." Jason said.

"Whyn't you get your nightie on." Dilsey said. She went and helped Caddy take off her bodice and drawers. "Just look at you." Dilsey said. She wadded the drawers and scrubbed Caddy behind with them. "It done soaked clean through onto you." she said. "But you wont get no bath this night. Here." She put Caddy's nightie on her and Caddy climbed into the bed and Dilsey went to the door and stood with her hand on the light. "You all be quiet now, you hear." she said.

"All right." Caddy said. "Mother's not coming in tonight." she said. "So we still have to mind me."

"Yes." Dilsey said. "Go to sleep, now."

"Mother's sick." Caddy said. "She and Da-muddy are both sick."

"Hush." Dilsey said. "You go to sleep."

The room went black, except the door. Then the door went black. Caddy said, "Hush, Maury," putting her hand on me. So I stayed hushed. We could hear us. We could hear the dark.

It went away, and Father looked at us. He looked at Quentin and Jason, then he came and kissed Caddy and put his hand on my head.

"Is Mother very sick." Caddy said.

"No." Father said. "Are you going to take good care of Maury."

"Yes." Caddy said.

Father went to the door and looked at us again. Then the dark came back, and he stood black in the door, and then the door turned black again. Caddy held me and I could hear us all, and the darkness, and something I could smell. And then I could see the windows, where the trees were buzzing. Then the dark began to go in smooth, bright shapes, like it always does, even when Caddy says that I have been asleep.

WHEN THE SHADOW OF THE SASH
appeared on the curtains it was between seven and
eight oclock and then I was in time again, hearing the
watch. It was Grandfather's and when Father gave it
to me he said, Quentin, I give you the mausoleum of
all hope and desire; it's rather excrutiating-ly apt
that you will use it to gain the reducto absurdum of
all human experience which can fit your individual
needs no better than it fitted his or his father's. I
give it to you not that you may remember time, but
that you might forget it now and then for a moment
and not spend all your breath trying to conquer it.
Because no battle is ever won he said. They are not
even fought. The field only reveals to man his own
folly and despair, and victory is an illusion of phi-
losophers and fools.

It was propped against the collar box and I lay
listening to it. Hearing it, that is. I dont suppose

anybody ever deliberately listens to a watch or a clock. You dont have to. You can be oblivious to the sound for a long while, then in a second of ticking it can create in the mind unbroken the long diminishing parade of time you didn't hear. Like Father said down the long and lonely light-rays you might see Jesus walking, like. And the good Saint Francis that said Little Sister Death, that never had a sister.

Through the wall I heard Shreve's bed-springs and then his slippers on the floor hishing. I got up and went to the dresser and slid my hand along it and touched the watch and turned it face-down and went back to bed. But the shadow of the sash was still there and I had learned to tell almost to the minute, so I'd have to turn my back to it, feeling the eyes animals used to have in the back of their heads when it was on top, itching. It's always the idle habits you acquire which you will regret. Father said that. That Christ was not crucified: he was worn away by a minute clicking of little wheels. That had no sister.

And so as soon as I knew I couldn't see it, I began to wonder what time it was. Father said that constant speculation regarding the position of mechanical hands on an arbitrary dial which is a symptom of mind-function. Excrement Father said like sweating. And I saying All right. Wonder. Go on and wonder.

If it had been cloudy I could have looked at the

window, thinking what he said about idle habits. Thinking it would be nice for them down at New London if the weather held up like this. Why shouldn't it? The month of brides, the voice that breathed *She ran right out of the mirror, out of the banked scent. Roses. Roses. Mr and Mrs Jason Richmond Compson announce the marriage of.* Roses. Not virgins like dogwood, milkweed. I said I have committed incest, Father I said. Roses. Cunning and serene. If you attend Harvard one year, but dont see the boat-race, there should be a refund. Let Jason have it. Give Jason a year at Harvard.

Shreve stood in the door, putting his collar on, his glasses glinting rosily, as though he had washed them with his face. "You taking a cut this morning?"

"Is it that late?"

He looked at his watch. "Bell in two minutes."

"I didn't know it was that late." He was still looking at the watch, his mouth shaping. "I'll have to hustle. I cant stand another cut. The dean told me last week——" He put the watch back into his pocket. Then I quit talking.

"You'd better slip on your pants and run," he said. He went out.

I got up and moved about, listening to him through the wall. He entered the sitting-room, toward the door.

"Aren't you ready yet?"

"Not yet. Run along. I'll make it."

He went out. The door closed. His feet went down the corridor. Then I could hear the watch again. I quit moving around and went to the window and drew the curtains aside and watched them running for chapel, the same ones fighting the same heaving coat-sleeves, the same books and flapping collars flushing past like debris on a flood, and Spoade. Calling Shreve my husband. Ah let him alone, Shreve said, if he's got better sense than to chase after the little dirty sluts, whose business. In the South you are ashamed of being a virgin. Boys. Men. They lie about it. Because it means less to women, Father said. He said it was men invented virginity not women. Father said it's like death: only a state in which the others are left and I said, But to believe it doesn't matter and he said, That's what's so sad about anything: not only virginity, and I said, Why couldn't it have been me and not her who is unvirgin and he said, That's why that's sad too; nothing is even worth the changing of it, and Shreve said if he's got better sense than to chase after the little dirty sluts and I said Did you ever have a sister? Did you? Did you?

Spoade was in the middle of them like a terrapin in a street full of scuttering dead leaves, his collar about his ears, moving at his customary unhurried walk. He was from South Carolina, a senior. It was his club's boast that he never ran for chapel, and had never got there on time and had never been absent in four years and had never made either chapel or first lecture with a shirt on his back and socks on his feet. About ten oclock he'd come in Thompson's, get two cups of coffee, sit down and take his socks out of his pocket and remove his shoes and put them on while the coffee cooled. About noon you'd see him with a shirt and collar on, like anybody else. The others passed him running, but he never increased his pace at all. After a while the quad was empty.

A sparrow slanted across the sunlight, onto the window ledge, and cocked his head at me. His eye was round and bright. First he'd watch me with one eye, then flick! and it would be the other one, his throat pumping faster than any pulse. The hour began to strike. The sparrow quit swapping eyes and watched me steadily with the same one until the chimes ceased, as if he were listening too. Then he flicked off the ledge and was gone.

It was a while before the last stroke ceased vibrating. It stayed in the air, more felt than heard, for a long time. Like all the bells that ever rang still ringing in the long dying light-rays and Jesus and Saint Francis talking about his sister. Because if it were just to hell; if that were all of it. Finished. If things just finished themselves. Nobody else there but her and me. If we could just have done something so dreadful that they would have fled hell except us. *I have committed incest I said Father it was*

97

I it was not Dalton Ames And when he put Dalton Ames. Dalton Ames. Dalton Ames. When he put the pistol in my hand I didn't. That's why I didn't. He would be there and she would and I would. Dalton Ames. Dalton Ames. Dalton Ames. If we could have just done something so dreadful and Father said That's sad too, people cannot do anything that dreadful they cannot do anything very dreadful at all they cannot even remember tomorrow what seemed dreadful today and I said, You can shirk all things and he said, Ah can you. And I will look down and see my murmuring bones and the deep water like wind, like a roof of wind, and after a long time they cannot distinguish even bones upon the lonely and inviolate sand. Until on the Day when He says Rise only the flat-iron would come floating up. It's not when you realise that nothing can help you — religion, pride, anything — it's when you realise that you dont need any aid. Dalton Ames. Dalton Ames. Dalton Ames. If I could have been his mother lying with open body lifted laughing, holding his father with my hand refraining, seeing, watching him die before he lived. *One minute she was standing in the door*

I went to the dresser and took up the watch, with the face still down. I tapped the crystal on the corner of the dresser and caught the fragments of glass in my hand and put them into the ashtray and twisted the hands off and put them in the tray. The watch ticked on. I turned the face up, the blank dial with little wheels clicking and clicking behind it, not knowing any better. Jesus walking on Galilee and Washington not telling lies. Father brought back a watch-charm from the Saint Louis Fair to Jason: a tiny opera glass into which you squinted with one eye and saw a skyscraper, a ferris wheel all spidery, Niagara Falls on a pinhead. There was a red smear on the dial. When I saw it my thumb began to smart. I put the watch down and went into Shreve's room and got the iodine and painted the cut. I cleaned the rest of the glass out of the rim with the towel.

I laid out two suits of underwear, with socks, shirts, collars and ties, and packed my trunk. I put in everything except my new suit and an old one and two pairs of shoes and two hats, and my books. I carried the books into the sitting-room and stacked them on the table, the ones I had brought from home and the ones *Father said it used to be a gentleman was known by his books; nowadays he is known by the ones he has not returned* and locked the trunk and addressed it. The quarter hour sounded. I stopped and listened to it until the chimes ceased.

I bathed and shaved. The water made my finger smart a little, so I painted it again. I put on my new suit and put my watch on and packed the other suit and the accessories and my razor and brushes in my hand bag, and wrapped the trunk key into a sheet of paper and put it in an envelope and addressed it to Father, and wrote the two notes and sealed them.

The shadow hadn't quite cleared the stoop. I stopped inside the door, watching the shadow move. It moved almost perceptibly, creeping back inside the door, driving the shadow back into the door. *Only she was running already when I heard it. In the mirror she was running before I knew what it was. That quick, her train caught up over her arm she ran out of the mirror like a cloud, her veil swirling in long glints her heels brittle and fast clutching her dress onto her shoulder with the other hand, running out of the mirror the smells roses roses the voice that breathed o'er Eden. Then she was across the porch I couldn't hear her heels then in the moonlight like a cloud, the floating shadow of the veil running across the grass, into the bellowing. She ran out of her dress, clutching her bridal, running into the bellowing where T. P. in the dew Whooey Sassprilluh Benjy under the box bellowing. Father had a V-shaped silver cuirass on his running chest*

Shreve said, "Well, you didn't. . . . Is it a wedding or a wake?"

"I couldn't make it," I said.

"Not with all that primping. What's the matter? You think this was Sunday?"

"I reckon the police wont get me for wearing my new suit one time," I said.

"I was thinking about the Square students. Have you got too proud to attend classes too?"

"I'm going to eat first." The shadow on the stoop was gone. I stepped into sunlight, finding my shadow again. I walked down the steps just ahead of it. The half hour went. Then the chimes ceased and died away.

Deacon wasn't at the postoffice either. I stamped the two envelopes and mailed the one to Father and put Shreve's in my inside pocket, and then I remembered where I had last seen the Deacon. It was on Decoration Day, in a G. A. R. uniform, in the middle of the parade. If you waited long enough on any corner you would see him in whatever parade came along. The one before was on Columbus' or Garibaldi's or somebody's birthday. He was in the Street Sweeper's section, in a stovepipe hat, carrying a two inch Italian flag, smoking a cigar among the brooms and scoops. But the last time was the G. A. R. one, because Shreve said:

"There now. Just look at what your grandpa did to that poor old nigger."

"Yes," I said, "Now he can spend day after day marching in parades. If it hadn't been for my grandfather, he'd have to work like whitefolks."

I didn't see him anywhere. But I never knew even a working nigger that you could find when you wanted him, let alone one that lived off the fat of the land. A car came along. I went over to town and went to Parker's and had a good breakfast. While I was eating I heard a clock strike the hour. But then I suppose it takes at least one hour to lose time in, who has been longer than history getting into the mechanical progression of it.

When I finished breakfast I bought a cigar. The girl said a fifty cent one was the best, so I took one and lit it and went out to the street. I stood there and took a couple of puffs, then I held it in my hand and went on toward the corner. I passed a jeweller's window, but I looked away in time. At the corner two bootblacks caught me, one on either side, shrill and raucous, like blackbirds. I gave the cigar to one of them, and the other one a nickel. Then they let me alone. The one with the cigar was trying to sell it to the other for the nickel.

There was a clock, high up in the sun, and I thought about how, when you dont want to do a thing, your body will try to trick you into doing it, sort of unawares. I could feel the muscles in the back of my neck, and then I could hear my watch ticking away in my pocket and after a while I had all the other sounds shut away, leaving only the watch in my pocket. I turned back up the street, to the window. He was working at the table behind the window. He was going bald. There was a glass in his eye — a metal tube screwed into his face. I went in.

The place was full of ticking, like crickets in September grass, and I could hear a big clock on the wall above his head. He looked up, his eye big and blurred and rushing beyond the glass. I took mine out and handed it to him.

" I broke my watch."

He flipped it over in his hand. " I should say you have. You must have stepped on it."

"Yes, sir. I knocked it off the dresser and stepped on it in the dark. It's still running though."

He pried the back open and squinted into it. "Seems to be all right. I cant tell until I go over it, though. I'll go into it this afternoon."

" I'll bring it back later," I said. " Would you mind telling me if any of those watches in the window are right? "

He held my watch on his palm and looked up at me with his blurred rushing eye.

" I made a bet with a fellow," I said, " And I forgot my glasses this morning."

" Why, all right," he said. He laid the watch down and half rose on his stool and looked over the barrier. Then he glanced up at the wall. " It's twen — "

" Dont tell me," I said, " please sir. Just tell me if any of them are right."

He looked at me again. He sat back on the stool and pushed the glass up onto his forehead. It left a red circle around his eye and when it was gone his whole face looked naked. " What're you celebrating today?" he said. "That boat race aint until next week, is it?"

"No, sir. This is just a private celebration. Birthday. Are any of them right?"

"No. But they haven't been regulated and set yet. If you're thinking of buying one of them —"

"No, sir. I dont need a watch. We have a clock in our sitting room. I'll have this one fixed when I do." I reached my hand.

"Better leave it now."

"I'll bring it back later." He gave me the watch. I put it in my pocket. I couldn't hear it now, above all the others. "I'm much obliged to you. I hope I haven't taken up your time."

"That's all right. Bring it in when you are ready. And you better put off this celebration until after we win that boat race."

"Yes, sir. I reckon I had."

I went out, shutting the door upon the ticking. I looked back into the window. He was watching me across the barrier. There were about a dozen watches in the window, a dozen different hours and each with the same assertive and contradictory assurance that mine had, without any hands at all. Contradicting one another. I could hear mine, ticking away inside my pocket, even though nobody could see it, even though it could tell nothing if anyone could.

And so I told myself to take that one. Because

Father said clocks slay time. He said time is dead as long as it is being clicked off by little wheels; only when the clock stops does time come to life. The hands were extended, slightly off the horizontal at a faint angle, like a gull tilting into the wind. Holding all I used to be sorry about like the new moon holding water, niggers say. The jeweler was working again, bent over his bench, the tube tunnelled into his face. His hair was parted in the center. The part ran up into the bald spot, like a drained marsh in December.

I saw the hardware store from across the street. I didn't know you bought flat-irons by the pound.

The clerk said, "These weigh ten pounds." Only they were bigger than I thought. So I got two six-pound little ones, because they would look like a pair of shoes wrapped up. They felt heavy enough together, but I thought again how Father had said about the reducto absurdum of human experience, thinking how the only opportunity I seemed to have for the application of Harvard. Maybe by next year; thinking maybe it takes two years in school to learn to do that properly.

But they felt heavy enough in the air. A street car came. I got on. I didn't see the placard on the front. It was full, mostly prosperous looking people reading newspapers. The only vacant seat was beside a nigger. He wore a derby and shined shoes and he was holding a dead cigar stub. I used to think that a

Southerner had to be always conscious of niggers. I thought that Northerners would expect him to. When I first came East I kept thinking You've got to remember to think of them as coloured people not niggers, and if it hadn't happened that I wasn't thrown with many of them, I'd have wasted a lot of time and trouble before I learned that the best way to take all people, black or white, is to take them for what they think they are, then leave them alone. That was when I realised that a nigger is not a person so much as a form of behaviour; a sort of obverse reflection of the white people he lives among. But I thought at first that I ought to miss having a lot of them around me because I thought that Northerners thought I did, but I didn't know that I really had missed Roskus and Dilsey and them until that morning in Virginia. The train was stopped when I waked and I raised the shade and looked out. The car was blocking a road crossing, where two white fences came down a hill and then sprayed outward and downward like part of the skeleton of a horn, and there was a nigger on a mule in the middle of the stiff ruts, waiting for the train to move. How long he had been there I didn't know, but he sat straddle of the mule, his head wrapped in a piece of blanket, as if they had been built there with the fence and the road, or with the hill, carved out of the hill itself, like a sign put there saying You are home again. He didn't have a saddle and his feet dangled almost to the ground. The mule looked like a rabbit. I raised the window.

"Hey, Uncle," I said, " Is this the way?"

"Suh?" He looked at me, then he loosened the blanket and lifted it away from his ear.

"Christmas gift!" I said.

"Sho comin, boss. You done caught me, aint you?"

"I'll let you off this time." I dragged my pants out of the little hammock and got a quarter out. "But look out next time. I'll be coming back through here two days after New Year, and look out then." I threw the quarter out the window. " Buy yourself some Santy Claus."

"Yes, suh," he said. He got down and picked up the quarter and rubbed it on his leg. "Thanky, young marster. Thanky." Then the train began to move. I leaned out the window, into the cold air, looking back. He stood there beside the gaunt rabbit of a mule, the two of them shabby and motionless and unimpatient. The train swung around the curve, the engine puffing with short, heavy blasts, and they passed smoothly from sight that way, with that quality about them of shabby and timeless patience, of static serenity: that blending of childlike and ready incompetence and paradoxical reliability that tends and protects them it loves out of all reason and robs them steadily and evades responsibility and obligations by means too barefaced to be called

107

subterfuge even and is taken in theft or evasion with only that frank and spontaneous admiration for the victor which a gentleman feels for anyone who beats him in a fair contest, and withal a fond and unflagging tolerance for whitefolks' vagaries like that of a grandparent for unpredictable and troublesome children, which I had forgotten. And all that day, while the train wound through rushing gaps and along ledges where movement was only a labouring sound of the exhaust and groaning wheels and the eternal mountains stood fading into the thick sky, I thought of home, of the bleak station and the mud and the niggers and country folks thronging slowly about the square, with toy monkeys and wagons and candy in sacks and roman candles sticking out, and my insides would move like they used to do in school when the bell rang.

I wouldn't begin counting until the clock struck three. Then I would begin, counting to sixty and folding down one finger and thinking of the other fourteen fingers waiting to be folded down, or thirteen or twelve or eight or seven, until all of a sudden I'd realise silence and the unwinking minds, and I'd say " Ma'am? " " Your name is Quentin, isn't it ? " Miss Laura said. Then more silence and the cruel unwinking minds and hands jerking into the silence. " Tell Quentin who discovered the Mississippi River, Henry." " DeSoto." Then the minds would go away, and after a while I'd be afraid I had gotten behind and I'd count fast and fold down another finger, then I'd be afraid I was going too fast and I'd slow up, then I'd get afraid and count fast again. So I never could come out even with the bell, and the released surging of feet moving already, feeling earth in the scuffed floor, and the day like a pane of glass struck a light, sharp blow, and my insides would move, sitting still. *Moving sitting still. One minute she was standing in the door. Benjy. Bellowing. Benjamin the child of mine old age bellowing. Caddy! Caddy!*

I'm going to run away. He began to cry she went and touched him. Hush. I'm not going to. Hush. He hushed. Dilsey.

He smell what you tell him when he want to. Dont have to listen nor talk.

Can he smell that new name they give him? Can he smell bad luck?

What he want to worry about luck for? Luck cant do him no hurt.

What they change his name for then if aint trying to help his luck?

The street car stopped, started, stopped again. Below the window I watched the crowns of people's heads passing beneath new straw hats not yet unbleached. There were women in the car now, with market baskets, and men in work-clothes were beginning to outnumber the shined shoes and collars.

The nigger touched my knee. " Pardon me," he said. I swung my legs out and let him pass. We were going beside a blank wall, the sound clattering back into the car, at the women with market baskets on their knees and a man in a stained hat with a pipe stuck in the band. I could smell water, and in a break in the wall I saw a glint of water and two masts, and a gull motionless in midair, like on an invisible wire between the masts, and I raised my hand and through my coat touched the letters I had written. When the car stopped I got off.

The bridge was open to let a schooner through. She was in tow, the tug nudging along under her quarter, trailing smoke, but the ship herself was like she was moving without visible means. A man naked to the waist was coiling down a line on the fo'c's'le head. His body was burned the colour of leaf tobacco. Another man in a straw hat without any crown was at the wheel. The ship went through the bridge, moving under bare poles like a ghost in broad day, with three gulls hovering above the stern like toys on invisible wires.

When it closed I crossed to the other side and leaned on the rail above the boathouses. The float was empty and the doors were closed. The crew just pulled in the late afternoon now, resting up before. The shadow of the bridge, the tiers of railing, my shadow leaning flat upon the water, so easily had I tricked it that would not quit me. At least fifty feet it was, and if I only had something to blot it into the water, holding it until it was drowned, the shadow of the package like two shoes wrapped up lying on the water. Niggers say a drowned man's shadow was watching for him in the water all the time. It twinkled and glinted, like breathing, the float slow like breathing too, and debris half submerged, healing out to the sea and the caverns and the grottoes of the sea. The displacement of water is equal to the something of something. Reducto absurdum of all human experience, and two six-pound flat-irons weigh more than one tailor's goose. What a sinful waste Dilsey would say. Benjy knew it when Damuddy died. He cried. *He smell hit. He smell hit.*

The tug came back downstream, the water shearing in long rolling cylinders, rocking the float at last with the echo of passage, the float lurching onto the rolling cylinder with a plopping sound and a long jarring noise as the door rolled back and two men emerged, carrying a shell. They set it in the water and a moment later Bland came out, with the sculls. He wore flannels, a grey jacket and a stiff straw hat. Either he or his mother had read somewhere that Oxford students pulled in flannels and stiff hats, so early one March they bought Gerald a one pair shell and in his flannels and stiff hat he went on the river. The folks at the boathouses threatened to call a policeman, but he went anyway. His mother came down in a hired auto, in a fur suit like an arctic ex-

plorer's, and saw him off in a twenty-five mile wind
and a steady drove of ice floes like dirty sheep. Ever
since then I have believed that God is not only a
gentleman and a sport; He is a Kentuckian too.
When he sailed away she made a detour and came
down to the river again and drove along parallel
with him, the car in low gear. They said you couldn't
have told they'd ever seen one another before, like
a King and Queen, not even looking at one another,
just moving side by side across Massachusetts on
parallel courses like a couple of planets.

He got in and pulled away. He pulled pretty well
now. He ought to. They said his mother tried to
make him give rowing up and do something else the
rest of his class couldn't or wouldn't do, but for once
he was stubborn. If you could call it stubbornness,
sitting in his attitudes of princely boredom, with his
curly yellow hair and his violet eyes and his eyelashes and his New York clothes, while his mamma
was telling us about Gerald's horses and Gerald's
niggers and Gerald's women. Husbands and fathers
in Kentucky must have been awful glad when she
carried Gerald off to Cambridge. She had an apartment over in town, and Gerald had one there too,
besides his rooms in college. She approved of Gerald
associating with me because I at least revealed a
blundering sense of noblesse oblige by getting myself
born below Mason and Dixon, and a few others
whose geography met the requirements (minimum)

Forgave, at least. Or condoned. But since she met Spoade coming out of chapel one He said she couldn't be a lady no lady would be out at that hour of the night she never had been able to forgive him for having five names, including that of a present English ducal house. I'm sure she solaced herself by being convinced that some misfit Maingault or Mortemar had got mixed up with the lodge-keeper's daughter. Which was quite probable, whether she invented it or not. Spoade was the world's champion sitter-a-round, no holds barred and gouging discretionary.

The shell was a speck now, the oars catching the sun in spaced glints, as if the hull were winking itself along. *Did you ever have a sister? No but they're all bitches. Did you ever have a sister? One minute she was. Bitches. Not bitch one minute she stood in the door* Dalton Ames. Dalton Ames. Dalton Shirts. I thought all the time they were khaki, army issue khaki, until I saw they were of heavy Chinese silk or finest flannel because they made his face so brown his eyes so blue. Dalton Ames. It just missed gentility. Theatrical fixture. Just papier-mache, then touch. Oh. Asbestos. Not quite bronze. *But wont see him at the house.*

Caddy's a woman too, remember. She must do things for women's reasons, too.

Why wont you bring him to the house, Caddy? Why must you do like nigger women do in the pas-

ture the ditches the dark woods hot hidden furious in the dark woods.

And after a while I had been hearing my watch for some time and I could feel the letters crackle through my coat, against the railing, and I leaned on the railing, watching my shadow, how I had tricked it. I moved along the rail, but my suit was dark too and I could wipe my hands, watching my shadow, how I had tricked it. I walked it into the shadow of the quai. Then I went east.

Harvard my Harvard boy Harvard harvard That pimple-faced infant she met at the field-meet with coloured ribbons. Skulking along the fence trying to whistle her out like a puppy. Because they couldn't cajole him into the diningroom Mother believed he had some sort of spell he was going to cast on her when he got her alone. Yet any blackguard *He was lying beside the box under the window bellowing* that could drive up in a limousine with a flower in his buttonhole. *Harvard. Quentin this is Herbert. My Harvard boy. Herbert will be a big brother has already promised Jason a position in the bank.*

Hearty, celluloid like a drummer. Face full of teeth white but not smiling. *I've heard of him up there.* All teeth but not smiling. *You going to drive?*

Get in Quentin.

You going to drive.

It's her car aren't you proud of your little sister owns first auto in town Herbert his present. Louis has been giving her lessons every morning didn't you get my letter Mr and Mrs Jason Richmond Compson announce the marriage of their daughter Candace to Mr Sydney Herbert Head on the twenty-fifth of April one thousand nine hundred and ten at Jefferson Mississippi. At home after the first of August number Something Something Avenue South Bend Indiana. Shreve said Aren't you even going to open it? *Three days. Times. Mr and Mrs Jason Richmond Compson* Young Lochinvar rode out of the west a little too soon, didn't he?

I'm from the south. You're funny, aren't you.

O yes I knew it was somewhere in the country.

You're funny, aren't you. You ought to join the circus.

I did. That's how I ruined my eyes watering the elephant's fleas. *Three times* These country girls. You cant even tell about them, can you. Well, anyway Byron never had his wish, thank God. *But not hit a man in glasses.* Aren't you even going to open it? *It lay on the table a candle burning at each corner upon the envelope tied in a soiled pink garter two artificial flowers. Not hit a man in glasses.*

Country people poor things they never saw an auto before lots of them honk the horn Candace so *She wouldn't look at me* they'll get out of the way *wouldn't look at me* your father wouldn't like it if you were to injure one of them I'll declare your father will simply have to get an auto now I'm almost sorry you brought it down Herbert I've enjoyed it so much of course there's the carriage but so often when I'd like to go out Mr Compson has the darkies doing something it would be worth my head to interrupt he insists that Roskus is at my call all the time but I know what that means I know how often people make promises just to satisfy their consciences are you going to treat my little baby girl that way Herbert but I know you wont Herbert has spoiled us all to death Quentin did I write you that he is going to take Jason into his bank when Jason finishes high school Jason will make a splendid banker he is the only one of my children with any practical sense you can thank me for that he takes after my people the others are all Compson *Jason furnished the flour. They made kites on the back porch and sold them for a nickle a piece, he and the Patterson boy. Jason was treasurer.*

There was no nigger in this street car, and the hats unbleached as yet flowing past under the window. Going to Harvard. We have sold Benjy's *He lay on the ground under the window, bellowing. We have sold Benjy's pasture so that Quentin may go to Harvard* a brother to you. Your little brother.

You should have a car it's done you no end of good dont you think so Quentin I call him Quentin at once you see I have heard so much about him from Candace.

Why shouldn't you I want my boys to be more

116

than friends yes Candace and Quentin more than friends *Father I have committed* what a pity you had no brother or sister *No sister no sister had no sister* Dont ask Quentin he and Mr Compson both feel a little insulted when I am strong enough to come down to the table I am going on nerve now I'll pay for it after it's all over and you have taken my little daughter away from me *My little sister had no. If I could say Mother. Mother*

Unless I do what I am tempted to and take you instead I dont think Mr Compson could overtake the car.

Ah Herbert Candace do you hear that *She wouldn't look at me soft stubborn jaw-angle not back-looking* You needn't be jealous though it's just an old woman he's flattering a grown married daughter I cant believe it.

Nonsense you look like a girl you are lots younger than Candace colour in your cheeks like a girl *A face reproachful tearful an odour of camphor and of tears a voice weeping steadily and softly beyond the twilit door the twilight-coloured smell of honeysuckle. Bringing empty trunks down the attic stairs they sounded like coffins French Lick. Found not death at the salt lick*

Hats not unbleached and not hats. In three years I can not wear a hat. I could not. Was. Will there be hats then since I was not and not Harvard then. Where the best of thought Father said clings like

117

dead ivy vines upon old dead brick. Not Harvard then. Not to me, anyway. Again. Sadder than was. Again. Saddest of all. Again.

Spoade had a shirt on; then it must be. When I can see my shadow again if not careful that I tricked into the water shall tread again upon my impervious shadow. But no sister. I wouldn't have done it. *I wont have my daughter spied on* I wouldn't have.

How can I control any of them when you have always taught them to have no respect for me and my wishes I know you look down on my people but is that any reason for teaching my children my own children I suffered for to have no respect Trampling my shadow's bones into the concrete with hard heels and then I was hearing the watch, and I touched the letters through my coat.

I will not have my daughter spied on by you or Quentin or anybody no matter what you think she has done

At least you agree there is reason for having her watched

I wouldn't have I wouldn't have. *I know you wouldn't I didn't mean to speak so sharply but women have no respect for each other for themselves*

But why did she The chimes began as I stepped on my shadow, but it was the quarter hour. The Deacon wasn't in sight anywhere. *think I would have could have*

She didn't mean that that's the way women do things its because she loves Caddy

The street lamps would go down the hill then rise toward town I walked upon the belly of my shadow. I could extend my hand beyond it. *feeling Father behind me beyond the rasping darkness of summer and August the street lamps* Father and I protect women from one another from themselves our women *Women are like that they dont acquire knowledge of people we are for that they are just born with a practical fertility of suspicion that makes a crop every so often and usually right they have an affinity for evil for supplying whatever the evil lacks in itself for drawing it about them instinctively as you do bedclothing in slumber fertilising the mind for it until the evil has served its purpose whether it ever existed or no* He was coming along between a couple of freshmen. He hadn't quite recovered from the parade, for he gave me a salute, a very superior-officerish kind.

"I want to see you a minute," I said, stopping.

"See me? All right. See you again, fellows," he said, stopping and turning back; "glad to have chatted with you." That was the Deacon, all over. Talk about your natural psychologists. They said he hadn't missed a train at the beginning of school in forty years, and that he could pick out a Southerner with one glance. He never missed, and once he had heard you speak, he could name your state. He had

a regular uniform he met trains in, a sort of Uncle
Tom's cabin outfit, patches and all.

"Yes, suh. Right dis way, young marster, hyer
we is," taking your bags. "Hyer, boy, come hyer
and git dese grips." Whereupon a moving mountain
of luggage would edge up, revealing a white boy of
about fifteen, and the Deacon would hang another
bag on him somehow and drive him off. "Now, den,
dont you drap hit. Yes, suh, young marster, jes give
de old nigger yo room number, and hit'll be done
got cold dar when you arrives."

From then on until he had you completely sub-
jugated he was always in or out of your room,
ubiquitous and garrulous, though his manner gradually moved northward as his raiment improved, until at last when he had bled you until you began to
learn better he was calling you Quentin or whatever, and when you saw him next he'd be wearing a
cast-off Brooks suit and a hat with a Princeton club
I forget which band that someone had given him and
which he was pleasantly and unshakably convinced
was a part of Abe Lincoln's military sash. Someone
spread the story years ago, when he first appeared
around college from wherever he came from, that
he was a graduate of the divinity school. And when
he came to understand what it meant he was so taken
with it that he began to retail the story himself, until at last he must come to believe he really had.
Anyway he related long pointless anecdotes of his

undergraduate days, speaking familiarly of dead and departed professors by their first names, usually incorrect ones. But he had been guide mentor and friend to unnumbered crops of innocent and lonely freshmen, and I suppose that with all his petty chicanery and hypocrisy he stank no higher in heaven's nostrils than any other.

"Haven't seen you in three-four days," he said, staring at me from his still military aura. "You been sick?"

"No. I've been all right. Working, I reckon. I've seen you, though."

"Yes?"

"In the parade the other day."

"Oh, that. Yes, I was there. I dont care nothing about that sort of thing, you understand, but the boys likes to have me with them, the vet'runs does. Ladies wants all the old vet'runs to turn out, you know. So I has to oblige them."

"And on that Wop holiday too," I said. "You were obliging the W. C. T. U. then, I reckon."

"That? I was doing that for my son-in-law. He aims to get a job on the city forces. Street cleaner. I tells him all he wants is a broom to sleep on. You saw me, did you?"

"Both times. Yes."

"I mean, in uniform. How'd I look?"

"You looked fine. You looked better than any of them. They ought to make you a general, Deacon."

He touched my arm, lightly, his hand that worn, gentle quality of niggers' hands. "Listen. This aint for outside talking. I dont mind telling you because you and me's the same folks, come long and short." He leaned a little to me, speaking rapidly, his eyes not looking at me. " I've got strings out, right now. Wait till next year. Just wait. Then see where I'm marching. I wont need to tell you how I'm fixing it; I say, just wait and see, my boy." He looked at me now and clapped me lightly on the shoulder and rocked back on his heels, nodding at me. " Yes, sir. I didnt turn Democrat three years ago for nothing. My son-in-law on the city; me — Yes, sir. If just turning Democrat'll make that son of a bitch go to work. . . . And me: just you stand on that corner yonder a year from two days ago, and see."

" I hope so. You deserve it, Deacon. And while I think about it — " I took the letter from my pocket. "Take this around to my room tomorrow and give it to Shreve. He'll have something for you. But not till tomorrow, mind."

He took the letter and examined it. " It's sealed up."

"Yes. And it's written inside, Not good until to-morrow."

" H'm," he said. He looked at the envelope, his mouth pursed. " Something for me, you say? "

" Yes. A present I'm making you."

He was looking at me now, the envelope white

in his black hand, in the sun. His eyes were soft and irisless and brown, and suddenly I saw Roskus watching me from behind all his whitefolks' claptrap of uniforms and politics and Harvard manner, diffident, secret, inarticulate and sad. "You aint playing a joke on the old nigger, is you?"

"You know I'm not. Did any Southerner ever play a joke on you?"

"You're right. They're fine folks. But you cant live with them."

"Did you ever try?" I said. But Roskus was gone. Once more he was that self he had long since taught himself to wear in the world's eye, pompous, spurious, not quite gross.

"I'll confer to your wishes, my boy."

"Not until tomorrow, remember."

"Sure," he said; "understood, my boy. Well—"

"I hope—" I said. He looked down at me, benignant, profound. Suddenly I held out my hand and we shook, he gravely, from the pompous height of his municipal and military dream. "You're a good fellow, Deacon. I hope. . . . You've helped a lot of young fellows, here and there."

"I've tried to treat all folks right," he said. "I draw no petty social lines. A man to me is a man, wherever I find him."

"I hope you'll always find as many friends as you've made."

"Young fellows. I get along with them. They dont

forget me, neither," he said, waving the envelope. He put it into his pocket and buttoned his coat. "Yes, sir," he said, "I've had good friends."

The chimes began again, the half hour. I stood in the belly of my shadow and listened to the strokes spaced and tranquil along the sunlight, among the thin, still little leaves. Spaced and peaceful and serene, with that quality of autumn always in bells even in the month of brides. *Lying on the ground under the window bellowing* He took one look at her and knew. Out of the mouths of babes. *The street lamps* The chimes ceased. I went back to the post-office, treading my shadow into pavement. *go down the hill then they rise toward town like lanterns hung one above another on a wall.* Father said because she loves Caddy she loves people through their shortcomings. Uncle Maury straddling his legs before the fire must remove one hand long enough to drink Christmas. Jason ran on, his hands in his pockets fell down and lay there like a trussed fowl until Versh set him up. *Whyn't you keep them hands outen your pockets when you running you could stand up then* Rolling his head in the cradle rolling it flat across the back. Caddy told Jason Versh said that the reason Uncle Maury didn't work was that he used to roll his head in the cradle when he was little.

Shreve was coming up the walk, shambling, fatly earnest, his glasses glinting beneath the running leaves like little pools.

"I gave Deacon a note for some things. I may not be in this afternoon, so dont you let him have anything until tomorrow, will you?"

"All right." He looked at me. "Say, what're you doing today, anyhow? All dressed up and mooning around like the prologue to a suttee. Did you go to Psychology this morning?"

"I'm not doing anything. Not until tomorrow, now."

"What's that you got there?"

"Nothing. Pair of shoes I had half-soled. Not until tomorrow, you hear?

"Sure. All right. Oh, by the way, did you get a letter off the table this morning?"

"No."

"It's there. From Semiramis. Chauffeur brought it before ten o'clock."

"All right. I'll get it. Wonder what she wants now."

"Another band recital, I guess. Tumpty ta ta Gerald blah. 'A little louder on the drum, Quentin.' God, I'm glad I'm not a gentleman." He went on, nursing a book, a little shapeless, fatly intent. *The street lamps* do you think so because one of our forefathers was a governor and three were generals and Mother's weren't

any live man is better than any dead man but no live or dead man is very much better than any other live or dead man *Done in Mother's mind though.*

Finished. Finished. Then we were all poisoned you are confusing sin and morality women dont do that your Mother is thinking of morality whether it be sin or not has not occurred to her

Jason I must go away you keep the others I'll take Jason and go where nobody knows us so he'll have a chance to grow up and forget all this the others dont love me they have never loved anything with that streak of Compson selfishness and false pride Jason was the only one my heart went out to without dread

nonsense Jason is all right I was thinking that as soon as you feel better you and Caddy might go up to French Lick

and leave Jason here with nobody but you and the darkies

she will forget him then all the talk will die away *found not death at the salt licks*

maybe I could find a husband for her *not death at the salt licks*

The car came up and stopped. The bells were still ringing the half hour. I got on and it went on again, blotting the half hour. No: the three quarters. Then it would be ten minutes anyway. To leave Harvard *your Mother's dream for sold Benjy's pasture for*

what have I done to have been given children like these Benjamin was punishment enough and now for her to have no more regard for me her own mother I've suffered for her dreamed and planned and sacri-

126

ficed I went down into the valley yet never since she opened her eyes has she given me one unselfish thought at times I look at her I wonder if she can be my child except Jason he has never given me one moment's sorrow since I first held him in my arms I knew then that he was to be my joy and my salvation I thought that Benjamin was punishment enough for any sins I have committed I thought he was my punishment for putting aside my pride and marrying a man who held himself above me I dont complain I loved him above all of them because of it because my duty though Jason pulling at my heart all the while but I see now that I have not suffered enough I see now that I must pay for your sins as well as mine what have you done what sins have your high and mighty people visited upon me but you'll take up for them you always have found excuses for your own blood only Jason can do wrong because he is more Bascomb than Compson while your own daughter my little daughter my baby girl she is she is no better than that when I was a girl I was unfortunate I was only a Bascomb I was taught that there is no halfway ground that a woman is either a lady or not but I never dreamed when I held her in my arms that any daughter of mine could let herself dont you know I can look at her eyes and tell you may think she'd tell you but she doesn't tell things she is secretive you dont know her I know things she's done that I'd die before I'd have you know that's it go on criticise Jason accuse me of setting him to watch her as if it were a crime while your own daughter can I know you dont love him that you wish to believe faults against him you never have yes ridicule him as you always have Maury you cannot hurt me any more than your children already have and then I'll be gone and Jason with no one to love him shield him from this I look at him every day dreading to see this Compson blood beginning to show in him at last with his sister slipping out to see what do you call it then have you ever laid eyes on him will you even let me try to find out who he is it's not for myself I couldn't bear to see him it's for your sake to protect you but who can fight against bad blood you wont let me try we are to sit back with our hands folded while she not only drags your name in the dirt but corrupts the very air your children breathe Jason you must let me go away I cannot stand it let me have Jason and you keep the others they're not my flesh and blood like he is strangers nothing of mine and I am afraid of them I can take Jason and go where we are not known I'll go down on my knees and pray for the absolution of my sins that he may escape this curse try to forget that the others ever were

 If that was the three quarters, not over ten minutes now. One car had just left, and people were already waiting for the next one. I asked, but he didn't know whether another one would leave before noon or not because you'd think that interurbans. So the first one was another trolley. I got on. You can feel noon. I wonder if even miners in the bowels of the earth. That's why whistles: because people that sweat, and if just far enough from sweat you wont hear whistles and in eight minutes you should be that far from sweat in Boston. Father said a man is the sum of his misfortunes. One day you'd think misfortune would get tired, but then time is your misfortune Father said. A gull on an invisible wire attached through space dragged. You carry the symbol of your frustration into eternity. Then the wings are bigger Father said only who can play a harp.

I could hear my watch whenever the car stopped, but not often they were already eating *Who would play a* Eating the business of eating inside of you space too space and time confused Stomach saying noon brain saying eat oclock All right I wonder what time it is what of it. People were getting out. The trolley didn't stop so often now, emptied by eating.

Then it was past. I got off and stood in my shadow and after a while a car came along and I got on and went back to the interurban station. There was a car ready to leave, and I found a seat next the window and it started and I watched it sort of frazzle out into slack tide flats, and then trees. Now and then I saw the river and I thought how nice it would be for them down at New London if the weather and Gerald's shell going solemnly up the glinting forenoon and I wondered what the old woman would be wanting now, sending me a note before ten oclock in the morning. What picture of Gerald I to be one of the *Dalton Ames   oh asbestos   Quentin has shot* background. Something with girls in it. Women do have *always his voice above the gabble voice that breathed* an affinity for evil, for believing that no woman is to be trusted, but that some men are too innocent to protect themselves. Plain girls. Remote cousins and family friends whom mere acquaintanceship invested with a sort of blood obligation noblesse oblige. And she sitting there telling us before their faces what a shame it was that Gerald should have all the family looks because a man didn't need it, was better off without it but without it a girl was simply lost. Telling us about Gerald's women in a *Quentin has shot Herbert he shot his voice through the floor of Caddy's room* tone of smug approbation. "When he was seventeen I said to him one day 'What a shame that you should have a mouth like that it should be on a girls face' and can you imagine *the curtains leaning in on the twilight upon the odour of the apple tree her head against the twilight her arms behind her head kimono-winged the voice that breathed o'er eden clothes upon the bed by the nose seen above the apple* what he said? just seventeen, mind. 'Mother' he said 'it often is.'" And him sitting there in attitudes regal watching two or three of

130

them through his eyelashes. They gushed like swallows swooping his eyelashes. Shreve said he always had *Are you going to look after Benjy and Father*

The less you say about Benjy and Father the better when have you ever considered them Caddy

Promise

You needn't worry about them you're getting out in good shape

Promise I'm sick you'll have to promise wondered who invented that joke but then he always had considered Mrs Bland a remarkably preserved woman he said she was grooming Gerald to seduce a duchess sometime. She called Shreve that fat Canadian youth twice she arranged a new room-mate for me without consulting me at all, once for me to move out, once for

He opened the door in the twilight. His face looked like a pumpkin pie.

"Well, I'll say a fond farewell. Cruel fate may part us, but I will never love another. Never."

"What are you talking about?"

"I'm talking about cruel fate in eight yards of apricot silk and more metal pound for pound than a galley slave and the sole owner and proprietor of the unchallenged peripatetic john of the late Confederacy." Then he told me how she had gone to the proctor to have him moved out and how the proctor had revealed enough low stubbornness to insist on consulting Shreve first. Then she suggested that he send for Shreve right off and do it, and he wouldnt do that, so after that she was hardly civil to Shreve. "I make it a point never to speak harshly of females," Shreve said, "but that woman has got more ways like a bitch than any lady in these sovereign states and dominions." and now Letter on the table by hand, command orchid scented coloured If she knew I had passed almost beneath the window knowing it there without My dear Madam I have not yet had an opportunity of receiving your communication but I beg in advance to be excused today or yesterday and tomorrow or when As I remember that the next one is to be how Gerald throws his nigger downstairs and how the nigger plead to be allowed to matriculate in the divinity school to be near marster marse gerald and How he ran all the way to the station beside the carriage with tears in his eyes when marse gerald rid away I will wait until the day for the one about the sawmill husband came to the kitchen door with a shotgun Gerald went down and bit the gun in two and handed it back and wiped his hands on a silk handkerchief threw the handkerchief in the stove I've only heard that one twice

shot him through the I saw you come in here so I watched my chance and came along thought we might get acquainted have a cigar

Thanks I dont smoke

No things must have changed up there since my day mind if I light up

132

Help yourself

Thanks I've heard a lot I guess your mother wont mind if I put the match behind the screen will she a lot about you Candace talked about you all the time up there at the Licks I got pretty jealous I says to myself who is this Quentin anyway I must see what this animal looks like because I was hit pretty hard see soon as I saw the little girl I dont mind telling you it never occurred to me it was her brother she kept talking about she couldnt have talked about you any more if you'd been the only man in the world husband wouldnt have been in it you wont change your mind and have a smoke

I dont smoke

In that case I wont insist even though it is a pretty fair weed cost me twenty-five bucks a hundred whole-sale friend in Havana yes I guess there are lots of changes up there I keep promising myself a visit but I never get around to it been hitting the ball now for ten years I cant get away from the bank during school fellow's habits change things that seem important to an undergraduate you know tell me about things up there

I'm not going to tell Father and Mother if that's what you are getting at

Not going to tell not going to oh that that's what you are talking about is it you understand that I dont give a damn whether you tell or not understand that a thing like that unfortunate but no police crime

I wasn't the first or the last I was just unlucky you might have been luckier

You lie

Keep your shirt on I'm not trying to make you tell anything you dont want to meant no offense of course a young fellow like you would consider a thing of that sort a lot more serious than you will in five years

I dont know but one way to consider cheating I dont think I'm likely to learn different at Harvard

We're better than a play you must have made the Dramat well you're right no need to tell them we'll let bygones be bygones eh no reason why you and I should let a little thing like that come between us I like you Quentin I like your appearance you dont look like these other hicks I'm glad we're going to hit it off like this I've promised your mother to do something for Jason but I would like to give you a hand too Jason would be just as well off here but there's no future in a hole like this for a young fellow like you

Thanks you'd better stick to Jason he'd suit you better than I would

I'm sorry about that business but a kid like I was then I never had a mother like yours to teach me the finer points it would just hurt her unnecessarily to know it yes you're right no need to that includes Candace of course

I said Mother and Father

Look here take a look at me how long do you think you'd last with me

I wont have to last long if you learned to fight up at school too   try and see how long I would

You damned little   what do you think you're getting at

Try and see

My God the cigar what would your mother say if she found a blister on her mantel just in time too look here Quentin we're about to do something we'll both regret I like you liked you as soon as I saw you I says he must be a damned good fellow whoever he is or Candace wouldnt be so keen on him listen I've been out in the world now for ten years things dont matter so much then you'll find that out let's you and I get together on this thing sons of old Harvard and all I guess I wouldnt know the place now best place for a young fellow in the world I'm going to send my sons there give them a better chance than I had wait dont go yet let's discuss this thing a young man gets these ideas and I'm all for them does him good while he's in school forms his character good for tradition the school but when he gets out into the world he'll have to get his the best way he can because he'll find that everybody else is doing the same thing and be damned to here let's shake hands and let bygones be bygones for your mother's sake remember her health come on give me your hand here look at it it's just out of

convent look not a blemish not even been creased
yet see here

To hell with your money

No no come on I belong to the family now see I
know how it is with a young fellow he has lots of private affairs it's always pretty hard to get the old man
to stump up for I know havent I been there and not
so long ago either but now I'm getting married and
all specially up there come on dont be a fool listen
when we get a chance for a real talk I want to tell
you about a little widow over in town

I've heard that too keep your damned money

Call it a loan then just shut your eyes a minute
and you'll be fifty

Keep your hands off of me you'd better get that
cigar off the mantel

Tell and be damned then see what it gets you if
you were not a damned fool you'd have seen that
I've got them too tight for any half-baked Galahad
of a brother your mother's told me about your sort
with your head swelled up come in oh come in dear
Quentin and I were just getting acquainted talking
about Harvard did you want me cant stay away from
the old man can she

Go out a minute Herbert I want to talk to
Quentin

Come in come in let's all have a gabfest and get acquainted I was just telling Quentin

Go on Herbert go out a while

Well all right then I suppose you and bubber do want to see one another once more eh

You'd better take that cigar off the mantel

Right as usual my boy then I'll toddle along let them order you around while they can Quentin after day after tomorrow it'll be pretty please to the old man wont it dear give us a kiss honey

Oh stop that save that for day after tomorrow

I'll want interest then dont let Quentin do anything he cant finish oh by the way did I tell Quentin the story about the man's parrot and what happened to it a sad story remind me of that think of it yourself ta-ta see you in the funnypaper

Well

Well

What are you up to now

Nothing

You're meddling in my business again didn't you get enough of that last summer

Caddy you've got fever *You're sick how are you sick*

I'm just sick. I cant ask.

Shot his voice through the

Not that blackguard Caddy

Now and then the river glinted beyond things in sort of swooping glints, across noon and after. Well after now, though we had passed where he was still pulling upstream majestical in the face of god gods. Better. Gods. God would be canaille too in Boston in Massachusetts. Or maybe just not a husband. The wet oars winking him along in bright winks and female palms. Adulant. Adulant if not a husband he'd ignore God. *That blackguard, Caddy* The river glinted away beyond a swooping curve.

I'm sick you'll have to promise

Sick how are you sick

I'm just sick I cant ask anybody yet promise you will

If they need any looking after it's because of you how are you sick Under the window we could hear the car leaving for the station, the 8:10 train. To bring back cousins. Heads. Increasing himself head by head but not barbers. Manicure girls. We had a blood horse once. In the stable yes, but under leather a cur. *Quentin has shot all of their voices through the floor of Caddy's room*

The car stopped. I got off, into the middle of my shadow. A road crossed the track. There was a wooden marquee with an old man eating something out of a paper bag, and then the car was out of hearing too. The road went into the trees, where it would be shady, but June foliage in New England not much thicker than April at home in Mississippi. I could see a smoke stack. I turned my back to it, tramping my shadow into the dust. *There was something terrible in me sometimes at night I could see it grinning at me I could see it through them grinning at me through their faces it's gone now and I'm sick*

138

Caddy
Dont touch me just promise
If you're sick you cant
Yes I can after that it'll be all right it wont matter dont let them send him to Jackson promise
I promise Caddy Caddy
Dont touch me dont touch me
What does it look like Caddy
What
That that grins at you that thing through them
I could still see the smoke stack. That's where the water would be, heading out to the sea and the peaceful grottoes. Tumbling peacefully they would, and when He said Rise only the flat irons. When Versh and I hunted all day we wouldn't take any lunch, and at twelve oclock I'd get hungry. I'd stay hungry until about one, then all of a sudden I'd even forget that I wasn't hungry anymore. *The street lamps go down the hill then heard the car go down the hill. The chair-arm flat cool smooth under my forehead shaping the chair the apple tree leaning on my hair above the eden clothes by the nose seen* You've got fever I felt it yesterday it's like being near a stove.

Dont touch me.

Caddy you cant do it if you are sick. That blackguard.

I've got to marry somebody. *Then they told me the bone would have to be broken again*

At last I couldn't see the smoke stack. The road

went beside a wall. Trees leaned over the wall, sprayed with sunlight. The stone was cool. Walking near it you could feel the coolness. Only our country was not like this country. There was something about just walking through it. A kind of still and violent fecundity that satisfied ever bread-hunger like. Flowing around you, not brooding and nursing every niggard stone. Like it were put to makeshift for enough green to go around among the trees and even the blue of distance not that rich chimaera. *told me the bone would have to be broken again and inside me it began to say Ah Ah Ah and I began to sweat. What do I care I know what a broken leg is all it is it wont be anything I'll just have to stay in the house a little longer that's all and my jaw-muscles getting numb and my mouth saying Wait Wait just a minute through the sweat ah ah ah behind my teeth and Father damn that horse damn that horse. Wait it's my fault. He came along the fence every morning with a basket toward the kitchen dragging a stick along the fence every morning I dragged myself to the window cast and all and laid for him with a piece of coal Dilsey said you goin to ruin yoself aint you got no mo sense than that not fo days since you bruck hit. Wait I'll get used to it in a minute wait just a minute I'll get*

Even sound seemed to fail in this air, like the air was worn out with carrying sounds so long. A dog's voice carries further than a train, in the darkness anyway. And some people's. Niggers. Louis Hatcher never even used his horn carrying it and that old lantern. I said, "Louis, when was the last time you cleaned that lantern?"

"I cleant hit a little while back. You member when all dat flood-watter wash dem folks away up yonder? I cleant hit dat ve'y day. Old woman and me settin fore de fire dat night and she say 'Louis, whut you gwine do ef dat flood git out dis fur?' and I say 'Dat's a fack. I reckon I had better clean dat lantun up.' So I cleant hit dat night."

"That flood was way up in Pennsylvania," I said. "It couldn't even have got down this far."

"Dat's whut you says," Louis said. "Watter kin git des ez high en wet in Jefferson ez hit kin in Pennsylvaney, I reckon. Hit's de folks dat says de high watter cant git dis fur dat comes floatin out on de ridge-pole, too."

"Did you and Martha get out that night?"

"We done jest that. I cleant dat lantun and me and her sot de balance of de night on top o dat knoll back de graveyard. En ef I'd a knowed of aihy one higher, we'd a been on hit instead."

"And you haven't cleaned that lantern since then."

"Whut I want to clean hit when dey aint no need?"

"You mean, until another flood comes along?"

"Hit kep us outen dat un."

"Oh, come on, Uncle Louis," I said.

"Yes, suh. You do you way en I do mine. Ef all I got to do to keep outen de high watter is to clean dis yere lantun, I wont quoil wid no man."

"Unc' Louis wouldn't ketch nothin wid a light he could see by," Versh said.

"I wuz huntin possums in dis country when dey was still drowndin nits in yo pappy's head wid coal oil, boy," Louis said. "Ketchin um, too."

"Dat's de troof," Versh said. "I reckon Unc' Louis done caught mo possums than aihy man in dis country."

"Yes, suh," Louis said, "I got plenty light fer possums to see, all right. I aint heard none o dem complainin. Hush, now. Dar he. Whooey. Hum awn, dawg." And we'd sit in the dry leaves that whispered a little with the slow respiration of our waiting and with the slow breathing of the earth and the windless October, the rank smell of the lantern fouling the brittle air, listening to the dogs and to the echo of Louis' voice dying away. He never raised it, yet on a still night we have heard it from our front porch. When he called the dogs in he sounded just like the horn he carried slung on his shoulder and never used, but clearer, mellower, as though his voice were a part of darkness and silence, coiling out of it, coiling into it again. WhoOoooo. WhoOoooo. WhoOoooo-oooooooooooo. *Got to marry somebody*

Have there been very many Caddy

142

*I dont know too many will you look after Benjy
and Father*

You dont know whose it is then does he know

*Dont touch me will you look after Benjy and
Father*

I began to feel the water before I came to the
bridge. The bridge was of grey stone, lichened, dappled with slow moisture where the fungus crept.
Beneath it the water was clear and still in the
shadow, whispering and clucking about the stone in
fading swirls of spinning sky. *Caddy that*

I've got to marry somebody Versh told me about
a man mutilated himself. He went into the woods
and did it with a razor, sitting in a ditch. A broken
razor flinging them backward over his shoulder the
same motion complete the jerked skein of blood
backward not looping. But that's not it. It's not not
having them. It's never to have had them then I
could say O That That's Chinese I dont know Chinese. And Father said it's because you are a virgin:
dont you see? Women are never virgins. Purity is a
negative state and therefore contrary to nature. It's
nature is hurting you not Caddy and I said That's
just words and he said So is virginity and I said you
dont know. You cant know and he said Yes. On the
instant when we come to realise that tragedy is
second-hand.

Where the shadow of the bridge fell I could see
down for a long way, but not as far as the bottom.

43

When you leave a leaf in water a long time after awhile the tissue will be gone and the delicate fibers waving slow as the motion of sleep. They dont touch one another, no matter how knotted up they once were, no matter how close they lay once to the bones. And maybe when He says Rise the eyes will come floating up too, out of the deep quiet and the sleep, to look on glory. And after awhile the flat irons would come floating up. I hid them under the end of the bridge and went back and leaned on the rail.

I could not see the bottom, but I could see a long way into the motion of the water before the eye gave out, and then I saw a shadow hanging like a fat arrow stemming into the current. Mayflies skimmed in and out of the shadow of the bridge just above the surface. *If it could just be a hell beyond that: the clean flame the two of us more than dead. Then you will have only me then only me then the two of us amid the pointing and the horror beyond the clean flame* The arrow increased without motion, then in a quick swirl the trout lipped a fly beneath the surface with that sort of gigantic delicacy of an elephant picking up a peanut. The fading vortex drifted away down stream and then I saw the arrow again, nose into the current, wavering delicately to the motion of the water above which the May flies slanted and poised. *Only you and me then amid the pointing and the horror walled by the clean flame*

The trout hung, delicate and motionless among the wavering shadows. Three boys with fishing poles came onto the bridge and we leaned on the rail and looked down at the trout. They knew the fish. He was a neighbourhood character.

"They've been trying to catch that trout for twenty-five years. There's a store in Boston offers a twenty-five dollar fishing rod to anybody that can catch him."

"Why dont you all catch him, then? Wouldnt you like to have a twenty-five dollar fishing rod?"

"Yes," they said. They leaned on the rail, looking down at the trout. "I sure would," one said.

"I wouldnt take the rod," the second said. "I'd take the money instead."

"Maybe they wouldnt do that," the first said. "I bet he'd make you take the rod."

"Then I'd sell it."

"You couldnt get twenty-five dollars for it."

"I'd take what I could get, then. I can catch just as many fish with this pole as I could with a twenty-five dollar one." Then they talked about what they would do with twenty-five dollars. They all talked at once, their voices insistent and contradictory and impatient, making of unreality a possibility, then a probability, then an incontrovertible fact, as people will when their desires become words.

"I'd buy a horse and wagon," the second said.

"Yes you would," the others said.

145

"I would. I know where I can buy one for twenty-five dollars. I know the man."

"Who is it?"

"That's all right who it is. I can buy it for twenty-five dollars."

"Yah," the others said, "He dont know any such thing. He's just talking."

"Do you think so?" the boy said. They continued to jeer at him, but he said nothing more. He leaned on the rail, looking down at the trout which he had already spent, and suddenly the acrimony, the conflict, was gone from their voices, as if to them too it was as though he had captured the fish and bought his horse and wagon, they too partaking of that adult trait of being convinced of anything by an assumption of silent superiority. I suppose that people, using themselves and each other so much by words, are at least consistent in attributing wisdom to a still tongue, and for a while I could feel the other two seeking swiftly for some means by which to cope with him, to rob him of his horse and wagon.

"You couldnt get twenty-five dollars for that pole," the first said. "I bet anything you couldnt."

"He hasnt caught that trout yet," the third said suddenly, then they both cried:

"Yah, wha'd I tell you? What's the man's name? I dare you to tell. There aint any such man."

"Ah, shut up," the second said. "Look, Here he comes again." They leaned on the rail, motionless, identical, their poles slanting slenderly in the sunlight, also identical. The trout rose without haste, a shadow in faint wavering increase; again the little vortex faded slowly downstream. "Gee," the first one murmured.

"We dont try to catch him anymore," he said. "We just watch Boston folks that come out and try."

"Is he the only fish in this pool?"

"Yes. He ran all the others out. The best place to fish around here is down at the Eddy."

"No it aint," the second said. "It's better at Bigelow's Mill two to one." Then they argued for a while about which was the best fishing and then left off all of a sudden to watch the trout rise again and the broken swirl of water suck down a little of the sky. I asked how far it was to the nearest town. They told me.

"But the closest car line is that way," the second said, pointing back down the road. "Where are you going?"

"Nowhere. Just walking."

"You from the college?"

"Yes. Are there any factories in that town?"

"Factories?" They looked at me.

"No," the second said. "Not there." They looked at my clothes. "You looking for work?"

"How about Bigelow's Mill?" the third said. "That's a factory."

"Factory my eye. He means a sure enough factory."

"One with a whistle," I said. "I havent heard any one oclock whistles yet."

"Oh," the second said. "There's a clock in the Unitarian steeple. You can find out the time from that. Havent you got a watch on that chain?"

"I broke it this morning." I showed them my watch. They examined it gravely.

"It's still running," the second said. "What does a watch like that cost?"

"It was a present," I said. "My father gave it to me when I graduated from high school."

"Are you a Canadian?" the third said. He had red hair.

"Canadian?"

"He dont talk like them," the second said. "I've heard them talk. He talks like they do in minstrel shows."

"Say," the third said, "Aint you afraid he'll hit you?"

"Hit me?"

"You said he talks like a coloured man."

"Ah, dry up," the second said. "You can see the steeple when you get over that hill there."

I thanked them. "I hope you have good luck. Only dont catch that old fellow down there. He deserves to be let alone."

"Cant anybody catch that fish," the first said. They leaned on the rail, looking down into the water, the three poles like three slanting threads of yellow fire in the sun. I walked upon my shadow, tramping it into the dappled shade of trees again. The road curved, mounting away from the water. It crossed the hill, then descended winding, carrying the eye, the mind on ahead beneath a still green tunnel, and the square cupola above the trees and the round eye of the clock but far enough. I sat down at the roadside. The grass was ankle deep, myriad. The shadows on the road were as still as if they had been put there with a stencil, with slanting pencils of sunlight. But it was only a train, and after a while it died away beyond the trees, the long sound, and then I could hear my watch and the train dying away, as though it were running through another month or another summer somewhere, rushing away under the poised gull and all things rushing. Except Gerald. He would be sort of grand too, pulling in lonely state across the noon, rowing himself right out of noon, up the long bright air like an apotheosis, mounting into a drowsing infinity where only he and the gull, the one terrifically motionless, the other in a steady and measured pull and recover that partook of inertia itself, the world punily beneath their shadows on the sun. Caddy that blackguard that blackguard Caddy

Their voices came over the hill, and the three

149

slender poles like balanced threads of running fire. They looked at me passing, not slowing.

"Well," I said, "I dont see him."

"We didnt try to catch him," the first said. "You cant catch that fish."

"There's the clock," the second said, pointing. "You can tell the time when you get a little closer."

"Yes," I said, "All right." I got up. "You all going to town?"

"We're going to the Eddy for chub," the first said.

"You cant catch anything at the Eddy," the second said.

"I guess you want to go to the mill, with a lot of fellows splashing and scaring all the fish away."

"You cant catch any fish at the Eddy."

"We wont catch none nowhere if we dont go on," the third said.

"I dont see why you keep on talking about the Eddy," the second said. "You cant catch anything there."

"You dont have to go," the first said. "You're not tied to me."

"Let's go to the mill and go swimming," the third said.

"I'm going to the Eddy and fish," the first said. "You can do as you please."

"Say, how long has it been since you heard of

anybody catching a fish at the Eddy?" the second said to the third.

"Let's go to the mill and go swimming," the third said. The cupola sank slowly beyond the trees, with the round face of the clock far enough yet. We went on in the dappled shade. We came to an orchard, pink and white. It was full of bees; already we could hear them.

"Let's go to the mill and go swimming," the third said. A lane turned off beside the orchard. The third boy slowed and halted. The first went on, flecks of sunlight slipping along the pole across his shoulder and down the back of his shirt. "Come on," the third said. The second boy stopped too. *Why must you marry somebody Caddy*

Do you want me to say it do you think that if I say it it wont be

"Let's go up to the mill," he said. "Come on."

The first boy went on. His bare feet made no sound, falling softer than leaves in the thin dust. In the orchard the bees sounded like a wind getting up, a sound caught by a spell just under crescendo and sustained. The lane went along the wall, arched over, shattered with bloom, dissolving into trees. Sunlight slanted into it, sparse and eager. Yellow butterflies flickered along the shade like flecks of sun.

"What do you want to go to the Eddy for?" the second boy said. "You can fish at the mill if you want to."

"Ah, let him go," the third said. They looked after the first boy. Sunlight slid patchily across his walking shoulders, glinting along the pole like yellow ants.

"Kenny," the second said. *Say it to Father will you I will am my fathers Progenitive I invented him created I him Say it to him it will not be for he will say I was not and then you and I since philoprogenitive*

"Ah, come on," the boy said, "They're already in." They looked after the first boy. "Yah," they said suddenly, "go on then, mamma's boy. If he goes swimming he'll get his head wet and then he'll get a licking." They turned into the lane and went on, the yellow butterflies slanting about them along the shade.

it is because there is nothing else I believe there is something else but there may not be and then I You will find that even injustice is scarcely worthy of what you believe yourself to be He paid me no attention, his jaw set in profile, his face turned a little away beneath his broken hat.

"Why dont you go swimming with them?" I said. *that blackguard Caddy*

Were you trying to pick a fight with him were you

A liar and a scoundrel Caddy was dropped from his club for cheating at cards got sent to Coventry caught cheating at midterm exams and expelled

152

*Well what about it I'm not going to play cards
with*

"Do you like fishing better than swimming?" I
said. The sound of the bees diminished, sustained
yet, as though instead of sinking into silence, silence
merely increased between us, as water rises. The
road curved again and became a street between shady
lawns with white houses. *Caddy that blackguard can
you think of Benjy and Father and do it not of me*

*What else can I think about what else have I
thought about* The boy turned from the street. He
climbed a picket fence without looking back and
crossed the lawn to a tree and laid the pole down and
climbed into the fork of the tree and sat there, his
back to the road and the dappled sun motionless at
last upon his white shirt. *Else have I thought about
I cant even cry I died last year I told you I had but I
didnt know then what I meant I didnt know what
I was saying* Some days in late August at home are
like this, the air thin and eager like this, with something in it sad and nostalgic and familiar. Man the
sum of his climatic experiences Father said. Man the
sum of what have you. A problem in impure proper-
ties carried tediously to an unvarying nil: stalemate
of dust and desire. *But now I know I'm dead I tell
you*

*Then why must you listen we can go away you
and Benjy and me where nobody knows us where* The
buggy was drawn by a white horse, his feet clopping

in the thin dust; spidery wheels chattering thin and dry, moving uphill beneath a rippling shawl of leaves. Elm. No: ellum. Ellum.

On what on your school money the money they sold the pasture for so you could go to Harvard dont you see you've got to finish now if you dont finish he'll have nothing

Sold the pasture His white shirt was motionless in the fork, in the flickering shade. The wheels were spidery. Beneath the sag of the buggy the hooves neatly rapid like the motions of a lady doing embroidery, diminishing without progress like a figure on a treadmill being drawn rapidly offstage. The street turned again. I could see the white cupola, the round stupid assertion of the clock. *Sold the pasture*

Father will be dead in a year they say if he doesnt stop drinking and he wont stop he cant stop since I since last summer and then they'll send Benjy to Jackson I cant cry I cant even cry one minute she was standing in the door the next minute he was pulling at her dress and bellowing his voice hammered back and forth between the walls in waves and she shrinking against the wall getting smaller and smaller with her white face her eyes like thumbs dug into it until he pushed her out of the room his voice hammering back and forth as though its own momentum would not let it stop as though there were no place for it in silence bellowing

154

When you opened the door a bell tinkled, but just once, high and clear and small in the neat obscurity above the door, as though it were gauged and tempered to make that single clear small sound so as not to wear the bell out nor to require the expenditure of too much silence in restoring it when the door opened upon the recent warm scent of baking; a little dirty child with eyes like a toy bear's and two patent-leather pig-tails.

"Hello, sister." Her face was like a cup of milk dashed with coffee in the sweet warm emptiness. "Anybody here?"

But she merely watched me until a door opened and the lady came. Above the counter where the ranks of crisp shapes behind the glass her neat grey face her hair tight and sparse from her neat grey skull, spectacles in neat grey rims riding approaching like something on a wire, like a cash box in a store. She looked like a librarian. Something among dusty shelves of ordered certitudes long divorced from reality, desiccating peacefully, as if a breath of that air which sees injustice done

"Two of these, please, ma'am."

From under the counter she produced a square cut from a newspaper and laid it on the counter and lifted the two buns out. The little girl watched them with still and unwinking eyes like two currants floating motionless in a cup of weak coffee Land of the kike home of the wop. Watching the bread, the neat

155

grey hands, a broad gold band on the left forefinger, knuckled there by a blue knuckle.

" Do you do your own baking, ma'am ? "

" Sir ? " she said. Like that. Sir ? Like on the stage. Sir ? " Five cents. Was there anything else ? "

" No, ma'am. Not for me. This lady wants something." She was not tall enough to see over the case, so she went to the end of the counter and looked at the little girl.

" Did you bring her in here ? "

" No, ma'am. She was here when I came."

" You little wretch," she said. She came out around the counter, but she didnt touch the little girl. " Have you got anything in your pockets ? "

" She hasnt got any pockets," I said. " She wasnt doing anything. She was just standing here, waiting for you."

" Why didnt the bell ring, then ? " She glared at me. She just needed a bunch of switches, a blackboard behind her 2 x 2 e 5. " She'll hide it under her dress and a body'd never know it. You, child. How'd you get in here ? "

The little girl said nothing. She looked at the woman, then she gave me a flying black glance and looked at the woman again, " Them foreigners," the woman said. " How'd she get in without the bell ringing ? "

" She came in when I opened the door," I said. " It rang once for both of us. She couldnt reach anything from here, anyway. Besides, I dont think she would. Would you, sister?" The little girl looked at me, secretive, contemplative. "What do you want? bread?"

She extended her fist. It uncurled upon a nickel, moist and dirty, moist dirt ridged into her flesh. The coin was damp and warm. I could smell it, faintly metallic.

"Have you got a five cent loaf, please, ma'am?"

From beneath the counter she produced a square cut from a newspaper sheet and laid it on the counter and wrapped a loaf into it. I laid the coin and another one on the counter. "And another one of those buns, please, ma'am."

She took another bun from the case. "Give me that parcel," she said. I gave it to her and she unwrapped it and put the third bun in and wrapped it and took up the coins and found two coppers in her apron and gave them to me. I handed them to the little girl. Her fingers closed about them, damp and hot, like worms.

"You going to give her that bun?" the woman said.

"Yessum," I said. "I expect your cooking smells as good to her as it does to me."

I took up the two packages and gave the bread to the little girl, the woman all iron-grey behind the counter, watching us with cold certitude. "You wait a minute," she said. She went to the rear. The door opened again and closed. The little girl watched me, holding the bread against her dirty dress.

"What's your name?" I said. She quit looking at me, but she was still motionless. She didnt even seem to breathe. The woman returned. She had a funny looking thing in her hand. She carried it sort of like it might have been a dead pet rat.

"Here," she said. The child looked at her. "Take it," the woman said, jabbing it at the little girl. "It just looks peculiar. I calculate you wont know the difference when you eat it. Here. I cant stand here all day." The child took it, still watching her. The woman rubbed her hands on her apron. "I got to have that bell fixed," she said. She went to the door and jerked it open. The little bell tinkled once, faint and clear and invisible. We moved toward the door and the woman's peering back.

"Thank you for the cake," I said.

"Them foreigners," she said, staring up into the obscurity where the bell tinkled. "Take my advice and stay clear of them, young man."

"Yessum," I said. "Come on, sister." We went out. "Thank you, ma'am."

She swung the door to, then jerked it open again, making the bell give forth its single small note. "Foreigners," she said, peering up at the bell.

We went on. "Well," I said, "How about some ice cream?" She was eating the gnarled cake. "Do you like ice cream?" She gave me a black still look, chewing. "Come on."

We came to the drugstore and had some ice cream. She wouldn't put the loaf down. "Why not put it down so you can eat better?" I said, offering to take it. But she held to it, chewing the ice cream like it was taffy. The bitten cake lay on the table. She ate the ice cream steadily, then she fell to on the cake again, looking about at the showcases. I finished mine and we went out.

"Which way do you live?" I said.

A buggy, the one with the white horse it was. Only Doc Peabody is fat. Three hundred pounds. You ride with him on the uphill side, holding on. Children. Walking easier than holding uphill. *Seen the doctor yet have you seen Caddy*

I dont have to I cant ask now afterward it will be all right it wont matter

Because women so delicate so mysterious Father said. Delicate equilibrium of periodical filth between two moons balanced. Moons he said full and yellow as harvest moons her hips thighs. Outside outside of them always but. Yellow. Feet soles with walking like. Then know that some man that all those mysterious and imperious concealed. With all that inside of them shapes an outward suavity waiting for a touch to. Liquid putrefaction like drowned things floating like pale rubber flabbily filled getting the odour of honeysuckle all mixed up.

"You'd better take your bread on home, hadnt you?"

She looked at me. She chewed quietly and steadily; at regular intervals a small distension passed smoothly down her throat. I opened my package and gave her one of the buns. "Goodbye," I said.

I went on. Then I looked back. She was behind me. "Do you live down this way?" She said nothing. She walked beside me, under my elbow sort of, eating. We went on. It was quiet, hardly anyone about *getting the odour of honeysuckle all mixed She would have told me not to let me sit there on the steps hearing her door twilight slamming hearing Benjy still crying Supper she would have to come down then getting honeysuckle all mixed up in it* We reached the corner.

"Well, I've got to go down this way," I said, "Goodbye." She stopped too. She swallowed the last of the cake, then she began on the bun, watching me across it. "Goodbye," I said. I turned into the street and went on, but I went to the next corner before I stopped.

"Which way do you live?" I said. "This way?" I pointed down the street. She just looked at me. "Do you live over that way? I bet you live close to the station, where the trains are. Dont you?" She just looked at me, serene and secret and chewing. The street was empty both ways, with quiet lawns and houses neat among the trees, but no one at all except back there. We turned and went back. Two men sat in chairs in front of a store.

"Do you all know this little girl? She sort of took up with me and I cant find where she lives."

They quit looking at me and looked at her.

"Must be one of them new Italian families," one said. He wore a rusty frock coat. "I've seen her before. What's your name, little girl?" She looked at them blackly for awhile, her jaws moving steadily. She swallowed without ceasing to chew.

"Maybe she cant speak English," the other said.

"They sent her after bread," I said. "She must be able to speak something."

"What's your pa's name?" the first said. "Pete? Joe? name John huh?" She took another bite from the bun.

"What must I do with her?" I said. "She just follows me. I've got to get back to Boston."

"You from the college?"

"Yes, sir. And I've got to get on back."

"You might go up the street and turn her over to Anse. He'll be up at the livery stable. The marshall."

"I reckon that's what I'll have to do," I said. "I've got to do something with her. Much obliged. Come on, sister."

We went up the street, on the shady side, where the shadow of the broken façade blotted slowly across the road. We came to the livery stable. The marshall wasnt there. A man sitting in a chair tilted in the broad low door, where a dark cool breeze smelling of ammonia blew among the ranked stalls, said to look at the postoffice. He didn't know her either.

"Them furriners. I cant tell one from another. You might take her across the tracks where they live, and maybe somebody'll claim her."

We went to the postoffice. It was back down the street. The man in the frock coat was opening a newspaper.

"Anse just drove out of town," he said. "I guess you'd better go down past the station and walk past them houses by the river. Somebody there'll know her."

"I guess I'll have to," I said. "Come on, sister." She pushed the last piece of the bun into her mouth and swallowed it. "Want another?" I said. She looked at me, chewing, her eyes black and unwinking and friendly. I took the other two buns out and gave her one and bit into the other. I asked a man where the station was and he showed me. "Come on, sister."

We reached the station and crossed the tracks, where the river was. A bridge crossed it, and a street of jumbled frame houses followed the river, backed onto it. A shabby street, but with an air heterogeneous and vivid too. In the center of an untrimmed plot enclosed by a fence of gaping and broken pickets stood an ancient lopsided surrey and a weathered house from an upper window of which hung a garment of vivid pink.

"Does that look like your house?" I said. She looked at me over the bun. "This one?" I said, pointing. She just chewed, but it seemed to me that I discerned something affirmative, acquiescent even if it wasn't eager, in her air. "This one?" I said. "Come on, then." I entered the broken gate. I looked back at her. "Here?" I said. "This look like your house?"

She nodded her head rapidly, looking at me, gnawing into the damp halfmoon of the bread. We went on. A walk of broken random flags, speared by fresh coarse blades of grass, led to the broken stoop. There was no movement about the house at all, and the pink garment hanging in no wind from the upper window. There was a bell pull with a porcelain knob, attached to about six feet of wire when I stopped pulling and knocked. The little girl had the crust edgeways in her chewing mouth.

A woman opened the door. She looked at me, then she spoke rapidly to the little girl in Italian, with a rising inflexion, then a pause, interrogatory. She spoke to her again, the little girl looking at her across the end of the crust, pushing it into her mouth with a dirty hand.

"She says she lives here," I said. "I met her down town. Is this your bread?"

"No spika," the woman said. She spoke to the

little girl again. The little girl just looked at her.

"No live here?" I said. I pointed to the girl, then at her, then at the door. The woman shook her head. She spoke rapidly. She came to the edge of the porch and pointed down the road, speaking.

I nodded violently too. "You come show?" I said. I took her arm, waving my other hand toward the road. She spoke swiftly, pointing. "You come show," I said, trying to lead her down the steps.

"Si, si," she said, holding back, showing me whatever it was. I nodded again.

"Thanks. Thanks. Thanks." I went down the steps and walked toward the gate, not running, but pretty fast. I reached the gate and stopped and looked at her for a while. The crust was gone now, and she looked at me with her black, friendly stare. The woman stood on the stoop, watching us.

"Come on, then," I said. "We'll have to find the right one sooner or later."

She moved along just under my elbow. We went on. The houses all seemed empty. Not a soul in sight. A sort of breathlessness that empty houses have. Yet they couldnt all be empty. All the different rooms, if you could just slice the walls away all of a sudden Madam, your daughter, if you please. No. Madam, for God's sake, your daughter. She moved along just under my elbow, her shiny tight pigtails, and then the last house played out and the road curved out

164

of sight beyond a wall, following the river. The woman was emerging from the broken gate, with a shawl over her head and clutched under her chin. The road curved on, empty. I found a coin and gave it to the little girl. A quarter. " Goodbye, sister," I said. Then I ran.

I ran fast, not looking back. Just before the road curved away I looked back. She stood in the road, a small figure clasping the loaf of bread to her filthy little dress, her eyes still and black and unwinking. I ran on.

A lane turned from the road. I entered it and after a while I slowed to a fast walk. The lane went between back premises — unpainted houses with more of those gay and startling coloured garments on lines, a barn broken-backed, decaying quietly among rank orchard trees, unpruned and weed-choked, pink and white and murmurous with sunlight and with bees. I looked back. The entrance to the lane was empty. I slowed still more, my shadow pacing me, dragging its head through the weeds that hid the fence.

The lane went back to a barred gate, became defunctive in grass, a mere path scarred quietly into new grass. I climbed the gate into a woodlot and crossed it and came to another wall and followed that one, my shadow behind me now. There were vines and creepers where at home would be honeysuckle. Coming and coming especially in the dusk when it rained, getting honeysuckle all mixed up in it as though it were not enough without that, not unbearable enough. *What did you let him for kiss kiss*

I didn't let him I made him watching me getting mad What do you think of that? Red print of my hand coming up through her face like turning a light on under your hand her eyes going bright

It's not for kissing I slapped you. Girl's elbows at fifteen Father said you swallow like you had a fishbone in your throat what's the matter with you and Caddy across the table not to look at me. It's for letting it be some darn town squirt I slapped you you will will you now I guess you say calf rope. My red hand coming up out of her face. What do you think of that scouring her head into the. Grass sticks crisscrossed into the flesh tingling scouring her head. Say calf rope say it

I didnt kiss a dirty girl like Natalie anyway The wall went into shadow, and then my shadow, I had tricked it again. I had forgot about the river curving along the road. I climbed the wall. And then she watched me jump down, holding the loaf against her dress.

I stood in the weeds and we looked at one another for a while.

"Why didnt you tell me you lived out this way, sister?" The loaf was wearing slowly out of the paper; already it needed a new one. "Well, come on then and show me the house." *not a dirty girl like*

Natalie. It was raining we could hear it on the roof, sighing through the high sweet emptiness of the barn.

There? touching her

Not there

There? not raining hard but we couldnt hear anything but the roof and as if it was my blood or her blood

She pushed me down the ladder and ran off and left me Caddy did

Was it there it hurt you when Caddy did ran off was it there

Oh She walked just under my elbow, the top of her patent leather head, the loaf fraying out of the newspaper.

"If you dont get home pretty soon you're going to wear that loaf out. And then what'll your mamma say?" *I bet I can lift you up*

You cant I'm too heavy

Did Caddy go away did she go to the house you cant see the barn from our house did you ever try to see the barn from

It was her fault she pushed me she ran away

I can lift you up see how I can

Oh her blood or my blood Oh We went on in the thin dust, our feet silent as rubber in the thin dust where pencils of sun slanted in the trees. And I could feel water again running swift and peaceful in the secret shade.

You live a long way, dont you. You're mighty smart to go this far to town by yourself." *It's like dancing sitting down did you ever dance sitting down? We could hear the rain, a rat in the crib, the empty barn vacant with horses. How do you hold to dance do you hold like this*

Oh

I used to hold like this you thought I wasnt strong enough didn't you

Oh Oh Oh Oh

I hold to use like this I mean did you hear what I said I said

oh oh oh oh

The road went on, still and empty, the sun slanting more and more. Her stiff little pigtails were bound at the tips with bits of crimson cloth. A corner of the wrapping flapped a little as she walked, the nose of the loaf naked. I stopped.

"Look here. Do you live down this road? We havent passed a house in a mile, almost."

She looked at me, black and secret and friendly.

"Where do you live, sister? Dont you live back there in town?"

There was a bird somewhere in the woods, beyond the broken and infrequent slanting of sunlight.

"Your papa's going to be worried about you. Dont you reckon you'll get a whipping for not coming straight home with that bread?"

The bird whistled again, invisible, a sound mean-

168

ingless and profound, inflexionless, ceasing as though cut off with the blow of a knife, and again, and that sense of water swift and peaceful above secret places, felt, not seen not heard.

"Oh, hell, sister." About half the paper hung limp. "That's not doing any good now." I tore it off and dropped it beside the road. "Come on. We'll have to go back to town. We'll go back along the river."

We left the road. Among the moss little pale flowers grew, and the sense of water mute and unseen. *I hold to use like this I mean I use to hold She stood in the door looking at us her hands on her hips*

You pushed me it was your fault it hurt me too

We were dancing sitting down I bet Caddy cant dance sitting down

Stop that stop that

I was just brushing the trash off the back of your dress

You keep your nasty old hands off of me it was your fault you pushed me down I'm mad at you

I dont care she looked at us stay mad she went away We began to hear the shouts, the splashings; I saw a brown body gleam for an instant.

Stay mad. My shirt was getting wet and my hair. Across the roof hearing the roof loud now I could see Natalie going through the garden among the rain. Get wet I hope you catch pneumonia go on home Cowface. I jumped hard as I could into the hog-

169

*wallow the mud yellowed up to my waist stinking I
kept on plunging until I fell down and rolled over
in it* "Hear them in swimming, sister? I wouldn't
mind doing that myself." If I had time. When I
have time. I could hear my watch. *mud was warmer
than the rain it smelled awful. She had her back
turned I went around in front of her. You know what
I was doing? She turned her back I went around in
front of her the rain creeping into the mud flatting
her bodice through her dress it smelled horrible. I
was hugging her that's what I was doing. She turned
her back I went around in front of her. I was hugging her I tell you.*

I dont give a damn what you were doing Caddy

*You dont you dont I'll make you I'll make you give
a damn. She hit my hands away I smeared mud on
her with the other hand I couldn't feel the wet smack-
ing of her hand I wiped mud from my legs smeared
it on her wet hard turning body hearing her fingers
going into my face but I couldn't feel it even when
the rain began to taste sweet on my lips*

They saw us from the water first, heads and shoulders. They yelled and one rose squatting and sprang
among them. They looked like beavers, the water
lipping about their chins, yelling.

"Take that girl away! What did you want to
bring a girl here for? Go on away!"

"She wont hurt you. We just want to watch you
for a while."

They squatted in the water. Their heads drew into a clump, watching us, then they broke and rushed toward us, hurling water with their hands. We moved quick.

"Look out, boys; she wont hurt you."

"Go on away, Harvard!" It was the second boy, the one that thought the horse and wagon back there at the bridge. "Splash them, fellows!"

"Let's get out and throw them in," another said. "I aint afraid of any girl."

"Splash them! Splash them!" They rushed toward us, hurling water. We moved back. "Go on away!" they yelled. "Go on away!"

We went away. They huddled just under the bank, their slick heads in a row against the bright water. We went on. "That's not for us, is it." The sun slanted through to the moss here and there, leveller. "Poor kid, you're just a girl." Little flowers grew among the moss, littler than I had ever seen. "You're just a girl. Poor kid." There was a path, curving along beside the water. Then the water was still again, dark and still and swift. "Nothing but a girl. Poor sister." *We lay in the wet grass panting the rain like cold shot on my back. Do you care now do you do you*

My Lord we sure are in a mess get up. Where the rain touched my forehead it began to smart my hand came red away streaking off pink in the rain. Does it hurt

Of course it does what do you reckon

I tried to scratch your eyes out my Lord we sure do stink we better try to wash it off in the branch "There's town again, sister. You'll have to go home now. I've got to get back to school. Look how late it's getting. You'll go home now, wont you?" But she just looked at me with her black, secret, friendly gaze, the half-naked loaf clutched to her breast. "It's wet. I thought we jumped back in time." I took my handkerchief and tried to wipe the loaf, but the crust began to come off, so I stopped. "We'll just have to let it dry itself. Hold it like this." She held it like that. It looked kind of like rats had been eating it now. *and the water building and building up the squatting back the sloughed mud stinking surfaceward pocking the pattering surface like grease on a hot stove. I told you I'd make you*

I dont give a goddam what you do

Then we heard the running and we stopped and looked back and saw him coming up the path running, the level shadows flicking upon his legs.

"He's in a hurry. We'd ——" then I saw another man, an oldish man running heavily, clutching a stick, and a boy naked from the waist up, clutching his pants as he ran.

"There's Julio," the little girl said, and then I saw his Italian face and his eyes as he sprang upon me. We went down. His hands were jabbing at my face and he was saying something and trying to bite me, I reckon, and then they hauled him off and held him heaving and thrashing and yelling and they held his arms and he tried to kick me until they dragged him back. The little girl was howling, holding the loaf in both arms. The half-naked boy was darting and jumping up and down, clutching his trousers and someone pulled me up in time to see another stark naked figure come around the tranquil bend in the path running and change direction in midstride and leap into the woods, a couple of garments rigid as boards behind it. Julio still struggled. The man who had pulled me up said, "Whoa, now. We got you." He wore a vest but no coat. Upon it was a metal shield. In his other hand he clutched a knotted, polished stick.

"You're Anse, aren't you?" I said. "I was looking for you. What's the matter?"

"I warn you that anything you say will be used against you," he said. "You're under arrest."

"I killa heem," Julio said. He struggled. Two men held him. The little girl howled steadily, holding the bread. "You steala my seester," Julio said. "Let go, meesters."

"Steal his sister?" I said. "Why, I've been——"

"Shet up," Anse said. "You can tell that to Squire."

"Steal his sister?" I said. Julio broke from the men and sprang at me again, but the marshall met him and they struggled until the other two pinioned his arms again. Anse released him, panting.

"You durn furriner," he said, "I've a good mind to take you up too, for assault and battery." He turned to me again. "Will you come peaceable, or do I handcuff you?"

"I'll come peaceable," I said. "Anything, just so I can find someone — do something with — Stole his sister," I said. "Stole his —"

"I've warned you," Anse said, "He aims to charge you with meditated criminal assault. Here, you, make that gal shut up that noise."

"Oh," I said. Then I began to laugh. Two more boys with plastered heads and round eyes came out of the bushes, buttoning shirts that had already dampened onto their shoulders and arms, and I tried to stop the laughter, but I couldnt.

"Watch him, Anse, he's crazy, I believe."

"I'll h-have to qu-quit," I said, "It'll stop in a mu-minute. The other time it said ah ah ah," I said, laughing. "Let me sit down a while." I sat down, they watching me, and the little girl with her streaked face and the gnawed looking loaf, and the water swift and peaceful below the path. After a while the laughter ran out. But my throat wouldnt quit trying to laugh, like retching after your stomach is empty.

"Whoa, now," Anse said. "Get a grip on yourself."

"Yes," I said, tightening my throat. There was another yellow butterfly, like one of the sunflecks had come loose. After a while I didnt have to hold my throat so tight. I got up. "I'm ready. Which way?"

We followed the path, the two others watching Julio and the little girl and the boys somewhere in the rear. The path went along the river to the bridge. We crossed it and the tracks, people coming to the doors to look at us and more boys materializing from somewhere until when we turned into the main street we had quite a procession. Before the drugstore stood an auto, a big one, but I didn't recognise them until Mrs Bland said,

"Why, Quentin! Quentin Compson!" Then I saw Gerald, and Spoade in the back seat, sitting on the back of his neck. And Shreve. I didnt know the two girls.

"Quentin Compson!" Mrs Bland said.

"Good afternoon," I said, raising my hat. "I'm under arrest. I'm sorry I didnt get your note. Did Shreve tell you?"

"Under arrest?" Shreve said. "Excuse me," he said. He heaved himself up and climbed over their feet and got out. He had on a pair of my flannel pants, like a glove. I didnt remember forgetting them. I didnt remember how many chins Mrs Bland had, either. The prettiest girl was with Gerald in front, too. They watched me through veils, with a

kind of delicate horror. "Who's under arrest?"
Shreve said. "What's this, mister?"

"Gerald," Mrs Bland said, "Send these people
away. You get in this car, Quentin."

Gerald got out. Spoade hadnt moved.

"What's he done, Cap?" he said. "Robbed a hen
house?"

"I warn you," Anse said. "Do you know the
prisoner?"

"Know him," Shreve said. "Look here——"

"Then you can come along to the squire's. You're
obstructing justice. Come along." He shook my
arm.

"Well, good afternoon," I said. "I'm glad to
have seen you all. Sorry I couldnt be with you."

"You, Gerald," Mrs Bland said.

"Look here, constable," Gerald said.

"I warn you you're interfering with an officer of
the law," Anse said. "If you've anything to say, you
can come to the squire's and make cognizance of the
prisoner." We went on. Quite a procession now,
Anse and I leading. I could hear them telling them
what it was, and Spoade asking questions, and then
Julio said something violently in Italian and I looked
back and saw the little girl standing at the curb,
looking at me with her friendly, inscrutable regard.

"Git on home," Julio shouted at her, "I beat hell
outa you."

We went down the street and turned into a bit of

lawn in which, set back from the street, stood a one storey building of brick trimmed with white. We went up the rock path to the door, where Anse halted everyone except us and made them remain outside. We entered a bare room smelling of stale tobacco. There was a sheet iron stove in the center of a wooden frame filled with sand, and a faded map on the wall and the dingy plat of a township. Behind a scarred littered table a man with a fierce roach of iron grey hair peered at us over steel spectacles.

" Got him, did ye, Anse ? " he said.

" Got him, Squire."

He opened a huge dusty book and drew it to him and dipped a foul pen into an inkwell filled with what looked like coal dust.

" Look here, mister," Shreve said.

" The prisoner's name," the squire said. I told him. He wrote it slowly into the book, the pen scratching with excruciating deliberation.

" Look here, mister," Shreve said, " We know this fellow. We — "

" Order in the court," Anse said.

" Shut up, bud," Spoade said. " Let him do it his way. He's going to anyhow."

" Age," the squire said. I told him. He wrote that, his mouth moving as he wrote. " Occupation." I told him. " Harvard student, hey ? " he said. He looked up at me, bowing his neck a little to see over the spectacles. His eyes were clear and cold, like a goat's.

" What are you up to, coming out here kidnapping children? "

" They're crazy, Squire," Shreve said. " Whoever says this boy's kidnapping — "

Julio moved violently. " Crazy? " he said. " Dont I catcha heem, eh? Dont I see weetha my own eyes — "

" You're a liar," Shreve said. " You never — "

" Order, order," Anse said, raising his voice.

" You fellers shet up," the squire said. " If they dont stay quiet, turn 'em out, Anse." They got quiet. The squire looked at Shreve, then at Spoade, then at Gerald. " You know this young man? " he said to Spoade.

" Yes, your honour," Spoade said. " He's just a country boy in school up there. He dont mean any harm. I think the marshall'll find it's a mistake. His father's a congregational minister."

" H'm," the squire said. " What was you doing, exactly? " I told him, he watching me with his cold, pale eyes. " How about it, Anse? "

" Might have been," Anse said. " Them durn furriners."

" I American," Julio said. " I gotta da pape'."

" Where's the gal? "

" He sent her home," Anse said.

" Was she scared or anything? "

" Not till Julio there jumped on the prisoner. They were just walking along the river path, towards town. Some boys swimming told us which way they went."

"It's a mistake, Squire," Spoade said. "Children and dogs are always taking up with him like that. He cant help it."

"H'm," the squire said. He looked out of the window for a while. We watched him. I could hear Julio scratching himself. The squire looked back.

"Air you satisfied the gal aint took any hurt, you, there?"

"No hurt now," Julio said sullenly.

"You quit work to hunt for her?"

"Sure I quit. I run. I run like hell. Looka here, looka there, then man tella me he seen him giva her she eat. She go weetha.

"H'm," the squire said. "Well, son, I calculate you owe Julio something for taking him away from his work."

"Yes, sir," I said. "How much?"

"Dollar, I calculate."

I gave Julio a dollar.

"Well," Spoade said, "If that's all — I reckon he's discharged, your honour?"

The squire didn't look at him. "How far'd you run him, Anse?"

"Two miles, at least. It was about two hours before we caught him."

"H'm," the squire said. He mused a while. We watched him, his stiff crest, the spectacles riding low on his nose. The yellow shape of the window grew slowly across the floor, reached the wall, climbing. Dust motes whirled and slanted. " Six dollars."

" Six dollars? " Shreve said. " What's that for? "

" Six dollars," the squire said. He looked at Shreve a moment, then at me again.

" Look here," Shreve said.

" Shut up," Spoade said. " Give it to him, bud, and let's get out of here. The ladies are waiting for us. You got six dollars? "

" Yes," I said. I gave him six dollars.

" Case dismissed," he said.

" You get a receipt," Shreve said. " You get a signed receipt for that money."

The squire looked at Shreve mildly. " Case dismissed," he said without raising his voice.

" I'll be damned — " Shreve said.

" Come on here," Spoade said, taking his arm. " Good afternoon, Judge. Much obliged." As we passed out the door Julio's voice rose again, violent, then ceased. Spoade was looking at me, his brown eyes quizzical, a little cold. " Well, bud, I reckon you'll do your girl chasing in Boston after this."

" You damned fool," Shreve said, " What the hell do you mean anyway, straggling off here, fooling with these damn wops? "

" Come on," Spoade said, " They must be getting impatient."

Mrs Bland was talking to them. They were Miss Holmes and Miss Daingerfield and they quit listening to her and looked at me again with that delicate and curious horror, their veils turned back upon their little white noses and their eyes fleeing and mysterious beneath the veils.

"Quentin Compson," Mrs Bland said, "What would your mother say? A young man naturally gets into scrapes, but to be arrested on foot by a country policeman. What did they think he'd done, Gerald?"

"Nothing," Gerald said.

"Nonsense. What was it, you, Spoade?"

"He was trying to kidnap that little dirty girl, but they caught him in time," Spoade said.

"Nonsense," Mrs Bland said, but her voice sort of died away and she stared at me for a moment, and the girls drew their breaths in with a soft concerted sound. "Fiddlesticks," Mrs Bland said briskly, "If that isn't just like these ignorant lowclass Yankees. Get in, Quentin."

Shreve and I sat on two small collapsible seats. Gerald cranked the car and got in and we started.

"Now, Quentin, you tell me what all this foolishness is about," Mrs Bland said. I told them, Shreve hunched and furious on his little seat and Spoade sitting again on the back of his neck beside Miss Daingerfield.

"And the joke is, all the time Quentin had us all fooled," Spoade said. "All the time we thought he was the model youth that anybody could trust a daughter with, until the police showed him up at his nefarious work."

" Hush up, Spoade," Mrs Bland said. We drove down the street and crossed the bridge and passed the house where the pink garment hung in the window. " That's what you get for not reading my note. Why didnt you come and get it? Mr MacKenzie says he told you it was there."

" Yessum. I intended to, but I never went back to the room."

" You'd have let us sit there waiting I dont know how long, if it hadnt been for Mr MacKenzie. When he said you hadnt come back, that left an extra place, so we asked him to come. We're very glad to have you anyway, Mr MacKenzie." Shreve said nothing. His arms were folded and he glared straight ahead past Gerald's cap. It was a cap for motoring in England. Mrs Bland said so. We passed that house, and three others, and another yard where the little girl stood by the gate. She didnt have the bread now, and her face looked like it had been streaked with coal-dust. I waved my hand, but she made no reply, only her head turned slowly as the car passed, following us with her unwinking gaze. Then we ran beside the wall, our shadows running along the wall, and after a while we passed a piece of torn newspaper lying beside the road and I began to laugh again. I could feel it in my throat and I looked off into the trees where the afternoon slanted, thinking of afternoon and of the bird and the boys in swimming. But still I couldnt stop it and then I knew that if I tried too hard to stop it I'd be crying and I thought about how I'd thought about I could not be a virgin, with so many of them walking along in the shadows and whispering with their soft girlvoices lingering in the shadowy places and the words coming out and perfume and eyes you could feel not see, but if it was that simple to do it wouldnt be anything and if it wasnt anything, what was I and then Mrs Bland said, " Quentin? Is he sick, Mr MacKenzie? " and then Shreve's fat hand touched my knee and Spoade began talking and I quit trying to stop it.

"If that hamper is in his way, Mr MacKenzie, move it over on your side. I brought a hamper of wine because I think young gentlemen should drink wine, although my father, Gerald's grandfather " *ever do that Have you ever done that In the grey darkness a little light her hands locked about*

"They do, when they can get it," Spoade said. "Hey, Shreve? " *her knees her face looking at the sky the smell of honeysuckle upon her face and throat*

"Beer, too," Shreve said. His hand touched my knee again. I moved my knee again. *like a thin wash of lilac coloured paint talking about him bringing*

"You're not a gentleman," Spoade said. *him*

between us until the shape of her blurred not with dark

"No. I'm Canadian," Shreve said. *talking about him the oar blades winking him along winking the Cap made for motoring in England and all 'time rushing beneath and they two blurred within the other forever more he had been in the army had killed men*

"I adore Canada," Miss Daingerfield said. "I think it's marvellous."

"Did you ever drink perfume?" Spoade said. *with one hand he could lift her to his shoulder and run with her running Running*

"No," Shreve said. *running the beast with two backs and she blurred in the winking oars running the swine of Euboeleus running coupled within how many Caddy*

"Neither did I," Spoade said. *I dont know too many there was something terrible in me terrible in me Father I have committed Have you ever done that We didnt we didnt do that did we do that*

"and Gerald's grandfather always picked his own mint before breakfast, while the dew was still on it. He wouldnt even let old Wilkie touch it do you remember Gerald but always gathered it himself and made his own julep. He was as crochety about his julep as an old maid, measuring everything by a recipe in his head. There was only one man he ever gave that recipe to; that was" *we did how can you*

184

*not know it if youll just wait I'll tell you how it was
it was a crime we did a terrible crime it cannot be hid
you think it can but wait   Poor Quentin youve never
done that have you   and I'll tell you how it was I'll
tell Father then itll have to be because you love
Father then we'll have to go away amid the pointing
and the horror the clean flame I'll make you say we
did I'm stronger than you I'll make you know we did
you thought it was them but it was me listen I fooled
you all the time it was me you thought I was in the
house where that damn honeysuckle trying not to
think the swing the cedars the secret surges the
breathing locked drinking the wild breath the yes
Yes Yes yes* "never be got to drink wine himself,
but he always said that a hamper what book did you
read that in the one where Geralds rowing suit of
wine was a necessary part of any gentlemen's picnic
basket" *did you love them Caddy did you love
them When they touched me I died*

one minute she was standing there the next he was
yelling and pulling at her dress they went into the
hall and up the stairs yelling and shoving at her up
the stairs to the bathroom door and stopped her back
against the door and her arm across her face yelling
and trying to shove her into the bathroom when she
came in to supper T. P. was feeding him he started
again just whimpering at first until she touched him
then he yelled she stood there her eyes like cornered
rats then I was running in the grey darkness it

185

smelled of rain and all flower scents the damp warm
air released and crickets sawing away in the grass
pacing me with a small travelling island of silence
Fancy watched me across the fence blotchy like a
quilt on a line I thought damn that nigger he forgot
to feed her again I ran down the hill in that vacuum
of crickets like a breath travelling across a mirror
she was lying in the water her head on the sand spit
the water flowing about her hips there was a little
more light in the water her skirt half saturated
flopped along her flanks to the waters motion in
heavy ripples going nowhere renewed themselves of
their own movement I stood on the bank I could
smell the honeysuckle on the water gap the air
seemed to drizzle with honeysuckle and with the
rasping of crickets a substance you could feel on the
flesh

  is Benjy still crying

  I dont know yes I dont know

  poor Benjy

I sat down on the bank the grass was damp a little
then I found my shoes wet

  get out of that water are you crazy

  but she didnt move her face was a white blur
framed out of the blur of the sand by her hair

  get out now

  she sat up then she rose her skirt flopped against
her draining she climbed the bank her clothes flop-
ping sat down

186

why dont you wring it out do you want to catch cold

yes

the water sucked and gurgled across the sand spit and on in the dark among the willows across the shallow the water rippled like a piece of cloth holding still a little light as water does

he's crossed all the oceans all around the world

then she talked about him clasping her wet knees her face tilted back in the grey light the smell of honeysuckle there was a light in mothers room and in Benjys where T. P. was putting him to bed

do you love him

her hand came out I didnt move it fumbled down my arm and she held my hand flat against her chest her heart thudding

no no

did he make you then he made you do it let him he was stronger than you and he tomorrow Ill kill him I swear I will father neednt know until afterward and then you and I nobody need ever know we can take my school money we can cancel my matriculation Caddy you hate him dont you dont you

she held my hand against her chest her heart thudding I turned and caught her arm

Caddy you hate him dont you

she moved my hand up against her throat her heart was hammering there

poor Quentin

her face looked at the sky it was low so low that all smells and sounds of night seemed to have been crowded down like under a slack tent especially the honeysuckle it had got into my breathing it was on her face and throat like paint her blood pounded against my hand I was leaning on my other arm it began to jerk and jump and I had to pant to get any air at all out of that thick grey honeysuckle

yes I hate him I would die for him I've already died for him I die for him over and over again everytime this goes

when I lifted my hand I could still feel crisscrossed twigs and grass burning into the palm

poor Quentin

she leaned back on her arms her hands locked about her knees

youve never done that have you *Caddy*

what done what *Quentin*

that what I have what I did *caddy*

yes yes lots of times with lots of girls

then I was crying her hand touched me again and I was crying against her damp blouse then she lying on her back looking past my head into the sky I could see a rim of white under her irises I opened my knife

do you remember the day damuddy died when you sat down in the water in your drawers *1898*

yes

I held the point of the knife at her throat

188

it wont take but a second just a second then I can
do mine I can do mine then
    all right can you do yours by yourself
    yes the blades long enough Benjys in bed by now
    yes
    it wont take but a second Ill try not to hurt
    all right
    will you close your eyes
    no like this youll have to push it harder
    touch your hand to it
    but she didnt move her eyes were wide open look-
ing past my head at the sky
    Caddy do you remember how Dilsey fussed at you
because your drawers were muddy
    dont cry
    Im not crying Caddy
    push it are you going to
    do you want me to
    yes push it
    touch your hand to it
    dont cry poor Quentin
    but I couldnt stop she held my head against her
damp hard breast I could hear her heart going firm
and slow now not hammering and the water gur-
gling among the willows in the dark and waves of
honeysuckle coming up the air my arm and shoulder
were twisted under me
    what is it what are you doing
    her muscles gathered I sat up

its my knife I dropped it
she sat up
what time is it
I dont know
she rose to her feet I fumbled along the ground
Im going let it go
I could feel her standing there I could smell her
damp clothes feeling her there
its right here somewhere
let it go you can find it tomorrow come on
wait a minute I'll find it
are you afraid to
here it is it was right here all the time
was it come on
I got up and followed we went up the hill the
crickets hushing before us
its funny how you can sit down and drop something and have to hunt all around for it
the grey it was grey with dew slanting up into
the grey sky then the trees beyond
damn that honeysuckle I wish it would stop
you used to like it
we crossed the crest and went on toward the trees
she walked into me she gave over a little the ditch
was a black scar on the grey grass she walked into
me again she looked at me and gave over we reached
the ditch
lets go this way
what for

lets see if you can still see Nancys bones I havent
thought to look in a long time have you
it was matted with vines and briers dark
they were right here you cant tell whether you see
them or not can you
stop Quentin
come on
the ditch narrowed closed she turned toward the
trees
stop Quentin
Caddy
I got in front of her again
Caddy
stop it
I held her
Im stronger than you
she was motionless hard unyielding but still
I wont fight stop youd better stop
Caddy dont Caddy
it wont do any good dont you know it wont let
me go
the honeysuckle drizzled and drizzled I could hear
the crickets watching us in a circle she moved back
went around me on toward the trees
you go on back to the house you neednt come
I went on
why dont you go on back to the house
damn that honeysuckle
we reached the fence she crawled through I

crawled through when I rose from stooping he was coming out of the trees into the grey toward us coming toward us tall and flat and still even moving like he was still she went to him

this is Quentin Im wet Im wet all over you dont have to if you dont want to

their shadows one shadow her head rose it was above his on the sky higher their two heads

you dont have to if you dont want to

then not two heads the darkness smelled of rain of damp grass and leaves the grey light drizzling like rain the honeysuckle coming up in damp waves I could see her face a blur against his shoulder he held her in one arm like she was no bigger than a child he extended his hand

glad to know you

we shook hands then we stood there her shadow high against his shadow one shadow

whatre you going to do Quentin

walk a while I think Ill go through the woods to the road and come back through town

I turned away going

goodnight

Quentin

I stopped

what do you want

in the woods the tree frogs were going smelling rain in the air they sounded like toy music boxes that were hard to turn and the honeysuckle come here

what do you want

come here Quentin

I went back she touched my shoulder leaning down her shadow the blur of her face leaning down from his high shadow I drew back

look out

you go on home

Im not sleepy Im going to take a walk

wait for me at the branch

Im going for a walk

Ill be there soon wait for me you wait

no Im going through the woods

I didnt look back the tree frogs didnt pay me any mind the grey light like moss in the trees drizzling but still it wouldnt rain after a while I turned went back to the edge of the woods as soon as I got there I began to smell honeysuckle again I could see the lights on the courthouse clock and the glare of town the square on the sky and the dark willows along the branch and the light in mothers windows the light still on in Benjys room and I stooped through the fence and went across the pasture running I ran in the grey grass among the crickets the honeysuckle getting stronger and stronger and the smell of water then I could see the water the colour of grey honey-suckle I lay down on the bank with my face close to the ground so I couldnt smell the honeysuckle I couldnt smell it then and I lay there feeling the earth

going through my clothes listening to the water and
after a while I wasnt breathing so hard and I lay
there thinking that if I didnt move my face I wouldnt
have to breathe hard and smell it and then I wasnt
thinking about anything at all she came along the
bank and stopped I didnt move

its late you go on home

what

you go on home its late

all right

her clothes rustled I didnt move they stopped
rustling

are you going in like I told you

I didnt hear anything

Caddy

yes I will if you want me to I will

I sat up she was sitting on the ground her hands
clasped about her knee

go on to the house like I told you

yes Ill do anything you want me to anything yes

she didnt even look at me I caught her shoulder
and shook her hard

you shut up

I shook her

you shut up you shut up

yes

she lifted her face then I saw she wasnt even looking at me at all I could see that white rim

get up

I pulled her she was limp I lifted her to her feet
go on now
was Benjy still crying when you left
go on
we crossed the branch the roof came in sight then
the windows upstairs
hes asleep now
I had to stop and fasten the gate she went on in
the grey light the smell of rain and still it wouldnt
rain and honeysuckle beginning to come from the
garden fence beginning she went into the shadow I
could hear her feet then
Caddy
I stopped at the steps I couldnt hear her feet
Caddy
I heard her feet then my hand touched her not
warm not cool just still her clothes a little damp still
do you love him now
not breathing except slow like far away breathing
Caddy do you love him now
I dont know
outside the grey light the shadows of things like
dead things in stagnant water
I wish you were dead
do you you coming in now
are you thinking about him now
I dont know
tell me what youre thinking about tell me
stop stop Quentin

you shut up you shut up you hear me you shut up
are you going to shut up
   all right I will stop we'll make too much noise
   Ill kill you do you hear
   lets go out to the swing theyll hear you here
   Im not crying do you say Im crying
   no hush now we'll wake Benjy up
   you go on into the house go on now
   I am dont cry Im bad anyway you cant help it
   theres a curse on us its not our fault is it our
fault
   hush come on and go to bed now
   you cant make me theres a curse on us
   finally I saw him he was just going into the barber-
shop he looked out I went on and waited
   Ive been looking for you two or three days
   you wanted to see me
   Im going to see you
   he rolled the cigarette quickly with about two motions he struck the match with his thumb
   we cant talk here suppose I meet you somewhere
   Ill come to your room are you at the hotel
   no thats not so good you know that bridge over the
creek in there back of
   yes all right
   at one oclock right
   yes
   I turned away
   Im obliged to you

196

look

I stopped looked back

she all right

he looked like he was made out of bronze his khaki shirt

she need me for anything now

I'll be there at one

she heard me tell T. P. to saddle Prince at one oclock she kept watching me not eating much she came too

what are you going to do

nothing cant I go for a ride if I want to

youre going to do something what is it

none of your business whore whore

T. P. had Prince at the side door

I wont want him Im going to walk

I went down the drive and out the gate I turned into the lane then I ran before I reached the bridge I saw him leaning on the rail the horse was hitched in the woods he looked over his shoulder then he turned his back he didnt look up until I came onto the bridge and stopped he had a piece of bark in his hands breaking pieces from it and dropping them over the rail into the water

I came to tell you to leave town

he broke a piece of bark deliberately dropped it carefully into the water watched it float away

I said you must leave town

he looked at me

did she send you to me

I say you must go not my father not anybody I say it

listen save this for a while I want to know if shes all right have they been bothering her up there

thats something you dont need to trouble yourself about

then I heard myself saying Ill give you until sundown to leave town

he broke a piece of bark and dropped it into the water then he laid the bark on the rail and rolled a cigarette with those two swift motions spun the match over the rail

what will you do if I dont leave

Ill kill you dont think that just because I look like a kid to you

the smoke flowed in two jets from his nostrils across his face

how old are you

I began to shake my hands were on the rail I thought if I hid them hed know why

Ill give you until tonight

listen buddy whats your name Benjys the natural isnt he you are

Quentin

my mouth said it I didnt say it at all

Ill give you till sundown

Quentin

he raked the cigarette ash carefully off against the

198

rail he did it slowly and carefully like sharpening a pencil my hands had quit shaking

listen no good taking it so hard its not your fault kid it would have been some other fellow

did you ever have a sister did you

no but theyre all bitches

I hit him my open hand beat the impulse to shut it to his face his hand moved as fast as mine the cigarette went over the rail I swung with the other hand he caught it too before the cigarette reached the water he held both my wrists in the same hand his other hand flicked to his armpit under his coat behind him the sun slanted and a bird singing somewhere beyond the sun we looked at one another while the bird singing he turned my hands loose

look here

he took the bark from the rail and dropped it into the water it bobbed up the current took it floated away his hand lay on the rail holding the pistol loosely we waited

you cant hit it now

no

it floated on it was quite still in the woods I heard the bird again and the water afterward the pistol came up he didnt aim at all the bark disappeared then pieces of it floated up spreading he hit two more of them pieces of bark no bigger than silver dollars

thats enough I guess

he swung the cylinder out and blew into the barrel a thin wisp of smoke dissolved he reloaded the three chambers shut the cylinder he handed it to me butt first

what for I wont try to beat that

youll need it from what you said Im giving you this one because youve seen what itll do

to hell with your gun

I hit him I was still trying to hit him long after he was holding my wrists but I still tried then it was like I was looking at him through a piece of coloured glass I could hear my blood and then I could see the sky again and branches against it and the sun slanting through them and he holding me on my feet

did you hit me Quentin

I couldnt hear

what

yes how do you feel

all right let go

he let me go I leaned against the rail

do you feel all right

let me alone Im all right

can you make it home all right

go on let me alone

youd better not try to walk take my horse

no you go on

you can hang the reins on the pommel and turn him loose he'll go back to the stable

let me alone you go on and let me alone

I leaned on the rail looking at the water I heard
him untie the horse and ride off and after a while I
couldnt hear anything but the water and then the
bird again I left the bridge and sat down with my
back against a tree and leaned my head against
the tree and shut my eyes a patch of sun came
through and fell across my eyes and I moved a
little further around the tree I heard the bird again
and the water and then everything sort of rolled
away and I didnt feel anything at all I felt almost
good after all those days and the nights with honeysuckle coming up out of the darkness into my room
where I was trying to sleep even when after a
while I knew that he hadnt hit me that he had
lied about that for her sake too and that I had just
passed out like a girl but even that didnt matter
anymore and I sat there against the tree with little
flecks of sunlight brushing across my face like yellow leaves on a twig listening to the water and not
thinking about anything at all even when I heard
the horse coming fast I sat there with my eyes
closed and heard its feet bunch scuttering the hiss-
ing sand and feet running and her hard running
hands

   fool fool are you hurt

   I opened my eyes her hands running on my face

   I didnt know which way until I heard the pistol I
didnt know where I didnt think he and you running
off slipping I didnt think he would have

she held my face between her hands bumping my
head against the tree
stop stop that
I caught her wrists
quit that quit it
I knew he wouldnt I knew he wouldnt
she tried to bump my head against the tree
I told him never to speak to me again I told
him
she tried to break her wrists free
let me go
stop it I'm stronger than you stop it now
let me go Ive got to catch him and ask his let me
go Quentin please let me go let me go
all at once she quit her wrists went lax
yes I can tell him I can make him believe anytime
I can make him
Caddy
she hadnt hitched Prince he was liable to strike out
for home if the notion took him
anytime he will believe me
do you love him Caddy
do I what
    she looked at me then everything emptied out of
her eyes and they looked like the eyes in the statues
blank and unseeing and serene
put your hand against my throat
she took my hand and held it flat against her
throat

202

now say his name

Dalton Ames

I felt the first surge of blood there it surged in strong accelerating beats

say it again

her face looked off into the trees where the sun slanted and where the bird

say it again

Dalton Ames

her blood surged steadily beating and beating against my hand

It kept on running for a long time, but my face felt cold and sort of dead, and my eye, and the cut place on my finger was smarting again. I could hear Shreve working the pump, then he came back with the basin and a round blob of twilight wobbling in it, with a yellow edge like a fading balloon, then my reflection. I tried to see my face in it.

"Has it stopped?" Shreve said. "Give me the rag." He tried to take it from my hand.

"Look out," I said, "I can do it. Yes, it's about stopped now." I dipped the rag again, breaking the balloon. The rag stained the water. " I wish I had a clean one."

"You need a piece of beefsteak for that eye," Shreve said. " Damn if you wont have a shiner tomorrow. The son of a bitch," he said.

"Did I hurt him any?" I wrung out the handkerchief and tried to clean the blood off of my vest.

"You cant get that off," Shreve said. "You'll have to send it to the cleaner's. Come on, hold it on your eye, why dont you."

"I can get some of it off," I said. But I wasn't doing much good. "What sort of shape is my collar in?"

"I dont know," Shreve said. "Hold it against your eye. Here."

"Look out," I said. "I can do it. Did I hurt him any?"

"You may have hit him. I may have looked away just then or blinked or something. He boxed the hell out of you. He boxed you all over the place. What did you want to fight him with your fists for? You goddamn fool. How do you feel?"

"I feel fine," I said. "I wonder if I can get something to clean my vest."

"Oh, forget your damn clothes. Does your eye hurt?"

"I feel fine," I said. Everything was sort of violet and still, the sky green paling into gold beyond the gable of the house and a plume of smoke rising from the chimney without any wind. I heard the pump again. A man was filling a pail, watching us across his pumping shoulder. A woman crossed the door, but she didnt look out. I could hear a cow lowing somewhere.

204

" Come on," Shreve said, " Let your clothes alone and put that rag on your eye. I'll send your suit out first thing tomorrow."

" All right. I'm sorry I didn't bleed on him a little, at least."

" Son of a bitch," Shreve said. Spoade came out of the house, talking to the woman I reckon, and crossed the yard. He looked at me with his cold, quizzical eyes.

" Well, bud," he said, looking at me, " I'll be damned if you dont go to a lot of trouble to have your fun. Kidnapping, then fighting. What do you do on your holidays ? burn houses ? "

" I'm all right," I said. " What did Mrs Bland say ? "

" She's giving Gerald hell for bloodying you up. She'll give you hell for letting him, when she sees you. She dont object to the fighting, it's the blood that annoys her. I think you lost caste with her a little by not holding your blood better. How do you feel ? "

" Sure," Shreve said, " If you cant be a Bland, the next best thing is to commit adultery with one or get drunk and fight him, as the case may be."

" Quite right," Spoade said. " But I didnt know Quentin was drunk."

" He wasnt," Shreve said. " Do you have to be drunk to want to hit that son of a bitch ? "

" Well, I think I'd have to be pretty drunk to

try it, after seeing how Quentin came out. Where'd
he learn to box?"

"He's been going to Mike's every day, over in
town," I said.

"He has?" Spoade said. "Did you know that
when you hit him?"

"I dont know," I said. "I guess so. Yes."

"Wet it again," Shreve said. "Want some fresh
water?"

"This is all right," I said. I dipped the cloth again
and held it to my eye. "Wish I had something to
clean my vest." Spoade was still watching me.

"Say," he said, "What did you hit him for? What
was it he said?"

"I dont know. I dont know why I did."

"The first I knew was when you jumped up all
of a sudden and said, 'Did you ever have a sister?
did you?' and when he said No, you hit him. I noticed you kept on looking at him, but you didnt seem
to be paying any attention to what anybody was
saying until you jumped up and asked him if he had
any sisters."

"Ah, he was blowing off as usual," Shreve said,
"about his women. You know: like he does, before
girls, so they dont know exactly what he's saying. All
his damn innuendo and lying and a lot of stuff that
dont make sense even. Telling us about some wench
that he made a date with to meet at a dance hall in
Atlantic City and stood her up and went to the hotel
206

and went to bed and how he lay there being sorry
for her waiting on the pier for him, without him
there to give her what she wanted. Talking about the
body's beauty and the sorry ends thereof and how
tough women have it, without anything else they can
do except lie on their backs. Leda lurking in the
bushes, whimpering and moaning for the swan, see.
The son of a bitch. I'd hit him myself. Only I'd
grabbed up her damn hamper of wine and done it if
it had been me."

"Oh," Spoade said, "the champion of dames.
Bud, you excite not only admiration, but horror."
He looked at me, cold and quizzical. "Good God,"
he said.

"I'm sorry I hit him," I said. "Do I look too bad
to go back and get it over with?"

"Apologies, hell," Shreve said, "Let them go
to hell. We're going to town."

"He ought to go back so they'll know he fights
like a gentleman," Spoade said. "Gets licked like
one, I mean."

"Like this?" Shreve said, "With his clothes all
over blood?"

"Why, all right," Spoade said, "You know best."

"He cant go around in his undershirt," Shreve
said, "He's not a senior yet. Come on, let's go to
town."

"You neednt come," I said. "You go on back
to the picnic."

"Hell with them," Shreve said. "Come on here."

"What'll I tell them?" Spoade said. "Tell them you and Quentin had a fight too?"

"Tell them nothing," Shreve said. "Tell her her option expired at sunset. Come on, Quentin. I'll ask that woman where the nearest interurban—"

"No," I said, "I'm not going back to town."

Shreve stopped, looking at me. Turning, his glasses looked like small yellow moons.

"What are you going to do?"

"I'm not going back to town yet. You go on back to the picnic. Tell them I wouldnt come back because my clothes were spoiled."

"Look here," he said, "What are you up to?"

"Nothing. I'm all right. You and Spoade go on back. I'll see you tomorrow." I went on across the yard, toward the road.

"Do you know where the station is?" Shreve said.

"I'll find it. I'll see you all tomorrow. Tell Mrs Bland I'm sorry I spoiled her party." They stood watching me. I went around the house. A rock path went down to the road. Roses grew on both sides of the path. I went through the gate, onto the road. It dropped downhill, toward the woods, and I could make out the auto beside the road. I went up the hill. The light increased as I mounted, and before I reached the top I heard a car. It sounded far away across the twilight and I stopped and listened to it.

I couldnt make out the auto any longer, but Shreve was standing in the road before the house, looking up the hill. Behind him the yellow light lay like a wash of paint on the roof of the house. I lifted my hand and went on over the hill, listening to the car. Then the house was gone and I stopped in the green and yellow light and heard the car growing louder and louder, until just as it began to die away it ceased all together. I waited until I heard it start again. Then I went on.

As I descended the light dwindled slowly, yet at the same time without altering its quality, as if I and not light were changing, decreasing, though even when the road ran into trees you could have read a newspaper. Pretty soon I came to a lane. I turned into it. It was closer and darker than the road, but when it came out at the trolley stop — another wooden marquee — the light was still unchanged. After the lane it seemed brighter, as though I had walked through night in the lane and come out into morning again. Pretty soon the car came. I got on it, they turning to look at my eye, and found a seat on the left side.

The lights were on in the car, so while we ran between trees I couldnt see anything except my own face and a woman across the aisle with a hat sitting right on top of her head, with a broken feather in it, but when we ran out of the trees I could see the twilight again, that quality of light as if time really had stopped for a while, with the sun hanging just under the horizon, and then we passed the marquee where the old man had been eating out of the sack, and the road going on under the twilight, into twilight and the sense of water peaceful and swift beyond. Then the car went on, the draught building steadily up in the open door until it was drawing steadily through the car with the odour of summer and darkness except honeysuckle. Honeysuckle was the saddest odour of all, I think. I remember lots of them. Wistaria was one. On the rainy days when Mother wasnt feeling quite bad enough to stay away from the windows we used to play under it. When Mother stayed in bed Dilsey would put old clothes on us and let us go out in the rain because she said rain never hurt young folks. But if Mother was up we always began by playing on the porch until she said we were making too much noise, then we went out and played under the wistaria frame.

This was where I saw the river for the last time this morning, about here. I could feel water beyond the twilight, smell. When it bloomed in the spring and it rained the smell was everywhere you didnt notice it so much at other times but when it rained the smell began to come into the house at twilight either it would rain more at twilight or there was something in the light itself but it always smelled strongest then until I would lie in bed thinking when will it stop when will it stop. The draft in the door smelled of water, a damp steady breath. Sometimes I could put myself to sleep saying that over and over until after the honeysuckle got all mixed up in it the whole thing came to symbolise night and unrest I seemed to be lying neither asleep nor awake looking down a long corridor of grey halflight where all stable things had become shadowy paradoxical all I had done shadows all I had felt suffered taking visible form antic and perverse mocking without relevance inherent themselves with the denial of the significance they should have affirmed thinking I was I was not who was not was not who.

I could smell the curves of the river beyond the dusk and I saw the last light supine and tranquil upon tideflats like pieces of broken mirror, then beyond them lights began in the pale clear air, trembling a little like butterflies hovering a long way off. Benjamin the child of. How he used to sit before that mirror. Refuge unfailing in which conflict tempered silenced reconciled. Benjamin the child of mine old age held hostage into Egypt. O Benjamin. Dilsey said it was because Mother was too proud for him. They come into white people's lives like that in sudden sharp black trickles that isolate white facts for an instant in unarguable truth like under a microscope; the rest of the time just voices that laugh when you see nothing to laugh at, tears when no reason for tears. They will bet on the odd or even number of mourners at a funeral. A brothel full of them in

Memphis went into a religious trance ran naked into the street. It took three policemen to subdue one of them. Yes Jesus O good man Jesus O that good man.

The car stopped. I got out, with them looking at my eye. When the trolley came it was full. I stopped on the back platform.

"Seats up front," the conductor said. I looked into the car. There were no seats on the left side.

"I'm not going far," I said. "I'll just stand here."

We crossed the river. The bridge, that is, arching slow and high into space, between silence and nothingness where lights — yellow and red and green — trembled in the clear air, repeating themselves.

"Better go up front and get a seat," the conductor said.

"I get off pretty soon," I said. "A couple of blocks."

I got off before we reached the postoffice. They'd all be sitting around somewhere by now though, and then I was hearing my watch and I began to listen for the chimes and I touched Shreve's letter through my coat, the bitten shadows of the elms flowing upon my hand. And then as I turned into the quad the chimes did begin and I went on while the notes came up like ripples on a pool and passed me and went on, saying Quarter to what? All right. Quarter to what.

Our windows were dark. The entrance was empty.

I walked close to the left wall when I entered, but it was empty: just the stairs curving up into shadows echoes of feet in the sad generations like light dust upon the shadows, my feet waking them like dust, lightly to settle again.

I could see the letter before I turned the light on, propped against a book on the table so I would see it. Calling him my husband. And then Spoade said they were going somewhere, would not be back until late, and Mrs Bland would need another cavalier. But I would have seen him and he cannot get another car for an hour because after six oclock. I took out my watch and listened to it clicking away, not knowing it couldnt even lie. Then I laid it face up on the table and took Mrs Bland's letter and tore it across and dropped the pieces into the waste basket and took off my coat, vest, collar, tie and shirt. The tie was spoiled too, but then niggers. Maybe a pattern of blood he could call that the one Christ was wearing. I found the gasoline in Shreve's room and spread the vest on the table, where it would be flat, and opened the gasoline.

the first car in town a girl Girl that's what Jason couldn't bear smell of gasoline making him sick then got madder than ever because a girl Girl had no sister but Benjamin Benjamin the child of my sorrowful if I'd just had a mother so I could say Mother Mother It took a lot of gasoline, and then I couldnt tell if it was still the stain or just the gasoline. It had

213

started the cut to smarting again so when I went to wash I hung the vest on a chair and lowered the light cord so that the bulb would be drying the splotch. I washed my face and hands, but even then I could smell it within the soap stinging, constricting the nostrils a little. Then I opened the bag and took the shirt and collar and tie out and put the bloody ones in and closed the bag, and dressed. While I was brushing my hair the half hour went. But there was until the three quarters anyway, except suppose *seeing on the rushing darkness only his own face no broken feather unless two of them but not two like that going to Boston the same night then my face his face for an instant across the crashing when out of darkness two lighted windows in rigid fleeing crash gone his face and mine just I see saw did I see not goodbye the marquee empty of eating the road empty in darkness in silence the bridge arching into silence darkness sleep the water* peaceful and swift not goodbye

I turned out the light and went into my bedroom, out of the gasoline but I could still smell it. I stood at the window the curtains moved slow out of the darkness touching my face like someone breathing asleep, breathing slow into the darkness again, leaving the touch. *After they had gone up stairs Mother lay back in her chair, the camphor handkerchief to her mouth. Father hadn't moved he still sat beside her holding her hand the bellowing hammering away like no place for it in silence* When I was little there was a picture in one of our books, a dark place into which a single weak ray of light came slanting upon two faces lifted out of the shadow. *You know what I'd do if I were King?* she never was a queen or a fairy she was always a king or a giant or a general *I'd break that place open and drag them out and I'd whip them good* It was torn out, jagged out. I was glad. I'd have to turn back to it until the dungeon was Mother herself she and Father upward into weak light holding hands and us lost somewhere below even them without even a ray of light. Then the honeysuckle got into it. As soon as I turned off the light and tried to go to sleep it would begin to come into the room in waves building and building up until I would have to pant to get any air at all out of it until I would have to get up and feel my way like when I was a little boy *hands can see touching in the mind shaping unseen door Door now nothing hands can see* My nose could see gasoline, the vest on the table, the door. The corridor was still empty of all the feet in sad generations seeking water. *yet the eyes unseeing clenched like teeth not disbelieving doubting even the absence of pain shin ankle knee the long invisible flowing of the stair-railing where a misstep in the darkness filled with sleeping Mother Father Caddy Jason Maury door I am not afraid only Mother Father Caddy Jason Maury getting so far ahead sleeping I will sleep fast when I*

215

door Door door It was empty too, the pipes, the porcelain, the stained quiet walls, the throne of contemplation. I had forgotten the glass, but I could *hands can see cooling fingers invisible swan-throat where less than Moses rod the glass touch tentative not to drumming lean cool throat drumming cooling the metal the glass full overfull cooling the glass the fingers flushing sleep leaving the taste of dampened sleep in the long silence of the throat* I returned up the corridor, waking the lost feet in whispering battalions in the silence, into the gasoline, the watch telling its furious lie on the dark table. Then the curtains breathing out of the dark upon my face, leaving the breathing upon my face. A quarter hour yet. And then I'll not be. The peacefullest words. Peacefullest words. *Non fui. Sum. Fui. Nom sum.* Somewhere I heard bells once. Mississippi or Massachusetts. I was. I am not. Massachusetts or Mississippi. Shreve has a bottle in his trunk. *Aren't you even going to open it* Mr and Mrs Jason Richmond Compson announce the *Three times. Days. Aren't you even going to open it* marriage of their daughter Candace *that liquor teaches you to confuse the means with the end.* I am. Drink. I was not. Let us sell Benjy's pasture so that Quentin may go to Harvard and I may knock my bones together and together. I will be dead in. Was it one year Caddy said. Shreve has a bottle in his trunk. Sir I will not need Shreve's I have sold Benjy's pasture and I can be dead in Harvard Caddy said in the caverns and the grottoes of the sea tumbling peacefully to the wavering tides because Harvard is such a fine sound forty acres is no high price for a fine sound. A fine dead sound we will swap Benjy's pasture for a fine dead sound. It will last him a long time because he cannot hear it unless he can smell it *as soon as she came in the door he began to cry* I thought all the time it was just one of those town squirts that Father was always teasing her about until. I didnt notice him any more than any other stranger drummer or what thought they were army shirts until all of a sudden I knew he wasn't thinking of me at all as a potential source of harm, but was thinking of her when he looked at me was looking at me through her like through a piece of coloured glass *why must you meddle with me dont you know it wont do any good I thought you'd have left that for Mother and Jason*

did Mother set Jason to spy on you I wouldnt have.

Women only use other people's codes of honour it's because she loves Caddy staying downstairs even when she was sick so Father couldnt kid Uncle Maury before Jason Father said Uncle Maury was too poor a classicist to risk the blind immortal boy in person he should have chosen Jason because Jason would have made only the same kind of blunder Uncle Maury himself would have made not one to get him a black eye the Patterson boy was smaller than Jason too they sold the kites for a nickel apiece until the trouble over finances Jason got a new partner still smaller one small enough anyway because T. P. said Jason still treasurer but Father said why should Uncle Maury work if he father could support five or six niggers that did nothing at all but sit with their feet in the oven he certainly could board and lodge Uncle Maury now and then and lend him a little money who kept his Father's belief in the celestial derivation of his own species at such a fine heat then Mother would cry and say that Father believed his people were better than hers that he was ridiculing Uncle Maury to teach us the same thing she couldnt see that Father was teaching us that all men are just accumulations dolls stuffed with sawdust swept up from the trash heaps where all previous dolls had been thrown away the sawdust flowing from what wound in what side that not for me died not. It used to be I thought of death as a man something like Grandfather a friend of his a kind of private and particular friend like we used to think of Grandfather's desk not to touch it not even to talk loud in the room where it was I always thought of them as being together somewhere all the time waiting for old Colonel Sartoris to come down and sit with them waiting on a high place beyond cedar trees Colonel Sartoris was on a still higher place looking out across at something and they were waiting for him to get done looking at it and come down

Grandfather wore his uniform and we could hear the murmur of their voices from beyond the cedars they were always talking and Grandfather was always right

The three quarters began. The first note sounded, measured and tranquil, serenely peremptory, emptying the unhurried silence for the next one and that's it if people could only change one another forever that way merge like a flame swirling up for an instant then blown cleanly out along the cool eternal dark instead of lying there trying not to think of the swing until all cedars came to have that vivid dead smell of perfume that Benjy hated so. Just by imagining the clump it seemed to me that I could hear whispers secret surges smell the beating of hot blood under wild unsecret flesh watching against red eyelids the swine untethered in pairs rushing coupled into the sea and he we must just stay awake and see evil done for a little while its not always and i it doesnt have to be even that long for a man of courage and he do you consider that courage and i yes sir dont you and he every man is the arbiter of his own virtues whether or not you consider it courageous is of more importance than the act itself than any act otherwise you could not be in earnest and i you dont believe i am serious and he i think you are too serious to give me any cause for alarm you wouldnt have felt driven to the expedient of telling me you have committed incest otherwise and i i wasnt

219

lying i wasnt lying and he you wanted to sublimate a piece of natural human folly into a horror and then exorcise it with truth and i it was to isolate her out of the loud world so that it would have to flee us of necessity and then the sound of it would be as though it had never been and he did you try to make her do it and i i was afraid to i was afraid she might and then it wouldnt have done any good but if i could tell you we did it would have been so and then the others wouldnt be so and then the world would roar away and he and now this other you are not lying now either but you are still blind to what is in yourself to that part of general truth the sequence of natural events and their causes which shadows every mans brow even benjys you are not thinking of finitude you are contemplating an apotheosis in which a temporary state of mind will become symmetrical above the flesh and aware both of itself and of the flesh it will not quite discard you will not even be dead and i temporary and he you cannot bear to think that someday it will no longer hurt you like this now were getting at it you seem to regard it merely as an experience that will whiten your hair overnight so to speak without altering your appearance at all you wont do it under these conditions it will be a gamble and the strange thing is that man who is conceived by accident and whose every breath is a fresh cast with dice already loaded against him will not face that final main which he knows

before hand he has assuredly to face without essay-
ing expedients ranging all the way from violence to
petty chicanery that would not deceive a child until
someday in very disgust he risks everything on a
single blind turn of a card no man ever does that
under the first fury of despair or remorse or bereavement he does it only when he has realised that even
the despair or remorse or bereavement is not particularly important to the dark diceman and i temporary and he it is hard believing to think that a
love or a sorrow is a bond purchased without design
and which matures willynilly and is recalled without
warning to be replaced by whatever issue the gods
happen to be floating at the time no you will not do
that until you come to believe that even she was not
quite worth despair perhaps and i i will never do that
nobody knows what i know and he i think youd
better go on up to cambridge right away you might
go up into maine for a month you can afford it if
you are careful it might be a good thing watching
pennies has healed more scars than jesus and i suppose i realise what you believe i will realise up there
next week or next month and he then you will remember that for you to go to harvard has been your
mothers dream since you were born and no compson
has ever disappointed a lady and i temporary it will
be better for me for all of us and he every man is the
arbiter of his own virtues but let no man prescribe
for another mans wellbeing and i temporary and

he was the saddest word of all there is nothing else in the world its not despair until time its not even time until it was

The last note sounded. At last it stopped vibrating and the darkness was still again. I entered the sitting room and turned on the light. I put my vest on. The gasoline was faint now, barely noticeable, and in the mirror the stain didnt show. Not like my eye did, anyway. I put on my coat. Shreve's letter crackled through the cloth and I took it out and examined the address, and put it in my side pocket. Then I carried the watch into Shreve's room and put it in his drawer and went to my room and got a fresh handkerchief and went to the door and put my hand on the light switch. Then I remembered I hadnt brushed my teeth, so I had to open the bag again. I found my toothbrush and got some of Shreve's paste and went out and brushed my teeth. I squeezed the brush as dry as I could and put it back in the bag and shut it, and went to the door again. Before I snapped the light out I looked around to see if there was anything else, then I saw that I had forgotten my hat. I'd have to go by the postoffice and I'd be sure to meet some of them, and they'd think I was a Harvard Square student making like he was a senior. I had forgotten to brush it too, but Shreve had a brush, so I didnt have to open the bag any more.

222

ONCE A BITCH ALWAYS A BITCH, what I say. I says you're lucky if her playing out of school is all that worries you. I says she ought to be down there in that kitchen right now, instead of up there in her room, gobbing paint on her face and waiting for six niggers that cant even stand up out of a chair unless they've got a pan full of bread and meat to balance them, to fix breakfast for her. And Mother says,

"But to have the school authorities think that I have no control over her, that I cant — "

"Well," I says, "You cant, can you? You never have tried to do anything with her," I says, "How do you expect to begin this late, when she's seventeen years old?"

She thought about that for a while.

"But to have them think that . . . I didn't even know she had a report card. She told me last fall that

they had quit using them this year. And now for
Professor Junkin to call me on the telephone and
tell me if she's absent one more time, she will have to
leave school. How does she do it? Where does she
go? You're down town all day; you ought to see her
if she stays on the streets."

"Yes," I says, "If she stayed on the streets. I
dont reckon she'd be playing out of school just to
do something she could do in public," I says.

"What do you mean?" she says.

"I dont mean anything," I says. "I just answered
your question." Then she begun to cry again, talking about how her own flesh and blood rose up to
curse her.

"You asked me," I says.

"I dont mean you," she says. "You are the only
one of them that isn't a reproach to me."

"Sure," I says, "I never had time to be. I never
had time to go to Harvard like Quentin or drink myself into the ground like Father. I had to work. But
of course if you want me to follow her around and
see what she does, I can quit the store and get a
job where I can work at night. Then I can watch her
during the day and you can use Ben for the night
shift."

"I know I'm just a trouble and a burden to you,"
she says, crying on the pillow.

"I ought to know it," I says. "You've been telling me that for thirty years. Even Ben ought to

224

know it now. Do you want me to say anything to her about it?"

"Do you think it will do any good?" she says.

"Not if you come down there interfering just when I get started," I says. "If you want me to control her, just say so and keep your hands off. Everytime I try to, you come butting in and then she gives both of us the laugh."

"Remember she's your own flesh and blood," she says.

"Sure," I says, "that's just what I'm thinking of —flesh. And a little blood too, if I had my way. When people act like niggers, no matter who they are the only thing to do is treat them like a nigger."

"I'm afraid you'll lose your temper with her," she says.

"Well," I says, "You haven't had much luck with your system. You want me to do anything about it, or not? Say one way or the other; I've got to get on to work."

"I know you have to slave your life away for us," she says. "You know if I had my way, you'd have an office of your own to go to, and hours that became a Bascomb. Because you are a Bascomb, despite your name. I know that if your father could have forseen—"

"Well," I says, "I reckon he's entitled to guess wrong now and then, like anybody else, even a Smith or a Jones." She begun to cry again.

" To hear you speak bitterly of your dead father," she says.

" All right," I says, " all right. Have it your way. But as I haven't got an office, I'll have to get on to what I have got. Do you want me to say anything to her? "

" I'm afraid you'll lose your temper with her," she says.

" All right," I says, " I wont say anything, then."

" But something must be done," she says. " To have people think I permit her to stay out of school and run about the streets, or that I cant prevent her doing it. . . . Jason, Jason," she says, " How could you. How could you leave me with these burdens."

" Now, now," I says, " You'll make yourself sick. Why dont you either lock her up all day too, or turn her over to me and quit worrying over her? "

" My own flesh and blood," she says, crying. So I says,

" All right. I'll tend to her. Quit crying, now."

" Dont lose your temper," she says. " She's just a child, remember."

" No," I says, " I wont." I went out, closing the door.

" Jason," she says. I didn't answer. I went down the hall. " Jason," she says beyond the door. I went on down stairs. There wasn't anybody in the dining-room, then I heard her in the kitchen. She was trying to make Dilsey let her have another cup of coffee. I went in.

"I reckon that's your school costume, is it?" I says. "Or maybe today's a holiday?"

"Just a half a cup, Dilsey," she says. "Please."

"No, suh," Dilsey says, "I aint gwine do it. You aint got no business wid mo'n one cup, a seventeen year old gal, let lone whut Miss Cahline say. You go on and git dressed for school, so you kin ride to town wid Jason. You fixin to be late again."

"No she's not," I says. "We're going to fix that right now." She looked at me, the cup in her hand. She brushed her hair back from her face, her kimono slipping off her shoulder. "You put that cup down and come in here a minute," I says.

"What for?" she says.

"Come on," I says. "Put that cup in the sink and come in here."

"What you up to now, Jason?" Dilsey says.

"You may think you can run over me like you do your grandmother and everybody else," I says, "But you'll find out different. I'll give you ten seconds to put that cup down like I told you."

She quit looking at me. She looked at Dilsey. "What time is it, Dilsey?" she says. "When it's ten seconds, you whistle. Just a half a cup. Dilsey, pl —"

I grabbed her by the arm. She dropped the cup. It broke on the floor and she jerked back, looking at me, but I held her arm. Dilsey got up from her chair.

227

"You, Jason," she says.

"You turn me loose," Quentin says, "I'll slap you."

"You will, will you?" I says, "You will will you?" She slapped at me. I caught that hand too and held her like a wildcat. "You will, will you?" I says. "You think you will?"

"You, Jason!" Dilsey says. I dragged her into the diningroom. Her kimono came unfastened, flapping about her, damn near naked. Dilsey came hobbling along. I turned and kicked the door shut in her face.

"You keep out of here," I says.

Quentin was leaning against the table, fastening her kimono. I looked at her.

"Now," I says, "I want to know what you mean, playing out of school and telling your grandmother lies and forging her name on your report and worrying her sick. What do you mean by it?"

She didn't say anything. She was fastening her kimono up under her chin, pulling it tight around her, looking at me. She hadn't got around to painting herself yet and her face looked like she had polished it with a gun rag. I went and grabbed her wrist. "What do you mean?" I says.

"None of your damn business," she says. "You turn me loose."

Dilsey came in the door. "You, Jason," she says.

"You get out of here, like I told you," I says, not

even looking back. "I want to know where you go when you play out of school," I says. "You keep off the streets, or I'd see you. Who do you play out with? Are you hiding out in the woods with one of those damn slick-headed jellybeans? Is that where you go?"

"You — you old goddamn!" she says. She fought, but I held her. "You damn old goddamn!" she says.

"I'll show you," I says. "You may can scare an old woman off, but I'll show you who's got hold of you now." I held her with one hand, then she quit fighting and watched me, her eyes getting wide and black.

"What are you going to do?" she says.

"You wait until I get this belt out and I'll show you," I says, pulling my belt out. Then Dilsey grabbed my arm.

"Jason," she says, "You, Jason! Aint you shamed of yourself."

"Dilsey," Quentin says, "Dilsey."

"I aint gwine let him," Dilsey says, "Dont you worry, honey." She held to my arm. Then the belt came out and I jerked loose and flung her away. She stumbled into the table. She was so old she couldn't do any more than move hardly. But that's all right: we need somebody in the kitchen to eat up the grub the young ones cant tote off. She came hobbling between us, trying to hold me again. "Hit me, den," she says, " ef nothin else but hittin somebody wont do you. Hit me," she says.

"You think I wont?" I says.

"I dont put no devilment beyond you," she says. Then I heard Mother on the stairs. I might have known she wasn't going to keep out of it. I let go. She stumbled back against the wall, holding her kimono shut.

"All right," I says, "We'll just put this off a while. But dont think you can run it over me. I'm not an old woman, nor an old half dead nigger, either. You damn little slut," I says.

"Dilsey," she says, " Dilsey, I want my mother."

Dilsey went to her. "Now, now," she says, "He aint gwine so much as lay his hand on you while Ise here." Mother came on down the stairs.

"Jason," she says, "Dilsey."

"Now, now," Dilsey says, "I aint gwine let him tech you." She put her hand on Quentin. She knocked it down.

"You damn old nigger," she says. She ran toward the door.

"Dilsey," Mother says on the stairs. Quentin ran up the stairs, passing her. "Quentin," Mother says, "You, Quentin." Quentin ran on. I could hear her when she reached the top, then in the hall. Then the door slammed.

Mother had stopped. Then she came on. "Dilsey," she says.

"All right," Dilsey says, "Ise comin. You go on and git dat car and wait now," she says, "so you kin cahy her to school."

"Dont you worry," I says. "I'll take her to school and I'm going to see that she stays there. I've started this thing, and I'm going through with it."

"Jason," Mother says on the stairs.

"Go on, now," Dilsey says, going toward the door. "You want to git her started too? Ise comin, Miss Cahline."

I went on out. I could hear them on the steps. "You go on back to bed now," Dilsey was saying, "Dont you know you aint feeling well enough to git up yet? Go on back, now. I'm gwine to see she gits to school in time."

I went on out the back to back the car out, then I had to go all the way round to the front before I found them.

"I thought I told you to put that tire on the back of the car," I says.

"I aint had time," Luster says. "Aint nobody to watch him till mammy git done in de kitchen."

"Yes," I says, "I feed a whole damn kitchen full of niggers to follow around after him, but if I want an automobile tire changed, I have to do it my-self."

"I aint had nobody to leave him wid," he says. Then he begun moaning and slobbering.

"Take him on round to the back," I says. "What

231

the hell makes you want to keep him around here where people can see him?" I made them go on, before he got started bellowing good. It's bad enough on Sundays, with that damn field full of people that haven't got a side show and six niggers to feed, knocking a damn oversize mothball around. He's going to keep on running up and down that fence and bellowing every time they come in sight until first thing I know they're going to begin charging me golf dues, then Mother and Dilsey'll have to get a couple of china door knobs and a walking stick and work it out, unless I play at night with a lantern. Then they'd send us all to Jackson, maybe. God knows, they'd hold Old Home week when that happpened.

I went on back to the garage. There was the tire, leaning against the wall, but be damned if I was going to put it on. I backed out and turned around. She was standing by the drive. I says,

"I know you haven't got any books: I just want to ask you what you did with them, if it's any of my business. Of course I haven't got any right to ask," I says, "I'm just the one that paid $11.65 for them last September."

"Mother buys my books," she says. "There's not a cent of your money on me. I'd starve first."

"Yes?" I says. "You tell your grandmother that and see what she says. You dont look all the way naked," I says, "even if that stuff on your face does hide more of you than anything else you've got on."

"Do you think your money or hers either paid for a cent of this?" she says.

"Ask your grandmother," I says. "Ask her what became of those checks. You saw her burn one of them, as I remember." She wasn't even listening, with her face all gummed up with paint and her eyes hard as a fice dog's.

"Do you know what I'd do if I thought your money or hers either bought one cent of this?" she says, putting her hand on her dress.

"What would you do?" I says, "Wear a barrel?"

"I'd tear it right off and throw it into the street," she says. "Dont you believe me?"

"Sure you would," I says. "You do it every time."

"See if I wouldn't," She says. She grabbed the neck of her dress in both hands and made like she would tear it.

"You tear that dress," I says, "And I'll give you a whipping right here that you'll remember all your life."

"See if I dont," she says. Then I saw that she really was trying to tear it, to tear it right off of her. By the time I got the car stopped and grabbed her hands there was about a dozen people looking. It made me so mad for a minute it kind of blinded me.

"You do a thing like that again and I'll make you sorry you ever drew breath," I says.

"I'm sorry now," she says. She quit, then her eyes

233

turned kind of funny and I says to myself if you cry here in this car, on the street, I'll whip you. I'll wear you out. Lucky for her she didn't, so I turned her wrists loose and drove on. Luckily we were near an alley, where I could turn into the back street and dodge the square. They were already putting the tent up in Beard's lot. Earl had already given me the two passes for our show windows. She sat there with her face turned away, chewing her lip. "I'm sorry now," she says. "I dont see why I was ever born."

"And I know of at least one other person that dont understand all he knows about that," I says. I stopped in front of the school house. The bell had rung, and the last of them were just going in. "You're on time for once, anyway," I says. "Are you going in there and stay there, or am I coming with you and make you?" She got out and banged the door. "Remember what I say," I says, "I mean it. Let me hear one more time that you are slipping up and down back alleys with one of those damn squirts."

She turned back at that. "I dont slip around," she says. "I dare anybody to know everything I do."

"And they all know it, too," I says. "Everybody in this town knows what you are. But I wont have it anymore, you hear? I dont care what you do, myself," I says, "But I've got a position in this town, and I'm not going to have any member of my family going on like a nigger wench. You hear me?"

234

"I dont care," she says, "I'm bad and I'm going to hell, and I dont care. I'd rather be in hell than anywhere where you are."

"If I hear one more time that you haven't been to school, you'll wish you were in hell," I says. She turned and ran on across the yard. "One more time, remember," I says. She didn't look back.

I went to the postoffice and got the mail and drove on to the store and parked. Earl looked at me when I came in. I gave him a chance to say something about my being late, but he just said,

"Those cultivators have come. You'd better help Uncle Job put them up."

I went on to the back, where old Job was uncrating them, at the rate of about three bolts to the hour.

"You ought to be working for me," I says. "Every other no-count nigger in town eats in my kitchen."

"I works to suit de man whut pays me Sat'dy night," he says. "When I does dat, it dont leave me a whole lot of time to please other folks." He screwed up a nut. "Aint nobody works much in dis country cep de boll-weevil, noways," he says.

"You'd better be glad you're not a boll-weevil waiting on those cultivators," I says. "You'd work yourself to death before they'd be ready to prevent you."

"Dat's de troof," he says, "Boll-weevil got tough time. Work ev'y day in de week out in de hot sun,

235

rain er shine. Aint got no front porch to set on en watch de wattermilyuns growin and Sat'dy dont mean nothin a-tall to him."

"Saturday wouldn't mean nothing to you, either," I says, "if it depended on me to pay you wages. Get those things out of the crates now and drag them inside."

I opened her letter first and took the check out. Just like a woman. Six days late. Yet they try to make men believe that they're capable of conducting a business. How long would a man that thought the first of the month came on the sixth last in business. And like as not, when they sent the bank statement out, she would want to know why I never deposited my salary until the sixth. Things like that never occur to a woman.

"I had no answer to my letter about Quentin's easter dress. Did it arrive all right? I've had no answer to the last two letters I wrote her, though the check in the second one was cashed with the other check. Is she sick? Let me know at once or I'll come there and see for myself. You promised you would let me know when she needed things. I will expect to hear from you before the 10th. No you'd better wire me at once. You are opening my letters to her. I know that as well as if I were looking at you. You'd better wire me at once about her to this address."

About that time Earl started yelling at Job, so I put them away and went over to try to put some life into him. What this country needs is white labour. Let these damn trifling niggers starve for a couple of years, then they'd see what a soft thing they have.

Along toward ten oclock I went up front. There was a drummer there. It was a couple of minutes to ten, and I invited him up the street to get a cocacola. We got to talking about crops.

"There's nothing to it," I says, "Cotton is a speculator's crop. They fill the farmer full of hot air and get him to raise a big crop for them to whipsaw on the market, to trim the suckers with. Do you think the farmer gets anything out of it except a red neck and a hump in his back? You think the man that sweats to put it into the ground gets a red cent more than a bare living," I says. "Let him make a big crop and it wont be worth picking; let him make a small crop and he wont have enough to gin. And what for? so a bunch of damn eastern jews, I'm not talking about men of the jewish religion," I says, "I've known some jews that were fine citizens. You might be one yourself," I says.

"No," he says, "I'm an American."

"No offense," I says. "I give every man his due, regardless of religion or anything else. I have nothing against jews as an individual," I says. "It's just the race. You'll admit that they produce nothing.

237

They follow the pioneers into a new country and sell them clothes."

"You're thinking of Armenians," he says, "aren't you. A pioneer wouldn't have any use for new clothes."

"No offense," I says. "I dont hold a man's religion against him."

"Sure," he says, "I'm an American. My folks have some French blood, why I have a nose like this. I'm an American, all right."

"So am I," I says. "Not many of us left. What I'm talking about is the fellows that sit up there in New York and trim the sucker gamblers."

"That's right," he says. "Nothing to gambling, for a poor man. There ought to be a law against it."

"Dont you think I'm right?" I says.

"Yes," he says, "I guess you're right. The farmer catches it coming and going."

"I know I'm right," I says. "It's a sucker game, unless a man gets inside information from somebody that knows what's going on. I happen to be associated with some people who're right there on the ground. They have one of the biggest manipulators in New York for an adviser. Way I do it," I says, "I never risk much at a time. It's the fellow that thinks he knows it all and is trying to make a killing with three dollars that they're laying for. That's why they are in the business."

Then it struck ten. I went up to the telegraph office. It opened up a little, just like they said. I went into the corner and took out the telegram again, just to be sure. While I was looking at it a report came in. It was up two points. They were all buying. I could tell that from what they were saying. Getting aboard. Like they didn't know it could go but one way. Like there was a law or something against doing anything but buying. Well, I reckon those eastern jews have got to live too. But I'll be damned if it hasn't come to a pretty pass when any damn foreigner that cant make a living in the country where God put him, can come to this one and take money right out of an American's pockets. It was up two points more. Four points. But hell, they were right there and knew what was going on. And if I wasn't going to take the advice, what was I paying them ten dollars a month for. I went out, then I remembered and came back and sent the wire. "All well. Q writing today."

"Q?" the operator says.

"Yes," I says, "Q. Cant you spell Q?"

"I just asked to be sure," he says.

"You send it like I wrote it and I'll guarantee you to be sure," I says. "Send it collect."

"What you sending, Jason?" Doc Wright says, looking over my shoulder. "Is that a code message to buy?"

"That's all right about that," I says. "You boys

239

use your own judgment. You know more about it than those New York folks do."

"Well, I ought to," Doc says, "I'd a saved money this year raising it at two cents a pound."

Another report came in. It was down a point.

"Jason's selling," Hopkins says. "Look at his face."

"That's all right about what I'm doing," I says. "You boys follow your own judgment. Those rich New York jews have got to live like everybody else," I says.

I went on back to the store. Earl was busy up front. I went on back to the desk and read Lorraine's letter. "Dear daddy wish you were here. No good parties when daddys out of town I miss my sweet daddy." I reckon she does. Last time I gave her forty dollars. Gave it to her. I never promise a woman anything nor let her know what I'm going to give her. That's the only way to manage them. Always keep them guessing. If you cant think of any other way to surprise them, give them a bust in the jaw.

I tore it up and burned it over the spittoon. I make it a rule never to keep a scrap of paper bearing a woman's hand, and I never write them at all. Lorraine is always after me to write to her but I says anything I forgot to tell you will save till I get to Memphis again but I says I dont mind you writing me now and then in a plain enevelope, but if you ever

240

try to call me up on the telephone, Memphis wont hold you I says. I says when I'm up there I'm one of the boys, but I'm not going to have any woman calling me on the telephone. Here I says, giving her the forty dollars. If you ever get drunk and take a notion to call me on the phone, just remember this and count ten before you do it.

"When'll that be?" she says.

"What?" I says.

"When you're coming back," she says.

"I'll let you know," I says. Then she tried to buy a beer, but I wouldn't let her. "Keep your money," I says. "Buy yourself a dress with it." I gave the maid a five, too. After all, like I say money has no value; it's just the way you spend it. It dont belong to anybody, so why try to hoard it. It just belongs to the man that can get it and keep it. There's a man right here in Jefferson made a lot of money selling rotten goods to niggers, lived in a room over the store about the size of a pigpen, and did his own cooking. About four or five years ago he was taken sick. Scared the hell out of him so that when he was up again he joined the church and bought himself a Chinese missionary, five thousand dollars a year. I often think how mad he'll be if he was to die and find out there's not any heaven, when he thinks about that five thousand a year. Like I say, he'd better go on and die now and save money.

When it was burned good I was just about to

shove the others into my coat when all of a sudden something told me to open Quentin's before I went home, but about that time Earl started yelling for me up front, so I put them away and went and waited on the damn redneck while he spent fifteen minutes deciding whether he wanted a twenty cent hame string or a thirty-five cent one.

"You'd better take that good one," I says. "How do you fellows ever expect to get ahead, trying to work with cheap equipment?"

"If this one aint any good," he says, "why have you got it on sale?"

"I didn't say it wasn't any good," I says, "I said it's not as good as that other one."

"How do you know it's not," he says. "You ever use airy one of them?"

"Because they dont ask thirty-five cents for it," I says. "That's how I know it's not as good."

He held the twenty cent one in his hands, drawing it through his fingers. "I reckon I'll take this hyer one," he says. I offered to take it and wrap it, but he rolled it up and put it in his overalls. Then he took out a tobacco sack and finally got it untied and shook some coins out. He handed me a quarter. "That fifteen cents will buy me a snack of dinner," he says.

"All right," I says, "You're the doctor. But dont come complaining to me next year when you have to buy a new outfit."

"I aint makin next year's crop yit," he says.

Finally I got rid of him, but every time I took that letter out something would come up. They were all in town for the show, coming in in droves to give their money to something that brought nothing to the town and wouldn't leave anything except what those grafters in the Mayor's office will split among themselves, and Earl chasing back and forth like a hen in a coop, saying "Yes, ma'am, Mr Compson will wait on you. Jason, show this lady a churn or a nickel's worth of screen hooks."

Well, Jason likes work. I says no I never had university advantages because at Harvard they teach you how to go for a swim at night without knowing how to swim and at Sewanee they dont even teach you what water is. I says you might send me to the state University; maybe I'll learn how to stop my clock with a nose spray and then you can send Ben to the Navy I says or to the cavalry anyway, they use geldings in the cavalry. Then when she sent Quentin home for me to feed too I says I guess that's right too, instead of me having to go way up north for a job they sent the job down here to me and then Mother begun to cry and I says it's not that I have any objection to having it here; if it's any satisfaction to you I'll quit work and nurse it myself and let you and Dilsey keep the flour barrel full, or Ben. Rent him out to a sideshow; there must be folks somewhere that would pay a dime to see him, then she cried more and kept saying my poor afflicted baby

243

and I says yes he'll be quite a help to you when he gets his growth not being more than one and a half times as high as me now and she says she'd be dead soon and then we'd all be better off and so I says all right, all right, have it your way. It's your grandchild, which is more than any other grandparents it's got can say for certain. Only I says it's only a question of time. If you believe she'll do what she says and not try to see it, you fool yourself because the first time that was that Mother kept on saying thank God you are not a Compson except in name, because you are all I have left now, you and Maury, and I says well I could spare Uncle Maury myself and then they came and said they were ready to start. Mother stopped crying then. She pulled her veil down and we went down stairs. Uncle Maury was coming out of the diningroom, his handkerchief to his mouth. They kind of made a lane and we went out the door just in time to see Dilsey driving Ben and T. P. back around the corner. We went down the steps and got in. Uncle Maury kept saying Poor little sister, poor little sister, talking around his mouth and patting Mother's hand. Talking around whatever it was.

"Have you got your band on?" she says. "Why dont they go on, before Benjamin comes out and makes a spectacle. Poor little boy. He doesn't know. He cant even realise."

"There, there," Uncle Maury says, patting her

hand, talking around his mouth. "It's better so. Let him be unaware of bereavement until he has to."

"Other women have their children to support them in times like this," Mother says.

"You have Jason and me," he says.

"It's so terrible to me," she says, "Having the two of them like this, in less than two years."

"There, there," he says. After a while he kind of sneaked his hand to his mouth and dropped them out the window. Then I knew what I had been smelling. Clove stems. I reckon he thought that the least he could do at Father's funeral or maybe the sideboard thought it was still Father and tripped him up when he passed. Like I say, if he had to sell something to send Quentin to Harvard we'd all been a damn sight better off if he'd sold that sideboard and bought himself a one-armed strait jacket with part of the money. I reckon the reason all the Compson gave out before it got to me like Mother says, is that he drank it up. At least I never heard of him offering to sell anything to send me to Harvard.

So he kept on patting her hand and saying "Poor little sister," patting her hand with one of the black gloves that we got the bill for four days later because it was the twenty-sixth because it was the same day one month that Father went up there and got it and brought it home and wouldn't tell anything about where she was or anything and Mother crying and saying "And you didn't even see him? You didn't even try to get him to make any provision for it?" and Father says "No she shall not touch his money not one cent of it" and Mother says "He can be forced to by law. He can prove nothing, unless — Jason Compson," she says, "Were you fool enough to tell — "

"Hush, Caroline," Father says, then he sent me to help Dilsey get that old cradle out of the attic and I says,

"Well, they brought my job home tonight" because all the time we kept hoping they'd get things straightened out and he'd keep her because Mother kept saying she would at least have enough regard for the family not to jeopardize my chance after she and Quentin had had theirs.

"And whar else do she belong?" Dilsey says, "Who else gwine raise her 'cep me? Aint I raised eve'y one of y'all?"

"And a damn fine job you made of it," I says. "Anyway it'll give her something to sure enough worry over now." So we carried the cradle down and Dilsey started to set it up in her old room. Then Mother started sure enough.

"Hush, Miss Cahline," Dilsey says, "You gwine wake her up."

"In there?" Mother says, "To be contaminated by that atmosphere? It'll be hard enough as it is, with the heritage she already has."

"Hush," Father says, "Dont be silly."

246

"Why aint she gwine sleep in here," Dilsey says, "In the same room whar I put her ma to bed ev'y night of her life since she was big enough to sleep by herself."

"You dont know," Mother says, "To have my own daughter cast off by her husband. Poor little innocent baby," she says, looking at Quentin. "You will never know the suffering you've caused."

"Hush, Caroline," Father says.

"What you want to go on like that fo Jason fer?" Dilsey says.

"I've tried to protect him," Mother says. "I've always tried to protect him from it. At least I can do my best to shield her."

"How sleepin in dis room gwine hurt her, I like to know," Dilsey says.

"I cant help it," Mother says. "I know I'm just a troublesome old woman. But I know that people cannot flout God's laws with impunity."

"Nonsense," Father said. "Fix it in Miss Caroline's room then, Dilsey."

"You can say nonsense," Mother says. "But she must never know. She must never even learn that name. Dilsey, I forbid you ever to speak that name in her hearing. If she could grow up never to know that she had a mother, I would thank God."

"Dont be a fool," Father says.

"I have never interfered with the way you brought them up," Mother says, "But now I cannot stand anymore. We must decide this now, tonight. Either that name is never to be spoken in her hearing, or she must go, or I will go. Take your choice."

"Hush," Father says, "You're just upset. Fix it in here, Dilsey."

"En you's about sick too," Dilsey says. "You looks like a hant. You git in bed and I'll fix you a toddy and see kin you sleep. I bet you aint had a full night's sleep since you lef."

"No," Mother says, "Dont you know what the doctor says? Why must you encourage him to drink? That's what's the matter with him now. Look at me, I suffer too, but I'm not so weak that I must kill myself with whiskey."

"Fiddlesticks," Father says, "What do doctors know? They make their livings advising people to do whatever they are not doing at the time, which is the extent of anyone's knowledge of the degenerate ape. You'll have a minister in to hold my hand next." Then Mother cried, and he went out. Went down stairs, and then I heard the sideboard. I woke up and heard him going down again. Mother had gone to sleep or something, because the house was quiet at last. He was trying to be quiet too, because I couldn't hear him, only the bottom of his nightshirt and his bare legs in front of the sideboard.

Dilsey fixed the cradle and undressed her and put her in it. She never had waked up since he brought her in the house.

"She pretty near too big fer hit," Dilsey says. "Dar now. I gwine spread me a pallet right acrost de hall, so you wont need to git up in de night."

"I wont sleep," Mother says. "You go on home. I wont mind. I'll be happy to give the rest of my life to her, if I can just prevent —"

"Hush, now," Dilsey says. "We gwine take keer of her. En you go on to bed too," she says to me, "You got to go to school tomorrow."

So I went out, then Mother called me back and cried on me awhile.

"You are my only hope," she says. "Every night I thank God for you." While we were waiting there for them to start she says Thank God if he had to be taken too, it is you left me and not Quentin. Thank God you are not a Compson, because all I have left now is you and Maury and I says, Well I could spare Uncle Maury myself. Well, he kept on patting her hand with his black glove, talking away from her. He took them off when his turn with the shovel came. He got up near the first, where they were holding the umbrellas over them, stamping every now and then and trying to kick the mud off their feet and sticking to the shovels so they'd have to knock it off, making a hollow sound when it fell on it, and when I stepped back around the hack I could see him behind a tombstone, taking another one out of a bottle. I thought he never was going to stop because I had on my new suit too, but it happened that there wasn't much mud on the wheels yet, only Mother saw it and says I dont know when you'll ever have another one and Uncle Maury says, " Now, now. Dont you worry at all. You have me to depend on, always."

And we have. Always. The fourth letter was from him. But there wasn't any need to open it. I could have written it myself, or recited it to her from memory, adding ten dollars just to be safe. But I had a hunch about that other letter. I just felt that it was about time she was up to some of her tricks again. She got pretty wise after that first time. She found out pretty quick that I was a different breed of cat from Father. When they begun to get it filled up toward the top Mother started crying sure enough, so Uncle Maury got in with her and drove off. He says You can come in with somebody; they'll be glad to give you a lift. I'll have to take your mother on and I thought about saying, Yes you ought to brought two bottles instead of just one only I thought about where we were, so I let them go on. Little they cared how wet I got, because then Mother could have a whale of a time being afraid I was taking pneumonia.

Well, I got to thinking about that and watching them throwing dirt into it, slapping it on anyway like they were making mortar or something or building a fence, and I began to feel sort of funny and so I decided to walk around a while. I thought that if I went toward town they'd catch up and be trying to make me get in one of them, so I went on back toward the nigger graveyard. I got under some cedars, where the rain didn't come much, only dripping now and then, where I could see when they got through and went away. After a while they were all gone and I waited a minute and came out.

I had to follow the path to keep out of the wet grass so I didn't see her until I was pretty near there, standing there in a black cloak, looking at the flowers. I knew who it was right off, before she turned and looked at me and lifted up her veil.

"Hello, Jason," she says, holding out her hand. We shook hands.

"What are you doing here?" I says. "I thought you promised her you wouldn't come back here. I thought you had more sense than that."

"Yes?" she says. She looked at the flowers again. There must have been fifty dollars' worth. Somebody had put one bunch on Quentin's. "You did?" she says.

"I'm not surprised though," I says. "I wouldn't put anything past you. You dont mind anybody. You dont give a damn about anybody."

"Oh," she says, "that job." She looked at the grave. "I'm sorry about that, Jason."

"I bet you are," I says. "You'll talk mighty meek now. But you needn't have come back. There's not anything left. Ask Uncle Maury, if you dont believe me."

"I dont want anything," she says. She looked at the grave. "Why didn't they let me know?" she says. "I just happened to see it in the paper. On the back page. Just happened to."

I didn't say anything. We stood there, looking at the grave, and then I got to thinking about when we were little and one thing and another and I got to feeling funny again, kind of mad or something, thinking about now we'd have Uncle Maury around the house all the time, running things like the way he left me to come home in the rain by myself. I says,

"A fine lot you care, sneaking in here soon as he's dead. But it wont do you any good. Dont think that you can take advantage of this to come sneaking back. If you cant stay on the horse you've got, you'll have to walk," I says. "We dont even know your name at that house," I says. "Do you know that? We don't even know you with him and Quentin," I says. "Do you know that?"

"I know it," she says. "Jason," she says, looking at the grave, "if you'll fix it so I can see her a minute I'll give you fifty dollars."

"You haven't got fifty dollars," I says.

"Will you?" she says, not looking at me.

"Let's see it," I says. "I dont believe you've got fifty dollars."

I could see where her hands were moving under

252

her cloak, then she held her hand out. Damn if it wasn't full of money. I could see two or three yellow ones.

" Does he still give you money? " I says. " How much does he send you? "

" I'll give you a hundred," she says. " Will you? "

" Just a minute," I says, " And just like I say. I wouldn't have her know it for a thousand dollars."

" Yes," she says. " Just like you say do it. Just so I see her a minute. I wont beg or do anything. I'll go right on away."

" Give me the money," I says.

" I'll give it to you afterward," she says.

" Dont you trust me? " I says.

" No," she says. " I know you. I grew up with you."

" You're a fine one to talk about trusting people," I says. " Well," I says, " I got to get on out of the rain. Goodbye." I made to go away.

" Jason," she says. I stopped.

" Yes? " I says. " Hurry up. I'm getting wet."

" All right," she says. " Here." There wasn't anybody in sight. I went back and took the money. She still held to it. " You'll do it? " she says, looking at me from under the veil, " You promise? "

" Let go," I says, " You want somebody to come along and see us? "

She let go. I put the money in my pocket. " You'll

do it, Jason?" she says. "I wouldn't ask you, if there was any other way."

"You're damn right there's no other way," I says. "Sure I'll do it. I said I would, didn't I? Only you'll have to do just like I say, now."

"Yes," she says, "I will." So I told her where to be, and went to the livery stable. I hurried and got there just as they were unhitching the hack. I asked if they had paid for it yet and he said No and I said Mrs Compson forgot something and wanted it again, so they let me take it. Mink was driving. I bought him a cigar, so we drove around until it begun to get dark on the back streets where they wouldn't see him. Then Mink said he'd have to take the team on back and so I said I'd buy him another cigar and so we drove into the lane and I went across the yard to the house. I stopped in the hall until I could hear Mother and Uncle Maury upstairs, then I went on back to the kitchen. She and Ben were there with Dilsey. I said Mother wanted her and I took her into the house. I found Uncle Maury's raincoat and put it around her and picked her up and went back to the lane and got in the hack. I told Mink to drive to the depot. He was afraid to pass the stable, so we had to go the back way and I saw her standing on the corner under the light and I told Mink to drive close to the walk and when I said Go on, to give the team a bat. Then I took the raincoat off of her and held her to the window and Caddy saw her and sort of jumped forward.

"Hit 'em, Mink!" I says, and Mink gave them a cut and we went past her like a fire engine. "Now get on that train like you promised," I says. I could see her running after us through the back window. "Hit 'em again," I says, "Let's get on home." When we turned the corner she was still running.

And so I counted the money again that night and put it away, and I didn't feel so bad. I says I reckon that'll show you. I reckon you'll know now that you cant beat me out of a job and get away with it. It never occurred to me she wouldn't keep her promise and take that train. But I didn't know much about them then; I didn't have any more sense than to believe what they said, because the next morning damn if she didn't walk right into the store, only she had sense enough to wear the veil and not speak to anybody. It was Saturday morning, because I was at the store, and she came right on back to the desk where I was, walking fast.

"Liar," she says, "Liar."

"Are you crazy?" I says. "What do you mean? coming in here like this?" She started in, but I shut her off. I says, "You already cost me one job; do you want me to lose this one too? If you've got anything to say to me, I'll meet you somewhere after dark. What have you got to say to me?" I says, "Didn't I do everything I said? I said see her a

255

minute, didn't I? Well, didn't you?" She just stood there looking at me, shaking like an ague-fit, her hands clenched and kind of jerking. "I did just what I said I would," I says, "You're the one that lied. You promised to take that train. Didn't you Didn't you promise? If you think you can get that money back, just try it," I says. "If it'd been a thousand dollars, you'd still owe me after the risk I took. And if I see or hear you're still in town after number 17 runs," I says, "I'll tell Mother and Uncle Maury. Then hold your breath until you see her again." She just stood there, looking at me, twisting her hands together.

"Damn you," she says, "Damn you."

"Sure," I says, "That's all right too. Mind what I say, now. After number 17, and I tell them."

After she was gone I felt better. I says I reckon you'll think twice before you deprive me of a job that was promised me. I was a kid then. I believed folks when they said they'd do things. I've learned better since. Besides, like I say I guess I dont need any man's help to get along I can stand on my own feet like I always have. Then all of a sudden I thought of Dilsey and Uncle Maury. I thought how she'd get around Dilsey and that Uncle Maury would do anything for ten dollars. And there I was, couldn't even get away from the store to protect my own Mother. Like she says, if one of you had to be taken, thank God it was you left me I can depend on you and I says well I dont reckon I'll ever get far enough from the store to get out of your reach. Somebody's got to hold on to what little we have left, I reckon.

So as soon as I got home I fixed Dilsey. I told Dilsey she had leprosy and I got the bible and read where a man's flesh rotted off and I told her that if she ever looked at her or Ben or Quentin they'd catch it too. So I thought I had everything all fixed until that day when I came home and found Ben bellowing. Raising hell and nobody could quiet him. Mother said, Well, get him the slipper then. Dilsey made out she didn't hear. Mother said it again and I says I'd go I couldn't stand that damn noise. Like I say I can stand lots of things I dont expect much from them but if I have to work all day long in a damn store damn if I dont think I deserve a little peace and quiet to eat dinner in. So I says I'd go and Dilsey says quick, " Jason! "

Well, like a flash I knew what was up, but just to make sure I went and got the slipper and brought it back, and just like I thought, when he saw it you'd thought we were killing him. So I made Dilsey own up, then I told Mother. We had to take her up to bed then, and after things got quieted down a little I put the fear of God into Dilsey. As much as you can into a nigger, that is. That's the trouble with nigger servants, when they've been with you for a long time they get so full of self importance that they're not worth a damn. Think they run the whole family.

"I like to know whut's de hurt in lettin dat po chile see her own baby," Dilsey says. "If Mr Jason was still here hit ud be different."

"Only Mr Jason's not here," I says. "I know you wont pay me any mind, but I reckon you'll do what Mother says. You keep on worrying her like this until you get her into the graveyard too, then you can fill the whole house full of ragtag and bobtail. But what did you want to let that damn idiot see her for?"

"You's a cold man, Jason, if man you is," she says. "I thank de Lawd I got mo heart dan dat, even ef hit is black."

"At least I'm man enough to keep that flour barrel full," I says. "And if you do that again, you wont be eating out of it either."

So the next time I told her that if she tried Dilsey again, Mother was going to fire Dilsey and send Ben to Jackson and take Quentin and go away. She looked at me for a while. There wasn't any street light close and I couldn't see her face much. But I could feel her looking at me. When we were little when she'd get mad and couldn't do anything about it her upper lip would begin to jump. Everytime it jumped it would leave a little more of her teeth showing, and all the time she'd be as still as a post, not a muscle moving except her lip jerking

258

higher and higher up her teeth. But she didn't say anything. She just said,

"All right. How much?"

"Well, if one look through a hack window was worth a hundred," I says. So after that she behaved pretty well, only one time she asked to see a statement of the bank account.

"I know they have Mother's indorsement on them," she says, "But I want to see the bank statement. I want to see myself where those checks go."

"That's in Mother's private business," I says. "If you think you have any right to pry into her private affairs I'll tell her you believe those checks are being misappropriated and you want an audit because you dont trust her."

She didn't say anything or move. I could hear her whispering Damn you oh damn you oh damn you.

"Say it out," I says, "I dont reckon it's any secret what you and I think of one another. Maybe you want the money back," I says.

"Listen, Jason," she says, "Dont lie to me now. About her. I wont ask to see anything. If that isn't enough, I'll send more each month. Just promise that she'll — that she — You can do that. Things for her. Be kind to her. Little things that I cant, they wont let. . . . But you wont. You never had a drop of warm blood in you. Listen," she says, "If you'll get Mother to let me have her back, I'll give you a thousand dollars."

259

"You haven't got a thousand dollars," I says, "I know you're lying now."

"Yes I have. I will have. I can get it."

"And I know how you'll get it," I says, "You'll get it the same way you got her. And when she gets big enough — " Then I thought she really was going to hit at me, and then I didn't know what she was going to do. She acted for a minute like some kind of a toy that's wound up too tight and about to burst all to pieces.

"Oh, I'm crazy," she says, "I'm insane. I can't take her. Keep her. What am I thinking of. Jason," she says, grabbing my arm. Her hands were hot as fever. "You'll have to promise to take care of her, to — She's kin to you; your own flesh and blood. Promise, Jason. You have Father's name: do you think I'd have to ask him twice? once, even?"

"That's so," I says, "He did leave me something. What do you want me to do," I says, "Buy an apron and a go-cart? I never got you into this," I says. "I run more risk than you do, because you haven't got anything at stake. So if you expect — "

"No," she says, then she begun to laugh and to try to hold it back all at the same time. "No. I have nothing at stake," she says, making that noise, putting her hands to her mouth, "Nuh-nuh-nothing," she says.

"Here," I says, "Stop that!"

"I'm tr-trying to," she says, holding her hands over her mouth. "Oh God, oh God."

"I'm going away from here," I says, "I cant be seen here. You get on out of town now, you hear?"

"Wait," she says, catching my arm. "I've stopped. I wont again. You promise, Jason?" she says, and me feeling her eyes almost like they were touching my face, "You promise? Mother — that money — if sometimes she needs things — If I send checks for her to you, other ones besides those, you'll give them to her? You wont tell? You'll see that she has things like other girls?"

"Sure," I says, "As long as you behave and do like I tell you."

And so when Earl came up front with his hat on he says, "I'm going to step up to Rogers' and get a snack. We wont have time to go home to dinner, I reckon."

"What's the matter we wont have time?" I says.

"With this show in town and all," he says. "They're going to give an afternoon performance too, and they'll all want to get done trading in time to go to it. So we'd better just run up to Rogers'."

"All right," I says, "It's your stomach. If you want to make a slave of yourself to your business, it's all right with me."

"I reckon you'll never be a slave to any business," he says.

"Not unless it's Jason Compson's business," I says.

So when I went back and opened it the only thing that surprised me was it was a money order not a check. Yes, sir. You cant trust a one of them. After all the risk I'd taken, risking Mother finding out about her coming down here once or twice a year sometimes, and me having to tell Mother lies about it. That's gratitude for you. And I wouldn't put it past her to try to notify the postoffice not to let anyone except her cash it. Giving a kid like that fifty dollars. Why I never saw fifty dollars until I was twenty-one years old, with all the other boys with the afternoon off and all day Saturday and me working in a store. Like I say, how can they expect anybody to control her, with her giving her money behind our backs. She has the same home you had I says, and the same raising. I reckon Mother is a better judge of what she needs than you are, that haven't even got a home. "If you want to give her money," I says, "You send it to Mother, dont be giving it to her. If I've got to run this risk every few months, you'll have to do like I say, or it's out."

And just about the time I got ready to begin on it because if Earl thought I was going to dash up the street and gobble two bits worth of indigestion on his account he was bad fooled. I may not be sitting with my feet on a mahogany desk but I am being paid for what I do inside this building and if I cant

262

manage to live a civilised life outside of it I'll go where I can. I can stand on my own feet; I dont need any man's mahogany desk to prop me up. So just about the time I got ready to start. I'd have to drop everything and run to sell some redneck a dime's worth of nails or something, and Earl up there gobbling a sandwich and half way back already, like as not, and then I found that all the blanks were gone. I remembered then that I had aimed to get some more, but it was too late now, and then I looked up and there Quentin came. In the back door. I heard her asking old Job if I was there. I just had time to stick them in the drawer and close it.

She came around to the desk. I looked at my watch.

"You been to dinner already?" I says. "It's just twelve; I just heard it strike. You must have flown home and back."

"I'm not going home to dinner," she says. "Did I get a letter today?"

"Were you expecting one?" I says. "Have you got a sweetie that can write?"

"From Mother," she says. "Did I get a letter from Mother?" she says, looking at me.

"Mother got one from her," I says. "I haven't opened it. You'll have to wait until she opens it. She'll let you see it, I imagine."

"Please, Jason," she says, not paying any attention, "Did I get one?"

" What's the matter? " I says. " I never knew you to be this anxious about anybody. You must expect some money from her."

" She said she — " she says. " Please, Jason," she says, " Did I? "

" You must have been to school today, after all," I says, " Somewhere where they taught you to say please. Wait a minute, while I wait on that customer."

I went and waited on him. When I turned to come back she was out of sight behind the desk. I ran. I ran around the desk and caught her as she jerked her hand out of the drawer. I took the letter away from her, beating her knuckles on the desk until she let go.

" You would, would you? " I says.

" Give it to me," she says, " You've already opened it. Give it to me. Please, Jason. It's mine. I saw the name."

" I'll take a hame string to you," I says. " That's what I'll give you. Going into my papers."

" Is there some money in it? " she says, reaching for it. " She said she would send me some money. She promised she would. Give it to me."

" What do you want with money? " I says.

" She said she would," she says, " Give it to me. Please, Jason. I wont ever ask you anything again, if you'll give it to me this time."

" I'm going to, if you'll give me time," I says. I took the letter and the money order out and gave her

264

the letter. She reached for the money order, not hardly glancing at the letter. "You'll have to sign it first," I says.

"How much is it?" she says.

"Read the letter," I says. "I reckon it'll say."

She read it fast, in about two looks.

"It dont say," she says, looking up. She dropped the letter to the floor. "How much is it?"

"It's ten dollars," I says.

"Ten dollars?" she says, staring at me.

"And you ought to be damn glad to get that," I says, "A kid like you. What are you in such a rush for money all of a sudden for?"

"Ten dollars?" she says, like she was talking in her sleep, "Just ten dollars?" She made a grab at the money order. "You're lying," she says. "Thief!" she says, "Thief!"

"You would, would you?" I says, holding her off.

"Give it to me!" she says, "It's mine. She sent it to me. I will see it. I will."

"You will?" I says, holding her, "How're you going to do it?"

"Just let me see it, Jason," she says, "Please. I wont ask you for anything again."

"Think I'm lying, do you?" I says. "Just for that you wont see it."

"But just ten dollars," she says, "She told me she — she told me — Jason, please please please. I've

265

got to have some money. I've just got to. Give it to me, Jason. I'll do anything if you will."

"Tell me what you've got to have money for," I says.

"I've got to have it," she says. She was looking at me. Then all of a sudden she quit looking at me without moving her eyes at all. I knew she was going to lie. "It's some money I owe," she says. "I've got to pay it. I've got to pay it today."

"Who to?" I says. Her hands were sort of twisting. I could watch her trying to think of a lie to tell. "Have you been charging things at stores again?" I says. "You needn't bother to tell me that. If you can find anybody in this town that'll charge anything to you after what I told them, I'll eat it."

"It's a girl," she says, "It's a girl. I borrowed some money from a girl. I've got to pay it back. Jason, give it to me. Please. I'll do anything. I've got to have it. Mother will pay you. I'll write to her to pay you and that I wont ever ask her for anything again. You can see the letter. Please, Jason. I've got to have it."

"Tell me what you want with it, and I'll see about it," I says. "Tell me." She just stood there, with her hands working against her dress. "All right," I says, "If ten dollars is too little for you, I'll just take it home to Mother, and you know what'll happen to it then. Of course, if you're so rich you dont need ten dollars — "

266

She stood there, looking at the floor, kind of mumbling to herself. "She said she would send me some money. She said she sends money here and you say she dont send any. She said she's sent a lot of money here. She says it's for me. That it's for me to have some of it. And you say we haven't got any money."

"You know as much about that as I do," I says. "You've seen what happens to those checks."

"Yes," she says, looking at the floor. "Ten dollars," she says, "Ten dollars."

"And you'd better thank your stars it's ten dollars," I says. "Here," I says. I put the money order face down on the desk, holding my hand on it, "Sign it."

"Will you let me see it?" she says. "I just want to look at it. Whatever it says, I wont ask for but ten dollars. You can have the rest. I just want to see it."

"Not after the way you've acted," I says. "You've got to learn one thing, and that is that when I tell you to do something, you've got it to do. You sign your name on that line."

She took the pen, but instead of signing it she just stood there with her head bent and the pen shaking in her hand. Just like her mother. "Oh, God," she says, "oh, God."

"Yes," I says, "That's one thing you'll have to learn if you never learn anything else. Sign it now, and get on out of here."

267

She signed it. "Where's the money?" she says. I took the order and blotted it and put it in my pocket. Then I gave her the ten dollars.

"Now you go on back to school this afternoon, you hear?" I says. She didn't answer. She crumpled the bill up in her hand like it was a rag or something and went on out the front door just as Earl came in. A customer came in with him and they stopped up front. I gathered up the things and put on my hat and went up front.

"Been much busy?" Earl says.

"Not much," I says. He looked out the door.

"That your car over yonder?" he says. "Better not try to go out home to dinner. We'll likely have another rush just before the show opens. Get you a lunch at Rogers' and put a ticket in the drawer."

"Much obliged," I says. "I can still manage to feed myself, I reckon."

And right there he'd stay, watching that door like a hawk until I came through it again. Well, he'd just have to watch it for a while; I was doing the best I could. The time before I says that's the last one now; you'll have to remember to get some more right away. But who can remember anything in all this hurrah. And now this damn show had to come here the one day I'd have to hunt all over town for a blank check, besides all the other things I had to do to keep the house running, and Earl watching the door like a hawk.

I went to the printing shop and told him I wanted to play a joke on a fellow, but he didn't have anything. Then he told me to have a look in the old opera house, where somebody had stored a lot of papers and junk out of the old Merchants' and Farmers' Bank when it failed, so I dodged up a few more alleys so Earl couldn't see me and finally found old man Simmons and got the key from him and went up there and dug around. At last I found a pad on a Saint Louis bank. And of course she'd pick this one time to look at it close. Well, it would have to do. I couldn't waste any more time now.

I went back to the store. " Forgot some papers Mother wants to go to the bank," I says. I went back to the desk and fixed the check. Trying to hurry and all, I says to myself it's a good thing her eyes are giving out, with that little whore in the house, a Christian forbearing woman like Mother. I says you know just as well as I do what she's going to grow up into but I says that's your business, if you want to keep her and raise her in your house just because of Father. Then she would begin to cry and say it was her own flesh and blood so I just says All right. Have it your way. I can stand it if you can.

I fixed the letter up again and glued it back and went out.

" Try not to be gone any longer than you can help," Earl says.

"All right," I says. I went to the telegraph office. The smart boys were all there.

"Any of you boys made your million yet?" I says.

"Who can do anything, with a market like that?" Doc says.

"What's it doing?" I says. I went in and looked. It was three points under the opening. "You boys are not going to let a little thing like the cotton market beat you, are you?" I says. "I thought you were too smart for that."

"Smart, hell," Doc says. "It was down twelve points at twelve o'clock. Cleaned me out."

"Twelve points?" I says. "Why the hell didn't somebody let me know? Why didn't you let me know?" I says to the operator.

"I take it as it comes in," he says. "I'm not running a bucket shop."

"You're smart, aren't you?" I says. "Seems to me, with the money I spend with you, you could take time to call me up. Or maybe your damn company's in a conspiracy with those damn eastern sharks."

He didn't say anything. He made like he was busy.

"You're getting a little too big for your pants," I says. "First thing you know you'll be working for a living."

"What's the matter with you?" Doc says. "You're still three points to the good."

"Yes," I says, "If I happened to be selling. I haven't mentioned that yet, I think. You boys all cleaned out?"

"I got caught twice," Doc says. "I switched just in time."

"Well," I. O. Snopes says, "I've picked hit; I reckon taint no more than fair fer hit to pick me once in a while."

So I left them buying and selling among themselves at a nickel a point. I found a nigger and sent him for my car and stood on the corner and waited. I couldn't see Earl looking up and down the street, with one eye on the clock, because I couldn't see the door from here. After about a week he got back with it.

"Where the hell have you been?" I says, "Riding around where the wenches could see you?"

"I come straight as I could," he says, "I had to drive clean around the square, wid all dem wagons."

I never found a nigger yet that didn't have an airtight alibi for whatever he did. But just turn one loose in a car and he's bound to show off. I got in and went on around the square. I caught a glimpse of Earl in the door across the square.

I went straight to the kitchen and told Dilsey to hurry up with dinner.

"Quentin aint come yit," she says.

"What of that?" I says. "You'll be telling me

next that Luster's not quite ready to eat yet. Quentin knows when meals are served in this house. Hurry up with it, now."

Mother was in her room. I gave her the letter. She opened it and took the check out and sat holding it in her hand. I went and got the shovel from the corner and gave her a match. "Come on," I says, "Get it over with. You'll be crying in a minute."

She took the match, but she didn't strike it. She sat there, looking at the check. Just like I said it would be.

"I hate to do it," she says, "To increase your burden by adding Quentin. . . ."

"I guess we'll get along," I says. "Come on. Get it over with."

But she just sat there, holding the check.

"This one is on a different bank," she says. "They have been on an Indianapolis bank."

"Yes," I says. "Women are allowed to do that too."

"Do what?" she says.

"Keep money in two different banks," I says.

"Oh," she says. She looked at the check a while. "I'm glad to know she's so . . . she has so much . . . God sees that I am doing right," she says.

"Come on," I says, "Finish it. Get the fun over."

"Fun?" she says, "When I think —"

"I thought you were burning this two hundred dollars a month for fun," I says. " Come on, now. Want me to strike the match?"

" I could bring myself to accept them," she says, " For my childrens' sake. I have no pride."

" You'd never be satisfied," I says, " You know you wouldn't. You've settled that once, let it stay settled. We can get along."

" I leave everything to you," she says. " But sometimes I become afraid that in doing this I am depriving you all of what is rightfully yours. Perhaps I shall be punished for it. If you want me to, I will smother my pride and accept them."

" What would be the good in beginning now, when you've been destroying them for fifteen years?" I says. " If you keep on doing it, you have lost nothing, but if you'd begin to take them now, you'll have lost fifty thousand dollars. We've got along so far, haven't we?" I says. " I haven't seen you in the poorhouse yet."

" Yes," she says, " We Bascombs need nobody's charity. Certainly not that of a fallen woman."

She struck the match and lit the check and put it in the shovel, and then the envelope, and watched them burn.

" You dont know what it is," she says, " Thank God you will never know what a mother feels."

" There are lots of women in this world no better than her," I says.

" But they are not my daughters," she says. " It's

273

not myself," she says, "I'd gladly take her back, sins and all, because she is my flesh and blood. It's for Quentin's sake."

Well, I could have said it wasn't much chance of anybody hurting Quentin much, but like I say I dont expect much but I do want to eat and sleep without a couple of women squabbling and crying in the house.

"And yours," she says. "I know how you feel toward her."

"Let her come back," I says, "far as I'm concerned."

"No," she says. "I owe that to your father's memory."

"When he was trying all the time to persuade you to let her come home when Herbert threw her out?" I says.

"You dont understand," she says. "I know you dont intend to make it more difficult for me. But it's my place to suffer for my children," she says. "I can bear it."

"Seems to me you go to a lot of unnecessary trouble doing it," I says. The paper burned out. I carried it to the grate and put it in. "It just seems a shame to me to burn up good money," I says.

"Let me never see the day when my children will have to accept that, the wages of sin," she says. "I'd rather see even you dead in your coffin first."

"Have it your way," I says. "Are we going to have dinner soon?" I says, "Because if we're not,

I'll have to go on back. We're pretty busy today."
She got up. "I've told her once," I says. "It seems
she's waiting on Quentin or Luster or somebody.
Here, I'll call her. Wait." But she went to the head
of the stairs and called.

"Quentin aint come yit," Dilsey says.

"Well, I'll have to get on back," I says. "I can
get a sandwich downtown. I dont want to interfere
with Dilsey's arrangements," I says. Well, that got
her started again, with Dilsey hobbling and mumbling back and forth, saying,

"All right, all right, Ise puttin hit on fast as I
kin."

"I try to please you all," Mother says, "I try to
make things as easy for you as I can."

"I'm not complaining, am I?" I says. "Have I
said a word except I had to go back to work?"

"I know," she says, "I know you haven't had the
chance the others had, that you've had to bury yourself in a little country store. I wanted you to get
ahead. I knew your father would never realise that
you were the only one who had any business sense,
and then when everything else failed I believed that
when she married, and Herbert . . . after his
promise . . ."

"Well, he was probably lying too," I says. "He
may not have even had a bank. And if he had, I dont
reckon he'd have to come all the way to Mississippi
to get a man for it."

We ate awhile. I could hear Ben in the kitchen, where Luster was feeding him. Like I say, if we've got to feed another mouth and she wont take that money, why not send him down to Jackson. He'll be happier there, with people like him. I says God knows there's little enough room for pride in this family, but it dont take much pride to not like to see a thirty year old man playing around the yard with a nigger boy, running up and down the fence and lowing like a cow whenever they play golf over there. I says if they'd sent him to Jackson at first we'd all be better off today. I says, you've done your duty by him; you've done all anybody can expect of you and more than most folks would do, so why not send him there and get that much benefit out of the taxes we pay. Then she says, " I'll be gone soon. I know I'm just a burden to you " and I says " You've been saying that so long that I'm beginning to believe you " only I says you'd better be sure and not let me know you're gone because I'll sure have him on number seventeen that night and I says I think I know a place where they'll take her too and the name of it's not Milk street and Honey avenue either. Then she begun to cry and I says All right all right I have as much pride about my kinfolks as anybody even if I dont always know where they come from.

We ate for awhile. Mother sent Dilsey to the front to look for Quentin again.

"I keep telling you she's not coming to dinner," I says.

"She knows better than that," Mother says, "She knows I dont permit her to run about the streets and not come home at meal time. Did you look good, Dilsey?"

"Dont let her, then," I says.

"What can I do," she says. "You have all of you flouted me. Always."

"If you wouldn't come interfering, I'd make her mind," I says. "It wouldn't take me but about one day to straighten her out."

"You'd be too brutal with her," she says. "You have your Uncle Maury's temper."

That reminded me of the letter. I took it out and handed it to her. "You wont have to open it," I says. "The bank will let you know how much it is this time."

"It's addressed to you," she says.

"Go on and open it," I says. She opened it and read it and handed it to me.

"'My dear young nephew,' it says,

'You will be glad to learn that I am now in a position to avail myself of an opportunity regarding which, for reasons which I shall make obvious to you, I shall not go into details until I have an opportunity to divulge it to you in a more secure manner. My business experience has taught me to be chary of committing anything of a confidential nature to any more concrete medium than speech, and my extreme precaution in this instance should give you some inkling of its value. Needless to say, I have just completed a most exhaustive examination of all its phases, and I feel no hesitancy in telling you that it is that sort of golden chance that comes but once in a lifetime, and I now see clearly before me that goal toward which I have long and unflaggingly striven: i.e., the ultimate solidification of my affairs by which I may restore to its rightful position that family of which I have the honour to be the sole remaining male descendant; that family in which I have ever included your lady mother and her children.

'As it so happens, I am not quite in a position to avail myself of this opportunity to the uttermost which it warrants, but rather than go out of the family to do so, I am today drawing upon your Mother's bank for the small sum necessary to complement my own initial investment, for which I herewith enclose, as a matter of formality, my note of hand at eight percent per annum. Needless to say, this is merely a formality, to secure your Mother in the event of that circumstance of which man is ever the plaything and sport. For naturally I shall employ this sum as though it were my own and so permit your Mother to avail herself of this opportunity which my exhaustive investigation has shown to be

278

a bonanza — if you will permit the vulgarism — of the first water and purest ray serene.

'This is in confidence, you will understand, from one business man to another; we will harvest our own vineyards, eh? And knowing your Mother's delicate health and that timorousness which such delicately nurtured Southern ladies would naturally feel regarding matters of business, and their charming proneness to divulge unwittingly such matters in conversation, I would suggest that you do not mention it to her at all. On second thought, I advise you not to do so. It might be better to simply restore this sum to the bank at some future date, say, in a lump sum with the other small sums for which I am indebted to her, and say nothing about it at all. It is our duty to shield her from the crass material world as much as possible.

'Your affectionate Uncle,
'Maury L. Bascomb.'"

"What do you want to do about it?" I says, flipping it across the table.

"I know you grudge what I give him," she says.

"It's your money," I says. "If you want to throw it to the birds even, it's your business."

"He's my own brother," Mother says. "He's the last Bascomb. When we are gone there wont be any more of them."

"That'll be hard on somebody, I guess," I says.

"All right, all right," I says, "It's your money. Do as you please with it. You want me to tell the bank to pay it?"

"I know you begrudge him," she says. "I realise the burden on your shoulders. When I'm gone it will be easier on you."

"I could make it easier right now," I says. "All right, all right, I wont mention it again. Move all bedlam in here if you want to."

"He's your own brother," she says, "Even if he is afflicted."

"I'll take your bank book," I says. "I'll draw my check today."

"He kept you waiting six days," she says. "Are you sure the business is sound? It seems strange to me that a solvent business cannot pay its employees promptly."

"He's all right," I says, "Safe as a bank. I tell him not to bother about mine until we get done collecting every month. That's why it's late sometimes."

"I just couldn't bear to have you lose the little I had to invest for you," she says. "I've often thought that Earl is not a good business man. I know he doesn't take you into his confidence to the extent that your investment in the business should warrant. I'm going to speak to him."

"No, you let him alone," I says. "It's his business."

280

"You have a thousand dollars in it."

"You let him alone," I says, "I'm watching things. I have your power of attorney. It'll be all right."

"You dont know what a comfort you are to me," she says. "You have always been my pride and joy, but when you came to me of your own accord and insisted on banking your salary each month in my name, I thanked God it was you left me if they had to be taken."

"They were all right," I says. "They did the best they could, I reckon."

"When you talk that way I know you are thinking bitterly of your father's memory," she says. "You have a right to, I suppose. But it breaks my heart to hear you."

I got up. "If you've got any crying to do," I says, "you'll have to do it alone, because I've got to get on back. I'll get the bank book."

"I'll get it," she says.

"Keep still," I says, "I'll get it." I went upstairs and got the bank book out of her desk and went back to town. I went to the bank and deposited the check and the money order and the other ten, and stopped at the telegraph office. It was one point above the opening. I had already lost thirteen points, all because she had to come helling in there at twelve, worrying me about that letter.

"What time did that report come in?" I says.

"About an hour ago," he says.

"An hour ago?" I says. "What are we paying you for?" I says, "Weekly reports? How do you expect a man to do anything? The whole damn top could blow off and we'd not know it."

"I dont expect you to do anything," he says. "They changed that law making folks play the cotton market."

"They have?" I says. "I hadn't heard. They must have sent the news out over the Western Union."

I went back to the store. Thirteen points. Damn if I believe anybody knows anything about the damn thing except the ones that sit back in those New York offices and watch the country suckers come up and beg them to take their money. Well, a man that just calls shows he has no faith in himself, and like I say if you aren't going to take the advice, what's the use in paying money for it. Besides, these people are right up there on the ground; they know everything that's going on. I could feel the telegram in my pocket. I'd just have to prove that they were using the telegraph company to defraud. That would constitute a bucket shop. And I wouldn't hesitate that long, either. Only be damned if it doesn't look like a company as big and rich as the Western Union could get a market report out on time. Half as quick as they'll get a wire to you saying Your account closed out. But what the hell do they care about the people. They're hand in glove with that New York crowd. Anybody could see that.

When I came in Earl looked at his watch. But he didn't say anything until the customer was gone. Then he says,

"You go home to dinner?"

"I had to go to the dentist," I says because it's not any of his business where I eat but I've got to be in the store with him all the afternoon. And with his jaw running off after all I've stood. You take a little two by four country storekeeper like I say it takes a man with just five hundred dollars to worry about it fifty thousand dollars' worth.

"You might have told me," he says. "I expected you back right away."

"I'll trade you this tooth and give you ten dollars to boot, any time," I says. "Our agreement was an hour for dinner," I says, "and if you dont like the way I do, you know what you can do about it."

"I've known that some time," he says. "If it hadn't been for your mother I'd have done it before now, too. She's a lady I've got a lot of sympathy for, Jason. Too bad some other folks I know cant say as much."

"Then you can keep it," I says. "When we need any sympathy I'll let you know in plenty of time."

"I've protected you about that business a long time, Jason," he says.

"Yes?" I says, letting him go on. Listening to what he would say before I shut him up.

"I believe I know more about where that automobile came from than she does."

"You think so, do you?" I says. "When are you going to spread the news that I stole it from my mother?"

"I dont say anything," he says, "I know you have her power of attorney. And I know she still believes that thousand dollars is in this business."

"All right," I says, "Since you know so much, I'll tell you a little more: go to the bank and ask them whose account I've been depositing a hundred and sixty dollars on the first of every month for twelve years."

"I dont say anything," he says, "I just ask you to be a little more careful after this."

I never said anything more. It doesn't do any good. I've found that when a man gets into a rut the best thing you can do is let him stay there. And when a man gets it in his head that he's got to tell something on you for your own good, good-night. I'm glad I haven't got the sort of conscience I've got to nurse like a sick puppy all the time. If I'd ever be as careful over anything as he is to keep his little shirt tail full of business from making him more than eight percent. I reckon he thinks they'd get him on the usury law if he netted more than eight percent. What the hell chance has a man got, tied down in a town like this and to a business like this. Why I could take his business in one year and fix him so he'd never have to work again, only he'd give it all away to the church or something. If there's one thing gets under my skin, it's a damn hypocrite. A man that thinks anything he dont understand all about must be crooked and that first chance he gets he's morally bound to tell the third party what's none of his business to tell. Like I say if I thought every time a man did something I didn't know all about he was bound to be a crook, I reckon I wouldn't have any trouble finding something back there on those books that you wouldn't see any use for running and telling somebody I thought ought to know about it, when for all I knew they might know a damn sight more about it now than I did, and if they didn't it was damn little of my business anyway and he says, "My books are open to anybody. Anybody that has any claim or believes she has any claim on this business can go back there and welcome."

"Sure, you wont tell," I says, "You couldn't square your conscience with that. You'll just take her back there and let her find it. You wont tell, yourself."

"I'm not trying to meddle in your business," he says. "I know you missed out on some things like Quentin had. But your mother has had a misfortunate life too, and if she was to come in here and ask me why you quit, I'd have to tell her. It aint that

thousand dollars. You know that. It's because a man
never gets anywhere if fact and his ledgers dont
square. And I'm not going to lie to anybody, for myself or anybody else."

"Well, then," I says, " I reckon that conscience
of yours is a more valuable clerk than I am; it dont
have to go home at noon to eat. Only dont let it interfere with my appetite," I says, because how the
hell can I do anything right, with that damn family
and her not making any effort to control her nor any
of them, like that time when she happened to see one
of them kissing Caddy and all next day she went
around the house in a black dress and a veil and even
Father couldn't get her to say a word except crying
and saying her little daughter was dead and Caddy
about fifteen then only in three years she'd been
wearing haircloth or probably sandpaper at that
rate. Do you think I can afford to have her running
about the streets with every drummer that comes to
town, I says, and them telling the new ones up and
down the road where to pick up a hot one when they
made Jefferson. I haven't got much pride, I can't
afford it with a kitchen full of niggers to feed and
robbing the state asylum of its star freshman.
Blood, I says, governors and generals. It's a damn
good thing we never had any kings and presidents;
we'd all be down there at Jackson chasing butterflies. I say it'd be bad enough if it was mine; I'd at
least be sure it was a bastard to begin with, and

286

now even the Lord doesn't know that for certain probably.

So after awhile I heard the band start up, and then they begun to clear out. Headed for the show, every one of them. Haggling over a twenty cent hame string to save fifteen cents, so they can give it to a bunch of Yankees that come in and pay maybe ten dollars for the privilege. I went on out to the back.

"Well," I says, "If you dont look out, that bolt will grow into your hand. And then I'm going to take an axe and chop it out. What do you reckon the boll-weevils'll eat if you dont get those cultivators in shape to raise them a crop?" I says, "sage grass?"

"Dem folks sho do play dem horns," he says. "Tell me man in dat show kin play a tune on a hand-saw. Pick hit like a banjo."

"Listen," I says. "Do you know how much that show'll spend in this town? About ten dollars," I says. "The ten dollars Buck Turpin has in his pocket right now."

"Whut dey give Mr Buck ten dollars fer?" he says.

"For the privilege of showing here," I says. "You can put the balance of what they'll spend in your eye."

"You mean dey pays ten dollars jest to give dey show here?" he says.

"That's all," I says. "And how much do you reckon . . ."

"Gret day," he says, "You mean to tell me dey chargin um to let um show here? I'd pay ten dollars to see dat man pick dat saw, ef I had to. I figures dat tomorrow mawnin I be still owin um nine dollars and six bits at dat rate."

And then a Yankee will talk your head off about niggers getting ahead. Get them ahead, what I say. Get them so far ahead you cant find one south of Louisville with a blood hound. Because when I told him about how they'd pick up Saturday night and carry off at least a thousand dollars out of the county, he says,

"I dont begrudge um. I kin sho afford my two bits."

"Two bits hell," I says. "That dont begin it. How about the dime or fifteen cents you'll spend for a damn two cent box of candy or something. How about the time you're wasting right now, listening to that band."

"Dat's de troof," he says. "Well, ef I lives twell night hit's gwine to be two bits mo dey takin out of town, dat's sho."

"Then you're a fool," I says.

"Well," he says, "I dont spute dat neither. Ef dat uz a crime, all chain-gangs wouldn't be black."

Well, just about that time I happened to look up the alley and saw her. When I stepped back and looked at my watch I didn't notice at the time who he was because I was looking at the watch. It was

288

just two thirty, forty-five minutes before anybody but me expected her to be out. So when I looked around the door the first thing I saw was the red tie he had on and I was thinking what the hell kind of a man would wear a red tie. But she was sneaking along the alley, watching the door, so I wasn't thinking anything about him until they had gone past. I was wondering if she'd have so little respect for me that she'd not only play out of school when I told her not to, but would walk right past the store, daring me not to see her. Only she couldn't see into the door because the sun fell straight into it and it was like trying to see through an automobile searchlight, so I stood there and watched her go on past, with her face painted up like a damn clown's and her hair all gummed and twisted and a dress that if a woman had come out doors even on Gayoso or Beale street when I was a young fellow with no more than that to cover her legs and behind, she'd been thrown in jail. I'll be damned if they dont dress like they were trying to make every man they passed on the street want to reach out and clap his hand on it. And so I was thinking what kind of a damn man would wear a red tie when all of a sudden I knew he was one of those show folks well as if she'd told me. Well, I can stand a lot; if I couldn't, damn if I wouldn't be in a hell of a fix, so when they turned the corner I jumped down and followed. Me, without any hat, in the middle of the afternoon, having to chase up and down back alleys because of my mother's good name. Like I say you cant do anything with a woman like that, if she's got it in her. If it's in her blood, you cant do anything with her. The only thing you can do is to get rid of her, let her go on and live with her own sort.

I went on to the street, but they were out of sight. And there I was, without any hat, looking like I was crazy too. Like a man would naturally think, one of them is crazy and another one drowned himself and the other one was turned out into the street by her husband, what's the reason the rest of them are not crazy too. All the time I could see them watching me like a hawk, waiting for a chance to say Well I'm not surprised I expected it all the time the whole family's crazy. Selling land to send him to Harvard and paying taxes to support a state University all the time that I never saw except twice at a baseball game and not letting her daughter's name be spoken on the place until after a while Father wouldn't even come down town anymore but just sat there all day with the decanter I could see the bottom of his nightshirt and his bare legs and hear the decanter clinking until finally T. P. had to pour it for him and she says You have no respect for your Father's memory and I says I dont know why not it sure is preserved well enough to last only if I'm crazy too God knows what I'll do about it just to look at water makes me sick and I'd just as soon swallow gasoline as a glass of whiskey and Lorraine telling them he may not drink but if you dont believe he's a man I can tell you how to find out she says If I catch you fooling with any of these whores you know what I'll do she says I'll whip her grabbing at her I'll whip her as long as I can find her she says and I says if I dont drink that's my business but have you ever found me short I says I'll buy you enough beer to take a bath in if you want it because I've got every respect for a good honest whore because with Mother's health and the position I try to uphold to have her with no more respect for what I try to do for her than to make her name and my name and my Mother's name a byword in the town.

She had dodged out of sight somewhere. Saw me coming and dodged into another alley, running up and down the alleys with a damn show man in a red tie that everybody would look at and think what kind of a damn man would wear a red tie. Well, the boy kept speaking to me and so I took the telegram without knowing I had taken it. I didn't realise what it was until I was signing for it, and I tore it open without even caring much what it was. I knew all the time what it would be, I reckon. That was the only thing else that could happen, especially holding it up until I had already had the check entered on the pass book.

I dont see how a city no bigger than New York can hold enough people to take the money away from us country suckers. Work like hell all day every day, send them your money and get a little piece of paper back, Your account closed at 20.62. Teasing you along, letting you pile up a little paper profit, then bang! Your account closed at 20.62. And if that wasn't enough, paying ten dollars a month to somebody to tell you how to lose it fast, that either dont know anything about it or is in cahoots with the telegraph company. Well, I'm done with them. They've sucked me in for the last time. Any fool except a fellow that hasn't got any more sense than to take a jew's word for anything could tell the market was going up all the time, with the whole damn delta about to be flooded again and the cotton washed right out of the ground like it was last year. Let it wash a man's crop out of the ground year after year, and them up there in Washington spending fifty thousand dollars a day keeping an army in Nicaragua or some place. Of course it'll overflow again, and then cotton'll be worth thirty cents a pound. Well, I just want to hit them one time and get my money back. I don't want a killing; only these small town gamblers are out for that, I just want my money back that these damn jews have gotten with all their guaranteed inside dope. Then I'm through; they can kiss my foot for every other red cent of mine they get.

I went back to the store. It was half past three almost. Damn little time to do anything in, but then

I am used to that. I never had to go to Harvard to learn that. The band had quit playing. Got them all inside now, and they wouldn't have to waste any more wind. Earl says,

"He found you, did he? He was in here with it a while ago. I thought you were out back somewhere."

"Yes," I says, "I got it. They couldn't keep it away from me all afternoon. The town's too small. I've got to go out home a minute," I says. "You can dock me if it'll make you feel any better."

"Go ahead," he says, "I can handle it now. No bad news, I hope."

"You'll have to go to the telegraph office and find that out," I says. "They'll have time to tell you. I haven't."

"I just asked," he says. "Your mother knows she can depend on me."

"She'll appreciate it," I says. "I wont be gone any longer than I have to."

"Take your time," he says. "I can handle it now. You go ahead."

I got the car and went home. Once this morning, twice at noon, and now again, with her and having to chase all over town and having to beg them to let me eat a little of the food I am paying for. Sometimes I think what's the use of anything. With the precedent I've been set I must be crazy to keep on. And now I reckon I'll get home just in time to take a nice long drive after a basket of tomatoes or something and then have to go back to town smelling like a camphor factory so my head wont explode right on my shoulders. I keep telling her there's not a damn thing in that aspirin except flour and water for imaginary invalids. I says you dont know what a headache is. I says you think I'd fool with that damn car at all if it depended on me. I says I can get along without one I've learned to get along without lots of things but if you want to risk yourself in that old wornout surrey with a halfgrown nigger boy all right because I says God looks after Ben's kind, God knows He ought to do something for him but if you think I'm going to trust a thousand dollars' worth of delicate machinery to a halfgrown nigger or a grown one either, you'd better buy him one yourself because I says you like to ride in the car and you know you do.

Dilsey said Mother was in the house. I went on into the hall and listened, but I didn't hear anything. I went up stairs, but just as I passed her door she called me.

"I just wanted to know who it was," she says. "I'm here alone so much that I hear every sound."

"You dont have to stay here," I says. "You could spend the whole day visiting like other women, if you wanted to." She came to the door.

"I thought maybe you were sick," she says. "Having to hurry through your dinner like you did."

"Better luck next time," I says. "What do you want?"

"Is anything wrong?" she says.

"What could be?" I says. "Cant I come home in the middle of the afternoon without upsetting the whole house?"

"Have you seen Quentin?" she says.

"She's in school," I says.

"It's after three," she says. "I heard the clock strike at least a half an hour ago. She ought to be home by now."

"Ought she?" I says. "When have you ever seen her before dark?"

"She ought to be home," she says. "When I was a girl . . ."

"You had somebody to make you behave yourself," I says. "She hasn't."

"I can't do anything with her," she says. "I've tried and I've tried."

"And you wont let me, for some reason," I says, "So you ought to be satisfied." I went on to my room. I turned the key easy and stood there until the knob turned. Then she says,

"Jason."

"What," I says.

"I just thought something was wrong."

"Not in here," I says. "You've come to the wrong place."

"I dont mean to worry you," she says.

"I'm glad to hear that," I says. "I wasn't sure. I thought I might have been mistaken. Do you want anything?"

After awhile she says, "No. Not any thing." Then she went away. I took the box down and counted out the money and hid the box again and unlocked the door and went out. I thought about the camphor, but it would be too late now, anyway. And I'd just have one more round trip. She was at her door, waiting.

"You want anything from town?" I says.

"No," she says. "I dont mean to meddle in your affairs. But I dont know what I'd do if anything happened to you, Jason."

"I'm all right," I says. "Just a headache."

"I wish you'd take some aspirin," she says. "I know you're not going to stop using the car."

"What's the car got to do with it?" I says. "How can a car give a man a headache?"

"You know gasoline always made you sick," she says. "Ever since you were a child. I wish you'd take some aspirin."

"Keep on wishing it," I says. "It wont hurt you."

I got in the car and started back to town. I had just turned onto the street when I saw a ford coming helling toward me. All of a sudden it stopped. I could hear the wheels sliding and it slewed around and backed and whirled and just as I was thinking what the hell they were up to, I saw that red tie.

Then I recognised her face looking back through the window. It whirled into the alley. I saw it turn again, but when I got to the back street it was just disappearing, running like hell.

I saw red. When I recognised that red tie, after all I had told her, I forgot about everything. I never thought about my head even until I came to the first forks and had to stop. Yet we spend money and spend money on roads and damn if it isn't like trying to drive over a sheet of corrugated iron roofing. I'd like to know how a man could be expected to keep up with even a wheelbarrow. I think too much of my car; I'm not going to hammer it to pieces like it was a ford. Chances were they had stolen it, anyway, so why should they give a damn. Like I say blood always tells. If you've got blood like that in you, you'll do anything. I says whatever claim you believe she has on you has already been discharged; I says from now on you have only yourself to blame because you know what any sensible person would do. I says if I've got to spend half my time being a damn detective, at least I'll go where I can get paid for it.

So I had to stop there at the forks. Then I remembered it. It felt like somebody was inside with a hammer, beating on it. I says I've tried to keep you from being worried by her; I says far as I'm concerned, let her go to hell as fast as she pleases and the sooner the better. I says what else do you expect except every drummer and cheap show that comes to

297

town because even these town jellybeans give her the go-by now. You dont know what goes on I says, you dont hear the talk that I hear and you can just bet I shut them up too. I says my people owned slaves here when you all were running little shirt tail country stores and farming land no nigger would look at on shares.

If they ever farmed it. It's a good thing the Lord did something for this country; the folks that live on it never have. Friday afternoon, and from right here I could see three miles of land that hadn't even been broken, and every able bodied man in the county in town at that show. I might have been a stranger starving to death, and there wasn't a soul in sight to ask which way to town even. And she trying to get me to take aspirin. I says when I eat bread I'll do it at the table. I says you always talking about how much you give up for us when you could buy ten new dresses a year on the money you spend for those damn patent medicines. It's not something to cure it I need it's just an even break not to have to have them but as long as I have to work ten hours a day to support a kitchen full of niggers in the style they're accustomed to and send them to the show with every other nigger in the county, only he was late already. By the time he got there it would be over.

After awhile he got up to the car and when I finally got it through his head if two people in a ford had passed him, he said yes. So I went on, and when I came to where the wagon road turned off I could see the tire tracks. Ab Russell was in his lot, but I didn't bother to ask him and I hadn't got out of sight of his barn hardly when I saw the ford. They had tried to hide it. Done about as well at it as she did at everything else she did. Like I say it's not that I object to so much; maybe she cant help that, it's because she hasn't even got enough consideration for her own family to have any discretion. I'm afraid all the time I'll run into them right in the middle of the street or under a wagon on the square, like a couple of dogs.

I parked and got out. And now I'd have to go way around and cross a plowed field, the only one I had seen since I left town, with every step like somebody was walking along behind me, hitting me on the head with a club. I kept thinking that when I got across the field at least I'd have something level to walk on, that wouldn't jolt me every step, but when I got into the woods it was full of underbrush and I had to twist around through it, and then I came to a ditch full of briers. I went along it for awhile, but it got thicker and thicker, and all the time Earl probably telephoning home about where I was and getting Mother all upset again.

When I finally got through I had had to wind around so much that I had to stop and figure out just where the car would be. I knew they wouldn't be far from it, just under the closest bush, so I turned and worked back toward the road. Then I couldn't tell just how far I was, so I'd have to stop and listen, and then with my legs not using so much blood, it all would go into my head like it would explode any minute, and the sun getting down just to where it could shine straight into my eyes and my ears ringing so I couldn't hear anything. I went on, trying to move quiet, then I heard a dog or something and I knew that when he scented me he'd have to come helling up, then it would be all off.

I had gotten beggar lice and twigs and stuff all over me, inside my clothes and shoes and all, and then I happened to look around and I had my hand right on a bunch of poison oak. The only thing I couldn't understand was why it was just poison oak and not a snake or something. So I didn't even bother to move it. I just stood there until the dog went away. Then I went on.

I didn't have any idea where the car was now. I couldn't think about anything except my head, and I'd just stand in one place and sort of wonder if I had really seen a ford even, and I didn't even care much whether I had or not. Like I say, let her lay out all day and all night with everything in town that wears pants, what do I care. I dont owe anything to anybody that has no more consideration for me, that wouldn't be a damn bit above planting that ford there and making me spend a whole afternoon and

Earl taking her back there and showing her the books just because he's too damn virtuous for this world. I says you'll have one hell of a time in heaven, without anybody's business to meddle in only dont you ever let me catch you at it I says, I close my eyes to it because of your grandmother, but just you let me catch you doing it one time on this place, where my mother lives. These damn little slick haired squirts, thinking they are raising so much hell, I'll show them something about hell I says, and you too. I'll make him think that damn red tie is the latch string to hell, if he thinks he can run the woods with my niece.

With the sun and all in my eyes and my blood going so I kept thinking every time my head would go on and burst and get it over with, with briers and things grabbing at me, then I came onto the sand ditch where they had been and I recognised the tree where the car was, and just as I got out of the ditch and started running I heard the car start. It went off fast, blowing the horn. They kept on blowing it, like it was saying Yah. Yah. Yaaahhhhhhhh, going out of sight. I got to the road just in time to see it go out of sight.

By the time I got up to where my car was, they were clean out of sight, the horn still blowing. Well, I never thought anything about it except I was saying Run. Run back to town. Run home and try to convince Mother that I never saw you in that car.

Try to make her believe that I dont know who he was. Try to make her believe that I didn't miss ten feet of catching you in that ditch. Try to make her believe you were standing up, too.

It kept on saying Yahhhhh, Yahhhhh, Yaaahhhhh-hhhh, getting fainter and fainter. Then it quit, and I could hear a cow lowing up at Russell's barn. And still I never thought. I went up to the door and opened it and raised my foot. I kind of thought then that the car was leaning a little more than the slant of the road would be, but I never found it out until I got in and started off.

Well, I just sat there. It was getting on toward sundown, and town was about five miles. They never even had guts enough to puncture it, to jab a hole in it. They just let the air out. I just stood there for awhile, thinking about that kitchen full of niggers and not one of them had time to lift a tire onto the rack and screw up a couple of bolts. It was kind of funny because even she couldn't have seen far enough ahead to take the pump out on purpose, unless she thought about it while he was letting out the air maybe. But what it probably was, was somebody took it out and gave it to Ben to play with for a squirt gun because they'd take the whole car to pieces if he wanted it and Dilsey says, Aint nobody teched yo car. What we want to fool with hit fer? and I says You're a nigger. You're lucky, do you know it? I says I'll swap with you any day because it takes a white man not to have anymore sense than to worry about what a little slut of a girl does.

I walked up to Russell's. He had a pump. That was just an oversight on their part, I reckon. Only I still couldn't believe she'd have had the nerve to. I kept thinking that. I dont know why it is I cant seem to learn that a woman'll do anything. I kept thinking, Let's forget for awhile how I feel toward you and how you feel toward me: I just wouldn't do you this way. I wouldn't do you this way no matter what you had done to me. Because like I say blood is blood and you cant get around it. It's not playing a joke that any eight year old boy could have thought of, it's letting your own uncle be laughed at by a man that would wear a red tie. They come into town and call us all a bunch of hicks and think it's too small to hold them. Well he doesn't know just how right he is. And her too. If that's the way she feels about it, she'd better keep right on going and a damn good riddance.

I stopped and returned Russell's pump and drove on to town. I went to the drugstore and got a coca-cola and then I went to the telegraph office. It had closed at 12.21, forty points down. Forty times five dollars; buy something with that if you can, and she'll say, I've got to have it I've just got to and I'll say that's too bad you'll have to try somebody else, I haven't got any money; I've been too busy to make any.

I just looked at him.

"I'll tell you some news," I says, "You'll be astonished to learn that I am interested in the cotton market," I says. "That never occurred to you, did it?"

"I did my best to deliver it," he says. "I tried the store twice and called up your house, but they didn't know where you were," he says, digging in the drawer.

"Deliver what?" I says. He handed me a telegram. "What time did this come?" I says.

"About half past three," he says.

"And now it's ten minutes past five," I says.

"I tried to deliver it," he says. "I couldn't find you."

"That's not my fault, is it?" I says. I opened it, just to see what kind of a lie they'd tell me this time. They must be in one hell of a shape if they've got to come all the way to Mississippi to steal ten dollars a month. Sell, it says. The market will be unstable, with a general downward tendency. Do not be alarmed following government report.

"How much would a message like this cost?" I says. He told me.

"They paid it," he says.

"Then I owe them that much," I says. "I already knew this. Send this collect," I says, taking a blank. Buy, I wrote, Market just on point of blowing its head off. Occasional flurries for purpose of hooking a few more country suckers who haven't got in to the telegraph office yet. Do not be alarmed. "Send that collect," I says.

He looked at the message, then he looked at the clock. "Market closed an hour ago," he says.

"Well," I says, "That's not my fault either. I didn't invent it; I just bought a little of it while under the impression that the telegraph company would keep me informed as to what it was doing."

"A report is posted whenever it comes in," he says.

"Yes," I says, "And in Memphis they have it on a blackboard every ten seconds," I says. "I was within sixty-seven miles of there once this after-noon."

He looked at the message. "You want to send this?" he says.

"I still haven't changed my mind," I says. I wrote the other one out and counted the money. "And this one too, if you're sure you can spell b-u-y."

I went back to the store. I could hear the band from down the street. Prohibition's a fine thing. Used to be they'd come in Saturday with just one pair of shoes in the family and him wearing them, and they'd go down to the express office and get his package; now they all go to the show barefooted, with the merchants in the door like a row of tigers or something in a cage, watching them pass. Earl says,

"I hope it wasn't anything serious."

"What?" I says. He looked at his watch. Then he went to the door and looked at the courthouse clock. "You ought to have a dollar watch," I says. "It wont cost you so much to believe it's lying each time."

"What?" he says.

"Nothing," I says. "Hope I haven't inconvenienced you."

"We were not busy much," he says. "They all went to the show. It's all right."

"If it's not all right," I says, "You know what you can do about it."

"I said it was all right," he says.

"I heard you," I says. "And if it's not all right, you know what you can do about it."

"Do you want to quit?" he says.

"It's not my business," I says. "My wishes dont matter. But dont get the idea that you are protecting me by keeping me."

"You'd be a good business man if you'd let yourself, Jason," he says.

"At least I can tend to my own business and let other peoples' alone," I says.

"I dont know why you are trying to make me fire you," he says. "You know you could quit anytime and there wouldn't be any hard feelings between us."

"Maybe that's why I dont quit," I says. "As long as I tend to my job, that's what you are paying me

306

for." I went on to the back and got a drink of water and went on out to the back door. Job had the cultivators all set up at last. It was quiet there, and pretty soon my head got a little easier. I could hear them singing now, and then the band played again. Well, let them get every quarter and dime in the county; it was no skin off my back. I've done what I could; a man that can live as long as I have and not know when to quit is a fool. Especially as it's no business of mine. If it was my own daughter now it would be different, because she wouldn't have time to; she'd have to work some to feed a few invalids and idiots and niggers, because how could I have the face to bring anybody there. I've too much respect for anybody to do that. I'm a man, I can stand it, it's my own flesh and blood and I'd like to see the colour of the man's eyes that would speak disrespectful of any woman that was my friend it's these damn good women that do it I'd like to see the good, church-going woman that's half as square as Lorraine, whore or no whore. Like I say if I was to get married you'd go up like a balloon and you know it and she says I want you to be happy to have a family of your own not to slave your life away for us. But I'll be gone soon and then you can take a wife but you'll never find a woman who is worthy of you and I says yes I could. You'd get right up out of your grave you know you would. I says no thank you I have all the women I can take care of now if I married a wife she'd prob-

307

ably turn out to be a hophead or something. That's all we lack in this family, I says.

The sun was down beyond the Methodist church now, and the pigeons were flying back and forth around the steeple, and when the band stopped I could hear them cooing. It hadn't been four months since Christmas, and yet they were almost as thick as ever. I reckon Parson Walthall was getting a belly full of them now. You'd have thought we were shooting people, with him making speeches and even holding onto a man's gun when they came over. Talking about peace on earth good will toward all and not a sparrow can fall to earth. But what does he care how thick they get, he hasn't got anything to do; what does he care what time it is. He pays no taxes, he doesn't have to see his money going every year to have the courthouse clock cleaned to where it'll run. They had to pay a man forty-five dollars to clean it. I counted over a hundred half-hatched pigeons on the ground. You'd think they'd have sense enough to leave town. It's a good thing I dont have any more ties than a pigeon, I'll say that.

The band was playing again, a loud fast tune, like they were breaking up. I reckon they'd be satisfied now. Maybe they'd have enough music to entertain them while they drove fourteen or fifteen miles home and unharnessed in the dark and fed the stock and milked. All they'd have to do would be to whistle the music and tell the jokes to the live stock in the barn, and then they could count up how much they'd made by not taking the stock to the show too. They could figure that if a man had five children and seven mules, he cleared a quarter by taking his family to the show. Just like that. Earl came back with a couple of packages.

"Here's some more stuff going out," he says. "Where's Uncle Job?"

"Gone to the show, I imagine," I says. "Unless you watched him."

"He doesn't slip off," he says. "I can depend on him."

"Meaning me by that," I says.

He went to the door and looked out, listening.

"That's a good band," he says. "It's about time they were breaking up, I'd say."

"Unless they're going to spend the night there," I says. The swallows had begun, and I could hear the sparrows beginning to swarm in the trees in the courthouse yard. Every once in a while a bunch of them would come swirling around in sight above the roof, then go away. They are as big a nuisance as the pigeons, to my notion. You cant even sit in the courthouse yard for them. First thing you know, bing. Right on your hat. But it would take a millionaire to afford to shoot them at five cents a shot. If they'd just put a little poison out there in the square, they'd get rid of them in a day, because if a merchant cant keep his stock from running around the square, he'd better try to deal in something besides chickens, something that dont eat, like plows or onions. And if a man dont keep his dogs up, he either dont want it or he hasn't any business with one. Like I say if all the businesses in a town are run like country businesses, you're going to have a country town.

"It wont do you any good if they have broke up," I says. "They'll have to hitch up and take out to get home by midnight as it is."

"Well," he says, "They enjoy it. Let them spend a little money on a show now and then. A hill farmer works pretty hard and gets mighty little for it."

"There's no law making them farm in the hills," I says, "Or anywhere else."

"Where would you and me be, if it wasn't for the farmers?" he says.

"I'd be home right now," I says, "Lying down, with an ice pack on my head."

"You have these headaches too often," he says. "Why dont you have your teeth examined good? Did he go over them all this morning?"

"Did who?" I says.

"You said you went to the dentist this morning."

"Do you object to my having the headache on your time?" I says. "Is that it?" They were crossing the alley now, coming up from the show.

"There they come," he says. "I reckon I better get up front." He went on. It's a curious thing how no matter what's wrong with you, a man'll tell you to have your teeth examined and a woman'll tell you to get married. It always takes a man that never made much at any thing to tell you how to run your business, though. Like these college professors without a whole pair of socks to their name, telling you how to make a million in ten years, and a woman that couldn't even get a husband can always tell you how to raise a family.

Old man Job came up with the wagon. After a while he got through wrapping the lines around the whip socket.

"Well," I says, "Was it a good show?"

"I aint been yit," he says. "But I kin be arrested in dat tent tonight, dough."

"Like hell you haven't," I says. "You've been away from here since three oclock. Mr Earl was just back here looking for you."

"I been tendin to my business," he says. "Mr Earl knows whar I been."

"You may can fool him," I says. "I wont tell on you."

"Den he's de onliest man here I'd try to fool," he says. "Whut I want to waste my time foolin a man whut I dont keer whether I sees him Sat'dy night er not? I wont try to fool you," he says. "You too smart fer me. Yes, suh," he says, looking busy as hell, putting five or six little packages into the wagon, "You's too smart fer me. Aint a man in dis town kin keep up wid you fer smartness. You fools a man whut so smart he cant even keep up wid hisself," he says, getting in the wagon and unwrapping the reins.

"Who's that?" I says.

"Dat's Mr Jason Compson," he says. "Git up dar, Dan!"

One of the wheels was just about to come off. I watched to see if he'd get out of the alley before it did. Just turn any vehicle over to a nigger, though. I says that old rattletrap's just an eyesore, yet you'll keep it standing there in the carriage house a hundred years just so that boy can ride to the cemetery once a week. I says he's not the first fellow that'll have to do things he doesn't want to. I'd make him ride in that car like a civilised man or stay at home. What does he know about where he goes or what he goes in, and us keeping a carriage and a horse so he can take a ride on Sunday afternoon.

A lot Job cared whether the wheel came off or not, long as he wouldn't have too far to walk back. Like I say the only place for them is in the field, where they'd have to work from sunup to sundown. They cant stand prosperity or an easy job. Let one stay around white people for a while and he's not worth killing. They get so they can outguess you about work before your very eyes, like Roskus the only mistake he ever made was he got careless one day and died. Shirking and stealing and giving you a little more lip and a little more lip until some day you have to lay them out with a scantling or something. Well, it's Earl's business. But I'd hate to have my business advertised over this town by an old doddering nigger and a wagon that you thought every time it turned a corner it would come all to pieces.

The sun was all high up in the air now, and inside it was beginning to get dark. I went up front. The square was empty. Earl was back closing the safe, and then the clock begun to strike.

"You lock the back door," he says. I went back and locked it and came back. "I suppose you're going to the show tonight," he says. "I gave you those passes yesterday, didn't I?"

"Yes," I said. "You want them back?"

"No, no," he says, "I just forgot whether I gave them to you or not. No sense in wasting them."

He locked the door and said Goodnight and went on. The sparrows were still rattling away in the trees, but the square was empty except for a few cars. There was a ford in front of the drugstore, but I didn't even look at it. I know when I've had enough of anything. I dont mind trying to help her, but I know when I've had enough. I guess I could teach Luster to drive it, then they could chase her all day long if they wanted to, and I could stay home and play with Ben.

I went in and got a couple of cigars. Then I thought I'd have another headache shot for luck, and I stood and talked with them awhile.

"Well," Mac says, "I reckon you've got your money on the Yankees this year."

"What for?" I says.

"The Pennant," he says. "Not anything in the League can beat them."

"Like hell there's not," I says. "They're shot," I says. "You think a team can be that lucky forever?"

"I dont call it luck," Mac says.

"I wouldn't bet on any team that fellow Ruth played on," I says. "Even if I knew it was going to win."

"Yes?" Mac says.

"I can name you a dozen men in either League who're more valuable than he is," I says.

"What have you got against Ruth?" Mac says.

"Nothing," I says. "I haven't got any thing against him. I dont even like to look at his picture." I went on out. The lights were coming on, and people going along the streets toward home. Sometimes the sparrows never got still until full dark. The night they turned on the new lights around the courthouse it waked them up and they were flying around and blundering into the lights all night long. They kept it up two or three nights, then one morning they were all gone. Then after about two months they all came back again.

I drove on home. There were no lights in the house yet, but they'd all be looking out the windows, and Dilsey jawing away in the kitchen like it was her own food she was having to keep hot until I got there. You'd think to hear her that there wasn't but one supper in the world, and that was the one she had to keep back a few minutes on my account. Well at least I could come home one time without finding Ben and that nigger hanging on the gate like a bear and a monkey in the same cage. Just let it come toward sundown and he'd head for the gate like a cow for the barn, hanging onto it and bobbing his head and sort of moaning to himself. That's a hog for punishment for you. If what had happened to him for fooling with open gates had happened to me, I never would want to see another one. I often wondered what he'd be thinking about, down there at the gate, watching the girls going home from school, trying to want something he couldn't even remember he didn't and couldn't want any longer. And what he'd think when they'd be undressing him and he'd happen to take a look at himself and begin to cry like he'd do. But like I say they never did enough of that. I says I know what you need, you need what they did to Ben then you'd behave. And if you dont know what that was I says, ask Dilsey to tell you.

There was a light in Mother's room. I put the car up and went on into the kitchen. Luster and Ben were there.

"Where's Dilsey?" I says. "Putting supper on?"

"She upstairs wid Miss Cahline," Luster says. "Dey been goin hit. Ever since Miss Quentin come home. Mammy up there keepin um fum fightin. Is dat show come, Mr Jason?"

"Yes," I says.

"I thought I heard de band," he says. "Wish I could go," he says. "I could ef I jes had a quarter."

Dilsey came in. "You come, is you?" she says. "Whut you been up to dis evenin? You knows how much work I got to do; whyn't you git here on time?"

"Maybe I went to the show," I says. "Is supper ready?"

"Wish I could go," Luster said. "I could ef I jes had a quarter."

"You aint got no business at no show," Dilsey says. "You go on in de house and set down," she says. "Dont you go up stairs and git um started again, now."

"What's the matter?" I says.

"Quentin come in a while ago and says you been follerin her around all evenin and den Miss Cahline jumped on her. Whyn't you let her alone? Cant you live in de same house wid you own blood niece widout quoilin?"

"I cant quarrel with her," I says, "because I haven't seen her since this morning. What does she say I've done now? made her go to school? That's pretty bad," I says.

"Well, you tend to yo business and let her alone," Dilsey says, "I'll take keer of her ef you'n Miss Cahline'll let me. Go on in dar now and behave yoself twell I git supper on."

"Ef I jes had a quarter," Luster says, "I could go to dat show."

"En ef you had wings you could fly to heaven," Dilsey says. "I dont want to hear another word about dat show."

"That reminds me," I says, "I've got a couple of tickets they gave me." I took them out of my coat.

"You fixin to use um?" Luster says.

"Not me," I says. "I wouldn't go to it for ten dollars."

"Gimme one of um, Mr Jason," he says.

"I'll sell you one," I says. "How about it?"

"I aint got no money," he says.

"That's too bad," I says. I made to go out.

"Gimme one of um, Mr Jason," he says. "You aint gwine need um bofe."

"Hush yo mouf," Dilsey says, "Dont you know he aint gwine give nothing away?"

"How much you want fer hit?" he says.

"Five cents," I says.

"I aint got dat much," he says.

"How much you got?" I says.

"I aint got nothing," he says.

"All right," I says. I went on.

"Mr Jason," he says.

"Whyn't you hush up?" Dilsey says. "He jes teasin you. He fixin to use dem tickets hisself. Go on, Jason, and let him lone."

"I dont want them," I says. I came back to the stove. "I came in here to burn them up. But if you want to buy one for a nickel?" I says, looking at him and opening the stove lid.

"I aint got dat much," he says.

"All right," I says. I dropped one of them in the stove.

"You, Jason," Dilsey says, "Aint you shamed?"

"Mr Jason," he says, "Please, suh. I'll fix dem tires ev'ry day fer a mont'."

"I need the cash," I says. "You can have it for a nickel."

"Hush, Luster," Dilsey says. She jerked him back. "Go on," she says, "Drop hit in. Go on. Git hit over with."

"You can have it for a nickel," I says.

"Go on," Dilsey says. "He aint got no nickel. Go on. Drop hit in."

"All right," I says. I dropped it in and Dilsey shut the stove.

"A big growed man like you," she says. "Git on outen my kitchen. Hush," she says to Luster. "Dont you git Benjy started. I'll git you a quarter fum Frony tonight and you kin go tomorrow night. Hush up, now."

I went on into the living room. I couldn't hear

318

anything from upstairs. I opened the paper. After awhile Ben and Luster came in. Ben went to the dark place on the wall where the mirror used to be, rubbing his hands on it and slobbering and moaning. Luster begun punching at the fire.

"What're you doing?" I says. "We dont need any fire tonight."

"I trying to keep him quiet," he says. "Hit always cold Easter," he says.

"Only this is not Easter," I says. "Let it alone."

He put the poker back and got the cushion out of Mother's chair and gave it to Ben, and he hunkered down in front of the fireplace and got quiet.

I read the paper. There hadn't been a sound from upstairs when Dilsey came in and sent Ben and Luster on to the kitchen and said supper was ready.

"All right," I says. She went out. I sat there, reading the paper. After a while I heard Dilsey looking in at the door.

"Whyn't you come on and eat?" she says.

"I'm waiting for supper," I says.

"Hit's on the table," she says. "I done told you."

"Is it?" I says. "Excuse me. I didn't hear anybody come down."

"They aint comin," she says. "You come on and eat, so I can take something up to them."

"Are they sick?" I says. "What did the doctor say it was? Not Smallpox, I hope."

"Come on here, Jason," she says, "So I kin git done."

"All right," I says, raising the paper again. "I'm waiting for supper now."

I could feel her watching me at the door. I read the paper.

"Whut you want to act like this fer?" she says. "When you knows how much bother I has anyway."

"If Mother is any sicker than she was when she came down to dinner, all right," I says. "But as long as I am buying food for people younger than I am, they'll have to come down to the table to eat it. Let me know when supper's ready," I says, reading the paper again. I heard her climbing the stairs, dragging her feet and grunting and groaning like they were straight up and three feet apart. I heard her at Mother's door, then I heard her calling Quentin, like the door was locked, then she went back to Mother's room and then Mother went and talked to Quentin. Then they came down stairs. I read the paper.

Dilsey came back to the door. "Come on," she says, "fo you kin think up some mo devilment. You just tryin yoself tonight."

I went to the diningroom. Quentin was sitting with her head bent. She had painted her face again. Her nose looked like a porcelain insulator.

"I'm glad you feel well enough to come down," I says to Mother.

"It's little enough I can do for you, to come to the table," she says. "No matter how I feel, I realise that when a man works all day he likes to be surrounded by his family at the supper table. I want to please you. I only wish you and Quentin got along better. It would be easier for me."

"We get along all right," I says. "I dont mind her staying locked up in her room all day if she wants to. But I cant have all this whoop-de-do and sulking at mealtimes. I know that's a lot to ask her, but I'm that way in my own house. Your house, I meant to say."

"It's yours," Mother says, "You are the head of it now."

Quentin hadn't looked up. I helped the plates and she begun to eat.

"Did you get a good piece of meat?" I says. "If you didn't, I'll try to find you a better one."

She didn't say anything.

"I say, did you get a good piece of meat?" I says.

"What?" she says. "Yes. It's all right."

"Will you have some more rice?" I says.

"No," she says.

"Better let me give you some more," I says.

"I dont want any more," she says.

"Not at all," I says, "You're welcome."

"Is your headache gone?" Mother says.

"Headache?" I says.

"I was afraid you were developing one," she says. "When you came in this afternoon."

"Oh," I says. "No, it didn't show up. We stayed so busy this afternoon I forgot about it."

"Was that why you were late?" Mother says. I could see Quentin listening. I looked at her. Her knife and fork were still going, but I caught her looking at me, then she looked at her plate again. I says,

"No. I loaned my car to a fellow about three o'clock and I had to wait until he got back with it." I ate for a while.

"Who was it?" Mother says.

"It was one of those show men," I says. "It seems his sister's husband was out riding with some town woman, and he was chasing them."

Quentin sat perfectly still, chewing.

"You ought not to lend your car to people like that," Mother says. "You are too generous with it. That's why I never call on you for it if I can help it."

"I was beginning to think that myself, for awhile," I says. "But he got back, all right. He says he found what he was looking for."

"Who was the woman?" Mother says.

"I'll tell you later," I says. "I dont like to talk about such things before Quentin."

Quentin had quit eating. Every once in a while she'd take a drink of water, then she'd sit there crumbling a biscuit up, her face bent over her plate.

"Yes," Mother says, "I suppose women who stay shut up like I do have no idea what goes on in this town."

"Yes," I says, "They dont."

"My life has been so different from that," Mother says. "Thank God I dont know about such wickedness. I dont even want to know about it. I'm not like most people."

I didn't say any more. Quentin sat there, crumbling the biscuit until I quit eating, then she says,

"Can I go now?" without looking at anybody.

"What?" I says. "Sure, you can go. Were you waiting on us?"

She looked at me. She had crumbled all the biscuit, but her hands still went on like they were crumbling it yet and her eyes looked like they were cornered or something and then she started biting her mouth like it ought to have poisoned her, with all that red lead.

"Grandmother," she says, "Grandmother —"

"Did you want something else to eat?" I says.

"Why does he treat me like this, Grandmother?" she says. "I never hurt him."

"I want you all to get along with one another," Mother says, "You are all that's left now, and I do want you all to get along better."

"It's his fault," she says, "He wont let me alone, and I have to. If he doesn't want me here, why wont he let me go back to —"

"That's enough," I says, "Not another word."

"Then why wont he let me alone?" she says. He — he just — "

"He is the nearest thing to a father you've ever had," Mother says. "It's his bread you and I eat. It's only right that he should expect obedience from you."

"It's his fault," she says. She jumped up. "He makes me do it. If he would just — " she looked at us, her eyes cornered, kind of jerking her arms against her sides.

"If I would just what?" I says.

"Whatever I do, it's your fault," she says. "If I'm bad, it's because I had to be. You made me. I wish I was dead. I wish we were all dead." Then she ran. We heard her run up the stairs. Then a door slammed.

"That's the first sensible thing she ever said," I says.

"She didn't go to school today," Mother says.

"How do you know?" I says. "Were you down town?"

"I just know," she says. "I wish you could be kinder to her."

"If I did that I'd have to arrange to see her more than once a day," I says. "You'll have to make her come to the table every meal. Then I could give her an extra piece of meat every time."

"There are little things you could do," she says.

324

"Like not paying any attention when you ask me to see that she goes to school?" I says.

"She didn't go to school today," she says. "I just know she didn't. She says she went for a car ride with one of the boys this afternoon and you followed her."

"How could I," I says, "When somebody had my car all afternoon? Whether or not she was in school today is already past," I says, "If you've got to worry about it, worry about next Monday."

"I wanted you and she to get along with one another," she says. "But she has inherited all of the headstrong traits. Quentin's too. I thought at the time, with the heritage she would already have, to give her that name, too. Sometimes I think she is the judgment of Caddy and Quentin upon me."

"Good Lord," I says, "You've got a fine mind. No wonder you kept yourself sick all the time."

"What?" she says. "I dont understand."

"I hope not," I says. "A good woman misses a lot she's better off without knowing."

"They were both that way," she says, "They would make interest with your father against me when I tried to correct them. He was always saying they didn't need controlling, that they already knew what cleanliness and honesty were, which was all that anyone could hope to be taught. And now I hope he's satisfied."

"You've got Ben to depend on," I says, "Cheer up."

"They deliberately shut me out of their lives," she says, "It was always her and Quentin. They were always conspiring against me. Against you too, though you were too young to realise it. They always looked on you and me as outsiders, like they did your Uncle Maury. I always told your father that they were allowed too much freedom, to be together too much. When Quentin started to school we had to let her go the next year, so she could be with him. She couldn't bear for any of you to do anything she couldn't. It was vanity in her, vanity and false pride. And then when her troubles began I knew that Quentin would feel that he had to do something just as bad. But I didn't believe that he would have been so selfish as to — I didn't dream that he — "

"Maybe he knew it was going to be a girl," I says, "And that one more of them would be more than he could stand."

"He could have controlled her," she says. "He seemed to be the only person she had any consideration for. But that is a part of the judgment too, I suppose."

"Yes," I says, "Too bad it wasn't me instead of him. You'd be a lot better off."

"You say things like that to hurt me," she says. "I deserve it though. When they began to sell the land to send Quentin to Harvard I told your father that he must make an equal provision for you. Then when Herbert offered to take you into the bank I said, Jason is provided for now, and when all the expense began to pile up and I was forced to sell our furniture and the rest of the pasture, I wrote her at once because I said she will realise that she and Quentin have had their share and part of Jason's too and that it depends on her now to compensate him. I said she will do that out of respect for her father. I believed that, then. But I'm just a poor old woman; I was raised to believe that people would deny themselves for their own flesh and blood. It's my fault. You were right to reproach me."

" Do you think I need any man's help to stand on my feet?" I says, "Let alone a woman that cant name the father of her own child."

" Jason," she says.

" All right," I says. " I didn't mean that. Of course not."

" If I believed that were possible, after all my suffering."

" Of course it's not," I says. " I didn't mean it."

" I hope that at least is spared me," she says.

" Sure it is," I says, " She's too much like both of them to doubt that."

" I couldn't bear that," she says.

" Then quit thinking about it," I says. " Has she been worrying you any more about getting out at night?"

"No. I made her realise that it was for her own good and that she'd thank me for it some day. She takes her books with her and studies after I lock the door. I see the light on as late as eleven oclock some nights."

"How do you know she's studying?" I says.

"I don't know what else she'd do in there alone," she says. "She never did read any."

"No," I says, "You wouldn't know. And you can thank your stars for that," I says. Only what would be the use in saying it aloud. It would just have her crying on me again.

I heard her go up stairs. Then she called Quentin and Quentin says What? through the door. "Goodnight," Mother says. Then I heard the key in the lock, and Mother went back to her room.

When I finished my cigar and went up, the light was still on. I could see the empty keyhole, but I couldn't hear a sound. She studied quiet. Maybe she learned that in school. I told Mother goodnight and went on to my room and got the box out and counted it again. I could hear the Great American Gelding snoring away like a planing mill. I read somewhere they'd fix men that way to give them women's voices. But maybe he didn't know what they'd done to him. I dont reckon he even knew what he had been trying to do, or why Mr Burgess knocked him out with the fence picket. And if they'd just sent him on to Jackson while he was under the ether, he'd never have

328

known the difference. But that would have been too simple for a Compson to think of. Not half complex enough. Having to wait to do it at all until he broke out and tried to run a little girl down on the street with her own father looking at him. Well, like I say they never started soon enough with their cutting, and they quit too quick. I know at least two more that needed something like that, and one of them not over a mile away, either. But then I dont reckon even that would do any good. Like I say once a bitch always a bitch. And just let me have twenty-four hours without any damn New York jew to advise me what it's going to do. I dont want to make a killing; save that to suck in the smart gamblers with. I just want an even chance to get my money back. And once I've done that they can bring all Beale Street and all bedlam in here and two of them can sleep in my bed and another one can have my place at the table too.

THE DAY DAWNED BLEAK AND CHILL,
a moving wall of grey light out of the northeast
which, instead of dissolving into moisture, seemed to
disintegrate into minute and venomous particles, like
dust that, when Dilsey opened the door of the cabin
and emerged, needled laterally into her flesh, pre-
cipitating not so much a moisture as a substance partaking of the quality of thin, not quite congealed oil.
She wore a stiff black straw hat perched upon her
turban, and a maroon velvet cape with a border of
mangy and anonymous fur above a dress of purple
silk, and she stood in the door for awhile with her
myriad and sunken face lifted to the weather, and
one gaunt hand flac-soled as the belly of a fish, then
she moved the cape aside and examined the bosom of
her gown.

The gown fell gauntly from her shoulders, across
her fallen breasts, then tightened upon her paunch

and fell again, ballooning a little above the nether garments which she would remove layer by layer as the spring accomplished and the warm days, in colour regal and moribund. She had been a big woman once but now her skeleton rose, draped loosely in unpadded skin that tightened again upon a paunch almost dropsical, as though muscle and tissue had been courage or fortitude which the days or the years had consumed until only the indomitable skeleton was left rising like a ruin or a landmark above the somnolent and impervious guts, and above that the collapsed face that gave the impression of the bones themselves being outside the flesh, lifted into the driving day with an expression at once fatalistic and of a child's astonished disappointment, until she turned and entered the house again and closed the door.

The earth immediately about the door was bare. It had a patina, as though from the soles of bare feet in generations, like old silver or the walls of Mexican houses which have been plastered by hand. Beside the house, shading it in summer, stood three mulberry trees, the fledged leaves that would later be broad and placid as the palms of hands streaming flatly undulant upon the driving air. A pair of jaybirds came up from nowhere, whirled up on the blast like gaudy scraps of cloth or paper and lodged in the mulberries, where they swung in raucous tilt and recover, screaming into the wind that ripped their harsh cries onward and away like scraps of paper or of cloth in turn. Then three more joined them and they swung and tilted in the wrung branches for a time, screaming. The door of the cabin opened and Dilsey emerged once more, this time in a man's felt hat and an army overcoat, beneath the frayed skirts of which her blue gingham dress fell in uneven balloonings, streaming too about her as she crossed the yard and mounted the steps to the kitchen door.

A moment later she emerged, carrying an open umbrella now, which she slanted ahead into the wind, and crossed to the woodpile and laid the umbrella down, still open. Immediately she caught at it and arrested it and held to it for a while, looking about her. Then she closed it and laid it down and stacked stovewood into her crooked arm, against her breast, and picked up the umbrella and got it open at last and returned to the steps and held the wood precariously balanced while she contrived to close the umbrella, which she propped in the corner just within the door. She dumped the wood into the box behind the stove. Then she removed the overcoat and hat and took a soiled apron down from the wall and put it on and built a fire in the stove. While she was doing so, rattling the grate bars and clattering the lids, Mrs Compson began to call her from the head of the stairs.

She wore a dressing gown of quilted black satin, holding it close under her chin. In the other hand she held a red rubber hot water bottle and she stood at the head of the back stairway, calling "Dilsey" at steady and inflectionless intervals into the quiet stairwell that descended into complete darkness, then opened again where a grey window fell across it. "Dilsey," she called, without inflection or emphasis or haste, as though she were not listening for a reply at all. "Dilsey."

Dilsey answered and ceased clattering the stove, but before she could cross the kitchen Mrs Compson called her again, and before she crossed the dining-room and brought her head into relief against the grey splash of the window, still again.

"All right," Dilsey said, "All right, here I is. I'll fill hit soon ez I git some hot water." She gathered up her skirts and mounted the stairs, wholly blotting the grey light. "Put hit down dar en g'awn back to bed."

"I couldn't understand what was the matter," Mrs Compson said. "I've been lying awake for an hour at least, without hearing a sound from the kitchen."

"You put hit down and g'awn back to bed," Dilsey said. She toiled painfully up the steps, shapeless, breathing heavily. "I'll have de fire gwine in a minute, en de water hot in two mo'."

"I've been lying there for an hour, at least," Mrs Compson said. "I thought maybe you were waiting for me to come down and start the fire."

Dilsey reached the top of the stairs and took the water bottle. "I'll fix hit in a minute," she said. "Luster overslep dis mawnin, up half de night at dat show. I gwine build de fire myself. Go on now, so you wont wake de others twell I ready."

"If you permit Luster to do things that interfere with his work, you'll have to suffer for it yourself," Mrs Compson said. "Jason wont like this if he hears about it. You know he wont."

"Twusn't none of Jason's money he went on," Dilsey said. "Dat's one thing sho." She went on down the stairs. Mrs Compson returned to her room. As she got into bed again she could hear Dilsey yet descending the stairs with a sort of painful and terrific slowness that would have become maddening had it not presently ceased beyond the flapping diminishment of the pantry door.

She entered the kitchen and built up the fire and began to prepare breakfast. In the midst of this she ceased and went to the window and looked out toward her cabin, then she went to the door and opened it and shouted into the driving weather.

"Luster!" she shouted, standing to listen, tilting her face from the wind, "You, Luster?" She listened, then as she prepared to shout again Luster appeared around the corner of the kitchen.

"Ma'am?" he said innocently, so innocently that

Dilsey looked down at him, for a moment motionless, with something more than mere surprise.

"Whar you at?" she said.

"Nowhere," he said. "Jes in de cellar."

"Whut you doin in de cellar?" she said. "Dont stand dar in de rain, fool," she said.

"Aint doin nothin," he said. He came up the steps.

"Dont you dare come in dis do widout a armful of wood," she said. "Here I done had to tote yo wood en build yo fire bofe. Didn't I tole you not to leave dis place last night befo dat woodbox wus full to de top?"

"I did," Luster said, "I filled hit."

"Whar hit gone to, den?"

"I dont know'm. I aint teched hit."

"Well, you git hit full up now," she said. "And git on up den en see bout Benjy."

She shut the door. Luster went to the woodpile. The five jaybirds whirled over the house, screaming, and into the mulberries again. He watched them. He picked up a rock and threw it. "Whoo," he said, "Git on back to hell, whar you belong at. 'Taint Monday yit."

He loaded himself mountainously with stove wood. He could not see over it, and he staggered to the steps and up them and blundered crashing against the door, shedding billets. Then Dilsey came and opened the door for him and he blundered across

335

the kitchen. " You, Luster! " she shouted, but he had already hurled the wood into the box with a thunderous crash. " Hah! " he said.

" Is you tryin to wake up de whole house? " Dilsey said. She hit him on the back of his head with the flat of her hand. " Go on up dar and git Benjy dressed, now."

" Yessum," he said. He went toward the outer door.

" Whar you gwine? " Dilsey said.

" I thought I better go round de house en in by de front, so I wont wake up Miss Cahline en dem."

" You go on up dem backstairs like I tole you en git Benjy's clothes on him," Dilsey said. " Go on, now."

" Yessum," Luster said. He returned and left by the diningroom door. After awhile it ceased to flap. Dilsey prepared to make biscuit. As she ground the sifter steadily above the bread board, she sang, to herself at first, something without particular tune or words, repetitive, mournful and plaintive, austere, as she ground a faint, steady snowing of flour onto the bread board. The stove had begun to heat the room and to fill it with murmurous minors of the fire, and presently she was singing louder, as if her voice too had been thawed out by the growing warmth, and then Mrs Compson called her name again from within the house. Dilsey raised her face as if her eyes could and did penetrate the walls and

336

ceiling and saw the old woman in her quilted dressing gown at the head of the stairs, calling her name with machinelike regularity.

"Oh, Lawd," Dilsey said. She set the sifter down and swept up the hem of her apron and wiped her hands and caught up the bottle from the chair on which she had laid it and gathered her apron about the handle of the kettle which was now jetting faintly. "Jes a minute," she called, "De water jes dis minute got hot."

It was not the bottle which Mrs Compson wanted, however, and clutching it by the neck like a dead hen Dilsey went to the foot of the stairs and looked upward.

"Aint Luster up dar wid him?" she said.

"Luster hasn't been in the house. I've been lying here listening for him. I knew he would be late, but I did hope he'd come in time to keep Benjamin from disturbing Jason on Jason's one day in the week to sleep in the morning."

"I dont see how you expect anybody to sleep, wid you standin in de hall, holl'in at folks fum de crack of dawn," Dilsey said. She began to mount the stairs, toiling heavily. "I sont dat boy up dar half hour ago."

Mrs Compson watched her, holding the dressing gown under her chin. "What are you going to do?" she said.

"Gwine git Benjy dressed en bring him down to

337

de kitchen, whar he wont wake Jason en Quentin,"
Dilsey said.

"Haven't you started breakfast yet?"

"I'll tend to dat too," Dilsey said. "You better
git back in bed twell Luster make yo fire. Hit cold
dis mawnin."

"I know it," Mrs Compson said. "My feet are
like ice. They were so cold they waked me up." She
watched Dilsey mount the stairs. It took her a long
while. "You know how it frets Jason when breakfast is late," Mrs Compson said.

"I cant do but one thing at a time," Dilsey said.
"You git on back to bed, fo I has you on my hands
dis mawnin too."

"If you're going to drop everything to dress Benjamin, I'd better come down and get breakfast. You
know as well as I do how Jason acts when it's late."

"En who gwine eat yo messin?" Dilsey said.
"Tell me dat. Go on now," she said, toiling upward.
Mrs Compson stood watching her as she mounted,
steadying herself against the wall with one hand,
holding her skirts up with the other.

"Are you going to wake him up just to dress
him?" she said.

Dilsey stopped. With her foot lifted to the next
step she stood there, her hand against the wall and
the grey splash of the window behind her, motionless
and shapeless she loomed.

"He aint awake den?" she said.

338

"He wasn't when I looked in," Mrs Compson said. "But it's past his time. He never does sleep after half past seven. You know he doesn't."

Dilsey said nothing. She made no further move, but though she could not see her save as a blobby shape without depth, Mrs Compson knew that she had lowered her face a little and that she stood now like a cow in the rain, as she held the empty water bottle by its neck.

"You're not the one who has to bear it," Mrs Compson said. "It's not your responsibility. You can go away. You dont have to bear the brunt of it day in and day out. You owe nothing to them, to Mr Compson's memory. I know you have never had any tenderness for Jason. You've never tried to conceal it."

Dilsey said nothing. She turned slowly and descended, lowering her body from step to step, as a small child does, her hand against the wall. "You go on and let him alone," she said. "Dont go in dar no mo, now. I'll send Luster up soon as I find him. Let him alone, now."

She returned to the kitchen. She looked into the stove, then she drew her apron over her head and donned the overcoat and opened the outer door and looked up and down the yard. The weather drove upon her flesh, harsh and minute, but the scene was empty of all else that moved. She descended the steps, gingerly, as if for silence, and went around the cor-

339

ner of the kitchen. As she did so Luster emerged quickly and innocently from the cellar door.

Dilsey stopped. " Whut you up to?" she said.

" Nothin," Luster said, " Mr Jason say fer me to find out whar dat water leak in de cellar fum."

" En when wus hit he say fer you to do dat?" Dilsey said. " Last New Year's day, wasn't hit?"

"I thought I jes be lookin whiles dey sleep," Luster said. Dilsey went to the cellar door. He stood aside and she peered down into the obscurity odorous of dank earth and mould and rubber.

" Huh," Dilsey said. She looked at Luster again. He met her gaze blandly, innocent and open. " I dont know whut you up to, but you aint got no business doin hit. You jes tryin me too dis mawnin cause de others is, aint you? You git on up dar en see to Benjy, you hear?"

" Yessum," Luster said. He went on toward the kitchen steps, swiftly.

" Here," Dilsey said, " You git me another armful of wood while I got you."

" Yessum," he said. He passed her on the steps and went to the woodpile. When he blundered again at the door a moment later, again invisible and blind within and beyond his wooden avatar, Dilsey opened the door and guided him across the kitchen with a firm hand.

" Jes thow hit at dat box again," she said, " Jes thow hit."

340

"I got to," Luster said, panting, "I cant put hit down no other way."

"Den you stand dar en hold hit a while," Dilsey said. She unloaded him a stick at a time. "Whut got into you dis mawnin? Here I sont you fer wood en you aint never brought mo'n six sticks at a time to save yo life twell today. Whut you fixin to ax me kin you do now? Aint dat show lef town yit?"

"Yessum. Hit done gone."

She put the last stick into the box. "Now you go on up dar wid Benjy, like I tole you befo," she said. "And I dont want nobody else yellin down dem stairs at me twell I rings de bell. You hear me."

"Yessum," Luster said. He vanished through the swing door. Dilsey put some more wood in the stove and returned to the bread board. Presently she began to sing again.

The room grew warmer. Soon Dilsey's skin had taken on a rich, lustrous quality as compared with that as of a faint dusting of wood ashes which both it and Luster's had worn, as she moved about the kitchen, gathering about her the raw materials of food, co-ordinating the meal. On the wall above a cupboard, invisible save at night, by lamp light and even then evincing an enigmatic profundity because it had but one hand, a cabinet clock ticked, then with a preliminary sound as if it had cleared its throat, struck five times.

Benjy

"Eight oclock," Dilsey said. She ceased and tilted her head upward, listening. But there was no sound save the clock and the fire. She opened the oven and looked at the pan of bread, then stooping she paused while someone descended the stairs. She heard the feet cross the diningroom, then the swing door opened and Luster entered, followed by a big man who appeared to have been shaped of some substance whose particles would not or did not cohere to one another or to the frame which supported it. His skin was dead looking and hairless; dropsical too, he moved with a shambling gait like a trained bear. His hair was pale and fine. It had been brushed smoothly down upon his brow like that of children in daguerrotypes. His eyes were clear, of the pale sweet blue of cornflowers, his thick mouth hung open, drooling a little.

"Is he cold?" Dilsey said. She wiped her hands on her apron and touched his hand.

"Ef he aint, I is," Luster said. "Always cold Easter. Aint never seen hit fail. Miss Cahline say ef you aint got time to fix her hot water bottle to never mind about hit."

"Oh, Lawd," Dilsey said. She drew a chair into the corner between the woodbox and the stove. The man went obediently and sat in it. "Look in de dinin room and see whar I laid dat bottle down," Dilsey said. Luster fetched the bottle from the diningroom and Dilsey filled it and gave it to him. "Hurry up,

342

now," she said. "See ef Jason wake now. Tell em hit's all ready."

Luster went out. Ben sat beside the stove. He sat loosely, utterly motionless save for his head, which made a continual bobbing sort of movement as he watched Dilsey with his sweet vague gaze as she moved about. Luster returned.

"He up," he said, " Miss Cahline say put hit on de table." He came to the stove and spread his hands palm down above the firebox. " He up, too," He said, " Gwine hit wid bofe feet dis mawnin."

"Whut's de matter now?" Dilsey said. "Git away fum dar. How kin I do anything wid you standin over de stove?"

"I cold," Luster said.

"You ought to thought about dat whiles you wus down dar in dat cellar," Dilsey said. "Whut de matter wid Jason?"

"Sayin me en Benjy broke dat winder in his room."

"Is dey one broke?" Dilsey said.

"Dat's whut he sayin," Luster said. "Say I broke hit."

"How could you, when he keep hit locked all day en night?"

"Say I broke hit chunkin rocks at hit," Luster said.

"En did you?"

"Nome," Luster said.

"Dont lie to me, boy," Dilsey said.

"I never done hit," Luster said. "Ask Benjy ef I did. I aint stud'in dat winder."

"Who could a broke hit, den?" Dilsey said. "He jes tryin hisself, to wake Quentin up," she said, taking the pan of biscuits out of the stove.

"Reckin so," Luster said. "Dese is funny folks. Glad I aint none of em."

"Aint none of who?" Dilsey said. "Lemme tell you somethin, nigger boy, you got jes es much Compson devilment in you es any of em. Is you right sho you never broke dat window?"

"Whut I want to break hit fur?"

"Whut you do any of yo devilment fur?" Dilsey said. "Watch him now, so he cant burn his hand again twell I git de table set."

She went to the diningroom, where they heard her moving about, then she returned and set a plate at the kitchen table and set food there. Ben watched her, slobbering, making a faint, eager sound.

"All right, honey," she said, "Here yo breakfast. Bring his chair, Luster." Luster moved the chair up and Ben sat down, whimpering and slobbering. Dilsey tied a cloth about his neck and wiped his mouth with the end of it. "And see kin you kep fum messin up his clothes one time," she said, handing Luster a spoon.

Ben ceased whimpering. He watched the spoon as it rose to his mouth. It was as if even eagerness

344

were muscle-bound in him too, and hunger itself inarticulate, not knowing it is hunger. Luster fed him with skill and detachment. Now and then his attention would return long enough to enable him to feint the spoon and cause Ben to close his mouth upon the empty air, but it was apparent that Luster's mind was elsewhere. His other hand lay on the back of the chair and upon that dead surface it moved tentatively, delicately, as if he were picking an inaudible tune out of the dead void, and once he even forgot to tease Ben with the spoon while his fingers teased out of the slain wood a soundless and involved arpeggio until Ben recalled him by whimpering again.

In the diningroom Dilsey moved back and forth. Presently she rang a small clear bell, then in the kitchen Luster heard Mrs Compson and Jason descending, and Jason's voice, and he rolled his eyes whitely with listening.

"Sure, I know they didn't break it," Jason said. "Sure, I know that. Maybe the change of weather broke it."

"I dont see how it could have," Mrs Compson said. "Your room stays locked all day long, just as you leave it when you go to town. None of us ever go in there except Sunday, to clean it. I dont want you to think that I would go where I'm not wanted, or that I would permit anyone else to."

"I never said you broke it, did I?" Jason said.

"I dont want to go in your room," Mrs Compson said. "I respect anybody's private affairs. I wouldn't put my foot over the threshold, even if I had a key."

"Yes," Jason said, "I know your keys wont fit. That's why I had the lock changed. What I want to know is, how that window got broken."

"Luster say he didn't do hit," Dilsey said.

"I knew that without asking him," Jason said. "Where's Quentin?" he said.

"Where she is ev'y Sunday mawnin," Dilsey said. "Whut got into you de last few days, anyhow?"

"Well, we're going to change all that," Jason said. "Go up and tell her breakfast is ready."

"You leave her alone now, Jason," Dilsey said. "She gits up fer breakfast ev'y week mawnin, en Cahline lets her stay in bed ev'y Sunday. You knows dat."

"I cant keep a kitchen full of niggers to wait on her pleasure, much as I'd like to," Jason said. "Go and tell her to come down to breakfast."

"Aint nobody have to wait on her," Dilsey said. "I puts her breakfast in de warmer en she —"

"Did you hear me?" Jason said.

"I hears you," Dilsey said. "All I been hearin, when you in de house. Ef hit aint Quentin er yo maw, hit's Luster en Benjy. Whut you let him go on dat way fer, Miss Cahline?"

"You'd better do as he says," Mrs Compson said, "He's head of the house now. It's his right to re-

346

quire us to respect his wishes. I try to do it, and if I can, you can too."

" 'Taint no sense in him bein so bad tempered he got to make Quentin git up jes to suit him," Dilsey said. "Maybe you think she broke dat window."

" She would, if she happened to think of it," Jason said. "You go and do what I told you."

" En I wouldn't blame her none ef she did," Dilsey said, going toward the stairs. "Wid you naggin at her all de blessed time you in de house."

" Hush, Dilsey," Mrs Compson said, " It's neither your place nor mine to tell Jason what to do. Sometimes I think he is wrong, but I try to obey his wishes for you alls' sakes. If I'm strong enough to come to the table, Quentin can too."

Dilsey went out. They heard her mounting the stairs. They heard her a long while on the stairs.

"You've got a prize set of servants," Jason said. He helped his mother and himself to food. " Did you ever have one that was worth killing? You must have had some before I was big enough to remember."

"I have to humour them," Mrs Compson said. "I have to depend on them so completely. It's not as if I were strong. I wish I were. I wish I could do all the house work myself. I could at least take that much off your shoulders."

" And a fine pigsty we'd live in, too," Jason said. "Hurry up, Dilsey," he shouted.

"I know you blame me," Mrs Compson said, "for letting them off to go to church today."

"Go where?" Jason said. "Hasn't that damn show left yet?"

"To church," Mrs Compson said. "The darkies are having a special Easter service. I promised Dilsey two weeks ago that they could get off."

"Which means we'll eat cold dinner," Jason said, "or none at all."

"I know it's my fault," Mrs Compson said. "I know you blame me."

"For what?" Jason said. "You never resurrected Christ, did you?"

They heard Dilsey mount the final stair, then her slow feet overhead.

"Quentin," she said. When she called the first time Jason laid his knife and fork down and he and his mother appeared to wait across the table from one another, in identical attitudes; the one cold and shrewd, with close-thatched brown hair curled into two stubborn hooks, one on either side of his forehead like a bartender in caricature, and hazel eyes with black-ringed irises like marbles, the other cold and querulous, with perfectly white hair and eyes pouched and baffled and so dark as to appear to be all pupil or all iris.

"Quentin," Dilsey said, "Get up, honey. Dey waitin breakfast on you."

"I cant understand how that window got broken,"

348

Mrs Compson said. " Are you sure it was done yesterday? It could have been like that a long time, with the warm weather. The upper sash, behind the shade like that."

" I've told you for the last time that it happened yesterday," Jason said. " Dont you reckon I know the room I live in? Do you reckon I could have lived in it a week with a hole in the window you could stick your hand — " his voice ceased, ebbed, left him staring at his mother with eyes that for an instant were quite empty of anything. It was as though his eyes were holding their breath, while his mother looked at him, her face flaccid and querulous, interminable, clairvoyant yet obtuse. As they sat so Dilsey said,

" Quentin. Dont play wid me, honey. Come on to breakfast, honey. Dey waitin fer you."

" I cant understand it," Mrs Compson said, " It's just as if somebody had tried to break into the house — " Jason sprang up. His chair crashed over backward. " What — " Mrs Compson said, staring at him as he ran past her and went jumping up the stairs, where he met Dilsey. His face was now in shadow, and Dilsey said,

" She sullin. Yo ma aint unlocked — " But Jason ran on past her and along the corridor to a door. He didn't call. He grasped the knob and tried it, then he stood with the knob in his hand and his head bent a little, as if he were listening to something much further away than the dimensioned room beyond the door, and which he already heard. His attitude was that of one who goes through the motions of listening in order to deceive himself as to what he already hears. Behind him Mrs Compson mounted the stairs, calling his name. Then she saw Dilsey and she quit calling him and began to call Dilsey instead.

"I told you she aint unlocked dat do' yit," Dilsey said.

When she spoke he turned and ran toward her, but his voice was quiet, matter of fact. "She carry the key with her?" he said. "Has she got it now, I mean, or will she have — "

"Dilsey," Mrs Compson said on the stairs.

"Is which?" Dilsey said. "Whyn't you let — "

"The key," Jason said, "To that room. Does she carry it with her all the time. Mother." Then he saw Mrs Compson and he went down the stairs and met her. "Give me the key," he said. He fell to pawing at the pockets of the rusty black dressing sacque she wore. She resisted.

"Jason," she said, "Jason! Are you and Dilsey trying to put me to bed again?" she said, trying to fend him off, "Cant you even let me have Sunday in peace?"

"The key," Jason said, pawing at her, "Give it here." He looked back at the door, as if he expected it to fly open before he could get back to it with the key he did not yet have.

"You, Dilsey!" Mrs Compson said, clutching her sacque about her.

"Give me the key, you old fool!" Jason cried suddenly. From her pocket he tugged a huge bunch of rusted keys on an iron ring like a mediaeval jailer's and ran back up the hall with the two women behind him.

"You, Jason!" Mrs Compson said. "He will never find the right one," she said, "You know I never let anyone take my keys, Dilsey," she said. She began to wail.

"Hush," Dilsey said, "He aint gwine do nothin to her. I aint gwine let him."

"But on Sunday morning, in my own house," Mrs Compson said, "When I've tried so hard to raise them Christians. Let me find the right key, Jason," she said. She put her hand on his arm. Then she began to struggle with him, but he flung her aside with a motion of his elbow and looked around at her for a moment, his eyes cold and harried, then he turned to the door again and the unwieldy keys.

"Hush," Dilsey said, "You, Jason!"

"Something terrible has happened," Mrs Compson said, wailing again, "I know it has. You, Jason," she said, grasping at him again. "He wont even let me find the key to a room in my own house!"

"Now, now," Dilsey said, "Whut kin happen? I right here. I aint gwine let him hurt her. Quentin,"

351

she said, raising her voice, " dont you be skeered, honey, I'se right here."

The door opened, swung inward. He stood in it for a moment, hiding the room, then he stepped aside. " Go in," he said in a thick, light voice. They went in. It was not a girl's room. It was not anybody's room, and the faint scent of cheap cosmetics and the few feminine objects and the other evidences of crude and hopeless efforts to feminize it but added to its anonymity, giving it that dead and stereotyped transience of rooms in assignation houses. The bed had not been disturbed. On the floor lay a soiled undergarment of cheap silk a little too pink; from a half open bureau drawer dangled a single stocking. The window was open. A pear tree grew there, close against the house. It was in bloom and the branches scraped and rasped against the house and the myriad air, driving in the window, brought into the room the forlorn scent of the blossoms.

" Dar now," Dilsey said, " Didn't I told you she all right?"

" All right?" Mrs Compson said. Dilsey followed her into the room and touched her.

" You come on and lay down, now," she said. " I find her in ten minutes."

Mrs Compson shook her off. " Find the note," she said. " Quentin left a note when he did it."

" All right," Dilsey said, " I'll find hit. You come on to yo room, now."

352

"I knew the minute they named her Quentin this would happen," Mrs Compson said. She went to the bureau and began to turn over the scattered objects there — scent bottles, a box of powder, a chewed pencil, a pair of scissors with one broken blade lying upon a darned scarf dusted with powder and stained with rouge. "Find the note," she said.

"I is," Dilsey said. "You come on, now. Me and Jason'll find hit. You come on to yo room."

"Jason," Mrs Compson said, "Where is he?" She went to the door. Dilsey followed her on down the hall, to another door. It was closed. "Jason," she called through the door. There was no answer. She tried the knob, then she called him again. But there was still no answer, for he was hurling things backward out of the closet: garments, shoes, a suitcase. Then he emerged carrying a sawn section of tongue-and-groove planking and laid it down and entered the closet again and emerged with a metal box. He set it on the bed and stood looking at the broken lock while he dug a key ring from his pocket and selected a key, and for a time longer he stood with the selected key in his hand, looking at the broken lock, then he put the keys back in his pocket and carefully tilted the contents of the box out upon the bed. Still carefully he sorted the papers, taking them up one at a time and shaking them. Then he up-ended the box and shook it too and slowly replaced

the papers and stood again, looking at the broken
lock, with the box in his hands and his head bent. Outside the window he heard some jaybirds swirl shriek-
ing past, and away, their cries whipping away along
the wind, and an automobile passed somewhere and
died away also. His mother spoke his name again beyond the door, but he didn't move. He heard Dilsey
lead her away up the hall, and then a door closed.
Then he replaced the box in the closet and flung
the garments back into it and went down stairs
to the telephone. While he stood there with the receiver to his ear, waiting, Dilsey came down the
stairs. She looked at him, without stopping, and
went on.

The wire opened. " This is Jason Compson," he
said, his voice so harsh and thick that he had to repeat himself. " Jason Compson," he said, controlling
his voice. " Have a car ready, with a deputy, if you
cant go, in ten minutes. I'll be there — What? —
Robbery. My house. I know who it — Robbery, I
say. Have a car read — What? Aren't you a paid
law enforcement — Yes, I'll be there in five minutes.
Have that car ready to leave at once. If you dont,
I'll report it to the governor."

He clapped the receiver back and crossed the diningroom, where the scarce-broken meal now lay cold
on the table, and entered the kitchen. Dilsey was
filling the hot water bottle. Ben sat, tranquil and
empty. Beside him Luster looked like a fice dog,

brightly watchful. He was eating something. Jason went on across the kitchen.

"Aint you going to eat no breakfast?" Dilsey said. He paid her no attention. "Go on and eat yo breakfast, Jason." He went on. The outer door banged behind him. Luster rose and went to the window and looked out.

"Whoo," he said, "Whut happenin up dar? He been beatin' Miss Quentin?"

"You hush yo mouf," Dilsey said. "You git Benjy started now en I beat yo head off. You keep him quiet es you kin twell I get back, now." She screwed the cap on the bottle and went out. They heard her go up the stairs, then they heard Jason pass the house in his car. Then there was no sound in the kitchen save the simmering murmur of the kettle and the clock.

"You know whut I bet?" Luster said. "I bet he beat her. I bet he knock her in de head en now he gone fer de doctor. Dat's whut I bet." The clock ticktocked, solemn and profound. It might have been the dry pulse of the decaying house itself; after a while it whirred and cleared its throat and struck six times. Ben looked up at it, then he looked at the bullet-like silhouette of Luster's head in the window and he begun to bob his head again, drooling. He whimpered.

"Hush up, loony," Luster said without turning. "Look like we aint gwine git to go to no church today." But Ben sat in the chair, his big soft hands dangling between his knees, moaning faintly. Suddenly he wept, a slow bellowing sound, meaningless and sustained. "Hush," Luster said. He turned and lifted his hand. "You want me to whup you?" But Ben looked at him, bellowing slowly with each expiration. Luster came and shook him. "You hush dis minute!" he shouted. "Here," he said. He hauled Ben out of the chair and dragged the chair around facing the stove and opened the door to the firebox and shoved Ben into the chair. They looked like a tug nudging at a clumsy tanker in a narrow dock. Ben sat down again facing the rosy door. He hushed. Then they heard the clock again, and Dilsey slow on the stairs. When she entered he began to whimper again. Then he lifted his voice.

"Whut you done to him?" Dilsey said. "Why cant you let him lone dis mawnin, of all times?"

"I aint doin nothin to him," Luster said. "Mr Jason skeered him, dat's whut hit is. He aint kilt Miss Quentin, is he?"

"Hush, Benjy," Dilsey said. He hushed. She went to the window and looked out. "Is it quit rainin?" she said.

"Yessum," Luster said. "Quit long time ago."

"Den y'all go out do's awhile," she said. "I jes got Miss Cahline quiet now."

"Is we gwine to church?" Luster said.

" I let you know bout dat when de time come. You keep him away fum de house twell I calls you."

" Kin we go to de pastuh ? " Luster said.

" All right. Only you keep him away fum de house. I done stood all I kin."

"Yessum," Luster said. " Whar Mr Jason gone, mammy ? "

" Dat's some mo of yo business, aint it ? " Dilsey said. She began to clear the table. " Hush, Benjy. Luster gwine take you out to play."

" Whut he done to Miss Quentin, mammy ? " Luster said.

" Aint done nothin to her. You all git on outen here ? "

" I bet she aint here," Luster said.

Dilsey looked at him. " How you know she aint here ?

" Me and Benjy seed her clamb out de window last night. Didn't us, Benjy ? "

" You did ? " Dilsey said, looking at him.

" We sees her doin hit ev'y night," Luster said, " Clamb right down dat pear tree."

" Dont you lie to me, nigger boy," Dilsey said.

" I aint lyin. Ask Benjy ef I is."

" Whyn't you say somethin about it, den ? "

" 'Twarn't none o my business," Luster said. " I aint gwine git mixed up in white folks' business. Come on here, Benjy, les go out do's."

They went out. Dilsey stood for awhile at the

table, then she went and cleared the breakfast things from the diningroom and ate her breakfast and cleaned up the kitchen. Then she removed her apron and hung it up and went to the foot of the stairs and listened for a moment. There was no sound. She donned the overcoat and the hat and went across to her cabin.

The rain had stopped. The air now drove out of the southeast, broken overhead into blue patches. Upon the crest of a hill beyond the trees and roofs and spires of town sunlight lay like a pale scrap of cloth, was blotted away. Upon the air a bell came, then as if at a signal, other bells took up the sound and repeated it.

The cabin door opened and Dilsey emerged, again in the maroon cape and the purple gown, and wearing soiled white elbow-length gloves and minus her headcloth now. She came into the yard and called Luster. She waited awhile, then she went to the house and around it to the cellar door, moving close to the wall, and looked into the door. Ben sat on the steps. Before him Luster squatted on the damp floor. He held a saw in his left hand, the blade sprung a little by pressure of his hand, and he was in the act of striking the blade with the worn wooden mallet with which she had been making beaten biscuit for more than thirty years. The saw gave forth a single sluggish twang that ceased with lifeless alacrity, leaving the blade in a thin clean curve between

358

Luster's hand and the floor. Still, inscrutable, it bellied.

"Dat's de way he done hit," Luster said. "I jes aint foun de right thing to hit it wid."

"Dat's whut you doin, is it?" Dilsey said. "Bring me dat mallet," she said.

"I aint hurt hit," Luster said.

"Bring hit here," Dilsey said. "Put dat saw whar you got hit first."

He put the saw away and brought the mallet to her. Then Ben wailed again, hopeless and prolonged. It was nothing. Just sound. It might have been all time and injustice and sorrow become vocal for an instant by a conjunction of planets.

"Listen at him," Luster said, "He been gwine on dat way ev'y since you sont us outen de house. I dont know whut got in to him dis mawnin."

"Bring him here," Dilsey said.

"Come on, Benjy," Luster said. He went back down the steps and took Ben's arm. He came obediently, wailing, that slow hoarse sound that ships make, that seems to begin before the sound itself has started, seems to cease before the sound itself has stopped.

"Run and git his cap," Dilsey said. "Dont make no noise Miss Cahline kin hear. Hurry, now. We already late."

"She gwine hear him anyhow, ef you dont stop him." Luster said.

359

"He stop when we git off de place," Dilsey said. "He smellin hit. Dat's whut hit is."

"Smell whut, mammy?" Luster said.

"You go git dat cap," Dilsey said. Luster went on. They stood in the cellar door, Ben one step below her. The sky was broken now into scudding patches that dragged their swift shadows up out of the shabby garden, over the broken fence and across the yard. Dilsey stroked Ben's head, slowly and steadily, smoothing the bang upon his brow. He wailed quietly, unhurriedly. "Hush," Dilsey said, "Hush, now. We be gone in a minute. Hush, now." He wailed quietly and steadily.

Luster returned, wearing a stiff new straw hat with a coloured band and carrying a cloth cap. The hat seemed to isolate Luster's skull, in the beholder's eye as a spotlight would, in all its individual planes and angles. So peculiarly individual was its shape that at first glance the hat appeared to be on the head of someone standing immediately behind Luster. Dilsey looked at the hat.

"Whyn't you wear yo old hat?" she said.

"Couldn't find hit," Luster said.

"I bet you couldn't. I bet you fixed hit last night so you couldn't find hit. You fixin to ruin dat un."

"Aw, mammy," Luster said, "Hit aint gwine rain."

"How you know? You go git dat old hat en put dat new un away."

360

" Aw, mammy."

" Den you go git de umbreller."

" Aw, mammy."

" Take yo choice," Dilsey said. " Git yo old hat, er de umbreller. I dont keer which."

Luster went to the cabin. Ben wailed quietly.

" Come on," Dilsey said, " Dey kin ketch up wid us. We gwine to hear de singin." They went around the house, toward the gate. " Hush," Dilsey said from time to time as they went down the drive. They reached the gate. Dilsey opened it. Luster was coming down the drive behind them, carrying the umbrella. A woman was with him. " Here dey come," Dilsey said. They passed out the gate. " Now, den," she said. Ben ceased. Luster and his mother overtook them. Frony wore a dress of bright blue silk and a flowered hat. She was a thin woman, with a flat, pleasant face.

" You got six weeks' work right dar on yo back," Dilsey said. " Whut you gwine do ef hit rain?"

" Git wet, I reckon," Frony said. " I aint never stopped no rain yit."

" Mammy always talkin bout hit gwine rain," Luster said.

" Ef I dont worry bout y'all, I dont know who is," Dilsey said. " Come on, we already late."

" Rev'un Shegog gwine preach today," Frony said.

" Is?" Dilsey said. " Who him?"

"He fum Saint Looey," Frony said. "Dat big preacher."

"Huh," Dilsey said, "Whut dey needs is a man kin put de fear of God into dese here triflin young niggers."

"Rev'un Shegog gwine preach today," Frony said. "So dey tells."

They went on along the street. Along its quiet length white people in bright clumps moved churchward, under the windy bells, walking now and then in the random and tentative sun. The wind was gusty, out of the southeast, chill and raw after the warm days.

"I wish you wouldn't keep on bringin him to church, mammy," Frony said. "Folks talkin."

"Whut folks?" Dilsey said.

"I hears em," Frony said.

"And I knows whut kind of folks," Dilsey said, "Trash white folks. Dat's who it is. Thinks he aint good enough fer white church, but nigger church aint good enough fer him."

"Dey talks, jes de same," Frony said.

"Den you send um to me," Dilsey said. "Tell um de good Lawd dont keer whether he smart er not. Dont nobody but white trash keer dat."

A street turned off at right angles, descending, and became a dirt road. On either hand the land dropped more sharply; a broad flat dotted with small cabins whose weathered roofs were on a level with the

362

crown of the road. They were set in small grassless plots littered with broken things, bricks, planks, crockery, things of a once utilitarian value. What growth there was consisted of rank weeds and the trees were mulberries and locusts and sycamores — trees that partook also of the foul desiccation which surrounded the houses; trees whose very burgeoning seemed to be the sad and stubborn remnant of September, as if even spring had passed them by, leaving them to feed upon the rich and unmistakable smell of negroes in which they grew.

From the doors negroes spoke to them as they passed, to Dilsey usually:

"Sis' Gibson! How you dis mawnin?"

"I'm well. Is you well?"

"I'm right well, I thank you."

They emerged from the cabins and struggled up the shading levee to the road — men in staid, hard brown or black, with gold watch chains and now and then a stick; young men in cheap violent blues or stripes and swaggering hats; women a little stiffly sibilant, and children in garments bought second hand of white people, who looked at Ben with the covertness of nocturnal animals:

"I bet you wont go up en tech him."

"How come I wont?"

"I bet you wont. I bet you skeered to."

"He wont hurt folks. He des a loony."

"How come a loony wont hurt folks?"

"Dat un wont. I teched him."

"I bet you wont now."

"Case Miss Dilsey lookin."

"You wont no ways."

"He dont hurt folks. He des a loony."

And steadily the older people speaking to Dilsey, though, unless they were quite old, Dilsey permitted Frony to respond.

"Mammy aint feelin well dis mawnin."

"Dat's too bad. But Rev'un Shegog'll cure dat. He'll give her de comfort en de unburdenin."

The road rose again, to a scene like a painted backdrop. Notched into a cut of red clay crowned with oaks the road appeared to stop short off, like a cut ribbon. Beside it a weathered church lifted its crazy steeple like a painted church, and the whole scene was as flat and without perspective as a painted cardboard set upon the ultimate edge of the flat earth, against the windy sunlight of space and April and a midmorning filled with bells. Toward the church they thronged with slow sabbath deliberation. The women and children went on in, the men stopped outside and talked in quiet groups until the bell ceased ringing. Then they too entered.

The church had been decorated, with sparse flowers from kitchen gardens and hedgerows, and with streamers of coloured crepe paper. Above the pulpit hung a battered Christmas bell, the accordian

364

sort that collapses. The pulpit was empty, though the choir was already in place, fanning themselves although it was not warm.

Most of the women were gathered on one side of the room. They were talking. Then the bell struck one time and they dispersed to their seats and the congregation sat for an instant, expectant. The bell struck again one time. The choir rose and began to sing and the congregation turned its head as one, as six small children — four girls with tight pigtails bound with small scraps of cloth like butterflies, and two boys with close napped heads, — entered and marched up the aisle, strung together in a harness of white ribbons and flowers, and followed by two men in single file. The second man was huge, of a light coffee colour, imposing in a frock coat and white tie. His head was magisterial and profound, his neck rolled above his collar in rich folds. But he was familiar to them, and so the heads were still reverted when he had passed, and it was not until the choir ceased singing that they realised that the visiting clergyman had already entered, and when they saw the man who had preceded their minister enter the pulpit still ahead of him an indescribable sound went up, a sigh, a sound of astonishment and disappointment.

The visitor was undersized, in a shabby alpaca coat. He had a wizened black face like a small, aged monkey. And all the while that the choir sang again and while the six children rose and sang in thin, frightened, tuneless whispers, they watched the insignificant looking man sitting dwarfed and countrified by the minister's imposing bulk, with something like consternation. They were still looking at him with consternation and unbelief when the minister rose and introduced him in rich, rolling tones whose very unction served to increase the visitor's insignificance.

" En dey brung dat all de way fum Saint Looey," Frony whispered.

" I've knowed de Lawd to use cuiser tools dan dat," Dilsey said. "Hush, now," she said to Ben, " Dey fixin to sing again in a minute."

When the visitor rose to speak he sounded like a white man. His voice was level and cold. It sounded too big to have come from him and they listened at first through curiosity, as they would have to a monkey talking. They began to watch him as they would a man on a tight rope. They even forgot his insignificant appearance in the virtuosity with which he ran and poised and swooped upon the cold inflectionless wire of his voice, so that at last, when with a sort of swooping glide he came to rest again beside the reading desk with one arm resting upon it at shoulder height and his monkey body as reft of all motion as a mummy or an emptied vessel, the congregation sighed as if it waked from a collective dream and moved a little in its seats. Behind the

366

pulpit the choir fanned steadily. Dilsey whispered, " Hush, now. Dey fixin to sing in a minute."

Then a voice said, " Brethren."

The preacher had not moved. His arm lay yet across the desk, and he still held that pose while the voice died in sonorous echoes between the walls. It was as different as day and dark from his former tone, with a sad, timbrous quality like an alto horn, sinking into their hearts and speaking there again when it had ceased in fading and cumulate echoes.

" Brethren and sisteren," it said again. The preacher removed his arm and be began to walk back and forth before the desk, his hands clasped behind him, a meagre figure, hunched over upon itself like that of one long immured in striving with the implacable earth, " I got the recollection and the blood of the Lamb ! " He tramped steadily back and forth beneath the twisted paper and the Christmas bell, hunched, his hands clasped behind him. He was like a worn small rock whelmed by the successive waves of his voice. With his body he seemed to feed the voice that, succubus like, had fleshed its teeth in him. And the congregation seemed to watch with its own eyes while the voice consumed him, until he was nothing and they were nothing and there was not even a voice but instead their hearts were speaking to one another in chanting measures beyond the need for words, so that when he came to rest against the read-

ing desk, his monkey face lifted and his whole
attitude that of a serene, tortured crucifix that tran-
scended its shabbiness and insignificance and made it
of no moment, a long moaning expulsion of breath
rose from them, and a woman's single soprano:
"Yes, Jesus!"

As the scudding day passed overhead the dingy
windows glowed and faded in ghostly retrograde.
A car passed along the road outside, labouring in the
sand, died away. Dilsey sat bolt upright, her hand
on Ben's knee. Two tears slid down her fallen cheeks,
in and out of the myriad coruscations of immolation
and abnegation and time.

"Brethren," the minister said in a harsh whisper,
without moving.

"Yes, Jesus!" the woman's voice said, hushed
yet.

"Breddren en sistuhn!" His voice rang again,
with the horns. He removed his arm and stood erect
and raised his hands. "I got de ricklickshun en de
blood of de Lamb!" They did not mark just when
his intonation, his pronunciation, became negroid,
they just sat swaying a little in their seats as the voice
took them into itself.

"When de long, cold — Oh, I tells you, breddren,
when de long, cold — I sees de light en I sees de
word, po sinner! Dey passed away in Egypt, de
swingin chariots; de generations passed away. Wus
a rich man: whar he now, O breddren? Wus a po

368

man: whar he now, O sistuhn? Oh I tells you, ef you
aint got de milk en de dew of de old salvation when
de long, cold years rolls away!"

"Yes, Jesus!"

"I tells you, breddren, en I tells you, sistuhn,
dey'll come a time. Po sinner sayin Let me lay down
wid de Lawd, lemme lay down my load. Den whut
Jesus gwine say, O breddren? O sistuhn? Is you got
de ricklickshun en de Blood of de Lamb? Case I aint
gwine load down heaven!"

He fumbled in his coat and took out a handkerchief
and mopped his face. A low concerted sound rose
from the congregation: "Mmmmmmmmmmmmm!
The woman's voice said, "Yes, Jesus! Jesus!"

"Breddren! Look at dem little chillen settin dar.
Jesus wus like dat once. He mammy suffered de
glory en de pangs. Sometime maybe she helt him
at de nightfall, whilst de angels singin him to sleep;
maybe she look out de do' en see de Roman po-lice
passin." He tramped back and forth, mopping his
face. "Listen, breddren! I sees de day. Ma'y settin
in de do' wid Jesus on her lap, de little Jesus. Like
dem chillen dar, de little Jesus. I hears de angels
singin de peaceful songs en de glory; I sees de closin
eyes; sees Mary jump up, sees de sojer face: We
gwine to kill! We gwine to kill! We gwine to kill yo
little Jesus! I hears de weepin en de lamentation of
de po mammy widout de salvation en de word of
God!"

" Mmmmmmmmmmmmmmmmmm ! Jesus ! Little
Jesus ! " and another voice, rising :

" I sees, O Jesus ! Oh I sees ! " and still another,
without words, like bubbles rising in water.

" I sees hit, breddren ! I sees hit ! Sees de blastin,
blindin sight ! I sees Calvary, wid de sacred trees,
sees de thief en de murderer en de least of dese ; I
hears de boasting en de braggin : Ef you be Jesus, lif
up yo tree en walk ! I hears de wailin of women en de
evenin lamentations ; I hears de weepin en de cryin
en de turnt-away face of God : dey done kilt Jesus ;
dey done kilt my Son ! "

" Mmmmmmmmmmmmmm. Jesus ! I sees, O
Jesus ! "

" O blind sinner ! Breddren, I tells you ; sistuhn, I
says to you, when de Lawd did turn His mighty face,
say, Aint gwine overload heaven ! I can see de
widowed God shet His do' ; I sees de whelmin flood
roll between ; I sees de darkness en de death ever-
lastin upon de generations. Den, lo ! Breddren ! Yes,
breddren ! Whut I see ? Whut I see, O sinner ? I sees
de resurrection en de light ; sees de meek Jesus sayin
Dey kilt Me dat ye shall live again ; I died dat dem
whut sees en believes shall never die. Breddren, O
breddren ! I sees de doom crack en hears de golden
horns shoutin down de glory, en de arisen dead whut
got de blood en de ricklickshun of de Lamb ! "

In the midst of the voices and the hands Ben sat,
rapt in his sweet blue gaze. Dilsey sat bolt upright

beside, crying rigidly and quietly in the annealment and the blood of the remembered Lamb.

As they walked through the bright noon, up the sandy road with the dispersing congregation talking easily again group to group, she continued to weep, unmindful of the talk.

"He sho a preacher, mon! He didn't look like much at first, but hush!"

"He seed de power en de glory."

"Yes, suh. He seed hit. Face to face he seed hit."

Dilsey made no sound, her face did not quiver as the tears took their sunken and devious courses, walking with her head up, making no effort to dry them away even.

"Whyn't you quit dat, mammy?" Frony said. "Wid all dese people lookin. We be passin white folks soon."

"I've seed de first en de last," Dilsey said. "Never you mind me."

"First en last whut?" Frony said.

"Never you mind," Dilsey said. "I seed de beginnin, en now I sees de endin."

Before they reached the street, though, she stopped and lifted her skirt and dried her eyes on the hem of her topmost underskirt. Then they went on. Ben shambled along beside Dilsey, watching Luster who anticked along ahead, the umbrella in his hand and his new straw hat slanted viciously in the sunlight, like a big foolish dog watching a small clever

371

one. They reached the gate and entered. Immediately Ben began to whimper again, and for a while all of them looked up the drive at the square, paintless house with its rotting portico.

"Whut's gwine on up dar today?" Frony said. "Something is."

"Nothin," Dilsey said. "You tend to yo business en let de white folks tend to deir'n."

"Somethin is," Frony said. "I heard him first thing dis mawnin. 'Taint none of my business, dough."

"En I knows whut, too," Luster said.

"You knows mo dan you got any use fer," Dilsey said. "Aint you jes heard Frony say hit aint none of yo business? You take Benjy on to de back and keep him quiet twell I put dinner on."

"I knows whar Miss Quentin is," Luster said.

"Den jes keep hit," Dilsey said. "Soon es Quentin need any of yo egvice, I'll let you know. Y'all g'awn en play in de back, now."

"You know whut gwine happen soon es dey start playin dat ball over yonder," Luster said.

"Dey wont start fer awhile yit. By dat time T.P. be here to take him ridin. Here, you gimme dat new hat."

Luster gave her the hat and he and Ben went on across the back yard. Ben was still whimpering, though not loud. Dilsey and Frony went to the cabin. After a while Dilsey emerged, again in the faded

calico dress, and went to the kitchen. The fire had
died down. There was no sound in the house. She put
on the apron and went up stairs. There was no sound
anywhere. Quentin's room was as they had left it.
She entered and picked up the undergarment and put
the stocking back in the drawer and closed it. Mrs
Compson's door was closed. Dilsey stood beside it
for a moment, listening. Then she opened it and entered, entered a pervading reek of camphor. The
shades were drawn, the room in halflight, and the
bed, so that at first she thought Mrs Compson was
asleep and was about to close the door when the
other spoke.

"Well?" she said, "What is it?"

"Hit's me," Dilsey said. "You want anything?"

Mrs Compson didn't answer. After awhile, without moving her head at all, she said: "Where's
Jason?"

"He aint come back yit," Dilsey said. "Whut you
want?"

Mrs Compson said nothing. Like so many cold,
weak people, when faced at last by the incontrovertible disaster she exhumed from somewhere a sort
of fortitude, strength. In her case it was an unshakable conviction regarding the yet unplumbed event.
"Well," she said presently, "Did you find it?"

"Find whut? Whut you talkin about?"

"The note. At least she would have enough consideration to leave a note. Even Quentin did that."

"Whut you talkin about?" Dilsey said, "Dont you know she all right? I bet she be walkin right in dis do' befo dark."

"Fiddlesticks," Mrs Compson said, "It's in the blood. Like uncle, like niece. Or mother. I dont know which would be worse. I dont seem to care."

"Whut you keep on talkin that way fur?" Dilsey said. "Whut she want to do anything like that fur?"

"I dont know. What reason did Quentin have? Under God's heaven what reason did he have? It cant be simply to flout and hurt me. Whoever God is, He would not permit that. I'm a lady. You might not believe that from my offspring, but I am."

"You des wait en see," Dilsey said. "She be here by night, right dar in her bed." Mrs Compson said nothing. The camphor-soaked cloth lay upon her brow. The black robe lay across the foot of the bed. Dilsey stood with her hand on the door knob.

"Well," Mrs Compson said. "What do you want? Are you going to fix some dinner for Jason and Benjamin, or not?"

"Jason aint come yit," Dilsey said. "I gwine fix somethin. You sho you dont want nothin? Yo bottle still hot enough?"

"You might hand me my Bible."

"I give hit to you dis mawnin, befo I left."

"You laid it on the edge of the bed. How long did you expect it to stay there?"

Dilsey crossed to the bed and groped among the

374

shadows beneath the edge of it and found the Bible, face down. She smoothed the bent pages and laid the book on the bed again. Mrs Compson didn't open her eyes. Her hair and the pillow were the same color, beneath the wimple of the medicated cloth she looked like an old nun praying. "Dont put it there again," she said, without opening her eyes. "That's where you put it before. Do you want me to have to get out of bed to pick it up?"

Dilsey reached the book across her and laid it on the broad side of the bed. "You cant see to read, noways," she said. "You want me to raise de shade a little?"

"No. Let them alone. Go on and fix Jason something to eat."

Dilsey went out. She closed the door and returned to the kitchen. The stove was almost cold. While she stood there the clock above the cupboard struck ten times. "One oclock," she said aloud, "Jason aint comin home. Ise seed de first en de last," she said, looking at the cold stove, "I seed de first en de last." She set out some cold food on a table. As she moved back and forth she sang a hymn. She sang the first two lines over and over to the complete tune. She arranged the meal and went to the door and called Luster, and after a time Luster and Ben entered. Ben was still moaning a little, as to himself.

"He aint never quit," Luster said.

"Y'all come on en eat," Dilsey said. "Jason aint

coming to dinner." They sat down at the table. Ben could manage solid food pretty well for himself, though even now, with cold food before him, Dilsey tied a cloth about his neck. He and Luster ate. Dilsey moved about the kitchen, singing the two lines of the hymn which she remembered. "Y'all kin g'awn en eat," she said, "Jason aint comin home."

He was twenty miles away at that time. When he left the house he drove rapidly to town, overreaching the slow sabbath groups and the peremptory bells along the broken air. He crossed the empty square and turned into a narrow street that was abruptly quieter even yet, and stopped before a frame house and went up the flower-bordered walk to the porch.

Beyond the screen door people were talking. As he lifted his hand to knock he heard steps, so he withheld his hand until a big man in black broad-cloth trousers and a stiff-bosomed white shirt without collar opened the door. He had vigorous untidy iron-grey hair and his grey eyes were round and shiny like a little boy's. He took Jason's hand and drew him into the house, still shaking it.

"Come right in," he said, "Come right in."

"You ready to go now?" Jason said.

"Walk right in," the other said, propelling him by the elbow into a room where a man and a woman sat. "You know Myrtle's husband, dont you? Jason Compson, Vernon."

"Yes," Jason said. He did not even look at the

376

man, and as the sheriff drew a chair across the room the man said,

"We'll go out so you can talk. Come on, Myrtle."

"No, no," the sheriff said, "You folks keep your seat. I reckon it aint that serious, Jason? Have a seat."

"I'll tell you as we go along," Jason said. "Get your hat and coat."

"We'll go out," the man said, rising.

"Keep your seat," the sheriff said. "Me and Jason will go out on the porch."

"You get your hat and coat," Jason said. "They've already got a twelve hour start." The sheriff led the way back to the porch. A man and a woman passing spoke to him. He responded with a hearty florid gesture. Bells were still ringing, from the direction of the section known as Nigger Hollow. "Get your hat, Sheriff," Jason said. The sheriff drew up two chairs.

"Have a seat and tell me what the trouble is."

"I told you over the phone," Jason said, standing. "I did that to save time. Am I going to have to go to law to compel you to do your sworn duty?"

"You sit down and tell me about it," the sheriff said. "I'll take care of you all right."

"Care, hell," Jason said. "Is this what you call taking care of me?"

"You're the one that's holding us up," the sheriff said. "You sit down and tell me about it."

Jason told him, his sense of injury and impotence feeding upon its own sound, so that after a time he forgot his haste in the violent cumulation of his self justification and his outrage. The sheriff watched him steadily with his cold shiny eyes.

"But you dont know they done it," he said. "You just think so."

"Dont know?" Jason said. "When I spent two damn days chasing her through alleys, trying to keep her away from him, after I told her what I'd do to her if I ever caught her with him, and you say I dont know that that little b—"

"Now, then," the sheriff said, "That'll do. That's enough of that." He looked out across the street, his hands in his pockets.

"And when I come to you, a commissioned officer of the law," Jason said.

"That show's in Mottson this week," the sheriff said.

"Yes," Jason said, "And if I could find a law officer that gave a solitary damn about protecting the people that elected him to office, I'd be there too by now." He repeated his story, harshly recapitulant, seeming to get an actual pleasure out of his outrage and impotence. The sheriff did not appear to be listening at all.

"Jason," he said, "What were you doing with three thousand dollars hid in the house?"

"What?" Jason said. "That's my business where

I keep my money. Your business is to help me get it back."

" Did your mother know you had that much on the place ? "

"Look here," Jason said, "My house has been robbed. I know who did it and I know where they are. I come to you as the commissioned officer of the law, and I ask you once more, are you going to make any effort to recover my property, or not ? "

"What do you aim to do with that girl, if you catch them ? "

"Nothing," Jason said, "Not anything. I wouldn't lay my hand on her. The bitch that cost me a job, the one chance I ever had to get ahead, that killed my father and is shortening my mother's life every day and made my name a laughing stock in the town. I wont do anything to her," he said. " Not anything."

"You drove that girl into running off, Jason," the sheriff said.

"How I conduct my family is no business of yours," Jason said. "Are you going to help me or not ? "

"You drove her away from home," the sheriff said. "And I have some suspicions about who that money belongs to that I dont reckon I'll ever know for certain."

Jason stood, slowly wringing the brim of his hat

379

in his hands. He said quietly: "You're not going to make any effort to catch them for me?"

"That's not any of my business, Jason. If you had any actual proof, I'd have to act. But without that I dont figger it's any of my business."

"That's your answer, is it?" Jason said. "Think well, now."

"That's it, Jason."

"All right," Jason said. He put his hat on. "You'll regret this. I wont be helpless. This is not Russia, where just because he wears a little metal badge, a man is immune to law." He went down the steps and got in his car and started the engine. The sheriff watched him drive away, turn, and rush past the house toward town.

The bells were ringing again, high in the scudding sunlight in bright disorderly tatters of sound. He stopped at a filling station and had his tires examined and the tank filled.

"Gwine on a trip, is you?" the negro asked him. He didn't answer. "Look like hit gwine fair off, after all," the negro said.

"Fair off, hell," Jason said, "It'll be raining like hell by twelve oclock." He looked at the sky, thinking about rain, about the slick clay roads, himself stalled somewhere miles from town. He thought about it with a sort of triumph, of the fact that he was going to miss dinner, that by starting now and so serving his compulsion of haste, he would be at

380

the greatest possible distance from both towns when noon came. It seemed to him that, in this, circumstance was giving him a break, so he said to the negro:

"What the hell are you doing? Has somebody paid you to keep this car standing here as long as you can?"

"Dis here ti' aint got no air a-tall in hit," the negro said.

"Then get the hell away from there and let me have that tube," Jason said.

"Hit up now," the negro said, rising. "You kin ride now."

Jason got in and started the engine and drove off. He went into second gear, the engine spluttering and gasping, and he raced the engine, jamming the throttle down and snapping the choker in and out savagely. "It's goin to rain," he said, "Get me half way there, and rain like hell." And he drove on out of the bells and out of town, thinking of himself slogging through the mud, hunting a team. "And every damn one of them will be at church." He thought of how he'd find a church at last and take a team and of the owner coming out, shouting at him and of himself striking the man down. "I'm Jason Compson. See if you can stop me. See if you can elect a man to office that can stop me," he said, thinking of himself entering the courthouse with a file of soldiers and dragging the sheriff out. "Thinks he

can sit with his hands folded and see me lose my job.
I'll show him about jobs." Of his niece he did not
think at all, nor of the arbitrary valuation of the
money. Neither of them had had entity or individu-
ality for him for ten years; together they merely
symbolized the job in the bank of which he had been
deprived before he ever got it.

The air brightened, the running shadow patches
were not the obverse, and it seemed to him that the
fact that the day was clearing was another cunning
stroke on the part of the foe, the fresh battle toward
which he was carrying ancient wounds. From time
to time he passed churches, unpainted frame buildings with sheet iron steeples, surrounded by tethered
teams and shabby motorcars, and it seemed to him
that each of them was a picket-post where the rear
guards of Circumstance peeped fleetingly back at
him. "And damn You, too," he said, "See if You
can stop me," thinking of himself, his file of soldiers
with the manacled sheriff in the rear, dragging Om-
nipotence down from His throne, if necessary; of the
embattled legions of both hell and heaven through
which he tore his way and put his hands at last on
his fleeing niece.

The wind was out of the southeast. It blew steadily
upon his cheek. It seemed that he could feel the prolonged blow of it sinking through his skull, and suddenly with an old premonition he clapped the brakes
on and stopped and sat perfectly still. Then he lifted

382

his hand to his neck and began to curse, and sat there, cursing in a harsh whisper. When it was necessary for him to drive for any length of time he fortified himself with a handkerchief soaked in camphor, which he would tie about his throat when clear of town, thus inhaling the fumes, and he got out and lifted the seat cushion on the chance that there might be a forgotten one there. He looked beneath both seats and stood again for a while, cursing, seeing himself mocked by his own triumphing. He closed his eyes, leaning on the door. He could return and get the forgotten camphor, or he could go on. In either case, his head would be splitting, but at home he could be sure of finding camphor on Sunday, while if he went on he could not be sure. But if he went back, he would be an hour and a half later in reaching Mottson. "Maybe I can drive slow," he said. "Maybe I can drive slow, thinking of something else — "

He got in and started. "I'll think of something else," he said, so he thought about Lorraine. He imagined himself in bed with her, only he was just lying beside her, pleading with her to help him, then he thought of the money again, and that he had been outwitted by a woman, a girl. If he could just believe it was the man who had robbed him. But to have been robbed of that which was to have compensated him for the lost job, which he had acquired through so much effort and risk, by the very symbol of the lost job itself, and worst of all, by a bitch of a girl. He drove on, shielding his face from the steady wind with the corner of his coat.

He could see the opposed forces of his destiny and his will drawing swiftly together now, toward a junction that would be irrevocable; he became cunning. I cant make a blunder, he told himself. There would be just one right thing, without alternatives: he must do that. He believed that both of them would know him on sight, while he'd have to trust to seeing her first, unless the man still wore the red tie. And the fact that he must depend on that red tie seemed to be the sum of the impending disaster; he could almost smell it, feel it above the throbbing of his head.

He crested the final hill. Smoke lay in the valley, and roofs, a spire or two above trees. He drove down the hill and into the town, slowing, telling himself again of the need for caution, to find where the tent was located first. He could not see very well now, and he knew that it was the disaster which kept telling him to go directly and get something for his head. At a filling station they told him that the tent was not up yet, but that the show cars were on a siding at the station. He drove there.

Two gaudily painted pullman cars stood on the track. He reconnoitred them before he got out. He was trying to breathe shallowly, so that the blood would not beat so in his skull. He got out and went along the station wall, watching the cars. A few garments hung out of the windows, limp and crinkled, as though they had been recently laundered. On the earth beside the steps of one sat three canvas chairs. But he saw no sign of life at all until a man in a dirty apron came to the door and emptied a pan of dishwater with a broad gesture, the sunlight glinting on the metal belly of the pan, then entered the car again.

Now I'll have to take him by surprise, before he can warn them, he thought. It never occurred to him that they might not be there, in the car. That they should not be there, that the whole result should not hinge on whether he saw them first or they saw him first, would be opposed to all nature and contrary to the whole rhythm of events. And more than that: he must see them first, get the money back, then what they did would be of no importance to him, while otherwise the whole world would know that he, Jason Compson, had been robbed by Quentin, his niece, a bitch.

He reconnoitred again. Then he went to the car and mounted the steps, swiftly and quietly, and paused at the door. The galley was dark, rank with stale food. The man was a white blur, singing in a cracked, shaky tenor. An old man, he thought, and not as big as I am. He entered the car as the man looked up.

"Hey?" the man said, stopping his song.

385

"Where are they?" Jason said. "Quick, now. In the sleeping car?"

"Where's who?" the man said.

"Dont lie to me," Jason said. He blundered on in the cluttered obscurity.

"What's that?" the other said, "Who you calling a liar?" And when Jason grasped his shoulder he exclaimed, "Look out, fellow!"

"Dont lie," Jason said, "Where are they?"

"Why, you bastard," the man said. His arm was frail and thin in Jason's grasp. He tried to wrench free, then he turned and fell to scrabbling on the littered table behind him.

"Come on," Jason said, "Where are they?"

"I'll tell you where they are," the man shrieked, "Lemme find my butcher knife."

"Here," Jason said, trying to hold the other, "I'm just asking you a question."

"You bastard," the other shrieked, scrabbling at the table. Jason tried to grasp him in both arms, trying to prison the puny fury of him. The man's body felt so old, so frail, yet so fatally single-purposed that for the first time Jason saw clear and unshadowed the disaster toward which he rushed.

"Quit it!" he said, "Here! Here! I'll get out. Give me time, and I'll get out."

"Call me a liar," the other wailed, "Lemme go. Lemme go just one minute. I'll show you."

386

Jason glared wildly about, holding the other. Outside it was now bright and sunny, swift and bright and empty, and he thought of the people soon to be going quietly home to Sunday dinner, decorously festive, and of himself trying to hold the fatal, furious little old man whom he dared not release long enough to turn his back and run.

"Will you quit long enough for me to get out?" he said, "Will you?" But the other still struggled, and Jason freed one hand and struck him on the head. A clumsy, hurried blow, and not hard, but the other slumped immediately and slid clattering among pans and buckets to the floor. Jason stood above him, panting, listening. Then he turned and ran from the car. At the door he restrained himself and descended more slowly and stood there again. His breath made a hah hah hah sound and he stood there trying to repress it, darting his gaze this way and that, when at a scuffling sound behind him he turned in time to see the little old man leaping awkwardly and furiously from the vestibule, a rusty hatchet high in his hand.

He grasped at the hatchet, feeling no shock but knowing that he was falling, thinking So this is how it'll end, and he believed that he was about to die and when something crashed against the back of his head he thought How did he hit me there? Only maybe he hit me a long time ago, he thought, And I just now felt it, and he thought Hurry. Hurry. Get it over with, and then a furious desire not to die seized him and he struggled, hearing the old man wailing and cursing in his cracked voice.

He still struggled when they hauled him to his feet, but they held him and he ceased.

"Am I bleeding much?" he said, "The back of my head. Am I bleeding?" He was still saying that while he felt himself being propelled rapidly away, heard the old man's thin furious voice dying away behind him. "Look at my head," he said, "Wait, I —"

"Wait, hell," the man who held him said, "That damn little wasp'll kill you. Keep going. You aint hurt."

"He hit me," Jason said. "Am I bleeding?"

"Keep going," the other said. He led Jason on around the corner of the station, to the empty platform where an express truck stood, where grass grew rigidly in a plot bordered with rigid flowers and a sign in electric lights: Keep your 👁 on Mottson, the gap filled by a human eye with an electric pupil. The man released him.

"Now," he said, "You get on out of here and stay out. What were you trying to do? Commit suicide?"

"I was looking for two people," Jason said. "I just asked him where they were."

"Who you looking for?"

"It's a girl," Jason said. "And a man. He had on

a red tie in Jefferson yesterday. With this show. They robbed me."

"Oh," the man said. "You're the one, are you. Well, they aint here."

"I reckon so," Jason said. He leaned against the wall and put his hand to the back of his head and looked at his palm. "I thought I was bleeding," he said. "I thought he hit me with that hatchet."

"You hit your head on the rail," the man said. "You better go on. They aint here."

"Yes. He said they were not here. I thought he was lying."

"Do you think I'm lying?" the man said.

"No," Jason said. "I know they're not here."

"I told him to get the hell out of there, both of them," the man said. "I wont have nothing like that in my show. I run a respectable show, with a respectable troupe."

"Yes," Jason said. "You dont know where they went?"

"No. And I dont want to know. No member of my show can pull a stunt like that. You her — brother?"

"No," Jason said. "It dont matter. I just wanted to see them. You sure he didn't hit me? No blood, I mean."

"There would have been blood if I hadn't got there when I did. You stay away from here, now.

That little bastard'll kill you. That your car yonder?"

"Yes."

"Well, you get in it and go back to Jefferson. If you find them, it wont be in my show. I run a respectable show. You say they robbed you?"

"No," Jason said, "It dont make any difference." He went to the car and got in. What is it I must do? he thought. Then he remembered. He started the engine and drove slowly up the street until he found a drugstore. The door was locked. He stood for a while with his hand on the knob and his head bent a little. Then he turned away and when a man came along after a while he asked if there was a drugstore open anywhere, but there was not. Then he asked when the northbound train ran, and the man told him at two thirty. He crossed the pavement and got in the car again and sat there. After a while two negro lads passed. He called to them.

"Can either of you boys drive a car?"

"Yes, suh."

"What'll you charge to drive me to Jefferson right away?"

They looked at one another, murmuring.

"I'll pay a dollar," Jason said.

They murmured again. "Couldn't go fer dat," one said.

"What will you go for?"

"Kin you go?" one said.

" I cant git off," the other said. " Whyn't you drive him up dar? You aint got nothin to do."

" Yes I is."

" Whut you got to do?"

They murmured again, laughing.

" I'll give you two dollars," Jason said. " Either of you."

" I cant git away neither," the first said.

" All right," Jason said. " Go on."

He sat there for sometime. He heard a clock strike the half hour, then people began to pass, in Sunday and Easter clothes. Some looked at him as they passed, at the man sitting quietly behind the wheel of a small car, with his invisible life ravelled out about him like a wornout sock. After a while a negro in overalls came up.

" Is you de one wants to go to Jefferson?" he said.

" Yes," Jason said. " What'll you charge me?"

" Fo dollars."

" Give you two."

" Cant go fer no less'n fo." The man in the car sat quietly. He wasn't even looking at him. The negro said, " You want me er not?"

" All right," Jason said, " Get in."

He moved over and the negro took the wheel. Jason closed his eyes. I can get something for it at Jefferson, he told himself, easing himself to the jolting, I can get something there. They drove on, along

391

the streets where people were turning peacefully into houses and Sunday dinners, and on out of town. He thought that. He wasn't thinking of home, where Ben and Luster were eating cold dinner at the kitchen table. Something — the absence of disaster, threat, in any constant evil — permitted him to forget Jefferson as any place which he had ever seen before, where his life must resume itself.

When Ben and Luster were done Dilsey sent them outdoors. "And see kin you keep let him alone twell fo oclock. T.P. be here den."

"Yessum," Luster said. They went out. Dilsey ate her dinner and cleared up the kitchen. Then she went to the foot of the stairs and listened, but there was no sound. She returned through the kitchen and out the outer door and stopped on the steps. Ben and Luster were not in sight, but while she stood there she heard another sluggish twang from the direction of the cellar door and she went to the door and looked down upon a repetition of the morning's scene.

"He done it jes dat way," Luster said. He contemplated the motionless saw with a kind of hopeful dejection. "I aint got de right thing to hit it wid yit," he said.

"En you aint gwine find hit down here, neither," Dilsey said. "You take him on out in de sun. You bofe get pneumonia down here on dis wet flo."

She waited and watched them cross the yard toward a clump of cedar trees near the fence. Then she went on to her cabin.

"Now, dont you git started," Luster said, "I had enough trouble wid you today." There was a hammock made of barrel staves slatted into woven wires. Luster lay down in the swing, but Ben went on vaguely and purposelessly. He began to whimper again. "Hush, now," Luster said, "I fixin to whup you." He lay back in the swing. Ben had stopped moving, but Luster could hear him whimpering. "Is you gwine hush, er aint you?" Luster said. He got up and followed and came upon Ben squatting before a small mound of earth. At either end of it an empty bottle of blue glass that once contained poison was fixed in the ground. In one was a withered stalk of jimson weed. Ben squatted before it, moaning, a slow, inarticulate sound. Still moaning he sought vaguely about and found a twig and put it in the other bottle. "Whyn't you hush?" Luster said, "You want me to give you somethin' to sho nough moan about? Sposin I does dis." He knelt and swept the bottle suddenly up and behind him. Ben ceased moaning. He squatted, looking at the small depression where the bottle had sat, then as he drew his lungs full Luster brought the bottle back into view. "Hush!" he hissed, "Dont you dast to beller! Dont you. Dar hit is. See? Here. You fixin to start ef you stays here. Come on, les go see ef dey started knockin ball yit." He took Ben's arm and drew him up and they went to the fence and stood side by side there, peering between the matted honeysuckle not yet in bloom.

"Dar," Luster said, "Dar come some. See um?"

They watched the foursome play onto the green and out, and move to the tee and drive. Ben watched, whimpering, slobbering. When the foursome went on he followed along the fence, bobbing and moaning. One said.

"Here, caddie. Bring the bag."

"Hush, Benjy," Luster said, but Ben went on at his shambling trot, clinging to the fence, wailing in his hoarse, hopeless voice. The man played and went on, Ben keeping pace with him until the fence turned at right angles, and he clung to the fence, watching the people move on and away.

"Will you hush now?" Luster said, "Will you hush now?" He shook Ben's arm. Ben clung to the fence, wailing steadily and hoarsely. "Aint you gwine stop?" Luster said, "Or is you?" Ben gazed through the fence. "All right, den," Luster said, "You want somethin to beller about?" He looked over his shoulder, toward the house. Then he whispered: "Caddy! Beller now. Caddy! Caddy! Caddy!"

A moment later, in the slow intervals of Ben's voice, Luster heard Dilsey calling. He took Ben by the arm and they crossed the yard toward her.

"I tole you he warn't gwine stay quiet," Luster said.

"You vilyun!" Dilsey said, "Whut you done to him?"

"I aint done nothin. I tole you when dem folks start playin, he git started up."

"You come on here," Dilsey said. "Hush, Benjy. Hush, now." But he wouldn't hush. They crossed the yard quickly and went to the cabin and entered. "Run git dat shoe," Dilsey said. "Dont you sturb Miss Cahline, now. Ef she say anything, tell her I got him. Go on, now; you kin sho do dat right, I reckon." Luster went out. Dilsey led Ben to the bed and drew him down beside her and she held him, rocking back and forth, wiping his drooling mouth upon the hem of her skirt. "Hush, now," she said, stroking his head, "Hush. Dilsey got you." But he bellowed slowly, abjectly, without tears; the grave hopeless sound of all voiceless misery under the sun. Luster returned, carrying a white satin slipper. It was yellow now, and cracked and soiled, and when they placed it into Ben's hand he hushed for a while. But he still whimpered, and soon he lifted his voice again.

"You reckon you kin find T. P.?" Dilsey said.

"He say yistiddy he gwine out to St John's today. Say he be back at fo."

Dilsey rocked back and forth, stroking Ben's head.

"Dis long time, O Jesus," she said, "Dis long time."

"I kin drive dat surrey, mammy," Luster said.

"You kill bofe y'all," Dilsey said, "You do hit fer devilment. I knows you got plenty sense to. But I cant trust you. Hush, now," she said. "Hush. Hush."

"Nome I wont," Luster said. "I drives wid T. P." Dilsey rocked back and forth, holding Ben. "Miss Cahline say ef you cant quiet him, she gwine git up en come down en do hit."

"Hush, honey," Dilsey said, stroking Ben's head. "Luster, honey," she said, "Will you think about yo ole mammy en drive dat surrey right?"

"Yessum," Luster said. "I drive hit jes like T. P."

Dilsey stroked Ben's head, rocking back and forth. "I does de bes I kin," she said, "Lawd knows dat. Go git it, den," she said, rising. Luster scuttled out. Ben held the slipper, crying. "Hush, now. Luster gone to git de surrey en take you to de graveyard. We aint gwine risk gittin yo cap," she said. She went to a closet contrived of a calico curtain hung across a corner of the room and got the felt hat she had worn. "We's down to worse'n dis, ef folks jes knowed," she said. "You's de Lawd's chile, anyway. En I be His'n too, fo long, praise Jesus. Here." She put the hat on his head and buttoned his coat. He wailed steadily. She took the slipper from him and put it away and they went out. Luster came up, with an ancient white horse in a battered and lopsided surrey.

"You gwine be careful, Luster?" she said.

"Yessum," Luster said. She helped Ben into the back seat. He had ceased crying, but now he began to whimper again.

"Hit's his flower," Luster said. "Wait, I'll git him one."

"You set right dar," Dilsey said. She went and took the cheekstrap. "Now, hurry en git him one." Luster ran around the house, toward the garden. He came back with a single narcissus.

"Dat un broke," Dilsey said, "Whyn't you git him a good un?"

"Hit de onliest one I could find," Luster said. "Y'all took all of um Friday to dec'rate de church. Wait, I'll fix hit." So while Dilsey held the horse Luster put a splint on the flower stalk with a twig and two bits of string and gave it to Ben. Then he mounted and took the reins. Dilsey still held the bridle.

"You knows de way now?" she said, "Up de street, round de square, to de graveyard, den straight back home."

"Yessum," Luster said, "Hum up, Queenie."

"You gwine be careful, now?"

"Yessum." Dilsey released the bridle.

"Hum up, Queenie," Luster said.

"Here," Dilsey said, "You han me dat whup."

"Aw, mammy," Luster said.

"Give hit here," Dilsey said, approaching the wheel. Luster gave it to her reluctantly.

"I wont never git Queenie started now."

"Never you mind about dat," Dilsey said. "Queenie know mo bout whar she gwine dan you does. All you got to do is set dar en hold dem reins. You knows de way, now?"

"Yessum. Same way T. P. goes ev'y Sunday."

"Den you do de same thing dis Sunday."

"Cose I is. Aint I drove fer T. P. mo'n a hund'ed times?"

"Den do hit again," Dilsey said. "G'awn, now. En ef you hurts Benjy, nigger boy, I dont know whut I do. You bound fer de chain gang, but I'll send you dar fo even chain gang ready fer you."

"Yessum," Luster said. "Hum up, Queenie."

He flapped the lines on Queenie's broad back and the surrey lurched into motion.

"You, Luster!" Dilsey said.

"Hum up, dar!" Luster said. He flapped the lines again. With subterranean rumblings Queenie jogged slowly down the drive and turned into the street, where Luster exhorted her into a gait resembling a prolonged and suspended fall in a forward direction.

Ben quit whimpering. He sat in the middle of the seat, holding the repaired flower upright in his fist,

398

his eyes serene and ineffable. Directly before him Luster's bullet head turned backward continually until the house passed from view, then he pulled to the side of the street and while Ben watched him he descended and broke a switch from a hedge. Queenie lowered her head and fell to cropping the grass until Luster mounted and hauled her head up and harried her into motion again, then he squared his elbows and with the switch and the reins held high he assumed a swaggering attitude out of all proportion to the sedate clopping of Queenie's hooves and the organlike basso of her internal accompaniment. Motors passed them, and pedestrians; once a group of half grown negroes:

"Dar Luster. Whar you gwine, Luster? To de boneyard?"

"Hi," Luster said, "Aint de same boneyard y'all headed fer. Hum up, elefump."

They approached the square, where the Confederate soldier gazed with empty eyes beneath his marble hand into wind and weather. Luster took still another notch in himself and gave the impervious Queenie a cut with the switch, casting his glance about the square. "Dar Mr Jason's car," he said then he spied another group of negroes. "Les show dem niggers how quality does, Benjy," he said, "Whut you say?" He looked back. Ben sat, holding the flower in his fist, his gaze empty and untroubled.

Luster hit Queenie again and swung her to the left at the monument.

For an instant Ben sat in an utter hiatus. Then he bellowed. Bellow on bellow, his voice mounted, with scarce interval for breath. There was more than astonishment in it, it was horror; shock; agony eyeless, tongueless; just sound, and Luster's eyes back-rolling for a white instant. "Gret God," he said, "Hush! Hush! Gret God!" He whirled again and struck Queenie with the switch. It broke and he cast it away and with Ben's voice mounting toward its unbelievable crescendo Luster caught up the end of the reins and leaned forward as Jason came jumping across the square and onto the step.

With a backhanded blow he hurled Luster aside and caught the reins and sawed Queenie about and doubled the reins back and slashed her across the hips. He cut her again and again, into a plunging gallop, while Ben's hoarse agony roared about them, and swung her about to the right of the monument. Then he struck Luster over the head with his fist.

"Dont you know any better than to take him to the left?" he said. He reached back and struck Ben, breaking the flower stalk again. "Shut up!" he said, "Shut up!" He jerked Queenie back and jumped down. "Get to hell on home with him. If you ever cross that gate with him again, I'll kill you!"

"Yes, suh!" Luster said. He took the reins and

hit Queenie with the end of them. "Git up! Git up, dar! Benjy, fer God's sake!"

Ben's voice roared and roared. Queenie moved again, her feet began to clop-clop steadily again, and at once Ben hushed. Luster looked quickly back over his shoulder, then he drove on. The broken flower drooped over Ben's fist and his eyes were empty and blue and serene again as cornice and façade flowed smoothly once more from left to right; post and tree, window and doorway, and signboard, each in its ordered place.

APPENDIX

COMPSON : 1699—1945

IKKEMOTUBBE. A dispossessed American king. Called "l'Homme" (and sometimes "de l'homme") by his fosterbrother, a Chevalier of France, who had he not been born too late could have been among the brightest in that glittering galaxy of knightly blackguards who were Napoleon's marshals, who thus translated the Chickasaw title meaning "The Man"; which translation Ikkemotubbe, himself a man of wit and imagination as well as a shrewd judge of character, including his own, carried one step further and anglicised it to "Doom." Who granted out of his vast lost domain a solid square mile of virgin North Mississippi dirt as truly angled as the four corners of a cardtable top (forested then because these were the old days before 1833 when the stars fell and Jefferson Mississippi was one long rambling onestorey mudchinked log building housing the Chickasaw Agent and his tradingpost store) to the grandson of a Scottish refugee who had lost his own birthright by casting his lot with a king who himself had been dispossessed. This in partial return for the right to proceed in peace, by whatever means he and his people saw fit, afoot or ahorse provided they were Chickasaw horses, to the wild western land presently to be called Oklahoma: not knowing then about the oil.

JACKSON. A Great White Father with a sword. (An old duellist, a brawling lean fierce mangy durable imperishable old lion who set the wellbeing of the nation above the White House and the health of his new political party above either and above them all set not his wife's honor but the principle that honor must be defended whether it was or not because defended it was whether or not.) Who patented sealed and countersigned the grant with his own hand in his gold tepee in Wassi Town, not knowing about the oil either: so that one day the homeless descendants of the dispossessed would ride supine with drink and splendidly comatose above the dusty allotted harborage of their bones in specially-built scarletpainted hearses and fire-engines.

These were Compsons:
QUENTIN MACLACHAN. Son of a Glasgow printer, orphaned and raised by his mother's people in the Perth highlands. Fled to Carolina from Culloden Moor with a claymore and the tartan he wore by day and slept under by night, and little else. At eighty, having fought once against an English king and lost, he would not make that mistake twice and

404

so fled again one night in 1779, with his infant grandson and the tartan (the claymore had vanished, along with his son, the grandson's father, from one of Tarleton's regiments on a Georgia battlefield about a year ago) into Kentucky, where a neighbor named Boon or Boone had already established a settlement.

CHARLES STUART. Attainted and proscribed by name and grade in his British regiment. Left for dead in a Georgia swamp by his own retreating army and then by the advancing American one, both of which were wrong. He still had the claymore even when on his home-made wooden leg he finally overtook his father and son four years later at Harrodsburg, Kentucky, just in time to bury the father and enter upon a long period of being a split personality while still trying to be the schoolteacher which he believed he wanted to be, until he gave up at last and became the gambler he actually was and which no Compson seemed to realize they all were provided the gambit was desperate and the odds long enough. Succeeded at last in risking not only his neck but the security of his family and the very integrity of the name he would leave behind him, by joining the confederation headed by an acquaintance named Wilkinson (a man of considerable talent and influence and intellect and power) in a plot to secede the whole Mississippi Valley from the United

States and join it to Spain. Fled in his turn when the bubble burst (as anyone except a Compson schoolteacher should have known it would), himself unique in being the only one of the plotters who had to flee the country: this not from the vengeance and retribution of the government which he had attempted to dismember, but from the furious revulsion of his late confederates now frantic for their own safety. He was not expelled from the United States, he talked himself countryless, his expulsion due not to the treason but to his having been so vocal and vociferant in the conduct of it, burning each bridge vocally behind him before he had even reached the place to build the next one: so that it was no provost marshal nor even a civic agency but his late coplotters themselves who put afoot the movement to evict him from Kentucky and the United States and, if they had caught him, probably from the world too. Fled by night, running true to family tradition, with his son and the old claymore and the tartan.

JASON LYCURGUS. Who, driven perhaps by the compulsion of the flamboyant name given him by the sardonic embittered woodenlegged indomitable father who perhaps still believed with his heart that what he wanted to be was a classicist schoolteacher, rode up the Natchez Trace one day in 1811 with a pair of fine pistols and one meagre saddlebag on a small lightwaisted but stronghocked mare which could do the first two furlongs in definitely under the halfminute and the next two in not appreciably more, though that was all. But it was enough: who reached the Chickasaw Agency at Okatoba (which in 1860 was still called Old Jefferson) and went no further. Who within six months was the Agent's clerk and within twelve his partner, officially still the clerk though actually halfowner of what was now a considerable store stocked with the mare's winnings in races against the horses of Ikkemotubbe's young men which he, Compson, was always careful to limit to a quarter or at most three furlongs; and in the next year it was Ikkemotubbe who owned the little mare and Compson owned the solid square mile of land which someday would be almost in the center of the town of Jefferson, forested then and still forested twenty years later though rather a park than a forest by that time, with its slavequarters and stables and kitchengardens and the formal lawns and promenades and pavilions laid out by the same architect who built the columned porticoed house furnished by steamboat from France and New Orleans, and still the square intact mile in 1840 (with not only the little white village called Jefferson beginning to enclose it but an entire white county about to surround it because in a few years now Ikkemotubbe's descendants and people would be gone, those remaining living not as warriors and hunters but as white men—as shiftless farmers or, here and there, the masters of what they too called plantations and the owners of shiftless slaves, a little dirtier than the white man, a little lazier, a little crueller—until at last even the wild blood itself would have vanished, to be seen only occasionally in the noseshape of a Negro on a cottonwagon or a white sawmill hand or trapper or locomotive fireman), known as the Compson Domain then, since now it was fit to breed princes, statesmen and generals and bishops, to avenge the dispossessed Compsons from Culloden and Carolina and Kentucky, then known as the Governor's house because sure enough in time it did produce or at least spawn a governor—Quentin MacLachan again, after the Culloden grandfather —and still known as the Old Governor's even after it had spawned (1861) a general—(called so by predetermined accord and agreement by the whole town and county, as though they knew even then and beforehand that the old governor was the last Compson who would not fail at everything he touched save longevity or suicide)—the Brigadier Jason Lycurgus II who failed at Shiloh in '62 and failed again though not so badly at Resaca in '64, who put the first mortgage on the still intact square mile to a New England carpetbagger in '66, after the old town had been burned by the Federal General Smith and the new little town, in time to be populated

408

mainly by the descendants not of Compsons but of Snopeses, had begun to encroach and then nibble at and into it as the failed brigadier spent the next forty years selling fragments of it off to keep up the mortgage on the remainder: until one day in 1900 he died quietly on an army cot in the hunting and fishing camp in the Tallahatchie River bottom where he passed most of the end of his days.

And even the old governor was forgotten now; what was left of the old square mile was now known merely as the Compson place—the weedchoked traces of the old ruined lawns and promenades, the house which had needed painting too long already, the scaling columns of the portico where Jason III (bred for a lawyer and indeed he kept an office up-stairs above the Square, where entombed in dusty filingcases some of the oldest names in the county—Holston and Sutpen, Grenier and Beauchamp and Coldfield—faded year by year among the bottom-less labyrinths of chancery: and who knows what dream in the perennial heart of his father, now com-pleting the third of his three avatars—the one as son of a brilliant and gallant statesman, the second as battleleader of brave and gallant men, the third as a sort of privileged pseudo-Daniel Boone-Robinson Crusoe, who had not returned to juvenility because actually he had never left it—that that lawyer's office might again be the anteroom to the governor's mansion and the old splendor) sat all day long with

a decanter of whiskey and a litter of dogeared
Horaces and Livys and Catulluses, composing (it
was said) caustic and satiric eulogies on both his
dead and his living fellowtownsmen, who sold the
last of the property, except that fragment containing
the house and the kitchengarden and the collapsing
stables and one servant's cabin in which Dilsey's
family lived, to a golfclub for the ready money with
which his daughter Candace could have her fine wedding in April and his son Quentin could finish one
year at Harvard and commit suicide in the following
June of 1910; already known as the Old Compson
place even while Compsons were still living in it on
that spring dusk in 1928 when the old governor's
doomed lost nameless seventeen-year-old greatgreat-
granddaughter robbed her last remaining sane male
relative (her uncle Jason IV) of his secret hoard of
money and climbed down a rainpipe and ran off with
a pitchman in a travelling streetshow, and still
known as the Old Compson place long after all
traces of Compsons were gone from it: after the
widowed mother died and Jason IV, no longer need-
ing to fear Dilsey now, committed his idiot brother,
Benjamin, to the State Asylum in Jackson and sold
the house to a countryman who operated it as a
boardinghouse for juries and horse- and mule-
traders, and still known as the Old Compson place
even after the boardinghouse (and presently the
golfcourse too) had vanished and the old square

mile was even intact again in row after row of small crowded jerrybuilt individuallyowned demiurban bungalows.

And these:

QUENTIN III. Who loved not his sister's body but some concept of Compson honor precariously and (he knew well) only temporarily supported by the minute fragile membrane of her maidenhead as a miniature replica of all the whole vast globy earth may be poised on the nose of a trained seal. Who loved not the idea of the incest which he would not commit, but some presbyterian concept of its eternal punishment: he, not God, could by that means cast himself and his sister both into hell, where he could guard her forever and keep her forevermore intact amid the eternal fires. But who loved death above all, who loved only death, loved and lived in a deliberate and almost perverted anticipation of death as a lover loves and deliberately refrains from the waiting willing friendly tender incredible body of his beloved, until he can no longer bear not the refraining but the restraint and so flings, hurls himself, relinquishing, drowning. Committed suicide in Cambridge, Massachusetts, June 1910, two months after his sister's wedding, waiting first to complete the current academic year and so get the full value of his paid-in-advance tuition, not because he had his old Culloden and Carolina and Kentucky grand-

411

fathers in him but because the remaining piece of the old Compson mile which had been sold to pay for his sister's wedding and his year at Harvard had been the one thing, excepting that same sister and the sight of an open fire, which his youngest brother, born an idiot, had loved.

CANDACE (CADDY). Doomed and knew it, accepted the doom without either seeking or fleeing it. Loved her brother despite him, loved not only him but loved in him that bitter prophet and inflexible corruptless judge of what he considered the family's honor and its doom, as he thought he loved but really hated in her what he considered the frail doomed vessel of its pride and the foul instrument of its disgrace; not only this, she loved him not only in spite of but because of the fact that he himself was incapable of love, accepting the fact that he must value above all not her but the virginity of which she was custodian and on which she placed no value whatever: the frail physical stricture which to her was no more than a hangnail would have been. Knew the brother loved death best of all and was not jealous, would (and perhaps in the calculation and deliberation of her marriage did) have handed him the hypothetical hemlock. Was two months pregnant with another man's child which regardless of what its sex would be she had already named Quentin after the brother whom they both (she and

412

the brother) knew was already the same as dead, when she married (1910) an extremely eligible young Indianian she and her mother had met while vacationing at French Lick the summer before. Divorced by him 1911. Married 1920 to a minor movingpicture magnate, Hollywood California. Divorced by mutual agreement, Mexico 1925. Vanished in Paris with the German occupation, 1940, still beautiful and probably still wealthy too since she did not look within fifteen years of her actual fortyeight, and was not heard of again. Except there was a woman in Jefferson, the county librarian, a mouse-sized and -colored woman who had never married, who had passed through the city schools in the same class with Candace Compson and then spent the rest of her life trying to keep *Forever Amber* in its orderly overlapping avatars and *Jurgen* and *Tom Jones* out of the hands of the highschool juniors and seniors who could reach them down without even having to tiptoe from the back shelves where she herself would have to stand on a box to hide them. One day in 1943, after a week of a distraction bordering on disintegration almost, during which those entering the library would find her always in the act of hurriedly closing her desk drawer and turning the key in it (so that the matrons, wives of the bankers and doctors and lawyers, some of whom had also been in that old highschool class, who came and went in the afternoons with the copies of the

413

Forever Ambers and the volumes of Thorne Smith
carefully wrapped from view in sheets of Memphis
and Jackson newspapers, believed she was on the
verge of illness or perhaps even loss of mind), she
closed and locked the library in the middle of the
afternoon and with her handbag clasped tightly
under her arm and two feverish spots of determina-
tion in her ordinarily colorless cheeks, she entered
the farmers' supply store where Jason IV had
started as a clerk and where he now owned his own
business as a buyer of and dealer in cotton, striding
on through that gloomy cavern which only men ever
entered—a cavern cluttered and walled and stalag-
mitehung with plows and discs and loops of trace-
chain and singletrees and mulecollars and sidemeat
and cheap shoes and horselinament and flour and
molasses, gloomy because the goods it contained
were not shown but hidden rather since those who
supplied Mississippi farmers or at least Negro
Mississippi farmers for a share of the crop did not
wish, until that crop was made and its value approximately computable, to show them what they could
learn to want but only to supply them on specific demand with what they could not help but need—and
strode on back to Jason's particular domain in the
rear: a railed enclosure cluttered with shelves and
pigeonholes bearing spiked dust-and-lintgathering
gin receipts and ledgers and cottonsamples and rank
with the blended smell of cheese and kerosene and

414

harnessoil and the tremendous iron stove against which chewed tobacco had been spat for almost a hundred years, and up to the long high sloping counter behind which Jason stood and, not looking again at the overalled men who had quietly stopped talking and even chewing when she entered, with a kind of fainting desperation she opened the handbag and fumbled something out of it and laid it open on the counter and stood trembling and breathing rapidly while Jason looked down at it—a picture, a photograph in color clipped obviously from a slick magazine—a picture filled with luxury and money and sunlight—a Cannebière backdrop of mountains and palms and cypresses and the sea, an open powerful expensive chromiumtrimmed sports car, the woman's face hatless between a rich scarf and a seal coat, ageless and beautiful, cold serene and damned; beside her a handsome lean man of middleage in the ribbons and tabs of a German staffgeneral —and the mousesized mousecolored spinster trembling and aghast at her own temerity, staring across it at the childless bachelor in whom ended that long line of men who had had something in them of decency and pride even after they had begun to fail at the integrity and the pride had become mostly vanity and selfpity: from the expatriate who had to flee his native land with little else except his life yet who still refused to accept defeat, through the man who gambled his life and his good name twice and lost twice and declined to accept that either, and the one who with only a clever small quarterhorse for tool avenged his dispossessed father and grand-father and gained a principality, and the brilliant and gallant governor and the general who though he failed at leading in battle brave and gallant men at least risked his own life too in the failing, to the cultured dipsomaniac who sold the last of his patri-mony not to buy drink but to give one of his descend-ants at least the best chance in life he could think of.

'It's Caddy!' the librarian whispered. 'We must save her!'

'It's Cad, all right,' Jason said. Then he began to laugh. He stood there laughing above the picture, above the cold beautiful face now creased and dog-eared from its week's sojourn in the desk drawer and the handbag. And the librarian knew why he was laughing, who had not called him anything but Mr Compson for thirty-two years now, ever since the day in 1911 when Candace, cast off by her hus-band, had brought her infant daughter home and left the child and departed by the next train, to return no more, and not only the Negro cook, Dil-sey, but the librarian too divined by simple instinct that Jason was somehow using the child's life and its illegitimacy both to blackmail the mother not only into staying away from Jefferson for the rest of her life but into appointing him sole unchallenge-able trustee of the money she would send for the child's maintenance, and had refused to speak to him at all since that day in 1928 when the daughter climbed down the rainpipe and ran away with the pitchman.

'Jason!' she cried. 'We must save her! Jason! Jason'——and still crying it even when he took up the picture between thumb and finger and threw it back across the counter toward her.

'That Candace?' he said. 'Don't make me laugh. This bitch aint thirty yet. The other one's fifty now.'

And the library was still locked all the next day too when at three oclock in the afternoon, footsore and spent yet still unflagging and still clasping the handbag tightly under her arm, she turned into a neat small yard in the Negro residence section of Memphis and mounted the steps of the neat small house and rang the bell and the door opened and a black woman of about her own age looked quietly out at her. 'It's Frony, isn't it?' the librarian said. 'Dont you remember me—— Melissa Meek, from Jefferson——'

'Yes,' the Negress said. 'Come in. You want to see Mama.' And she entered the room, the neat yet cluttered bedroom of an old Negro, rank with the smell of old people, old women, old Negroes, where the old woman herself sat in a rocker beside the hearth where even though it was June a fire smoldered—a big woman once, in faded clean calico and an immaculate turban wound round her head

above the bleared and now apparently almost sightless eyes—and put the dogeared clipping into the
black hands which, like the women of her race, were
still as supple and delicately shaped as they had been
when she was thirty or twenty or even seventeen.

'It's Caddy!' the librarian said. 'It is! Dilsey!
Dilsey!'

'What did he say?' the old Negress said. And the
librarian knew whom she meant by 'he', nor did the
librarian marvel, not only that the old Negress
would know that she (the librarian) would know
whom she meant by the 'he', but that the old Negress
would know at once that she had already shown the
picture to Jason.

'Dont you know what he said?' she cried. 'When
he realised she was in danger, he said it was her,
even if I hadn't even had a picture to show him. But
as soon as he realised that somebody, anybody, even
just me, wanted to save her, would try to save her,
he said it wasn't. But it is! Look at it!'

'Look at my eyes,' the old Negress said. 'How
can I see that picture?'

'Call Frony!' the librarian cried. 'She will know
her!' But already the old Negress was folding the
clipping carefully back into its old creases, handing
it back.

'My eyes aint any good anymore,' she said. 'I cant
see it.'

And that was all. At six oclock she fought her

418

way through the crowded bus terminal, the bag
clutched under one arm and the return half of her
roundtrip ticket in the other hand, and was swept
out onto the roaring platform on the diurnal tide of
a few middleaged civilians but mostly soldiers and
sailors enroute either to leave or to death and the
homeless young women, their companions, who for
two years now had lived from day to day in pull-
mans and hotels when they were lucky and in day-
coaches and busses and stations and lobbies and
public restrooms when not, pausing only long enough
to drop their foals in charity wards or policestations
and then move on again, and fought her way into
the bus, smaller than any other there so that her
feet touched the floor only occasionally until a shape
(a man in khaki; she couldn't see him at all because
she was already crying) rose and picked her up
bodily and set her into a seat next the window,
where still crying quietly she could look out upon
the fleeing city as it streaked past and then was behind and presently now she would be home again,
safe in Jefferson where life lived too with all its
incomprehensible passion and turmoil and grief and
fury and despair, but here at six oclock you could
close the covers on it and even the weightless hand
of a child could put it back among its unfeatured
kindred on the quiet eternal shelves and turn the
key upon it for the whole and dreamless night. *Yes*
she thought, crying quietly *that was it she didn't*

419

want to see it know whether it was Caddy or not because she knows Caddy doesn't want to be saved hasn't anything anymore worth being saved for nothing worth being lost that she can lose

JASON IV.   The first sane Compson since before Culloden and (a childless bachelor) hence the last. Logical rational contained and even a philosopher in the old stoic tradition: thinking nothing whatever of God one way or the other and simply considering the police and so fearing and respecting only the Negro woman, his sworn enemy since his birth and his mortal one since that day in 1911 when she too divined by simple clairvoyance that he was somehow using his infant niece's illegitimacy to blackmail its mother, who cooked the food he ate. Who not only fended off and held his own with Compsons but competed and held his own with the Snopeses who took over the little town following the turn of the century as the Compsons and Sartorises and their ilk faded from it (no Snopes, but Jason Compson himself who as soon as his mother died—the niece had already climbed down the rainpipe and vanished so Dilsey no longer had either of these clubs to hold over him —committed his idiot younger brother to the state and vacated the old house, first chopping up the vast oncesplendid rooms into what he called apartments and selling the whole thing to a countryman who opened a boardinghouse in it), though this was

420

not difficult since to him all the rest of the town and the world and the human race too except himself were Compsons, inexplicable yet quite predictable in that they were in no sense whatever to be trusted. Who, all the money from the sale of the pasture having gone for his sister's wedding and his brother's course at Harvard, used his own niggard savings out of his meagre wages as a storeclerk to send himself to a Memphis school where he learned to class and grade cotton, and so established his own business with which, following his dipsomaniac father's death, he assumed the entire burden of the rotting family in the rotting house, supporting his idiot brother because of their mother, sacrificing what pleasures might have been the right and just due and even the necessity of a thirty-year-old bachelor, so that his mother's life might continue as nearly as possible to what it had been; this not because he loved her but (a sane man always) simply because he was afraid of the Negro cook whom he could not even force to leave, even when he tried to stop paying her weekly wages; and who despite all this, still managed to save almost three thousand dollars ($2840.50) as he reported it on the night his niece stole it; in niggard and agonised dimes and quarters and halfdollars, which hoard he kept in no bank because to him a banker too was just one more Compson, but hid in a locked bureau drawer in his bedroom whose bed he made and changed himself since he kept the bedroom door locked all the time save when he was passing through it. Who, following a fumbling abortive attempt by his idiot brother on a passing female child, had himself appointed the idiot's guardian without letting their mother know and so was able to have the creature castrated before the mother even knew it was out of the house, and who following the mother's death in 1933 was able to free himself forever not only from the idiot brother and the house but from the Negro woman too, moving into a pair of offices up a flight of stairs above the supplystore containing his cotton ledgers and samples, which he had converted into a bedroom-kitchen-bath, in and out of which on weekends there would be seen a big plain friendly brazenhaired pleasantfaced woman no longer very young, in round picture hats and (in its season) an imitation fur coat, the two of them, the middleaged cottonbuyer and the woman whom the town called, simply, his friend from Memphis, seen at the local picture show on Saturday night and on Sunday morning mounting the apartment stairs with paper bags from the grocer's containing loaves and eggs and oranges and cans of soup, domestic, uxorious, connubial, until the late afternoon bus carried her back to Memphis. He was emancipated now. He was free. 'In 1865,' he would say, 'Abe Lincoln freed the niggers from the Compsons. In 1933, Jason Compson freed the Compsons from the niggers.'

422

BENJAMIN. Born Maury, after his mother's only brother: a handsome flashing swaggering workless bachelor who borrowed money from almost anyone, even Dilsey although she was a Negro, explaining to her as he withdrew his hand from his pocket that she was not only in his eyes the same as a member of his sister's family, she would be considered a born lady anywhere in any eyes. Who, when at last even his mother realised what he was and insisted weeping that his name must be changed, was rechristened Benjamin by his brother Quentin (Benjamin, our lastborn, sold into Egypt). Who loved three things: the pasture which was sold to pay for Candace's wedding and to send Quentin to Harvard, his sister Candace, firelight. Who lost none of them because he could not remember his sister but only the loss of her, and firelight was the same bright shape as going to sleep, and the pasture was even better sold than before because now he and TP could not only follow timeless along the fence the motions which it did not even matter to him were humanbeings swinging golfsticks, TP could lead them to clumps of grass or weeds where there would appear suddenly in TP's hand small white spherules which competed with and even conquered what he did not even know was gravity and all the immutable laws when released from the hand toward plank floor or smokehouse wall or concrete sidewalk. Gelded 1913. Committed to the State

Asylum, Jackson 1933. Lost nothing then either because, as with his sister, he remembered not the pasture but only its loss, and firelight was still the same bright shape of sleep.

QUENTIN. The last. Candace's daughter. Fatherless nine months before her birth, nameless at birth and already doomed to be unwed from the instant the dividing egg determined its sex. Who at seventeen, on the one thousand eight hundred ninetyfifth anniversary of the day before the resurrection of Our Lord, swung herself by a rainpipe from the window of the room in which her uncle had locked her at noon, to the locked window of his own locked and empty bedroom and broke a pane and entered the window and with the uncle's firepoker burst open the locked bureau drawer and took the money (it was not $2840.50 either, it was almost seven thousand dollars and this was Jason's rage, the red unbearable fury which on that night and at intervals recurring with little or no diminishment for the next five years, made him seriously believe would at some unwarned instant destroy him, kill him as instantaneously dead as a bullet or a lightningbolt: that although he had been robbed not of a mere petty three thousand dollars but of almost seven thousand he couldn't even tell anybody; because he had been robbed of seven thousand dollars instead of just three he could not only never receive

justification—he did not want sympathy—from
other men unlucky enough to have one bitch for a
sister and another for a niece, he couldn't even go
to the police; because he had lost four thousand
dollars which did not belong to him he couldn't even
recover the three thousand which did since those
first four thousand dollars were not only the legal
property of his niece as a part of the money supplied
for her support and maintenance by her mother
over the last sixteen years, they did not exist at all,
having been officially recorded as expended and consumed in the annual reports he submitted to the
district Chancellor, as required of him as guardian
and trustee by his bondsmen: so that he had been
robbed not only of his thievings but his savings too,
and by his own victim; he had been robbed not only
of the four thousand dollars which he had risked
jail to acquire but of the three thousand which he
had hoarded at the price of sacrifice and denial,
almost a nickel and a dime at a time, over a period
of almost twenty years: and this not only by his own
victim but by a child who did it at one blow, without
premeditation or plan, not even knowing or even
caring how much she would find when she broke the
drawer open; and now he couldn't even go to the
police for help: he who had considered the police
always, never given them any trouble, had paid the
taxes for years which supported them in parasitic
and sadistic idleness; not only that, he didn't dare

pursue the girl himself because he might catch her and she would talk, so that his only recourse was a vain dream which kept him tossing and sweating on nights two and three and even four years after the event, when he should have forgotten about it: of catching her without warning, springing on her out of the dark, before she had spent all the money, and murder her before she had time to open her mouth) and climbed down the same rainpipe in the dusk and ran away with the pitchman who was already under sentence for bigamy. And so vanished; whatever occupation overtook her would have arrived in no chromium Mercedes; whatever snapshot would have contained no general of staff.

And that was all. These others were not Compsons. They were black:

TP. Who wore on Memphis's Beale Street the fine bright cheap intransigent clothes manufactured specifically for him by the owners of Chicago and New York sweatshops.

FRONY. Who married a pullman porter and went to St Louis to live and later moved back to Memphis to make a home for her mother since Dilsey refused to go further than that.

LUSTER. A man, aged 14. Who was not only capable of the complete care and security of an idiot twice his age and three times his size, but could keep him entertained.

DILSEY.
They endured.

WILLIAM FAULKNER, born New Albany, Mississippi, September 25, 1897—died July 6, 1962. Attended University of Mississippi. Enlisted Royal Air Force, Canada, 1918. Traveled in Europe 1925-1926. Resident of Oxford, Mississippi, where he held various jobs while trying to establish himself as a writer. First published novel, *Soldiers' Pay,* 1926. Writer in Residence at the University of Virginia 1957-1958. Awarded the Nobel Prize for Literature 1950.

THE SOUND AND THE FURY, published October 7, 1929, was Faulkner's fourth novel. Though it immediately became famous in literary circles, it did not achieve a wide American audience until after it was added to the Modern Library in 1946. The plates for the text of this new edition were produced photographically from a copy of the first printing, which has fewer errors than the 1946 setting.

MODEL LIBRARY COLLEGE EDITIONS

The Best of the World's Best Books
COMPLETE LIST OF TITLES IN
THE MODERN LIBRARY

A series of handsome, cloth-bound books, formerly available only in expensive editions.

MODERN LIBRARY

MODERN LIBRARY

MODERN LIBRARY

MISCELLANEOUS